King Sorrow

ALSO BY JOE HILL

Full Throttle (story collection)

Strange Weather (story collection)

The Fireman

NOS4A2

Horns

Heart-Shaped Box

20th Century Ghosts (story collection)

GRAPHIC NOVELS

Locke & Key, Volumes 1–7
(with Gabriel Rodríguez)

Locke & Key: The Golden Age
(with Gabriel Rodríguez)

Wraith (with Charles Paul Wilson III)

Basketful of Heads (with Leomacs)

Plunge (with Stuart Immonen)

JOE HILL

King Sorrow

HEADLINE

Copyright © Joe Hill 2025

"We Are The Champions" by Freddie Mercury. © 1977 Queen Music Ltd. All rights administered by Sony Music Publishing (US) LLC, 1005 17th Avenue South, Suite 800, Nashville, TN, 37212. All rights reserved. Used by permission.

The right of Joe Hill to be identified as the Author of the Work has been asserted by him in accordance with the Copyright, Designs and Patents Act 1988.

First published in the United States in 2025 by William Morrow, an imprint of HarperCollins Publishers

Published in 2025 by Headline Publishing Group Limited

3

Apart from any use permitted under UK copyright law, this publication may only be reproduced, stored, or transmitted, in any form, or by any means, with prior permission in writing of the publishers or, in the case of reprographic production, in accordance with the terms of licences issued by the Copyright Licensing Agency.

All characters in this publication are fictitious and any resemblance to real persons, living or dead, is purely coincidental.

Cataloguing in Publication Data is available from the British Library

Hardback ISBN 978 1 0354 3429 9
Trade Paperback ISBN 978 1 0354 3430 5

Offset in 11.55/15.22pt FreightText Pro by Six Red Marbles UK, Thetford, Norfolk

Printed and bound in Great Britain by Clays Ltd, Elcograf S.p.A.

Designed by Leah Carlson-Stanisic

Grateful acknowledgement is given to Gabriel Rodríguez for the dragon rampant illustration that graces these pages (@gr_comics).

Headline's policy is to use papers that are natural, renewable and recyclable products and made from wood grown in well-managed forests and other controlled sources. The logging and manufacturing processes are expected to conform to the environmental regulations of the country of origin.

Headline Publishing Group Limited
An Hachette UK Company
Carmelite House
50 Victoria Embankment
London EC4Y 0DZ

The authorised representative in the EEA is Hachette Ireland, 8 Castlecourt Centre, Dublin 15, D15 XTP3, Ireland (email: info@hbgi.ie)

www.headline.co.uk
www.hachette.co.uk

For Gillian

Gillian, my love

A thousand times Gillian

HC SVNT DRACONES

KING
Sorrow

Book One

THE BRIARS

1989

ONE

On the first weekend in September, Arthur Oakes drove west to see his mother in the House of Correction. It was a trip of more than two hundred miles, across the southern half of Maine, the chimney pipe of New Hampshire, and into Vermont, and it ended, as it always did, in a line of cars waiting to pass through a twelve-foot-high gate topped with barbed wire.

Arthur always thought the House of Correction looked like a high school: a three-story block of sandstone brick, with narrow slots for windows. He slowed to a stop behind a Ford Ranchero disgorging oily black smoke from the exhaust pipe. A bumper sticker read: NO FREE RIDES—GAS, GRASS, OR ASS. There was a bumper sticker a man could respect. Arthur's VW had been his mother's ride before it was his, and the Rabbit had bumper stickers too . . . a lot of them. His mother hadn't let a square inch of the rear end go to waste. One said ARE YOU FOLLOWING JESUS THIS CLOSE? Another showed a picture of Gandhi and said AN EYE FOR AN EYE MAKES THE WHOLE WORLD BLIND. They should've locked her up for crimes against her own car. It grated on him, parking his inherited Christmobile in a lot full of vehicles that had probably seen action as getaway cars.

If the exterior of the Black Cricket Women's House of Correction looked like a big public high school, the lobby resembled a cramped ER waiting room. Fluorescent lights buzzed and cast a dispiriting, impoverished glow. A TV set played daytime talk.

A guard, a heavyset woman with a butch haircut, piloted a rolling office chair behind a scratched, dirty window. Arthur joined the queue, behind a couple in their mid-twenties and a teenage girl. The guy wore black jeans, tight to his stovepipe legs, a sleeveless black Harley tee, and a do-rag. His lady leaned against him, a woman with hard, bony features that she had tried to soften with blusher and bubblegum-pink lipstick. The teenager stood close by, head down, face hidden behind her own unwashed yellow hair. She had on a Guns N' Roses tee that was too small for her, exposing her midriff. Her acid-washed jeans sagged to reveal the top of her shiny black thong. Arthur looked away, felt somehow it was indecent to have noticed.

"She can't go in there wearing that shirt," said the officer behind the window. She pointed at the teenager.

The girl craned her neck to peer down at her GN'R shirt, as if to hunt for an offensive stain, and Arthur realized, with a jolt, that he knew her . . . not by name but by profession. She delivered pizzas for Shut-Up-And-Eat-It Pizza in Podomaquassy—and marijuana or 'shrooms as well, if you knew what to order, and Arthur's roommate, Donovan McBride, did. She turned up at their off-campus student housing once or twice a month to bring Van a sausage pie and a baggie of green. Arthur figured she hooked half the campus up with weed and indigestion.

"What's wrong with it?" the pizza girl asked.

"No references to firearms. Cover it up or take it off."

"You'd like that, wouldn't you?" the older sister asked. She put the pizza girl in a headlock and squeezed one breast. "Get an eyeful of Tana's melons." Tana shrieked and twisted free.

The guard let her bored gaze drift away. "The rules are right there on the wall."

Tana rubbed her breast and said, "It's a concert shirt."

"I see a pair of crossed pistols. Garments displaying drugs, weapons, or obscenities are not allowed in the House of Correction. Volpe, Nighswander, you're cleared to enter. Your sister will have to stay here." The guard tipped her head toward the double doors on the left.

"My sis is coming with us, lez," said the older sister.

"What's that?" asked the officer. She cocked her head, turning her ear to the glass. Arthur thought it possible she genuinely hadn't heard.

"Jayne," Tana said, "I'll wait in the truck. Whatever. You and Ronnie can talk to Mom. You don't need—"

"Don't start tellin' me what I need. You're the whole reason we're here," Jayne Nighswander said. She turned her attention back to the officer. "I hadda get up at six in the goddamn morning to drive Tana here so she could explain her latest fuck-up to our mother. And you're gonna make her sit in the truck because you don't like her shirt?"

The officer stood. One hand fell to the baton on her belt.

"You want to spend time with your mother," she said, "keep running your mouth. We might be able to arrange a cell right next to her."

"Six in the mornin'," Jayne went on. "Three-hour drive and I gotta knock heads with a fascist dy—"

"She can have my hoodie," Arthur spoke over her before she could say *dyke* and get her pointy, narrow head knocked in.

It was the girl, Tana, who impelled him to pipe up. She had shut her eyes, lowered her chin to her chest, and hunched her shoulders like a kid listening to Mom and Dad fight. In that moment, she looked not nineteen, but a terrorized nine, and Arthur couldn't bear it.

Jayne Nighswander looked Arthur over. Arthur couldn't quite track the emotions that flickered through her pale blue eyes. He saw something like curiosity, an instant of cold reptilian calculation, and finally, a gleam of amusement.

The ugly color began to drain from the security guard's face and she settled back into her chair. "As long as I don't see guns, I don't see a problem."

Arthur wriggled out of his hoodie and slipped it off. It had belonged to his mother and he still sometimes imagined it smelled of her, the smell of the chapel: old hymnals and pine pews. On the back was an outline of Africa with Steve Biko's face peering out from within.

Tana Nighswander didn't thank him. She kept her head down as she pulled it on, never even looked at him. The boyfriend, Ronnie Volpe, admired the back of the sweatshirt and then said, in a hoarse, smoker's voice, "Eddie Murphy! I love that absurd motherfucker."

The security officer jerked a thumb at the door. "Go on. Next."

As the three of them moved away, Jayne Nighswander looked back at him and flashed a wolfish grin. "That was damn big of you, bud. We'll have to pay you back someday." She ushered Volpe and her sister through the doors and out of sight.

The guard behind the Plexiglas window was shaking her head, her jaw tight.

"I'm here to see my mother, Dr. Erin Oakes," Arthur said.

"Yeah, I know who you're here to see. The holy mother." She pushed a clipboard at him. "Sign here, dumbass." She muttered this last bit to herself, but Arthur caught it all the same, and then wondered if he had misheard.

"What?"

"Why'd you do that?" she asked him. She sounded genuinely aggrieved. "Why'n't you mind your own business?"

"Oh," Arthur said, "I don't know. Just trying to help. It's what my mother would've done."

"Buddy," said the security guard, "if your mother made such great choices, do you think she'd be in here?"

TWO

The family room held half a dozen stainless steel tables bolted to a sticky tile floor. Arthur took his usual seat, only peripherally aware of the Nighswanders at the next table over. His mother was one of the first inmates through the door, limber and easy in her prison blues, her hair clipped short.

Erin Oakes dropped into the seat across from him, kissed the tip of her pointer finger, and touched it to his. Physical contact wasn't allowed in the family room, but if any of the guards saw, they declined to object. Erin and Arthur sat across from each other, the slender white woman serving seven for manslaughter, and her son, the long-limbed and gangly Black kid finishing up a four-year stretch himself in the one of the whitest colleges on the East Coast—where he was on the dean's list every semester, in case anyone had any questions about his right to be there.

"I missed you all summer long," she said. "How was Old Blighty?"

"It's the only country in the world where they think Spam is one of the five major food groups," Arthur said.

Arthur spent his summers in the UK, with his paternal grandparents, who were Windrush generation, shipped over from Jamaica in the 1950s to rebuild what the Krauts had bombed into rubble. Arthur's father was there too, in Kent. He had the newest marble monument in a graveyard full of mossy, tilting, four-hundred-year-old headstones.

"Do anything fun?"

"I spent an afternoon in the British Library looking at illustrated manuscripts. I think I'm going to write about them in my 'Book as Object' class this semester."

"I was hoping you screwed a red-headed Scottish barmaid out of her plaid socks and got arrested protesting Margaret Thatcher's criminal incompetence. Maybe you'll get around to busty barmaids when you're into Magdalen."

"*If* I get into Magdalen," he said. He shrank from even talking about it, the school where his father had earned his master's in English literature. As a teenager, Arthur had done his homework under a framed poster of C. S. Lewis and had experimented with wearing tweed. Dark days. "And I'm not going if you're still in here."

"February," she said.

"February," he repeated—the date of her first parole hearing. In February she would know about early release, and not long after he would know if Oxford wanted him or not.

"What about your summer? Shank anyone in the prison yard?" Arthur asked.

"No, but I did start a book club! We voted on our first book yesterday."

"Oh yeah? What was the winner? *How to Win Friends and Influence Your Parole Board*? *How to Escape in Ten Easy Lessons*?"

"I suggested *Capitalist Patriarchy and the Case for Socialist Feminism*—"

"Bet that racked up the votes."

"—but I was shot down in favor of Jackie Collins. *Hollywood Wives*. Which is fine. I can work with that. It's still an opportunity to talk about the way the culture strips women of their personhood. It's right there in the title—women defined by their marriages instead of their ideas."

"You think that's why they want to read Jackie Collins?"

"Naw. They want to read it 'cause it's the smuttiest book in the prison library." She lowered her voice to a mock whisper. "There's three copies going around and they all smell like countach."

"Shit," Arthur said. "That reminds me, though. I had my picture in the paper. They did a profile on some of the rare books in the school library and they quoted me." In his final year at Rackham College, Arthur had been made the senior student librarian and tasked with making a digital inventory of the books in the rare collection—copying them to big floppy disks in the library's new computer. It was the card catalog of the future and a good reason for *The Podomaquassy Record* to do a fluff piece about the most peculiar items held in the special collection: a letter from Walt Whitman, an early typed draft of *Our Town*, and, of course, the Enoch Crane journal. No way anyone was going to do an article about the Special Collection at Rackham College without talking about Enoch Crane.

Arthur sat up and patted his pockets—then sat back down. "Shit," he said again. "I musta left it in the car."

"I just think it's great one of us got in the paper and it wasn't in the police blotter," she said. "I'm so proud of my little boy."

Someone cleared their throat. Arthur looked back and saw Jayne Nighswander standing behind him, her sister at her side. Jayne had a hand on the nape of Tana's neck in what was either a gesture of comfort or a way to keep her pinned.

"'Scuse me. Dr. Oakes, isn't it? Am I correct in saying you are a sort of political prisoner here? You were *convicted* for your *convictions*, so to speak." She laughed at this fine bit of wordplay.

"I was convicted for trespassing and damaging federal property."

"And manslaughter."

Erin shifted her gaze from Jayne to Tana and back. Tana's face was once again hidden behind her lank strands of hair. Ronnie Volpe and Tana's mother watched from the next table over. The eldest Nighswander was a tiny woman with lean, haggard features and hair that was some colorless hue between blond and gray.

"A man died, yes," Erin said. "Although we came unarmed, and in a spirit of nonviolence, there was an accident. A security guard lost control of his weapon and was shot."

"And you stuck around?"

"To put pressure on the wound."

"And he died anyway, huh? You ever think you woulda been better off if you just legged it?"

"Sometimes. But then I would've been in a different kind of prison. A mental one."

Jayne wagged a finger at her. "Uh-huh. Now we're getting to it. You didn't mean for anyone to die. But you made a choice to break into federal property and someone did."

"Sorry," Arthur said. "But if it's all right with you, my mom and I are trying to have a quiet visit."

Jayne paid him no mind. She went on, "You were a priest of some kind, weren'tcha? Or was you a professor?"

"I taught practical ethics and theology at Dartmouth. I'm also a pastor with the Episcopalian Church."

"They don't defrock you for manslaughter?"

"They haven't got around to it yet." Arthur's mother narrowed her eyes and tried a smile on Tana. "Are you all right, honey? I love your Biko sweatshirt. I have one just like it."

"That *is* your sweatshirt," Arthur said, but it was like he was talking to himself; no one even glanced at him.

"She's fine," Jayne said. "So you've done enough ethical professorin' to help us puzzle something out. You set out to do a good thing, only there's a freak accident in the process of breakin' and enterin' and some poor fella eats it. You didn't want it. But you're responsible for it, all the same."

"I think that's true. When you choose a course of action, you accept the consequences—those you intended and those you didn't."

"There you go," Jayne said, lowering her head to look into Tana's face. "See? Voice of educated reason, right there."

Tana lifted her chin and glared at Erin with wet, reddened eyes.

"Screw this," she said. "Screw her and screw you. I'm going to the car."

She twitched out of her sister's grip and started toward the exit. Her path took her past her mother, and as she walked by, the elder Nighswander kicked Tana behind her left knee.

Her leg folded and Tana dropped behind the table. There was a guard a few yards away, but he was staring at the TV hanging from a bracket in one corner of the room.

"You burned up my shit, you fuckin' flake," Tana's mother yelled, rising from her chair. "An' Imma have it back, every cent. I don't care if Jayne gotta rent you out to hobos for ten bucks a pop." She had a paper cup of coffee in one hand and she threw it at her daughter's head. "Drink up, you thirsty bitch."

Arthur didn't remember coming to his feet. He was, simply, suddenly, between them. It was the kind of leap in time one often made in dreams, but it was the first time he could ever recall it happening in waking life.

He had his back to Tana's mother, to help Tana off the floor. He sensed Mama Nighswander rising from her chair, and he held one hand out behind him, palm raised, like an officer trying to stop traffic. He meant no harm by it. He reached with his other hand to take Tana by the elbow.

"Fuck off me," Tana hissed, and pushed him away.

The sudden motion rocked him backward, off balance, and he slammed the heel of his extended hand into Mama Nighswander's face. The impact snapped the older woman's head back. Her calves struck the chair behind her and she toppled. The chairs were bolted to the floor, same as the table, and had no give. She crashed across it and went sprawling.

"My node!" she cried, blood spouting from her small, hard, bony nose . . . a nose that looked suddenly, disturbingly crooked. "You mudderfugger!"

The elder Nighswander sprang to her feet and lunged, but before she could get her hands on Arthur's neck, a prison guard caught her in both arms and lifted her right off the floor. Jayne shouldered Arthur aside, sinking her fingers into Tana's upper arm. Jayne turned a furious glare upon Arthur. "The fuck you think you're doing, sticking your oar in?"

The guard was retreating with Mama Nighswander in his arms while she kicked her legs helplessly in the air. Two more prison guards smacked through the doors at the back of the room. One of them caught Mama Nighswander by the thrashing feet, and then they were carrying her out like a pair of movers with a rolled-up rug. The third guard unsheathed a nightstick and began to strike it against an iron radiator.

"Inmates, line up against the far wall! Do it now! Visiting's over. Visitors, move to the exits."

Mama Nighswander writhed and arced her hips, bucking in the arms of her captors. She howled—a scream of fury that was cut off as they carried her out. Arthur's own mother moved slowly toward the far wall with the other inmates. She kissed her fingertip and pointed at him, smiling with a kind of tired resignation.

Jayne Nighswander was cursing and marching her sister across the room. Ronnie tossed Arthur a wink before he followed them out. "You got some touch with the ladies, pardner. At my absolute best, I never pissed off more'n two at a time. I think you just collected the whole set."

Arthur was another forty minutes in the waiting room, filling out an incident report. He looked for the Nighswanders when he left, with a touch of anxiety, but they were long gone.

He was halfway home before he realized Tana Nighswander still had his Biko hoodie. And as for the article he had wanted to show his mother, the one about the Brooks Library at school, it was a week before he had cause to think of it again.

THREE

Van McBride was surrounded.

Arthur went looking for him in Arundel Hall and found him at one of the cafeteria tables, sitting across from Donna McBride and Allie Shiner . . . a girl so beautiful, Arthur believed it was unsafe to look at her directly. People suddenly got clumsy around Allie—Arthur had seen it happen. It happened to Van all the time. Once, Van had glanced at Allie before trying to leave a room, missed the door, smashed into the doorframe headfirst, and had to go to the student infirmary for a cold compress.

Donna wasn't too shabby herself, though Arthur couldn't imagine making out with her. She looked too much like Van. She was three minutes older than her twin brother and could easily be mistaken for him in low light. Only last spring, one of Donna's boyfriends had sat down next to Van in the gloom of the student union and slipped a hand onto his thigh before realizing he was fondling the wrong McBride. "Carry on, son," Van told him. "This is the most action I've had in months."

Perhaps a dozen undergrads were gathered around Allie and the McBride twins. Donna had half a deck of cards in front of her and Van had the other half, like they were playing a game of War. Arthur watched as Donna lifted the top card from her deck and peered down at it, keeping it hidden from her brother. They locked eyes.

"Three of spades," Van said.

Donna flipped the card onto the table, face up, so everyone could see the three of spades. There were whoops and yells of satisfaction.

Van lifted a card off his own deck and gave it a cursory look.

"Black. It's black," Donna said. "I'm picturing a cruel son of a bitch, someone used to being served. A king? The king of clubs?"

"Oh, listen to this baloney," said Allie.

Van dumped the king of clubs face up on the table.

Donna hardly glanced at her next card before Van shook his head and muttered, "Four of diamonds."

Donna tossed it in the air. A pimply freshman caught it and showed the other onlookers: four of diamonds.

"Can you read *my* mind?" asked the student on Arthur's left. Arthur looked around and saw he was standing next to a fellow senior, name of Colin Wren. Colin slid a card off Van's deck and looked at it.

"No. It only works with Van. It's a twin thing."

"Now you gonna tell them how we've been twins before," Van drawled.

Donna nodded. "That's right."

"Before?" Someone in the audience cackled. "Before what?"

"Before this life. We were siblings in Salem. They killed us because we loved the devil." Donna reported this as a matter of simple fact.

"Ugh," groaned a girl at one corner of the table. "*So* creepy. People act like the devil's some big joke. They don't ever think it could happen to them."

"Don't ever think *what* could happen to them?" asked Colin.

"Damnation," the girl said. She plucked at a gold cross around her neck. "They think the devil is just a story. But there's a preschool in California where the teachers made all the kids have sex with each other and then stab a goat. Satan is coming back in a big way."

Van said, "So are bell-bottoms. Just goes to show, no great evil is ever truly laid to rest."

The girl wrinkled her nose, shook her head, and took off.

"You've got a lot going on," Colin said. "Twin telepathy and reincarnation, with a sprig of Satan worship to add flavor. I like it."

Colin had the angular build of a coffin, broad shoulders and narrow hips. His bald scalp gleamed beneath the dining hall's chandeliers. Arthur had seen Colin at school fundraisers, in the company of his grandfather, a professor emeritus in psychology, a bright-eyed old man who wore bow ties and was never without a pocket square in his double-breasted coat. Colin lived with his grandfather on a vast estate just off campus, called The Briars, on the headland. Arthur found Colin vaguely intimidating, more like a professor himself than a student.

"How long have you been able to read each other's minds?" Colin asked.

"Since we were little," Donna said. "We had our own language too. Do you remember, Van? Di biyah?"

"Di kisa? Manjay mwen," Van replied.

Arthur looked away. Maybe that sounded like a secret twin language to everyone else, but it sounded like a Louisiana Creole to him, and the McBrides were from Pensacola.

Colin said, "I *love* this stuff. I have a lot of theories. Have you ever seen Zener cards? My grandfather has a deck."

"What's a Zener deck?" Donna asked.

"It's a way to test for the presence of psychic potential. You should come by my place sometime. I'd be interested to measure the full extent of your power under controlled conditions."

"Can I come?" Arthur asked. "I'd like to see you measure the full extent of Van's power."

"It's already been measured," Van said. "Tenth grade, me 'n' the boys passed a ruler around the locker room. Seven lousy inches. Proof there may be a devil—but there sure isn't a God."

FOUR

In their third year at Rackham College, Arthur and Van had moved off campus and into a Colonial Revival, half a mile from school. At some point in the seventies the house had been painted an unnatural shade of aqua green that looked like it should glow in the dark and had been divided into a pair of student apartments, one unit upstairs, one down. Three girls had the place above them. Early in the semester the girls had partied hard, blasting Frankie Goes to Hollywood loud enough to shake the windows, jumping off the furniture while they screamed along. But by late September, the upstairs apartment exuded an air of exhaustion and abandonment. One of the girls had tumbled out of a window at a campus rave, broken her back, and been sent home. Another was dating a boy attending the University of Maine and was never around anymore. The third was majoring in marine biology and spent three days of every four on a boat. Van said he missed them, that it was nice having loud, happy, probably horny girls nearby; it stimulated the imagination and cheered the heart.

Arthur didn't mind the new stillness, though, and when the phone rang he was taking advantage of the quiet to solve some riddles in Old English. He loved it, had always loved it, the way an ancient word felt in the brain, in the mouth. *Heartache* was an okay word but *bitre breostcaere*—bitter breast-care—caught at something else, something more deeply felt, from a time when people lived in their bodies, not in their heads. Sometimes, when he had been reading Old English for a while, he found himself *thinking* in it. He might've been a Dorset monk copying out a manuscript before vespers.

He reached for the phone, mounted on the wall above the kitchen table, and answered on the second ring. A girl with a stiff Yankee accent spoke without preamble. "You want this hoodie back?"

He needed a moment to figure out who he was talking to and what they were talking about. "Biko?"

"I know who he is. Like from the Peter Gabriel song. I'm not stupid just because I'm a townie."

"I never said—sorry. What's your name again?"

"Tana Nighswander. You know where to find Shut-Up-And-Eat-It? It's on the corner of McDonald and Lang. Come by around seven, when I finish my shift. You can grab it then."

"I guess I can do that."

"You guess," she said, with an inexplicable contempt. "If you didn't lend me your sweatshirt, I wouldn't'a got in to see my mother. I can't thank you enough. Tell you what, though. Dinner's on me tonight." She made it sound like a threat.

Shut-Up-And-Eat-It was a mile away, in Gogan, the next town over, but the late afternoon was so pleasant—*splendid* was the word that came to mind—Arthur decided to leave the Christmobile in the driveway and walk it. Those last days of September lingered with one foot in summer and the other in autumn. In the early evening, the sunlight spilled across the face of the earth in a warm, golden haze. The leaves were splashed with streaks of autumnal color and the air was as crisp and sweet as a bite from a fresh-picked apple.

Arthur found Shut-Up-And-Eat-It in a strip mall between a check-cashing place and a liquor store. He pushed through a Plexiglas door and into a long room, unromantically lit by fluorescent lights, pizzas turning on a stack of platters under heat lamps. Ms. Pac-Man squawked against one wall. Tana Nighswander was on the till.

"Can I get a steak bomb, a large Coke, and a lightly worn Biko sweatshirt?" he asked.

He thought it was a pretty smooth line—he had practiced it on the walk over—but she just stoically punched in his order. "I'm off in fifteen. Your hoodie's in the car, out back. Grab it now if you want."

He hung out long enough to collect his sandwich—when he offered a ten-dollar bill she shook her head—then followed a dimly lit hallway into the back, past a bathroom and a dark storeroom. He punched through a fire door and into the gravel parking lot out back.

Arthur hadn't figured on company and was surprised to see Ronnie and Tana's older sister, Jayne, hanging out by a Ford Ranchero. Arthur recognized it at once from Black Cricket. NO FREE RIDES—GAS, GRASS, OR ASS. Ronnie had a cigarette between his lips and his head cocked back to blow smoke into the night. Jayne wore the Biko hoodie unzipped over a clinging white tank top. She sat on the hood with a sweating bottle of beer between her thighs.

The two of them were passing Polaroids back and forth and it took a moment for them to acknowledge him.

"Oh hey! It's Arthur Oakes! How they hangin'?" Ronnie asked him.

That surprised Arthur—he hadn't given his full name to any of them. He still wasn't sure how Tana had known who to call. He nodded at Jayne. "Nice sweatshirt."

"Yeah, it's growing on me," she said.

Arthur didn't care if it was growing on her. He was more worried about what might be growing on *it*.

He knew they were waiting for him to ask what they were looking at and he didn't feel like playing along. He didn't feel like asking for the sweatshirt either. Asking for anything felt as if he would be placing himself at their mercy. His appetite had gone, but he unwrapped his sandwich and had a bite anyway.

Jayne said, "Hey, man, wanna see a hot piece of ass? Check it out."

She frisbeed a Polaroid at him. He clapped it to his chest with one hand. His mouth was caked and dry, even before he looked at it.

It was a poorly lit shot. He was looking at a woman's round rear end in a pair of white cotton panties. Someone held the handle of a spoon into the frame, just barely poking one buttock with the tip. That end of the spoon had been scraped and burned to a blackened point. Arthur's single bite of sandwich sat in his stomach, a gluey, indigestible lump of paste.

"Your mom got a sweet little can, huh?" Jayne asked. "I know she's a woman of the cloth, but you see a rump like that, hard not to dwell on sinful thoughts."

He wanted to throw it back at her. Instead, he stood there, holding the photo and staring stupidly at Ronnie and Jayne.

"Maybe you don't think that's really her. I guess I'd be worried about you if you could recognize your mom from a glance at her ass. Here. You can see her face in this one."

She set her bottle of Coors aside and slid off the hood to offer him another Polaroid. He took one corner of it. She held on to the other while he peered down at it.

In this photograph, his mother was on her side, eyes shut, head crushed into her thin pillow. Someone's hand extended into the shot, holding the spoon-handle shiv. The tip was directly below her right eyeball.

Jayne snapped the Polaroid away from him. Arthur stared at her, feeling hot in the face, as if he had been slapped.

Ronnie said, "Whoo! He angry now. Boy! Look at him."

"He ain't angry. He gonna cry," Jayne said. "That right, Artie? You gonna cry?"

"You're making a big fucking mistake," he said, but the mistake was his, speaking at all. His voice came out in such a thin, strangled squeak that Jayne and Ronnie disintegrated into laughter. Jayne laughed so hard she lost her balance and had to steady herself against the hood of the Ranchero.

She wiped her streaming eyes on the sleeve of his Biko sweatshirt. "Oh, Artie. That's funny. That's *so* funny."

"If your mother goes anywhere near my mom—" Arthur began, but Jayne cut him off.

"No fear of that. My mother caught a month in solitary 'cause you had to pull your white knight act. She's got lights shining on her twenty-four hours a day. She takes a shit, someone's watching her through a camera." Jayne gestured with the Polaroid. "This ain't *my* mother with the knife. Daphne Nighswander hasn't gone anywhere near your mom and doesn't need to. See, unlike *your* mother, Daphne's got *friends*. *My* mother isn't a condescending college bitch, thinks she smarter than everyone else. My mother doesn't start book clubs. She was doin' her time and you made sure she can kiss her first shot at parole goodbye. But it's all right! We ain't the kind of people to hold a grudge. You know what my mother says? Every problem is an opportunity."

"Hey," Ronnie said. "You going to eat that?" He pointed at Arthur's steak bomb.

Arthur shook his head, afraid to speak, afraid he might start making Alvin and the Chipmunk noises again. Ronnie eased the cheesesteak out of his hands.

"Deep breaths, Artie," Jayne said. "No one's hurt your mommy. She don't know a thing about this and she don't need to. But you want her to cruise through the rest of her days inside, you gotta work with us."

She pushed her hand into one pocket of the Biko hoodie and produced a folded sheet of newsprint. She unfolded it and narrowed her eyes to read.

"'The future comes to Rackham College,'" she read, and Arthur's dread intensified into something like horror. She turned the sheet of newspaper around so he could see the photo that accompanied the piece. Mr. Meckfessel, the head librarian of the Brooks Library, had one hand on the monitor of their new IBM, patting it like it was the head of a small and obedient child. Several of the student librarians stood behind him, smiling for the camera. Arthur was the most prominent of them, waiting with arms crossed, chin lifted, hint of a smile, looking every inch the nerd in his Mister Rogers sweater. "Were you gonna show your momma how you got your face in the paper? That's cute. Says here you're the head student librarian. Says here you got *access* to what you call a special collection, because you're doing an *in*-ven-tory, putting it all in a computer. Is it true they got a first edition of *Huckleberry Finn* in that room? How much is something like that worth, anyway?"

"I don't know," Arthur said. His insides felt cramped and sick. "Probably not much. There's a lot of them out there."

Jayne nodded, in a resigned sort of way, then stepped up, put her hand on his forehead, and shoved. His skull rapped against the bricks behind him. He dropped his bottle of Coke. It hit the ground and foamed.

"Try six *grand*, shit for brains," Jayne said. "Don't play games with me. I can get a crack addict to face-fuck your mother with a shiv while a guard keeps watch to make sure no one interrupts them. You want her to come home fucking *blind*?"

"That's a lie," Arthur said, but his voice came out pitched barely above a whisper.

"Which part don't you believe? About the crack addict or about the guard? Who do you think handed me these Polaroids? There's plenty of men in blue, happy to make a couple bucks on the side and watch some crazy bitches rip each other up. Prison guard pay is even worse than cop pay, and I got a couple cops in my employ too, bitch. There's officers come in to Shut-Up-And-Eat-It for a slice of pizza, a large Coke, and two hundred bucks under the table so we can run weed and PCP through this place."

The rear door to Shut-Up-And-Eat-It swung open, and Tana came out. She cast a disinterested look at Arthur as she went by.

"My shift's done," she said. "Can we go? I got shit to do."

Jayne caught her by one arm and whirled her around to face Arthur. "Soon."

Tana didn't look at Arthur, but Jayne held her arm and kept her standing there. "Hey, Artie, I get you're angry. You want to wallop someone, you can give my sis a few lumps. If it wasn't for her, we wouldn't bother you. This twerp here saw police pulling up in front a the house four weeks ago—state police, not our friendly local guys—and jammed sixty grand of rocket fuel into the woodstove."

"Rocket fuel?" Arthur asked. Arthur could read Old English, Welsh, and some Irish, but Jayne was speaking a language he didn't know.

"Angel dust. PCP. Sixty grand *at least*. Might've been able to stretch it to three times that once it was cut. Our momma was pretty steamed, I'll tell you." Jayne peered down at the article Arthur had clipped from *The Podomaquassy Record*. "What about a letter from Walter Whitman? He famous, right?"

"I can't," he said.

"I think you can. It's not like this stuff is locked up in a vault. And besides. It says right here in the article, you got *access*." She said this last word with tremendous relish, as if it had erotic connotations.

"But you can't even sell something like the Whitman letter. Buyers don't buy rare and valuable literary goods unless they know where they came from. It's called provenance."

"Not the *Huck Finn*," Ronnie said, around a mouthful of cheesesteak. "First editions? Lotta those on the market. The Walt Shitman, that might be harder to move, but I know an old lady in Boston, she says she can—"

"Hey, Ronnie," Jayne said. "Put another bite of that sandwich in your mouth and shut the fuck up."

Ronnie waved one hand in a lazy apology.

Jayne said, "We can move whatever you get us. And we aren't greedy. We need to make things right with a guy and he's going to give us the time we need to raise the money. Soon as he's got sixty large, your mom is off the hook."

"You want me to steal . . . sixty *thousand* dollars of rare books from the Brooks Library?" he asked. His lungs tingled with panic. "I can't do that. Someone will catch me."

"No one's going to catch you. No one is even going to notice. It's like when they bury someone with their jewels and rings and shit. Why do they do that anyhow? It can't do anyone any good under the dirt. The books on this list? They're buried in the library. That's the *real* crime. Money sitting on the shelves, collecting dust. Get something by this weekend. Something good. Tana will pop by your place on Sunday afternoon, take whatever you collect off your hands. Get her the right books, we could probably settle up by Christmas." Jayne patted her sister on the head, then spun her and shoved her toward the car. Tana opened the passenger door of the Ranchero, folded the seat forward, and scrambled into the rear without a look back. Jayne stood holding the open door. "Hey! You know how your mom has her own book club, sharing the riches of literature with dangerous reprobates? You'll be doing the same.

This will be like *your* book club—you'll be enriching *us* with every pick. It's not a crime! It's a public service."

Ronnie had polished off the sandwich. He drained the last of his bottle of beer and slung the empty at a streetlamp. It was an incongruous bit of street furniture, a lamp that looked like it belonged in the London of Sherlock Holmes, not next to a dumpster behind a strip mall. The bottle hit with a satisfying crunch.

Ronnie stretched and looked through the windshield at the girls waiting in the Ranchero. He glanced back at Arthur with a sly grin and shook his head. "Well, I got to take the ladies home. Don't look too blue, Artie. Things could be worse. You could hafta live with them."

The Ranchero peeled out so hard, the tires threw rocks. A couple of pebbles struck the wall around Arthur. One stung his shin. He didn't flinch, didn't know he had been hurt until he took off his shoes later and found one sock soaked in blood.

Insult to injury: it didn't cross his mind until the next morning that Jayne Nighswander had kept his hoodie.

FIVE

For most of the next thirty-six hours, Arthur felt stunned, as if he had a fever. Everything he ate smelled wrong and tasted spoiled. He sat in hour-long lectures and walked out having heard nothing, learned nothing; he could not have said what was discussed.

Arthur had a shift at the library on Wednesday but begged off, pleading sickness. It wasn't much of a lie. His stomach knotted up on him whenever he imagined walking into the vast, marble-floored reception, footsteps echoing off the domed ceiling.

His next rotation, though, was the Friday one-to-seven slot, and he didn't think he could avoid the place any longer. When he entered the Brooks Library through the battered twenty-foot-high bronze doors, he paused and cast a look in the direction of the Special Collection.

To reach the Special Collection, one had to pass behind the walnut counter at the far end of reception and climb a twisting wrought-iron staircase to a Juliet balcony one floor above. Up there on the second floor, a whole wall of leaded glass panes looked into the room itself, the glass old and melty, so anyone moving around behind it looked like a figure swimming beneath rippling water.

The room on the other side was a large, rectangular space with a blue slate floor and loophole windows, as if archers might be required to repel the illiterate hordes. The walls were lined with valuable books . . . although the most irreplaceable volumes were locked in a barred cabinet. These included Rackham College's most notorious possession, the memoirs of Enoch Crane, who had been executed in New Hampshire "for trafficking with the devyll" in 1701. At Crane's request, the book had been bound in his own tanned and dried skin after he was hanged. There were only five other volumes encased in human hide in all of New England: two at Harvard, one in the Boston Athenaeum, one at Dartmouth, one at UMO. Arthur, who loved a good word when he came across one—he chewed on them like caramels—even knew the formal term for such books, *anthropodermic bibliopegy*, language both scientific and somehow vaguely dirty, as if it described a perversion instead of an object.

In the first weeks of term, he had spent a fair amount of time alone in the Special Collection, wearing white cotton gloves and dusting down the books, inspecting them for silverfish, book lice, and mold. Anything in bad shape was marked for repair and restoration. He had the index to the complete collection in a blue binder and as senior student librarian had earned the glamorous job of copying everything into the new IBM DOS computer, with updated notes on the condition of each volume. *The Podomaquassy Record* had made the work sound like something out of *WarGames*, akin to hacking the Pentagon. In fact, it was a task only slightly more rewarding than cleaning a floor with a toothbrush.

He had no intention of entering the Special Collection today, didn't want to be anywhere near the valuable old books. He wanted to keep them safe from him, felt he was a far greater threat than bugs or mildew. Arthur checked himself in and spent an hour pushing a cart around, returning books to their proper places on the shelves. While he was wandering the aisles, he located a hardcover copy of *The Killer Angels* by Michael Shaara, one of three on the shelf. He checked, confirmed it was the second printing with the battlefield maps on the endpapers, and put it on the cart. In another ten minutes he had collected a mint first of Katherine Anne Porter's *Collected Stories* and a slightly battered first of Percy's *The Moviegoer*. He figured altogether it was five hundred dollars' worth of books. Better still, there were multiple copies of everything he intended to steal. The liberated editions might not be noticed for years.

When he was back behind the checkout counter, he used an X-Acto knife to peel the magnetic strips out of the spines of the books he had selected. He packed them into his school backpack and went on with his duties. By six in the evening, he had the library almost to himself, most of the students in the cafeteria. At the end of his shift, Arthur slipped away to Periodicals, to do a little homework that had nothing to do with his classes.

The microfiche machines—big blocks of brushed steel and glass—were in a darkened alcove. He collected half a dozen reels containing every issue of the *Portland Press Herald* from 1987 to 1989 and sat down with them. His mother had been in prison for three years, but he had not come across the Nighswanders until this September. That suggested Daphne Nighswander had only been locked up there a few months.

Arthur threaded the first reel, May–June 1989, and twisted the dial. History whirred past, like the windows of a brightly lit train flickering by at night. Grainy black-and-white photographs: George Bush, Manuel Noriega, Danny DeVito, Arnold Schwarzenegger. *Coke—you can't beat the feeling. Army—be all you can be. Sega Genesis—your world will never be the same.*

He was prepared to spend an hour scanning articles, but he had only been blurring through the pages for a minute when he got his first hit, in the back pages of the *Herald*'s June 11 issue.

POSTAL ASSAILANT RECEIVES MAX SENTENCE

Augusta, ME.—The sentencing hearing was scheduled to begin at 2PM. It took less than ten minutes for Justice Levon Skelton to make his decision, and sentence Daphne Nighswander to serve not less than ten years, for firing a 9mm pistol into the leg of postman Albert Frown on March 15. Additional state charges are pending in the matter of the nearly twelve-hour stand-off with law enforcement that followed the shooting . . .

Arthur found the tape for March–April. The reels shrilled, spinning forward to March 16. He read the first report—it was a front-page story, but light on details—then the more fully fleshed-out piece that followed the day after.

Daphne Nighswander had been in her kitchen, listening to the radio and sorting a pound of PCP into individual plastic baggies—mixing it with baking powder as she went along—when postal officer Albert Frown reached her door. Frown's hands were full with a bulky package and the doorbell hadn't worked for at least two years. So instead of knocking, he thumped at it with his knee. Frown was a new hire and it was his first time delivering to houses on Reddy Lane in Gogan. And he was Black.

Daphne's Massachusetts supplier had recently exchanged words—and gunfire—with the Intervale Posse, the gang that moved most of the hard drugs in the Boston area, and that aimed to control the entire flow of angel dust in New England. Daphne's connection had cautioned her to watch out for "a slick n***** who would flash a badge to get inside her house and then lay waste to her hillbilly ass." Nighswander looked at a twenty-three-year-old Black man in a blue uniform, holding a long brown package in both arms, and saw an Intervale Posse shooter with a shotgun in a box. She aimed her 9mm at Albert Frown's head, missed, and put three bullets into his knee, shin, and ankle instead.

She held the police off for most of the day, promising to execute the first Barney Fife motherf***** through the door. She didn't surrender until channel 5 announced the Powerball numbers that evening, at 9:30 p.m. She checked her tickets, determined she wasn't a winner, and came out with her hands up, saying it just wasn't her day.

Arthur was reading about the prospects for Albert Frown's recovery (good, although he'd probably always have the limp) when he heard Van's voice from behind him.

"You ever been to a house with a name before? Shit, it's not even a house. It's an *estate*."

Arthur started and swiveled around. Van was leaning in, narrowing his eyes to examine the screen of the microfiche machine. Arthur casually put his thumb down on the button to rewind the tape.

"What are you talking about?" he asked.

Van straightened up. "Colin Wren. Come on. The girls are outside. We're going over to his place. He wants to run some tests on

Donna and me, find out how psychic we are. You and Allie got to be there too."

"Why's that?" Arthur popped the microfiche cassette out of the machine. If he was going to talk to anyone about his predicament, it would be Van. But he wasn't ready yet. He was in a filthy mess and had some obscure dread of getting the grime on anyone else . . . maybe especially a friend. And then there was this: to discuss it would make it more real. The situation was already too real as it was.

"He said he needs two people without any psychic talent for a control group. I said you were the least talented person I know," Van told him.

"Can't argue with that. But why Allie? You have no idea the extent of her powers. For all you know, she's the female Uri Geller."

"Shit. That girl can't read minds. If she could read mine, she'd never talk to me again."

"Oh, Van," Arthur said. "She knows."

"Shit," Van said, and actually blushed.

SIX

Colin's house didn't have a yard—it had *grounds*. A fieldstone wall that was almost eight feet high surrounded the sprawling, wooded property. The briars that gave the house its name were piled up against the inside of that wall, black, thorny, and bare this late in the year. Arthur steered the Christmobile between the stone columns flanking the drive. A pair of wrought-iron dragons squatted atop them. Later, Arthur wondered if that was a coincidence.

For all that, the house was surprisingly modest: a two-story brick Federal-style building, barely large enough for a family of eight and a dozen servants. The slate roof was exactly the same icy gray-blue as the ocean, which was visible in glints through the trees behind the house.

They piled out, Arthur, Van, and the girls, and mounted the sort of granite steps one usually finds at the entrance of a nineteenth-century courthouse. Colin opened the front door before they could pound the big brass knocker. He was wearing a black turtleneck, tucked into his jeans, his head as sleek as a bullet.

Arthur craned his neck, taking in the white Doric columns holding up the roof of the portico and the great fan-shaped window above the front door, which looked like it might be Tiffany. "Does your granddad have a lot of money?" he asked. A tactless thing to say, and he knew it the moment it was out of his mouth.

Colin wasn't bothered. "Enough is as good as a feast," he said, and let them into the lobby.

That was what it felt like, not a front room, but a lobby. The floor was done in large, rough flagstones. A grand staircase of darkest mahogany wound upstairs to a gallery above.

"What did your granddad do?" Donna asked.

"He wrote a book that's never been out of print," Colin said, "but I don't know that he made a lot of money on it."

"What about?" Arthur asked.

"The art of brainwashing," Colin said.

"How to resist it?"

"No," Colin said. "How to apply it. He was a psychologist for the military during Vietnam. He literally wrote the textbook on how to obliterate someone psychologically."

They followed Colin Wren into a kitchen large enough to serve a good-size restaurant. A woman in her mid-forties was unloading an industrial-size dishwasher. A girl sat at the center island, bent over a mess of books and papers. Gwen Underfoot—Arthur didn't know her name then—wore a chambray shirt over a V-neck tee, and a pair of enormous glasses with black plastic frames. Arthur figured her for a high school kid. Her unlaced Dr. J Converse high-tops looked old enough to be in high school themselves. She had a precalculus textbook open in front of her, but she had put her homework aside to pick at a crossword.

Colin greeted the woman at the stove, who had to be the girl's mother. She was built the same, if twenty pounds heavier and twenty years older, with a matching pair of specs on the end of her nose. She kissed Colin on the cheek as if she was *his* mother, put the kettle on, and asked if anyone wanted tea or hot chocolate.

"Who's this, Colin?" asked the girl, without looking up from her puzzle. "Your Bible study group?"

"Psychics, Gwen," Colin said. "Donna and Van here can read each other's minds."

"Try not to get ectoplasm all over the house, 'cause if you do, you'll have to clean it up yourself. I'm driving Mom home as soon as the spice cake is out of the oven." So her mother was the help and Gwen was at least old enough to drive, which made Arthur feel a little better about admiring the fine line of her neck, and the way she wiggled her bottom getting comfortable on her stool. Even her smudgy cheap glasses were adorable—he wanted to pull them off her face and wipe 'em clean on his shirttail.

Arthur got as far as the door to the hallway, then looked back at Gwen and said, "Strip."

She blinked at him. "Never on a first date, pal."

"No." He shook his head. "Twelve down. Five letters? 'Something funny on Sunday.' The answer is 'strip.' You know, like *Garfield*."

"Oh!" she said, and filled it in. "Thanks."

"Anytime," he said, and got out of there.

One wall of the library was lined with cherry bookcases that had to be twelve feet high. The opposite wall was a bank of French windows looking out onto the stony headland and the chilly blue of the bay, creaming with whitecaps. The only break in the French windows was a stone hearth. A curious upright piano stood against the wall to the right of the door; a panel was open above the keys to show a spool of paper, fed through studded iron drums, like the insides of the world's biggest music box. The wall above the piano was crowded with black shadow boxes, two or three butterflies mounted in each one. Butterflies with wings like beaten bronze, butterflies with iridescent wings of silver and chrome.

Unsure where to plant himself, Arthur settled on the piano bench, beneath that beautifully displayed butterfly holocaust. His mental calculations made him the brokest person in the room. Allie Shiner's father had played for the Dallas Cowboys and spent ten years in Congress before becoming some kind of lobbyist; he owned a summer house in Kennebunkport, a town house in DC, and a mansion in Houston. The McBrides came from money too—a bit of it, anyway. Their father owned a TV station and a few regional newspapers in the Deep South.

One end of the library was occupied by a massive desk made of cherry, with a leather surface. Donna wandered behind it to inspect a tall wooden case with glass doors. Arthur thought the items on display within were probably rare, likely valuable, and certainly not for touching. But Donna was the sort of person who thought it was better to ask forgiveness than permission—although, come to think of it, she rarely bothered to ask for either. She threw open the doors, removed a helmet, and clapped it on her head. It was a rust-spotted olive with a red star in the center. She dug around in the cabinet some more and produced a ball-peen hammer with a cork handle. Donna gave it an experimental slash through the air. "Which army did you say your granddad fought for?" Donna abruptly went ramrod stiff, clapped her heels together, and threw the Nazi salute. Her other hand pressed the hammer to her breast as if it were an army rifle. "Sieg Fail!"

"That's not Nazi, it's Russian. It belonged to Wolf Messing, Stalin's personal seer. Although he may never have worn it. The hammer was the murder weapon at the Los Feliz murder house. It's famously—and violently—haunted. The house, not the hammer. I think my granddad was hoping it would have a little malevolent sparkle on it but, alas, nothing."

Donna grimaced and set the hammer back in the cabinet.

"What the hell is all this stuff?" she asked, bending to explore the lower shelves.

"My grandfather's Cabinet of Curiosities. He's always on the hunt for haunted dolls and UFO photos, stuff like that. He's sort of a weird shit enthusiast, after years of being a professor of weird shit and researching weird shit for the government."

"How'd you wind up living with your granddad, anyway?" Van asked.

Colin said, "My mother was going to leave my father, and made the mistake of telling him while they were in the Porsche. So he drove them off a cliff at a hundred and ten miles an hour. Or at least that's the theory. Obviously, no one can know for certain. Maybe he was swatting at a mosquito and lost control."

"Jesus," Van said. "I'm so sorry. That's fucking awful."

Colin nodded. "The Porsche was a classic."

Donna picked up a reel of film in its battered can. She squinted to read the faded label. "Visit. From. Corporal. Hondo." She glanced up. "This your granddaddy's gay porn, Colin?"

Colin said, mildly, "My grandfather *is* a homosexual, in fact." That produced a moment of startled silence. Colin pointed to the reel and went on: "That's film from one of the later Philip Experiments, the ones conducted by the military, here in America. Inspired by the work Whitton and Owen were doing in Canada."

"What's a Philip Experiment?" Allie asked.

"A team of researchers in Toronto in the 1970s got together to invent a ghost. They made up a character, Philip Aylesford, invented a whole made-up history for him, full of intentional errors and rubbish. Then they tried to contact him with a séance. Only it worked. Philip could make the table levitate. He could dim the lights, slam the shutters on the windows, drop the temperature by ten, twenty degrees. This is all true—look it up. Never debunked. My granddad repeated the experiments with his research group in Langley. They dreamt up a fun-loving ghost of their own named Corporal Elwood Hondo."

"What'd Hondo do?"

"It's on the film. We should watch it sometime."

While they were talking about ghosts, Arthur was poking at the piano. It had an iron lever that moved back and forth between OFF and PLAY and another for TEMPO. Arthur prodded the lever and without warning the piano keys began to crash, producing a chipper, maniacal sonata. He gave a choked cry and almost fell off the bench. The keys went on rising and falling for another moment or two, the sound steadily dwindling, as if the coked-up poltergeist was beginning to wipe out, slide away into a coma.

"He's here!" shouted Van, and he dived behind the desk, grabbing Allie and hauling her down with him. "Hondo is among us!" Allie shrieked, but she didn't sound scared—closer to delighted.

"That's a player piano," Colin said. "You pump the pedals to keep it playing. There are different scrolls for it, if you don't care for Mozart. I think Granddad even has some boogie-woogie." By now, Colin had moved behind a games table with a green felt surface that wouldn't have looked out of place in a European casino. He had a deck of cards and was shuffling them with one hand in a tricksy sort of way. "Come on, let's begin. If we all focus, we ought to be able to prove the existence of ESP by the time the spice cake is out of the oven."

Donna and Van settled at opposite ends of the games table and tried to read each other's minds. The Zener deck had symbols on the cards: a square, a circle, a star, some wiggly lines, a plus sign. Van would draw one and stare intently at it and Donna would tell him what she thought it was, while Colin kept a score of hits and misses on a notepad.

At first Donna and Van didn't have it. Allie stood behind Donna, massaging her shoulders. "It's okay. Some days Satan is with you and some days he isn't."

"Triangle," Donna said.

"There are no triangles in this deck, bitch," Van said wearily.

Donna put on a pair of mirrored shades and tapped one temple. "Headache. I wouldn't be surprised if I get a nosebleed. Telepathy is always giving people with psychic powers nosebleeds. A well-known fact established by many, many movies."

Donna took her turn drawing the cards and, after a couple misses, the twins went on a run, ten in a row.

"There it is," Colin said. "You're finding it. Van, do you feel like you're inside your sister's head . . . or is it more like she's pushing her thoughts into *yours*?"

"Or—and I'm just throwing this out there," Arthur said, "does it feel like you're seeing the cards reflected in Donna's sunglasses?"

Van reached across the table, grabbed the deck of cards, and threw them at Arthur.

Colin wasn't fazed. "Ah, of course. It's obvious now that Arthur points it out. But you had *something* going on that day in the cafeteria."

"Sure," Arthur said. "A better way to cheat. Hey, Van? How do you say 'We're full of shit' in your secret twin language? The one that sounds a lot like Louisiana Creole?"

"Kass twa," Van said.

"This is disappointing," Colin said, not sounding disappointed at all. "I was hoping to have scientific proof of ESP by now."

"I'll try the Zener deck," Arthur said. He hardly knew himself. He had forgotten, in the last few days, what happiness was like. "I'm ready to read someone's deepest, darkest secrets."

"We'll see about that," said Gwen. She stood in the door holding a tray with the spice cake and mugs of cocoa upon it.

"Guys, this is Gwen Underfoot," Colin said.

"Ignore him," Van said. "You're not underfoot, babe. Bring that cake right over."

"That's her *name*, dipshit," Donna said. "Don't talk to her like she's the fucking help."

"I *am* the help," Gwen said.

"No, you aren't," Colin said. "Your *mother* is the housekeeper."

"It's only a matter of time," Gwen said. "My grandmother was the housekeeper before her. Whenever a Wren needs to wipe his ass, there's usually an Underfoot standing nearby with the toilet paper."

She put the tray down on the card table and everyone helped themselves. There was a single marshmallow in each mug—they were big blocks the size of Rubik's Cubes. Those marshmallows were like everything else at The Briars: magnificently grand and vaguely implausible at the same time.

"Go on, Oakes," Colin said. "You and Gwen have a try."

The piano began to play. It was Allie at the keys and she was *actually* playing, not pumping the pedals. The werewolves were roaming London.

"Pretty bold, doing the Friday *New York Times* crossword in pen," Arthur said, as he picked Zener cards off the floor.

"If that's your idea of bold, I bet you're a wild date," Gwen said.

Donna yelled with laughter. "She's got your number, Arthur. Allie, what are the odds Oakes is still a virgin?"

"Maybe you've got Arthur's number," Van said, "but Allie's got all the others. She's been taking graduate courses in statistics since she was seventeen. Personally, I find that offensive. You shouldn't be better looking than your friends *and* smarter than them . . . they'll lose heart and look for companionship more on their level."

"You don't need psychic powers if you've got statistics," Allie said. "A big data set is way more reliable than tarot cards." She began to sing.

I saw a werewolf with a Chinese menu in his hand
sixty percent chance he'll order the moo goo gai pan!
I saw a werewolf with a blue-collar job in Michigan
eighty-five percent chance he voted for Reagan!

"That's," Van stammered, "that's—not the rhyme scheme, Allie—*stop*—I love Warren Zevon—you're hurting me—" He squeezed his head between his hands.

Donna greeted Gwen with a little wave. "Donna McBride. My homunculus over there is Donovan."

"We're twins," Van said. "I meant to eat her in the womb, I swear."

"I'm Allison Shiner," Allie sang, "of east Texas, by the bayou. And there's a ninety-three percent chance I'm gonna like you."

"Shall we?" Arthur asked, holding up the Zener deck. It rubbed him wrong that he had to share Gwen with the others and that they were more entertaining than him. He wasn't funny like Donna and Van, wasn't dazzling like Allie, wasn't a sophisticated alien intelligence like Colin. It was tiring to have remarkable friends.

But Gwen grinned at him and thumbed her glasses up her nose. "All right, then. Let's see if I've got in your head yet, Arthur Oakes."

"I don't think that's in question," Arthur said, and looked at the top card. Then he looked up and met Gwen's eyes. He couldn't hold her gaze for more than a moment. It made him short of breath. He blinked down at the card again.

"Star," she said.

He looked down at a plus sign. "No."

"I meant to say *you're* a star, obviously. Square?"

"No, sorry."

"I haven't activated my powers yet. I was asking if *you're* square."

"Yes. I read medieval French for fun."

"Good," she said. "I'm a square too. But you already knew that. I do *The New York Times* crossword puzzle in pen."

He laughed. He couldn't help it. "Come on, old buddy. Make a real guess."

"Cirrrr—" He shook his head at her. "—rrrrr plus sign!"

"That's it."

Colin said, "Wow. The psychic charge between you two is off the charts."

Colin was ribbing them, but Gwen got the next one right (square) and the one after (plus sign). They got five in a row before Arthur risked meeting her gaze again.

She was studying him: a thing both terrifying and lovely. Her eyes weren't brown exactly. They were green at the outer edges, a very pale green, like looking through the side of a Coke bottle. But there were threads in them of what almost looked like gold foil. He inhaled deeply, feeling good, then thought about someone holding a knife under his mother's eye in a photograph, and was stricken with guilt for feeling even a moment's pleasure.

"Polaroid," she said.

"Huh?"

Gwen shook her head. "Sorry. For a moment I was picturing an undeveloped Polaroid. Let's try again. Wavy lines?"

"Mm-hm," Arthur said, feeling numb.

"You're doing well," Colin said. "You're up to six in a row now. We're approaching statistical relevance. This is really sexy. You're undressing him with your mind, Gwen."

"Keep your innuendos to yourself, Wren," she said.

Gwen called nine of the next twelve correctly, but Arthur didn't need to draw another card to know that she could read him like a book.

SEVEN

Arthur spent his Sunday afternoon in a state of mounting suspense, struggling to work through a straightforward translation of *The Life of Saint Aubin*. Sentences lost their coherence halfway through. He went from one word to the next and found himself unable to string them together into anything that made sense. His stolen books sat in a stack to one side of the kitchen table, hovering at the periphery of his vision.

Jayne had promised that Tana would come for the loot on Sunday afternoon, but she had not said when. The longer he waited, the worse he felt. He forgot to turn on the lights and went on working while the tide of late-day shadows rose high enough to drown him in gloom. Finally, he could no longer read the words on the page. The light switch was just out of reach. He didn't get up to turn it on. He was too old to slip into his bedroom and hide under the covers, but sitting quietly in the dark of the kitchen felt like the next best thing.

When someone rapped at the front door, his throat clenched up so tightly, he thought he might not be able to breathe. Tana Nighswander waited on the porch, a pizza box balanced in one hand and a look of disinterest slapped across her foxy, freckled face.

"You had dinner?" she asked.

"No," he said.

She offered him the box.

"Boneless wings," she said. "All yours."

"I don't know if I can eat 'em," he said. "I feel sick."

"Your appetite will come back," she said. "Doesn't really matter what you've done. Or had done to you." She spoke like one discussing something that had been learned firsthand.

"Thanks."

He put the pizza box on the cast-iron radiator to the left of the door and returned to the kitchen to get the books. It felt like picking up a bundle of dynamite—*old* dynamite, sweating amber beads of nitroglycerin, ready to go off at one wrong jolt. Tana was waiting where he had left her in the hall.

"I'll be back next Sunday," she said. "Don't be empty-handed."

Van emerged from his bedroom just as she left, the screen door smacking shut behind her. He peered out at her as she crossed the street to a dumpy Civic with the Shut-Up-And-Eat-It light box mounted on the roof. Arthur wondered if he noted the books under her arm. Van's head swung around and his gaze lit upon the box of wings.

"You ordered from Shut-Up-And-Eat-It and you didn't even ask if I wanted something?" Van asked. "I thought you cared."

"They're yours," Arthur said. "I don't even know why I ordered them. I got no appetite."

A frown line appeared across Van's pale brow. "You okay? You don't look so hot."

"Too many translations, too little time," Arthur said.

Van stroked his nonexistent beard. "You need to do something to relax. That little Gwen Underfoot maybe."

Arthur opened his mouth and closed it and then turned back to the kitchen. Van cawed like a crow.

On the Friday following, Arthur Oakes lifted first editions of Malamud's *Dubin's Lives*, Rothstein's *The Runner*, and Sontag's *The Benefactor*. The week after that, it was a hardback first of Edward Abbey's *Good News*, a copy of Baum's *Patchwork Girl of Oz* that at least *looked* old, and a handsome fifth edition of Tolkien's *Farmer Giles of Ham*. It hurt him to swipe this last, a slender, well-kept hardcover with a fantastical tree on the dust jacket, but there were five copies in stock. No one would miss it.

By then it was the middle of October. Tana turned up on Sunday night to make the third pickup. That time she had a cold Hawaiian pizza for him. She took the books and considered their spines.

"These worth anything?" she asked.

"*Farmer Giles* is priceless, as far as I'm concerned."

"The last bunch were duds," she said, hefting them in one hand. "Jayne was bitchin' they were hardly worth the gas to drive 'em to Boston."

"Maybe whoever Jayne is selling to figures she's easy to cheat. It's hard to know what a book is worth when you've never read one."

Tana's eyes flashed. "My sister doesn't need to *read* a phone book to beat your face in with one. That'd be an education for you."

After she was gone, he sat at the kitchen table, picking pineapple off a cold slice. He was wondering what sort of masochist wanted fruit on their pizza when the phone rang.

"Hey," Colin said, without so much as a *hello*. "Want to see something *really* scary?"

EIGHT

Llewellyn Wren threaded the movie reel himself. It turned out they weren't watching *any* scary movie . . . but one starring Llewellyn himself.

Colin's grandfather was not always, or even often, a part of their get-togethers in the study. Years later, though, when Arthur thought back on their almost daily gatherings at The Briars to do schoolwork, or share a meal, or test each other for psychic powers, it seemed to him the old man often wandered among them for a while, warming himself by the hearth of their enthusiasms. Or maybe that had it backward and they warmed themselves by his.

He was a spare, slight man who said things like "Hot dog!" or "Swell!" as if he were a 1940s newsboy stuck in an old man's body. To remove an object from his Cabinet of Curiosities was to invite an hour of exuberant conversation, full of digressions into history, psychology, and literature. One night, Donna found a jade box, filigreed with gold. She slid open a drawer in the side to reveal a collection of small, dusty ivory pieces. It was an Egyptian game of Set, which Llewellyn said represented a voyage from one world to the next. They had been playing for nearly an hour before the old man casually mentioned the pieces were an infant's finger bones.

Another time Donna removed a long-barreled rifle and sighted down the length of the room with it. Llewellyn was at his desk, where he had a candy jar full of Excedrin, which he tossed back like M&Ms. His eyes brightened and his eyebrows rose at the sight of the gun.

"Who'd this belong to? Lee Harvey Oswald?" Donna asked,

cheek pressed to the stock as if she planned to put a slug into the player piano.

"Close," Llewellyn said. "A substitute English teacher with a history of mental illness attempted to assassinate a Congressional candidate, Greg Stillson, with that gun. The shooter, John Smith, supposedly suffered from the gift of prophecy. He for sure suffered from a brain tumor. They found a cancerous mass as big as your fist at his autopsy. Golly—wouldn't that be something for the Cabinet? John Smith's brain tumor! I wonder if it's pickled in a jar somewhere."

"My parents *loved* Greg Stillson," Allie said. "My dad did a couple of events with him, said he could've been president. He was polling *great* with independents and white evangelicals. It was *so* sad. He had such terrible PTSD after the assassination attempt, he killed himself. John Smith might as *well* have shot him."

"Do you think the baby had PTSD too?" Van wondered. "The one Stillson was using as a human shield when John Smith drew down on him?"

"Ignore him," Donna said. "That's a lot of Van's leftie bullshit. Stillson was *trying* to throw the baby to safety. Rush Limbaugh had a pretty good breakdown of what really happened."

Arthur didn't have any comment. His mother had been arrested protesting outside a Stillson rally and was of the opinion that Greg Stillson pretty much *ate* babies.

Llewellyn's seventy-year-old mind was itself a kind of cabinet of curiosities. There was no end to the things he knew. He collected butterflies and reels for his player piano. He was casually fluent on the current thinking in psychology . . . and Swedish film, cheese-making, and the spiritual beliefs of the !Kung bushmen. He preferred Jung to Freud, and claimed, with an unnerving certainty, that extraterrestrials had been present as neutral observers at Los Alamos on the day Oppenheimer lit the Bomb.

Today, Llewellyn and Colin were behind an iron Bell & Howell projector from the 1960s and Allie was rolling down a small classroom movie screen in front of the desk. Donna and Gwen were rearranging the stools from the card table into a kind of seating area. Van sprawled on the piano bench, smoking one of Llewellyn's Sobranies, watching the smoke trickle toward the ceiling.

Colin ran an extension cord to the projector while Llewellyn threaded the reel. Llewellyn spoke as he worked, offering them a sort of prologue to the film at hand.

"I gather Colin has already told you something of Dr. Whitton's Philip Experiment in Toronto. Joel Whitton was well read on the Victorian séance, and while the spiritualists of that day were easy marks for hoaxers, it was clear that many séances had produced phenomena worth exploring: voices, abrupt changes in temperature, levitation in plain daylight. Whitton believed if you could get a group with a shared belief system into a relaxed, creative state, they could throw reality for a bit of a wobble. So he and a gang of merry sociologists and psychologists came up with an experiment. They invented the fictional Philip Aylesford and began to hold séances to see if they could contact him."

"Even though they made him up?" Gwen asked, pushing her glasses up her nose. Her mother had sent her in with mugs of tea and then she had stayed, Colin inviting her to join them with as little as a glance at an empty chair.

"Even though. Dr. Whitton felt that Philip was simply a magnifying glass to focus their directed unconscious. And by the fall of 1972, Philip was showing up at every séance. Division 19—the branch of the US military concerned with psychological research—figured it warranted further investigation, and as their in-house researcher, I was tasked with replicating Whitton's work. Our ghost was one Elwood Hondo, who died in the chair after strangling several young men in Florida. I had a theory that a killer would produce a more aggressive and hence more measurable response."

"A *made-up* killer," Donna said. "You *made up* a homicidal maniac because you thought he'd be more likely to do violent ghost shit."

"We certainly didn't want a ghost too polite to rattle his chains," Llewellyn said. "Ask any novelist—an unstable, violent personality is a wonderful thing for advancing the plot."

The projector began to chatter, and Colin shut off the lights. A square of brightness appeared on the pull-down screen. The image was fuzzy for a moment, then Llewellyn adjusted something and the picture sprang into focus.

Half a dozen men and two women were squeezed in around a folding card table. Arthur recognized Llewellyn straight off, although he had a tidy black mustache and wore a thick burgundy turtleneck that was as much of the era as lava lamps and disco. None of the men were in uniform. A bull-necked Black man wore mirrored sunglasses, even though the group was indoors and there were no visible windows. The women were in their late forties or early fifties, with hairstyles straight off *The Brady Bunch*. *All of them sit with fingertips lightly touching the table's surface. A low bookshelf crammed with textbooks runs the length of the wall behind them. A reel-to-reel tape recorder sits on top of it, spools turning slowly. Normally, this would be a briefing room, but today, maybe thirty bare metal chairs have been folded up and stacked against the wall to one side.*

Several of the people around the table are murmuring to one another, as if they are gathered at a suburban cocktail party. Llewellyn's voice rises above them all, clear and playful:

"Corporal Hondo? Are you with us tonight? Elwood? I have a whole folder of dirty pictures here. If you can be a good boy and give us a knock, I'll show them to you."

"Give us a knock," shouts a woman, and one of the men joins in, "Give us a couple raps, Elwood!"

"C'mon, Elwood boy," says the Black man in the mirrored shades. "You know you want a look in that folder. Got one of some skinny ol' white boy just chokin' on a dick. You gonna love it."

1970s-Llewellyn flips open the folder and turns over a photograph within. The photo cannot be seen from the camera's fixed angle. "Do you want to see one, as a sort of appetizer? Feast your eyes, dear boy. And if you like *this, there's more and better where that came from. But if you want to view the others, you'll have to give us a sign. Give us a good old rap on the table and say hello."*

One of the women begins to sing "We Are the Champions" at the top of her voice. Several others join in. They have made it through a bit of the first verse when a metal folding chair falls over with a sharp clap of steel on concrete and

Donna screamed and almost fell over in her own chair. Arthur, who was right behind her, reached to steady her. Colin laughed, a teenager going over the first drop on a fast roller coaster, high on his own velocity. On the screen the

revelers look around. The sing-along hitches, falters . . . and then they throw themselves back into it, louder than before, WEEEeeeEEE'LL KEEEEEEEP *on* fffIIIIIIIIGHTIN' . . .

Another folding chair falls with a crash, followed by another. They collapse with one shocking steel bang after another. Then a chair goes flying, as if thrown. A second follows it. Something flings a whole stack of them. At the séance table, Llewellyn and the women erupt into manic laughter. The man in the sunglasses begins to withdraw his hands from the table, catches a cautionary glance from Llewellyn, and puts his fingertips back. All of them are twisting in their seats to watch the folding chairs tumble and crash. One of the folding chairs opens itself up and then begins to walk *across the room, opening and closing, hitching itself along.*

Suddenly the members of the séance are rising unsteadily to their feet. They have *to stand if they want to keep their fingers on the tabletop, because the card table is coming loose from the floor, wobbling drunkenly into the air, and someone cries out—*

"That's where I'd get the fuck out of the room," Van said.

"Not me," Gwen said. The glow of the movie screen lit up her glasses, turned them to circles of ghost-colored light. "I think I'd stay. You don't turn your back on a guy like Elwood Hondo."

"A make-believe guy?" Arthur asked.

"He's pickin' up the table and chuckin' around chairs," Gwen said. "You catch a flying chair in the head, I figure the concussion would be real enough to suit you."

The table clunks down onto the floor, and the revelers at the séance whoop and sit. Most of them whoop, anyway. The man in the sunglasses flinches as if he has borne witness to a gruesome act of violence.

Behind them, on the bookshelf, something is happening to the reel-to-reel tape recorder. One of the chunky buttons goes thud and the reels stop moving. Another button clunks down. The reels scream in reverse. Thunk! goes another button. The reels stop. A final button bangs down and the recorder begins to play.

Voices rise from the tape recording, the guests at the séance singing a snippet of Queen:

Ba-a-a-a-a-a-ad mistakes!

The stop button thuds. The reels whine backward, stop. Play again.

Ba-a-a-a-a-a-A-A-Aad miIstaAkes!

Thump, whir, again.

Ba-a-a-a-a-a-A-A-A-A-W-W-d miISSstaAAkes!

It's playing the same snippet, again and again, a little slower each time. Their shared harmony has become a single, deep, slurring voice:

BA-A-A-A-A-A-A-AW-AW-AW-AWW-D MII-I-ISTAAA-AAA-AKES.

The reels whir and thud and play.

I'VE COME THROUGH

wheeeeee vvvvvvvvv

THUD.

I'VE.

COME.

THROOOOOUGH.

The tape begins to play backward, at high speed, producing a sound like the tittering voice of a hysteric. As the reels spin, a new sound begins to rise. It sounds like laughter . . . sick, demented laughter. Or maybe sobbing. On the screen, the Black man looks over his shoulder, removing his sunglasses at last. The tape comes off one of the reels completely and then the machine abruptly reverses direction and begins to spew threads of black tape into the air.

The Black man recoils and looks away—looks toward the camera—and his eyes are covered in scribbles, a mess of weird quivering lines sketched right onto the picture, and he opens his mouth to say

"*Fuck.* THIS!" Donna shouted and leapt to her feet. She struck the light switch with the palm of her hand. The lights came on in the library . . . and then the bulb in the sconce directly above her exploded with a white flash.

Donna screamed. Van toppled backward and would've dropped to the floor if Allie hadn't reached to steady him. Arthur wasn't sure if he shouted too. He had an idea his voice got caught in his throat. Gwen jumped into his lap, striking him with a hard curve of round hip, then quickly slid back into her seat. Only Llewellyn seemed unsurprised, looking mildly around, eyebrows raised in a good-humored sort of way. And like that, the film ended. The reels kept spinning, but one of them was empty, the tail end of the film slap-slap-slapping free.

Llewellyn clapped his hands to his knees and rocked forward out of his chair to stand. He gave the wall sconce a long, musing look. The lightbulb hadn't just blown. It was blackened and cracked, a silky trickle of white smoke spilling in a ribbon from the split in the glass.

"Oh, Elwood, that was very rude," Llewellyn said, and slipped out of the room.

For a few moments all of them were silent, while Colin rethreaded the spent reel and began to rewind the film.

"The last time I watched this," Colin said, "a bird flew into the window and killed itself. Llewellyn says a little Elwood is stuck on the film: he almost always says hi before it's over."

Donna glared at him. "That wasn't *real*. If it was real, it would be all over CNN. Those black lines over the guy's eyes? Someone scratched that right on the celluloid. I've never seen anything so fake."

Colin popped the reel off the camera and held it out to her. "You're welcome to look over the film yourself to see if anyone tampered with it."

She didn't take it. "I mean, I believe it's *something*, okay? I believe it's psyops. Isn't that what you said Llewellyn was into? I believe it was filmed to make, I don't know—foreign powers believe the US government was going to enlist an army of ghosts. Let a copy of the film loose behind the Iron Curtain so Moscow can shit their pants over America's arsenal of weaponized poltergeists."

"Moscow was quite a bit ahead of us, I'm afraid," Llewellyn said, returning to the room with a fresh lightbulb for the sconce. "They had been inventing ghosts since the fifties. They called it the Goblin Scheme, and they gave it up in 1965, after Andreev, their lead researcher, stuck a screwdriver into his ear and lobotomized himself. His wife said he was trying to stop 'the little whisperer.' The problem with inviting the unnatural into your life is it might decide to stay. Can I pour any of you a Scotch? Nothing complements a taste of the occult like a swallow of single-malt."

"That's a yes," said Van. "Actually, I think it's a hell, yes."

"Mr. Wren, can I ask about something at the end of the film?"

"Yes, Gwen?"

"The man in the sunglasses. The one who had scribbles over his eyes. He died . . . didn't he?" When she said it, Arthur realized he had known too, at the first sight of those black squiggles, that the big Black man in the turtleneck was a goner. They had all known.

"George Lane. Three weeks after we shot that film. He hit a fawn on his way into base. It came right through his windshield and kicked his head in." Llewellyn began to hand around glasses of Scotch. "Elwood went quiet after that." He gestured at the wall sconce. "Though sometimes he rolls over and murmurs in his sleep."

Arthur had his first-ever swallow of whiskey. It tasted like a mouthful of dragon's flame.

NINE

It wasn't all digging around in Llewellyn's Cabinet of Curiosities and scaring themselves silly with ghost stories. That fall they watched a lot of *Unsolved Mysteries* together. The McBrides had a passion for it, couldn't bear to miss an episode. Donna fixated on the subhuman creeps who hurt children. She had a yen for cruel retribution. She didn't just believe in the death penalty—she thought sex murderers should be castrated first, with a rusty machete. Van, on the other hand, had a fascination with people who got away with it: Jack the Ripper, D. B. Cooper, the Unabomber.

It could give you whiplash, listening to the two of them. Van thought college should be free and national health care a law. Donna wanted the Central Park Five executed by firing squad. Arthur had always assumed twins would agree on everything. It was a source of amusement to all of them that Donna—who was president of Rackham College's young conservative club—was the identical twin of a hayseed socialist who thought the Democrats were too far to the right. Van had claimed he was going to vote for Willie Nelson as a write-in candidate in the 1988 presidential election. Willie would legalize pot and the taxes on marijuana sales would pay for national day care. Donna said she would vote for George Bush twice if she was allowed. In the end, though, neither of them voted—they forgot to register in the state of Maine.

"What are the chances they'll ever get him?" Arthur asked. "The Unabomber?"

"They'll get him," Colin said. "They'll use a computer to construct a database about him. Everything he does reveals who he is: the people he kills, the way he writes the address on the package, the materials he uses to create the bombs. People leave information behind them like snails leave slime. You can follow it right to them."

Colin had a Commodore 64, which he could use to talk to people scattered all over the world. He used a device called a modem, which made an awful squeal and shriek as it tried to connect with other computers through the telephone line plugged into the back. That shrill grinding sound was, Arthur thought, the voice of the future: inhuman, idiotic, and *loud*, so loud it drowned out all other sound. But then Arthur had spent a fair amount of the fall copying catalog information into the library's IBM, a task of obliterating dullness, and came by his dislike of such machines honestly.

"Do you think you're going to do something smart with computers someday?" Allie asked Colin.

Colin said, "I'd like to use them to predict the future."

"I don't think computers are going to develop ESP anytime soon," Arthur said.

"I think they're more likely to develop reliable ESP than people. Pretty soon they'll be able to recognize us. Your computer will point a camera in your face to figure out who you are. It'll be able to recognize if you're dangerous in one glance."

"I bet," Gwen said, "it'll take one glance and if you've got a Black face, it'll call the cops."

Arthur held out his hand and Gwen slapped him five without even looking at him.

"Computers can't be racist," Colin said with a quizzical smile. "How could they be?"

Allie said, "You inspire me, Colin. I want to learn to do things with computers too. I want to know what people do before they do it too. I want to know what they aren't telling me. That's why I love statistics."

Van said, "No one's keeping secrets from you. *I'm* not. I'm an open book."

"Everyone keeps secrets," Allie said. "We can't help ourselves.

And I'm very nosy, even if the secrets aren't important. Like who wants to have sex with me, for example."

"Everyone," Van said. "Especially me."

Allie ignored that. "I want to know if I'm going to be fat, if I'm going to be sad. I'd like to know what all of you are going to do after college and if we're going to stay friends, or if I should harden my heart and prepare for losing you."

Gwen said, "It's easier to imagine you shaving your head than hardening your heart, Allie, so I guess we'd better all stay friends."

"Allie is going to do clever things with math," Donna said. "Colin is going to do clever things with computers. I'm going to be on TV and famous. Van is going to be on drugs and broke. What are you going to do, Arthur?"

Van answered for him. "He'll do what he does best—bore people to death. He'll become the world's expert in ancient Hungarian and memorize ancient Hungarian texts about the best way to grow potatoes. All of us will graduate from college but Arthur never will, not really. He'll just go from wanting to molest the co-eds to teaching them."

"He'll still want to molest them," Donna said.

"No," Van said. "He's too boring to be insidious. At thirty he'll begin to smell like cobwebs. By forty, rumors will spread that he's a ghost of himself. Eventually he'll just be another ghost haunting the stone catacombs of Oxford University."

"Oxford?" Gwen asked, slanting her eyes to look sidelong at Arthur.

"Mm," he said, surprised by the sudden eye contact—surprised and confused. He had the wild idea, in that moment, that Gwen's gaze had an unhappy quality, as if the news disturbed her.

"His father studied there. Arthur is secretly British, didn't you know that?"

"Funny, I missed the accent," Gwen said, smiling now.

"He only talks like an American to fool people, but don't believe it: Marmite runs in his veins. I once caught him masturbating over Anglo-Saxon word roots in the *Oxford English Dictionary*."

Of all of them, it was hardest to see what Gwen might become, or how she fit in—or even if she was one of them at all. She was the only one of them who wasn't attending Rackham; she was a high school student, for Chrissake. Arthur had finally worked up the nerve to ask her age, posing the question to Colin on a walk across campus. Arthur had inquired in a tone that suggested a random curiosity. He fooled no one. The McBrides were strolling along behind them and immediately began to howl and shove each other.

"Jailbait! Arthur wants to bang some fuckin' jailbait! I knew it!" Van yelled, grabbing Arthur's shoulders from behind and shaking him back and forth.

"Gwen is eighteen," Colin said. "Legal in this state. But I wouldn't let that be a salve to your conscience, Arthur. The law is no replacement for a moral code."

So Gwen was in high school, and the rest of them were in college, but that was by no means the only complication. Gwen Underfoot was also a townie. You could tell it just looking at the enormous men's flannel shirts she got from the free box at the Episcopal church. She lived in Gogan, a place no sensible Rackham College student went unless they were looking for pills, pussy, or trouble (NO FREE RIDES in Gogan, Arthur reflected; GAS, GRASS, OR ASS). There had been incidents, clashes, between Rackham students and the local kids, going back decades. Arthur was uncomfortably aware he would've never even met Gwen if her mother wasn't cook and housekeeper at The Briars.

Gwen usually turned up at the house after school got out, to do homework in the peace of the Wren kitchen until her mother finished making dinner, at which point Gwen would drive her home. Often, when Arthur wandered in, Gwen was already at the kitchen island with her schoolwork and the newspaper scattered around her, the crossword puzzle two-thirds finished. She liked crosswords, said it was like playing Tetris with language and you didn't need to own a computer. Sometimes they sat and did the crossword together.

"You working on your college apps yet?" Arthur asked her one day, while they were polishing off the easy *USA Today* crossword.

(He filled in the answer to "prisoners and problems": CONS. She filled in the answer to "visually loaded 38s": BRA.)

"I'm going to apply to Kennebec." She shrugged.

"Kennebec has a college?" He already knew it couldn't be a good one.

"Community," she said. "But they've got EMT training. That's what I want to do. I think I'd be a steady hand at that sort of thing—ambalance work—and I like the idea of being there for someone when they're at their most frightened. Seeing someone across the fear, and on to where they know they'll be okay. I don't scare easy myself, I'm not grossed out by blood, and my family aren't what you'd call excitable sorts. Also, I hate waiting in traffic and when you've got an ambalance you can run all the reds."

The six of them were flopped on pillows in front of *Unsolved Mysteries* when he found the backbone to ask her about applying to Rackham. She frowned and began to feel around in the pockets of her baggy jeans.

"Hang on a minute," she said, brow creasing with concentration.

"What are you looking for?" he asked her.

"A quarter of a million dollars," she replied, then turned her empty pockets inside out. "Nope. Didn't think so. Don't suppose *you* got a couple hundred grand to spare?"

Arthur did not. What he did have was the trust his father had established for his education, a trust funded by an insurance policy that had paid out nearly three hundred thousand pounds upon his father's death at the age of thirty-nine. The best thing Oliver Oakes had ever done for Arthur was not visit the A&E after falling and striking his head against a stone curb. He had died of an epidural hematoma in his sleep six hours later. Between the trust and a partial scholarship, Arthur had enough for Rackham, and for Magdalen College at Oxford after. It wasn't a bottomless fortune, but he was painfully aware that he had exponentially more than Gwen Underfoot.

"I thought your father worked at Rackham." Arthur had learned this fact from Colin a few days before.

"In the grounds department. He's not faculty. He's the help. It's not the same."

It wasn't? The thought grated on him . . . and induced a queer feeling of guilt. The whole pack of them were suddenly awkwardly intent on the TV, working overtime to avoid making eye contact with her.

"Look at all of you," Gwen said. "You look like I told you it's my life's dream to live in a trailer and raise nine or ten kids while working part-time at a strip club. There are a *few* options open to me."

"Like being an EMT," Arthur offered. "Keeping someone alive to the hospital. I get it."

"Or I could see myself doing something in criminal justice," she said. "I'm never gonna be a lawyer, but I could be a paralegal. Help people who are broke get representation. Work for the kind of people who always get fucked over by the system. Or become a parole officer."

"I love that," Allie said. "When Arthur's mother gets out of jail you could be *her* parole officer! I bet that'd be really nice for both of you."

There was a moment of stunned silence. Allie wasn't joking—her tone was completely sincere. It was the first time Arthur allowed himself to understand that they all knew. *Of course* they all knew. He had talked to Van about it; Van kept nothing from his sister; Donna and Allie were roommates; and the information would've passed effortlessly, like a head cold, on to Colin and Gwen. Gwen looked around, eyes bright, worried for him. Her hand found his and squeezed, while her eyes said: *Are you all right?*

Arthur opened his mouth to reply—and laughed. It was such a fabulously Allie Shiner thing to have said. She spoke of Gwen becoming his mother's parole officer as if this were a delightful bonding opportunity, like going shopping for shoes. Arthur cackled and set the rest of them off. All except Allie, who frowned in a pretty sort of way, no idea what she had said that was so funny. They fell all over each other, the pack of them roaring together, no one laughing harder than Arthur himself, who suddenly found himself choking on something close to sobs, tears running down his face.

As he laughed—harder and then harder still—the others began to drop into silence. His lungs couldn't get enough air. He wasn't sure when he began crying, but at some point, Gwen let go of his hand and began to rub his back. Donna put a hand on his knee. Allie slid across the carpet and gently wrapped her arms around his neck.

"Ah, shit," Arthur said. "Shit, shit, shit. I'm sorry."

Van was the first to reply. He cleared his throat and said, "It's all right, man. For what it's worth, if my mom got locked up for the bullshit your momma got locked up for, I'd cry like a pussy too."

There was another stunned silence . . . and then they were all laughing again, even Arthur. Laughing while big, fat tears plopped off his chin. Gwen gave Van's head a playful shove.

"You carry around a lot of weight," Colin said to Arthur when the howls died down. "And you never show it. I wish we could take some of it off you. I hope you know, if there's anything any of us can do to make it easier . . . and I don't know what that would be . . . we got you."

"We got you," Allie said, squeezing him hard.

It was one thing to be hugged by Allie . . . and another to feel Van put his arms around him. Donna slipped in between Allie and Van both and embraced him around the waist. Somehow, they were all hugging him. He didn't know which of them kissed the top of his head. He lowered his face so none of them could see him fighting fresh tears, although probably they knew anyway.

One by one they began to release him until only Gwen remained pressed to his side, her head on his shoulder. That felt good. Better even than he imagined, which was saying something.

"That's right," Gwen said. "You need us to break your mom out, we'll start digging the tunnel tomorrow. My daddy has all the tools we'd need."

"I don't think we have to go that far," Arthur said, relieved his voice was steady and not choked with emotion. "She'll walk out on her own two feet in twelve months. Maybe four if she catches a break at her parole hearing."

Unless he fell out of favor with Jayne Nighswander and someone up at Black Cricket stuck a sharpened spoon in Erin's throat. In which case she would come out of prison a lot sooner.

On a stretcher. Or in a bag.

TEN

Arthur spent nearly four hours on Halloween morning decorating the Brooks Library for the "Ghosts of Shakespeare" party, an annual fête that had been held since the 1950s. By the time he and the other student librarians were done, the halls were decked out with flickering electric candles and the shelves were draped in fake cobwebs. After dark, the drama club kids would emerge from balconies and out of darkened nooks to perform sinister snippets of *Hamlet* and *Macbeth* while the audience wandered around in the gloom, tittering nervously. When Van learned Arthur wasn't planning to attend, he looked horrified and astonished—as if Arthur had told him Johnny Cash was dead. It was one of Rackham's most popular yearly events, and the idea of Arthur avoiding the library on Halloween night was like imagining the Vatican on Easter without the pope.

"We're all going!" Van said. "Allie and Donna are going to sneak Gwen in, and she'll probably be dressed as a slutty witch or something. You telling me you can bear to miss that? What are you going to do instead? Stay in the apartment and study the Scrabble dictionary?"

Arthur hated the idea of Gwen having fun with the others and not being there to see it. But after stealing two thousand dollars' worth of books from the library, he could hardly bear to spend one more minute there than was necessary. Walking into the place now made his teeth ache. It was as if the library had become toxic to him . . . only that had it backward. The library wasn't poison. He was. Every time he stole a book for Jayne, he polluted the place a little more with his existence.

He hit the 7-Eleven on the way back to the apartment. Unsurprisingly, the candy aisle was pretty well wiped out. He scrounged through what was left and picked up a large bag of circus peanuts. When he was back at the apartment, he poured them into a bowl and left it on the porch, hoping kids would help themselves and let him be. He parked himself at his usual spot in the kitchen to polish off a translation.

Not long after full dark, there came a rap at the door, urgent and sharp, and he pushed away his copy of *The Exeter Book*. He still had a half-full bag of circus peanuts and carried it to the door with him, thinking the bowl must already be empty, and kids these days were turning into pigs.

Only it wasn't a pack of children at all. Instead, he found the Mystery Gang waiting for him: Fred, Daphne, Shaggy, Scooby, and, of course, Velma. It was Gwen in Velma Dinkley's fuzzy carrot-colored sweater and the pleated skirt that ended midthigh, orange socks pulled to her knees. She looked at him merrily through her glasses, which he now saw had always been exactly the sort of black-framed chunky glasses Velma wore.

"Jinkies," she said. "We were looking for someone with a clue. Boy, did we come to the wrong place!"

Allie waved both hands and jumped up and down in excitement. She looked great as Fred, an orange silk ascot around her throat, bell-bottoms flaring around her platform sandals. Her boyishly short blond hair was swept back Fred-style.

"Zoinks!" she cried. "Love your costume, Arthur! You're all dressed up as someone who doesn't know how to have fun."

"Chrissakes," Van said. He was hanging off Allie's arm. "Have you ever *seen* an episode of *Scooby-Doo*? How deprived *were* you as a child? Shaggy's the one who says 'Zoinks.'" Van wore a shoulder-length copper wig, a purple dress, and trashy black stockings. At first glance, Arthur had assumed he was Donna. Donna was to the right of him, though, in Shaggy's loose green tee and baggy trousers.

"You might not want to pretend to be some big expert in Scooby-Doo, strutting around in a pair of fishnets like those," Arthur said. "Daphne never wore stockings like that."

"She does now," Van told him. "How the fuck do you think they pay for the Scooby-Doo lifestyle?"

"Fred Jones doesn't need to prostitute his girlfriends," Colin said, looking unselfconscious and easy in his own skin, even if he was wearing a Great Dane costume—his face sticking out from under Scooby's jaw. "They're financed by the CIA. How else do you think the Mystery Gang can communicate with a dog? They were all part of the MK-Ultra experiments: hammered with experimental drugs until they heard animals speaking to them."

They found their way to Arthur's bedroom, which, in an earlier era, had been someone's parlor. One half of the room had been made over into a sort of living area, with beanbags arranged around Arthur's small Zenith TV set. Van flipped it on without asking. Freddy was leaving body parts all over Elm Street. Donna led Colin in by the leash and tugged him down onto a beanbag beside her.

Van sprawled on his belly, slow-kicking his own bottom with his transparent stripper heels. "Be honest, guys. Is Allie checking out my moneymaker? She was undressing me with her eyes the whole walk over. I'm pretty amped—I don't think she's ever ogled me before."

Gwen had to pound Allie on the back. She had a circus peanut stuck in her throat.

Gwen's hand, striking Allie between the shoulder blades, sounded like a fist banging on a door. Only the knocking continued after she stopped. Arthur snatched the bag of circus peanuts away from Donna and went to investigate.

He opened the front door and stepped onto the porch without looking to see who was there. He found a trio of trolls waiting for him, two guys and a girl, all of them too old for trick-or-treat. The girl was visibly pregnant, her cheap purple tank top stretched over a front porch of her own. All three of them wore identical rubber masks. Tusks protruded from leathery, snarling mouths. Foreheads bulged, Frankenstein-style.

A wiry guy in a jean jacket and a wifebeater, with the lean hips of a fencer, stood in front of the other two. He held a big hardcover in one hand, down at his side. Arthur was surprised, didn't think the average trick-or-treater went out with reading material. He crooked his neck to read the title on the spine: *The Patchwork Girl of Oz*. A sick, paralyzing chill began to spread behind his breastbone.

By the time Arthur realized the guy wasn't a guy at all, Jayne Nighswander was on top of him, smacking him upside the head with the book. He stumbled backward and she hit him again, the flat of the book across his nose. He felt something pop, staggered, and sat down, blinking at tears.

"Fuck is this?" Jayne said, squatting to get eye to eye with him and waving the hardcover in his face. She hooked one thumb under the bottom of her mask and lifted it up so he could see her flushed face. "*Patchwork Girl of Oz*? Not even signed? My Boston buyer said she'd give me thirty bucks for it. Thirty fucking bucks? That barely covers the gas to Boston and back. We need *sixty grand*, fuckface." She smacked him with the book again, turning his head halfway around.

He was trying to get an arm up to defend himself when Ronnie caught her wrist and pulled her up. "Come on, babe. Look at him. He's starting to cry. He's just a kid." Arthur had dropped the bag of circus peanuts, throwing a scatter of them across the porch. Ronnie bent to pick one up and pop it in his mouth. "Man, I love these! They're like Halloween crack!"

The screen door opened behind Arthur. He came drunkenly to his feet as Colin stepped onto the porch, blinking at the trolls from the hole in Scooby's chest. "What's up, folks?"

His leash was dangling. Jayne stepped forward, grabbed it, and yanked him toward her. Colin almost fell into her before she shoved him the other way. His heels skidded out from under him and he crashed into the wall, falling to the floor amid the circus peanuts.

"Who the hell is this?" Jayne asked.

"This is the fuckin' cavalry," Donna said, moving into the doorway, glancing from Colin to Jayne. "Yo, bitch. Put your mask back on before you scare someone."

"Arthur, are you all right?" Gwen asked, ducking past Donna to get to him.

Allie was in the hall, peering out past Donna's shoulder. She said, "I'll call the police," and turned toward the hall phone.

Jayne moved. Donna stepped into her path to slow her down and Jayne slammed the spine of the hardcover into her throat. Donna's hands flew to her neck and she made a sound somewhere between a gag and a cough. She reeled back and fell over Colin, who was still on the ground.

Allie got one step down the hall and then Jayne had her by the ascot, was dragging her onto the porch. Allie took three tottering steps back in her platform sandals before her heels hit the jamb and she toppled, falling on top of Donna and Colin.

Jayne was staring at the squirming pile of college students at her feet when Van lunged out of the dark of the hallway, driving his right shoulder into Jayne's bony chest, slamming her back into Ronnie and sending the book flying. Jayne was wiry and slender, maybe 115 pounds, and her legs went. She sagged, as if to sit down, but Ronnie got his left arm around her waist to hold her up. His right hand came out from behind his back to level an automatic pistol in Van's face.

"Whoa there, cowboy," Ronnie said.

Jayne's eyes were cold and unfocused. She righted herself and Ronnie let her go.

Van looked frightened now, patches of color in his cheeks, his hands up, palms out. "*Hey*. What the fuck's with the gun? That's not cool, man."

Jayne took a step toward him. "You think you got big balls. Shove a woman? Do you got big balls, kiddo?" She shoved a hand under his skirt, grabbed him by the crotch, and squeezed. Van's knees bent and drew together. He began to double over, crying out softly. "They don't feel that big to me. They feel like li'l ol' jellybeans." When she let him go, he keeled over, hitting the porch so hard it shook the windows in their frames.

"Check it out, Jayne! I think Fred has boobies!" Ronnie cried.

Allie had crawled off Colin and Donna and was now on her hands and knees at Ronnie's feet. She gave him her most winsome smile. "Hey, man. Point that somewhere else, okay? Please."

Ronnie stuck the gun in the waistband of his jeans, settling it at the small of his back. Up until this time, Tana had not moved or spoken. Now, though, she lifted her mask to reveal her face. Tana handed Gwen a plastic package of Kleenex, which she had produced from a cheap pink plastic clutch.

"For his nose," she said, nodding to Arthur. Arthur stared back at her, his gaze shifting to her ripening abdomen and back to her pretty, freckled, snub-nosed face.

"Thanks, Tana," Gwen said. "I don't think it's broken. Colin, can Donna breathe?"

"Well enough," Colin said, rubbing Donna's back while she gasped. "You two know each other?" Nodding from Gwen to Tana.

"We worked in Dunkin' Donuts together a couple years ago," Gwen said.

"Dunkin' Donuts is where Tana got that sweet fat ass of hers," Jayne said, and gave her sister an open-handed whap on the bottom.

If this bothered Tana in any way at all, her face didn't show it. Instead, she gave Arthur a calm, considering look. He had to stare down the length of his nose to meet her gaze, his chin tipped back, Gwen pressing tissues to his nostrils. "Arthur? I know what you're doing. It's been obvious for a while. You're trying not to steal anything too valuable from the library. I get it. You don't want to do anything really terrible. But trust me, it's better to get it over with. Just close your eyes and do what they want and then put it behind you. Don't think about it. With a little practice, it can be like it never happened at all."

"Hey, babe," Ronnie said to Allie. "Do me a favor? Will you pick up the circus peanuts and put 'em in the bag? That shit is *good*. We're taking them with us."

Allie began to crawl around on all fours, collecting circus peanuts. Ronnie smiled, studying the sway of her rear end.

Donna lifted her chin. Her cheeks were puffy, swollen from

crying, and her black lashes were gummed with tears. Colin had a hand on her shoulder—whether to steady her or restrain her, Arthur couldn't have said.

"Stop picking them up!" Donna screamed at Allie, her voice a painful rasp. "Stop crawling around for them!"

Allie ignored her. She finished collecting the circus peanuts and then offered Ronnie the bag from her knees, her face level with his crotch.

Ronnie put a hand under her chin, tipping her head back. With his other hand he took the bag of circus peanuts. "Thank you, honey. These are almost as sweet as you."

Ronnie dropped his hand and Allie crawled to Van, who was curled in the fetal position on his side. She cradled his head in her lap, his wig long gone.

"Quit nibbling around with the little shit, Artie," Jayne said. "Next time Tana comes by to collect, you better hand her books worth their weight in gold. You don't want to know what's gonna happen to your mother if you don't."

"You're fucking disgusting," Donna rasped. "You're fucking disgusting human beings."

"Lot of people, they only get to be monsters one night of the year," Jayne said, tugging her troll mask back down over her face. "Which is a real shame. It's much more fun when you make it a way of life."

ELEVEN

They gathered in the dimness of Arthur's bedroom, with the TV off, and Gwen saw to them all. She slipped into the kitchen and returned with a bag of frozen kernel corn for Donovan's mashed nuts. He sprawled on the floor, head in Allie's lap, and held the bag to his crotch. Gwen disappeared again and returned a moment later with a bottle of Advil and another of Tylenol. Donna and Van took two of each, while Arthur settled for three Tylenol. They swallowed them down with cans of Milwaukee's Best, which was Van's favorite beer, because it was cheap.

"Have you ever heard how Milwaukee's Best is like sex in a canoe?" Colin asked. "They're both fucking close to water." The way Colin said *fucking*, it sounded less like an obscenity, more like a technical term. No one laughed.

Gwen settled in a beanbag, with Arthur between her legs, his head tipped back against her shoulder. She held a washcloth filled with ice to his nose, lifting it now and then so he could speak. In a thick, congested voice, he told them about the Nighswanders and his mother and the books he had been swiping from the library. As bad as the evening had been, it felt good to tell. He had not realized until that night how exhausting it had been to deal with the Nighswanders alone.

Donna kept clearing her throat, making shallow wet coughs that were not far removed from sobs. Gwen said, "Do you want some lemon and honey tea? For your throat?"

"I'll tell you what I want," Donna said, in a hoarse whisper. "I want to catch those gruesome motherfuckers on the interstate.

Drop a brick off an overpass into their windshield. Watch 'em fly off the road at seventy miles an hour."

"I'm not sure staking out overpasses is the most effective way to deal with people of Jayne Nighswander's stripe," Colin said.

"What would you do, Colin?" Allie asked.

"I know what *you'd* do, Allie," Donna snapped, before he could reply. "You'd suck that guy's cock and thank him for the pleasure. Jesus. Crawling around on your hands and knees to collect his fucking circus peanuts. Why would you do that? Why would you humiliate yourself that way?"

"So they wouldn't hurt you again," Allie said.

"Well, I didn't need your fucking protection and I didn't need you kissing his ass after he—after he—" Donna had to stop, pinching the bridge of her nose, gritting her teeth to fight back tears. Arthur had never seen someone fight off tears that way—through sheer rage.

"I guess calling the police is out of the question," Allie said.

Van gave that suggestion a thumbs-down.

"No, I don't think we can do that," Arthur agreed. "What *would* you do, Colin?"

"Just pay them," Colin said. "If your mother was going to be locked up another decade, it would be different. But she's out in—what is it, Arthur? A year?"

"A year, yes. Maybe sooner. She has a hearing in February. She might not get her parole . . . though I think she will. She started a book club, she offers spiritual counseling . . . she's more like a prison social worker than an inmate."

"So we're looking at four to twelve months," Colin said. "I say pay Nighswander off. I can get you four grand this month—that's what I've got socked away—and another six hundred dollars, every month, until your mother is free."

Van pushed out a pained breath and said, "Yo, son. Where you going to get six hundred dollars every month?"

"My allowance," Colin said.

"You have an allowance of six hundred dollars a month?"

Colin said, "No . . . it's quite a bit more. I receive two hundred dollars a week. But I have to keep *some* money to spend, if only to avoid awkward questions from my grandfather."

Allie said, "I can do a thousand a month. That's the most I can take off the credit card without getting a hassle from my father."

Van said, "I can't give you any dough, Arthur. I'm going to need every spare cent for surgery on my ruptured testicles."

Arthur was about to tell them he couldn't take their money— but Gwen spoke first.

"How did any of you get into college? That's what I'd like to know."

"What?" Donna asked.

"I thought you had to be smart to get into Rackham," Gwen said. "Don't you see? They'll take your money . . . and *still* tell Arthur to steal books for them."

"Why would they do that?" Colin asked. It was, Arthur thought, the first time he had ever seen him perplexed.

"Because it's *fun*," Gwen said. "Because they're getting off on it! Do you think they'll be *done* when they have sixty thousand dollars? They won't be done until Arthur's mother is out and they can't touch her. Don't give them a single thing they haven't asked for. You can't horse-trade with these people."

"We've got to do something to help Arthur, though," Allie said. "Don't we?"

"You're already doing it," Arthur said. "How do you think I got through the last eight weeks of my life? How do you think I'm going to get through the next eight, while I'm busy stealing sixty thousand dollars of books for a pair of orcs?"

They had nothing to say to that. Gwen bent and placed a light kiss on top of his head. The feathery sensation of her lips against his hair gave him a shiver.

"There is *one* thing we can do," Colin said, "besides just being your emotional support system."

"What's that?" Arthur asked.

"We can make sure you never get caught," Colin said.

But then Van was asking if Allie could help him to the bathroom so he could throw up, and Donna began pulling off her fake Shaggy beard in angry fistfuls, and Gwen had to collect some fresh ice for Arthur's nose, and so Colin never got around to explaining what he had in mind.

TWELVE

On the following Wednesday afternoon, Arthur reported for his usual shift at the Brooks Library. At the first quiet moment, he left another student librarian to watch the checkout counter and climbed the winding wrought-iron staircase to the Juliet balcony above. He let himself into a cool, shady room that had not changed much in over a century. Shelves lined walls to either side. Unlike the rest of the library, which was organized according to the Dewey Decimal system, here the shelves were marked FICTION, BIOLOGY, HISTORY, and so forth. The only windows were set three feet deep in stone embrasures. A Norman archer with a full quiver and a Bible could hold off a band of Vikings from here. And in fact all that cold stone *had* defended the place well enough, not from Norsemen, but from the fire of 1840 that had reduced the rest of the original Rackham College to a scorch mark three hundred acres wide.

With such small medieval windows, there was always something crepuscular about the Special Collection, no matter how bright the day. There was only the one door in and out. A barred cabinet holding the most valuable rarities stood against a walnut column in the middle of the room. The bars were thick battered iron, laid across one another in a grid. Arthur didn't give it a second look. He wasn't touching anything in there. Not that day, anyway.

He had every right to be there. Indeed, he was expected to spend at least some of his working hours in there, to complete the annual inspection and copy the updated Special Collection catalog into the IBM that sat on a lectern in one corner of the room. He took a moment now to flip the chunky switch on the back of the computer. While the machine was warming up, he hunted along the

FICTION shelf until he found what he was looking for: a first edition of Jack London's *White Fang*, a little foxed on the spine, some black speckling on the back cover that might've been mold, and London's signature on the title page. A scan of SPORTS/OUTDOORS produced a limited first of *The Compleat Angler*, with an original Cosway binding. As Arthur put the books in his school bag, his gaze was fixed upon one of the embrasure windows. A fine rain speckled the old glass. It was as if, somehow, his right hand was engaged in theft while the rest of him was occupied elsewhere.

It was still raining when he got off work six hours later. He walked out of the library with eight thousand dollars' worth of books in his backpack. A cherry '49 Cadillac convertible with the ragtop up idled alongside the curb. The passenger-side window was down and a silky film of smoke spilled through the opening. Arthur had spied Llewellyn's car once or twice at The Briars, but he had never sat in it before. As he approached, Van got out of the passenger side and pulled the seat forward so Arthur could duck his head and scramble into the back with Donna and Allie.

Van climbed back in and thumped his door shut. Colin sat behind the front seat with a fat blunt. The smoke that hazed the inside of the car was peppery and sweet.

"Want a hit?" Colin asked him, offering the joint over the back of his seat. "It's blue. Lovely feminized strain, one of the sativa-heavy lines."

Arthur had never heard of blue marijuana, and the rest of what Colin had said was like a different language, one he had somehow never encountered. He laughed—and was surprised at himself. He had not thought there could be any laughter in him on such a day. Colin's breezy exuberance and his almost professorial desire to share what he knew—to recite an entry from his mental catalog of the peculiar and profane—cheered Arthur to no end.

"I'll pass, but thanks," Arthur said to Colin.

Donna helped herself, leaned back into the old leather seat, and took an assertive drag.

"Straight arrow?" Colin asked him.

"Tragically. Aren't you worried your granddad will smell it on you?"

"Who do you think I got it from? He's my supplier . . . and he gets it straight from the US government."

"No way," Arthur and Donna said at the same time.

"They're the biggest grower in North America. Granddad smokes it for his appetite."

"Oh," Arthur said. "Is he sick with something?"

"Yes," Colin told him. "AIDS."

THIRTEEN

When Tana turned up at the door of Arthur's apartment the following Sunday afternoon, she had a pizza and something in a brown paper bag, and she was wearing the Biko hoodie. It was two sizes too big for her and she swam inside it. Looking at her in it now, Arthur never would've guessed she was pregnant.

He stood aside to let her carry the pizza down the hall to the kitchen. He hadn't had much appetite since looting the Special Collection—aka the treasure room—at the library, but a good-smelling steam was trickling around the lid of the box, a savory odor of melted cheese and sauce.

"Van here?" she asked.

Arthur shook his head. He found it difficult to speak. His throat had closed up with emotion the moment he opened the door and saw her standing there.

"Too bad," she said. "I get a sense that's one kid hates to miss out on a free meal. We'll just have to eat it without him. Something to wash it down?"

She took a six of Michelob out of the brown paper bag and put it on the table, next to *White Fang* and *The Compleat Angler*. She popped a can and handed it to him, popped another and had a swig. He didn't tell her pregnant women weren't supposed to drink.

"Sorry my sister ruined your Halloween," Tana said. "I'm sorry about the whole fucked-up mess."

He waited to feel something and found he didn't. He wasn't grateful for her apology. He wasn't angry or despairing either. He had discovered what waited beyond anger and despair: numbness. Un-feeling.

"That's my mom's Biko sweatshirt," he said, gesturing to it with his can of beer. In a remote, disinterested sort of way, he thought his whole life had hinged on one act, which at the time he had thought was simple decency. If he had not offered her the hoodie then he would not be a thief now, and there would not be eight thousand dollars' worth of rare books sitting on the kitchen table next to the pizza.

She looked down at it. "Oh. Yeah. Here. You want it back?"

As she pulled the hoodie off over her head, her T-shirt rode up with it, rising to reveal the tender pink swell of her stomach. Arthur saw she had the top button of her jeans undone, could see the satin black-and-pink lace strap of her panties.

Tana saw him staring and smiled. There was a kind of bemused curiosity in that smile, which just touched the corners of her lips. After a moment she pulled the T-shirt the rest of the way off and dropped it on the table, covering the books. She stood in front of him in her bra and jeans.

He looked her over, feeling something at last. It was a sharp click of desire, but it wasn't *just* desire; it was mingled with something that felt almost like grief. He felt bad about himself for looking at her while she was half undressed. He felt bad about himself for wanting to reach out and tug down her denims.

"Did Jayne tell you to do this? Throw me a little something to keep me in line?" he asked.

"Does it matter?" She had her thumbs in the loops of her jeans and was smiling just a little and rocking her hips from side to side, letting him look her over.

Arthur *wanted* it to matter. He wanted to be the kind of person to whom such a thing would matter. Maybe he even had been that kind of person, a few months ago.

But he wasn't that kind of person anymore. He reached for the waistband of her jeans and pulled her toward him.

At some point they made their way to one of the beanbags in his bedroom—the beanbag Gwen had sat in, on Halloween night.

When they were done, he rolled off her and sat on the floor. She stretched out with her ankles crossed. She was still wearing her socks, but nothing else, had left her jeans in the hall and her panties on the threshold to his room. It was now dark and the streetlight threw the shadows of raindrops against the far wall.

He wondered how many men Jayne Nighswander had made her sister sleep with and if he was now one of them. He had been assaulted, threatened, and blackmailed, and after all that, it felt like he deserved something for himself. So he had taken Tana because he could, and now he worried he was no better than Jayne or Ronnie. He had hated them for months. Now he could hate himself too.

"Have you really had to sleep with people because your sister owes them money?"

"Among other things," she said.

They didn't look at each other. He got up and went naked into the kitchen for their beers and came back.

"Is that why we did this?" He couldn't leave it alone, needed to know one way or another.

"What do you think?" she asked, taking her can when he held it out for her. Then she said, "I hope it's not a girl." It took him a moment to realize she was talking about her baby. "I'd run away from Jayne, but I don't know how we'd live. I can't make rent by delivering pizzas, and Jayne takes the money anyway. Most of it. I've got a little tucked away." She had a swallow of beer and sighed. "Sometimes I think it'll be okay. Sometimes I think someone will kill Jayne and make it okay. Someone she owes money to. Or someone will stick her up for drugs and things will go bad. When I'm feeling down, I remind myself it could end at any time. Someone could kill her or she could kill me."

"What if you went to the police?" he asked.

She laughed—a dry, caustic sound—and did not dignify this question with a reply.

"So you don't want a girl?" he asked.

"No," Tana said. "I don't want to have a girl and have my sister let guys fuck her when she's eleven. A boy would be better. Jayne would have a harder time figuring out how to make money off a little boy."

"Is the father going to help out?" Arthur asked.

"Not sure who it is," she said. "I'll have to see if the kid is Black. That'll narrow it down." She laughed. There was no humor or happiness in it. "I hope it's a boy and he does something good with his life. Someone who rescues cats from trees instead of swerving to hit them. Ronnie does that. He keeps score on his dashboard. Two points for a cat, four for a dog."

The rain ticked on the windows.

"If you get ahold of Gwen Underfoot," Tana said suddenly, "you want to make sure she don't wriggle free. That year the two of us worked at Dunkin', she was my Secret Santa. She gave me a new pair of sneakers. Best gift I ever got. Everyone else got joke presents or five-dollar gift cards. Me, I unwrap brand-new Reeboks. She had noticed my old sneaks were held together with duct tape. I know you'll probably be tempted to find someone else—some college girl, someone who spends the summer down the Cape and listens to James Taylor and doesn't get her hair done at Supercuts—but take it from me. She's the best you're going to find."

"You might be right," he said. "But do you think I'm the best *she's* going to find?"

"No," Tana said. "I'm sure she can do better."

He was too.

They sat together in the gloom listening to the rain, and at some point he took her hand. He even kissed her knuckles. She laughed.

"For what it's worth, Arthur," she said, "you aren't a completely shitty lay."

It was his turn to laugh. "You want a slice of that pizza? It might not be cold yet."

"Okay," she said. "That would be all right."

He stood and glanced back at her. The shadows of raindrops trickled down her bare stomach, over her breasts, down one side of her face. With her head turned toward him, she looked older, had the fatigued beauty of a young and harried woman in her mid-thirties. It was the first he ever really noticed that she was beautiful, with her freckles and tired eyes.

"Hey, Arthur. You could make both our lives easier and kill my sister yourself." She stared idly at the ceiling, watching shadows trickle across the plaster. "Something to think about."

FOURTEEN

In the second week of November, Arthur stole a 1765 treatise on shipbuilding, bound in calfskin, printed on linen rag, and worth around two grand. In Germany, college students were taking sledgehammers to the Berlin Wall, climbing up onto the ruins to wave flags and pump their fists. Communism had imploded in East Germany, an event that shook the world; Arthur hardly noticed.

In the third week, he lifted an 1818 first edition of *Frankenstein* off the shelves, a book so exquisite, and so valuable, it would wipe out a third of what Jayne Nighswander said he had to pay. But then, as he slid the book into his backpack, a queer lightheaded sensation rolled over him and he began to feel sick. His heart quailed at the thought of stealing something so precious. It was too much. He grabbed a first edition of *All the Sad Young Men* by Fitzgerald instead.

He had considered taking sixty thousand dollars of books all in one go, but Gwen had cautioned him against it. "Tell them you can't take too much too quickly. Tell them there's always other students around and that you have to be careful. Give 'em one book worth a grand, another worth two."

"But I could pay off everything I owe by Thanksgiving."

"And what do you think happens then?" she asked him. "You think they'll shake your hand, say it was a pleasure doing business, and you'll never hear from them again? You think they're the kind of people who get tired of free money?"

He drove to Black Cricket to visit his mother the weekend before Thanksgiving. Arthur was braced to see the Nighswanders—more than 150 visitors were there for an afternoon holiday dinner with their incarcerated relatives—but they didn't show.

The buffet was in the prison gym: lukewarm turkey, congealing brown gravy, and a yam casserole under a half-inch of toasted marshmallows. Folding tables had been set up for the families, red-and-white-checked cloths thrown over them for a touch of class, white cards to indicate where people should sit. Maybe half of the families in the room were Black. There was a certain grim, nihilistic comedy in it, he thought. At a prison get-together, he blended right in; at the college where he hoped to graduate with honors, he was the only Black face in the whole cafeteria, unless the janitor had been summoned to mop up a spill. Arthur found their table without seeing any sign of his mother. He was antsy, wondering if he should ask a guard if she was being held up for some reason, when Erin mounted the low stage at the far end of the room. She wore her usual prison jumpsuit, with her clerical stole tossed over her shoulders. It had fallen to her to say grace. When she smiled down at them, Arthur felt like he had turned his face into the first warm rays of spring.

"Aren't we the lucky ones," she said, and there was a bit of laughter—families sitting with loved ones doing ten years for arson, twenty for transporting, thirty for homicide. "Most of the women in this room never expected to live this long. Most of our families never thought we would either. Most of us have done things we'd give anything to take back, but somehow people have decided to love us anyway, and they're here with us today . . . though we've put them through plenty of sorrow . . . and believe me, folks, we aren't done yet. You haven't tasted sorrow till you've tried prison cafeteria turkey." This time the laughter was almost raucous. His mother had always been good at this, at finding her way to the words others needed to hear. "You don't have to be in prison to feel trapped. You don't have to receive a sentence to feel like you're serving life. Most of us weren't free before we were locked up. We were already serving time, the worst kind of time, locked away with our own guilt while doing things that made us hate ourselves. Your own head can be solitary confinement. But here we are now, and it's Thanksgiving and the people we love are with us still, serving our sentences with us. Counting the days with us. Their love is our parole. Let's bow our heads and say thanks for them, thanks for our good luck. Because we are loved, prison doesn't have to be where freedom ends . . . it might be where freedom begins. Amen and God bless."

By the time she stepped from the podium, Arthur was fighting tears, blinking furiously to hold them back.

Oh, Mom, he thought. *No parole for me. I have been found guilty of being a helpless chickenshit and my warden is Jayne Nighswander.*

His mother reached the table, touched his cheek with one finger, brushing away a tear.

"Damn," she said, trying to make a joke of it. "I knew I was good, but I didn't think I was *that* good." Then, in a gentler voice, she said, "You all right?"

For a moment he was close to telling her. But if he told, *she'd* tell. And then what? In the absolute best-case scenario, she would be placed under protection, and the police would round up Jayne, Ronnie . . . and Tana. Tana would have that baby in a prison hospital, and it would be both the first and last time she ever held her infant in her arms.

And that was only if everything went exactly right. If anything went sideways, his mother would be stabbed to death in the exercise yard and Tana would *still* have her baby ripped away from her. No. He was committed now. He would steal books until he got caught or Erin got parole and set them both free.

He rubbed roughly at his eyes with the back of his hand.

"Look around, Ma," he said, gesturing at the wet-eyed families and choked-up convicts seated at the other tables. "You killed 'em. It's a massacre. Someone ought to call the cops."

FIFTEEN

On the last Friday before Christmas break, Arthur took a signed first of John O'Hara's *Appointment in Samarra* out of the treasure room. He had stolen more expensive items, but when he stuck that one in his messenger bag, Arthur knew it was the most important book he had taken so far. He was going to learn something now. A question was about to be answered. He wasn't in much doubt about the nature of that answer, not anymore, but that didn't stop his stomach from bunching up in a nervous knot of anticipation.

When he was back in his apartment, he called Shut-Up-And-Eat-It to arrange a meeting with Jayne.

"I need to get with your sister," he said when Tana picked up. "Tomorrow?"

"Yeah, I don't see why not. Come by around four? If she can't make it, I'll call back. Is that it? I got food to deliver."

"That's it. Don't keep people waiting on the best part of their day."

"Ha," she said. "You must think I fuck *all* of 'em." And she hung up.

He didn't think that. She had made three pickups since that one time they screwed, but had not stayed, had not even come in the door. She had just accepted the books and left.

He wished he hadn't done it and he couldn't stop thinking about it and wanting to do it again. He remembered the breathless way she had laughed when he roughly yanked down her jeans. He remembered the way she cajoled him—*come on, big guy, do me like you wanna do your little Gwennie*—and was both aroused and stricken. Arthur had felt he deserved *something* for himself after being terrorized for months; that he had *earned* the right to fuck Tana Nighswander. Yet another part of him, even then, had known he shouldn't do it, that it was a deeper sort of wrong than stealing books from the library. Jayne was happy to offer her sister to the men with whom she did business; she did it as casually as she'd offer a guest a beer. Those men were weapons Jayne had used to abuse her sister and now Arthur was one of them. He didn't know if Tana could forgive him, and maybe it didn't matter—he was already certain he could not forgive himself. The worst part of it was that if Tana came by the house and offered herself to him again, he doubted he could say no.

When he got to Shut-Up-And-Eat-It, it was dusk. Jayne was already in the parking lot out back, sitting on the hood of her Ranchero. Ronnie sat in the passenger seat, the door open, smoking a number.

"What did I tell you about bringing us this nickel-and-dime junk?" Jayne asked, casting her cold gaze across *Appointment in Samarra*. "This looks like a handful of crap. If this was in the quarter box at a yard sale I wouldn't give it a second look."

"I bet you wouldn't. But if your buyer knows her twat from her Twain she'll have a cardiac arrest when she sees it. That's a mint Harcourt and Brace first edition. Good luck finding a copy for anything less than seventy-five hundred dollars."

She took the hardcover from him and tossed it to Ronnie.

"What's it about?" Ronnie asked, gazing blankly at the cover.

"A guy who can't escape his fate," Arthur said.

"So, basically, your memoir," Jayne said.

"You got that wrong," Arthur said. "I've been doing the math. You said you needed sixty thousand dollars. With the O'Hara, I've stolen closer to sixty-five. So we're done now. Right?"

Jayne shook her head, looking sad for him. "Wrong. Maybe what you've took is worth sixty-five grand on the open market. But moving stolen goods is different. You can't ask for top dollar. You said this one is worth seventy-five hundred dollars? Well. I'll get two grand for it."

"Two grand?" Arthur cried. He had expected her to jerk him

around, had mentally braced for it, but felt shock lance through him all the same. "Two fucking grand?"

Jayne nodded. "I know. Highway robbery, right? And she won't sell 'em for full value either. They're too hot. She has to sell through private channels, mostly abroad. It's a long line of crooks, each one sticking up the last. By the way. Speaking of my old Boston bookworm, there's one she wants in particular. She'll go twelve grand for it. Take that next and you can fuck my sister in the ass."

Arthur felt sick.

"Leave your sister out of it," he said.

Jayne grinned. "It's a bit late for chivalry, King Arthur." *Chivalry*, there was a word he wouldn't have expected her to know.

But if she's so dumb and you're so smart, why is she the one giving the marching orders? Arthur thought then. *Gwen is the only one who doesn't underestimate her because Gwen is the only one who doesn't dismiss her as a dumb townie. How did you wind up like the others, Arthur? How did you wind up a Rackham College asshole, a know-it-all who doesn't know a thing?*

"What book?" he asked.

Some part of him already knew.

"I can't remember the exact name," Jayne said. "The skin book."

"No."

Jayne didn't seem to hear him, went on talking. "I guess the guy who wrote it was some lunatic from the days of the witch trials. They hung him for his crimes, then used his own fuckin' hide to bind his journal."

"That book is priceless. There are literally only five works of anthropodermic bibliopegy in all of New England, and—"

Ronnie hooted, puffed smoke from the corners of his mouth. "What the fuck you say, boy? Anthropo-fuckin' biblio-whatsis sounds like some shit you catch from a ten-dollar hoor."

Jayne shook her head again. "You've got it all wrong, Artie. No *book* is priceless. Your mother. *She's* priceless. You remember that."

"I *can't* take it," he said. "They keep it locked up."

"I'm sure they trust you with the key," Jayne told him.

"Yeah, they *do*. And pretty much *only* me. Which is why when they realize it's missing they're going to know *I* took it."

Jayne said, "Stick it on your roommate. He buys drugs. Say he got the key off you and stole that book for drug money. You could fix him up for it easy. Steal a couple other books and hide 'em in his room."

"He's my friend," Arthur said.

"Friends are nice. Alibis are better, though."

"I can't do anything for the next month. The library is about to close for Christmas break. School is back in session on January 15 and I can get you more books then. Not that one, though—forget about the Crane journal—but I can grab you plenty of other books worth real money."

Jayne studied him, head cocked to the side, then turned her face and blew a long rippling stream of white fog into the cold air, as if she were smoking.

"Yeah. Okay, Artie. To be honest, the feeling's mutual. I've only spent five minutes with you and that's about all of your miserable Black face I can stand for one month."

Arthur wasn't surprised to hear it. He was only surprised he hadn't heard something like it sooner. Jayne didn't seem like the kind of person who would miss the low-hanging racist fruit. And yet he felt his vision tunneling ever so slightly, going dark and strange at the edges.

"There we go. We finally got there," Arthur said, his voice flat, toneless.

Jayne slid off the hood of the Ranchero.

"Next time I see you—say the end of January—you'd better have that book for me." She spoke over her shoulder as she moved around to the driver's seat. Ronnie pulled his legs into the car. "No excuses, no bullshit. My connection in Boston has her heart set and is going to give me top dollar. Think of it as your own *Appointment in Samarra*. You don't miss an appointment like that, do you, Arthur?"

He didn't reply as she got behind the wheel, slammed the door, and peeled out.

When something wet kissed his cheek, he thought, for half a second, that he was crying. But it was only a snowflake. By the time he reached the street it was coming down in earnest, and it didn't let up for three days.

SIXTEEN

Arthur slept as poorly as he could ever remember, nodding off in snatches, then coming awake with the feeling of boiling in his own skin. He tossed off the covers and dozed again. When next he lurched awake, he was a-tremble in a cold, rotten sweat.

He dreamt about helping Gwen with a college application, which for some reason had to be turned in on a strip of human skin, red at the edges. Her personal information had to be tattooed on, but when he took the needle to that ribbon of skin it twitched and wrinkled and tried to squirm away. Now and then he'd lurch awake, but soon he'd slip back down into sleep once more, and always, the dream would be waiting for him, picking right up where it had left off. He dreamt that fucking dream all night long.

He gave up a little after five in the morning. The world outside was dim and cottony, and the snow fell in great wet wads. He put on three layers and tramped out. He felt like he had a fever, felt the snow should sizzle, like spit on a stovetop, when it flew into his face.

The Brooks Library was open twenty-four hours for finals week, but at 6:00 a.m. there were only a few other students there and a single student librarian on duty. Arthur did not ask to enter the Special Collection. It was the first time in months he had showed up at the library without theft on his mind.

He spent an hour in a carrel with a cup of tea from the student center and the bylaws of Rackham College, latest edition, 1982. He picked through nearly three hundred badly Xeroxed pages in a three-ring binder before he found what he was looking for, what he had half suspected would be there all along. A good liberal arts college in the Northeast, famous for its early support of abolition and women's suffrage, of course it was there. When he finally found it, he was conscious of the feverish feeling finally passing, leaving him achy, tired . . . but not unhappy.

In the afternoon he climbed into the Christmobile. He threw on the headlights—it was already dark at 4:00 p.m.—and drove to Gogan.

Gogan was only the next town over, but he didn't know the roads and in a short time was lost. The Underfoot family were in the phone book, and he had located their rough address in the grainy map helpfully printed in the back of the Yellow Pages. But between the dark and the falling snow it was easy for a person to lose his way, and once he got off Gogan's main drag, it was a twisty maze of narrow lanes. The way the snow was falling, he didn't dare do much more than fifteen miles an hour. Once, a pack of three dogs chased his car, barking hysterically, for almost two blocks. He was keenly aware that Gogan was not Podomaquassy.

Finally, feeling he was close, he slowed the car alongside a steep hill behind an abandoned brick mill. Kids sailed down the hill on plastic sleds, whooping as they raced to the bottom of the nearly quarter-mile slope, which ended amid a tumble of rusting auto parts. It looked like a great way to fly headlong into a case of tetanus, but Arthur thought maybe some of the parents standing at the top of the hill could tell him where to find the Underfoots. There was a gravel lot up there, with a few parked cars in it, headlights throwing illumination onto the sledding hill. He turned in and was surprised to see a plow with a Rackham College decal on the driver's-side door, the amber caution light revolving on the roof of the cab. He parked and got out.

"Arthur!" Gwen hollered, and she held up a red plastic sled. "What are you doing out here! Did you get lost looking for a place to score drugs?"

"Gwen Underfoot!" said Gwen's mother. "You're the one musta got lost. Went and got lost looking for your manners."

Gwen didn't pay her any mind. Mrs. Underfoot looked like a Lego figure in her puffy parka and snow pants, square hood over her head. Arthur saw her almost every day at The Briars, and she routinely brought him and the others cocoa and lemon-coconut cake and peach-strawberry pie, and it occurred to him now he had no idea of her first name. Gwen's father was Martin, Arthur knew, because he had looked him up in the school directory, where he was listed among the groundskeepers in the back.

Her old man shook Arthur's hand, his dark, bloodshot eyes both wary and weary.

"Mr. Underfoot," Arthur said. "Pleasure to meet you."

"*Mhm*," he said, which Arthur later realized was quite verbose for him.

"Where are the rest of them?" asked Mrs. Underfoot.

"It's just me tonight."

"Did you come to watch me break my neck?" she wanted to know. "Sorry to disappoint you."

"She won't go," Gwen said. "She says sleds are for kids, but what she really means is that *fun* is for kids. It kills me. Come on, Mom. We'll go together. Just imagine it! The thrill of the speed! The darkness racing by!"

Mrs. Underfoot glanced down the hill. "I'm imaginin' a burst spleen and a buncha hospital bills we can't pay. I didn't give up on fun, Gwennie. I gave up on being a hundred-and-ten-pound girl made of rubber. You go. I'll stay up here with the first aid kit."

"I'll go with you, Gwen," Arthur said.

When Gwen turned her face to his, it shone with a mixture of delight and surprise. Her pleasure was so immediate and so undisguised, he couldn't help feeling a fresh, bitter spasm of shame. He didn't deserve a look like that—a look of such gladness.

"Climb on," she said, and dropped her cheap plastic sled on the snow. She settled herself in the front end. "You can be the big spoon." He got on behind her and put his legs to either side of her waist, his knees jutting over the sides.

"Anyone ever get hurt doing this?"

"All the time. Scott Carson from school hit the half-buried blade from someone's table saw when he was nine. Took off two fingers. Which is a reminder to keep your hands inside the sled at all times.

If we dump, try and throw yourself on top of me. That way at least I can cop a feel before I die. You ready, old pal?"

"Ready as I'll ever be, old buddy."

He put his knuckles into the snow and pushed them forward, a foot at a time—but it was Mr. Underfoot who leaned in, gripped the back of the sled, and launched them into the night. In less than ten seconds they were doing thirty miles an hour and screaming their heads off.

At the bottom they ground to a slow, squeaky halt amid the litter of auto parts. They sat in the sled for a while, watching kids half their age come rocketing down, howling all the way, sometimes toppling out while the sleds were still moving at high speed. Finally, they climbed out and Arthur took the rope at the front of the sled to drag it while they trudged up the slope.

"We hit that one bump so hard," Arthur said, "I thought I was going to accidentally take your virginity."

"Ha ha," she said. "More like I'd accidentally take yours, Arthur."

He thought of Tana and a sick feeling pulsed through him. He took a deep scouring breath of cold air and pushed his guilt away.

He bumped her shoulder with his. "How are the college applications going?"

She gave him a sharp-eyed sidelong glance. "Polished and done. Kennebec, Husson, University of Southern Maine."

"Not Rackham?"

When she spoke again, he thought she was clamping down on annoyance. "*No*, Arthur. It costs fifty thousand dollars a year to go to Rackham College. That's more than my father's annual salary, and I don't have the grades for a scholarship. You know this."

"Unless one of your parents is faculty. Then you're eligible for one of three different payment plans, all at massively reduced rates."

"My father isn't a teacher. He plows the roads. In the summer, he pilots the riding mower."

"Doesn't matter."

"Says who?"

"Says the college's own bylaws. I've got a photocopy of the relevant clauses in the car if you want to look."

Gwen thought it over, then shrugged.

"I doubt I have the grades. You wouldn't believe how I've struggled in Spanish. I'll be lucky to pull a C minus in Spanish III."

"I can help you with Spanish. And one grade doesn't matter that much. Especially when you've done five years of volunteering with the Big Sisters of America."

"I didn't do that to impress the admissions department of Rackham College," she said, with some heat.

"I know you didn't. But they'll take it into account all the same."

"They don't take townies."

"Oh, will you quit with that college kids vs. the people who clean their floors bullshit?" he said, with an edge that surprised both of them. "Makes you sound like Jayne Nighswander. All that matters is whether you got something in you worth building up or not. And you do. You're smarter than all of us put together. Can't you at least try? What are the odds I'm going to talk you into this?"

"About the same odds that you can get my mother to sled down this hill."

"Copy that," he said, and quickened his pace.

"Arthur?" she asked, hustling to keep up with him.

He didn't speak until they were on top of the hill, both of them breathing hard, vapor steaming from their lips.

"Mrs. Underfoot?" Arthur asked. "Will you sled down this hill with me? I'll take care not to steer us into anything that can give you hepatitis."

"Arthur Oakes, have you been drinking?"

"I'm dead sober, Mrs. Underfoot. What if I told you your daughter's future happiness depends on the two of us taking this sled down this hill, right now?"

Gwen said, "Do you have any shame at all?"

"None," he said. "Mrs. Underfoot? I will not let you be hurt."

Mrs. Underfoot cocked her head, studying him intently. "That's not my concern. My question is whether Gwen is gonna wind up hurt?"

He thought of Tana, tasted bile in the back of his mouth, and swallowed it down. "Not a chance."

Mrs. Underfoot stared at him a moment longer, a faint smile touching her lips.

"Arthur," Gwen said, "for the record, you are an absolute rat."

"He better not be," Mrs. Underfoot said, and sat down in the sled. She looked back at her husband. "If I don't come back, Martin, return the videos to the corner store. They're on the table by the TV. I don't want no more late fees. And there's frozen mac and cheese in the icebox."

"*Mhm*," he said, and when Arthur sat behind Mrs. Underfoot, Martin took the back of the sled and began to run, thrusting them into the darkness.

Mrs. Underfoot screamed and took Arthur's hand as they fell off the edge of the world. She screamed so loudly, Arthur almost couldn't hear Gwen laughing behind them.

SEVENTEEN

Van and Donna flew back to the panhandle on the Friday before Christmas. Allie was already gone, had left for Texas after taking her last final in the middle of the week.

"Are you going to have Christmas with *anyone*?" Allie had wanted to know. Allie loved Christmas, had worn Christmas sweaters all month long, and attended choir practice at the campus chapel like it was a full-time job. Arthur could see it horrified her, the thought that he'd spend the holiday alone in his off-campus apartment.

"He's going to spend it with me," Colin said, putting an arm over Arthur's shoulders. "We're going to drink my granddad's oldest whiskey and I'm going to beat his ass at chess."

"I'd have to drink quite a bit before I start losing to you, Colin," Arthur said. He felt a glow of happy warmth spreading through his chest, as if he had already had his first swallow of Scotch. It was the first he knew he was expected at The Briars on Christmas morning, the first he knew he had something to look forward to.

He had made no firm plans beyond visiting his mother on Christmas Eve. He pointed the Christmobile toward Black Cricket early on the morning of the twenty-fourth. The defroster labored on full but couldn't keep up with the bitter cold outside. Arthur didn't see the Ranchero behind him until he was halfway to Black Cricket, and then he couldn't stop glancing at it in the rearview mirror.

The Ranchero rolled into an empty slot while he was walking toward the visitor's entrance. He looked back, waiting for Jayne and Ronnie to get out, but the truck just sat there. The sun glanced off the windshield in a dazzling blue glare, obscuring everything behind it.

He scuffed into the waiting room and made his way to the security window.

"'S not happening today, kid," said the CO behind the glass. "I'm real sorry. Your mother was moved to isolation this morning. Fight in the cafeteria."

"My mother . . . got in a fight?" Arthur said. "My mother is a pacifist."

"Oh, yeah? That why she's in here? Too much pacifism?"

"Has she been hurt?" In his mind's eye he saw a close-up of someone pounding the shiv into the small of her back, once, twice, a third time, *thump, thump, thump.*

"If she was hurt, she wouldn't be in isolation, she'd be in the infirmary."

He forced the vision of a lunch-hall knifing out of his head. "Ma'am, I drove three hours to see her. It's Christmas tomorrow."

"I hear you. I get it. You must be crushed. I would be too." And she sounded like she meant it. "But there was an incident in the cafeteria and your ma was right in the middle of it. A search of her cell produced contraband—"

"What contraband?" Arthur asked.

"I'm not free to share that information."

"Please. What contraband?"

The guard tapped the clipboard against the edge of the desk. "A spoon with the handle sharpened to a blade."

Arthur was aware of a bitter taste in his mouth, as if he had just bitten down on copper wire.

"I will tell you," the guard said, "the fight is one thing, fights happen. A knife is another. It's sure to come up in her parole hearing. I'm real sorry."

She was still talking when Arthur pivoted on his heel and headed for the exit. He punched through the Plexiglas doors and plunged into the bitter, stinging cold. The Ranchero idled, a hundred feet away.

"You happy?" Arthur shouted.

The Ranchero began to creep forward. He stalked toward it, but it was already turning away from him in a slow U.

"You happy, motherfuckers?" he shouted again, but the Ranchero was accelerating now, back toward the security checkpoint and the state highway. He couldn't read the NO FREE RIDES bumper sticker—it was hidden under months of road filth—but it didn't matter, he got the message all the same.

EIGHTEEN

Although classes would not resume until January 15, the library reopened on Thursday the eleventh, and Arthur went in the following afternoon. The place had a closed feel, lights off in both wings, the carrels empty, the vast central room submerged in chilly blue shadows.

The Special Collection was dark and desolate. When he looked around, Arthur thought it was obvious that books were missing. The shelves seemed less densely packed, hardcovers tipped against one another. It was probably just his imagination.

The steel cabinet that held the most valuable books stood three inches off the ground on feet sculpted to look like reptilian talons. The lock was a nineteenth-century beauty, crafted in the shape of a heart as big as a man's hand. The key slid into it with a smooth, oiled click and it sprang open with a snap.

Rows of ancient books bound in worn pebbled leather crowded the cabinet's three shelves. The volume he needed was on the middle shelf, preserved inside a large, handsome Solander box. Arthur pulled out the box, tugged on a blue silk ribbon to open the clamshell case, and there it was: the Crane journal. He had been possessed by the morbid idea that it would look like the Necronomicon in *The Evil Dead*, a book bound in wrinkled flesh, with a tormented face bulging from the front cover. But it was merely an oversize leather volume like any other, saddle-colored, worn and nicked with age.

He removed it from the box and returned the empty clamshell to the shelf. On a cursory glance, the book might not be missed. He pushed the door of the safe shut and refastened the lock. He knew of only three keys that could open the safe, and he knew who had each. Mr. Meckfessel, the head librarian, had the original. One of the two dupes was with campus security. The other was with him: one of only three Black kids at Rackham college, and the only student whose mother was serving time for murder.

Sooner or later, the book would be discovered missing, and they wouldn't have to scratch their heads for long to figure out who had taken it. It was only a matter of time.

NINETEEN

Later, Arthur could not quite remember the chronology of events—none of them could.

Later, they could not even agree how long they worked at bringing King Sorrow over from the Long Dark. Donna and Van thought everything happened that Friday night. Gwen said it was the night after, on Scatterday evening—Gwen insisted that Scatterday was the secret day hidden between Friday and Saturday. Colin liked the idea of Scatterday . . . a pocket in time crammed full of junk, like a small child's pocket, only instead of marbles and string it held dragons and trolls and sorcery. Allie said not only did Scatterday exist, but there was an extra number between midnight and one: dragonedy. She insisted it had been ten after dragonedy when King Sorrow first spoke to them.

He had worked his full shift at the library and walked out of the place a little after six, with the Crane journal in his messenger bag. Twenty minutes later he walked into The Briars. The others were waiting for him in the kitchen. Gwen was on her usual stool at the kitchen island and knew at a glance that he had stolen the awful book Jayne had commanded him to take—understanding passed between them without a word. All of them knew.

They gathered in front of the TV to watch *America's Most Wanted*—not as good as *Unsolved Mysteries*, but it would do in a pinch—settling in the big second-floor room at the back of the house, a den with aromatic cedar beams and the quality of a refinished attic. Colin left them during the first commercial break and returned with a package of mottled white paper, soft as unprocessed cotton, which he unfolded to reveal a clear plastic bag of bright sapphire leaves.

He rolled a joint for Van, who took a long sucking hit and then casually passed it to Allie. He rolled another for himself but gave it up when Donna wordlessly reached for it. Then he tossed back the flap of Arthur's messenger bag and helped himself to the Crane journal. Colin settled in one corner of the couch, reading by the light of the TV. Later that seemed significant: memory began to fragment and splinter—for all of them—as soon as he cracked the cover of the book. Of course, it wasn't just reality that went hazy right around then. The air was so fogged with ganja smoke, the room was turning into a Navajo sweat lodge. It swirled in serpentine patterns, as if invisible snakes moved in the air.

"He branded himself. With a hot cross. Right between the eyes. To make the devil's voice go away," Colin said, without looking up from the book.

"How old was he?" Gwen asked.

"Thirteen."

"Sounds like adolescent schizophrenia," Allie said, without looking from the TV. "Onset is usually thirteen. It affects less than one percent of children and is more common in boys."

"Allie," Van said, "you know the percentages on everything. What are the odds you'll smoke enough of this shit to get horny and want to ride a cowboy?"

"About the same odds as you ever being a cowboy," Donna answered for her. "Zero."

Colin brightened. "He branded the Cobbett sisters too! One of them wanted it and one of them didn't. The one who didn't was nine. They held her down and branded her on the stomach. They all had devils in them, bossing them around."

"What were the devils telling them to do?" Donna asked.

"The usual devil shit. Dance naked in the woods. Butcher their mothers like hogs. Denounce Christ and bow before the rulers of hell. Baal. Ereshkigal. Father Ruin."

"I'm pretty sure Father Ruin is on tour with Ratt next summer," Van said.

"And King Sorrow," Colin said, his finger moving along the page. "They had to swear fealty to His Majesty King Sorrow. We don't want to forget him."

"How could we forget King Sorrow?" Arthur asked. "Give me some of that." Donna passed him the blunt.

"I didn't know you smoked weed," Gwen said.

Arthur said, "I didn't know I committed felonies. Turns out I'm full of surprises."

TWENTY

Colin turned another page and a crease appeared across his wide brow.

"Uh-oh. Something bad is happening here. Jane Cobbett took Crane by the hand and led him to the barn and showed him her secret black contra punctum," Colin said.

"Is that a book of spells?" Donna asked.

"It might be a ward against the devil," Colin said. "Like a pentagram."

"Nope," Arthur said, inhaling deeply off the joint, feeling like his head was full of drifting sparks instead of thoughts. "Pretty sure that's her pussy."

TWENTY-ONE

"Yep!" Colin announced three minutes or three hours later. "It *was* her pussy."

"Men have a hundred words for it," Arthur said. "Like Eskimos describing snow."

TWENTY-TWO

"How's it going with Enoch Crane?" Van asked. "He stick it in anyone's contrawhatum lately?"

"Every chance he gets," Colin said, still reading.

It was after midnight and they had put *America's Most Wanted* behind them. They were on to MTV now, *Headbangers Ball*. The window was open because the blue fug had started to make their eyes water and it was as hot as being under a pile of blankets together. Allie hung her head out into the night.

"What about burning down his neighbor's house? They going to hang him for it?" Van croaked. Van was smoking like a house afire himself, blue haze spilling from his lips, from his nostrils, from his clothes.

"He says that was King Sorrow."

"Who's King Sorrow again?" Gwen asked.

"A creature summoned from the Long Dark, sort of a demon. No—a *dragon*. Enoch Crane calls him all kinds of things: proud worm, cunning serpent, armored devil. But I think he's describing a conventional dragon, your basic Smaug-class creature. Sired by Father Ruin, the most ancient and powerful of dragons."

"How do you summon a dragon?" Donna asked.

Colin turned another thick, cottony page. "They made their own spell from scratch. All magic, it turns out, is *particular* magic. Unique to the people casting the spell. Enoch Crane would starve himself for a week and then eat cakes made from binder weed seeds, which I assume was your basic backwoods hallucinogen."

"Morning glory, I bet," Van said. "Hillbilly LSD."

Colin said, "Then he'd fill a pail with water and talk to his reflection. He called it the Other Face. The Other Face knew all about sorcery. He told Crane that reality is a brightly lit cage, everyone kept in their own cell. The Long Dark is on the other side of the bars, an infinite space full of frolicking spirits. Those bars aren't there to keep us prisoner. They're there to keep us *safe* from the stuff out in the Long Dark. The creatures that dwell there are irresistibly drawn to reality. They envy our actuality. If you want to open the cage and let them in, you need to make a kind of magical key, and everyone's lock is different. Crane cast spells with these Cobbett sisters. To summon King Sorrow, one of the sisters carried a dead crow in her arms until it flew. The other sister went around with a bonnet full of eggs, describing everything she saw to them. Then she cracked them one by one and the last one held an eyeball. Crane opened his chest as if it were a cabinet, removed one of his kidneys, and made a meal of it, an offering for the King. Once they had each broken reality in their own individual fashion, they joined in a circle and the world went dim and they bargained with King Sorrow."

"Sounds like they made a Philip," Gwen said. "An Elwood Hondo."

"Yes. I surmised much the same thing." Colin turned another page.

"Allie? Allie, are you sick?" Gwen asked, stirring, sitting up.

Allie had been leaning her head and shoulders out the window for almost the entire conversation.

"There's some guy walking through the backyard," Allie said.

Van drifted to the window, put his hand on the small of Allie's back, and looked out. "What's up, man? Yo!"

Allie and Van pulled their heads back into the room at the same time.

"He disappeared around the corner of the house," Allie said. "Wonder where he's going."

"At two in the goddamn morning?" Donna asked. "In the middle of the goddamn Maine winter? There's nothing out here to walk to."

On the TV someone played a guitar with sparks flying out of the neck. No one could seem to sustain any interest in the man who had crossed through the yard.

"So are we gonna go for it?" Van said.

"Go for what?" Arthur asked.

Gwen shifted her gaze to him. "What we've been talking about for the last however many hours—summoning King Sorrow. What do you say, Arthur? Do you want to bargain with a real live dragon?"

TWENTY-THREE

At some point they made their way to the study and fell into their usual stools around the card table. Arthur wasn't sure when. He remembered telling Gwen he *did* want to see a real live dragon . . . and then nothing until they were all sitting around the study, underneath that wall of bright butterflies in their shadow boxes. They were all stoned and determined to stay that way. Later, he believed they stayed high to give themselves moral cover, so they could say they were baked and being silly, and never thought it would work.

Of course they thought it would work.

"King Sorrow was sired by Father Ruin, the oldest of all the dragons to visit Midgard, land of men," Colin told them, while he poured whiskeys. "He was the only one of his brood not eaten by his mother, Old Char. Sorrow persuaded her that he was too scrawny to eat, that she would choke on his bones. Instead, he said, 'Eat father while he's sleeping,' and handed Old Char her own plump tail, and she devoured herself."

"The old ouroboros trick," Arthur said, which got him some looks.

"Dragons usually only come to Midgard to lay eggs—like a migratory bird—but they live in the Long Dark, where they feed on nightmares for most of their long lives. They dream of our world and we dream of theirs. That's a bit of an ouroboros right there, Arthur," Colin said.

"Why do you keep talking about the Northern Lights?" Allie asked.

"Not the aurora borealis," Arthur said. "An *ouroboros* is the ancient symbol of a snake eating its own tail."

"What's that a symbol of?"

"I think it means what goes around comes around," Gwen said.

"Oh," Allie said. "Well, I've always wanted to see the Northern Lights. I think they're romantic. Take me somewhere I can see the Northern Lights sometime, Van?"

"Okay," Van said. "It's a plan."

"King Sorrow has often visited Earth to serve the wicked ends of men," Colin continued. "His bargains entail having someone to slay or he claims his right to slay *you*. He may even have served Herod, who died after he drank a goblet of King Sorrow's tears, a swift poison."

"You mean Herod from *Jesus Christ Superstar*?" Donna said.

"And other notable Christian texts," Arthur said.

"Before that he was with Mithridates," Colin said. "And afterward with Genghis Khan."

"Sounds like if your aspiration is to be one of the world's great mass murderers, King Sorrow is your guy," Van said.

"Or if you want to be one of the world's winners," Donna said.

Colin went on: "Dragons like riddles and wordplay, and King Sorrow is no exception. They enjoy games but have been known to throw terrible tantrums when they lose. Beating a dragon in checkers is a great way to end up with a flattened barn and a whole mess of charred sheep. But they eat pain, not flesh. Oh, they'll inhale a cow or a family of four, but it's not really satisfying. The pain and the fear of their prey is the feast."

"Pretty sure Jayne Nighswander is on the same meal plan," Gwen said.

Van drummed on the edge of the card table. "Come on. How do we get this clown show started?"

"We've already started," Colin said, looking at each of them in turn, his eyes brilliant with pleasure and purpose. "We needed a story to believe and now we've got one. Some of what I just told you is from the journal and some I made up . . . but I knew it was true when I said it."

"So what now?" Arthur asked.

"There's a radio dish in Puerto Rico, the Arecibo Observatory, as big as a lake. They use it for radio astronomy. It can detect the faintest signals from hundreds of millions of miles away and transmit as far. That's what we want to be now. We're a circle, like that radio dish, and we're transmitting a signal into the Long Dark. Put the fingers of both hands on the table. Don't lift them. Then we start asking King Sorrow to make himself available to us. Like when my grandfather and his friends invited Elwood Hondo to say hello."

"Yo, King Sorrow," Van said, setting his fingers on the table. "Where you at, bitch?"

"King Sorrow? Can you give us a rap and let us know you're here?"

"Hello! Calling Radio Dragon, do you copy?"

"Hey! Hey! King Sorrow! Give us a knock!"

So they began, talking over one another, jeering and pleading and requesting his presence with mock formality. At first it felt stupid and Arthur didn't participate. Donna was roaring, "Come on, you cold-blooded fuck, we're waiting—give your scales a shake and come on down!" and he stared at the green felt tabletop, fingertips pressed to the surface, and the half-full tumbler of whiskey next to his left hand. His throat was hoarse from all the weed, and he was wondering if anyone would care if he lifted his hand for a sip. He was looking into the tumbler and a reflection of his left eye stared back from the surface of his eighteen-year Talisker . . . then closed in a slow, sly wink.

A tingle of shock spread through his chest and for a moment he was struggling to breathe.

"Water," he croaked.

"What's that?" Gwen asked.

"We need a bowl of water," he said. "To see the Other Face. It worked for Enoch Crane and it will work for us."

Colin crossed the room to the Cabinet of Curiosities and returned a moment later with the olive-colored helmet that had once belonged to the Russian seer, Wolf Messing. He carried it into the bathroom, and when he returned it was sloshing with water. "If we're going to attempt lecanomancy, we should use a basin with some power in it."

"Lecanomancy," Van said. "I thought we were trying to raise a dragon, not turn someone into a werewolf."

"Lecanomancy is the art of contacting other worlds through water, usually collected in a sacred dish. The helmet of a Jewish psychic ought to do." Colin set it in front of Arthur, who looked into the water: a jade darkness. "Let's try again. Hands on the table."

This time Arthur was the first to speak. "King Sorrow, will you speak to us? Will you tell us how we may bring you closer?"

"Paging King Sorrow!" Allie cried. "Paging King Sorrow, cleanup on aisle six."

"C'mon, King Sorrow," Gwen said. "We have snacks."

Arthur stared hard at his own reflection, waiting to see the face in the water come to life on its own. The air felt dry, charged. Arthur thought if he touched Gwen, sitting on his left, he would give her the mother of all static electricity zaps.

After a few minutes he shook his head in frustration. "Nothing. This isn't working."

"Let me try," Allie said. He handed her the great, spiny, bleached conch shell (conch shell? Wasn't it supposed to be a Russian helmet?) and she held it to the side of her face and began to speak into it as if it were a telephone receiver. "King Sorrow? Hello? Operator, can you put me through to King Sorrow?"

"C'mon, you fuckin' snake," Donna said. "Slither out of your hole already. The door's wide open, so come the fuck—"

The door to the hallway slammed shut as if someone had kicked it. Donna screamed and jerked her hands off the table. Arthur almost fell off his stool.

"Fuck my! . . . Fuckin'! . . . *Ass!*" Donna stammered. "Who did that?"

"I think we know who," Colin said. Arthur wondered how he could sound so calm. Arthur's own heart was on a rampage, whamming furiously in his chest.

"Put your fingers back, girl," Gwen said. "You don't do something like this halfway."

Donna gave Gwen a startled, unhappy stare, but put her fingers back on the table.

"I thought twins had identical reactions to things," Arthur said. "How come you didn't jump up, Van?"

"Couldn't," Van said, his face a rigid blank. "Shit my pants."

The doorknob turned. The sight gripped Arthur with a dreadful fascination: he could not have been more horrified if he had been watching someone approach him with an ax. He didn't think he could bear to find out who was on the other side, but when at last the door eased open, it showed only the dimly lit hallway beyond.

"This isn't funny," Donna said.

"Never was," Gwen said.

The door slammed shut again. Donna flinched. Colin didn't react, his gaze fixed on Allie. She didn't react either, was listening intently to the great conch shell—yes, she was definitely holding a conch, Arthur didn't know what had happened to Wolf Messing's helmet—her eyes remote and far away.

Across the room the doorknob began to turn again.

"No no no!" Donna said. "Don't come in."

"Yes!" Arthur shouted over her. "Yes, do. King Sorrow, we invite you in."

The house groaned and creaked as if it had been struck by a great blast of wind, although outside the night was still. Arthur was briefly gripped with the queerest sensation, a feeling like some giant hand had reached down and given the whole house a sudden sharp twist, as if The Briars itself was a doorknob rotating in a great claw. His stomach turned with it. The others felt it too. He saw Van and Gwen grab the edge of the card table as if they might be flung from their seats. Colin wobbled for balance on his dealer's stool. The door on the far side of the room sailed gently open . . . only the lights had gone out in the hall and now there was nothing on the other side except (*the Long Dark*) impenetrable blackness.

Allie passed the hand mirror across the table to Donna (*Hand mirror? Wasn't it a conch shell? What happened to the conch?* Arthur wondered. *What happened to the helmet?*) and stood. Her face was tranquil and empty, her eyes unfocused. She crossed to the player piano, arranged herself on the bench, and began to play. Arthur recognized the theme straight away: "Puff the Magic Dragon."

The door slammed once more. Donna jumped, almost fell off her stool.

"This is fucked," she said.

"Look in the mirror," Van told her. "See what you see."

"I don't want to," Donna said. "I don't like where this is going."

"You aren't Cady Lewis, sis," Van said, a name Arthur had never heard before. "We're here. *I'm* here. I'm with you no matter what happens. All of us."

Donna lifted the mirror—it had a jagged Y-shaped crack running up the middle that split her face into three misaligned segments—and stared raptly at her own wan reflection.

Behind her, the doorknob began to turn once more. Arthur's skin crawled and he thought, *Make it stop*, but he did nothing to make it stop, not even when the house groaned and shifted again, seemed to rotate beneath them once more. A few books fell off the shelf behind him. Donna came jerkily to her feet, shoving the mirror across the table toward Colin. Van rose a moment later, using the table to push himself unsteadily up. When Arthur looked at him, Van had a pair of white sand dollars placed over his eyes, like coins on the eyes of a corpse. But then he walked around the table, passed behind Colin, and when he came out on the other side his eyes were just his eyes.

The door threw itself open and there was a featureless darkness where the hallway belonged and then an eye the size of a headlight opened sleepily in the darkness. It was a golden eye, stained an infected red, and Arthur found himself choking back a scream—*Oh, God! He sees us! He sees us all the way from the Long Dark!*—and the eye closed again and the darkness was absolute and the door closed very gently once more.

Only Colin and Gwen and Arthur remained at the table now and Arthur's brow pricked with a rotten sweat and Colin was staring into the helmet filled with water, no sign of the mirror now (or the conch—wasn't there a conch?). The house lurched. The doorknob was turning again. He didn't want to see what was in the hall now. Instead, he looked out the French windows . . . and saw himself walk past in the snow out beyond the patio. The sight gave him a jarring sense of dislocation. He began to pant and he shook his head to clear it. *I'm not there, I'm here, I'm here, dammit,* he told himself, but it didn't feel true. Later, the others told him he had been the first to leave the table, and he thought probably they were right and he had left some ghost of himself behind to observe the proceedings. A terrible, sickening notion. A terrifying one, to think the soul could so casually be spilled from the body, knocked out of it like whiskey from an overturned tumbler.

The sight of himself was the worst thing yet, and so he turned his gaze away from the window and was immediately sorry. The door yawned wide and the eye all but filled it, was as big as the tire on a tractor. The golden iris was stitched with crimson threads, slit up the middle by the long black line of the pupil. Arthur shut his eyes so he wouldn't have to see it.

When he opened them again, the door was closed. Colin had placed the helmet brimming with water in front of him. Arthur looked down at his reflection and his reflection gazed blankly back. When the face in the water began to speak—lips moving, although only Arthur heard the voice in his mind, a voice that was not his own—the tongue that flickered out was black and forked.

Arthur stared fixedly into the water and learned what was expected of him.

TWENTY-FOUR

The dark man fled across the snow and Arthur Oakes followed.

They each had a job to do, although Arthur was only vaguely aware of what was expected of the others—music and courtiers for the King, a proclamation to announce his arrival, incense to honor the royal presence. Arthur was required to prepare the King's meal, which meant catching the dark man who was carrying it. It didn't look like he was carrying anything, but he had it on him, Arthur knew it.

He had tried to run him down at first, had run shouting—*Wait, wait, motherfucker, shit!*—but the dark man could run too and didn't seem to get tired. When Arthur slowed to a walk, so did his quarry. Instead, Arthur decided to try and gain on him in subtle increments.

He had gone outside in his sneakers, without a coat, and by the third trip around the house, he was very cold. That was part of it, he thought. He wasn't allowed to go back inside and get a coat. If he did, the fleeing man would escape. And so the dark figure—who he was fairly sure was Enoch Crane himself—walked and Arthur followed in the deadly chill.

Their path took them in a rough ellipse around The Briars, through a stand of birch, past a family graveyard, over hillocks, along a narrow path through bunches of wild thorns armored in ice. Fairy tale country, Arthur thought.

His winding course took him past the open French windows. The library within was lit up like a theater. Colin sat on a purple pillow with a water bong, facing the stone patio and blowing smoke rings, looking like Alice's caterpillar. Allie hunched over the piano, mechanically banging out "Puff the Magic Dragon." The keys were smeared with blood. She meant to play it until her fingers were smashed down to the bone. Arthur could distantly glimpse Van and Donna sitting on the floor across from each other. It looked like they were playing cards. *You aren't Cady Lewis, sis*, Van said, and somehow Arthur thought he already knew who she was. Cady Lewis was the reason Donna thought sex offenders should be executed by firing squad.

And Gwen? Arthur didn't know what task she had been given. *Please let her be all right*, he thought. *Don't let her get hurt because I dragged her into this.*

Colin saw him passing. He exhaled three fat, trembling rings, then called out, "Keep going, Arthur! The King will expect a hot dinner after his long cold journey!"

The dark man fled across the white desert and Arthur followed.

A little hill led up to a stand of birch on the southern edge of the property. That was where the dark man slipped for the first time and went to one knee. When he rose, Arthur had shaved at least twenty feet off the distance between them . . . close enough to see his quarry was shirtless. Arthur had thought he was wearing some kind of crude, ugly tunic, but now he could see his arms were bare, and there was something wrong with his back, some very precise disfigurement. A broad square of glistening darkness rose from the small of his back to midway up his shoulder blades.

The disfigured man limped on. He stumbled again, coming out of the icy thicket of blackberry bushes, a thorny snare hooking his arm and half turning him, causing him to reel. By the time he recovered, Arthur was close enough to hit him with the toss of a football. Close enough to realize the other man was barefoot. Arthur almost pitied him.

They circled the house again. "Puff the Magic Dragon" was still playing, but when Arthur glanced through the French windows this time he saw Allie dancing to it, head down, hair in her face, arms waving over her head, so who the hell was playing? No one sat at the piano. He was still trying to figure that out when he heard Donna cry: "Dragon! Dragon and that's game!" She leapt up from her card game with Van, who held a fistful of cards. He threw them into the air and they exploded in a shower of flames.

The dark man fled across the cold desert and Arthur Oakes followed.

He felt as if he would be chasing Enoch Crane for the rest of his life. Arthur's breath exploded from his lips in a white smoke. When he checked the sky again it seemed the moon was stuck in place, couldn't sink to the horizon and disappear, not until they finished the spell.

"Come on, man," Arthur told him. "Aren't your feet cold? Let's get this over with."

"I can bear it a while longer. My feet ha' been cold since I struck the end of a rope in the year of your Lord 1789." Crane's voice was a raw, deep slur from another century.

"I can do this all night, brother. It's no skin off my back. Which is more than I can say for you."

When Arthur next crossed the flagstones behind the house, Colin's rings of smoke hung improbably still in the air. Colin blew another smoke shape from his bong: a dragon, no larger than a kitten. It opened its wings and began to fly, darting through each ring of smoke. Colin lifted his head to watch it go, and as he did, a storm of butterflies poured from the open doors, following the smoke dragon up into the stars. Gwen appeared behind Colin, staring after them.

"Go on!" Gwen called. "Fly to the land of Honalee and bring him back!"

Crane was limping now. He had slipped again in the snow and gone down hard on one knee. Arthur thought he had twisted the leg. It pleased Arthur to run him to earth—he felt the simple murderous joy of the hawk falling on the hare.

When they were on the narrow, winding trail in the frozen-over blackberry thicket, Arthur began to run. The path twisted and meandered and Crane could not see him closing in. When Arthur burst from the bushes, the dead man was not ten feet away. He tried to put on some speed, but it was too late. Arthur lunged and took Crane around the waist, carried him down into the snow.

Crane didn't struggle as Arthur flung him onto his back. He had a patchy beard and bad teeth and the flesh of his chest had been peeled off as well, in a square that reached from nipples to navel. Where there should've been a cage of bloody ribs there was, instead, a walnut cabinet with an ornate dragon carved in the center of a Celtic labyrinth. Arthur should've felt surprise or wonder or horror, but instead, at the sight of this cabinet, he was gripped with a euphoric, wordless triumph. There was only a single word in the entire English language that could express that feeling: *mine*.

"Aye," Crane said, as if Arthur had spoken aloud. "Yours. A meal fit for a king and help yourself to it. Mark me, though. What you claim now is but an appetizer. He'll have your anguish for his mains. See if he don't."

Arthur opened the cupboard door in Enoch Crane's chest to discover a Cabinet of Curiosities within. Its wooden shelves and cubbies held all kinds of clutter. Arthur saw an airplane ticket on one shelf, with Allie's name printed on it. There was a sand dollar, as white as a bleached bone, a bloody thumbprint stamped upon it. At the sight of it he thought of Donovan. There was a paperweight showing the Twin Towers in New York City. For some reason, they were both spilling clouds of smoke like some homage to *King Kong*, when the big ape had scaled the towers carrying Jessica Lange. There was a postcard of a mossy stone bridge in a green country—the sight of it made Arthur's heart ache, and he was gripped with a sudden urge to apologize to Gwen Underfoot, although he could not have said what for.

And on a shelf in the upper right corner of the cabinet was a human heart. Enoch Crane's heart. It was beating furiously until the moment Arthur removed it, coming free at his touch, cold as a raw steak from the fridge.

"He promised me 'e'd have it," Enoch Crane said. "And 'e'll have yours too, Arthur. One way or another: 'e'll eat it or he'll stop it. Either way, King Sorrow wins."

Arthur closed the cupboard. The heart in his hand stained his palm with blood but did not drip. He stood too quickly and darkness squeezed his vision from either side. He needed to throw his head back and fill his chest with air to keep from falling. He glanced at the night sky, feeling lightheaded. A vast black shape flitted across the stars. When he looked down, Crane was gone, leaving behind a dirty, man-shaped indentation in the snow, stamped with a square of blood.

He lowered his head, feeling the cold, and started walking again. The butterflies returned from the Long Dark as he crossed the flagstones to the French doors. Only now they were burning—a flurry of billowing, flaming confetti, spreading an ugly stink.

As Arthur entered the library, the overhead lights flickered, brightened, then went out. The music was over, the room still, the silence loud with suspense. That silence was a roar. He approached the card table, holding a man's heart, and when Gwen saw what he carried she left the room. She returned a moment later with a gold-edged platter. Fine china for a king. Arthur set the heart upon it and sat at the card table, Gwen on his left, Van on his right.

The upside-down helmet, filled with water, was rocking in the center of the table, the water slapping one side of the steel basin and then the other. The helmet rocked this way and that and abruptly flipped in the air, as if someone had struck the rim. It landed right-side up, its contents soaking the table. The front of the helmet bent upward slightly, like a lip lifted in a sneer. Beneath was darkness.

"What's this?" came a voice from inside the helmet: deep, plummy, resonant, good-humored. "Is it a party? Oh, loverly. Will there be fun and games? I hope so. In fact," King Sorrow told them, "if we put our minds to it, I think we can have a bit of both."

TWENTY-FIVE

Van found his voice first. "You're smaller'n I expected, son. Somehow I didn't think you'd fit under a helmet."

"Small as an evil thought, a worm in the brain," King Sorrow said. A puff of blue smoke rippled out from beneath the dented rim of the helmet. "Even a small notion can burn down a whole city. One such as myself expects to be addressed with the honorifics that are his due, Donovan McBride . . . but I s'pose every king must have his fool and a fool need not bother with the niceties of court."

"How does one as magnificent as yourself expect to be addressed, my lord?" Gwen asked.

"His Excellency. His Most Glorious Majesty. Crucifier of the Catholics, perpetrator of the pogroms, mass murderer of the Muslims. Or, Underfoot, simply *Lord* will do." Another streamer of smoke and then he added, "Gwendolyn and Arthur. I knew a Gwen and an Arthur once. She was a whore. He was worse."

"Oh? Tell us, Lord—what's worse than a hoor?" Gwen asked.

"An idealist."

"Your gracious sovereign," Colin said. "We humbly petition you to defend us in our hour of need—and to this end we have performed great deeds and are prepared to make sacrifice."

"We have brought you a heart to feast on," Arthur said, putting two fingers on the edge of the gold-rimmed platter.

"I have a better idea," said King Sorrow. "Let's *riddle* instead. If any of you can stump me, I'll pile that plate high with gold chain."

"And what if you stump *us*?" Allie asked.

"Then I will tear out your tongues and make a necklace of them, so your mewling voices will never disturb me again. You woke me from a deep sleep and a fine dream."

"Of what do dragons dream?" Arthur asked.

"Fire," King Sorrow said. "What else? Did you know that the obese will not burn so much as *melt*? They bubble away like a tallow candle. When a modern woman burns, she smells like bacon steeped in maple syrup. I don't remember women of the ancient world smelling so sweet, but that's refined sugars for you. Your modern diet, you know, is almost as bad for the health as knowing *me*, mate."

"I'm too baked for riddles," Allie said.

"Hah," King Sorrow replied. "You aren't baked yet but lose a few riddles to me and you will be."

"Thank you, no, m'lord," Colin said. "We honor you with a human heart and ask only that you rid us of our meddlesome foes."

Two fine tendrils of smoke streamed from the darkness beneath the helmet.

"If you promise me a life, I expect to receive one," King Sorrow said. "All arrangements are final, no substitutions acceptable . . . unless you offer to substitute *yourself*. Know that I require time to come through from the Long Dark to the thin light of your world. As you can see, I am now only a shadow of myself. But given time I will wax like the moon. With time, I will crack the fragile shell of your reality like an egg and be born into it in all my splendor. Upon Easter morning whomsoever you name will cease to trouble you: your enemies and all who would defend them. There will be no safe shelter for them. No army will shield them from me."

King Sorrow never said *kill*, but Arthur could not pretend—not then, not later—that they didn't all understand what he meant.

"What if they come for us before you're ready?" Donna asked, her voice harsh, ready to be angry. "Fat lot of good you'd do us then."

"Are you afraid your enemies will take you like Cady, Donna McBride?" King Sorrow asked. "Take you to die in terror and pain?"

"Don't you dare mock Cady Lewis," Donna said.

"You think I would mock a poor dead child? If only she had been one of my subjects, Donna. I would've skinned the men who hurt her, while they were alive." He paused. The helmet seemed to wobble this way and that, ringing faintly. "If you assent, I will mark you all . . . invisibly. You will only see my mark when you *need* to see it. The mark of a serpent, twining its way around you in a protective sheath. Touch two fingers to the serpent's head—one touch!—and I will leap from the Long Dark to protect you from any man or woman who would do you harm. Although, I suppose you might still be killed by ambush. There are limits even to my regal powers. But console yourself! If one of you were to fall, struck down by a cowardly attack from behind, five would remain to call me down upon your assassin."

"That's not as consoling as you might think," Van said.

"Take heart. It is surprisingly difficult to truly catch an adversary unawares, Donovan. The fox always hears the blast of the horn and the yaps of the approaching dogs. Perhaps not one victim in a thousand fails to see it coming, and such sorry souls are almost always distracted with some perverse business of their own—the thief counting his money while his accomplice readies the ax. That will have to be enough . . . and if it isn't, then goodbye and good night to you."

"It's enough for me," Colin said, glancing around the table at the others. Arthur moved his chin in agreement, saw the others nodding from the edges of his vision.

"I get aggravated pretty easily," Donna said. "I usually want to kill three or four people a day. How often is too often to use this mark you're talking about?"

"I advise you to employ it sparingly. To strike before I am ready, I must draw from your internal energies, your own will and life force. I can fight a *war* for you, Donna McBride. But to use the mark in your own defense will leave you as aged and weary as if you had fought the war yourself. Is this acceptable to you? Your liege swears his protection and in turn you offer me a sacrifice on Easter day. Are we agreed?"

"The people we're talking about," Colin said, "are a pointless evil, like AIDS. I can't speak for anyone else, but for myself, I would see them gone. Blasted from the face of the Earth."

"I'd see them gone," Gwen said, "and my friend Arthur safe from them."

"Hell, yes," Donna said.

"I'm in," Van said.

"Do it," Allie agreed.

A moment's silence followed.

"And you, Arthur Oakes?" King Sorrow asked. "I take it the enemies who haunt all of you are your own particular curse. Do you agree to my terms, with a full heart?"

"With gratitude, Lord," Arthur said. "As for a full heart, it's here for you when you're ready to dine." Touching the plate again.

There was a bassy rumble of laughter. "You understand, should you lose your nerve, only one of your own lives will do as a replacement for those you name."

"If it's them or me," Arthur said, "I choose them. Jayne Nighswander and Ronnie Volpe."

"My precious subjects," King Sorrow said, "I live only to serve you."

"Possibly for dinner," Gwen said, and King Sorrow laughed again.

Another blue stream of smoke came from beneath the helmet... followed an instant later by something that at first glance looked like a garter snake escaping across the green felt of the card table. When it unwound, slipping rapidly toward the china dish, Arthur had to repress a cry of revulsion. It was a *tongue*, forked at the end, glistening with spit, and at the sight he flashed to a memory of his own face, reflected in water, and a tongue just like it spilling from his own mouth.

The tongue flicked at the heart on the plate, delicately tasting it—then coiled around it and pulled it across the table, leaving a wet, brown smear on the felt. The helmet rocked, tipped back just enough to drag the heart into the darkness beneath. As the tongue vanished, Arthur thought he saw the eye again, peering out at him from beneath the helmet, small now, no bigger than his own fist. It was the same eye he had seen through the open door: a golden iris slit by the vertical pupil of a snake. The eye blinked like the shutter of a camera snapping shut and springing open again, fixed upon him. Arthur's chest tingled with horror. He wanted to scream. Instead, he grabbed the lid of the helmet and flipped it over. It thudded softly on the felt, in the watery light of early morning.

Arthur stared as the helmet rocked back and forth. It was hard to think, as if he had just been jolted awake from a nightmare. It had been Scatterday night when he grabbed the edge of the helmet to flip it over, but it was well after dawn by the time it landed upside down. Wolf Messing's helmet looked like it had been used as an ashtray, a few burnt roaches and some fragrant ash in the bottom.

He peered around him, to see if anyone else had noticed how suddenly the morning had come, springing upon them like a tiger from the tall grass.

Arthur was alone at the card table. Van sat on the couch in his boxers and a T-shirt, a hand clapped over his face. Allie was behind him, massaging his neck. Gwen stood over Van with a glass of water and some Excedrin from the candy jar on Llewellyn's desk.

"I feel like I swallowed a live snake," Van said, and Arthur almost laughed and thought, *Be glad it didn't swallow you.* "I ain't had the spins like this since I drank a pitcher of beer and climbed on a mechanical bull one time."

The door behind the desk—the door into the spare bedroom—was open and Colin stood in it, in a white T-shirt and white jockeys. He was stringy and fit, not an ounce of extra fat on him, and his skull had recently been shaved. He came upon every day fresh made, as if he had been stamped out by a machine. Movement behind him caught Arthur's eye, and he saw Donna roll over in the tangle of sheets, yawning, in a halter top and a G-string. She struggled out of bed, wrapping herself in the sheet, and joined Colin at the door.

"Nothing makes a weekend like a bale of primo weed and a black mass," Colin said.

"Ugh," Donna said. "So this is what Saturday morning looks like. I hate it."

But she was wrong. It wasn't Saturday. It was Sunday. Saturday was gone—had vanished with King Sorrow. Twenty-four hours of their lives, gone in one bite.

TWENTY-SIX

He made arrangements through Tana to meet with Jayne that afternoon.

"Yeah, that's just as well," Tana told him over the phone. "If you took the thing she wanted, I don't want to touch it. I ain't what anyone would call a delicate girl, but just the thought of it gives me the willies. Makes my skin wanna crawl right off my back."

"Just think: if that happened, maybe someone would make a book out of you," Arthur told her.

"Ugh," Tana said. Then she laughed and said, "I wonder what the title would be. How about 'Bad Life Choices: The Tana Nighswander Story'?"

"How about 'She Deserved Better: A Girl's Life in Gogan'?"

Tana laughed again. "You know something, Arthur? You ain't as terrible a person as you like to think you are."

He took the Christmobile from his apartment and drove south into Gogan. The sky was pitilessly blue and bright and every snowbank threw a blinding dazzle of reflected sunlight. He did not think about Enoch Crane or King Sorrow or a human heart sitting on fine china. By then he had already dismissed most of his rapidly fading recollections of the weekend—which felt like three days, not two. *Scatterday*, he thought, and laughed. It was cold in the car and his breath gushed from his mouth in a golden smoke, as if he were preparing to exhale a blast of fire.

If someone asked him what he had done with his weekend (some kindly and imaginary confessor to whom he could admit everything), he would've said he stole a book worth more money than most people made in a year. He didn't want to do it but had been made to, to keep his incarcerated mother from being assaulted by a gang of moral imbeciles. His own crime made him sick . . . so sick, he spent the weekend fucked up in front of MTV, smoking blunt after blunt, an act that was wildly out of character for him. He had dreamt pot-crazed dreams about the Philip Experiment and dragons. He had spent hours chasing a dead man with a cabinet door for a chest, and if that wasn't the stuff of fantasy, he didn't know what was.

He got to Shut-Up-And-Eat-It ahead of Jayne, parked out back, and sat in the Christmobile holding his hands up to the heaters. They were only just beginning to produce a trickle of lukewarm air when the Ranchero slowed to turn into the lot. He climbed out into a sadistic cold that brought tears to his eyes and then froze them on his eyelashes.

Jayne slewed her ride to a messy stop, spraying rocks. Ronnie was slumped against the passenger-side door in a snow parka, the hood pulled up, so Arthur couldn't see his face, only a dark hole where his face belonged. That parka was the exact shiny black of a body bag. He looked like he'd been zipped in and heaped carelessly into the passenger seat.

Arthur reached back into the Christmobile for the Crane journal and walked around to the driver's side of the Ranchero. Jayne rolled down the window and stuck her hand out. Whatever he had been planning to say went out of his mind the moment he saw her face.

"What's wrong with you?" Arthur asked.

There were bluish circles under her eyes and her color was bad and her lips were so chapped they were peeling. She looked like she was fighting off a flu. She looked like death.

"Couldn't sleep last night. Bad dreams. Probably because I knew I was going to have to deal with your sorry ass today, Oakes."

"Was a lot worse'n bad dreams," Ronnie said. His voice was muffled from inside the hood of his parka. "Bitch got wasted and passed out with a lit cigarette in her mouth. Lucky she didn't burn her face off. Or burn down the whole house."

"I told you, fuckhead, I wasn't smoking."

Ronnie pushed his hood back and Arthur twitched. He looked bad too. Beneath his whiskers, his skin was cheesy, almost translucent, and his eyes glittered from dark hollows.

"Why'd you wake up coughing smoke then? I swear you were coughing sparks."

The fine hairs on the nape of Arthur's neck stirred with a gentle unease.

"So where was the fucking cigarette?" she yelped at him.

"You probably swallowed it. You were so wasted, I wouldn't be surprised if you ate the whole pack and thought it was a sammidge."

She exhaled a thin, harsh breath through pursed lips, and looked back at Arthur. They each held one end of Enoch Crane's journal. She turned it slightly to examine it.

"I thought it would have a nipple on the cover or something," Jayne said. "This just looks like any other old book."

"Well, it isn't. It's worth more than all the other books I brought you put together." She tugged on it—but he didn't let go. Instead, he bent slightly to meet her gaze directly. "Jayne. Ask your buyer for *thirty*. Not twelve. *Thirty*."

Jayne's eyes were watery and bloodshot, and there were deep lines etched around her mouth, the sort of lines one expected to see in a woman twice her age.

She lives hard, Arthur said to himself. *She won't live long going the way she does.*

Then he thought, *I wouldn't give her past Easter*, a thought that gave him a shudder. Hadn't there been something about Easter in his weed-stoked dream of dragons?

"I got no other place to take it, and she knows it. I've never budged her a penny. Miserable old bitch. I tried to argue her up once and she looked at me like I was dog puke on the sidewalk. Stopped answering my calls for two weeks. In the end I got less'n her first offer and had to take it."

Arthur said, "If she doesn't want it for thirty, tell her to think on it. Tell her she can have a week, and then you're going to start tearing pages out and using them for toilet paper. She'll come up. Maybe not to thirty. But at least to twenty. Maybe twenty-five."

Jayne's eyes were fogged with exhaustion, but one corner of her mouth twitched at that. "Gosh, you're bold today. I hope this isn't because you want something out of Tana she hasn't given you yet. That what you want? You want anal?"

A sliver of disgust—for himself as much as for Jayne—lanced right through him, an emotion that felt like a stabbing. He said, "No. I want to be left alone until after February break."

Her wide lips twitched in another suggestion of a smile. "Your momma got a parole hearing then, don't she? End of February?"

"Yes, she does. And I'm going up there to testify on her behalf." To grovel, if he had to.

"Too bad they found a shiv in her cell. That probably scotches that. A concealed weapon, that's a serious thing. Looks to me like she's going to have to do her full stretch. Don't get your hopes up, Arthur. They pass her over, she's in there another year. Dr. Oakes won't graduate until 1991, and neither will you. You and me still got a lot more business to do, I think."

He felt ill at the thought of being caught, ruined, arrested. But he felt worse at the thought of continuing to get away with it, stealing for Jayne month after month, with no hope of reprieve.

"No," he said. "You forget. I graduate. I won't have access anymore."

"You're friends with that shiny-headed rich bastid the Underfoots work for, ain't you? Wren? In his house all the time? You don't have access to the school library anymore, you'll still be able to get into The Briars. Colin Wren's grandfather is a rich ol' queen. I bet there's plenty to take in there."

A sick throb pulsed in the side of his neck, up into his jaw. He shook his head. "Can't. I'll be gone, Jayne. I leave for the UK in the middle of July to see my grandparents, and this year, I'm not coming back. I'm enrolling at Magdalen College in Oxford to get my master's degree." When he thought of Oxford, it was with the desperation of a man who finds himself in freezing seas, a mile from shore, battling against the force of the tides.

Jayne smirked and looked away. "We can talk about that later, I guess."

"Talk about what?"

"Your post-graduation plans. I'm thinking that's something we probably ought to decide together. If your mom is still in the clink then, I figure you'd want to put off going to England and stay right close, for emotional support. Hell, if you were to leave, who knows what would happen to her? She might get so heart-broke she decides to kill herself in her cell."

His legs felt weak. He wondered if they'd give out on him, if he'd just sit down now on the frozen blacktop.

"They skinned a fella to make this," Jayne said, considering the book now. "Think of that. I guess books and men aren't so different. They're both red after they're opened up." She tossed it into Ronnie's lap. He had pulled his hood back up, might've gone to sleep. She said, "If my Boston connection really does go to twenty, you can have a break till the end of February. But then we're back in business, Artie. I'm getting a lot out of our little book club. Aren't you?"

He straightened. She was laughing when she rolled up her window. The inside of the window was steamed over from condensation, so she looked like a ghost of herself, seen through the glass. She looked like a drowning victim, submerged beneath a layer of ice.

Arthur never stole another thing for Jayne Nighswander.

TWENTY-SEVEN

When Arthur returned to The Briars that evening, he found the French doors thrown open wide in the study. The patio was littered with broken branches. A trail of pine needles led through the snow to the rock shelf above the water, where Colin and the others were gathered around the corpse of the Christmas tree. Arthur crunched across the snow, through the piercing, bitter cold, under the blackest and clearest night sky he had ever seen. He paused when he crossed a set of tracks, his own, from the night before (*no, Arthur, those are from Scatterday*). Just one. Whatever he had chased out here had existed only in his head.

The others had not bothered with jackets, but stood around with tumblers, singing "Nothin' but a Good Time." Donna was pretending a can of lighter fluid was a penis. She groaned ecstatically as she urinated petroleum onto the tree. Allie's cheeks were so pink, it looked as if she had been slapped, and she was laughing so hard, she tottered from the force of her own hilarity and suddenly sat down in the snow. She was happily drunk . . . and it crossed Arthur's mind that Allie usually *was* by this time of the evening. Donovan was smoking a cigarette—tobacco, not weed, which was a relief, because Arthur thought if he smelled ganja he might retch. Colin had two glasses of Glenfiddich in his hands, and he passed one to Arthur.

They stood on a granite ledge, ten feet above a wide strand of stinking mud and driftwood. Fifty yards away, across the salt flats, the ocean gasped. The sea air had a refreshing, salty bite and it felt good to fill his lungs with it. It felt even better when Gwen Underfoot bumped her shoulder against his.

"You all right, old chum?" she asked.

"As rain, old buddy," he said, and tried to smile. Gwen wasn't fooled and gave him a concerned, interrogatory look. He shook his head to indicate they could talk about it later, or, preferably, never.

"It's time to burn last year to the motherfucking ground," Colin said. "Who wants to do the honors?"

Van flicked his cigarette at the Christmas tree. The twelve-foot pine was right at his feet but somehow he contrived to miss. Donna had just helped Allie to her feet, but at this they both roared with laughter, and this time when Allie's legs gave, she pulled Donna down on top of her. Donna sprawled between her legs, her head on Allie's chest, like an inebriated lover. Gwen bent, picked Van's smoldering butt out of the snow, and sailed it onto the tree.

The blue spruce ignited with a great, hushed, concussive whump and a flash of heat that drove Arthur and Gwen back. One of her heels slipped in the snow and he got a hand on her waist to steady her. She captured his chest between her arms; he felt her tumbler pressing into his back. She looked up into his face, a new question in her gaze, and this one was affectionate and hopeful. Her lips were slightly parted and her breathing was soft and her curls tumbled loose from under the band of her watch cap. He drew a deep breath and the air was so cold it made the inside of his chest ache.

He wanted to kiss her, but in that moment he flashed to a memory of yanking down Tana Nighswander's jeans in the kitchen while Tana egged him on. Jayne peddled her sister to men to keep them happy and compliant, and in a moment of moral blindness, Arthur had let himself become one of them and put himself under Jayne's power forever. He didn't want Gwen anywhere near the sort of man he was now. He prayed with all his heart she never found out the sort of man he was.

And even if he hadn't helped himself to Tana, there was the problem of Oxford and Magdalen College. If he kissed her now, wouldn't he be making a kind of promise? And wasn't it one he couldn't keep? Come August, he meant to be gone, and if he wasn't, then either he would still be working for Jayne Nighswander or he would be headed to jail himself. He wanted to hold Gwen, to kiss and be kissed, to hear her soft laughter and feel her soft breath on his neck. He wanted those things deeply. But he *needed* England—he needed to get the fuck out of this country as soon as he could. He needed to get across the ocean like a sick man needs medicine.

Gwen Underfoot was a silver pin that would stick him to America like a butterfly to velvet if he let her. If he fell into her embrace now, he would certainly be impaled and mortally wounded by his own want. He could be her friend, could want the best for her. If Gwen got into Rackham and escaped working for the Wrens, it would even be a kind of atonement for what he had done with Tana. He could walk away with an almost clear conscience. He drew back from her slightly, feeling he had only narrowly escaped being run through.

Gwen waited, watching one emotion and then another moving across his features. She narrowed her eyes slightly and then seemed to nod to herself. She straightened and stepped out of his arms. He cleared his throat, feeling as if he had swallowed something sticky and salty that hadn't gone all the way down.

"So that's up in smoke," she said, in a warm, comradely tone, but whether she was talking about their future or the Christmas tree, he didn't know and didn't ask.

TWENTY-EIGHT

He was just letting himself into the apartment, back home after his Wednesday Anglo-Saxon seminar, when the phone jangled in the kitchen. He tromped in without getting out of his parka and caught it on the third ring. It was Tana.

"My sis wanted me to let you know you're off the hook a while," Tana said.

"Boston gave in," Arthur said, "didn't they?"

"I don't know anything about that. The only time Jayne talks money with me is when she's decided I owe her some. She just said it turned out like you said it would and you earned yourself till February." She paused a moment and then said something that made the fine hairs stir on the back of Arthur's forearms. "I think that book scared her. She didn't like having it in the house. Been givin' her nightmares. I woke up the other night because I thought she was screaming at Ronnie. Only Ronnie wasn't even home. He was up to Capehart to move some product. She was all alone. She was screaming in her sleep." Tana laughed—the hoarsened laugh of an old smoker. "Arthur Oakes has his revenge at last."

She laughed again. Arthur didn't laugh with her.

TWENTY-NINE

Gwen banged on the door but didn't wait for him to answer. She let herself in, calling his name.

"Here," he called and she hurried into the kitchen, yanking herself out of her peacoat. It was the first week of February, a day of dazzling brilliance and bitter cold, and she had her hands clapped together, puffing on them to warm them.

Arthur was crouched in front of the open oven. He had just been checking on a pair of Hungry-Man TV dinners—fried chicken for Van, Salisbury steak for himself. They needed to bake another ten minutes. At the age of twenty, Arthur's idea of home cooking ran the gamut from peanut butter on toast to beans on toast, with space in between for chipped corned beef on toast. When they ran out of toast, they ate TV dinners. Donovan and Arthur did all their shopping at the 7-Eleven. Arthur hadn't been inside a supermarket since his mother had gone to prison.

"You need to look at something," Gwen said. She reached for the hem of her Maine Black Bears hoodie and pulled it off over her head. The T-shirt beneath rose to the cups of her bra. His pulse quickened at that sight of smooth bare stomach. Alongside a sudden, intense throb of desire, he had a disorientating sensation of time doubling back on itself, something stronger than garden variety déjà vu. It had been less than half a year since the day Tana walked into his kitchen and tugged off the Biko hoodie to give it back to him. The rest of her clothes had followed, a memory that thrilled and provoked regret in equal measure.

He straightened and pushed the oven shut with his foot. Gwen grabbed his hand and towed him out of the kitchen and down the hall.

"Are you okay?" he asked.

"No, I'm going crazy and I'm scared out of my mind." She towed him into the dark of his room, turned, and without pausing, stripped off her T-shirt.

She was breathing hard. The swell of her breasts shuddered in the pale violet cups of a worn-out bra. It was cold in his room, and her torso was already prickling with goose bumps. Arthur's pulse quickened and he thought of a silver pin again, pushing through a butterfly and pinning it to black velvet. The needle was ready to sink into him now, and he wasn't sure he could flutter away this time.

"Do you crazy kids need some time alone?" Van asked them from the hallway, peering in through the half-open door. "I could run some errands, head down to the Nite Owl to pick up some beer or . . . lube or . . . whatever? I'm here to help."

"Get in here, Van," she said. "I need you too."

Arthur blanched.

"Oh, wow," Van said. "Oh, WOW." His voice softened, acquired an almost reverent tone. "I just never thought this would happen to me."

"No," she said. "Not for *that*. I need both of you to tell me I'm not losing my mind. I just about want to throw up. Or sit down and cry. And I am not a throw-up-and-start-crying kind of girl. Both of you, just—" She grabbed one of Arthur's hands and one of Van's and hauled them farther into the room. She positioned both of them so they stood with their backs to the bed. "Sit down? Please?" She hugged herself, arms crossed over her chest, and Arthur realized she was trembling.

He sat down. Van sank onto the edge of the mattress beside him.

"Whatever happens next," Van murmured to Arthur, "I'm willing to put a hand on your butt or something, but nothing more than that."

"Shut up, Van," Arthur said. He was unnerved himself by then, had never seen Gwen afraid before. He felt instinctively that whatever she wanted to show them was something he didn't want to see.

Gwen went around the side of the bed and turned on the lamp. Then she returned to stand before them. Her pupils were dilated from the dimness of the room. Her breathing was shallow and fast.

"Please tell me you're seeing this too," she said and lifted a hand to her left breast.

"I don't . . ." Arthur began, his gaze sweeping the length of her torso once, and again . . . and then he pushed himself back and away from her, his skin crawling.

Van made an unhappy sound in his throat, close to a moan. His gaunt hands clenched the sheets of Arthur's bed and squeezed into fists, bunching up the fabric.

The tattoo faded in from her waist upwards, a serpent in black and red, winding all the way around her waist, disappearing behind her back, then reemerging high on her ribs. Its spade-shaped head rested across the top of her left breast, not an inch from the two fingers she was pressing into her skin. She let out a pained breath and bent slightly, as if it hurt.

"You see it," she said. "You both see it." She sounded weak, and scared, but also relieved.

"That's not real," Arthur said.

"Yes, it is," Van whispered. "I've got one too."

At that, Gwen's eyes widened. "You—*what'd* you say there?"

"I've got one just like it," Van told her. His voice was pitched only slightly above a whisper.

"What the hell do you mean, you got one just like it?" Arthur asked. He was tingling all over, as chilled as if he were the one who had pulled off his shirt in this cold room.

"I saw it four days ago, when I got out of the shower. I was so freaked out I did some mescaline to calm myself down, and then later, I told myself it was a peyote hallucination. Even though when I got out of the shower, I was cold sober. And I didn't look again because I was scared shitless of it coming back."

Gwen's hand dropped from her breast and the tattoo began to vanish, disappearing from the head backward, erasing itself from her skin. In a moment it was as if it had never been there at all. Gwen dropped onto one of the beanbags. Arthur had an idea her legs had gone out on her.

"Are you both fucking with me?" Arthur asked. His voice had discovered a new, higher register.

"Would I fuck, son?" Van asked him. "He said he was going to mark us."

"Who said?"

"King Sorrow. The dragon."

Arthur felt a sense of dislocation so profound, it dizzied him. He flashed to a recollection of chasing a dead man with a skinned back across the snow; he recalled a voice speaking from beneath a battered Russian helmet. A part of him knew those things had happened. Another part of him refused to know it. It was like experiencing double vision, the world splitting and separating into overlapping images, then swimming back together—only it wasn't double vision, it was double memory.

Van shifted his gaze to look at him sidelong. "You remember. I know you remember. You fed him a heart on a china plate. Not the kind of thing a person forgets."

Arthur let out a short gasping breath. "That's not funny."

"It was never funny," Van said. He looked to Gwen. "*You* remember."

Gwen was still topless, aside from her bra, but whatever erotic charge had been present was long gone. She had her T-shirt in her lap but seemed to have forgotten about it. The hand that had touched her breast now rose to her left temple and began to move in small circles there.

"I remember I was really drunk, maybe for the first time in my life. Drunk, and I s'pose I had a contact high too. I remember I took the butterflies off the wall and I unpinned them and told them to fly away while they had a chance. Fly to the land of Honalee and bring back Puff the Magic Dragon."

"'Fraid they came back with a nastier lizard altogether, hon."

"Why are *we* cloudy on what happened and *you* aren't?" Gwen asked.

"I always thought someday I'd make contact with something from the astral realm," Van said, "if I smoked enough of the good shit. Matter of time, really."

While they spoke, Arthur began to pull himself out of his shirt with leaden arms. He let it drop to the floor and considered his sunken torso in the poor light. All he had to do was lift his hand to his heart, but he found himself strangely unwilling, as unwilling as he would've been to reach into a gaping chest wound. (*You were plenty willing to reach into an open chest not so long ago, Arthur, don't kid yourself you weren't.*)

"Go on, Arthur," Gwen said. "We're here. We're in this together. Go on and do it."

He touched his chest above his left nipple and the tattoo faded in from his waist upward, winding itself around his torso. His sides prickled, as if he were being kissed by a rope of thorns.

"What happens if I touch the—"

"Don't," Gwen said, and Van said, "He comes through. He comes through and lays waste."

"Lays waste to what?"

"Us, most likely."

Arthur's hand dropped from his chest and the ink dropped from his skin, the lines unwriting themselves from his chest. They sat in silence together. Gwen was at his feet, had a hand on his knee, and was looking into his face with frightened eyes.

"There's one bright side to this," Van said.

"What's that?" Gwen asked.

"I'm going to have to drop in on Allie and Donna now and tell them about this and there is a practical certainty Allie is going to take her shirt off."

The fire alarm went off, a stammering electronic shriek that went right through Arthur's head. *It's him!* he thought in that first wild instant. *He's come through!* Believing the alarm was the alien shriek of a four-hundred-ton reptile from a J.R.R. Tolkien novel.

He leapt up, adrenaline gunning his heart, and then almost tumbled over Gwen. She caught his waist to steady him. There was a haze of smoke in the hallway.

"Fuck," Arthur said, running into the kitchen, where the smoke was thick enough to sting his eyes. "Fuck fuck fuck." He jumped and stabbed the button on the fire alarm to shut it off.

Arthur got a towel and waved it at the smoke. It caught in his lungs and he began to cough, helplessly. He ran for the oven and threw it open and a black gush of smoke billowed into his face, driving him back, and he

sits up in bed, heart beating too fast, beating like after a blast of cheap, shitty cocaine. There's someone in the house, someone moving around.

There's no way to tell what time it is. The digital clock by the bedside blinks 12:00. *It's been blinking* 12:00 *for days. Neither of them has bothered to reset it.*

The door lolls open a crack. A ghost-colored light flickers in the hall. At the bottom of the doorway, Jayne can see a black shadow. As she watches, it shifts, moves, and disappears . . . as if someone had been standing there and is only now backing away.

"Tana?" Jayne whispers. "You up?"

Ronnie sleeps on his stomach, the bedsheets kicked back. He wears white Fruit-of-the-Looms, so old they've assumed a certain transparency, his ass visible through the old fabric, and his face is half-buried in his bloodstained pillow. He gets nosebleeds after too much coke and uses the pillowcase to wipe. She wants to club him one, wake him up, but he usually hits back, and she's not in the mood for a punch-up tonight.

The TV is running. That's what's casting the spectral blue light glimmering in the hallway. She can hear SportsCenter. *Then there's a snapping sound and a hiss of static. A moment passes and there's another snap and Jayne can hear MTV,* Headbangers Ball, *Ozzy Osbourne pouring himself a suicide solution. Tana. Has to be Tana. She can't sleep either.*

Still, when she slips out of the bed, she reaches for the shotgun, leaning against the wall beside the end table.

It's a single-barrel Ithaca pump and it was her daddy's gun. It's older than Tana, a slam-fire model. They literally don't make 'em like this anymore. Hold the trigger down and the Ithaca will fire as fast as you can pump shells into the chamber. It's not quite an automatic weapon, but it's perfectly possible to squeeze off four rounds in four seconds.

She nudges the bedroom door open with the barrel of the gun and considers the short corridor to the living room. Tana's bedroom door is ajar on the left. The door to the bathroom stands open on the right, looking into maximum darkness.

Jayne creeps sidelong down the hall and peers through the open crack of Tana's bedroom door. The sight sends a paralytic tingle of alarm through her. It can't be Tana in the living room because Tana is right there, *asleep on her side, one hand cupping the swollen curve of her belly and a copy of* What to Expect When You're Expecting *on the bed beside her. She snores delicately, her hair across her face.*

In the living room the TV clunks to a new channel. The TV is ten years old, and when someone changes the channel, it sounds like slamming a fresh magazine into a gun. A studio audience roars with unhinged laughter.

"Who's there?" she cries. Without waiting for an answer, she shouts, "I have a gun!"

The audience laughs and laughs, as if that was the funniest thing ever. Tana makes a small muttering sound in her bedroom, and then says Jayne's name, but she isn't all the way awake, Jayne can tell from her tone.

She moves, has *to move, can't be still any longer. She ducks into the living room, lifting the Ithaca, swinging the barrel to cover the couch. As she does the TV turns itself off with another loud clunk.*

Light collapses to a dot in the center of the screen. In its fading glow, Jayne can see the remote on the armrest of the couch. It is not a large living room and there is nowhere to hide. She can see in a glance she's alone. The empty sofa, angled to face the TV, takes up most of the space. She wheels toward the front door. A black overcoat hanging from a peg looks like a man slouching against the wall, and for a microsecond Jayne is thi-i-i-i-i-sss *close to emptying a barrel into Ronnie's favorite duster.*

Then she realizes she's moved too far into the living room and has her back to the open archway of the kitchen. She pivots on her heel to cover the tiny kitchen . . . and sees a white, gaping corpse face, staring at her through the window over the sink. She catches herself before she can blast away, realizes she's been tricked by her own reflection in the glass.

Jayne's hands are shaking as she revolves to face the living room once again. And now, for the first time, she can dimly see an image of something squirming across the television screen. Jayne hits the wall switch and lights the room up.

The TV screen has become a glass window looking into a dry aquarium, and there's a fucking snake stuffed in there, a snake as thick as a firehose, knotted and tangled on itself. It shifts and twists, slowly, hardly enough room inside the boxy old TV for it. That's an anaconda, *she thinks,* there is a fucking South American anaconda in the TV, *and then she sees it has* arms. Scaly arms, and black talons, and one of those claws draws three white scratches across the inside of the glass with a faint, almost musical whine. Its face presses to the glass, staring out at her with one golden eye, the pupil a vertical black slit.

"Who says there's nothin' on the telly this hour of the night," remarks the thing inside the television, in a voice that reminds her of the sailor in Jaws, what was his name, Quint. "You never know when you might find a good creature feature, babe. Even better than that, Jayney. Sometimes, in the wee hours, a creature feature finds you." A black forked tongue flickers from the dragon's thin-lipped mouth and that one staring eye closes in a slow wink.

Jayne screams. She has never screamed so loudly in her entire life. And even so, she can barely hear herself over the thunderous boom of the shotgun. Her hands are shaking, but the shot is true. The curved screen of her ten-year-old TV erupts. The back of the TV explodes outward, blowing capacitors and diodes straight through the wall.

She advances on the television, coming around the sofa. She racks another shell into the pipe and because she's still depressing the trigger, the Ithaca booms again, this time punching a hole in the floor in front of the television. The sudden detonation scares her so badly, she takes a stumbling step backward. Her calves strike the couch and *she abruptly sits down. Through the droning in her ears, she hears her sister screaming and Ronnie falling out of bed.*

Jayne stares at the smoking wreck of her TV, looking for the black ruin of the snake, the thing that spoke to her, but he's gone, he's gone now, which should be a relief, but she's fighting for breath and there's a terrible thought cycling through her head, a paranoid chant, the worst thought of her life, he knows my name, he knows my name, he knows my NAME, he

—knows my name," Van muttered, coughing weakly.

Arthur came back to himself, sitting on the floor, back to the wall. The haze was clearing—Gwen stood in the open back door, one foot out on the step—but the room remained blurry with smoke. He swung his head heavily toward Van, who was on all fours near the oven. Van looked back at him and his eyes were white and hideous, covered with a filmy, semi-transparent, nictating membrane. He blinked and the membrane was gone.

"You were there too?" Arthur asked him.

That was how it seemed to him. He had not had a vision—it was more powerful than that. For a time he had simply left the kitchen and gone to live in Jayne Nighswander's head. The inside of her head was a dreadful place to find oneself, about the worst place he had ever been. Prison would be better.

Van gazed blankly back at him and Arthur knew he hadn't heard the question. He was still making his way back from Jayne's head to his own. Arthur peered across the room.

"Gwen, did you—?" Arthur began. He didn't need to finish. The answer was in her face.

"What did we do, Arthur?" she asked. "What in God's name did we do?"

"I don't know," he told her. "But whatever we did, we have to find a way to stop it."

THIRTY

Colin stood behind the card table, and the rest of them sat across from him, spread out along the curved leather bumper as if they were there to play blackjack and he was there to deal. He offered them whiskey but none of them wanted to be drunk. Gwen made tea instead.

Arthur took in his friends' faces. Gwen had recovered herself—a little. Her face had a washed-out, colorless quality, as if she had recently come in from the cold or was recovering from a flu. Van perched awkwardly on the edge of his stool, a hungover cowboy barely able to stay in the saddle. Allie waited in a state of almost military readiness, back straight, knees together, little spots of color in her cheeks. Donna sat hunched and flushed beside her. The two of them were holding hands under the table.

In the end, Arthur, Van, and Gwen had all gone together to the dorm room Allie and Donna shared on campus. When Allie had seen her own tattoo blooming across her pale, delicate skin, she had begun to laugh hysterically, laughter that sounded dangerously like screaming. Donna hadn't laughed. Donna had hardly said anything in three hours. Arthur thought nothing made Donna angrier than being afraid.

Only Colin was his usual self, serene and smiling, his bald Mr. Clean dome looking as if it had been recently waxed.

"How long have you known?" Arthur asked.

"I thought we all knew. I thought we had just silently agreed never to speak of it." Colin paused, then shook his head. "No, wait. I take that back. I thought some of you had blacked it out on purpose. Or decided it was something you dreamt. The mind resists knowing some things. The mind is an estate far bigger than The Briars, and it's quite possible to switch the lights off in one room, shut the door, and never go there again. We all smoked a lot of weed. We all drank too much Scotch. Intoxication is a useful way to redact uncomfortable memories."

"But *you* didn't black it out or forget," Gwen said.

"No."

"And it doesn't scare the shit out of you?" Arthur asked him.

Colin's eyes shone with inspiration, like an evangelical at his own baptism. "We brought a creature of the imagination out of some realm of the impossible and into the real world. We smashed reality like throwing a rock through a window. I consider the night we summoned King Sorrow to be the most important experience of my life. The most meaningful. I know how my grandfather must've felt now, that first time Elwood Hondo came through."

"But Elwood Hondo went away, didn't he? This thing isn't going anywhere. It's getting stronger." No, that wasn't quite right, Arthur thought. It wasn't getting stronger . . . or at least, it wasn't *just* getting stronger. It was getting *closer*.

Easter, he thought, and shivered.

"Yes. And you know why. You know what we asked him to do."

"Jayne," Van said, in a gravelly voice.

"And Ronnie," Arthur said.

No one spoke for a moment. Donna exhaled, a thin, fuming breath. It was like sitting next to a teakettle in which the water has come to such a high boil, the kettle has started to rattle on the stovetop.

"But we're not going to let him obliterate Jayne Nighswander," Arthur said. "We're going to take it back, aren't we?"

Colin poked his tongue into one cheek and seemed to consider this. "I think I'll have a whiskey, even if no one else wants one."

Van said, "Deal me in."

Colin busied himself at the bar. Ice clinked in glasses. He brought back a double for himself and a double for Van. He swirled the liquid round and round, then tipped his head back and had a taste.

"You asked if we can take it back. Let's set that aside for the moment and ask a different, better question: Why would we want to? Jayne Nighswander and Ronnie Volpe forced you to steal thousands of dollars of books from the school library. They blackmailed you and abused you psychologically, not to mention physically. They assaulted us all. They threatened to maim and blind your mother. They said they would kill her if you failed to keep them happy. I regard them in much the same way I'd regard biting ants. All they're ever going to do is bite and ruin picnics and make little ants. They're going to go on hurting people, humiliating and degrading others, until one of these nights Jayne will climb into her car while she's loaded on coke and steer it into oncoming traffic. It might happen a year from now or ten years. Sooner would be preferable, since it would limit how much damage she does to others in the meantime. If we set something against her that wipes her out before she can do more harm? We've probably saved lives." He swirled the amber liquid again, watching it eddy. "Morality has its own arithmetic. Two lives for ten is a good exchange. You know Nighswander and Volpe are slinging PCP. I wonder how many people have already overdosed on their drugs. Besides . . . animals have to eat. I wouldn't feel bad if I read a newspaper report about both of them being eaten by a shark. I'm not going to feel bad if they're chewed up by our imaginary dragon either."

"You can't aim a shark at someone like a rifle."

"What changed, Arthur? Why are you having second thoughts? Is it because it's not pretend anymore? I'm not criticizing. I'm genuinely curious. What happened?"

What happened is he had felt her fear. He had walked into the smoke-filled kitchen and somehow passed straight through into Jayne's head, to live through something she had experienced only a few nights before. He had felt her terror as she crept through the dark with her shotgun, afraid of what she was going to find. When she screamed, he had felt it in his own throat.

"Now I know what it's doing to her," Arthur said. "I saw it, somehow. I told you I saw it. I was in her head. We all were: Van and Gwen and I. She's not just going to be killed. She's being tortured first. I don't want that on my conscience. I've got enough guilt already."

"But we *can't* stop it, can we?" Gwen said. "The only way we can save Ronnie and Jayne is for one of us to die in their place. And that's not happening." She looked toward Arthur with a mixture of warning and affection. *You don't get to sacrifice yourself, old buddy. Not for the likes of Jayne Nighswander.* He understood her as clearly as if she said it aloud. They were good at reading each other. They had been good at it since the beginning, when she had known what was on each Zener card as soon as he glanced at it.

"Well," Colin said. "Wait a minute."

"What?"

"I'm not certain there's no way out for them. To be clear, I'm *sure* there's no backing out of our arrangement with King Sorrow. All sales are final. But I have doubts about the extent of his powers. My grandfather thinks an egregore has a practical range."

Van said, "How often do I gotta tell you to speak American, goddamn it?"

Colin said, "An egregore is a Philip. A noncorporeal being created by communal belief. Elwood Hondo couldn't go far from the people who generated him. It's true, when one views the Hondo film, sometimes it seems to throw a little glitch into reality. A bird will fly into a window, or a lightbulb will explode. But the people watching the film have expanded the circle of belief. It's still basically a local, close-range phenomenon. If Jayne and Ronnie get far enough away from *us*, they might also slip beyond King Sorrow's reach."

"Every king has his kingdom," Van said.

"That's right. And King Sorrow's might—I only say *might*—be confined to our immediate stomping grounds. If Jayne and Ronnie got fifty, a hundred miles away from us . . ." He moved his bony shoulders in a shrug. "Who could say for sure?"

"If Jayne slips out of reach, what's to stop the dragon from taking one of us in her place?" Gwen asked.

"We have an agreement, and it binds him as surely as it binds us. We gave him Jayne and Ronnie. If they *escape* him, escape his wrath—well, then we didn't disappoint him, he disappointed *us*. We aren't to blame for what he can't do."

"Are you sure of that?" Arthur asked.

"Which part?"

"If he can't reach them, he won't turn around and chow down on one of us?"

Colin thought it over. "Yes-*s*-*s*. That part of the contract seems clear enough."

"And you think if Ronnie and Jayne run far enough," Allie said, "they'll be okay?"

"Oh, not at all! That part is *highly* doubtful. But I think it would be fun to see them try!"

"What if we cast another spell?" Arthur asked. "To make King Sorrow go away? When we summoned him, we made the spell up as we went along. You said all magic is particular magic. Can't we just make up another spell to send him back to the Long Dark?"

A small dent appeared between Colin's eyebrows. "Even if that was the case—and I'm not sure it is—there'd still be a problem. Bringing him over involved magic *particular to us*. Sending him home would involve all of us working together again . . . *including* King Sorrow. He'd have to be a willing part of any ceremony. And I'd guess he won't be so willing."

"What about the book?" Gwen asked. "Was there anything in the Crane journal about getting rid of him?"

For the briefest moment, Arthur thought Colin's eyes flashed with something like irritation. Arthur was struck suddenly with the idea that Colin *liked* having a dragon and that all this talk of sending him away was threatening to ruin his fun. But when Colin spoke, his voice was musing and reasonable. "Not that I recall. But I wasn't really reading to see how to *banish* a dragon. I was trying to figure out how to summon one. I suppose there might be something. If we still had the book . . . but it's gone in the wind." Colin finished his whiskey and set down his tumbler. "So do we try and save Jayne or not? We could take a show of hands, but personally, my conscience isn't up for a vote. Arthur, if you want to try and help her, then I think that's what we should do. If that's what you *really* want."

Arthur looked at Gwen . . . and Gwen surprised him by reaching across the table to take his hand.

"Save her," Gwen said. "Save her if we can. I don't like her—I *hate* what she's done to Arthur—but I don't want to be the reason she dies." She moved her thumb across his knuckles, just once, and let him go.

"But you aren't going to be the reason she dies," Donna said, speaking for the first time since they had gathered in the study. "King Sorrow is."

"Who will rid me of this meddlesome priest?" Arthur murmured. Everyone except Colin looked perplexed.

"No, hon. It's on all of us," Gwen said. "One way or t'other and there's no fiddling around about it. If we dropped her in a pit of alligators, they wouldn't send the gators to jail for eatin' her. They'd send us."

"But we aren't going to go to jail—no jury in America would convict us of having a pet dragon—so I say bon appétit," Donna said. "Fuck Jayne Nighswander. This bitch buys time to pay off her debts by letting men fuck her kid sister. She can roast. And as far as I'm concerned, every man who ever fucked Tana can roast with her."

Arthur felt a prickling across his torso that had nothing to do with the mark King Sorrow had put on him and everything to do with the memory of Tana's body against his.

Colin said, "Allie? You haven't weighed in. I'm afraid we don't have the polling data on the morality of feeding one's enemies to a dragon. Any thoughts?"

Allie said, "One thought, yeah. I keep thinking about this great old joke. You ever hear the one about the two guys who go camping, only when they get up in the morning, there's a giant grizzly bear getting ready to attack them? And the one guy, he starts lacing up his sneakers, and the other guy says, what are you doing, you can't outrun a grizzly! And the first guy says, I know, but I don't need to outrun the bear, I need to get ready to go home with her, and pour her a nice drink, and watch some comfort TV with her until she feels better."

Colin stared, perplexed.

"I'm Donna's roommate," Allie said. "Whatever she votes, that's how I vote. I have to lace up my sneakers and go home with the grizzly."

"What say you, Van?" Colin asked.

"You don't point a gun at someone and *then* decide if you want to shoot 'em," Van said. "That's something you ought to decide before the gun is in your hand. But if you don't want her to die, Arthur, then that's that. We'll have to try and save her." Then he looked across Allie at his sister. "Come on, Donna. It's fine to kill Jayne, but if we don't do something, it's gonna fuckin' kill Arthur, and that's a whole 'nother ball of cheese."

Donna glared at him with watery eyes. "Fine. Let's locate this nasty bitch and tell her to get the hell out of Dodge while she's got a chance."

"Call her, Arthur," Colin said. "We'll back your play. As it happens, there might be something else to be gained, on a personal level, from reaching out to Jayne and Ronnie. But if we're going to meet with them—and I think we should all be there—it isn't going to be like Halloween. Not this time."

"No," Arthur said. "This time, we're the monsters."

THIRTY-ONE

Arthur was leaning against the brick wall behind Shut-Up-And-Eat-It when Jayne and Ronnie pulled in. He had told them he wanted to meet at seven thirty, but he had been there since seven so he could be there when they arrived. He'd left the message with the sleepy-sounding bro who was taking orders, and quite intentionally picked a night when Tana was off work. He didn't want her there for this.

The Ranchero ground in across the dirt lot, raising a cloud of white chalk, faintly luminescent in the light from that out-of-place lamppost. It settled into the empty spot almost directly in front of Arthur. Jayne sat in the passenger seat. In the aquamarine glow of the dash she looked more like a drowned corpse than ever. She stayed where she was while Ronnie threw open the driver's-side door and hauled himself wearily out. He left the door open, and music thundered into the night. "Dr. Feelgood" was on a rampage, blasting from the speakers. Good. If there were shouts—if there were screams—the music might drown them out. Arthur pushed himself off the brick wall and started toward him.

"This about, Artie?" Ronnie asked, in a tone that approximated his usual stoner's charm, but did not quite disguise the faint note of irascibility beneath it. "You wanted till the end of February, we gave it to you, and I think we were all enjoying the break from each other. Unless maybe you been missing when Tana comes around to collect and—"

Then he clocked that Arthur was still closing in on him. Arthur had the hammer up one sleeve of his black parka: the ball-peen hammer found in the Los Feliz murder house, one of the prizes of Llewellyn's Cabinet of Curiosities. As he closed the distance between them, Arthur let it slide down his sleeve and into his fist. Ronnie tried to get his hands out of the pockets of his denim jacket, but it was too late. Arthur swiped the hammer into the side of his knee. It connected with a bony crack.

Ronnie howled, grabbed the knee, and began to hop on one leg. Arthur drove his shoulder into his chest and the little man tipped over, hit the side of the Ranchero, and fell into the slush.

"You fuck," Ronnie shrieked. "You motherfuck, are you out of your goddamn—"

Jayne threw open the passenger-side door. She had the gun in one hand, the 9mm Ronnie had carried Halloween night. She got one foot out, started to rise, and Gwen came up from behind the next car over. Gwen threw herself into the passenger-side door and it slammed on Jayne's face. Jayne sagged into the passenger seat. Her arm, and the gun, still hung out into the night. Arthur's heart jammed itself in his throat: he wanted to scream, *Get down, get down, Gwen.* He clenched up, waiting for the gun to go off and rip a hole in the night.

It never fired. Gwen gave the door a kick, smashing it into Jayne's bicep. Her grip loosened on the gun. Gwen wrenched at the 9mm and Jayne was dragged out of the car in her attempt to hold on to it. Jayne went down hard in the gray, wintery slime and Gwen stepped away, trembling, with the pistol in both hands. Arthur thought it might be three or four days before his heart slowed down.

Gwen passed the nine back to Donna McBride, who had been crouched out of sight next to her, behind Gwen's road-dirty Civic. Donna knew more about guns than any of them, had been going to the range since she was thirteen, had fired everything from revolvers to an M16. She racked the slide and a brass shell leapt into the night. She caught the bullet in one hand, examined it briefly, and ejected the entire magazine.

"Cop killers," she said. "The ammunition choice of dirtbags

nationwide. You know how stupid it is to keep a bullet in the chamber? You jam it down the front of your pants, feeling gangsta, and wind up blowing your twat off. Self-inflicted crotch wounds are surprisingly common."

"You're dead!" Jayne screamed at them. "Every last fucking one of you!"

Arthur had looked away from Ronnie, his attention drawn by the brief grapple over the gun. He didn't see the knife, hardly registered the steely click of it snapping open. But before Ronnie could lunge to his feet and stick it into him, Colin stepped past Arthur and trod on his wrist, pinning his arm to the ground. Ronnie yelped. The butterfly knife fell to the wet tarmac.

"No one needs to get hurt tonight," Colin said. "Not much, anyway. Believe it or not, we're here out of human concern."

Van emerged from behind the parked Christmobile, where he had been hiding with Colin. He kicked the knife clattering under the Ranchero, then leaned into the front seat and turned down the volume on the radio. As he dipped back out of the car, Van said, "Sorry, man. Enough people been terrorized tonight without inflicting the Crüe on innocent bystanders."

Jayne struggled up to one knee. She looked bad—worse than in that brief glimpse Arthur had of her through the windshield. She had lost ten pounds she didn't have to lose and her coke-bright eyes glittered in dark hollows. Her hair had lost its vibrancy, looked fragile and pale. Maybe it was even thinning. In the light from the streetlamp Arthur could see her scalp through the strands.

She laughed angrily. "Hey, Artie. Your little piece of ass here? I'm not going to kill her, 'cause she's only a kid. I'm gonna cut off her nose. I'm going to make her too ugly to fuck." It was hard to tell if the bright shine in her eyes was a product of drugs, excitement, or panic, but she turned her gaze on Gwen with a kind of triumph. "You hear that? When I'm done with you, the only way he'll be able to fuck you is with a bag over your head."

Gwen sank down in front of Jayne, and when she reached out with one hand, Jayne flinched, as if she expected to be struck.

Instead, Gwen caught some of Jayne's pale, washed-out hair and rubbed it between two fingers. In the reflected glare of the Ranchero's headlights, Arthur could see some of it had turned white.

"I'm sorry," Gwen said. "Awful as you are, if I could take it back, I would."

Jayne flinched again. "Don't you pity me—don't you *dare*. You aren't better than me. You think these people are your friends? You're a hot piece of townie ass for Arthur to bang while he's on his four-year college vacation. He's got a taste for that kind of thing." Arthur's insides cramped and he thought, *Here it comes, here's where she spills it about Tana.*

But Jayne never got to it. Allie had drifted over to stand next to Gwen, and now she helped Gwen to her feet. "I can think of one way Gwen is better than you."

"Yeah? What's that?"

"The person holding the gun is on her side," Allie said. "That's a lot better."

"This might be hard for you to believe," Colin said, "what with both of you knocked on your asses in the slush, but we got together tonight to try to *help* you."

It was a marvel, how Colin Wren was so completely Colin, all day long. It was hard to imagine him frightened. It was difficult to imagine him raising his voice.

"Some among us think you deserve a chance to . . . I don't know, exactly. Start your lives again? Do better? For myself, I can't be troubled. You're a pair of junkies who sell hard drugs to other junkies. You live revolting lives. Everything you touch, everyone you meet, is stained by you. If Arthur didn't cooperate with you, you threatened to have his mother beaten and blinded. How revolting is that?"

"Man," Ronnie said, a whine in his voice. "Man, you think we really woulda done that to her? Or even coulda? We were ninety percent fucking with him. We were—"

He never got out the rest. Donna had moved around the front of the Ranchero to stand by Colin, and now she smacked the butt of the gun across his mouth. It struck with a wet thud. He screamed, started to get up, and Van put a boot on his shoulder and shoved him back down.

Donna said, "Open your dirty germ hole again and you're going to be holding the rest of your teeth in your hand."

Colin seemed to have lost his place. Van spoke next.

"What my pal here is saying, it's time to saddle up and ride out of town."

"What?" Jayne said. She sounded incredulous.

"Take off. Make like a banana and split," Allie said. "Make like a tree and leave. Get in that butt-ugly car of yours and make it walk and talk. The sooner the better. I don't know how far you need to go. Maybe just put the pedal down and keep driving until you hit Mexico. You should try Cancún. I read a thing in the paper about all the garbage and medical waste washing up on the beach. The Gulf Coast current pushes all the trash there. You'll fit right in."

"Run for it," Colin said. "That's your best chance. Possibly your only chance."

"Or *what*?" Jayne asked. "Or you fucking twerps are going to hassle us again?"

"No," Arthur said. "It'll be King Sorrow next time."

Jayne shrank back into the side of the car, and her hands came up a little, as if one of them had threatened to cut up her face.

"What are you talking about?"

"You know what," Arthur said. "He's getting closer all the time. You've heard him moving around your house at night."

"*You*," Jayne cried. "Did you hire someone to come after us?"

"Not . . . *someone*," Colin said.

"You've seen him, Jayne. He spoke to you. You blew up your TV because you thought he was inside it."

"How do you know that, man?" Ronnie asked, although with one hand clapped over his smashed mouth, it came out more like *How a you no da, mang?* "Are you watching our house?"

No one paid him any mind.

"Easter," Jayne whispered.

"Yes," Arthur said. "You only have till Easter. Did he tell you that?"

She gestured with one hand at the back of the car. "He scratched it into the rear window of the Ranchero. I found it a couple days ago."

Arthur had to see for himself. He walked around to the back of the car, and there it was, etched jaggedly across the rear window:

EASTER

He felt ill at heart at the sight. "We can't stop him. King Sorrow. But we think maybe—if you run—if you go very far away—he might not be able to follow you."

Jayne repeated the name with something like reverence. "King Sorrow."

"Yes." It was Colin now. "If he draws his power from us, he should have an effective range. On the other hand, if he existed *before* us, and all we did was open a door to him . . . then it probably doesn't matter where you go. I'm interested to see which it is." Then he said something else, something none of them expected. "There's *another* possible defense . . . just a little thing. It probably won't work, but if I was in your position, I'd want to try everything."

"What?" Jayne asked.

Colin shook his head. "I'll tell you, but first you have to do a favor for us. In a week, Arthur's mother has a parole hearing. By the time that happens, someone at Black Cricket has to take credit for planting a shiv in her cell. Clear her name and I'll share the other thing I know."

"You can't hold out on me," Jayne said. "You can't. Yesterday afternoon—he was under the bed. I was trying to take a nap and he woke me with a claw on my ankle. I thought my heart was going to stop. I *felt* it stop for a moment—seize up like I was going into vapor lock."

"I've heard of that," Colin said mildly. "People dying of fear. Terrible. Help us. So I can help you. Get Arthur's mother off the hook and I'll share the other piece of what I know. Could be a game changer."

"What the fuck are you all talking about?" Ronnie shouted. Maybe he wanted to sound threatening, but his voice was the adenoidal squeak of a twelve-year-old going through puberty. "Are you all high on crack? There's no dragon. There's no fucking dragon."

"Who said King Sorrow is a dragon?" Allie asked. "I don't believe any of us mentioned that."

"I guess ol' Ronnie has been seeing him too," Van said. "And don't want to admit it."

Ronnie shook his head, a gesture that seemed to indicate panic more than disagreement. His eyes rolled, showing the whites, like a terrified horse.

"Sure, Ronnie's seen him," Jayne said. "King Sorrow was in the sky tonight. He followed us here."

"You shut up, bitch," Ronnie said, his voice piping and small.

"The dragon passed in front of the moon," Jayne said. "And I saw him in the passenger-side mirror. He was . . . huge. There for a moment and gone. And you saw him too, Ronnie. I know you did. You just about jumped out of your skin and your ciggy fell in your lap and nearly burned your prick off." Jayne swiveled her head to face Arthur. Her eyes were enormous in her gaunt face. "Call it off. Call it off and I'll suck your dick. I'll do it right now." She laughed harshly. "And Ronnie can suck off your friends, if that's what you want. Just call it off."

"We can't," Arthur said. "All you can do now is run. I'm sorry."

Allie said, "Give her gun back, Donna."

Donna looked as if Allie had suggested a group hug. "The fuck would I do that?"

"We're under King Sorrow's protection," Allie said. She plucked the gun out of Donna's hand—Donna was too amazed to stop her—and tossed it at Ronnie. Ronnie caught it with one hand and clapped it to his chest with a yelp. The barrel was pointing straight down, and Arthur twitched at a sudden vision of the gun spouting flame and putting a bullet into Ronnie's nuts. *Self-inflicted crotch wounds are surprisingly common.* "There you go. You can't use it on us. Our dragon will eat you if you try."

Ronnie looked up at them, grinning—or grimacing—with bloody

teeth. "You're crazy! You're all fucking crazy!" Then he looked at Allie with a violent satisfaction. "And you most of all if you think I won't kill every fucking one of you." He lifted the gun and pointed it at Arthur's face.

There was a gunshot crack and Arthur's insides bunched up painfully in shock for the second time in five minutes. But it wasn't the pistol going off. It was the sodium-vapor bulb in that faux-nineteenth-century streetlamp. It erupted in a shower of yellowish-white sparks, which fell sizzling to the pavement. Ronnie twisted at the waist with a cry, looking around at the suddenly darkened corner of the lot. But it was Jayne who screamed.

"Her eyes!" Jayne shrieked. "Look at her eyes, Ronnie!"

Ronnie didn't—Ronnie ignored her completely—but Arthur looked. Allie's right hand had slipped under her fuzzy cardigan. She was not quite touching her heart, but Arthur thought her fingers were stroking the edge of the serpent tattoo upon her breast . . . and her eyes had filmed over with the white nictating membrane of a snake. Van's eyes had been just the same, when he was coming out of his King Sorrow trance in the smoky kitchen. *Somehow he's inside us now*, Arthur thought. *Incubating.*

Steel groaned. The top of the streetlamp began to *bend*, as if some great weight was pressing down upon it. The brushed steel creaked and buckled.

"What's happening?" Ronnie screamed. "What the fuck is happening?"

"Shoot it!" Jayne screamed. "Shoot the fucking thing!"

"I don't see anything!"

"There!" she screamed and pointed her finger into the stars, into the sky, at nothing. She was pointing at the darkness directly above the streetlamp. "*There!* How do you not see it?"

The streetlamp strained and deformed, sinking lower, the top bending into a hook.

"There's nothing there!" Ronnie cried.

Arthur didn't see anything either—not exactly. But it seemed to him the shadows above the buckling streetlamp had *thickened* into the vague shape of a dragon, a bit larger than a full-grown gorilla.

The darkest part of the darkness was folded on itself in a way that brought to mind bat-like wings.

"Oh, God, Arthur," Gwen said, and Arthur felt her hand on his arm. "What did we do?"

The streetlamp was wrenched steadily downward until it formed a question mark. Ronnie screamed wordlessly and pointed his nine and squeezed the trigger. The action clapped down with a dry click. He pulled again and again, producing a whole series of those dry clicks.

"It's not loaded, asshole," Donna said, holding up the magazine. "How dumb do you think I am?"

"Her eyes, Ronnie!" Jayne shrieked, pointing at Allie, and at last Ronnie looked wildly around. When he saw Allie standing there, eyes white and blind, he sobbed.

Allie's eyes moved behind that wet, white, terrible membrane, and she smiled dreamily. "*His* eyes," she said, ever so softly. "*His* eyes now, Jayne."

The membrane slid back. The eyes behind them were crimson, shot with threads of gold, the pupils vertical slits.

"FUCK THIS!" Ronnie screamed. "I'M NOT PART OF THIS! I WAS NEVER PART OF IT! IT WAS ALL HER IDEA! *TAKE HER!* TAKE HER AND LEAVE ME OUT OF IT!" He yanked himself into the Ranchero and began to back up without even closing the driver's-side door. Backing away and leaving Jayne behind.

"Wait!" Jayne cried. "Don't leave me!"

Arthur thought he would've though, if he hadn't backed straight into the dumpster on the far side of the lot, colliding with a thunderous clang. Arthur saw Ronnie's head bounce off the steering wheel. The impact stunned the gangly stoner and he sat there for a moment, blank eyed, hand to his forehead . . . long enough for Jayne to reach the passenger side of the Ranchero. Her door was still hanging open and she scrambled in while Ronnie dumbly shut his own door. Arthur wondered if he would try to push her out of the car, but the steering wheel had knocked the fight out of him. He merely put the car into drive and took off.

The tires rumbled and threw rocks as the car slewed around in the parking lot. Jayne thudded her door shut as they passed under another streetlamp. As they headed for the street, Arthur glimpsed that word gouged into the rear window again. The letters glinted and flashed as if dusted with diamonds. *Easter*.

The Ranchero bounced as it hit the street. The bumper struck the blacktop and threw sparks. It was gone from sight a moment later, although Arthur could hear its tires shrieking on Ballard Street as it raced away.

Arthur glanced around in time to see Allie's hand fall to her side, out from under her sweater. She was blinking rapidly and smiling in a dazed sort of way, swaying slightly. Her eyes were her own again. Her cheeks were flushed and there was a pretty strand of hair stuck to her brow. Donna reached over, in an affectionate, sisterly sort of way, to peel it free.

"Wow," Allie said. "They really couldn't touch us. It worked. I wasn't sure it would work. Turns out it's good to be friends with the King."

I don't think we're his friends, Arthur wanted to say, but his throat was dry, and he was short of breath, and he couldn't get it out.

"That's impossible," Donna said, staring at the mangled streetlamp.

Van flicked one hand at the iron question mark on the far side of the lot. The darkness above it seemed perfectly ordinary now, nothing dragon-shaped about it. "Don't gimme that. I hate the part in movies when someone sees something crazy and then everyone argues about whether they imagined it. We can skip that shit. Look at it. I mean—just look at it." Then he pointed a scowl at Colin. "What's this other thing you figured out? You said you know something else Jayne and Ronnie can do to protect themselves from King Sorrow?"

"Hm?" Colin asked, pulling his gaze away from the deformed streetlamp with some effort. "What? Oh. I was shitting her. There isn't anything. I'll have to make something up. I just wanted to make sure Arthur's mom has a fair chance in her parole hearing. I told you there was something to be gained from this meeting, whether we're able to save them or not." He lowered his eyes and seemed to quietly reflect for a moment. "Maybe I'll tell her to wear a necklace made out of garlic. Like what you do for a vampire. If she's going to be King Sorrow's dinner, she might as well smell like it."

The gang stared at him in shocked, silent disbelief... and then Donna snorted, a rumble of amusement, and put her head on Allie's shoulder. Van looked away and laughed wearily and rubbed the back of his neck.

Arthur felt Gwen's small hand stealing into his. He squeezed it gently. They stood together, staring at the ruined lamppost. The air smelled sharply of ozone and superheated copper wire. Something shorted inside the lamp and it vomited another burst of bright sparks—a final blazing shower before the light died out for good.

THIRTY-TWO

On the last Sunday in February, Van climbed behind the wheel of the Christmobile and drove Arthur west to Yorrick, Vermont, for his mother's parole hearing.

"I can find the way myself, you know," Arthur had told him.

"Friends don't let friends drink alone," Van replied. "Besides, I wasn't invited to Texas." Donna was flying to El Paso with Allie, where they planned to spend their break licking salt off the rims of their margarita glasses.

"How do you know we're going to be drinking? We don't know how it's going to turn out."

"It's going to turn out one of two ways, my son," Van told him. "And either way is going to require some drinking."

They got a room with two beds in a Best Western, located a short drive from the penitentiary. It was the only hotel in town, and the clientele consisted almost entirely of people visiting their incarcerated loved ones. The picture window in their room had a view of a buckled asphalt parking lot, the four-lane highway beyond, and, across the road, a 7-Eleven and a permanently closed Dairy Queen with plywood nailed up in the windows. A view like that belonged on a calendar, Arthur thought, for devotees of New England's peaceful, rural beauty.

A little after 10:00 p.m., Van began nagging Arthur to cross the street and get them some Doritos. He didn't want to go himself. He had his jeans off and said he didn't like to get dressed again once he had relaxed for the evening. He was persistent, and finally, when he began to lob balled-up socks at Arthur's head, Arthur pulled on his Biko hoodie and made his way across all four lanes through the blowing wet. He was three minutes at the checkout, in full view of the security camera, the footage time-stamped, providing him with an unshakable alibi for the evening. As it happened, it was an alibi no one ever felt the need to check—a source of great disappointment to Colin.

In the morning, Arthur showered, shaved, slapped on some Bay Rum cologne, and threw on the blue blazer that made him look like the musty professor of medieval literature he hadn't yet become. He let himself out of the room without waking Van and drove to Black Cricket alone. The parking lot at the penitentiary was the emptiest he had ever seen it. But then he had never been there outside scheduled visiting hours.

His mother's parole hearing was in the west wing, on the second floor, at the end of a corridor lined with administrative offices. Walking down that hall reminded him of being sent to the principal's office to answer for some offense or other, and he thought again how Black Cricket resembled a high school from the outside.

Somehow, he had thought his mother would be there, that they would sit side by side during the course of his interview, perhaps be allowed to hold hands. But of course she wasn't there. Her own interview was scheduled for later in the day.

The parole board—a psychologist, a priest, a retired attorney general, a retired officer of the state police, and a former state congresswoman—sat behind a long walnut table. The former congresswoman had silver hair blown out in the style of Murphy Brown, and she wore a scarlet power suit with squared-off shoulders. She ran the proceedings. She said she was glad Arthur could join them and asked him if he'd like a cup of coffee or tea. He said a cup of tea would be fine and was provided with a small paper cup of lukewarm water with a bag of Tetley floating in it. He never touched it. The congresswoman asked if Arthur had prepared some remarks. Arthur had. He read a two-page statement, emphasizing his mother's work with battered women, both before and during her incarceration; the spiritual counsel she had offered other prisoners; her work for peace and against apartheid; and her role in his life as his only surviving parent, a woman he loved and looked up to.

The congresswoman asked him how he had managed while she was locked up, and he told her about his studies at Rackham, his summers in England with his father's people. She asked him if his mother had ever apologized to him, or expressed any remorse at all, for leaving him to fend for himself while she served her time. Arthur replied in a patient, measured tone that she had told him she would never be done apologizing and trying to make amends, not just to him, but also to the family of the late Officer Jason Einaudi.

At that, the retired state policeman spoke up.

"How *do* you make amends for getting a man killed?" he asked. He studied Arthur with watering, hostile eyes.

"Can anyone ever?" Arthur asked. "Is another twelve months going to make anyone hurt any less? My mother is going to try and help people whether she's in here or out there. I didn't come to ask you to give *her* life back. I came here to ask you for *mine*."

The congresswoman closed her binder and thanked him for his time.

As Arthur rose, the congresswoman said, "We haven't made a decision yet, and we won't for several days. I don't want to give you false reasons for optimism. Your mother is responsible for the death of a law officer, which occurred while she was committing trespass on federal land, with the intent of destroying government property. It's not a speeding ticket. But we won't see another prisoner with a record like hers—a record of service to others and unfailing compassion—all year. I'd add that in retrospect, it's surprising anyone ever believed a pacifist and ordained priest was hiding a weapon in her cell."

"Ma'am?" Arthur asked, his heart doing a soft jog in his chest.

"I think you know she was placed into isolation after a weapon was discovered in her pillowcase? A spoon with a handle sharpened into a knife. Planted, apparently, by a lifer who had a grudge. Seems your mother vetoed her pick for the book club." One corner of her mouth moved in the hint of a smirk. "A book club in a place like this. Your mother does like her noble wastes of time, doesn't she? No, don't answer that, Arthur. Stay out of trouble yourself, hm?"

The wind was blowing when he crossed to the Christmobile. Serpents of white snow hissed across the blacktop. That last line—*stay out of trouble yourself*—grated on him, as if his family was prone to acts of homicide. Then he thought of Jayne and Ronnie and reflected that maybe they were.

Van was sitting shoeless on the edge of his bed when Arthur got back to the Best Western. His eyes were bright in the gloom, glinting like new-minted quarters.

"You better call your boss," Van said. "Back at school."

"Boss?"

"Meckfessel. At the library. I was just talking to Colin. I guess there was a break-in while we were away. Someone stole some expensive books. Fuckin' shame. Fuckin' outrage! Someone's head is gonna roll." Van grinned. "Not yours, though."

THIRTY-THREE

Townies—that was what the insurance investigators concluded.

The townies waited for February break, when most of the students were away and campus security was half-staffed. At some point between midnight and 4:00 a.m., they had come through Rackham's Wood, an area of almost forty forested acres on the western side of campus. They emerged from the woods at the parking lot behind the library. The lot was normally under the watchful eye of a security camera, mounted twenty feet off the ground on a lamppost. But a couple of weeks earlier, some girls—Allison Shiner and Donna McBride—had had a contest to see if either of them could hit it with a snowball, and it turned out they could. It hadn't been repaired yet.

That was a little convenient, the camera getting wiped out a few weeks before the break-in, but there had been something of a sport all winter long of nailing the cameras with snowballs. There had been anonymous leaflets about living in a surveillance society and outrageous suggestions that security used the cameras to ogle girls. Snowballing a camera had become something of a way to prove one was a good feminist. By early February only about eight of the twenty on-campus security cameras were in good working order. Allison and Donna were never serious suspects. They were in Texas at the time of the robbery and couldn't reasonably have had anything to do with the break-in. In fact, no Rackham students were ever questioned about a possible role in the theft, and why would they have been? It occurred during February break, and 80 percent of the student body wasn't even in-state.

The thieves had smashed a cellar window and squirmed through into a women's room on the basement level. They left an empty bottle of Ripple, in a brown paper bag, in one of the bathroom stalls. The receipt was still in the bag, and the police traced the purchase to a Chinese takeout in Gogan. The staff had poor English and worse memories and couldn't say who they might've sold the bottle to—and in any event, they moved a lot of Ripple and Wild Irish Rose in a town like Gogan.

The thieves had also abandoned a set of bolt cutters in the library's Special Collection (the price tag was still on the handle; it had been purchased at the Ace Hardware in Gogan; *Sorry, officer, we sell one or two of those every day, and most of our customers buy in cash*). The townies used the bolt cutters to clip the lock on the safe where the most expensive books were kept and had cleared it out, took it all. They helped themselves to a sack of rarities off the shelves as well. The real point of the trip appeared to be vandalism, however. Someone had spray-painted RACKHAM GIRLS ARE STUCK-UP BICHES on the walnut checkout counter. ("Did you really have to misspell it?" Gwen asked Colin with a weary sigh. Colin said, "If local law enforcement is going to hold prejudices, I'm going to take advantage of them. That's on them, not me.")

Many of the most valuable books were recovered a few days later. An anonymous tip pointed police to a burned-out 1970 Chevy Monte Carlo, located at the We-Buy-Your-Wreck in west Gogan. Something like thirty books were found in the trunk (along with a sizable quantity of high-grade blue marijuana), although several valuable volumes (Enoch Crane's journal among them) were never recovered.

It was notable that We-Buy-Your-Wreck *did* have functioning security cameras, and one of them offered a good view of the Monte Carlo. There was no video of the heisters stashing their stolen goods. We-Buy-Your-Wreck reused the same videotapes over and over, recording for twenty-four hours, then rewinding and starting over. They hadn't saved any of the footage from the day the library was looted. But there was video from Wednesday night, taped just ten hours before the police were tipped off that they could find some of the books at the junkyard.

In the recording, a gangly man with pale hair, wearing baggy carpenter jeans and a flannel jacket, wandered through the yard of wrecks and then sat down on the trunk of the Monte Carlo. He lifted his chin and stared directly into the camera. He patted the trunk and smirked and lifted a hand in a wave hello. His eyes were black holes in his narrow, country-boy face. They ran the footage on the local news: *Do you know this man?* It was an unsettling forty seconds of video. The image hiccupped and jumped, so one instant the man in the image would be sitting on the trunk, and in the next he'd be on his feet, peering straight into the camera's lens. Sometimes he seemed like he was six feet tall . . . and sometimes he stretched like an image in a fun house mirror. His hands were white blurs. The quality of the video was badly degraded (no surprise, given how often the junkyard recycled their tapes) so that the shadows around him seemed to simmer and twitch with a life of their own.

"Who the hell is that?" Arthur asked, when they were all gathered in The Briars, watching the late local news together.

"I don't know," Colin said, but he was smiling. "Maybe it's the conscientious fellow who called in the tip."

"*You* called in the tip," Van said.

"Oh, that's right," Colin said. "I remember now. I *did*. I also remember what I was doing, the evening before I called the tip in . . . the night this weirdo walked into the junkyard. I was transferring the Elwood Hondo footage to VHS, wanted to be able to watch it without setting up the projector. Maybe that's who it is. Maybe Elwood wanted to say hello."

"What a crock of shit," Donna said.

"We pulled a dragon out of the Long Dark through the sheer power of belief," Colin said. "You accept that but you can't believe Elwood Hondo might've slipped out of an old film to give us a wink and a wave? Look at him. Look right now at the guy in the security footage. Are you completely sure he isn't looking back at you?"

On the TV the gaunt man grinned into the camera, gazing with black, bottomless eye sockets. Arthur sank into the couch, putting his shoulder against Gwen's. He didn't like the sudden sensation of being stared at. Not one bit.

There was a flaw in the security tape. The whole image bent and twisted to one side then jumped forward a few seconds in time. When the image clarified, the junkyard wanderer was gone. It was less as if he had walked out of the frame and more as if he had simply dissolved. He was never identified.

THIRTY-FOUR

When Arthur answered the phone, there was a click and a hiss, and then a prerecorded message began to play. A somewhat robotic female voice informed him that he had a call from Erin Oakes at the Black Cricket Women's House of Correction, that the call would be recorded and monitored, and that if he did not wish to speak to this prisoner, he should hang up now. He did not hang up.

"Well," she said, and there was happiness and relief in her voice, and he knew the rest without her saying anything. When he drew his next breath, it felt like the first time he had been able to properly fill his lungs in four years.

"Well," he replied, a little word that was doing a lot of work, because it meant "I love you," and "Oh thank God," and also "When can I come get you?"

Saturday, it turned out. That Saturday, Dr. Erin Oakes walked out of the House of Correction with Arthur at her side.

THIRTY-FIVE

It seemed absurd to Arthur, but his mother was required to complete her sentence in a residential reentry center, a fancy term for a halfway house—as if a woman who had taught ethics at Dartmouth and was an ordained minister might spend her first days of freedom scoring meth, booze, and a scorching hot case of gonorrhea.

"Stop that," his mother said. "This is exactly the right place for me. This is exactly where I need to be."

"It is?" Arthur asked, giving her side-eye. He was pushing a shopping cart at the time. They were in Wal-Mart, buying sheets for her bed, a toothbrush, shampoo, and other necessities. "You don't want to get back to Dartmouth College and resume living your life? If you don't want to teach anymore, you could move to Podomaquassy. We could have a place together." He felt almost embarrassed saying it—it came dangerously close to revealing how alone and afraid and unmoored he had felt since the day of her arrest. It was alarmingly close to saying, *I want you with me, where I can keep an eye on you and know that you're safe.*

His mother said, "I know where my work is now, and it isn't at Dartmouth."

Because of course she wasn't done with Black Cricket. There were people she cared about there. There were some who would never get out. She had already put in an application to join the Chaplaincy Services Branch of the Federal Bureau of Prisons so she could return to Black Cricket, not as an inmate, but as a spiritual counselor. She wanted to do advocacy and social work. "Do you know how many battered women are in there for shooting their abuser?" she asked him. "Do you know how many were forced into abortions they didn't want or forced to carry babies they didn't want or got into drugs because of a lifetime of sexual abuse?"

He knew all about it, but that didn't make her decision any easier to swallow. In the days and weeks to follow they argued—no, that wasn't quite right. It was more accurate to say *he* argued and she listened. He didn't want her anywhere near the place, anywhere near Daphne Nighswander, Daphne Nighswander's friends, and the on-the-take security guards who had allowed someone to take a Polaroid of his sleeping mother while someone menaced her with a shiv. He didn't talk about the Nighswanders, though. He didn't know if he'd ever be ready to talk about them.

"It blows my mind," he told her once, at the end of an especially fraught phone call. His voice was patient and reasonable, the way it always got when he was quaking with fury. "How little it matters to you what I might want. It didn't matter to you the day you got locked up. It didn't matter you had a seventeen-year-old in boarding school. It didn't matter that I couldn't look anyone else in the eye the whole last five months I was there. It didn't matter what I had to go through for four years, walking into Black Cricket every month to visit you. I wouldn't want my feelings to get in the way of your newest self-improvement project. Just remember that the last time you threw yourself into a big act of spiritual activism, a guy got killed."

"Oh, Arthur—" she began, but he told her he had to go, and he hung up, a sick upwelling of emotion in his breast.

That had been an awful thing to say, throwing the dead man in her face. Officer Einaudi had been killed in the most freakish of freak accidents, and only a fool or the American legal system could ever have blamed her for it. In this case, though, his mother was the fool—Arthur knew she had been *grateful* for prison, grateful to be punished, felt that any suffering at all on her part would be a good start. He sat at his little kitchen table, feeling tremulous with unhappiness. It had been an awful thing to say, yes, but he had done and said worse things in the last few months. He was getting acclimated to the idea that he wasn't the good guy in the story.

The phone rang again and he grabbed for it, thinking it was Erin, and she would be soothing and understanding and he would apologize, and they would make it better together. Only it wasn't Erin. It was Tana.

"What the fuck did you do?" Tana barked into Arthur's ear. "What the fuck did you *do* to them? And did you give me a single goddamn thought before you did it?"

Her fury rattled and startled him—startled him so thoroughly, he needed a moment to collect his thoughts. He exhaled slowly, shifting gears from the Erin Oakes problem to the Tana Nighswander problem. When he finally replied, his pulse was jacked, but his tone was calm. "Slow down. What happened?"

Ronnie and Jayne killed themselves, he thought. *That's what happened. Murder-suicide, to be more specific. Jayne took the Ithaca and pumped one into Ronnie, then deep-throated the barrel herself. You drove them to it, Arthur.*

"They're gone! They took the Ranchero and took off. I don't know how the fuck I'm even gonna get to the grocery store. I am eight goddamn months pregnant, you dumb fuck. They were my *ride*. How am I going to get to *work*? How am I going to get to the *hospital*?"

"Do you know where they went?" he asked.

"Out west," she said. "Nevada maybe? Ronnie has a cousin there. She took all her money and she took all of mine too. I had cash in the box spring of my bed. I didn't think she knew. I should've known I couldn't keep anything from her. There's nothing I have she won't take."

"Not anymore," he said, and that quieted her. "If it comes to it, Tana, I'll drive you to the hospital myself when you're ready to deliver. As for work . . . you didn't use the Ranchero to make your deliveries. Shut-Up-And-Eat-It has cars."

"Yeah, well, they aren't loaners," she spat.

"I'll think of something. I'll help you through this. And you won't have to give anyone a blow job or a lay this week to keep them happy either." *Including me*, he thought, but didn't say. "That part of your life is over, Tana. Whatever else I fucked up for you, that part of it I feel good about."

He listened to her breathing on the other end of the line.

"Did Jayne say anything before she left?"

"No," Tana said. "But Ronnie said to tell you he's sorry. That he's never been more sorry in his whole life. I used to imagine what it would be like—to see them both like that. Freaking the fuck out. Helpless. It wasn't as good as I imagined."

They were both silent, listening to the phone hiss.

"Gwen," Tana said, finally. "Gwen can drive me. She has her own car and she only lives a few blocks from my place. You owe me that."

"I can ask her. But . . . Tana." He felt an intense discomfort that made it hard to say the next part. "If she helps you out, I need you to help *me* out. I'd be grateful if you didn't tell her."

Even as he said it, he felt something inside him writhing with shame. What did it matter if she told? He had no claim on Gwen. He didn't want Gwen to have a claim on him. He was afraid of his own need, his own wish to have her in his arms, afraid his longing would take Oxford away from him. If Gwen knew the truth about him, it would make it that much easier to go, but he didn't want her to know the truth, he wanted her to go on looking at him with fondness and pleasure. He liked when she leaned against him, when she bumped her head on his shoulder, had grown used to it, and felt ill at the thought of losing it.

A part of him was astonished at himself, the way he could bully his mother one moment, and wheedle and whine at Tana the next. He had possessed a functioning sense of shame once.

"Tell her what?" Tana asked. There was a taunting edge in her voice, and for a moment she sounded like Jayne.

"You know what."

"Say it."

"That we had sex."

She was silent.

"Tana . . ." He knew it was a mistake to ask and couldn't help himself. "Did Jayne make you? To keep me happy?"

Tana laughed: a harsh caw. "What do you think?"

"If I ask Gwen to drive you . . ."

"You'll just have to wonder what us girls talk about when you aren't around. You think I *want* her help? It sucks. And if it's going to suck for me, it's going to suck for *you*, Arthur."

He shut his eyes and rested his head against the wall. She laughed again.

"Have her give me a call," Tana said. "Tell her I'd appreciate it. Tell her it'd be real sisterly. I'm already looking forward to it. I don't get nearly enough girl talk. And Gwen and I have so much in common. We're both the kind of uneducated townies Arthur Oakes gets hard for. Lucky us."

THIRTY-SIX

Of course, Gwen was glad to drive Tana. And on the first day she took Tana to work, she dropped by The Briars straight after and knocked on the doorframe to the study.

Arthur was sitting across the chessboard from Colin. Arthur knew he had no great gift for the game, but he had been in the chess club in junior high and later at Fryeburg Academy, and he had done the reading. He approached all his interests in much the same plodding, methodical way, making up for a lack of talent with a tireless capacity for study. For months, he had pounded Colin without pity or apology, believed it was condescending to offer pointers or encouragement. But Colin could do the reading too. He had started to win games over Christmas break, and Arthur now had the uneasy sense that all his early dominance was slipping away. Colin had a knack for setting traps and Arthur had one for walking into them. He was studying the board with a sense of acute dismay, conscious he had just wandered into another, when he saw Gwen at the door and all thoughts of the game went out of his head.

Her eyes wouldn't meet his, and when he stood up, there was so much adrenaline zipping inside him, his legs felt watery and loose. He supposed Tana had told her everything. He decided to accept whatever Gwen thought of him without argument. If she hated him now, then he had at least earned her contempt honestly. *When I get to Oxford, I can start again*, he thought, although it felt like a hollow consolation.

He stepped into the hall. Gwen put her hands in her back pockets and leaned against the wall.

"You don't know how long I've been practicing this in my head," she said.

He nodded and braced for it.

"My senior prom," she said, and stopped and started again. "Bracken McLeod asked me this afternoon. I love Bracken, but the only thing he ever talks about is graduating and going to work with his dad selling tractor parts, and I don't care about farm machinery. If you don't want to—and why would you want to? You're in college. You've moved past this juvenile shit."

The words were coming in a rush, but he was slow piecing them together, couldn't figure out what any of it had to do with Tana. Finally, it came to him that she wasn't talking about Tana at all.

She put her face in her hands. "Christ. Say something?"

"Are you asking if I want to take you to your senior prom?"

She peeked between her fingers. "Katrina Ward is taking a kid from Bates. Sarah Pinners is dating a dude who *graduated* from UMO—he's six years older than her! It isn't totally weird."

Then he understood that Tana hadn't said anything, that she wasn't going to say anything, and if a part of him was still ashamed, another part of him felt as if an elephant had lifted a foot off his chest. He was so relieved, he leaned toward her, thought he would hug her, rest his chin on her head. Only she leaned toward him at the same time, and he looked into her face and quite naturally her mouth found his. He did not know if she decided to kiss him or if he decided to kiss her, only that her lips were warm and gentle and to feel them against his sent a ringing electrical shock of pleasure through his whole body. A needle of happiness speared him through and stuck him in place. His hands were around Gwen's waist. Hers were lightly pressed to his chest.

"Huh," he said, when he drew back.

She laughed. She wore a pretty flush on her round face.

"So, anyway," she said. "About that dance."

"About that dance," he said. "Sure. Sounds fun. I just want to apologize in advance for my car. I didn't put all those Jesus bumper stickers on it, that was my mom. I'll park a couple blocks from the dance so no one has to see you getting out of it."

"Fuck that!" Colin called from the study. "Take the Caddy. If it's warm you can put the top down. Also, you're three moves from check."

"Thank you and I surrender," Arthur called. Gwen laughed again, a low ripple of mirth that gave him a shivery, pleasant feeling. She rose on her tiptoes to kiss him again, and this time he took off her glasses first. That second kiss was longer and slower and left his heart racing.

She found her fit in his arms, her head right under his chin. It felt good. If there was a karmic opposite to the ugly triumph of revenge, this was it, Arthur thought.

With his chin resting on her head he said, "Did you and Tana talk about anything?"

"She asked me if I thought she oughta switch to light beer since she's pregnant," Gwen said. "And I said that's probably an all right idea. We're going grocery shopping after she gets out of work. She ain't so bad. Little rough around the edges, but anyone who's been trampled like she has will get that way." Gwen looked into his face, eyes shining with happiness. "At least you were nice to her. She said that almost first thing. She said you were one of the nicest people she knew, and I have to say, I couldn't agree more."

They kissed a third time then, but a worm of shame squirmed in Arthur's heart, to let him know it was there—it would always be there.

THIRTY-SEVEN

The night before Easter Sunday, Arthur couldn't sleep. There was a bitter taste in his mouth like he had been chewing on a copper wire. He felt the next day was his own execution, not Jayne's. Finally, at three in the morning, he got out of bed, knelt next to the mattress, and prayed, as his mother had showed him how to pray. He prayed to God to let Jayne and Ronnie live.

THIRTY-EIGHT

The tension wore on him all day. It *stacked*, like thunderclouds mounting along the horizon, bringing with them a building sense of pressure and darkness, a throb of electrical potential. Only the pressure and throb built inside his head and the stabs of lightning were firing behind his eyes. By midafternoon his headache was so intense he couldn't study. The words on the page surged and eddied like a cloud of sparrows.

He was bent over a book he couldn't read in the kitchen, late into the day, darting nervous looks at the telephone. He expected it to ring, felt, somehow, that if Jayne Nighswander was dead, someone would call. Maybe King Sorrow would call himself! If such a thing occurred, Arthur thought dragon smoke would trickle through the listening holes in the receiver.

When it did finally ring, he almost screamed. But it was only the March of Dimes, asking if he could give five dollars to change a life.

THIRTY-NINE

There was no relief from it, not that day, not the next. It was a thunderstorm that refused to break. He thought often of a summer heat dome, the air pregnant with a suffocating warmth and a liquid weight, lightning flitting along the horizon, and everything still, waiting for the storm to erupt at last and tear open the sky in cannonades of thunder.

Arthur saw that tension in the others. He walked to the campus with Van, whose face was whey colored and eyes glassy, and who often made it halfway to his classes before realizing he was carrying the wrong books. He saw it in Allie and Donna. Allie seemed to have lost her hairbrush and went around with her cornsilk hair stirred into a staticky, weightless tangle. Sometimes she would begin to tunelessly hum "Puff the Magic Dragon." Whenever Donna noticed what Allie was doing she would scream at her to shut up—would scream so loudly, with such hostility, it made everyone jump. Arthur saw it in Gwen too. He often turned up at The Briars in the late afternoon, when Gwen could usually be found doing her homework at the kitchen island. Gwen shot him a look as he walked in, the same look every day, a glance that expressed dismay and anxiety. That look said: *Nothing yet, still nothing, how long until we know what happened, how long, and how are we supposed to wait?* He would hug her while she sat on her stool, her face pressed hard to his chest, and the slightest tremor in the hands pressed to his back. Only Colin seemed his usual self—and Arthur wasn't even sure about that. Colin seemed more distracted than usual and had become compulsive about straightening things, moving books and papers so they aligned with the edge of his grandfather's desk, adjusting throw pillows so they sat neatly on the couch in the study.

It went on and on—the not-knowing, the terrible not-knowing. They began meeting in the student center for Jell-O Pudding Pops and desultory games of Trivial Pursuit. The Briars wasn't always the best place for them anymore. Gwen's mother had noticed the mood and begun jabbing at them with irritable, suspicious questions: *Why are you all as jumpy as cats?* and *You better not be doing drugs, you five, my daughter looks up to you.* Getting together on campus meant doing without Gwen, which Arthur didn't love. But Colin counseled it was for the best.

"Arthur," Colin told him, tenderly, "you are a terrible, nervous liar and none of us can bear to see you even in the same room with Arlene Underfoot. We're doing this for you, because we love you, and we all want Gwen to hurry up and take your virginity."

"Arlene," Arthur muttered in reply. "I was wondering about her first name."

Colin was best at the Science and Nature categories, Arthur couldn't be stumped by any of the Art and Literature problems, Donna was strongest at History, and Allie, whose father had been an All-American, seemed to know everything about Sports without the slightest interest in the subject. Van alone refused to care—he said the pursuit of the trivial went to the rot at the core of America's consumer culture—and played primarily to make his sister lose her shit.

"What is America's number-one pain reliever?" he read off one card.

"Tylenol!" Donna shouted.

"Wrong!" Van shouted back. "America's number-one pain reliever is the fat blunt I have to smoke to get through another one of these fucking games."

Donna had her arm cocked back to throw a fistful of dice at her brother when Gwen came looking for them. The moment Arthur saw the look on her face, he sprang out of his chair. She was waxen, eyes bright and stunned. That would've been enough to alarm him but was secondary to the bigger shock: she had sought them out *on campus*, a place he had never before seen her.

His first thought was, *It's the King, she's seen the King, he couldn't get Jayne Nighswander because she slipped out of range, and he's pissed, he's boiling, he wants us to pick someone to die in Jayne's place. He wants one of us now.* The idea was like a swallowed shard of glass. They were all rising from their chairs by then. Allie came around the table to give Gwen a hug. He noticed then that Gwen had a letter in one hand, folded into thirds, but as Allie embraced her, she dropped the sheet of paper on the game board. Arthur saw the header, *Rackham College*, and some of the tension went out of him. She wasn't here about the King after all—she was here because they had rejected her, of course they had, and it had been stupid of him, stupid and even a little cruel, to get her hopes up. He was so sick of being wrong.

But he was seeing the letter upside down and Donna wasn't. She took one glance, stepped around the table, and gave Gwen a hard swat on the ass. "You clever bitch. I knew they'd take you."

Arthur turned the letter around to read it properly. Words jumped out at him: "honored," "extraordinary," "proud addition to our student body," "family of faculty rate, provisional on academic excellence." Then he was up, standing on his chair, holding his fists over his head, shouting loud enough so everyone in the student center was looking at him.

"The glorious goddamn Gwen Underfoot just got into the ninety-eighth best small liberal arts college in America!" he shouted. "How do you like that, Rackham?"

This announcement was met by a scattering of derisive cheers.

Van said, "Oh, baby, we are going to get you so drunk tonight, you're going to need to apply for a scholarship to Alcoholics Anonymous."

Arthur jumped off the chair and Gwen found her way into his arms.

"It turned out all right," she said into his neck. "And now I get to be one of you."

"Oh, sweetest," Allie said. "You think you needed to get into this dump to be one of us?"

Arthur kissed the top of her head.

"Look at that," he said. "Sometimes the good guys win."

FORTY

They agreed to decamp to The Briars and get into the good stuff. Colin said you couldn't drink beer to celebrate a day like this, you had to have Scotch like a civilized human being, and anyway, Llewellyn would want to drink with them. He had written one of Gwen's recommendation letters. By some agreement, the McBrides and Allie went with Colin, crammed into his granddaddy's cherry Caddy, which was over in student parking. Arthur left with Gwen to ride in her Civic. She had left her car in the staff lot, behind the student center, where the custodians and cafeteria services parked.

Gwen grabbed his hands and spun him and they kissed—a wonderful, sloppy kiss, clinging tight to one another, staggering and rebalancing and laughing. They broke and he led her across the lot toward her car. They made it three steps before he saw Tana Nighswander.

She had spotted them at the same time, had just climbed out of the Shut-Up-And-Eat-It delivery car, holding a stack of pizza boxes. Her round face was a dull, dark-eyed blank, pink from the evening chill. Arthur gently pulled himself free of Gwen. Gwen glanced past him, saw Tana, and touched her mouth, embarrassed. Tana stood with the pizza boxes in both hands and resting on the shelf of her distended belly.

"Tana," Gwen said. "How are you?"

Tana stared with glazed eyes, swaying as if she were under the influence of *something*.

"My sister is dead," Tana said. "She burned to death. How are you?"

"What?" Arthur asked. "When?" Some disassociated part of

himself noted that his heartbeat hardly accelerated, that in this moment there was no physical sense of shock at all.

"Easter. They found her in the Ranchero with her driver's license in her purse. They called my mother and she called me. They're checking Jayne's dental records to confirm, but it's her. She knew she was going to die. She called me from the road, a few days before. She told me. She said she wasn't going to make it."

Gwen walked across the pitted gravel, took the pizzas, and set them on the top of the car. She took Tana in her arms and Tana put her head on Gwen's shoulder and began to cry. Gwen stroked her hair while Tana wept. Arthur waited to feel something, but nothing came. He had heard that when one suffered a serious injury it was much the same—that men who had legs suddenly blown off very rarely registered any immediate pain.

"Will you stay with me after work, Gwen?" Tana asked. "Will you stay with me? I feel awful bad. I don't want to be home alone. Not while it's dark."

"Long as you need, darlin'," Gwen said.

"She was a bad person," Tana whispered. "But she was *my* person."

"I can be your person tonight," Gwen said. "I'd be glad to. Should you be working?"

Tana caught a hitching breath and put a hand against her belly. "Gonna have to pay for diapers somehow."

Gwen didn't argue with her. "I'll pick you up after work and stay as long as you need."

Arthur had been walking toward them and now he placed a tentative hand on Tana's back.

"I'm sorry," he said.

"I'm not," Tana said. "Why do you think I feel so bad?"

FORTY-ONE

They parked at The Briars, behind the Caddy, and let themselves in. Gwen had wept for a while, in the dark of the car, but had mastered herself by the time they arrived—although anyone who looked at her could see she had been in tears. Arthur hadn't wept himself. He was too full of a stunned emptiness to feel anything like heartbreak or horror or shame or whatever you were supposed to feel after someone you hated was burned to death by your command. The others were in the library, Colin hunched down to arrange logs for a fire, and when they walked in Allie whooped:

"Hey, college girl, your education begins ton*iiiiiiiiiiiii*ght!" Then she saw Gwen's face and clapped a hand over her mouth.

Colin remained crouched by the hearth but regarded them with bright, avid eyes.

"King Sorrow," Colin said. "He got her. Didn't he? He caught up to them."

Gwen nodded, walked shakily to the card table, and sat down.

"How did it happen?" Colin asked.

Arthur reported the little that Tana had told them. Colin went on constructing his fire, setting a match to fine cedar shavings and newspaper, feeding it a few sticks to build it up. At last, he rose and went to the bar and poured Scotch.

"Well," Donna said, when Arthur finished. "Now we've got two things to celebrate."

Arthur looked at her, genuinely surprised. "You really don't care?"

"I care. About *you*. And *us*." Gesturing with her hand to indicate everyone in the room. "I've got my limits. I never pretended otherwise."

"I'm not sorry either," Van said. "Not really. I'm only bummed we had to find out now, because it ruined Gwen's special day."

Colin handed Gwen a Scotch rocks. She drank half in one swallow, then shut her eyes and rested her wrists against the card table's leather bumper. Colin sat on one side of her, Arthur on the other. Van took Colin's usual spot, on the dealer's stool, and began to shuffle.

Colin squinted through his own glass of Scotch, peering into the firelight, enjoying the play of the light through the whiskey. A small, philosophical smile played at the corners of his mouth. At last, he said, "We financed a war in Biafra to secure access to their oil fields. By the time we were done, the whole country was littered with bodies. Half a million dead."

Allie slipped up behind Gwen, put her arms around her, and rested her chin on her head. Gwen leaned back into her embrace and shut her eyes. Allie said, "I guess I'm crossing Biafra off my list of future spring break possibilities. We'll have to go someplace safer. Like Nicaragua."

"I know what you're getting at, Colin," Arthur told him.

"I'll say it anyway: none of *us*—the six of us in this room—directly killed anyone in Biafra. But our country did. The CIA did. They did it for us, so we could live in peace and security. No one rips themselves up with guilt about it every time they fill the tank."

"Maybe we should. Ever think that?" Gwen asked him.

"Maybe. But if we started hating ourselves for Biafra, I'm not sure where we'd stop. Because most of the good things in our lives were purchased in blood. We don't think about it, but any number of things we enjoy and take for granted—starting, first and foremost, with each other—are held at the cost of other lives. If you unfocus your eyes, Gwen, it's possible to see Jayne Nighswander's death in that context . . . the red backdrop of American life. The slave labor in Indonesia that made Donovan's sneakers. The miner dying of black lung so we can turn on the lights. The construction worker who fell off a high girder so the World Trade towers could kiss the sky. Because we care about each other, we make peace with a certain level of horror."

"Is that what we have to do?" Gwen asked. "Unfocus our eyes so we can't see who we hurt? Walking around with your eyes unfocused sounds like a good way to get hurt yourself."

"Oh, fuck this," Donna said. "Fuck this feel-bad *bullshit*. Jayne Nighswander was rancid and murderous trash. I'm not going to feel sorry for her now. Fuck that. Let's play poker. Deal the cards, Van."

Van dealt them their cards and then turned over the flop: a queen of spades, a king of hearts, and a dragon of diamonds.

For a moment no one besides Arthur seemed to notice. They were all looking at the hands they had been dealt. Then Gwen cried out and dropped her cards. She had a dragon of clubs. Instead of a king or a queen, it showed a skinny golden reptile with a sly smile and gold whiskers suggesting a dapper mustache.

Allie coughed and waved at a blue haze in the air. "Colin, the fire's backing up. My lungs are full of smoke."

"You get used to it," King Sorrow said, as the lights went out.

FORTY-TWO

Arthur sucked a breath to shout for Gwen and inhaled a chest full of choking smoke. He coughed, a harsh, racking cough that felt like it was going to pry bones apart in his chest. Without thinking, he dropped from the stool, searching for air close to the floor.

He heard shouts. A stool fell. He crawled away from the card table and thumped heads with Allie.

"It's so dark," Allie said. "What happened to the fire?"

"Swallowed it, luv," King Sorrow said. "A little amuse-bouche before the mains."

At first Arthur didn't know where King Sorrow's voice had come from. Then he had a nasty idea—he thought it was possible he *himself* had spoken in King Sorrow's voice. In fact, he thought *all* of them had replied to Allie as King Sorrow, speaking together. It would explain the way the dragon's words seemed to reverberate from every corner of the room.

Arthur made his way along on hands and knees, calling for Gwen. She grabbed his hand in the smoke and the darkness, her fingers cold, her grip almost painful.

"He can't hurt us," Arthur told her. "He's just trying to scare us. He already had his feast."

The smoke replied: "Fair play, Arthur. But a dragon on a diet can still look at a menu."

Gwen tugged on Arthur's hand. "Come on," she said, and let go. He followed the sound of her clambering away, until he spied a long straight silver line of moonglow on his right. Arthur thought it was the space between the floor and the curtains pulled across the French windows. Night—and cold, clean air—waited on the other

side. He managed the last yard, felt the rough fabric of the curtain brushing his face, pushed it aside, and looked out onto
the bright glare of late morning under a western sun, so dazzling that it hurts his eyes.

This is Reno. He doesn't know how he knows, although he can see he's on a four-lane street, with casinos on two corners and a gentleman's club on a third. At this hour of the day, the avenue could not look any more cheap or run-down.

Jayne Nighswander's eyes are bright with sleeplessness. She wears a tank top with the words CINDERELLA CITY written across the chest in a glittery Disney-fied cursive and a rattling necklace of what looks like pale pink seashells. Cinderella City was in Colorado. They had ice cream there at a place called Farrell's. Jayne had a scoop of peppermint, Ronnie had a chocolate sundae he didn't eat. He smoked a cigarette and watched it melt. Later that night, Jayne was in the motel bathroom, trying to take a dump, when she saw a shape rise behind the shower curtain, a serpentine figure as thick as a Japanese elm, with a great frill that opened around its head. She screamed and jumped up and pulled the curtain aside. There was nothing there, but she threw up anyway: a peppermint-flavored mouthful of puke. Arthur knows all of this as if he were there, wearing her skin, when it happened.

Cinderella City was the last she had seen of King Sorrow, and that was three days ago. She had not smelled his filthy smoke since; he had not woken her with one of his sly bons mots in the middle of the night; she had not seen his shadow or his scaly claw, nor sensed him sailing through the night, a thousand feet above the car, when they drove after dark. At some point, late Friday afternoon, it had come to her that they had managed to get clear. Those Rackham trust fund assholes had been right . . . about that part, at least. She fingered the necklace around her neck and Arthur saw now that it was half a dozen dried-out garlic bulbs on a plain white thread. After the Oakes woman won her parole, the bald-headed cyborg named Wren had reached out to Jayne and told her to try garlic, that sometimes garlic repelled creatures that thrived on human fear. She thought now he had been fucking with her head and having a laugh at the same time.

As far as she could tell, the great serpent took no notice of the garlic at all, though she went on wearing it, had got used to its persistent faint perfume. Garlic didn't make a difference, but distance did. The dragon hadn't been able to follow them west of the mountains. They had left him at last on the other side of the Colorado back range.

Probably.

Just in case she's wrong about that, Jayne spent thirty minutes working on a letter at the little desk in the motel room. Now she stops in front of a blue mailbox and taps the edge of the envelope against it.

(On his hands and knees in The Briars, Arthur gave his head an unconscious little shake, as if a biting insect were humming around his face. He couldn't see far enough into Jayne's mind to learn anything more about the letter in her right hand. It bothered him not to know what was in it and who it was for. In the next moment it struck him that the King was happy to show them most of his cards, his dragon of clubs, his dragon of diamonds . . . but he had decided to keep this one back, a bad thought.)

"You aren't the only one with a pet dragon, bitch," *she says, and drops the letter in and closes the hatch on the big blue postal box.*

She doesn't hear the envelope sliding down the chute, so she opens the hatch again, to make sure it dropped, and an enormous scaly claw, big as her head, reaches up from inside the darkness and SLAMS down against the open steel drawer. Talons big as meat hooks punch through the steel. Jayne screams and the hatch slaps shut.

Claws bunched into a fist crash against the inside of the mailbox, creating a great mushroom-shaped dent in the side, and Jayne screams again and steps off the curb into traffic. A horn wails and she jumps and a panel truck swerves to avoid her. It whips past so close, the slipstream sucks the air out of her mouth. She staggers back onto the curb. Inside the mailbox, the dragon smashes his tail against the inner walls. The rivets burst along one side of the container and a drift of letters pours out. Jayne turns and runs. One cheap plastic flip-flop falls off her right foot. She doesn't go back for it, can't go back, and she wants to cry, wants to shout Not fair! We drove two thousand miles! They said you couldn't follow me that far and I'm wearing this fucking garlic necklace and it's NOT FAIR! *but* she doesn't have the breath for it and her eyes blur and she bangs into someone, careens off him, spins and—

—twelve minutes later falls through the door into the dim of their motel room. Ronnie is still asleep. She grabs his hands, pulls him into a sitting position. His head rolls limply on his neck, his eyelids fluttering. He's naked except for his jockeys and his own dried-out and crumbling garlic necklace.

"Wake up," says Jayne. "It's here. We have to go. Right now."

He mewls in his sleep. He's been dipping into their swiftly diminishing supply of Percocet this last week to take the edge off his terror. She slaps him—she's been doing a lot of that lately—to bring him around. She hits him hard enough to leave a pink handprint on his cheek.

"The fuck, bitch?" he asks, listlessly.

"We have to go. It's coming."

He stares at her glassily. "Where we going to go, babe? Wherever we go is gonna be Samarra. Don't you know that?"

She doesn't have any idea what he's talking about and doesn't care.

"I will *leave you here*," she says. "I will leave you in his path and hope that buys me a few days."

That gets him moving. Five minutes later, they're back on the road, with a quarter of a tank of gas and a little less than ten dollars between them.

"Where to, darlin'?" Ronnie asks, but she shakes her head and points a finger and he steers them—

—east and south and east again, stitching a line back and forth across the Nevada/California border. They are only 140 miles from Los Angeles when the engine begins to make a hollow knocking sound. A half hour later, fluffy white steam begins to seethe up around the edges of the hood. By then, Jayne has come to believe if they can get to LA, they might survive another night. She reckons they can get themselves arrested and brought to a major lockup. She would like to see King Sorrow come get them through concrete walls, past a hundred cops with access to riot gear and machine guns.

When the car goes, it happens suddenly. Something shrieks like a teakettle under the hood. Then there is a sudden wham, like someone firing the Ithaca that Jayne pawned for fifty dollars in Pennsylvania. The car begins to hitch along in little jolts.

"There goes the belt," Ronnie says, with perfect calm.

"No," Jayne says. "No, no, no. There's nothing out here."

"There's a drive-in," he says, and nods at a billboard.

THE AMERICAN DRIVE-IN
ONE MILE
YOU'RE ALMOST THERE
HAPPY ENDINGS GUARANTEED!

But when they reach the American—by then they are coasting, slowing steadily—it's abandoned. Even before Ronnie stops the car, Jayne knows this is where it will end. He turns them onto a narrow dirt road, weedy and overgrown. The tires thump over a rusty chain that once barred the way but has long since fallen to the ground.

They pull through the sequoias into a scruffy meadow with the drive-in screen at one end. The canvas is dirty and there's a twelve-foot-wide hole in one corner revealing the strut work behind. The exposed wooden beams look like crosses waiting for the condemned. At the other end of the field is a concrete pillbox that once served as the projection booth. The great field is filled with even rows of rusting pipes. Once upon a time, speakers sat on top of those pipes, but they've long since been removed.

Ronnie rolls to a stop in one of the rear slots and puts the Ranchero into park. The dusk reverberates with insect song.

"I don't understand what happened to the Ranchero," Jayne says.

"It's like that thing about bankruptcy," Ronnie says. "It happens gradually, then all at once. I read that somewhere. Maybe in Hustler."

"Do you think there's a phone nearby?"

"Who would we call? 1-800-We're-Fucked?" He laughs again and looks in the rearview mirror at the projection booth. "I gotta piss. I'll check out the projection booth. I wonder if we can barricade ourselves in there."

He climbs out of the car but then pauses to lean back in through the window. His useless, dried-out garlic necklace rustles at his throat. He grins at her, and for a moment it is possible to remember why she fell for him. He has a grin like a ten-year-old boy on the first day of summer vacation.

"It was a damn short movie, wasn't it, babe?" he says, and laughs his smoker's laugh and claps a hand against the inside of the door. He sets out for the low concrete building, a gangly, scrawny man with the rolling gait of a pirate. Soon he has disappeared into the gloom.

Jayne watches the last of the light drain from the sky. She draws her knees to her chest and hugs herself. She tries to catalog what she is feeling. Resentment and terror, yes. But also a kind of giddy hilarity. Of all the ways she thought she might die, being run to earth and butchered by a dragon had not been on her list. She takes a long deep breath and smells garlic and thinks suddenly that she is wearing a garnish, she is garnished and ready to be served.

Mars burns red above one corner of the movie screen and she wonders what's taking Ronnie so long. She's just started to sit up straighter in her seat when the movie screen goes bright. A projector switches itself on, throwing a vast rectangle of white brilliance onto the blank screen.

A shadow uncoils across it. King Sorrow's head appears first, crowned with that spreading, regal fan. It rises from a neck that goes on and on, long as a telephone pole and sinewy as a cobra. Wings unfold. At their full extent they blot out the light entirely.

Jayne begins to laugh. It is a shrill, hysterical sound, very close to a scream.

Suddenly the shadow soars straight upward and disappears, giving her a last, long look at a tail that seems to trail on for most of a minute. Then the darkness has moved on and the screen is bright again, as white and empty as oblivion.

A gust of wind strikes the Ranchero and rocks it up and down on its springs.

A moment later, Ronnie Volpe hits the hood, falling from a height of at least a hundred feet. He strikes with enough force to collapse the front end of the car, landing with a concussive iron BANG! that jumps the rear tires off the ground. Jayne's laughter turns to a wail. She's staring at the reddened, clawed stump of his neck.

Ronnie's head comes through the windshield a moment later. It hits the driver's seat and rolls, comes to a stop against her hip, staring up at her. His mouth is open and stuffed with bulbs of garlic. Splinters of broken glass glint in his curly hair.

Jayne scrabbles for the latch but before she can get the door open, something—perhaps one of King Sorrow's hind feet—descends slowly on the Ranchero's roof and crushes it in and down. The side windows splinter and crack, erupt outward. The entire frame of the car deforms under the massive weight and Jayne finds she can't force her door open, not even when she throws all her weight against it.

"Stop!" she screams. "Stop! Stop! Please! PLEASE!"

The chassis groans. The roof continues to sink toward her. The gap where the windshield belongs is narrowing, closing out the view of the movie screen.

With an infinite slowness, King Sorrow lowers his head from above, to put both of his black, scaly nostrils into the open space. His breath stinks of a campfire.

"Manners," King Sorrow says. "Manners at last. You see, Jayne, it's never too late to learn something new."

He inhales deeply, so deeply that road rubbish—empty wax cups, hamburger wrappers—whirls about the inside of the car in a fantastic eddy. Then he exhales, great flowers of flame, and Jayne tries to scream but her lungs have already ignited in her chest, burning up in an instant like paper bags touched with a torch. Before her eyes explode in her head, she has time to see the flesh and sinew blasted off the hands she has raised to protect her face. With her last breath, she can smell the seared pork-and-garlic odor of her own frying skin. She missed lunch and dinner, and the smell, in that last dreadful instant of her life, makes her stomach tighten with hunger.

Arthur jerked his head back from the flash of heat on his face, eyes blurring with tears from the smoke. He blinked rapidly to clear his vision. When he could see again, he reached out to shove the heavy drapes aside. The brick patio and the yard beyond were lit by icy moonlight.

"It's over," he told Gwen, squeezing her hand. At some point in the last few moments, he had found it again. With his other hand, he fumbled for the latch and pushed the door open. The air that billowed in was unexpectedly summery and sweet. "He's gone."

She squeezed his hand in acknowledgment and he looked down and it wasn't Gwen's hand at all, it was a reptile's claw, a fine black webbing between hard bony fingers. Arthur shouted and let go and the hand shrank back into the darkness.

"This meeting of the Get Even Club," King Sorrow told them, "has been adjourned."

FORTY-THREE

Three days later, he was pulling on a pair of khakis in his bedroom when he heard a papery, rasping sound in the front hall, followed by a whap of steel: someone dropping a letter through the mail slot. *Her* letter, he knew, a chill spreading into his blood. *Jayne's letter*.

He stepped into the doorway, holding his unbuttoned pants up with one hand. Van got to the letter first, though, squatted down, picked a cream-colored envelope up off the floor, turned it over and looked at the front.

"It's for you," Van said, his face calm and blank, nothing in his eyes.

Arthur took it out of his hands, tore it open, unfolded the letter within, and read his future.

FORTY-FOUR

Gwen was not herself.

It would've been normal, the most normal thing in the world, if she was distressed. Arthur knew a thing or two about feeling distressed. Two days after he saw Jayne Nighswander die, he stopped at the Rackham cafeteria for a cup of tea on his way to a morning lecture. Breakfast was laid out buffet-style in stainless steel serving dishes. He glanced into a pan full of sausage patties, flat discs of charred meat glistening with dewy drops of grease, drew a breath, and smelled Jayne burning. Arthur turned on his heel, swiftly exited the cafeteria, and vomited into a hedge. A student on his way by glanced at him sidelong and sighed, "Another satisfied customer."

But Gwen didn't seem *distressed* to Arthur so much as distracted. Whenever he popped by The Briars, he found her in her regular place at the kitchen island, holding her glasses in one hand—she was usually chewing on the part that hooked over her ear—and staring fixedly into space, as if she were trying to puzzle out an especially maddening clue in a Sunday crossword. Only there was no crossword spread out before her and sometimes no homework either.

"I don't know what you're thinking about," he said, "but the way you're frowning, I hope it isn't me."

"Never, old chum," she told him, and smiled weakly . . . and said no more.

Even when they were all together, they weren't all together. Once upon a time, Gwen had told Arthur that the distance between Rackham College and Gogan, Maine, was farther than it looked on paper. It wasn't a mile and a half; it was a thousand miles and a half. At the time, he felt he knew what she meant—but he understood her even better now, when he could sit down next to her and still feel they weren't even in the same room. The essential Gwen had gone somewhere far beyond the call of his voice. The thought made him despair, just a little. There were no more breathtaking kisses, no more holding on to one another as they had the night she was accepted to Rackham. It was funny, the way double murder put a damper on romance.

And anyway, there was the matter of the letter he had received, and what was in the letter. He could not find a way to tell her. Didn't have the stomach.

And then, five days before Gwen's prom, Llewellyn Wren missed a step on his way down the front stairs.

ARTHUR GOT THE WHOLE STORY later from Colin.

Gwen's mother came in a little before eight on a Wednesday morning, as was her habit, and was just lifting a tray of biscuits out of the oven when she heard a sound like someone firing a rifle in the front hallway. She dropped the pan and came running. She found Llewellyn Wren at the bottom of the stairs, grimacing and clutching his right leg. The old man had been on his way down when the thigh bone suddenly snapped. An ambulance took him to Eastern Maine Medical, where an X-ray revealed a femur with the inner consistency of honeycomb. His ribs were likewise hollowed out by osteopenia and were as fragile as eggshell. He had smashed four of them.

"I didn't know the virus could do that," Colin told Arthur later, looking uncharacteristically nonplussed. "I didn't know it could even make your bones sick."

The leg required surgery, and the first doctor consulted refused to operate on a patient who had developed full-blown AIDS. By the following day, Llewellyn's fever had spiked, he could not stop trembling in nervous pulses, and his right foot was turning an ominous shade of blue; it was the sort of color one saw in a dead body as blood pooled in the low points. A surgeon was brought in from Brigham and Women's, a skinny and expressionless Bostonian with colorless eyes who had no fear of HIV; he himself had been living with the virus for two years. The operation to reset the fragmented bone was managed in a few hours. A course of antibiotics took out the infection—and left Llewellyn desperately weak, in the grip of dehydration, diarrhea, and vicious stomach cramps. Colin arranged for a hospital bed to be shipped to The Briars.

"It's stage three," Colin told Arthur, on the night Llewellyn returned to The Briars. "And this elevator only goes four floors."

They were in the kitchen, then, just the two of them. Arlene Underfoot was upstairs, where a nurse was demonstrating how to safely care for the catheter in Llewellyn's left arm. Gwen had joined them. Arthur wasn't sure why—maybe to make sure her mother understood everything. He hoped Gwen wouldn't try to help. It wasn't very noble of him, but the thought of her accidentally exposing herself to Llewellyn's illness made his insides squirm with nervousness.

"They find new medicines every day," Arthur said, a line that sounded pathetic even to his own ears.

Colin smiled sadly. "Don't do that, Arthur. It doesn't suit you."

"What doesn't suit me?"

"The language of false comfort. Maybe that kind of talk doesn't suit *any* of us anymore. Not after what we did." He paused, poking at a slice of cold pizza without any appetite. "When it comes to evil, King Sorrow is an absolute prince compared to AIDS."

"You think?" Arthur asked.

"I do," Colin told him. "If there has to be evil in the world, then I'd at least like to be in charge of it."

Arthur did not think it was the proper moment to point out what was obvious, at least to him: they hadn't been in charge of anything. King Sorrow had let them *feel* they were in charge, because it pleased him, but he had never been playing their game—they had been playing his. He was a king, after all, and they his subjects.

No one was ever in charge of a dragon. Some snakes were too big to catch by the tail.

DRIVING THE '49 CADILLAC was like steering a float in a parade, it was that big. Arthur pointed it into Gogan, and rolled with the canvas top down and warm, summery air blasting in over him. Gogan was Gogan. Someone had left a mildewed couch out on the curb. Every fourth shop was boarded up and the plywood in the windows had been tagged with bad graffiti, big black cocks and big black boobs. He loved it anyway. He loved the cat that stood in the middle of the street and wouldn't move, so he had to drive around it. He loved the loud bars, the doors flung open, and the smell of fresh beer and stale cigarettes wafting out. He loved the bras and the underwear hanging from the branches of the trees like an eccentric's notion of Christmas decorations.

With Gwen's careful instructions, the Caddy wound unerringly through the maze of narrow streets and on to the Underhill house, a narrow, three-story place with a foot-wide strip of grass for a front yard. She sat on the top step, waiting for him, and at the sight of her, he rose up behind the steering wheel, his heart going light and funny in his chest. She stood and gave him a shy little wave. Her prom dress was a soft, blushing shade of peach, a work of bewildering feminine complexity, with a loose, see-through layer wrapped around a sleek, almost shiny sheath beneath. A cat's cradle of straps laced up across her bare back. Something about it brought to mind the sort of paper lantern that would float weightlessly into the stars, once someone had set a candle within it.

She wobbled coming down the step and nearly twisted an ankle. He was already out of the car and kept her from falling on her face, one hand on her hip, another on her shoulder.

"Tell me the purpose of high heels," she said, laughing.

"They were invented to make it easier for a girl to stumble into the arms of someone tall, dark, and handsome."

"Arthur Oakes," she said. "If I didn't know better, I'd think you just tried out a line on me."

"I didn't spend six years of my life studying romance languages for nothin'," he told her.

Two hours later, they were dancing to Simply Red, "If You Don't Know Me by Now," and his hands were on her hips and her face was turned up to his. The prom was held in her high school's gymnasium, and there was an unmistakable fragrance of sweaty jockstraps and rotten sneakers. But the space was dramatically lit by banks of aquamarine light, and they kicked through an inch of glittering fluff, and Gwen's eyes were as luminous as her dress. He was readying himself for a kiss when a girl who was obviously drunk lurched into them and smashed a plastic cup of cherry punch into Gwen's chest.

The drunk, a skinny chick with smeared lipstick, shouted, "Oh, jeez, I'm such an asshole, sorry!" and reeled away into the milling bodies. Gwen said it was all right, she could dry her boobs off with the lap blanket in the back of the Caddy and she had brought a cardigan she could pull over her top to hide the stain.

He led her by the hand, out into the acres of parking lot that surrounded a two-story brick fortress of a school that might've been designed by the same architect who dreamt up the Black Cricket Women's House of Correction. They found the car and Gwen fetched a threadbare pea-colored cardigan from the passenger seat. Just as she finished buttoning it over her gown, Arthur drew her into his arms again. The fire door to the gym was open and the music carried. The DJ put on Sinéad O'Connor, "Nothing Compares 2 U," and the Irish girl's voice rang out across the warm evening. There were no stars to see, the constellations blotted out by the yellow-tinged glare of the titanium streetlamps. They hardly danced, just held each other and rocked. Her hair smelled like summer.

Arthur wanted her—wanted to find the body under the gown, to find his mouth with hers—but there was no playful friskiness in either of them. Jayne Nighswander was only two weeks dead and they had both lost something, something deeper and more meaningful than virginity. Once you murdered someone you had to carry it forever. You went to bed with it and it was with you when you woke up. He had dreamt of Gwen in his bed for months, but it was Jayne he came home to at night. Jayne was always there in the dark, grinning at him from her charred and blackened face.

"Is Van in the apartment?" Gwen asked, her face close to his neck, so he couldn't see her expression, and he did not need her to explain why she was asking.

"He's out tonight. He had some studying to do."

"Oh, he did, did he?" Gwen asked and dared a glance into his face. She was struggling not to smile. "I'm not surprised, a young man of his scholarly inclinations. What's he studying?"

"The bottom of one of Colin Wren's Scotch glasses, I believe, and a hand of poker."

"Good. How much longer do we have to dance before we can get the hell out of here? I've had about all of high school I can stand, and my parents don't expect me home until the witching hour."

"Gwen," he said, a discomfort and a hesitancy in his voice. "Gwen, I got a letter a few days ago."

"Yes," she said. Her face still turned to his, her eyes unblinking behind her glasses. "And I know what was in it."

"You do?" he asked, briefly flummoxed.

"Van told Donna and Donna told me. It isn't a surprise, Arthur. I knew you were going. I knew they would accept you. When do you leave for Oxford?"

"The fall term—they call it Michaelmas—begins in September. But . . . I'll go at the beginning of August. I have family there, my father's family. They'll help me move in, and—I try to spend some time with them every year. It seems important to know them. Since I can't know him." He took her hands in his and dropped his head. She put her hand under his chin and lifted his face back up.

"We can still steal something just for us, can't we?" Gwen asked. "Before you go? Is that so wrong?" She smiled fondly at him.

It was hard to speak. Maybe that was why he took to studying languages—he kept hoping to find one that would make it easier to talk about what he felt. "I'm a little attached, Gwennie," he said in a whisper. "That's the thing."

"I'm a little attached too," she said, still smiling, but blinking suddenly at tears. "I'm not like Donna or Van. I have to feel attached to do the next thing. But I also know you're going—and you need to go. I know it means the world to you, although I don't know why. I know and I'm okay with it. I wouldn't be okay if you tried to change your mind because of me. I'm not asking to have you forever, Arthur. Just tonight." She laughed and brushed at a bright gem on her cheek. "Arthur, old pal, we have solved at least fifty crosswords together. How much more of this smoking hot foreplay do you expect an ordinary girl like me to take?"

"I don't think there's anything ordinary about Gwen Underfoot," he said. He smiled and kissed one cheek and the other and then the mouth in between.

When they pulled up in front of the house, the porch and the windows were dark, and with the car switched off, the night seemed to throb with cricket song. Arthur wished suddenly he had thought ahead, had bought flowers and left them on one pillow for her, or had put a bottle of champagne in the fridge to chill. But he had not made such preparations because he had not allowed himself to imagine the night ending here, had even advised himself not to bring her home. *Be better than that*, he had told himself. But if the last half year had shown him anything, it was his own capacity to do worse than expected.

"Do you like champagne?" he asked.

"Tickles my nose," she said.

"Oh, whew," he said. "I didn't buy any."

The engine ticked as it cooled.

"I've never done this before, old sport," she said.

"Me neither," he said, and when he said it, it felt entirely true. It *was* true. He had never made love with someone he adored, someone who could make him feel almost heartsick with happiness.

They went up the path, bumping shoulders. In psychological time, it took him approximately seven and a half hours to find the key while she waited patiently behind him, although in real time he supposed it was only half a minute. While he was fumbling for the light in the front hall, he reached back to take her hand—and for an instant imagined he would find King Sorrow's cold and scaly claw instead. *What do you say to a threesome, mate*, the dragon purred in his mind.

Gwen stopped him before he could flip the light switch. "Leave it off." The door was still open to the street behind her when she unbuttoned her sweater, then shrugged off one shoulder strap of her dress.

"The door," he said, his voice suddenly rough.

"No one is looking," she said. "And no one can see. And the air feels good on my back." The gown dropped with a dry rustle and swish around her heels. She bit her lower lip while she worked to unclasp her bra. "This damned thing."

"Christ," he said, and got an arm around her while he shoved the door shut with the other hand.

She was tight and they had to be patient, working at it slowly and gently. He took his time to be sure it was all right, while she urged him on, whispering it was fine, it didn't hurt, although later, tired and happy, she admitted it had, just a little. For a long time afterward, he lay on his side next to her, enjoying the flush across her chest and throat, moving his fingers between her breasts to feel the trip-trap of her hurrying heart. Her hand closed over his after a while and held his palm to her breastbone.

"It's still there, you know," she said.

"What is?" he asked.

"The tattoo," she told him. "I can show you, if you want."

"No," he said, his sides prickling with goose bumps. "No, thanks."

"You haven't noticed?"

He shook his head.

"Isn't that funny? He left his mark on all of us. Do you think it's an invitation? To call him back sometime?"

"He's not coming back. Not ever. That's over now." He didn't want to talk about it. He got up and went into the bathroom to get rid of his condom. Grotesque little things, like the shed skin of a snake—he found them distasteful, but between Tana's pregnancy and Llewellyn's illness, he was persuaded they were necessary until such time as they weren't.

"I won't get it, you know," she said to him when he came back to bed.

"Get what?"

"AIDS," she said. "I won't get it looking after Llewellyn." As if she had read his mind on the subject of prophylactics, and maybe she had—she had been half reading his thoughts since the beginning.

He furrowed his brow. "But you aren't looking after him. Your mother is. You're starting school in a few months."

Gwen looked at the ceiling—she was still smiling, still easy, no tension in her body at all—but she sighed in a way that suggested there was a sticky conversation ahead of them. Arthur felt a sudden tug of unease, but before the conversation could proceed, the phone rang in the kitchen. They listened to the brash clamor of the bell, three, four, five times.

"Probably Van, wanting to know if he can come home yet," Arthur said.

"Can he?"

"No," Arthur said. "I've many more wicked designs for your tender and innocent flesh."

"Not so innocent flesh now!" she said merrily.

The phone stopped ringing. His hand slid down to her navel. The phone began to ring again.

"You should get one of those machines," she said.

On the fifth ring he threw the sheets back and stalked naked into the kitchen and grabbed the phone.

"I'm in the middle of doing something," he said.

"Yeah," Tana Nighswander said, "and I know *who* you're doing too, but pull your dick out of her and get dressed. You two are my goddamn ride to the goddamn hospital and we need to go because I'm having this goddamn baby whether I goddamn want to or not."

MAINE MEDICAL WAS A COLLECTION of smart, five-story towers made of brick and glass, surrounded by a green collegiate campus and parking garages. Arthur cruised around and around it, looking for signs to the family center with an increasing sense of desperation, while Gwen and Tana sat in the back of the Caddy.

"Take your time, sport," Tana said. "I'll just be back here emptying my birth canal all over these nice leather seats." Then she made an angry sound and doubled over, clutching her abdomen, while Gwen stroked her between the shoulder blades. "Did a baby just fall outta me?"

Gwen leaned forward to squint into the footwell. "Nope. Not yet."

He found the entrance to the family center at last and slowed at the curb. Gwen helped Tana out of the back. Tana was hunched over, one hand resting on her great globe of a stomach, her legs pipestems beneath. She grimaced as if stepping into a face full of cold wind.

"Thanks for driving me, Arthur," Tana said. "That's the nicest car I've ever rode in. I felt like an absolute princess. Next time I'm in a car that nice, it'll probably be a hearst."

He watched them walk in through the automatic doors and then took off to find a place to park the Caddy. Ten minutes later he was in the maternity ward, a warren of antiseptic corridors, bedrooms, and offices, managed by a quartet of chippy nurses in soothing pink smocks. When Arthur said he was looking for Gwen and Tana Nighswander, one of the nurses invited him to have a seat in Family Room B. Family Room B turned out to be a lounge with a few worn-out recliners in it and a TV tuned to CNN. The windows offered a view of some air-conditioning units and, across the street, a dumpster. Arthur stood at the window and watched a pair of raccoons digging through the trash. One of them sniffed a diaper and discarded it with unmistakable and very human revulsion.

He was still at the window, long after the raccoons had gone on their way, when he saw Gwen reflected in the glass. She had a hospital smock on over her prom gown now. She looked wide-eyed with exhaustion, although it wasn't yet midnight.

"How's it going?" Arthur asked.

She had to clamp down on a quiver of emotion. "Not so well. They're going to do a C-section. Some girls get all the luck."

"Oh," he said. "Why?"

"The baby is turned the wrong way and they can't shift him. The longer he's stuck, the more risk to his life. So they're reaching for the can opener."

"She's in good hands here. This is what they do. Come back in the morning?"

"I can't, Arthur. I told her I'd stay. She doesn't have anyone and she talks tough, but she's scared out of her wits. You might as well go. They can't let you in the room. She's only allowed one person."

"And you're her person."

"I am tonight."

He had had plenty of time to think, all on his own in Family Room B, and had arrived at some ideas that he didn't much care for.

"What about tomorrow?" he asked. "Are you going to be her person tomorrow? Or will you be taking a shift with Llewellyn instead?"

She sighed for the second time that evening and fitted her small hand inside his large one. She rested her head on his shoulder.

"He offered me forty-five thousand dollars," she said. "Just to see him through the end. He can promise me forty hours a week, minimum."

"Why would he do that?" Arthur said. "You aren't a nurse. He needs a nurse."

"He'll have one. More than one. For nights and weekends and regular visits. He'll have my mother and me for the rest." She squeezed his hand. "There's no reason to be afraid. I understand the precautions. I can't get the disease from handling his dirty dishes and I won't get it from handling his dirty diapers. I'll wear gloves and I'll be careful."

"I'm not afraid," he said, which was a lie. "I'm worried for you. How are you going to look after a sick old man and manage Rackham? Forty hours a week, plus a full slate of classes? It was thoughtless of him to pressure you into it."

"He didn't pressure me—Arthur. I offered. *I* suggested it."

"You—why?"

She didn't reply.

"Maybe," he said, "you should talk to admissions at Rackham and see how they'd feel if you only attended part-time in your first year."

"I'm not going to Rackham. I've already put my deposit down at the University of Southern Maine in Portland. I'm going to study to be an EMT. It's two years of work and then they ease you right into a job with one of the ambalance companies. Caring for Llewellyn will be good training for that too. Please don't be mad with me."

He felt a cold anesthetized sensation spreading through him, a kind of numbness in the extremities, not unlike being plunged into icy water. It took him a moment to identify this sensation not as shock but as rage.

"Why? I need to know why."

"Don't you already know?"

He shook his head.

"I want to help people, Arthur. Right *now*, not later. I need to. *Need*. The way a person needs to breathe when someone is holding their head underwater. You and the others gotta find absolution your way. This is mine. I can do something for Mr. Wren. I can make the last months of his life bearable. I can look after Tana too. She's going to need to get in the social service system, and I can help with that. I'm patient and I wear bureaucracies down. And when she goes back to work, she's going to need childcare, and I can offer her some. Tana and Mr. Wren don't know this, but they're my way back. If I can do enough good for them, maybe someday, in a few years, I'll be able to look at myself in the mirror again and see something besides an evil tattoo. I want to *like* myself again, Arthur. Can't you understand that?"

"You can help more people with a degree." He thought his own voice sounded both mulish and childish.

"I could help them later, and by then Llewellyn will be in the ground and Tana's child will be in foster care, and I'm carrying around enough regret already."

"If you aren't going to Rackham, maybe I shouldn't go to Oxford," he said. "I could stay here. Help with the old man. Learn ambulance stuff. We could work together."

Even as he said it, he knew he wouldn't. He didn't have the courage for dramatic gestures and he didn't know anything but the study of literature. It frightened him, to imagine his life without a syllabus. He felt safest with an assignment to finish, a paper to write—he felt safe in the classroom, was comforted by the smell of chalk dust, reassured by the respectful give-and-take of a directed conversation.

Gwen laughed at him—warmly and affectionately, knuckles lightly brushing his chest.

"Didn't we just talk about this? Someday, I'm going to meet your mother. And if I'm the reason you don't go to Oxford, she's going to look at me like I'm trash. You want that? You want her to hate me?"

"I don't care," he said.

"I *do*. Maybe you don't know the difference between what you want and what you need, but I do. You need Oxford. And I need this—Tana, the old guy, and emergency work. I wanna save lives, not ruin them. Let's start with yours."

"Ms. Underfoot?" said a nurse, leaning into the room. "Tana is asking for you. They're moving her into the surgical theater."

"Yes," Gwen said, and she rose on her tiptoes and kissed the corner of Arthur's mouth. "Are you going to be okay? Don't stay. I'll get a ride back from my mom later."

"Go on," he said. She was already turning away, but he patted her bum, and when she glanced back he made himself smile. "Go be her person."

She grinned and went with the nurse, briskly moving away down a dimly lit corridor. In her medical smock, Gwen already looked a bit like a hospital employee herself. Arthur watched her hurry away to Tana, thinking there was some kind of cold moral logic in it, thinking he had not lost Gwen tonight, or on the day Gwen was accepted to EMT classes at the University of Southern Maine. He had lost her months ago. He had lost her when he took Tana to his bedroom. That didn't make any logical sense at all, but somehow it was still true.

Later that morning Gwen called to tell him it was a boy.

FORTY-FIVE

The others scattered after finals, leaving Gwen and Arthur to each other.

Van and Donna went back to the panhandle to work for their father, Van at the old man's newspaper, Donna at his TV station. Van caught the thankless job of covering local town meetings, sitting in stuffy hearing rooms while selectmen debated budget amendments and sewage repair. Donna interned with makeup for a while, but by the middle of the summer was sometimes doing on-camera fluff pieces on slow nights: a local family offering children rides on their pet ostrich, an elderly woman who would clean houses topless for twenty dollars an hour.

It peeves me something good to know my sister is going to get famous before I do, Van wrote Arthur.

Just because she has tits and no shame. The thing holding me back right now is my general lack of a work ethic and any discernible talents. My poor prospects for the future have left me depressed. My gloom has driven me to the bottle. I'm drunk most days by lunch. Fortunately I'm a high-functioning drunk. Shit. I guess that's my talent. How do you like that, old son?

Donna wrote Arthur too.

I'm hoping Van will pull out of it before Allie comes to visit for July 4th. He smells like feet and has started chewing tobacco and getting brown spittle on his shirt. Also he's learned how to play the

A chord on the guitar and he sits at the dinner table playing it over and over and staring at everyone with bloodshot eyes. If it keeps up, I'm going to garrote him with a guitar string. Oh, I had my third TV spot yesterday! I wore a light summery emerald top and didn't realize the lighting made it as transparent as green cling wrap, so basically I did a live report in my bra. I looked damn good though.

Allie sent postcards from Martha's Vineyard, Rome, Houston, and Panama City, where she stayed with the McBrides for two weeks in July. Her cards usually contained at least one interesting statistical observation.

I have told Van I will consider a kiss (w/tongue) if he can give up chewing tobacco, he has cut his usage by 70% in three days, so I am getting my tonsils ready.

And:

Donna and I are shopping for miniskirts that are 30% shorter, she has noted a correlation between hem length and invitations to appear onscreen. This is a foul, fallen world, isn't it? On the other hand, she has SUCH great legs it is a shame to hide them.

And:

I can't believe you won't be in Maine this fall, I am going to miss you 100% of the time.

She was returning in the fall for her junior year; Donna and Van would be back at Rackham as seniors. Only Colin and Arthur had graduated.

Colin also left Maine behind for the summer, after he concluded his grandfather wasn't going to die on him in the next few months. He took a ten-week internship in New York City with a company called America Online. People who signed up could send letters electronically. They were called emails and they were delivered instantly, anywhere in the world, for free.

You would've received this letter days ago if you had a computer, you beautiful, silly luddite, Colin wrote him. *They're learning how to play chess, you know—the computers. Someday they'll be even better at thrashing you than I am.*

Gwen read that letter aloud to Arthur while they were in his bed together, the windows open so the cross-breeze cooled the sweat on their bare bodies. She laughed and said, "Colin Wren is the sort of patient, reasonable scientist who invents teleportation and accidentally turns himself into a big fly."

His ground-floor apartment, a few blocks from Rackham, had no air-conditioning, and that summer it was oppressively hot inside—a humid, smothering swelter that made the idea of wearing clothes ridiculous. He had never imagined he could adore another human body as much as he adored Gwen's, as much as he adored the slope of her hip and the dimples in the small of her back and her sweet little round tum. They had eight weeks that summer, both of them boiling for each other in his bedroom, the smell of hot blacktop and fresh-cut grass seeping in around the drapes, from the open windows. The slight airlessness of the place made orgasms keener—when Arthur first read about autoerotic asphyxiation, he got it right away, because that summer it was sometimes hard to breathe, it was so hot in his little bedroom.

Every life has to have a best part, and later he understood that was his. They spent a long weekend in Vermont, helping his mother move out of the halfway house and into a cottage in Montpelier, a one-floor, two-bedroom place with blue siding and white trim, and roses growing in beds along the foundation. It was a forty-five-minute drive from Black Cricket, and fifteen minutes from an Episcopalian retreat where Erin would offer workshops on counseling the incarcerated.

There were skylights in Erin's bedroom. The ex-convict stood on her bed and opened them, then climbed out onto the roof. She shouted for Arthur to get the iced tea. All three of them finished the day sprawled on the hot tar paper shingles of the roof, beneath a cloudless, intensely blue sky. The White Mountains were mounded up on the horizon, so pale, so faded, they were like ghosts of mountains. Arthur sat up on his elbows, ice clinking softly in his glass, and looked sidelong, over Gwen, at his mother, who was flat on her back, eyes shut.

"How do you feel?" he asked her.

"I've had ten thousand showers since I got out of Black Cricket," Erin said, "but this is the first time I've felt like I washed it off me. Turns out I didn't need a shower. I just needed this sun."

They shared a bottle of pinot grigio that night, the wine so bright and clear, it was as if someone had distilled the afternoon sunlight instead of grapes. They drank a little too much and laughed a little too hard and ate a homemade macaroni and cheese that Gwen had brought from Maine. When Gwen's hand stole into Arthur's, Erin noticed, and she narrowed her eyes with pleasure and gentle approval. Gwen and Arthur made love that night in the guest room with the curtains pushed back and the sky still faintly glowing a pale shade of peach, the color of her prom dress—even at 10:00 p.m., the sun refused to entirely quit the earth.

"I hate that it's going to get dark and we have to go to sleep and tomorrow there'll be one day less," Arthur said.

"But tomorrow," Gwen said, her lips close to his ear, "we also get one day more."

FORTY-SIX

Almost half a year later, on the twenty-third of December, Arthur flew from Heathrow to Logan Airport. Colin Wren was waiting for him on the other side of customs. They crossed the skybridge to the six-story parking garage and Arthur threw his suitcase in the trunk of the '49 Caddy convertible. Colin put the car in gear and pointed them at Maine.

The plan was to spend the night with Colin and the others, and then go on to Montpelier for Christmas Eve with his mother. They listened to NPR most of the way, driving into the dusk, through whirling white flakes of snow. The US was building up its forces in Saudi Arabia, to drive a tinpot dictator out of Kuwait. The US First Light Armored was already over there, and the United Kingdom's First Armored Division was right next to them, everyone getting ready to tally-ho across the desert, there's a good lad, back to Baghdad with you.

When they got to The Briars the others were there, except for Gwen, who was driving a plow for her father and would be over later. Donna had already built up a crackling fire in the hearth, and there was a two-story blue spruce waiting to be decorated. Van poured the Scotch.

They were hanging a string of lights that looked like giant snowflakes when Gwen came in, her face gray and her mouth tight. She had not bothered to take off her boots and had tracked in white footprints. She shivered. Arthur was five steps up a ladder—the only reason he didn't catch her at the door and pull her into his arms. He opened his mouth to call to her . . . and then shut it again when he saw her expression.

"Llewellyn had a good night," Colin told her. "He got almost six hours' sleep. And now he's watching the PBS *Sherlock Holmes* on video. I think Jeremy Brett reminds him of himself. Are you all right? You look like you ran someone down on the way over here. I hope no one's dead."

"Not yet," Gwen said. "But someone's going to be. King Sorrow was at my house this morning—under the stairs, in the basement. He says it's that time of year again. He says a deal's a deal. He says we have to decide who we're going to kill next."

First Interlude

GWEN, UNDERFOOT

1990

I.

"I was always good with a knife," the old man told her one day, his breath stinking, the inside of his mouth white and soft with thrush. He grinned, and in the dark of his bedroom she could see the yellow of his teeth. He was like the Cheshire Cat in *Alice*, Gwen thought, if the cat was rotting from the inside out. "I took naturally to close fighting. I suffered from some debility of the imagination. I could never take it seriously when someone wanted to kill me. It always felt like we were both playacting, only pretending we were going to do something bad to each other. It gave me the psychological freedom to bring a certain sense of play to acts of homicide. Near the end of the fighting in Italy, we surprised a boy hiding in a haystack—he looked about twelve, although I suppose he was older, the Germans weren't desperate enough to draft children *then*—and he went at me with a bayonet. I was trying not to laugh the whole time."

"You should rest," Gwen said.

He didn't seem to hear her.

"Even when I cut his throat," Llewellyn Wren said. "And he

fell flopping into the frozen dirt, his head hanging crooked off his neck. The blade went so deep I half decapitated him. Even then, I was fighting back giggles. I couldn't take it seriously. Not his life. Not mine."

2.

It started snowing on Wednesday afternoon and didn't stop until early on Thursday morning. Her father made a pit stop home just after 6:00 a.m. to fill his thermos and eat chipped beef on toast, standing up at the kitchen counter. He didn't take his knit cap off. He had been out all night plowing the campus.

"You're on your own for dinner," Gwen told him. "Momma is cleaning up after the dean's Christmas party and I've got the baby."

"Mhm. How much is Tana paying you for childcare again?"

"Jett's got an evil rash on his bottom. You can't imagine how he cries."

"That's right," he said. "You do it for pleasure. Front walk is shoveled out. Put down some rock salt so your tired mother don't snap her neck coming in."

After he left, Gwen stayed at the kitchen table, drinking her tea and working on the crossword. She finished half and did no more. She thought of the unfinished bit as Arthur's half. He was always the answer to the parts of the puzzle she couldn't solve. She would see him before the day was out, for the first time in months. A thought that gave her a funny tickle of excitement in the pit of her stomach.

The basement door was under the stairs and only four and a half feet high. When Gwen was small, her aunt Ethelyn had promised her that Alamagüslen lived behind little doors like that, a shrunken old man who was as old as rivers, and who liked to suck the sweet flesh off children's bones. Gwen hated going through that door into the basement, even now, but the rock salt wasn't going to bring itself upstairs.

The basement had a soil floor and plastered walls, the plaster falling away in jagged flakes to show the stone behind. She was two steps from the bottom when King Sorrow reached through the space between steps to grasp her ankle.

She tottered, let go of the rail, fell, and hit the dirt floor on her elbows, then bounced her chin off it. Her teeth clacked. A darkness lurched up behind her eyes.

The hand still had her ankle. She twisted onto her side and looked at it: four scaly fingers, a delicate black webbing between them, golden talons curving at their tips. King Sorrow released her and his claws slid away beneath the stairs. A pair of polluted red eyes with slitted pupils peered out from the darkness.

"When you were small," he said, "you were scared to come down here, weren't you? Because, like all children, you secretly believed there was something hungry and evil waiting for you in the basement. And like all children, you were right."

Gwen opened her mouth to scream, then thought how pointless that would be. She was alone in the house. The closest neighbor, Thomas Nadler, was eighty-nine and deaf.

So when she spoke, her voice was level. "Go away."

"Whatever you say, luv. Just tell me where to go."

"I don't care, you old snake. It isn't up to me."

"Oh, Gwen," he said. "*It is.*"

3.

"Are you all right?" Colin asked. "You look like you ran someone down on the way over here. I hope no one's dead."

"Not yet," Gwen said. "But someone's going to be. King Sorrow was in my basement this morning. He says it's that time of year again. He says a deal's a deal. He says we have to decide who we're going to kill next."

Arthur was on a ladder, hanging enormous blue crystals, big as softballs, on the towering pine in a corner of the study. Colin was on the floor by a box of ornaments, handing the globes up to him. Donna and Van had a tinsel rope and were winding it around and around Allie. But when Gwen said King Sorrow's name they all stopped and looked at her as if she had arrived covered in blood.

"If you're trying to be funny," Van said, "then I hope you weren't planning a career in stand-up. Because your material sucks."

"Easter," Gwen told them. "Someone has to die at Easter."

Allie, still bound by the twinkling loops, said, "*Last* Easter. The deal was someone had to die *last* Easter."

"No. *Every* Easter. Either we pick someone to die or one of us dies instead. Last year it was up to Arthur who died. This year, he seems to have decided it's me."

Donna said, "He . . . he can't *do* that. He can't make us—it was a *one*-time deal."

"That's not how he sees it. You want to argue with him, Donna? Maybe we could take him to court." Gwen's voice was not quite steady. "We can tell the judge we never agreed to yearly contract killings. Our deal was strictly for two murders, no more."

Arthur found his way down the ladder and crossed the room. He took her hands in his. There. That was better.

"Are you sure . . ." Arthur began. "Is there any chance . . . shit. Is there any chance you . . . dreamt it?"

His face was so serious it loosened something in her chest and she found she could almost smile. "I'd love that. I'd love it so much. But tell me, Arthur, do I have a bruise on my chin? Just a little one?"

She lifted her head and let him look.

He nodded. "And a little cut."

"Then I guess I didn't dream it, because I did that falling on my face when he grabbed my ankle from under the stairs."

Colin unfolded his legs and rose from the floor. Something

about the way he moved made Gwen think of one of those insects that resemble sticks.

"Maybe we should have a drink," Colin said.

"King Sorrow's a bit of a lawyer, isn't he?" Colin said when she was done telling her story again. "He was very particular about the wording when we made our deal. 'Your liege swears his protection and in turn you offer me a sacrifice on Easter day.' Isn't that what he told us?"

"I've been reading about them," Arthur said. "Dragons."

Of course he had been reading about them. Gwen didn't know anyone who was so inclined to turn everything into homework. One of the things she loved about him was his quiet, even dull, devotion to study. He wasn't brilliant like Colin. He was a born toiler—someone who dug his way out of problems one shovel load at a time.

"Have you drawn any conclusions from your research?" Colin asked. It was hard to tell if he was teasing or not.

"A few. For starters, it's a bad idea to make a deal with them. Language is one of their weapons . . . as much as the fire they breathe or the tail that can knock down a house."

"Thanks for the insight, Sigmund," Van said. "We could've used that pearl of wisdom twelve months ago."

Arthur ignored him. "Someone tells you, 'Christmas is in December,' you understand they mean *every* December. Not just *that* December."

"What a crock of balls. Fuck him. We don't have to give him shit," Donna said.

"Yes, we do. We have to give him Gwen," Colin said. "Unless we nominate someone to die in her place." He bowed his head and considered in silence. At last he nodded to himself. "Okay. It's not so bad."

"What the hell do you mean it's not so bad?" Gwen asked. "He's going to kill someone. *Again*. And force us to be a part of it."

"There's a lot of bad fellows in the world. All we have to do is pick one of them. Any of them. Right now our country is gearing up to send people to die in the sand for us. We could wipe out Saddam Hussein and save everyone a whole lot of trouble."

"Or the Toolbox Killers," Donna said, her voice suddenly hushed. "Bittaker and Norris. I can't remember how many girls they killed—but I know they raped and tortured their victims first. They should burn alive for what they did, but they'll probably live another thirty years, eating Jell-O paid for by the taxpayer and enjoying free health care. Fuckers."

"What we need is an Enemies List," Colin said. "A list of people who are absolutely irredeemable and whose continued existence is toxic. So—in fact—probably *not* Bittaker or Norris. Because they *are* in jail and can't hurt anyone else now. Maybe not even Saddam, since he's about to get a bunker-busting missile dropped on his head. We want to deal with the tinpot dictators and serial murderers who have *evaded* retribution and accountability. People who get away with it. I'll make a spreadsheet. Best to collect an array of candidates, and then after Christmas we can discuss the pros and cons of each."

"Why do we need a spreadsheet? We only need one name," Arthur said.

"Sure. *This* year," Gwen replied.

That shut them up for a bit. It was going to keep going. This Easter. Next Easter. They might still be choosing victims for King Sorrow when Gwen was sixty.

"We could fight him," Arthur said softly.

"He bent a lamppost into a question mark. And if you didn't notice, by the time he comes through into our world, he's the size of an attack helicopter," Van said.

"Sure, he'd tear us apart if we tried to go toe-to-toe with him. But there are other ways to battle dragons."

Colin said, "Do you want to riddle with him, Arthur? I get the impression he's fond of riddling contests. Do you think you know any he hasn't already heard in the last three thousand years?" When Arthur didn't reply, Colin went on: "This is how I parse it: we can make a desperate play to outfight him and wind up like Jayne Nighswander, or we can sacrifice a serial killer to him, a Ted Bundy type, and do a little good. Put another way, if we go to war against King Sorrow, we would essentially be risking our lives to *protect* a guy like Ted Bundy." He glanced sidelong at Gwen, as if it had been her arguing instead of Arthur. "You have to decide who's worth more to the world, Gwen. Us, or some sick serial murderer somewhere."

"But Colin," Gwen said, "we're serial murderers too."

5.

It wasn't her shift, but she went in to check on the old man. The evening nurse, Eddy, sat in a chair over by the windows, under the only lit lamp, working at a book of word searches. Llewellyn slept with one gaunt hand curled on his chest and his mouth open slightly, and, in his black satin pajamas with the red piping, projected something of a Dracula vibe. When he exhaled, Gwen had the idea she could smell his insides dying . . . a ridiculous notion, and yet she was sure it was true. Eddy waved; Gwen nodded and went back out.

She almost fell over Arthur. He was sitting on the staircase, his elbows on the top step, a glass of Colin's good Scotch in one hand. Gwen glanced down the hall and saw the door to the guest room open, the sheets rumpled up, and felt a nervous tickle in the pit of her stomach. It would be the easiest thing in the world to take him by the hand, put a finger to her lips to shush him, and tow him down the hall to his bedroom. The others were still downstairs and would guess what they were up to and have a good laugh at them when they reappeared, and she didn't care.

But she did care about Jett and had to be at Tana's in forty minutes, so instead of taking him by the hand and hauling him to bed, she sat on the step next to him. He bumped his shoulder against hers and smiled.

"Hell of a Christmas present," he said.

"Hell of a thing to come back to," she agreed. "Right about now you probably wish you'd stayed."

"No. I don't wish I'd stayed. I wish I'd come back sooner. I almost did a couple times. I'd have these moments when I'd begin doing the math . . . how long it takes to get from Oxford to London by train, how long it would take to get to Heathrow, how long I'd be waiting for my flight. I'd get excited just thinking about it. I could imagine leaving all my stuff, not even bothering to pack."

"What about your classes?"

He shrugged. "What about them? I'd just go. I figured out I only needed twenty hours to get to Maine. I could have you in bed within a day."

She laughed at that, a loud, healthy shout of hilarity that echoed in the reception hall. Her face went hot.

"Pretty cocky," she said. "How do you know I haven't moved on? How do you know I haven't been running a whole parade of men in and out of my bed?"

"Have you?" he asked, earnestly. "Have you met someone?"

His eyes were bright in the dark and he took her hand in his. The funny tickling sensation of nervousness and longing was in her chest now.

"No, Arthur," was all she said. "Tell me one thing you love about Oxford."

"The school hosted a literary gala for graduate students—champagne and fancy cheeses—and three different white kids asked if I was the coat check boy. I loved that."

"Oh, no, Arthur."

"I try to remind myself it was much harder for my father when he attended Magdalen."

"Is that why you wanted to go? Because he studied there?"

"I wanted to go because he should've *taught* there. He should've been made chair of medieval and Renaissance literature. He applied to teach. He applied three times. He was told he lacked the qualifications. He spoke and read six languages. Maybe if he had learned seven, huh? The best he could do was a job writing for *The Guardian*. They sent him to South Africa to cover apartheid, and he died there."

"He was killed for writing about apartheid?" Gwen asked.

"I wish. That would be so cool. He had a few drinks with some friends, then fell running to catch a bus in the rain and hit his head on the curb. He went back to his little apartment to sleep off his headache and died of an epidural hematoma instead. He wasn't killed by the apartheid state. Maybe you could say he was killed by Oxford. If they'd hired him, he'd be alive now." Arthur considered the sharp crease in his trousers. "Magdalen hired a Black woman recently. First-ever Black educator. Progress comes for us all."

She put her hand inside of his and they were quiet together on the stairs for a while.

"Did I see you peeking into my bedroom?" he asked her. "Were you thinking thoughts?"

She chortled and hid her face against his chest.

"When are you back from your mother's?" she asked.

He rested his chin on the top of her head.

"Not nearly soon enough," he said. "When do you leave for Tana's?"

"Too soon," she said.

"Story of our lives," he told her.

6.

They all remembered bringing King Sorrow into the world differently. Colin and Arthur believed there had been a helmet filled with water, and they had passed it around and around, looking into it for some hint of dragons. But Gwen never saw a helmet. She remembered a cracked hand mirror with a mother-of-pearl handle and a Y-shaped fissure in the glass, so reflections appeared as a triptych. It had belonged to Maria Romanov before her murder. Colin said her executioner had told her to calm herself, to brush her hair, everything would be fine, and so she was staring into it when he raised the gun to shoot her in the back of the head. It was just a story, no one could prove it, but Gwen could see that Colin relished the idea. He said they could use it as a scrying mirror and Van said, "If I had your face, I'd cry every time I looked in a mirror too," and Colin smiled indulgently and said he was talking about catoptromancy and Van said, "I don't want to do nothin' that's going to trigger catalepsy, I already have trouble staying awake in my goddamn classes."

"Catoptromancy is the art of using a reflective surface as a window to see into other worlds. I figure the hand mirror of a murdered Russian princess will do," Colin said as he offered the mirror to Arthur, handle first.

They had passed the mirror and called for the King. Gwen promised him snacks. Allie pretended she was working the desk in an airport. "Paging King Sorrow. Your American Airlines flight to Podomaquassy, Maine, and other points on Earth is fully boarded, please get your scaly ass in your seat."

"Come on in," Arthur said. "The door is open."

The door to the hall flew open behind them, as if flung wide by a sudden gust. Air blew papers across the desk at the far end of the room, ruffled the pages of an open book. Before anyone could react, the door slammed itself shut. Donna screamed and yanked her hands off the table.

"Fuck this!"

"Come on in," Colin said. "We're waiting."

The door opened again and slammed so hard it knocked some of the framed shadow boxes on the wall askew, the boxes that contained Llewellyn's collection of dead, glittering, brooch-like butterflies. A hundred corpses, precisely impaled by Llewellyn Wren's silver pins, lovingly embalmed with Llewellyn Wren's poisons.

7.

"None of these poisons will kill the virus," Llewellyn told her, "but if we give them time, Gwen, they might kill *me*. It's a race to see what I die of first: my infections or my medicine."

They were in the dark of his bedroom and she was passing him the paper cups with his pills in them, one at a time.

The shades were drawn against the last of the daylight. Llewellyn couldn't bear the sunshine any longer. His eyes had gone the color of filthy dishwater from a cytomegalovirus, eyelids red and inflamed. His face was a death mask; his nose had a great winestain sarcoma on the end of it, ruining what had been a genial, affectionate face.

She handed him another paper thimble of tablets. "Keep swallowing."

"That's what the boys said to me, my first Friday night belowdecks on a destroyer," Llewellyn said. "God, that was a good time. There was a lot of excellent fagging about in the North Atlantic in those days." He swallowed three more pills and grimaced. "Tasty. I think I said something about the war the other night. Was I rambling, Gwen?"

Gwen noted, with interest, his almost sly undertone.

"Which war?"

"Well, precisely," he sighed. "I did have a hand in quite a few of them . . . including the one upon us now. I wrote a psychological profile on Saddam. Terrifically uninteresting fellow. Generic gangster mentality. Thinks there's nothing classier than shitting on a gold toilet."

Gwen spooned up some porridge. She fed him with care, using the spoon to catch anything that didn't make his lips and nudging it back in.

"Thank you, my love," he said. "But I *did* talk to you, didn't I? About one of my wars? What did I say?"

"Just a bunch of malarkey," Gwen said. "You talked about important men you wanted to screw, important men who wanted to screw you. Who knew you had such a torrid imagination, you filthy old fairy. Ought to be ashamed of yourself. I'm an innocent and untutored girl of the Christian faith. I feel despoiled every time I walk out of here."

"Nothing about Vietnam?" he asked her. "Nothing about my instruction manual or my research in Saigon?"

Something in his tone unsettled her—his slow, probing curiosity.

"No," she said.

He sighed again. She fed him another spoonful.

"You are right," he said, suddenly. "It *is* all malarkey. You mustn't believe anything I say when I am not myself, my dearest. It may sound real but be sure of it: it is nothing more than horrible fantasy born of a lurid imagination. This will come as no surprise to you. You have seen my Cabinet of Curiosities. You must forget whatever I say and never repeat it to anyone. I wouldn't want anyone to think less of me. To hear how I raved, or what peculiar ideas I held at the end." But he said all this in a light tone that approached glee.

She scraped the spoon around the inside of the bowl and put it to his lips, and he ate.

"Wonderful," he said. "Thank you."

But it came back up twenty minutes later. He twisted on his side, suddenly, as if he had been gut-shot, and vomited into her lap.

"Oh, God," he said. "Oh, no. Oh, Gwen. I'm so sorry." He was trying not to cry.

"Never you mind," she said, rising to her feet. She had a cloth, much like one of the rags she used to burp Jett, and began to clean it up.

"I didn't mean to," he said.

"Of course you didn't. You weren't even awake. It came up on you while you were drifting. I'll change the sheets."

He vomited again.

"Get it all out," she said, his puke beginning to dry on her jeans. "Get it out and you can start to feel better."

"I don't think there is better," he said, panting heavily. "Not from here on. Only worse. I had endurance training in the army. Before the war and after. In one . . . test . . . of our stamina . . . we would stand in foxholes filled with icy water. To see how long we could take it. I could take it longer than just about anyone. I'm going to last a long time, Gwen. I'm going to rot right off my bones while I'm still alive." He gave her a glaucous look. "You must change those jeans right away."

"First your sheets, then my jeans."

When he stopped shaking, she helped him into the wheelchair and made his bed with fresh sheets.

She had spare clothes in her gym bag, and she took them into his palatial bathroom to change. She left the door open between them. If he wasn't half-blind by then, he could've watched her undress. Maybe he would've enjoyed it! Homosexual or not, she thought, Llewellyn had a cheerfully lascivious streak and relished a good naked body of any gender. He had been married for years and had a child himself, so he had got it up at least once for a bit of female tail. She had seen some of the dirty books of hardcover fetish photography on his shelves, the Mapplethorpe, the Helmut Newton. And then there was his novel, an unpublished pulp soldier-of-fortune thing Llewellyn had written in the late sixties, full of sadism and submission and unlikely couplings, both hetero- and homosexual in nature. He kept a copy of the manuscript in the library. She had started reading it, usually with her eyebrows raised as high as they would go, in a mixture of admiring horror and bemused shock. Maybe she would try to finish it one of these days.

"I wanted to see the spring. Sit out back in the wheelchair with the sun on my face and smell the dogwoods. Maybe if I was having a good day, you'd let me have a cigar and a whiskey."

"Not only would I get you a cigar and a whiskey, I'd drink one with you."

"I'd like that." His voice was soft in the dark. "I'm glad you spent so much of your childhood in this house, Gwen. It did me good to have your sturdy kindness in my life. My son, Colin's father, was a terrible person. He was good at everything he put his hand to—polo, sailing, selling, modeling—but couldn't bear to work at anything. He only ever did one honorable thing: he died—took his mouse of a wife with him—before he could ruin Colin. And that's how I got a second chance to be a father. I must not have done so badly this time around. Colin has good friends. He has you."

She eased him back into bed. He found her hand.

"But if I have a choice," he said, "if I can have anyone beside me at the end, I want you there instead of him, Gwen. I know how selfish that is. But I know you'd . . . help me through the hard bits. I never imagined dying could be such hard work."

"What makes you so sure you'll go first?" Gwen said. "You'll probably talk me to death, you ol' bastard."

He didn't just laugh at that. He *roared*.

8.

When Jayne Nighswander unloaded her daddy's shotgun into her own TV set, she had peppered the wall behind it with shot, and in the new year, Gwen resolved to replaster and repaint so Tana didn't raise her boy in a place that had bullet holes in the walls. Gwen left Jett cooing and frog-kicking in his crib and wandered into the kitchen to see if there were pliers in the junk drawer. She could start tonight by picking the iron pellets out of the wall.

There were no pliers amid the mess of acid-caked old batteries, rusting screwdrivers, and rubber bands. She gave up and closed the drawer—Jett was beginning to make grizzling sounds, he was going to want a bottle soon—and then slid it open again for another look. Gwen felt she had spied something important; seen it without *knowing* she had seen it. She sorted through the dried-up ballpoint pens and broken clothespins until her gaze settled on a stained and crumpled napkin from Dunkin' Donuts. Someone had written on it in jagged cursive. There was a 617 number—that was Boston—followed by the words *Katherine Porter—Moviegoer, Killer Angel*. Gwen wondered if Katherine Porter was a friend of Ronnie Volpe's, one of the strippers he knew and sold drugs to. Killer Angel might be the name she used when she was grinding the pole. Moviegoer could be Ronnie's way of saying she also did porno.

Only . . . that didn't feel right. Why would Ronnie write her whole name out that way, so formally? And a moviegoer wasn't *in* films, they *watched* films. Gwen didn't know why the old note bothered her, only that it did.

Jett began to bleat in a goaty sort of way and she had to let it go.

He had all of one bottle and most of a second before he calmed and she was able to rock him into a slumber. Then she left him in his crib and went onto the back stoop to get a lungful of fresh air and clear her head. She watched a plane rise from Portland International, red lights blinking on its wingtips. Gwen had never been any farther out of state than Boston. She and her father attended a single Red Sox game every summer, usually after the home team was out of contention and the seats were at their cheapest. She wanted to go with Arthur to London someday, see a place where people had dwelt for a thousand years. She wanted to see *Arthur's* London, his cafés, his parks . . . his bookshops.

It hit her then. "They're book titles. Katherine Porter. *Killer Angels*. Dammit, they're books, aren't they?"

The night offered no opinion on the matter.

Gwen returned to the darkened kitchen, picked the phone off the wall, and dialed the 617 number on the napkin. It rang five times and then there was a click and a thunk and she was listening to the prerecorded message on an answering machine.

"This is Bridget Fleming, and you've reached Fleming Antiquarian Books, specializing in signed editions, rare firsts, vintage erotica, and literary ephemera." The woman on the machine paused to hack a wet smoker's cough, then went on in her creaking North Boston voice. "Our collection is open by appointment only, details available through our mailing list. If you're looking for something specific, leave your number after the tone and let me know what you're looking for. If I don't have it, I can find it. Sheldon, do *not* leave any more messages. You need a therapist. If I see you in front of my apartment again, I'm calling your mother—or the goddamn cops." There was a beep. Gwen did not leave a message.

She stood in the stillness and shadows of the empty kitchen, her pulse as quick in her as if she had just run up a flight of stairs. Bridget Fleming was a dealer, like Ronnie and Jayne. Only they dealt angel dust and Bridget Fleming dealt fairy dust: old books, old stories, Granddaddy's sepia-tinted pornography. Had they sold the stolen books to her? Did she still have them? Did she still have the Enoch Crane journal? Because Enoch Crane had a lot to say about King Sorrow. He had explained how to invite him into their world and how to keep him fed.

Maybe he had also written something about how to make him go away.

9.

When the hand mirror made its way around to her, Gwen and Arthur were the only ones still sitting at the card table. Colin had seen something in the mirror (only he insisted later it had been a helmet filled with water), got up from the table, and gone to perform some necessary part of the ritual.

Gwen and Arthur held hands and she stared into murdered Maria's mother-of-pearl inlaid mirror, gripping it in her right hand so she could see herself and Arthur and Allie playing piano beneath the framed shadow boxes of Llewellyn's prize butterflies. The door to one side of the piano gaped wide, looking into an impenetrable darkness. A great pale eye opened slowly in that darkness, an infected eye with a vertical slit for a pupil, an eye as golden as a harvest moon. Opened . . . and then slowly, dreamily, shut again and was gone.

Arthur called out in a loud, clear voice, "Your subjects beseech their king for his protection. We call our king down from the Long Dark."

In the mirror, Gwen watched the door to the hallway slam shut once more. It crashed shut so loudly, Gwen fumbled, almost dropped the mirror in her own lap. Curiously, she didn't think Allie so much as flinched. Allie was bent over the keys, maniacally banging away at "Puff the Magic Dragon." She was somewhere else. Deep in the dream of the song.

When Gwen righted the mirror, she had a queer sensation of dislocation, a wooziness that she felt in the spot right between her eyes. The mirror was splintered into three big shards, split by a Y-shaped crack that ran up the center. In the shard on her left she saw Arthur, only he wore a black gauze blindfold and he was no longer holding her hand. Instead, he held the shining silver hilt of a sword, the sword of a king, and his chin rested upon it. The blade was pointed straight down, probably buried in the floor. The black muslin over his eyes was semitransparent, and he seemed to be drowsing. His tunic was made of the same rough, black stuff.

In the big shard on the right-hand side she could see the door to the hall, slowly yawning open once more. A night sky waited on the other side, a vast darkness filled with cold, ancient stars. The butterflies in the shadow boxes began to twitch and shiver, and then one by one they lifted free, sliding off their pins and flying in a bright, whispering storm to escape into the Long Dark. And that was when she knew her task. She had to look after the dead until they were ready to carry a message of fire to King Sorrow.

In the sliver of glass in the crotch of the Y, she could see herself, and her eyes had become the yellow, slitted eyes of the serpent. Her reflection threw her a wink and sent her on her way.

10.

Colin had a twelve-page handout, stapled at one corner, for each of them. The first page was a spreadsheet, with a row of names running down the left. Other columns noted age, current place of residence (if known), crimes suspected or confirmed, and a number ranging from 1 to 100 that described "Ongoing Threat Valence." Most were in the 90s, although a small number were in the middle 50s, and one, an incarcerated child murderer, scored a mere 12.

He was brisk, sunny, and all business. Gwen's mother had made a pot of tea and fluffy, buttery biscuits for their "study session." The curtains were pulled back from the French windows and the room was flooded with daylight. The way they sat around the card table, they might've been at a meeting for a charitable foundation, gathered to decide how best to distribute their money.

Arthur, just back from Vermont that morning, began turning through the pages with a crease of concentration—or maybe bewilderment—between his eyebrows. He looked as if he had been presented with an exam for which he had, uncharacteristically, forgotten to prepare.

Van pushed the handout away. "I'm too sober for this."

Colin looked amused. "It's one in the afternoon."

"No, it isn't," Van said. "It's murder o'clock. Drinkin' time."

"Dragonedy o'clock," Allie murmured.

Van walked around to the bar. "Anyone else?"

"Me too! Me too!" Allie bounced on her stool and waved one hand.

Van found beers in the mini-fridge and opened them with his back to the rest of the group.

Donna said, "Gilbert Carmichael Quinn. Let's do him."

Colin frowned, looked at the first page of the handout.

"He's not on the list," Colin said.

"No," Donna said. "He's in Powledge Prison, in Texas, for possession of child pornography. Back in 1979 he kidnapped my best friend, raped and strangled her, and left her in a ditch."

Van drank half a Dos Equis, then lowered the bottle and said, "Fuck he did."

Donna turned odd, watery, burning eyes on her brother. "He confessed. Told one of his cellmates all the details."

"Jailhouse snitch don't mean nothin'. Some old boy looking to knock a couple years off his sentence by throwing a perv under the bus. I mean, you want to blast this Quinn dude off the face of the earth, be my guest. He's sixty-two, he's got diabetes so bad they had to amputate one foot, and he's never getting out of jail, but suit yourself. Only don't kid yourself he's the one took Cady. It was looked into. Twelve hours before Cady got took, Quinn was in Los Angeles, hitching his semi to a load of bananas going to Denver." He said it *Los Anga-lees*.

"If he didn't do it to her, he did it to some other child," Donna said. "Count on it."

Van shrugged. "Whatever."

Allie snuck her hand over to take Donna's, but Donna twisted her wrist and pulled away.

"How do we do this?" Arthur asked. He went back to the beginning of the handout and then slowly leafed through the pages once more. "Do we hold a vote? Are we all going to raise our hands for the person we most want to see dead?"

"We could put their pictures on the wall and throw darts," Allie said.

"You go to church every weekend, Allie. You sing in the choir. You believe in salvation and mercy. How do you stay so damn perky?"

Allie said, "Alcohol."

"Should we go through," Colin said, "and discuss each in turn?"

Donna looked at Gwen. "My vote is for Gilbert Carmichael Quinn." She tossed the handout, got to her feet, and went around to the bar to fix herself a drink.

Colin looked forlorn. "Gee, I worked on this thing all week. How dumb am I?" He looked at Arthur and Gwen hopefully. "Do you guys want to talk through the options?"

"It's a lot to take in," Arthur said, in a slow, unhappy voice. "You've definitely found some first-rate bastards here. And all men!"

"I thought this first time," Colin said, "it might be too psychologically stressful to wipe out another woman. Maybe in a few years?"

"A few years," Arthur repeated, dismally. "A few years of picking people to die."

For once Colin looked fatigued. "It's the nature of the beast . . . quite literally, Arthur. There's no good option here, only the possibility of settling on a bad option we can live with. There's no such thing as an ethical murder. Might as well believe in unicorns."

"Or dragons," Arthur said, and laughed without humor.

Gwen folded up the handout. "Thank you, Colin. I know you worked hard on this. I'm going to give it a good close look now."

Colin offered her a smile that seemed to mix gratitude and relief. "I hope it helps. In the end, I suppose it's going to be up to you."

22.

Gwen was putting their teacups in the dishwasher when Arthur came looking for her.

"Did you just clean up after us?" he asked.

"I had to come through here anyway before I go up to sit with Mr. Wren."

"Colin and them treat you like the help," he said. He glanced past her into the dishwasher and saw his own mug. "Christ. *I* treat you like the help."

"I'm on the payroll now," she said. Like her mother. Like her mother before her and her mother before *her*.

"Who are you going to pick?"

"I don't know. How could I know? Colin just gave me twelve pages of homework."

"Maybe I can help. Maybe we can find someplace to do your homework together?"

"With our clothes off?" she asked.

"Shit," he said, and looked away and laughed.

"I can't," Gwen said. "I have to sit with Mr. Wren until five, then get out to Gogan so Tana can get to work."

"Are we still a thing?" he asked, without looking at her.

Her insides seemed to squeeze together in a sudden shock of feeling. She wanted to hug him, she wanted to kiss him, she was scared of him, she was scared of the future, she wanted to be pressed naked against him, she wanted to be holding his hand, she wanted to know the right thing to say, she wanted to think, she couldn't think. Being in love was such a complication of emotion, it made a person feel half-drunk and half-sick and half-giddy, which was three halves, but math went to shit when you cared for someone the way she cared for Arthur.

He had written her two letters a month for almost half a year. She kept them all together, folded into the front of a book of Sunday crosswords, and sometimes when she was feeling lonesome had to get them out and look at them again, even though they made her eyes sting with emotion. He signed all those letters "love." She knew that was a formality, like signing a letter "regards" or "best," but she wanted to believe it meant more, felt it was his way of saying it without really risking saying it, which suited her fine. She didn't dare say it herself.

"You're there and I'm here," she said. "But there's still an 'us,' if that's what you're asking."

"Oxford was a mistake," he said, quietly. "It's the kind of mistake you can only stumble into when you figured your life out at twelve years old and refuse to deviate from the plan. I was going to show them they fucked up when they didn't hire my father. I was going to get my master's and then I was going to get hired there and then I was going to have the chair they should've given my dad, the chair they gave C. S. Lewis. I could see it in my head, how it would be. Psyching myself up. But when I was twelve I didn't know about you. I don't think I'm going to finish my thesis."

"You have to," she said. "You'll regret it if you don't."

"I've had five months to learn plenty about what I regret."

She had not felt so lightheaded, so muddled up, since the night she caught a contact high off Colin's blue weed and they summoned the serpent. She was telling him to stay because it felt like the right thing to do, but she didn't want him to stay, didn't care about Oxford. In her mind, the whole school smelled like an old man: farts and wet tweed.

"What's your thesis about, anyway?" she asked.

"Dragons," he said, and laughed. "They're everywhere, when you start to look for them, especially in England. They're on money and flags and stained-glass windows. What I was wondering, is there a way to stop King Sorrow from hurting anyone ever again? I was just curious, but suddenly it seems like something we might want to know. Maybe I'll find some old book leading me to a sword jammed into a stone."

"You want to read up on dragons," Gwen said, "you might want to make a stop in Boston before you sally back to Old Blighty."

"What's in Boston?"

"The Enoch Crane journal," she said, and then, when she saw the look on his face, added, "*Maybe*. There's some old bag, Bridget Fleming, slings books out of her apartment. She sounds like if lung cancer had a Boston accent."

Arthur looked taken aback. She might've just told him she had decided to marry Colin.

"There was more in that book," Arthur said.

"I know there was."

Neither of them said what they were both thinking: that Enoch Crane had written about how to drive King Sorrow away, be rid of him. Maybe even how to kill him.

"Shit," Arthur said. "She won't still have it. She got rid of all those books as soon as the news broke about the thefts at Rackham. It was too hot to hold on to them."

"Maybe it was too hot to *unload* them, ever think about that?"

"Shit." He shut his eyes, tried to think. "I don't even have a car."

"I do," Colin said, standing in the swinging door behind them.

"When do we leave?" Van asked, standing behind him.

12.

They were waiting in the driveway, breathing white smoke, when Colin steered the big red Caddy out of the carriage house and down the lane to them. Once upon a time, some Wren of old had kept his barouche and Morgan horses in that carriage house . . . and some Underfoot type had probably kept the nags brushed out and the axles oiled.

The five of them piled in, Arthur up front with Colin, the rest of them on the cream leather couch in the back. It should've been tight, but Allie was skinny as a boy, and Van was skinny as a scarecrow. Allie sat between Van's legs and he put his arms around her waist.

"I hope you're on the pill," Van told her. "If we hit a pothole, we're going to need protection."

They hauled ass for Boston in the dying light, the sun burning a bronze pinhole in the cold, austere blue of the sky. When the Caddy got up to sixty-five, the wind roaring over the canvas top was so loud, they had to shout to talk.

"I WISH WE HAD A GUN," Donna shouted.

"THANK GOD WE DON'T HAVE A GUN," Arthur yelled back.

"BARREL RIGHT IN HER FACE," Donna exclaimed. "WE'RE THE LIBRARY POLICE, BITCH, AND YOU'RE SITTING ON OVERDUE BOOKS."

"What do we need a gun for? We have a dragon," Van said, in a normal tone of voice, which they were all able to hear, but which allowed them to ignore his contribution to the conversation.

"I LOVE GOING ON ADVENTURES WITH MY FRIENDS," Allie hollered. "AFTER WE ASSAULT THIS OLD LADY, WE SHOULD GET TACOS!"

Fleming Antiquarian Books was downslope from the Bunker Hill Monument, on a narrow one-way street. The big Caddy had to inch along between the cars parked on either side, crowding the road. There hardly seemed room to thread a bicycle, let alone a car, and there was no place to park. Nor could they be sure which was Bridget Fleming's town house. There was no bookstore awning, no words stenciled in gold on a window. Colin circled the block and, when no parking spot materialized, made a circuit around the whole general neighborhood. Finally, he parked the Caddy in the lot beside a dark, closed Bank of Boston.

They walk-huddled close for warmth, a shuffling mass of Arthur-Gwen-Donna-Allie-Van-Colin, shoulders pressed together, breathing on their hands. They got lost, couldn't find the right street, and stumbled into a French patisserie to thaw out and re-orient themselves. It was crowded and Gwen's glasses fogged over in the steamy heat. They got coffees and golden, flaky croissants, and crowded around a marble-topped, chest-high table for two. It was hard to take even a single step without bumping into someone. Gwen knew when she was among her people: this crowd were townies, all of 'em. The girls were painted into their jeans, cheap denim dazzled up with rhinestones on the back pockets. The boys wore flannel jackets and watch caps and called each other *dude*.

"Where the hell is this fucking bookstore?" Donna asked. "Allie is freezing her tits off and she hardly has any tits to freeze."

"I think I saw it," Colin said, "the last time we went up Cordis Street. But I don't know if Fleming is home. It looked pretty dark."

"Are you looking for Fleming Antiquarian?" someone said from over Gwen's shoulder.

Gwen twisted her head and looked around at a scrawny gomer, a foot taller than she, his bony Adam's apple right in her face. His shirt was half-unbuttoned to show the Iron Maiden tee beneath. He smelled like pizza, and his glasses were so greasy he had to squint to see through them. He was looking down Gwen's top.

"Too true, son," Van said. "Do you know where it is? Hey. Hey! My eyes are up here, babe." Snapping his fingers, pointing into his own eyes.

The gomer looked reluctantly away from Gwen's bosom. "Fleming probably won't see you if you don't have an appointment."

Allie said, "If you could take us over there, we'd love you forever. My date would pay for your coffee!"

"Which of us is her date?" Van murmured to his sister.

The gomer let the McBrides get him a coffee and led them back out into the bitter cold, along the crooked brick sidewalk toward Bunker Hill. He lugged a brown paper bag of paperbacks. Gwen was struck with a sudden notion about who was leading them to Bridget Fleming's house.

"Did you say your name was Sheldon?" she asked, even though he hadn't said.

He nodded lazily and shook a Golden Light free from its box. He put it in the corner of his mouth . . . and then lit it with a handheld butane torch in a blast of blue flame. Van cried out in delight.

"He's got a goddamn flamethrower!"

"Do you always walk around with an incendiary device in your pocket?" Colin asked.

Sheldon shrugged. "I wash dishes at the Radisson. The dessert chef uses it for the crème brûlée. I keep it with me because I like it." The coal of his cigarette bobbed in the corner of his mouth. "What's your name, kid?" he asked Gwen.

She told him and then nodded at his bag of paperbacks. "What's that?"

"These books made me sick," Sheldon told her. "Some books carry illness in them. Did you know that? Some books, they damage you."

"Yes," Gwen said. "I think that's true."

"I wish it wasn't," Arthur added. "But if you believe a book can change the world for the better, you have to be open to the possibility they could also change it for the worse."

"*Mein Kampf*," Colin said.

Arthur nodded. "*Protocols of the Elders of Zion*."

Van stroked the red wisps of mustache at the corners of his mouth. "Don't forget those books about fuckin' Garfield the cat. Garfield is a cancer."

"Ms. Fleming got me addicted to these novels and now she has to take them back," Sheldon said. "I borrowed money to buy them. From my mother. Only I didn't ask, so that's stealing. My stepfather will have me arrested again if I don't get the money back, and I'm too old for juvie now. Ms. Fleming was wrong to sell them to me in the first place. She knows I've got compulsions. She took advantage. And these goddamn books, they put some bad ideas in my head. This is it. We're here."

They had arrived at a brownstone with a grand black door under a stone arch, at the top of three granite steps. Only Sheldon led them past the front door to a steep flight of stairs leading below the street. A second, very narrow door, like the lid of a coffin, waited at the bottom. Sheldon let them pile past him, and Gwen gave him an inquisitive look when she saw him lingering on the sidewalk.

"It's better if you all stand in front of me," Sheldon said. "She's got a beef with me because I want my money back and she's a cheap rhymes-with-witch. Last time I tried to talk to her, she almost broke my foot."

Gwen didn't get a chance to ask *how* she had almost broken his foot. Colin was using the knocker, a blackened iron owl. Gwen heard bronchial coughing from within.

"What is it?" came a voice Gwen recognized from the answering machine.

"Fleming Antiquarian?" Colin asked. The door remained shut.

"Closed! Call for an appointment!"

"Fed Ex, just need a signature. Something from Charing Cross Road, London?"

"From—what the hell? Who's gonna spend a fortune on postage now when I'm there in April for Firsts? Are you—"

The door opened on the chain. Colin smiled at her. She tried to close it and he jammed a foot into the opening.

"Get your foot out my door or I'll call the law," said a short woman with severe black bangs. Gwen could see past her into a little mudroom. A collection of walking sticks stuck out of the brass casing of a bazooka shell. There was a marble end table, with a sloppy pile of mail on it.

"By all means, give the police a ring. We can all talk about Jayne Nighswander together."

Fleming hesitated for a beat too long. "I don't know any Jayne Nighswhatever."

"We just want it back," Colin told her.

"Get your foot out my door, Kojak, or you're gonna develop a real bad limp."

Donna said, "Give us what we want, lady. We can be reasonable! We can also be *un*reasonable. Just ask Jayne."

"I don't know what you want!" Fleming squawked.

"The Crane journal," Arthur said. "That book is all kinds of trouble."

"I have nothing to hide. I'm not afraid of cops."

"I was talking about trouble worse than cops," Arthur said. "I was talking about us."

Gwen hardly recognized the dull, almost clinical calm in his voice. This was a different Arthur, an Arthur who knew what he could do, how far he could go, and had accepted it. Fleming retreated ever so slightly, took a half-step backward, and had to steady herself by placing a hand on the side table piled with mail.

"I don't have any fuckin' idea—" Fleming sputtered, then added, "I never—okay, okay, wait. Wait. There *was* a fuckin' skank bitch from down Portland, tried to sell me some books last year. Yeah, I remember now. She said it was stuff from her grandfather's library . . . like she come from a family where any of them fuckin' read books. I don't deal in hot goods and I told her where she could fuckin' put 'em."

"You can tell when she's lying," Sheldon muttered. "That's when she starts throwing around the F-word."

He spoke in a low voice, but Fleming heard him and her eyes widened, staring past them, up the stairs.

"It's you! The little masturbator! I should've known! I'm not buying back your fuckin' John Norman first editions! Those Gor books got cum stains in them now! I can't resell something with the pages stuck together! I told you, Sheldon, if you come back again, I'll call your goddamn mother."

Colin looked away, up the stairs, which was when Fleming made her move. She snatched a walking stick with a steel tip and poked it at him. She missed his eye and struck his cheekbone. His head went back and she brought the tip down on his foot with a fleshy thump. Colin screamed and fell back into Donna. The door slammed.

"I *WILL* call the cops, you little fucks," she shouted from the other side. "I'm doing it now! You think I won't?"

Colin had one hand clapped to his face while he hopped on his left foot. Donna seized his elbow to keep him from falling over.

"We should go," Van said. "In case she really does call someone. I'm holding."

"You're *what*?" Donna cried.

He shrugged. "It's not like I've got a pocket full of black tar heroin. It's just 'shrooms. But at fifty bucks an ounce, I'm not going to chuck 'em in the gutter."

"I might have to hit urgent care anyway," Colin said. "There's a small chance she broke my foot."

They were climbing up the stairs, but Sheldon was moving in the other direction, squeezing between them to get to that absurdly narrow door. Colin limped. Donna and Allie helped him along.

Gwen trailed behind the others, head down, going back over what had just happened. When she answered the door, Fleming had been wondering why a package would come from the United Kingdom, when she was headed to London herself in just a few months. She was going abroad at almost the same time King Sorrow would be notching up his next kill. She'd be gone—and her apartment would be empty. Gwen kept this thought to herself. She tried to think who she knew in Gogan who could get her in through the window. It was a surprisingly fulsome list.

Sheldon stumbled to the bottom of the steps and began to beat on the door.

"Mrs. Fleming! Mrs. Fleming? You got to take 'em back. I'm asking nice! I'm asking *so* nice! Please? Pretty please?"

Then he began to bang his head against the door. Gwen paused to look back, anxious for him. Sheldon drew his head back and snapped it forward, once, again. As he beat his head on the door, he began to laugh.

"Pretty please with brains on it? Pretty please with brains all over your door? Pretty *please* pretty *please* pretty *please*," smashing his head into the door on each *please* while Fleming screamed from inside, screamed the police were coming, which was probably true.

Sheldon paused, turned his head, and grinned up the steps at Gwen. Blood drooled from a welt in the center of his forehead. There was some blood in his teeth.

"I been trying to get some real bad ideas out of my head," Sheldon told her. "Think if I keep beatin' my head against this door, I finally will?"

Arthur squeezed Gwen's hand and drew her away, down the sidewalk, into the icy darkness. She could hear Sheldon slamming his head against Fleming's door and laughing, all the way to the end of the block.

23.

Llewellyn liked to suck on little pieces of ice. It numbed his sore mouth, and the cold trickle of water into his throat made it easier to bear the fever. Gwen knew all this without being told. When he wouldn't drink his dinner—a nutrient shake—she spooned him ice, a few crunchy pieces at a time. Colin drank the shake instead, sipping at it now and then, while he watched the TV at the foot of the bed, the only light in the dark. Jeremy Brett in a top hat, carrying a cane, stalked the wicked in a sunlit London that never was. Llewellyn couldn't see the TV anymore, but he could hear the carriage wheels clacking over cobblestones and Brett's clipped, precise observations. How they resembled one another, Llewellyn a decayed and wasted version of the great detective.

"We used ice water," he said. "In Saigon. But not on the asset. Never on the asset. It was best if they had a wife. Or children. We had designed a kind of theater in the debriefing room: a window with a red velvet curtain, tied back with a gold rope, at the back of what had been a French cabaret. Once upon a time men could pay to enter the room and view a private dance. It served much the same purpose for us, only the curtain was drawn back to reveal the asset's wife. Or daughter. Or son. Always naked. It was a room made for nakedness. There was a big steel washtub filled with ice water. One of us would plunge them in head and shoulders and hold them underwater, their hands tied behind their backs. A man never lied after seeing his naked, screaming daughter half-drowned. Sometimes I asked the questions and sometimes I held the fish. Love shatters the best of us. This is the heart of my book on interrogation, which is still studied and shared among field agents to this day."

She offered him a spoonful of ice.

"You should rest," she said.

"Do you know how I want to die, Colin?"

"Tell me," Colin said, without looking from the TV.

"I want to be drowned in ice water with my hands bound behind my back, and a man forcing my head into the basin."

"Is that how you want to die," Colin said, "or is that your idea of foreplay?"

The old man cackled. His laughter turned to coughing, until blood flecked his lips, and then a bronchial wheeze that shook his whole frame. Gwen put on latex gloves and dabbed him clean with a tissue. When she was done, she paused, looking at the stained paper, thinking how fully death was concentrated in those few drops of blood.

Calm again, Llewellyn's bony, withered hand found Gwen's in the dark, a claw not unlike the one that had gripped her from beneath the basement stairs.

"My blood is full of the most evil poison," he whispered. "But you cleaned it up anyway, without a flinch. You're a good girl, Gwen. So brave. So easy around death. You were born for this—to show people to the last door and to hold it open for them. I know, because I was too."

24.

When Llewellyn was at last asleep, she opened the door into darkness and crept out along the gallery over the reception hall, leaving him with Colin. Her eyes were still adjusting to the gloom when Arthur's hand slipped into hers and her heart throbbed. His other hand found the waistband of her sweatpants and tugged her toward him. In his black turtleneck and cinder-colored jeans, it was as if the shadows had sprung to life and reached out and caught her.

They didn't talk, and the guest room was only a few steps away. Even after, they hardly said a word.

25.

Gwen climbed in behind the wheel of the car, wondering if it would start. The night was so cold, the windshield was a blind eye, frosted over with a thousand overlapping feathers of ice. It was less like getting into a Honda Civic, more like finding herself in a cave of ice. The chill was thrilling, or maybe she was just highly sensitized; her body was still ringing like a struck bell.

She bent to stick the key in the ignition, turned it over—a gentle whinny and it sprang to life—and sat up again, which was when one claw gripped her right arm from behind. Another reached forward from the dark and took her left, pinning her to her seat.

Gwen looked in the rearview mirror.

Nothing.

"I am *hungry*," King Sorrow said. "As far as I can see, this misbegotten parcel of the American States specializes in exactly two crops: potatoes and fatty little Underfoots. And I'm offa chips, luv, I'm watching my waistline. There's a lot of it to watch. Thirty-eight feet of it."

"You didn't eat Jayne Nighswander. She wasn't food."

"Not her flesh," a cold, rasping tongue trilled at her earlobe. "I supped on her dying anguish. It saturated her blood—all that misery, all that terror—and made it as sweet as the sweetest Riesling. I could *never* resist that. Give me a taste and I *have* to have every drop. I need it like Donovan needs a drink, like Allie needs pussy, like Arthur needs *you*. I has cravings, I has, and you has to satisfy them. You have Colin Wren's list of names. Pick someone off the menu."

"Tell me something. Say I do pick someone for you. Do you *have* to persecute them? Terrify them? Tease them like you do?"

"Sweet meat must have sour sauce," he crooned. "It's the marinade that flavors the flesh."

"What if I didn't want you to torment them before you kill them?"

"What if the damned want ice water in hell?" he said and laughed.

"I'd riddle for it," she said. "For you to extend that mercy."

"Oh," he said—almost sighed. "I *do* enjoy a good riddling contest. You'd risk a riddle with me . . . just so I don't haunt the chosen before their sacrifice?"

"I'd want more than that. Tell me about King Herod."

"I slew babies for Herod. As they say, young flesh and old fish are best."

"Way I heard it, you missed the only one he wanted."

"I got the ones *I* wanted, which suits me well enough. And in the end I got Herod too—he drank my tears from a golden goblet. Which was better than he deserved."

"It was painful?"

"Not at all. When he died he was filled with a sweet feeling of incandescence, which eased him out of this life on wings of flame. All his suffering came in the months *before* he drank from my cup. He had picked up a disease from a whore. His cock was black and when he pissed, he pissed blood."

"Kind of you to give him a gentle end," she said. "Why was that?"

"He paid me with a fine puzzle. Perhaps it pains you, to learn a wicked man chose the terms of his own ending? But it is the finest of all riddles: Why are the best among us nailed to crosses to die while the cruel live long enough to grow bored of their harems?"

"How does it work? The riddling contest?"

"I give you a riddle, and if you answer it, you get what's coming to you."

"What do you want if I can't answer?"

"I want you to tell Arthur you do not love him and never did. You are not to sleep with him again, not ever—you are never to care for each other that way. Fail on this point and your life is forfeit . . . and his too. Prince Charming's kiss brought Beauty back to life, but *your* kiss, Gwendolyn, will condemn your beloved to death."

Gwen felt her shock as a stone hardness in the pit of her stomach. She had anticipated some macabre cruelty. He would want to claw her face off; he would want to cripple her; he would want to harm her parents. She had not imagined he would want to play some kind of game with the simplest bit of happiness she had left to her: Arthur's easy affection, his arms around her, his head on her shoulder. She was not fifteen minutes from Arthur's gentle kisses, not fifteen minutes from Arthur's warm, bare body.

"That's fucked," she said, and King Sorrow laughed again. A little smoke, smelling almost of incense, gushed into the front seat.

"He'll know something is up," Gwen said. "I wouldn't just tell him I don't love him."

"Then tell him it's because he fucked Tana Nighswander

against her will. Fucked her because he could. Because her older sister *made* her give Arthur a little sweetener to keep him on the hook."

"That's not true."

"Ask him."

"He wouldn't do that."

"He *did* do that. He felt he was owed, and it was revenge, and Tana was just a bit of townie trash to him. You don't imagine he thinks any differently of you, do you?" King Sorrow shifted in the back seat and the Honda rocked on its springs. "Hm, p'raps I've *already* won my prize! But that's no fun. We *have* to riddle."

Gwen couldn't think. It was like being knocked down a flight of stairs. For a moment all she could do was sit there, stunned, trying to figure out if anything had been broken. She struggled to determine if this was a thing that could be forgiven . . . then pushed such considerations aside.

"How long do I have to answer your riddle?" Her tongue felt numb and heavy.

"Till a star falls from the sky. That's long enough."

"Till there's a shooting star? That could be hours."

"Or moments." He paused. "How much do you want it, Gwen? Do we have a game?"

"I need . . . I need a few minutes."

"No. We play now or not at all. Conversing with you this way, before I've fully come through from the Long Dark, is a pleasure, but also tiring. It's now or never."

She stared at the windshield, a sheet of brushed chrome. The defroster roared, melting the hoarfrost at the bottom of the glass in circles. The stars were out there. Who knew when the next would fall.

"All right then. Let's hear your riddle."

"Sometimes I taste bitter, sometimes I taste sweet," he said gleefully. "I hate to be held but I loved mother's teat."

Gwen stared into the night, her mind a bewildered, terrifying blank. The ice melted from the windshield and she gazed helplessly into dim and distant stars.

She shouted her answer just as one of them dropped like a tear, guessing wildly. "A toddler! Or hope."

"Neither," he sneered. "*Your tongue*, luv. And it would've been better if you held yours, don't you think? You just talked yourself out of Arthur's love. I can't wait to see his face. I *will* see it, you know. I see you *all*, often, as through a blurred sheet of glass. The six of you come more and more into focus as Easter approaches."

She sank forward, putting her brow against the steering wheel, thinking *Stupid stupid stupid damn townie*. She hurt through the middle as if she had been struck in the chest. He was going to take the best thing she had from her and she would win nothing.

"Wait," she said. "I didn't get to ask you a riddle. And you want a riddle."

"We'd have to agree on terms. I won't give you Arthur back. That's off the table, my joy. But if you can stump me—if I can't answer before the next star falls—I'll give you what you asked for first, an easy ending for your sacrifice."

"What if I can't—"

"Then you'll fuck Colin Wren and write Arthur a letter about how good he was." King Sorrow cackled.

"No," she whispered, through cracked lips.

"Very well. I suppose this concludes the business of the evening and I expect soon enough to know who I am going to kill this—"

"All right," she said, frantic now, her breath shooting out of her. A part of her was still tumbling down that first flight of stairs. *Tana was just a bit of townie trash* and *I want you to tell Arthur you do not love him*. She was tumbling and she did not know what would happen to her when she struck bottom. She took a ragged breath. "What do I have in my pock—"

"No, *no*. That's not a riddle, it's a question. And weren't you listening to me? I see you *all*. You've got two nickels in one front pocket of your overalls and a baby's pacifier in the other. I saw you putting things in those pockets when you hardly knew what your hands were doing. Try again. Make it good, Gwen. How you would delight me if you could outwit me. You may not believe that, but it's true."

She should've prepared. Why hadn't she prepared? How had she somehow imagined she could wing this? She should've studied like Arthur. She should've buried herself in the Rackham College library and read every book she could find on riddles, ancient and modern. Although maybe even that wouldn't have helped her. King Sorrow had heard a thousand-thousand riddles. He knew them all, had heard all the good ones, all the classic ones.

"Gwen," he said. "I'm waiting."

"Why is sex in a canoe like Milwaukee's Best?" she blurted without thinking.

They sat in the silence, the car idling in darkness.

"Why is—" King Sorrow began and his voice trailed off. At last, he said: "Is this *really* a riddle, Gwen Underfoot?"

"That's the sort of thing a person asks," she said, "when they don't know the answer."

They sat in darkness and Gwen watched the stars, her pulse thumping in her neck.

16.

Two days before Arthur's flight back to London, Gwen was in the library, stripping decorations off Colin's tree, when Arthur wandered in from the kitchen with two mugs of tea. She looked at him and then quickly looked away. Arthur looked good, in a waffled hoodie and a pair of carpenter jeans, a big man who slouched and lumbered, bearlike. The sight of him twisted up her insides and it took an almost physical effort to keep her face a careful blank, to fight off the sudden stinging sensation in the backs of her eyes.

"Want me to help dispose of the body?" he asked.

"Nothing stopping you," she said, her voice stilted and stiff. He didn't seem to notice.

He handed her a mug of good, hot, strong tea, and it was easy, with the first sip, to imagine being with him all day, basking in his quiet attention. It was a morning for pajamas, pancakes, sex on the couch, and lazy TV, but they weren't going to get any of that. Not today, not ever.

She sent him to get their coats and opened the French doors. The sun glared off the humped and cracked ice in the little bay, and she could smell the rotting seaweed tang of low tide. Some despised that smell, but she had always liked it, liked the salty perfume of sea-scrubbed rock and cold ocean.

"We hauling it down to the water?" Arthur asked.

Gwen started to reply and her throat was too tight. She swallowed, and tried again, and her voice seemed almost normal to her. "Like last year. You guys will have to burn it down without me, though. Tana is working. I'm looking after the baby." This was a lie, but when she thought about what was coming, she knew she couldn't be there tonight, with the others, pretending everything was fine, pretending she wasn't stricken, almost numb with hurt.

They shuffled out through the open doors, into the sharp air and the dazzle of light glancing off snow. It was big but not heavy, and the only real effort was stepping through the snow, which was almost a foot deep, glazed on the surface, soft powder beneath.

"I'm out of here in forty-eight hours," he said, as if she didn't know. "We should do something tomorrow evening." In a diffident tone he added, "Colin said we could borrow the Caddy. We could get something to eat and maybe drive down to Portland." Letting her know they could have the night together and it wouldn't have to be under anyone's nose. He wouldn't have to bring her back to The Briars, she wouldn't have to sneak him into her house.

Best, she thought, to get it done, now, today. To drink off her own goblet of dragon tears.

"You could just get us a pizza from Shut-Up-And-Eat-It," Gwen said. "If Tana's working, she could give you a freebee. Didn't she used to do that? A free pizza now and then, when it was time to pick up the books? You ever take anything else from her, free of charge, Arthur?"

He didn't reply. His face was set in an expression of the mildest calm, the professor surveying the class while they worked at a test. They crunched along through the snow, with the carcass of the Christmas tree between them, and she had the angry thought that he was planning a lie.

They crossed a hundred yards, to the edge of a fissured stony embankment, and set the tree down. It was as good a spot as any to burn something to the ground. A mile of frozen bay lay before them, great plates of ice broken in crooked lines and piled up against each other in jagged ridges. Out past the edge of the floe, the water was blue and choppy.

"I thought Tana would tell you sometime," he said.

"Thought? Or worried?"

He looked out to sea, staring into the eastern waters. When he spoke, his voice was as reasonable as his expression. "I wish I could take it back. I was angry and I was scared."

"I wish you could take it back too. She was prostituted by her sister. To drug dealers. To people they owed money. And to you."

At that he flinched—but did not reply.

"I'm sorry," he said, without looking at her.

"Me too." She wanted to touch him. She wanted to turn his face back to her and hold it against her shoulder. She didn't know what dragon tears tasted like, but she knew the flavor of her own well enough. She brushed them away, dashing one hand, then the other, across her cheeks. "I understand why you did it. A part of me, Arthur, cares about you too much to hold it against you. But I am not your girl. I am never going to be your girl again. I can be your friend, but not your lover. I am not going to solve half the crossword for you anymore. Whatever we almost had is going to remain an *almost*."

"I love you," he said.

"I know. But I don't love you."

There. It was done.

Or it should've been.

He frowned. "This stinks. None of this smells right. This isn't how you deal with things, Gwen."

He turned his head suddenly and examined her with such a searching curiosity, it was almost alarming.

"What?" she said. "You expected me to be a doormat? Or did you think I wouldn't care, because Tana's trash?"

"Tana isn't trash. I'm pretty sure you know I don't think she is. I mean—" He struggled with a thought in silence, then shook his head. "I don't know what I mean. Just . . . this doesn't feel like you."

"I guess it's going around. Because fucking a girl who can't say no doesn't feel like you."

He nodded. A wind, cutting across the bay, raised towers of snow and let them collapse.

"Okay," he said. "I get it. I feel what I feel for you, Gwen. I can't help that. But I understand that you don't. I was wrong to take advantage of Tana. And I'll tell her that. She needs to hear it even more than you. I'll speak to her before I go home tomorrow."

She had never heard him call the UK home before, and in that instant she knew he wasn't coming back after he graduated. He would stay there, make a place in the world for himself there. Maybe Arthur didn't know that himself yet . . . but he was giving up America as well as her. The thought made her heartsick but was also a relief. A few thousand miles of ocean between them might make the next few months—the next few years—easier to stomach.

"Don't bother," Gwen said. "Tana doesn't want to talk to you."

And wasn't that a laugh—that Gwen had expected Arthur to lie, but instead she was the one who didn't dare the truth. She didn't want him talking to Tana. Tana would tell him she hadn't said anything to Gwen, and then Arthur would naturally wonder who did.

He nodded. "If that's what you recommend."

"It is."

Arthur stood with his hands in his pockets, watching a couple of seagulls struggle over the wreckage of a dead, frozen fish, out on the ice. Gwen decided maybe he wanted to be alone. She wanted to be alone herself, somewhere she could have a good cry without being bothered.

She was walking away when he called out to her.

"Have you decided who you're going to give to him?" he asked her. "To the King?"

"Yes," she said. "It wasn't so hard."

He gave her a grin. "Let me know if it's me? I've got six courses hanging over me next semester—I don't want to do all that homework if I don't have to."

17.

Things took a turn for the worse in the early spring, and Llewellyn had a three-week stay in Eastern Maine Medical. But he rallied after his doctors eliminated one prescription and added two others, and at the end of March they sent him home. He had lost weight, and most of his teeth. By then he was 108 pounds. He turned seventy-two in the middle of March, and Colin had spent the money to get him the right birthday present. After the cake, Llewellyn unwrapped a bottle of 1912 Heidsieck & Co. Metropole Gout Americain, the same champagne that had been on the menu on the *Titanic*.

"Thought it would be fitting," Colin said. "The *Titanic* wasn't the only thing to go down in 1912. Isn't that when you discovered the Yale glee club?"

"I had them all singing falsetto by the time I was done," Llewellyn cried, chortling, and never mind he hadn't been born until 1919. "They never sounded better."

They didn't drink it, though. Llewellyn wasn't allowed. It went into the Cabinet of Curiosities, between a videotape exploring the red room in the haunted Amityville house and a megalodon's tooth.

But there was whiskey waiting when Gwen wheeled Llewellyn out onto the flagstone patio two weeks later, into the warm, almost damp air, perfumed with the smell of the sea and the pines. When she closed her eyes she smelled those firs and thought of Christmas, thought of carrying the tree across the snowy yard with Arthur, her heart thudding too quickly in her chest.

Llewellyn didn't see the decanter of Scotch, didn't know it was there. His sight was entirely gone by then. The tide was coming in and Gwen could hear the gentle, reassuring crash of it, thudding into the stones, and the satisfied hiss as it drew away. The old man had a blanket across his legs. He got cold so easily, even though it was almost T-shirt weather. Gwen stopped him by the metal table and put the brake on his wheelchair. She sat down with him and gently opened the wooden humidor next to the cut-crystal decanter.

His nearly toothless mouth gaped. He looked starved. He seemed only vaguely aware of where he was. Gwen thought he looked like one of those photos of the men rescued from the concentration camps at the end of the war. Llewellyn had not been in Europe to do the rescuing, although he had helped refugees relocate lost family members, as part of his role with the army in the postwar reconstruction. Gwen had gone looking for his records weeks before, in his meticulously kept files in the study. It was something to do when she wasn't reading his unpublished novel, the manuscript pages yellowing and so dry the pages flaked at the edges. It turned out he had enlisted just two months before Hiroshima. So much for knifing boys in Italy.

"I suppose you intend to ruin a perfectly delightful afternoon by forcing me to take my medicine," he said.

"I came with just what the doctor ordered," Gwen said. "Want to start with a few chips of ice?"

"Yes, please. My mouth. Ugh. I lost another tooth yesterday and the socket is all dry throb. If I had saved all the teeth that have fallen out in the last six months, I could make a savage necklace out of them. You could wear it! A trophy taken from your suffering victim."

She poured a trickle of Scotch into a glass of crushed ice and passed it to him. "Can you handle that?"

"I suppose," he said, and lifted it to his lips . . . and then paused, raising one shaggy eyebrow. He swirled the glass, inhaling the scent. A slow sly smile touched the corners of his thin-lipped mouth.

"This is whiskey," he said. "Glen Garioch, the '78. That smell! Like burnt moss and sin. What manner of sadism is this, Underfoot? I never took you for cruel tricks."

"Colin says it's your favorite."

"It is, isn't it?" Colin said, from the doorway, his voice coming from the dark of the study behind them. "It's the best of them?"

Llewellyn cocked his head. He hadn't heard his grandson approaching. The smile remained—that knowing, ironic smile that so made him look like Jeremy Brett.

"You know it is. What are you both about? What is this?"

Colin didn't speak. He couldn't, Gwen thought. It was hard enough for him just to breathe, to swallow one gulp of air after another. She had never seen him struggle with an emotion before.

Gwen clipped the fragrant end off one of Llewellyn's cigars and was a while lighting it, rolling it slowly between her fingers while she held the flame of a brass lighter to the tip. The lighter was from the Cabinet of Curiosities. It had been in Charles Whitman's pocket when he was killed in 1966.

"I promised you this," she said at last, "if you stuck around. Do you remember?" Handing him his cigar. "Go easy with that. You don't want to set off a coughing fit."

He took it and held it in one hand, his whiskey in the other, smiling in a way that seemed both unbelieving and indecently grateful at the same time. His milky eyes shifted sightlessly in her direction.

"You'll drink too?"

"Yes, I will," she said, and poured a quarter inch for herself and a bit more for Colin. Colin didn't take it, though. He couldn't seem to move from the study. He was leaning against the doorframe, his breath hitching now and then.

Llewellyn inhaled, gently, and shut his eyes in pleasure.

"I often felt a great tenderness for someone," the old man said, the words coming out in a gush of sweet smoke. "After I broke them for information. I drank with many of them, after I had forced them to betray their countries, their oaths, their lovers."

"No," Gwen said, "you didn't."

His eyes opened.

"You didn't drown children in ice water," Gwen said, "except in your unpublished fiction. When you told me the story about knife-fighting in Italy, I thought I had come across it somewhere before. I had—that's in your novel too. The one you wrote but never published. And it wasn't based on personal experience either. The fighting in Italy was over by the time you enlisted. You taught at Rackham for most of the Vietnam War. The CIA *did* employ you as a consultant, beginning in 1967, and you *did* write a widely distributed manual on interrogation—including an examination of methods you condemned as immoral and warned would inspire the enemy. But you never left the States. You never tortured anyone in the Mekong Delta. You pretended to have dementia and told us a lot of make-believe."

"Pretended?" he asked, his mouth agape, but his face had a humorous cast.

"If you were suffering from dementia, you'd be taking medication for it. You think I didn't take the time to research what your medications are for?"

"Why would I pretend?"

"Why would you rave cruel secrets to make us hate you? So

we could justify holding a pillow over your face, you old bastard." And as she said it, she clinked her glass to his and sipped. It burned going down, a delicious swallow of heat.

Colin made a choked sound from the open French windows.

"Why you are crying, m'boy?" Llewellyn asked, lifting his head querulously, his clouded eyes brightening.

Colin said, "I—" and choked again and turned his face away.

Gwen said, "I know you want it to be done, Llewellyn. I know you're exhausted. And embarrassed by the way your body has started to betray you, although Lord knows you've no reason to be. I know this isn't how you want Colin to remember you. I love you, old man. We all do. And if you're ready, there's a glass of something harder for you after you finish your whiskey."

"No," he whispered. "You mustn't. Not like that. A poison will be discovered."

"Not *this* poison."

Llewellyn tilted his head to one side, lips parted slightly, his lean Sherlockian visage alive with interest. "Oh? What bitter concoction have you discovered, Gwen Underfoot? I never took you for a mistress of poisons."

"You wouldn't believe me," she said. "So you'll just have to trust me instead."

"The dragon," Llewellyn whispered.

She hadn't seen that one coming and needed a moment to process it.

"You know about King Sorrow."

"Yes." It was Colin who spoke, not Llewellyn. Colin's voice was hoarse with emotion, but he took one step toward them now. "I told him most of it, over the last few months. I only left out the part about King Sorrow's return, that we have to kill again. I didn't want him to worry about us." And then, to Llewellyn, he said: "You had enough to deal with. It turns out we have to pick someone *every* Easter. Not just last Easter. It's not a one-and-done. It goes on and on."

"Until?"

"We've had enough, I guess."

"Ah," Llewellyn said. "And you chose *me*. Well. You couldn't have chosen better. And he gave you . . . a poison to finish me off? He isn't going to visit me like he visited Ms. Nighswander and her confederate? He isn't going to fall on me in a crash of claws and f-f-flame?" He began to cough then, a dry, splintering sound that doubled him over. He set the cigar on the edge of the table with a shaking hand.

Gwen got up to pat and stroke his back while he gasped. Before she sat back down, she reached over the table and moved the decanter aside. The goblet was behind it: a dusky gold chalice studded with ancient emeralds and rubies. There was a comical sheet of Saran Wrap over the top to keep the contents from spilling. It was very full. There was enough there to poison an army. King Sorrow told her the last person to drink from it was Ivan IV. *Keep it when you're done*, King Sorrow told her. *On the house.*

"No. We had a riddling contest. After I stumped him, he had to make some concessions." She sat back down with the chalice in one hand. "I'm told it won't hurt. But you have to drink it tonight, before midnight."

"Or . . ." Llewellyn asked, cocking one eyebrow.

"Or Gwen will have to drink it for you," Colin answered.

"Ah," Llewellyn said. "Well, we shan't let that come to pass."

"Do you . . . have anything you want to do first?" Gwen asked. "Anyone you want to call? Anything that needs finishing?"

"Besides this whiskey? No. It was all done ages ago. I've been in hell's waiting room for months. Maybe I didn't drown children. But I wrote a guide that said threatening a man's loved ones would be a most effective application of pressure. That was true. The work I did for the Shop in the seventies and eighties—that was true too. This is lovely whiskey—the loveliest thing I have had in months." He drank off the last of it and closed his eyes to savor it. "Lovely. Colin, will you hold my hand? I am not afraid. But I would like you with me. You were the best thing in my life."

Colin sank to one knee and took Llewellyn's right hand like a drowning man grabbing for someone who could pull him out of the current. Gwen had never seen Colin crying before, and never saw him cry again.

"Do you want another whiskey?" Gwen asked him. "We still have a quarter of the decanter."

"No. I might get too attached to my own life again. I've had my shot. Where's my chaser?"

Her hand shook when she handed him the goblet. He put his slender nose to the rim and inhaled.

"Smells like the sea," he said. "Is it . . . venom?"

"Tears."

"Dragon tears?" He seemed pleased by the idea. "You're a good girl, Gwen. I hope you will give my regards and my thanks to Mrs. Underfoot for decades of excellent service." He squeezed Colin's hand with his right, holding the goblet in his left. "Look after all of this money for me, Colin. And look after your friends."

Colin couldn't reply. He pressed his wet face to the old man's hand.

Llewellyn lifted the goblet in Gwen's general direction. "Here's to pornography, whiskey, long walks, and good books. Make sure you get plenty of all four." He shut his eyes and drank swiftly, one swallow and then another.

When he set the goblet back down, it was still three-quarters full. But his eyes had widened in surprise. He put his free hand to his breastbone.

"Fascinating," he said, and smoke seethed out of his lips. "It tastes like the power and the glory. I almost mean that literally." He let out a short, hard, panting breath, and sparks flew from his mouth. "I think my soul is burning. Who knew it would feel so good? Makes the whiskey seem like weak tea." He exhaled again: a lick of blue fire. Gwen nearly leapt up in surprise, stayed in her chair only by a great force of will. "Who knew the soul could burn so hot, Gwendolyn? Who knew . . . that we were made to burn eternal? Who." Only this last word was not a word at all, only a sound, as he blew a smoke ring into the gathering darkness.

He sat very still, head cocked to one side, his eyes open. Colin made little choked sounds, his head pressed into Llewellyn's forearm. The ocean went *boom-sssissssh*.

After a while, Gwen poured out what was left of the whiskey. She used the decanter to keep what was left of the dragon tears, and she put it in her car before she called emergency services.

28.

The memorial was on Friday, in the Rackham College chapel—piles of hothouse orchids in front of the altar and World War II–era swing music from the college jazz orchestra—and then a reception at The Briars. One would've thought Donna and Gwen were hosting the reception. Colin couldn't stand to be there, couldn't smile, shake hands, and chuckle at anecdotes about Llewellyn's years as a teacher, his sexual adventures, his psychological studies, his thousand small acts of kindness and generosity.

"They stayed away while he suffered and died," Colin told Gwen, in a voice that ever so slightly shook with disgust. "All of them. As if they could catch AIDS just by looking at him, or by sitting with him while he watched *Sherlock Holmes*. I hope to God I never get sick, never get weak, never get old. That's not how I want to find out how few people really love me."

Donna had held Colin for a while, put her head to his, and said, "Fuck 'em, fuck all of 'em. We got this. You go."

He helped himself to four Excedrin out of the plastic cube on Llewellyn's desk and got out of there, left in the cherry Caddy, sliding out past the line of parked cars running up the mile-long drive. No one saw him again for days.

Gwen did her social duty until the last of the mourners were gone, then stayed another hour to clean with her mother. It was going on five in the afternoon when she finally climbed back into her Honda. She told her mother she was off to watch Jett, which was kind of true. But when she got to Gogan, Tana emerged carrying the baby car seat in one hand and a brown paper bag from Ace Hardware in the other. The two women were a few minutes locking the baby seat into Gwen's car and buckling Jett into it, then Tana dropped herself into the passenger seat, paper bag between her legs. In the bag was a putty knife, a can of quick-release agent that would undo almost any epoxy, a suction cup, and latex gloves.

"This is a first," Tana said.

"You've never done this before? A little B and E?"

"Oh, I've stolen shit before," Tana said. "But this is the first time I brought a baby to a felony."

"You can really use that stuff to pull out a windowpane and get us in? What if she has an alarm?"

"I'm not scairt of her alarm. I wouldn't look forward to meeting her over a twelve-gauge, though. I get my ass blown away tonight, try and make sure Jett eats his vegimals."

"She's in London for a book fair. That's why we're doing this now."

"You sure of that?"

"Pretty sure," Gwen said. "But just in case, I'll go in first. I know what I'm looking for and Jett needs his mother."

But as they approached the Bunker Hill Memorial, through the gathering dark, Gwen heard the piercing shriek and wail of first one siren and then another. Tana gave her a nervous sidelong look.

"Shit," Tana said. "They can't arrest us, we ain't done no crimes yet."

Gwen didn't reply. She had a sudden bad feeling, a clammy,

crawling sensation at the nape of her neck. She put the window down a few inches and breathed in the warm spring air. She smelled smoke, wondered if someone had a bonfire going.

They got to Bridget Fleming's town house ahead of the first fire trucks, but by then the blaze was all the way to the third floor. Lurid tongues of red fire spurted through windows that had exploded outward from the heat. A black tower of smoke boiled up from the roof. Neighbors had come out on their steps to stare, their faces lit in shades of yellow and crimson by the glow of the flames. Someone was dancing in the street in front of Fleming's, jigging about in untied work boots and flailing his arms like he was in the mosh pit at a Jane's Addiction show.

Gwen slowed to a crawl as she went around the dancer in the street, and when Sheldon glanced over his shoulder, he didn't appear to recognize her. His glasses were smeared over with soot. One tail of his shirt had come out of his filthy corduroys. He had the crème brûlée butane torch in one hand, and he squeezed the trigger and blue flame spurted into the darkness. His tongue hung out, like a dog after a crazed run.

"Keep going, Gwen," Tana told her. "Just keep driving."

Sheldon turned to watch them drive away, dancing all the while to music only he could hear. Maybe, Gwen thought, he had recognized her after all—she could see him staring after her in the driver's-side mirror, his eyes wide with fascination. He had been more attentive that night than anyone had realized, and not just to her. He had heard Bridget Fleming muttering about Firsts, the antiquarian book fair too. The bitch had underestimated him, and in more ways than one. Later he told the police he hadn't needed to use his lighter to burn the place down, that he had been able to start the fire just by *thinking* about it— through the sheer power of his hate—which was probably why he was remanded to a wing for the mentally ill in Bridgewater State Hospital.

Gwen hit her blinker, turned the corner, and Cordis Street was gone. But she could see the reflected light of the fire for a long time, the glow of the flames illuminating that coil of rising smoke. That tower of sparks and cinders could be seen for miles... almost as if King Sorrow had paid the neighborhood a visit.

29.

APRIL 23, 1990

The letter was the first Daphne Nighswander had received during her entire incarceration. She had served just over a year so far. Twenty-four more to go.

She read the letter from her eldest daughter once, her lips moving, and then again, sitting cross-legged on the bed in her cell, while other inmates catcalled one another, cussed and jabbered and laughed, their voices echoing in the concrete halls. Somewhere music was playing an old-fashioned calypso full of horns and rattling hothouse drums. A man with a fruity Caribbean accent sang about the graveyard. I nearly bus' my head runnin from the dead, *he sang. The Trinidadians in Black Cricket loved their old jigaboo island tunes, laughed and sang along, like anyone in that joint had anything to be happy about.*

Dear Momma,

Well I'm out Nevada way with Ronnie. Business went south before we did. Long story. We got out of town like there were wild dogs chasing us. Seriously, I thought if I stayed one more day in Maine I was going to DIE of boredom. Ronnie's cousin is out here and might be able to hook us up with something.

We left in such a hurry, I forgot to say goodbye to a few friends. If things don't work out for us here, you might get back to Gogan sooner than I do. If that's what happens, maybe YOU could say goodbye to them for me: Colin Wren, Donna and

Donovan McBride, Allison Shiner, Gwen Underfoot, and especially Arthur Oakes. You remember his mom. The Holy Mother. Best, I think, to forget you ever knew her. Trust me on that. But remember her kid, for later. It would mean the world to me if you could send him my love. Oh, hey, I think Tana likes him. Art's a fun guy—he's pulled a couple funny ones on me! Real prankster, that one!—but he's not right for her, and I hope you'll tell her so. I hope you'll look after our Tana. God knows she can't look after herself. She's too easily swayed by bad influences.

When she was little, Tana was always scared there was something bad hiding in the dark at the back of her closet. I used to laugh at her but it turns out she was right. Pretty funny, huh?

From Reno,
Jayne

Daphne's attention was like an ant, crawling slowly from word to word, sentence to sentence. When her mind had finished its second crawl across the expanse of words, she folded the letter and put it under her pillow. But she continued to go over it in her mind: what the letter said, and more important, what it hadn't. Down the hall she heard a breathy, throaty exchange of accusations, a clash of steel on concrete, a desperate scuffle, a hoarse eruption of victorious laughter, and a desperate, groveling voice making desperate, groveling promises. Bitches being bitches. Daphne had lukewarm noodle soup for supper. A nervous little born-again went down on her in the last half hour before lights out and Daphne made sure she got a little paper envelope of sticky black heroin for debasing herself in the eyes of her Lord. And even while the scrawny little white girl was down between her legs, Daphne's mind was half on the letter, and the names in it.

A week later a guard came for her after lunch to say the social worker, Ms. Adams, wanted to speak with her. The guard was new, a kid with a feather-down brown mustache and big eyelashes, and he hadn't learned to hide anything yet. He regarded her with compassion and sorrow.

"I can't tell you what it's about, so don't ask," he told her.

"I know what it's about," Daphne Nighswander said, and pulled herself out of bed and went to find out where her eldest daughter had died and how.

Some women in grief said the rosary, but Daphne didn't grieve, she got even, and on the walk to the social worker's office, she didn't bother reciting the Apostle's Creed. She said the names to herself instead, feeling each one almost as a stone in the mouth, resting on the tongue.

Colin Wren.
Donna McBride.
Donovan McBride.
Allison Shiner.
Gwen Underfoot.
Arthur Oakes.

Book Two

FLIGHT OR FRIGHT

1995

3:55 p.m. (EST)

8 hours and 5 minutes to dragonedy o'clock

Allie unclamped the hatch on the front of the dryer, paying no mind to what she was doing. She had half a jelly jar of white wine in her right hand, had opened a bottle at lunch, and somehow she was drinking the last of it now. Dinner was still two hours off, but what the frack, it was Saturday. She thrust her arm into the machine for her laundry and her hand settled on a pile of cold, scaly loops, thick as a python. She screamed and yanked her hand back, but King Sorrow was faster, and caught her wrist with one claw before she could get away.

"Time flies, Allie," said the thing that both was and wasn't inside her machine. "It's almost Easter again. And you know what else flies? Men who are running for their lives. Men like Horation Matthews."

"*Huh*—Horation Matthews?" Allie asked, and King Sorrow let go of her and she fell back, sat down hard on the yellow linoleum. His claw slipped away into the warm darkness.

"He's headed to London tonight, via New York City. Come midnight he'll be on British Airways out of JFK. You've heard people complain about their in-flight meals, but you won't hear any of that rot out of me, luv. I'm already licking my chops."

"I don't understand. Why would he do that? There'll be other people on that plane. There'll be *hundreds* of other people." She felt shaky and weak, too weak to stand. She wished she hadn't had so much wine. But then she always needed to stay drunk to get through Easter.

"Maybe that's the idea. Maybe he wants to die in company. I'm sure the plane will be full of the sort of people he hates: atheists and Jews and Black people and taxpayers and gays and people with hard-to-pronounce last names and college graduates and women with jobs. Maybe he believes their death will give his meaning. Or maybe he's running, like Jayne ran, like so many of them run at the end."

"Why are you telling me this?" Allie said.

"He was your pick, Allie. I thought you'd enjoy a sneak preview of the grand finale. I thought you'd appreciate knowing that none of this would be possible . . . if not for you."

"You're saying they'll die because of me," Allie whispered. "But really they'll die because of *you*. And you want to rub my face in it."

"Oh, Allie." King Sorrow spoke from the darkness in the dryer, even though he was really in the darkness inside her head. "What a hurtful thing to say. And unfair! I didn't have to tell you anything. But now you know where Horation will be at dragonedy o'clock—in the air, over the North Atlantic. And you can still do something about it. I'm giving you a chance to save everyone, because—you may doubt this, but it's true—when you're carrying so much guilt already, it didn't seem fair to pile on. What with breaking Van's heart and breaking your own. That's enough for anyone. You know, Allie, the plane won't take off for another two and a half hours. If you want to save those people, all you have to do is be on it. Get yourself on that plane, darling, and *no one* but Horation Matthews has to die tonight."

4:09 p.m. (EST)

7 hours and 51 minutes to dragonedy o'clock

Allison Shiner came off the ramp doing eighty, steering with one hand, punching numbers into her flip phone with the other.

"*Collllllin! Hel-lllloooo?!* Pick up!" she shouted at his answering machine. "We got a problem, smart guy, so stop waxing your head and call me back. It's four p.m. on Saturday afternoon, and everything is *scr-eww-ewww-ed*." She sang the last word in her finest choir girl alto.

She disconnected, then had to yank the steering wheel to keep from rear-ending an oil tanker. She cut into the left lane, nearly sideswiping a boxy Chevy Blazer, which slammed on the brakes and laid on the horn. Allie couldn't sweat it. If the day ended with just one or two fatalities, she'd be doing great.

She dialed Donna next. Donna was already in Manhattan, even closer to the airport than Allie.

"What'chu doin', babe?" Donna said when she picked up.

"I'm on my way to the airport!" Allie sang gaily. She always sang when she was stressed, as Donna would've known if she ever paid attention, which she didn't. "I'm flying to London and you'll never guess with who!"

Donna let out a sigh. "You and Van worked out your shit? I knew when you didn't give back the ring—*well*. If he was gonna take you somewhere romantic, I would've suggested Capri, but tickets to London were probably less expensive, the cheap bastard."

"Not Van," Allie said. "Horation Matthews. He's on the six forty out of JFK to Heathrow."

Donna needed a moment to process that. When she spoke again, her voice was lower, husky with strain. "Why the fuck is *he* going to England? I thought that Jesus freak never left his compound."

"They run. You know they run. Jayne ran. And you said it yourself. *Arthur* is in England."

"He doesn't know anything about Arthur. He can't know."

"Yes, he can. He could've riddled for Arthur's name. He could've riddled for *all* our names. This is a guy who thinks in Old Testament terms. For all we know he's headed to the UK to do something biblical to our Arthur."

"Yeah, but . . . it's going to be Easter morning in eight hours. What happens if he's on the flight when—" Donna's voice trailed off, as she figured it out for herself. "Fuck. Fuck, *fuck*, fuck, FUCK."

"Now you're singing my song."

As Allie blew past an eighteen-wheeler the mud flaps threw a filthy, rattling spray across her windshield. For a few moments the road was a brownish blur. She told herself to slow down but instead her foot mashed the pedal closer to the floor.

"Do you think Matthews has any idea what could happen?" Donna asked. "Not just to him but to everyone he's flying with?"

"I didn't pick Horation Matthews off a list of nice, socially responsible role models, Donna. The dude watched TV while his wife roasted to death two hundred feet away. Probably not even good TV. I bet it was one of those fishing shows on ESPN, where fat guys in camouflage get breathless about hooking a trout. But does he know? If he does, he doesn't care."

"How do *you* know all this?"

"How do you think? King Sorrow was in my gosh-darn dryer, having a chuckle that four hundred innocent people are going to die and it's all my fault."

"Hang the fuck on, that's a good point. They're all going to die. Did I hear you say you're getting on the plane too? The fuck you wanna do that for?"

"If I'm on the plane, King Sorrow can't touch Matthews. Remember? He swore to protect us. He has to follow the rules too. He won't be able to touch the guy until we land."

"Are you sure?"

"One hundred percent," she said. She was going to add that King Sorrow had told her so himself, but she had to bang on her brakes to keep from rear-ending a HEARSE and the words went out of her head. No doubt about it: the day was determined to stay on theme.

"I don't want you on that flight. I don't want you anywhere near Matthews. He's a dangerous goddamn paramilitary psychopath, and for all you know he's planning to hijack the fucking plane. There's got to be other options. Call in a bomb threat."

"So they look for a bomb and they don't find it and the flight takes off anyway and then King Sorrow blows it up? And as a bonus, the FBI has an audiotape somewhere with my voice on it, and I go to jail for a million years. Or! Or: they delay the flight and King Sorrow takes out a whole terminal like someone dropped a bunker buster on it. Instead of four hundred dead, you got a thousand corpses. Maybe more."

"Can he *do* that?"

"He says he leveled a few Hungarian shtetls. Are those bigger than airports?"

"You'd have to ask Arthur about shtetls. I wouldn't even know how to spell it."

"There's another way, Donna. You could meet me at the airport. We could waylay him in the bar and offer him a threesome, make him skip his flight that way."

"Don't make jokes. You know you aren't funny. You've never been funny."

"Who's being funny? Meet me at the airport." Allie felt a surge of almost desperate need to have Donna with her, to be in this together. If Donna was with her, Allie wouldn't need to be brave. Donna was always brave enough for both of them.

"I can't do that," Donna said. "I have to be on the air at six."

"Oh. *Oh*. *Well*. That's fine. You go on TV. Do your thing and let me worry about the men, women, children who are about to burn to death and fall out of the sky. Hey, if I screw this up, do you think they'll let you cover the whole air disaster thing on the eleven o'clock?"

But you couldn't guilt-trip Donna—her lack of shame made her immune to such appeals.

"Call Van," Donna said. "Get him to meet you at the terminal."

It was in Allie's head to say *he doesn't want to talk to me*. It was in her head to say *he can't bear to look at me anymore, never mind talk to me*. Instead she said, "I don't think Horation Matthews is going to want a threesome with Van."

"Not for a threesome. Stop talking about threesomes. For help. For support. You're shook up and you're scared and how much have you had to drink?"

Not enough, Allie didn't say. When she switched lanes too quickly, she could actually hear the gin sloshing in the bottle of Gordon's she had pushed into her purse on her way out the door.

"Call Van," Donna repeated, when Allie didn't reply. "He'd never let you face this alone."

"Donna," Allie said, and licked her lips, and tried again, "Donna. I . . . you don't know how I left things. How badly I messed it up. I think it would be easier to face a terrorist at thirty thousand feet than Van over a drink."

Donna didn't say anything.

"Oh, God, what did he tell you?" Allie said. "Did he tell you I'm in love with you? I'm not. I mean, I *am*, I *love* you, you're my best friend, but I don't . . . I'm not like that. When I get drunk, really drunk, I say stupid things. Everyone does. It doesn't mean I want— God, I can't even say it. It's so embarrassing. Please say something to me."

Donna answered with stony silence.

"Please don't hate me," Allie whispered. "I don't know what's wrong with me. I went to a camp to fix it when I was sixteen but sometimes it comes unfixed again. Please, say anything. I couldn't bear it if you shut me out. Please, Donna? Donna? Hello?"

She didn't know AT&T had dropped her call until she looked at her phone. When she looked up, she was about to rear-end a station wagon loaded with kids. She had to swerve into the breakdown lane to get around it, and the woman behind the wheel laid on the horn, a long furious wail of rage and terror. Allie gave her a Queen Elizabeth wave of acknowledgment, couldn't help feeling better. In a worst-case scenario, she'd be dead by sunrise, in which case, she'd never have to find out how much Donna had just heard. Even death had an upside.

4:29 p.m. (EST)

7 hours and 31 minutes to dragonedy o'clock

No one could spot a bad idea faster than Gwen—so Allie tried her next, punching in the number with her thumb as soon as she had a couple of bars on her Nokia. By then traffic had forced her to slow down and she was creeping along at an agonizing forty miles an hour, hemmed in on all sides.

When Gwen didn't answer at home, Allie tried Tana Nighswander. Gwen spent as much time there as she did at her own place, looking after the baby while Tana worked.

Only Tana was at home and picked up on the second ring.

"Tana? It's Allie, Allison Shiner? I'm Gwen's friend, in New York?"

"Oh, right. You're Donovan's lady. Did you guys set a date yet?"

Any reply to that question would end in tears, and Allie couldn't afford tears right now, so she pretended she hadn't heard. "Is Gwen there? I'm having a little emergency."

"You're outta luck. She's out there dealing with everyone else's emergencies today. She's riding in the ambalance this afternoon."

"When will she be back?"

"She don't get off her shift till midnight. What's wrong? Can you tell me?"

"I'm just . . . fleeing the country like my life depends on it. Like someone's life depends on it, anyway." She laughed. It sounded like a sob.

"Aw, c'mon, getting married to the McBride kid can't be that bad."

Allie opened her mouth to reply that it wasn't that, it was nothing to do with Van—and something tightened in her throat, made it impossible to force out any sound. And for an instant she was back with Van in the hospital after he cracked his head and he was half turned away from her. *You coulda died, you big dumb idiot*, she said, trying to be sweet and funny and angry with him at the same time. *My parents already put a deposit down on the venue. Think how steamed they'd be if we had to use it for your funeral instead of our wedding.*

On the bright side, he said, without looking at her, *maybe after the funeral Donna would throw you a pity fuck. A little comfort for the grieving widow. I don't think Donna is gay, but she's pretty much up for anything when she's drunk.*

When Tana spoke again—after a long and awkward silence—she sounded awed. "No. *Way*. Is this real runaway-bride-type shit? Come on, girl. Don't hold back. I gotta have some details. The only romantic misadventures in these parts is when the batteries die in my vibrator."

Allie shouted with laughter. The cry of her own voice was so loud she shocked herself and almost fumbled her phone. She hadn't known she could laugh on a day like this.

"It's not like that," Allie said. "I mean, I'm not running away. I already ran away. Van learned some things about me—what I'm really like, behind closed doors—and it ruined me for him." She let out a breathless, choked laugh and said, "I'm glad for him in a way. There never was a sunnier fella than Van. He deserves better."

"Oh, for fuck's sake," Tana Nighswander said. "What could he find out to ruin you for him? Did you have a pussy hair out of place one night or something?"

Allie laughed again, almost a scream of laughter. "Jesus! I never heard such smut. Do you kiss your mother with that mouth?"

"Probably best not to kiss *my* mother. Likely get an STD from her, fuckin' skag."

It was the unlikeliest of all things, in that moment: to find herself on the edge of giggles, on the edge of tears. Tana's rude mouth shocked and inspired her. Allie had always admired people who did not need to look at polling data to have an opinion, that 30 percent of people who were unafraid to say the wrong thing. Allie always felt best when agreeing with others herself. Her father said, with a kind of gentle sadness, as if discussing a disability, that she was a compulsive pleaser. She always found it thrilling to be in the company of someone with views of their own. She liked to mold herself to them, to make herself the thing that made them happy. Of course, if she hadn't tried so hard to be the things Van wanted her to be, she might've saved them all a lot of unhappiness.

Allie saw the exit for the airport coming up on her right, hit her blinker, and began crossing from one lane to the next, jamming herself into any opening, horns wailing and squalling in a chorus of disdain.

"What's going on?" Tana said. "Did you just drive by a traffic accident?"

"Trying not to cause one," Allie said.

"Do you want to leave a message for Gwen? Can she call you back? I know midnight is late, but—"

"I'll be on a plane by then. I hope. There's a flight to London in two hours and I have to be on it. It's kinda life or death."

"Oh," Tana said. Then she said, "Arthur's in London. The old man. I love that dude to pieces—no one ever paid a higher price for loaning a girl a hoodie."

"I'll let him know you wished him well," Allie said. She didn't add, *if I'm still alive tomorrow*.

"You got a message you want me to pass on to Gwen?" Tana asked again.

"Tell her—" Allie struggled to think of a message she could safely pass through the medium of Tana Nighswander, some way to alert Gwen about Horation Matthews and the threat to BA 238 to London. But she didn't have the wit for it, not after a bottle of wine and forty minutes of driving faster than she had ever driven in her life. She said, "Tell Gwen I said 'Happy Easter,' and I'll try to call her from the other side of the pond."

"Okay," Tana said uncertainly. "I wish I could help, whatever it is. I wish you felt okay talking about it with me. But I won't keep after you, and I'll let Gwen know. Tell you what, Easter isn't really her holiday. She always gets moody around this time of year. Withdrawn, you know? You'd think they were going to crucify Christ all over again. And someone hired her to pound in the nails."

5:32 p.m. EST

6 hours and 28 minutes until dragonedy o'clock

She had her ticket and was through security twenty minutes before boarding began. There was a crowd in the seating area by the gate, but Allie wasn't ready to plunge in, could hardly look at them. One of those passengers had killed his wife and killed her slow. He had killed his stepdaughter too and plotted the murders of FBI agents and abortion doctors, and for his many crimes he had been marked for death, sentence to be carried out by a large lizard. Allie wasn't sure she'd know him if she saw him. She had only ever seen one photograph, and that was a grainy photocopy from a newspaper article. In the picture, taken after the homicide charges were dismissed, he looked every inch the soldier: dark crew cut, narrow, hooded eyes, cheeks cratered with acne scars, blunt-fingered butcher's hands. Put that guy on the stand if you wanted, all you were going to get was name, rank, and serial number.

Allie had to sit down, had to slow her heart rate, take a moment to breathe. She found a stool in a darkened bar directly across from the gate, a place called Dickens' Authentic English Pub, full of the odor of stale beer.

They had framed pictures of Dickens, Orwell, and James Joyce on the walls (though Allie was pretty sure Joyce was Irish), a barroom piano against one wall, and microwaved sausage pies on the menu. If she kept her back to the Jetway, she could almost pretend she was in a London tourist trap . . . at least until the bartender came to take her order. He had a mullet, a Jersey accent, and a spray-on tan. He brought her white wine in a glass roughly the size of a bathroom sink. She had a tremor in her hand when she lifted the glass to her lips.

She thought about Horation Matthews, the former marine and Christian fundamentalist who fantasized about bringing down the government. Allie had babbled about waylaying him in a bar, offering him a threesome with Donna to keep him from boarding the flight. In her mind that was possible, because Donna could talk a man into bed, and Allie could stand next to her while she did it. She wondered what she'd do if Horation walked in here right now, if Allie could put the moves on him herself. The thought nearly made her cough wine back up her nose. Horation Matthews believed interracial marriage was a plot to water down Christian male bloodlines and that the IRS was as bad as the Gestapo. How did you get someone like that hot and bothered? Whisper in his ear that she had always wanted to be spanked with the federal tax code? *Hey, pal, wanna have a few beers and then go somewhere you can do domestic terrorism to my body?* Or maybe you went the religious route. Ask him to biblically smite her girl parts, part her legs like the Red Sea.

Someone stroked the keys of the barroom piano over against the wall. By the time Allie looked around to see who, the guy was already settling onto the stool next to her. She wasn't sure she'd recognize Horation Matthews, but she knew when someone *wasn't* Horation Matthews, and he wasn't. From the waist down he was a skinny guy in new-looking jeans with stovepipe legs. From the waist up he was built like John Candy, a fat man in a cheap sports coat, frayed at the cuffs. His eyes were sharp, though—dark brown, humorous, and clever.

"Did he let you down?" he said.

"Mhm?" Allie asked, twisting around on her stool.

"You look like a woman been stood up," he said. "Tell Frank Heck all about it."

"Heck?" she asked, thinking she must've heard wrong.

"As in what the heck."

"Or: heck no."

He shot a finger at her to say she had the right idea. He asked the bartender for an old-fashioned and to get another glass for Allie while he was at it. Allie was surprised to see her first was already gone.

"Maybe I'm the one who let him down," she said, suddenly, her thumb twisting the engagement ring that she really had no business still wearing.

He saw the diamond flash and smirked. "I wish more of my disappointments looked like you. A man could start to enjoy the feeling of regret. Where you headed, hun?"

"London," she said.

"The six forty? Maybe we'll sit together. What takes you there?"

"Off to see a friend. He's a lot smarter than me, and I need someone smart to figure out what I'm doing with my life. What about you, Mr. Heck? What do you do?"

"Make money and spend it on women who look like you."

"Ah! That's a good line. I've never had a line."

"Girl like you don't need a line."

Allie had now finished off most of two glasses of wine in just a few minutes and her head was swimmy. "What about you? Why are you going to London?"

"Well, now, I'm developing a few propositions. Like the Churchill Atlantic Commander One-Piece Sleeping Costume for Men. Did you know Churchill designed his own pajamas? Like a jumpsuit with booties on it, made him look a little like, who's the guy in the McDonald's commercials? Big purple guy?"

"Grimace."

"Right, Grimace. Shoot, what *is* Grimace, anyway? Is he a big potato? Or, like, a giant raisin?"

"He's a tumor. He represents what grows inside you if you eat too much McDonald's."

"That explains how I wound up in this state," Frank Heck said, and smacked his belly. "Maybe it's not fat at all. Could be a tumor."

"That's what got my brother. Cancer," she said, and then wished she could take it back. Theo wasn't the stuff of casual pub conversation with a stranger.

"I'm sorry to hear that. What was his name?"

"Theodore. They never made a better man." *Enough*, she told herself. The problem with wine was it made you emotional. The problem without wine was sobriety.

"Let's drink to Theo then," said Frank Heck. "Let me buy you another."

"No, thank you," she said, and felt a sudden surge of emotion, a great swell of pride in her own forceful resolve. *No*. She would *not* have another glass of wine. Not until she was in her seat on the plane, and then a little one would be fine. "One drink is polite, but a second with a strange man would be inappropriate." And this time she flashed the engagement ring deliberately.

"Well, then, b'God, we should drink to holy matrimony. That's not inappropriate." He nodded to the bartender, who was already there to fill her glass, and she gave in, didn't want to be rude. Heck said, "I guess he must have faith in you, let you go off to London all by your lonesome. How's he know you won't meet a pajama salesman and decide not to come home?"

"I never wear pajamas," she said, and Heck fanned his face with a paper napkin and rolled his eyes.

"Hun, don't say them kind of things. Man carrying as much weight as me, my heart could go at any time."

Allie laughed and for a moment almost liked the pushy fat man who was trying his luck with the only single woman in the bar. He had brass, and brass counted for something with Allie.

The flight announced preboarding for families traveling with children and anyone else who needed extra time. She began to dig in her purse for her credit card. Heck glanced down into the open crochet bag in time to see the bottle of Gordon's in the bottom, half-full (not half-empty . . . Allie was an optimist). She was too buzzed to be embarrassed. He put his hand on hers.

"Let me," he said. "Buying a pretty woman a glass of wine is what I call a smart investment."

"Well, aren't you sweet as heck," she said, and he threw her a broad wink.

She slipped off her stool while he was turned away, raising his hand to get the bartender's attention—New Jersey had moved down to the end of the counter to unload the dishwasher. But she glanced back when she was halfway across the pub and saw him watching her go. The look in his eyes gave her a nasty chill. There was something hard and bright in his stare, an almost clinical curiosity that didn't go with his easy talk and down-home twang. His finger was moving around the rim of his old-fashioned, but he hadn't touched it. Not a drop.

She smiled uncertainly back and, as she passed the piano, played her left hand across it, saying goodbye to him the way he had said hello—her nimble fingers finding the first few notes of "Give Me That Old-Time Religion." He raised the glass in acknowledgment.

But then—as she tottered away, a heel wobbling beneath her, so that she came close to turning an ankle—the piano played on, sounding out the first five notes of "Puff the Magic Dragon," keys rising and falling on their own for a moment. She hip-checked a table and had to grab a chair to keep from falling on her face. No one else seemed to have noticed. But then no one else was *supposed* to notice. It was a little joke intended for her alone. King Sorrow had his failings—mass murder among them—but no one could say he didn't have a sense of humor.

1:02 a.m. EST

5 years, 3 months, 2 days, and 16 hours before dragonedy o'clock

"What are we going to do with that?" Van asked, when Colin came back to the table with a bleached, pitted conch shell bigger than a football and prickling with spines.

"We're going to listen to it," Colin told him. "The tradition of conchomancy was old before Christ was born. It goes back thousands of years in South America. This is an Aztec speaking trumpet, employed in the days before Cortés. The quiquizoani called spirits to sacrifice by blowing into it—like a dinner bell for their gods, let them know they were serving up a beating heart. Then they turned it around and listened to it for instructions. That's what we're going to do. We're going to take turns blowing into it, to call King Sorrow to us, and then we'll listen and see what sacrifice he demands."

"The quiquizoani?" Van said. "Sounds like something you'd order from a pizza place."

Or at least that was how Allie remembered it. No one else remembered the conch. Gwen and the McBrides remembered passing a pearl-handled mirror. Colin and Arthur said it had been a World War II–era helmet filled with water, which they used as a scrying bowl.

And no one but Allie remembered dragonedy o'clock.

They passed the conch and blew into it and called for King Sorrow. Doors slammed. Donna screamed. Gwen told her to keep her hands on the table. At one point the door to the hallway flew open and it was just a starry night out there, like the sky over the desert.

Allie had seen a sky like that before, when she was on the Outback Highway in Australia. She would never forget it, just a hundred miles from Ayers Rock. The sky was so big, and so full of stars, you didn't dare look into it for long or your head would get dizzy and strange. Her parents had taken them on a trade mission to the Pacific Rim nations. It was all good memories, that trip. Theo had been in remission—they all believed he had beaten it. Eighty-five percent of adolescents with his cancer did. With his yellow hair and cleft chin and faraway blue eyes, her older brother looked like the stout-hearted, headstrong hero of a young adult novel. He argued with their father at every turn—about politics, theology, ethics—but patiently, with a grin, and their father grinned back, both of them enjoying it. When they argued Allie always took her father's side, although he was indifferent to her help and Theo wouldn't argue with her, would only look at her fondly, proudly. He was two years older but had always called her "kid." A few months after Ayers Rock, the cancer surged back, and Theo was dead by seventeen. Her mother stopped going to church after that, while Allie became more serious about attending weekly services, if only to see the graffiti Theo had scratched in the pew with his pocketknife. JESUS SAVES BUT ALLIE INVESTS and IS IT A SIN TO FART WHILE PRAYING?

Allie had seen stars in the hallway as she lifted the conch to her lips like a boy-savage preparing to address the tribe. She blew a breathy blat and wondered for the thousandth time if it *was* a sin to fart while praying.

"Paging King Sorrow," she called, as she lowered the conch. "King Sorrow, proceed to your gate, your flight from the big nowhere to Earth is preparing to depart."

She lifted the big old Aztec shell to her ear and shut her eyes. For the longest time there was only that mindless susurration that people said sounded like the sea, but which to her was closer to the sound a TV made when it was tuned to a dead channel, receiving only static. She listened so hard her ears started to ring.

No—wait. It wasn't a ringing in her ears. It was a single lingering note, a high G. Allie had been singing in choir since she was six and had a good ear, an *educated* ear, could harmonize in an instant with a note played on a piano. The high G she could hear now had no beginning. It had always been there and she had gradually picked it out of the ceaseless shush. Then it dropped to an F sharp. And dropped again, and then climbed, in a melancholy strain. She only needed three notes to recognize "Puff the Magic Dragon," one of the first songs she had ever learned to play on the piano. It came from a maddening distance, was so faint it was less like hearing a song and more like *imagining* it, and it died away just before the very last note. It came to her then, what she had to do: King Sorrow wanted her to play for him. She rose straightaway, thoughtlessly passing the cracked mirror to Donna (now *that* was odd, that she remembered passing Donna a mirror and not the pitted old seashell), and went to the player piano.

There were cartridges for the player piano. Big scrolls with holes punched in them, not all that different from the hole-punched metal scrolls inside a child's music box. Mr. Wren had a couple dozen tucked inside the piano bench, but Allie didn't look for "Puff the Magic Dragon," already knew it wasn't there among the ragtime and early blues numbers. Instead she began to play the ever so slightly out-of-tune piano, fingers falling on the keys, notes rising into the air.

She played.

She played until her arms ached, until her fingers ached, until she tried to lift her hands and found she *couldn't*, which was when she realized the piano was playing *her*. The keys yanked her fingers up-down-down-down-up-down. She knew the others were no longer sitting together at the card table. She sensed them moving through the room, each under the power of some unnatural idea of their own. *Witched* was the word that came to mind, although maybe that was wrong, maybe they had been *dragoned*. She played faster. She smashed a fingernail, and the ring finger on her left hand began to bleed. First the keys were smeared with blood. Then they were slick with it.

At some point, Allie lifted her head and saw Gwen taking framed butterflies down from the wall above the piano. Gwen had been freeing them for a while before Allie noticed, but then it was easy not to see Gwen, she was the most unseeable girl Allie had ever met. Gwen was only *almost* pretty, but she had kind eyes, eyes that promised that if something was broken, you would mend it together. They were the green of old sea glass, the sort of sea glass that might wash up on the shores of Honalee, and how long had Allie been playing this song? She caught a glimpse of her watch and saw it was five past dragonedy. Dragonedy was a number, a bit like the number two, only it was a dragon with a lowered head.

When Allie looked up a second time, smoke was trickling from under the lid of the piano, and suddenly the keys released her hands. The song went on, the bloody keys flashing and depressing and springing back up, her red fingerprints all over them. Allie threw the lid open to see if something was burning in there, waving a hand back and forth to clear away the faintly spicy-smelling haze. No fire, but she could see a cartridge plugged into the machine, the scroll feeding itself through the sprockets. She saw a yellowing, peeling label which identified the song as "Blaec Wyrm the Magic Dragon." The fallboard clapped shut over the keys with a bang and startled Allie so badly she stepped back and her legs struck the bench and she had to sit down.

Allie had never listened to a seashell since. She was afraid of what she might hear.

6:25 p.m. EST

5 hours and 35 minutes until dragonedy o'clock

She stepped aboard, entering the galley at the waist of the plane and making the unfamiliar right turn into economy. By the time she got to the airport, her nerves had been too jangled to think about where she sat, and she had just asked for a seat on the next available flight to Heathrow. No—maybe there had been more to it than that. Some anxious part of her had the wild thought that somehow Horation Matthews would *know* her if he saw her, would somehow magically recognize in a glance one of the people who had set the dragon against him. She did not want to find him on the plane or be found by him, and it seemed to her it would be easier to hide in the crowd of people in the cheap seats.

She wondered if this was the first time she had ever flown in economy and supposed it was. She was curious to see how else she'd be willing to debase herself in this desperate hour. Maybe she would drink a Fresca and eat something plebeian, like a hot dog.

Allie made her way into the rear, along the starboard aisle. A kid in a black hoodie, with black fingernail polish, occupied the window seat. The aisle seat contained one of the most striking-looking women Allie had ever seen—not beautiful but arresting, with a wide, bold mouth, lips glossed to a high shine, and hair blown out in the style of late-seventies Farrah Fawcett. Only when Allie was standing right over her, she saw that the woman in the flower-print dress had an Adam's apple. Wouldn't it be fucked up, she thought, if Horation Matthews had boarded the plane dressed as a woman? This wasn't Horation Matthews, though, but a cross-dresser of about forty—did you call them cross-dressers? She didn't think so.

Other than Van, she had never met a man who would wear a dress in a public place. Allie's seat was sandwiched between the goth and the—what? Transvestite? No, that wasn't right either. She had a stern thought, then, in Colin Wren's voice: *He's not a man in a dress, Allie, she's a woman in a man's body.*

The woman in the man's body stood up to let her past and said, in a posh English accent, "Squeeze by, darling, there you are. Don't be alarmed if you think you hear a noise like birds getting sucked into the engine on our flight, that's just how I sound when I start to snore. Robin Fellows."

"I won't mind, I think even snoring sounds more elegant in an English accent," Allie said, charmed in an instant, the way she was always charmed by someone who so obviously enjoyed being exactly themselves. She never thought of Robin Fellows as a man again.

"What's your thing, love?" Robin asked, leaning into Allie. She had a great scent on, a spicy tingle of wildflowers and whiskey. "What do you do?"

"Polls," Allie said, absent-mindedly, glancing around for anyone who resembled Matthews. No one. "Grinding polls."

Robin arched one eyebrow. "Well, you've got the body for it, God bless. There was a time I did a little burlesque myself, but I didn't have the body for it even then. Bit embarrassing to remember now. I was a cliché and didn't know it. If one of my writers put twenty-five-year-old me in a book, I would've told them I was trite."

"Are you an editor then? What sort of books?"

"Bit of this, bit of that. Mysteries mostly, but I've done true crime and a couple of rock bios, which are not so different from true crime. At least not the good ones—drugs, jailbait, and hopefully a few corpses."

"I wish my fiancé was here, you'd have so much to talk about." It had slipped out before she could help herself, calling Van her fiancé. She wasn't used to not having a future with him yet. Her thumb found the engagement ring again and began to play with it. "He writes for *Rolling Stone*. I promise I won't pitch you on his work until you've had something to drink."

"And did you meet in the strip club?"

"Hm? I don't think I've ever been in a strip club. No, that's not true. I went to Chippendales with Donna once. She's his sister. She looks like him, only sexy."

Robin frowned. "So do you *teach* pole-dance then? Are such things taught?"

"*Oh*," Allie said. "Oh, I can't dance. I wish I could. I just flail around and hit people with my elbows. No, I'm a *pollster*. I grind out surveys for polling firms. I like having a reason to call people up and ask them random questions. It's amazing what strangers will tell you. I love calling old women with surveys about sex. Old women can be really dirty, especially if you get them around wine o'clock. I remember one old lady saying she always thought a Coke tasted better after sucking her husband off."

Robin lowered her eyes and coughed into her hand. "I couldn't offer an opinion."

A flight attendant appeared beside them and tried to get the slumped goth's attention. It took a few tries before the kid in the black hoodie plucked the headphones off his ears.

"Would you be Charlie Schow?" the flight attendant asked. "Mr. Schow, I'm sorry to say we've managed to overbook economy and have to ask you to change seats." The kid stiffened in alarm and the attendant hurried on: "We're upgrading a select few passengers and have a new seat for you up in Club World!"

The goth un-Slinky-ed himself from his seat, the alarm gone in an instant, and almost bounced to his heels. Allie and Robin half stood to let him squeeze by.

"I'm glad they didn't come for me," Robin said, as she sat again. "Traveling in economy builds moral fiber. Like rolling out of bed and going for a five-kilometer jog first thing in the morning. It's the discomfort that builds character."

"I hate running," Allie said. "If you slow down there are insects, which is bad, and if you don't slow down, you're running, which is worse."

"*So* much worse. But we're happy here. We don't need their silver platters of chilled crab or their luxurious seats. We've got each other."

"You wouldn't rather have chilled crab?"

"The flight is off to such a good start," Robin said. "Let's pretend you didn't ask that."

A flight attendant wheeled a trolley through the cabin, offering passengers bubbly in plastic flutes. Allie took one and looked into it at the little fizzing circle of golden champagne and hated the idea of drinking it and knew she had to. It was lonesome business, getting drunk without Van or Donna. Only, no—she was *already* drunk. But she was going to have to work at it to stay that way, and the thought of the effort ahead made her very sad. It was necessary. She needed to stay drunk, because if she didn't drown her anxiety, she might start shaking.

For a while, on the parkway, she hadn't been sure she would get on this flight at all, had been terrified she would not arrive at JFK in time. She had not stopped moving since King Sorrow had grabbed her wrist as she reached into the dryer, had been moving at eighty miles an hour even before she got in her car. All that speed, that rush, had offered her a kind of mental security: the acceleration had swept aside any doubts. Now that she was on the flight, she had come to a standstill, and she felt clammy and a little woozy with dread. Now she had to sit and think her thoughts, and what she kept thinking was that she had missed something obvious and crucial. It was like wondering if she had left the oven on when she left the house, only worse.

She had not felt this bad since she let Mona Kennedy kiss her at the Christmas party, let Mona lead her by the hand into the stairwell, kiss her there, and put a hand under her skirt. She had been so drunk then. It didn't count—letting Mona finger her, while people sometimes walked by and paused to watch—because she had been almost too drunk to remember it the next day. Allie had not felt this bad since she had called Mona to tell her it had to stop, three times was three times too many, and she had not known Van was in the kitchen, listening in on the extension. *I just got engaged and I don't want to be a cheat*, she said and Mona said, *You just got engaged and you don't want to be gay, but you are. I swear you're wet right now, thinking about what I can do to you* and Allie couldn't answer because all the breath went out of her and then Van spoke up on the line and said, *Hey, Allie, let me know when you're off the phone, I was going to order pizza. Mona, good luck with your fantasy football team this weekend.*

The worst of it was that she cherished Van, who loved her without qualification, who made her waffles when she was hungover and picked her laundry up off the floor and talked sports with her father and celebrity gossip with her mother and looked at her, sometimes, the way a child looks at the ocean for the first time: with a wonder that is inseparable from joy. No one had cherished her since Theo died. After they buried him, she had never expected to be cherished again. She thought the least she could do for Donovan—for the person who loved her, she supposed, more than anyone ever had or ever would—was to avoid letting co-workers finger her in the stairwell at office parties. She hated the impulse anyway, had long wanted to rip it out of herself. In truth, she *knew* she wasn't really gay at all, but only self-destructive, and rebelling against Jesus for taking her brother too young . . . all facts she had learned at the summer camp her parents sent her to, after she sent some silly love letters to a girl in her English class. A youth pastor named Chuck had helped her see why she was deluding herself she was a homosexual and had *proved* she could enjoy natural sex by fucking her several times before the summer was done. She was wishing for Van, for his stoner's sangfroid, even more than she was wishing for another glass of champagne—while she was brooding, she had swallowed down the first—and so when she saw him push through the curtain at the waist of the plane, she thought, for a few moments, she was imagining him. It was as if she had forced him to materialize by thinking about him, a bit of wizardry every bit as mind-boggling as summoning a dragon from the Long Dark.

He looked good, in shredded denims and the blue chambray shirt she loved so much. She had worn that shirt herself sometimes, for a nightdress. He had his copper hair up in a man bun, which she didn't love; it was better down. He had a Nike bag slung over one shoulder, as if he were off to the gym—as if either of them ever went to the gym, hahaha—and wore his trademark smirk.

The flight attendant who had ushered the goth into business class pointed at Allie, and Van's smirk blossomed into a shit-eating grin.

She rose, surprised to find her legs trembling. Robin noticed as well, looked up in alarm. Allie understood the goth's business-class upgrade had been a ploy to open up the seat beside her, one Van had set in motion himself, and she was so glad to see him, glad not to have to go into the sky alone. She wanted him beside her, had a thousand things to tell him. He reached across Robin Fellows to take Allie's hands as Robin looked from one to the other in bewilderment. He leaned in to kiss her; she leaned in to kiss him; his forehead smacked her nose; his mouth missed and he kissed her chin as her lips found his ear.

"You stupid panhandle hick," she whispered, clutching him tightly, "what the poop are you doing on this plane?"

"What the poop," he whispered back. "I adore you and your whole Hallmark card vocabulary. You're like dating a two-hour Christian holiday special. Pretend you're happy."

"I don't have to pretend."

"Pretend you're even happier."

"Why?"

"Because we need a cover story, and I've got one that's perfect," he said. And then he drew away from her and raised his voice so the whole cabin could hear and said, "I love you so goddamn much, Allison Shiner, say that you'll elope with me. Let's get married tomorrow."

People laughed. Some rose from their seats for a better look at the excitement. Over Van's shoulder she saw, for the first time, Frank Heck, sitting just two rows up on the left, staring back at her with one eyebrow raised in wry amusement.

She had never been able to resist giving a crowd what they wanted. Of course she said yes.

6:45 p.m. EST

5 hours and 15 minutes until dragonedy o'clock

A freckly college student put his fingers in his mouth and whistled, and that set off most of the economy cabin, who began to applaud—a little raucously, many of them already finished with that first complimentary drink. Allie felt a tingling flush of excitement that made absolutely no sense at all, given the situation. Say one thing about Van, he had never suffered from shyness—he and his sister both knew how to seize a moment.

Someone farther back shouted, *kiss her!* and Van obliged, and Allie kissed him back. Someone else shouted, "Introducing tonight's nominees for the mile-high club!" to general laughter. Allie blushed on cue.

The flight attendant was standing in the aisle right behind them, with fresh glasses of champagne for the happy couple. He was a balding man with the slim hips of a fencer, but with a blue five o'clock shadow that gave him just a touch of a thug in an alley. When he passed the drinks over, he cried, "I'm so happy for you!" with a clear undertone of *get the fuck in your seats*. Robin twisted to get her legs out of the way and Van squeezed into the window seat, pausing to put his hands on Allie's hips and press his chest to hers.

Allie leaned into him, as if to neck, and whispered, "Donna Donna fricking Donna she told you why did she tell?"

"Because she loves you."

"Why are you here?"

"Because *I* love you," Van whispered back. "And there was never any chance I would let you do this alone."

She felt like she wanted to cry. He had caught her cheating with another woman, but here he was. She had almost got him killed, but he had come running. She didn't deserve him, she thought. She never had.

A voice came over the public address system, asking all passengers on BA 238 to give the safety video their full attention, and Allie was suddenly frightened for them both, her grip on his arm going white-knuckled. *Fifty percent of marriages in the US end in divorce. One hundred percent of deals with King Sorrow end in disaster.* "Frick. *Frick.* What are we going to do? Horation Matthews is on this flight."

"Well," he said, slyly, flashing that shit-eating grin again, "first, who cares? Because you're right. King Sorrow can't do anything to this flight with us on it. The big lizard swore to protect us, and he has to honor the deal. But there's another thing. Matthews *isn't* on the flight. You've been sadly misinformed. I know, because when I got on board, the flight attendant let me look at the manifest to see where you were sitting. Guess who pussied out and never got on this flight at all?"

"You're sure?" Allie asked, hardly daring to believe it.

He nodded. "You think I'd miss a name like 'Horation'?"

6:58 p.m. EST

5 hours and 2 minutes until dragonedy o'clock

"Congratulations are in order!" Robin said to Allie. "We must bury a bottle of white in your honor. I'm a schmuck for romance and so love a good elopement. I'm sorry you didn't get one, dear. You could be headed to the South of France or Venice or Crete, but unfortunately you'll be celebrating your nuptials with cold drizzle and bad food."

"The in-flight drinks cart is probably the greatest invention in aviation since they moved from biplanes to single-wing aircraft," Van said, and introduced himself to her.

"I wouldn't want to dirty one of the happiest nights of your young lives with cheap airline plonk," Robin said, and reached into the giant beaded bag stashed beneath the seat in front of her. "Not when I've been to the duty-free." She held up a bottle of white wine. Allie looked once—and then again. It was from a Napa vineyard called Dragon Yard. A green ribbon bound a complimentary corkscrew to the neck: a silver, handsome instrument with a dragon unwinding itself around the handle. Allie threw a wild look at Van and they both erupted into ever so slightly hysterical laughter. Robin produced a pleasant, puzzled little frown.

"It's a pinot gris," Van said, "which I jauntily called penis grease on our first date and then wondered why Allison didn't call me back."

This was a bald-faced lie, but Allie admired how smoothly it came off his tongue. His gift for invention was really underutilized in his life as a journalist, where he was, on occasion, forced to traffic in facts.

"Your betrothed already mentioned your elegance with language," Robin said.

"It's a gift."

Allie's knit satchel was by her feet, and as the plane turned for the runway, something thrummed inside it. She almost didn't notice—the whole plane was thrumming. But a minute later it thrummed again, and this time it caught her attention. She pulled the bag into her lap and dug through the contents for her flip phone. She had 1 VOICEMAIL.

She frowned, flipped the phone open, and pressed the star button to hear her voicemail. The plane began to accelerate.

It was Colin. His tone was brisk and calm, but not without urgency.

"Allie. I'm sorry I missed your calls. I was at Langley today, and they take my phone when I check in. I'm only going home now. Listen: Horation Matthews won't be traveling under that name—it's the baptismal name he received from his church. You want to look for a Randy Mathers. That's his birth name, that's what'll be on his passport. *If* he's using his passport. I wouldn't be entirely surprised if he managed to lay his hands on false papers." He breathed out and said, "I have it from Donna that you are going to try and get on the plane with him and that Van is going to join you. That for some reason you believe if you're on the plane, King Sorrow can't attack it. That isn't true. You *cannot* protect the plane by being on it. *Get off that flight.* Let whatever happens happen. This isn't our fault. We couldn't have known. Delete this message after you've listened to it. And call me when you can."

4:13 p.m. EST

January 3, 1995

102 days, 7 hours, and 47 minutes until dragonedy o'clock

"They all take a new name when they're baptized into the church," Colin told them, over tumblers of good Scotch. "Which is how Ella Gresch became Faith Matthews—the third of Horation's three wives—and her daughter June became Chastity. It's Ella Gresch on the death certificate, though."

It was Allie's turn to choose someone for King Sorrow. The others had each gone before her, beginning with Arthur in 1990. It had been Colin's turn most recently, in '94—he had sent King Sorrow after the commander of a Serbian brigade who had filled a pit with corpses in the rocky crags beyond Sarajevo. As it happened, the brigade commander didn't last until Easter. He leapt off the tenth-floor balcony of a hotel in Hungary in early March—leapt shrieking to escape the eyes of the dragon he had seen in his closet. King Sorrow was almost sulky about it. He hated it when the mouse died before he was done playing with it. *War criminals*, he complained. *They don't make 'em like they used to.*

There had been twenty-four candidates on Colin's spreadsheet the day before. Allie had narrowed it down to three: the Middle Eastern mastermind of a 1993 attempt to bomb the World Trade Center, a Hutu extremist who financed genocidal militias in Rwanda, and this last, Horation Matthews.

"Ella wedded him in 1990, on the nine-thousand-acre compound in Iowa that Matthews calls home. He's got company: there's another hundred people sharing his spread, largely composed of seven sprawling, heavily armed families. The glue that holds them together is their own personal religion, the Scripture of the Kingdom Church, a branch of Christian Identity theology."

"Christian Identity theology—is that those freaks who handle snakes?" Gwen asked.

"Allie will give them a snake to handle," Donna said. "She'll give them all the snake they can take."

"No, the Christian Identity types are white supremacists," Van said. "Their favorite cross is the one burning in a Black man's front yard."

"In theory," Colin continued, "they're led by their pastor, an elderly preacher named Jacob Weyland. Weyland ministers to them in person but addresses an audience of another thirty thousand through his Sunday morning services on shortwave radio. A few AM stations carry his broadcast too.

"But Horation is the power behind the pulpit. The property is all in his name—his legal name, Mathers—and he's the one who figured out how to keep them all fiscally solvent. Publicly, they claim to be living an agrarian lifestyle according to the dictums of scripture. But their real crop is guns. They've done especially good business turning select-fire rifles into fully automatic weapons and selling them outside gun shows."

"This is what happens," Donna said, "when you ban something that shouldn't be banned. You create a black market so scumbags like Horation Matthews can get rich."

"Exactly my point," Van said, "about marijuana. So glad you finally agree with me, Donna. You'll be signing my petition to legalize it right after we're done here, yeah?"

"Might sign your ass," Donna said, "with my bootheel."

Arthur said, "Tell us about Ella Gresch."

"And her daughter June," Gwen added.

"In November of 1992, one of Horation's three stepdaughters, Chastity—June to us—turned up at her grandmother's house, in a thin blouse and jeans, shaking uncontrollably from the cold, and her feet clad in moccasins worn to rags. She had walked and hitched nearly forty miles in them after escaping the compound.

June told her grandmother that Ella was dead and had been dead since August. June said her mother boiled to death."

In the summer, Ella/Faith had learned Horation was screwing June—raping his sixteen-year-old stepdaughter—and had made plans to slip away by night. She had the bags all packed and the bus tickets paid for when Horation found out. Ella was confined to the House of Reflection for five days to meditate upon her own faithlessness. The House of Reflection was a stone box, too small to stand up in, with an iron floor and an iron hatch that locked from the outside. Faith started screaming on day three. She was quiet again by the afternoon of day four. She had no voice left by then. Day four was the hottest of the week, 98 degrees outside, and almost 160 inside the House of Reflection, which was little more than a kiln. The dimensions of the box forced Faith to remain kneeling, forehead almost touching the floor. When they hauled her out, she was not just a wasted corpse, she was leathery from most of a week of slow roasting. Her death went unreported. Her corpse was buried on the compound, in the family graveyard.

"For the love of Christ," Gwen said.

"Well, yes," Colin said. "That's exactly how Horation viewed it. After her mother's death, June spent a day in the House of Reflection as well, to calm her hysteria. Horation wouldn't let her call her grandmother to tell her what happened. There's only the one landline in the compound, and only men are allowed to use it. No cell phones, obviously. It's still roughly 1975 in that part of the country."

Colin had got them all phones for Christmas, sleek Nokias in brushed stainless steel, a different shade for each of them. Arthur had been utterly baffled by his.

"I already have a phone," he had said. "In my kitchen. And another in my office, on campus."

"Yes, but what if you want to talk to one of us while you're out on a walk?" Colin asked.

Arthur had regarded Colin with true bewilderment. "If I'm out on a walk, couldn't I just . . . walk to a phone?"

"You can send text messages with it," Colin added, starting to sound a little desperate.

Arthur said, "But . . . if I have a phone in my hand . . . why would I text you?"

Colin considered Arthur with a mix of amazement and horror. "It's kind of beautiful. It's like the future bounces right off you."

"How's a motherfucker like Horation Matthews cook a woman to death and walk away like he burned some cookies in the oven?" Van asked.

"Well, basically, the First Amendment," Colin said. "But since we're talking about things getting burned up, who wants to go ignite the Christmas tree? It's dark enough now."

They were twenty minutes packing themselves into boots and puffy snow jackets and gloves. Colin led them—like Christopher Robin leading Pooh and the other stuffed animals—out across a snowscape swept into pearly dunes by the wind off the bay. The sun was a glow of infected red light behind the black pines in the west. In the freezing, salty air coming off the water in pulses, Allie felt almost like a human being again. When she looked around, she noticed that Gwen and Arthur lagged behind, walking together, but not talking. Sometimes they made her think of parents who had lost a child years before and were more tightly bound by their silent grief than any vow. It was hard to believe they *weren't* married, the way it seemed they sometimes held whole conversations between one another in a glance. Allie didn't have that with Van. She wondered if she ever would.

Colin was talking again. "Turns out, everyone on the compound had spent time in the House of Reflection, for one crime or another against God or their community. Horation spent a weekend in there himself, kneeling on nails, to punish himself for putting off work. He had the scars to prove it." The Christmas tree, fourteen feet high and smelling sweetly of the season, sprawled on the edge of the stony embankment. Driftwood had been piled around it for a bigger blaze. "Furthermore, it turned out Father Weyland, not Horation, was the one who commanded Ella to climb into the House of Reflection . . . and in his deposition he insisted she entered with her eyes shining to God, and that when she screamed, they were screams of joy. The House of Reflection represented a cruel, dangerous, barbaric form of punishment, but its use was entirely protected by the First Amendment's promise to allow the free exercise of religion."

"Does the First Amendment protect Horation's right to fuck his underage stepdaughter?" Donna said, her voice choked, and Allie wanted to put her arms around her.

"Charges were never brought. Chastity—sorry, June—was killed behind the wheel of her grandmother's car before they could set a trial date. She sideswiped a tree at nearly seventy miles an hour and got her head crushed in. No one could say why she was driving so fast. There were no witnesses to the accident. She left a statement that Horation Matthews had been raping her since she was fourteen. But her arms were scarred from wrist to elbow with cuts she admitted administering to herself, and in her diary, she talked about being visited by angels, and once of traveling to Jerusalem and back in a single night, carried on a cloud. Several of Horation's sons were prepared to testify that Chastity was mentally unwell and had claimed she was raped by demons, the postman, and Bill Clinton."

"She was probably telling the truth about Bill Clinton," Donna said, in a husky voice.

"You mentioned Horation has other stepdaughters?" Gwen asked.

Colin nodded. "As it happens, Horation did spend six weeks in jail, after a long standoff with state police. They wanted child protective services to interview his other children, and he wouldn't let them. He was eventually brought in under arrest, and the two surviving girls, eleven and nine, were interviewed separately. They both agreed Horation was a lovely father, and that they were happy and learning how to go to heaven." He paused, lifted an eyebrow. "The one in the cast insisted she had broken her arm falling out of a tree."

Donna's lips were pressed so tightly together they were white, which was when Allie decided.

"All right," Allie said. "Let's do him. Before the other girls are old enough for Daddy."

Donna looked at her with such gratitude, Allie felt her heart might fail her.

"Are you sure?" Colin said, his breath smoking in the darkness. "There are strong cases for the other candidates. Matthews hasn't done anything like what the Hutu militias did in Rwanda last spring. I guess the worst of it is over now, but for a few months the rivers were choked with bodies."

"No single money guy is to blame for all that murder," Donna said. "It would be like getting even with Jack the Ripper by killing his banker."

"And we can't undo a genocide," Allie said. "We missed our window to make a difference there. It isn't too late to stop Matthews. As for the other guy on the short list—what was his name? Usama bin Layden?"

"Laden."

"A nutcase who thought he was going to bring down the World Trade Center with a bomb in a van? Better luck next time."

"Gwen, can I have that box of matches?" Colin asked.

He produced a can of bear spray with a festive green ribbon tied around it; Donna had bought them all bear spray for Christmas, said it was better than Mace, better than pepper spray. He lit three sturdy kitchen matches with one hand, held them together, pointed the can, and depressed the trigger. There was a whoosh and a roar and a tongue of flame eight feet long blasted out across the Christmas tree. The branches of dried pine erupted into fire.

"Fuckin' metal!" Van cried, rising up on one foot and playing a few licks on an air guitar, and then they were all taking turns using their cans of bear spray as makeshift flamethrowers, pouring fire down on the vast tangle of branches, until the flames were twenty feet high and they had to step back from the heat.

Allie looked around at her friends, the people she loved most in the world. Their faces were damp with sweat and aglow in the infernal light of the bonfire. Colin grinned—he was often happy, but he was frugal with grins. Van was breathing hard, as if he had run up some stairs, and rubbing his nose, and Allie knew he was thinking of the cocaine zipped into the inside pocket of his parka. He liked to do lines off her stomach and from between her breasts. He said if he couldn't be in a band, he could at least do drugs like a rock star. It was his favorite form of foreplay. The glow of the flames played across Donna's bold, handsome, confident features. In the gathering dark she looked like the better version of her brother, the surer version. Gwen held a glass of Scotch in one mittened hand, taking little sips, her eyes merry in the firelight. Arthur seemed to have retreated farthest from the fire, and he alone seemed to take no cheer from it. He was contemplating Colin, appeared almost to be reading his friend's face, as he might've studied an illuminated manuscript. When he spoke, though, he spoke to Allie.

"You said it's not too late to stop him, Allison—but stop him from doing what?" Arthur said. "We know he creeps on adolescent girls. But unlike Bin Laden and the Rwandan militias, do we know he presents a threat on a large scale?"

"I think we do," Colin said, answering for her. "Him and his whole community, which King Sorrow may well destroy while he's taking out Matthews—we can hope, right? Horation has an online manifesto where he talks about crucifying federal officers and IRS agents. He writes approvingly of the Unabomber and lists the addresses of doctors who perform abortions in case 'anyone wants to pay one of these guys a visit.' I couldn't prove the manifesto is his in a court of law, but I know it's him. It was uploaded from his compound's ISP and he has consistent misspellings, favorite phrases."

"What's an ISP?" Van wanted to know.

"Who allowed him to post a manifesto online?" Arthur asked.

Colin glanced at Arthur with real surprise. "An ISP is your computer's fingerprint, and anyone can post *anything* online. Including essays threatening the wholesale slaughter of government officials."

"And AOL will just let you do that?" Arthur asked, outraged.

"He didn't post it on AOL. He posted it on the World Wide Web." Colin absorbed Arthur's baffled look and said, "Think of AOL as a medieval city. The Web is the uncivilized wasteland beyond the castle walls."

"What's out there?" Arthur asked.

"Mostly racists and pictures of cats," Colin said. "Porn is next. Soon as people get faster connections. Historical note: every new leap in technology is powered by people's desire to talk about their cats, start race wars, and look at other people fucking."

Allie said, "I don't think Tipper Gore is going to allow porn on the internet. She doesn't even like Twisted Sister. How are tits going to get past her?"

"Tits always find a way," said Donna.

"Thank God," Van said. He raised his can of bear spray and shot a great blast of dragon's breath into the night.

7:05 p.m. EST

4 hours and 55 minutes until dragonedy o'clock

Flight had always been one of Allie's simplest pleasures. She loved the feel of acceleration as a jet sped to the end of the runway, had always felt a thrill at the moment of lift, when the wheels kissed the tarmac goodbye and sprang into the air. Flying after dark was best, the way a big aircraft would slide itself effortlessly into the night.

But she hardly noticed the 747 taking off, was not aware they were in the sky until the plane banked and she glimpsed Manhattan off the starboard wing. Towers bristled from the island, blades of glass and steel, and the surrounding mist glowed with their lights. The plane rose and rose, and all the while Allie was thinking, *We're in trouble, we're in trouble, oh, God, we're in so much fucking trouble.*

Robin pinned the bottle of Dragon Yard between her thighs—an unconscious slip back into a former self, Allie thought, because that was the way a man would do it—and buried the screw deep into the cork. She worked at it with a tanned, straining forearm, and the cork thumped free, drawing the citrusy tang of the wine along behind it. Allie and Van had finished off their complimentary drinks and held out their empty champagne glasses for a healthy splash.

"To connubial bliss," Robin said, after she had poured for herself and lifted her cup to them.

Allie drank her entire glass in three burning swallows.

"Did you *know* he was going to be on this flight?" Robin asked, narrowing her eyes at Allie.

For a moment Allie thought she was talking about Horation

Matthews. Her heart kicked like a rabbit in a snare. Then she realized, from Robin's sly smile and sidelong look, that she meant Van.

"Daydreamed," Allie said, and put her head against Van's chest.

"Drink, drink," Robin said. "There's more where that came from, and you need it. You're shaking like a leaf."

"Excitement," Allie said.

The jet juddered like a pickup truck going over a washboarded dirt road as Robin lifted her own cup to her mouth. Wine slopped into her lap and she cursed floridly. No one in all the world, Allie thought, cursed with the vigor of the English. Lights flickered. Nervous laughter rippled across the cabin.

"Folks, this is Captain Lucas Vanhoenacker, welcoming you from the flight deck on behalf of the whole crew here on BA 238," came a voice over the PA. "We'll be ascending to thirty-one thousand feet, to reach some clear air, but we still expect to experience some turbulence for the first hour or two. There's a large storm system churning over this part of the Atlantic. With that in mind, I'm going to leave the seat belt light on and ask you to remain in your seats. The good news is that we've got a strong tailwind and expect to touch down in London Heathrow ahead of schedule. In the meantime, our best-in-class cabin crew will keep you comfortable for the flight. So sit back and relax—"

The plane whammed over a pocket of air, slewed sideways, and dropped hard enough to open a couple of luggage compartments. Someone squeaked. A few passengers gasped. The two men in the seats right in front of Allie grabbed each other's shoulders and laughed.

When the pilot's voice came back, he sounded close to laughing himself. "So sorry about that, folks. Try not to worry about the bumps, and thanks again for flying with British Airways."

Robin Fellows, for one, clearly viewed the seat belt light as a suggestion rather than a command. She pushed herself up and handed the half-full bottle of wine to Allie.

"I entrust this to your care," Robin said. "And I'll be disappointed if it's not a bit lighter by the time I get back, loves. I have to see if I can save this skirt, it's a Helmut Lang."

She made her way up the aisle, swaying, touching the backs of seats to steady herself.

"The fuck's going on?" Van asked. "You had a voicemail and it was like someone knifed you."

"Colin tried to get us before the flight took off." Allie turned her face to his, as if to whisper sweet nothings into his ear, and said, "Horation Matthews *is* on board."

"No," Van murmured. "I saw the flight manifest. He can't be."

"He can. He is. But he's not flying under that name. He's flying under the *other* name, his *old* name. Something Mathis, like the singer."

"Randy Mathers. But even if he is on board, it doesn't matter. As long as we're on the flight King Sorrow can't touch it. He can't hurt us. That's the rule."

"That's what I thought too," Allie told him. "That's what he told me. But Colin said not to believe it."

"What do you mean? *Who* told you the flight would be safe if you were on board?" Looking at her with sudden horror.

"King Sorrow. He told me if I was on the flight tonight, no one had to die but Horation."

"You—you decided to get on the plane because *King Sorrow* told you to?" Van asked. What little color was left in his face drained out of it. He reached for the wine, tugged it out of her hand, and drank straight from the bottle.

She pulled it away from him and jammed the cork back into it, worked the corkscrew free. That corkscrew was a reassuring weight in her hand, the silver length of the dragon pressing into her palm like a rosary, like a holy medallion.

Van shook his head. "No. *No*. We've got a deal. King Sorrow *swore* he would protect us. I *remember*. It was a few years ago, and I was stoned as fuck, but I remember that much."

This was wrong *wrong* WRONG WRONG. They had fucked it up—of course they had fucked it up, a drunk and a cokehead, there had never been any hope they could get it right. She didn't know how they had fucked it up, but somehow they had. She knew it in her stomach. They were Jayne Nighswander and Ronnie Volpe in the Ranchero, on a one-way trip to the incinerator. And only *they* could've fucked it up so badly, her and Van. Gwen would have somehow avoided the danger. Colin would've seen King Sorrow was laying a trap—because that's what it was, Allie understood that now, and she had run straight into it, as fast as her little legs could carry her—and found a way to invert it, use the lizard's own scheme against him.

And Arthur . . . Arthur would never take anything King Sorrow said at face value. What had Arthur told them once? Words were a dragon's weapon, every bit as much as fire.

Then Robin was back and it was Allie's turn to move. She couldn't stay in her seat anymore. Her anxiety was a loaded spring, ready to punch her to her feet. She undid the seat belt and plunged into the aisle, past Robin, started toward the waist of the plane.

No sooner had she started moving toward the front than the plane banged and shook and pitched her to one side. She reached out to steady herself before she could go down, wound up putting her hand on the crotch of the man sitting in the row in front of her, as if grabbing for his balls.

"Oh, jeez!" she cried, pulling away.

He smiled sociably up at her. "No worries. Usually, I'd have to buy a lady a couple drinks to get that far."

He was forty-ish, with a round pleasant face and a head of curly mouse-colored hair. Kindly eyes blinked behind a pair of gold-framed square glasses. The man sitting next to him, in the window seat, was in every way his twin, except he was thirty years older at least. The older man smiled up at her, the corners of his very blue eyes etched with fine wrinkles.

"Excuse him," the older man said. "He has a childish sense of humor. He got it from me." His eyes narrowed. "Are you all right? Are you going to be sick?"

None of us are all right, she wanted to say. *This plane is never going to land*, she wanted to tell him, and the moment she thought it she knew it was true. She had never had a truer thought in all her life.

"I never get airsick," she said. "I'm a very good flyer. I'm just a bad walker. So sorry, hope I didn't squash anything."

"Only my romantic hopes," said the forty-year-old, clapping a hand to his chest. "I may have overheard you're getting married tomorrow. When they bring the drinks around, I'll raise a glass of rum and coke to you."

"I *hope* I'm getting married tomorrow. He may not want me if I wet myself."

She pushed herself upright again and swayed on down the aisle, while the plane rattled and rumbled. At the edge of her vision she saw Frank Heck watching her stagger along, his eyelids heavy and the eyes beneath them watchful and sly.

She swatted through the curtain into the darkened compartment at the waist of the plane. The gloom already smelled faintly of the lavatory, an antiseptic odor that only somewhat covered the stronger scent of urine. Curtains blocked the view into the front of the plane. A carpeted staircase climbed to a second floor. The gangly flight attendant with the bristly chin was on his feet, doing something with the microwave. He caught her eye as she made for the head.

"Ma'am, this isn't the best time to be out of your seat—"

"Need the little girl's room, *bad*," Allie said and clapped the door shut behind her.

She dropped the lid and collapsed onto the toilet just as the plane hit the next burst of rough air. This turbulence was of an entirely different order than any that had come before. It was as if flak were exploding outside the jet, buffeting it from either side. The plane shook and shook, and the light went out, and in the total darkness she braced herself against the walls. One of the cabinets under the sink popped open, banged shut, swung open again.

"I hope they've got something tasty for tonight's in-flight meal," King Sorrow said from the black hole under the sink. "I know I'm looking forward to mine."

His great eye opened and stared out at her: yellow sclera, with an infected red shot all through it, and a black pupil as big as a mail slot. The plane jolted and the fluorescent lights flickered back on and for an instant he was gone. Then the plane took another hit and the light went out again and that eye reappeared.

"I thought the seats in coach were bad," Allie said. "How's it under the sink?"

King Sorrow laughed. "I'm not really here. You know that. There's a part of me inside you . . . inside all of you. That's what you're seeing now. The real me is a mile or two off your starboard wing. More or less. I've almost come all the way through. I'm dropping in and out of your reality like a stone skipping across the surface of a loch. They've got me on radar, flicking in and out of sight. Not just your pilots. NORAD. They might scramble F-16s. I'd enjoy that. I've never fought a modern fighter jet. I was over Dresden in World War II, but the German air defenses were of a far cruder nature."

"You fought for the Allies?" Allie heard herself asking, as if it mattered.

"I fought for Joe Stalin. Well. Not Joe. For his mystic. Wolf Messing. Less of a wolf, more of a goose, I'm afraid, and in the end, his goose was well cooked. But the firebombing of Dresden? Oh, that was a good night." He paused, then said, "Come to think of it, I've never obliterated a passenger jet before. This plane is bigger than me! The secret to a happy life is always finding new challenges."

"You can't touch this plane. Van and I are aboard, and you made a promise. You swore to protect us. You swore that this plane would be safe, as long as I was on it."

King Sorrow's unblinking eye looked amused. "Oh, darling, how could you misunderstand me so? I said if you were on this plane, no one but Horation needed to die. And I meant it! No one else needs to die . . . as long as you kill Horation yourself before midnight!"

"That's . . . that's not fair. You can't. You swore to protect us."

"I swore to protect you from ENEMIES, my love, not gravity." Now he did chuckle. "I told you I would protect you from any man or woman who stood against you. But I am neither man nor woman. I also told you that come Easter morning, I will have the life I am promised, or I will have one of your lives as forfeit. If I am required to claim the latter to win the former, I am content I have still kept my word to you."

"There are children aboard."

"Oh, Allie. I had a sympathetic, loving heart once—it was delicious."

"Please. I'll riddle with you."

"But we're *already* riddling, Allison. Don't you see? If Horation Matthews is alive, aboard this 747, when it crosses an international time line into midnight, I will tear this fucking aircraft out of the sky and send four hundred and one souls to their doom, yours and Donovan's included. But you can save them! The power lies in your nimble, piano-playing hands. The only question is how. That's the riddle before you this evening: How are you going to murder the man on this crowded flight, at thirty thousand feet, before someone stops you?" He closed his eye in a slow wink, then opened it again. "It isn't all bad, Allie. It is the fondest wish of Donovan McBride's heart to live the rest of his life with you at his side. And the way tonight is going, I think he's going to get what he wanted. Who says dreams don't come true?"

The plane struck turbulence again, and this time the light flickered on and off as the whole superstructure shook. Unhappy cries rose from beyond the bathroom door. Then, abruptly, they skated into still air. The light in the lavatory came on and stayed on. The door beneath the sink flapped back and forth, showing the shallow, empty space behind.

7:30 EST

4 hours and 30 minutes until dragonedy o'clock

When Allie emerged from the lavatory, she found she had the waist of the plane to herself. The first thing she did was find an adorably small bottle of Jack Daniels in the drinks cart, screw off the top, and throw it back. It hit hard, and she swayed on her heels, and for a moment she felt like an inflatable girl, a plastic woman full of sweet emptiness and air, so weightless she might've lifted right out of her shoes.

When her eyes stopped watering, she twitched the curtain two inches to one side, to inspect economy, what BA called "World Traveller." There had to be almost three hundred people back there—they called them souls when you were aloft, three hundred souls—and flight attendants moving among them. Allie couldn't possibly take in all of them, could hardly see to the back of the cabin. Her eyes stung at the hopelessness of finding Horation Matthews among all the rest. It couldn't be done. For all she knew he was in disguise, wearing a wig, a fake mustache. She hardly knew what he looked like *un*disguised, and a figure came back to her, that people only recognize a familiar face out of context 8 percent of the time.

But then she looked, *really looked*. Her gaze began to flick from face to face, registering each for a moment, no more. She saw: a young Black man, dressed in office casual; his children; his wife, leaning over the kids to help them with a *Mad Libs*; an old man with a Ken Follett novel, his wife pressed to his side, her hand resting gently, unconsciously, on his thigh; a bald woman with her head in a pastel silk wrap. Allie studied her for an extra moment, wondering if she could be a Christian nationalist with a shaved skull and lipstick, but there was no psychopathy in this woman, only cancer. Allie's gaze drifted on, sorting passengers as she sorted numbers on a spreadsheet, pushing aside the thought that in a few hours they'd all be dead. That child there would die with half her face burned off her skull. That laughing teenage girl would hit the ocean hard enough to be liquefied herself.

She looked and looked, but it was going too slowly, it was taking too long, and desperation chased all the patience out of her. She let the curtain fall back into place. In the next moment, the desperation ebbed, and a wild certainty took its place. She couldn't spot him in the back of the plane because he *wasn't* in the back of the plane. She had only ever seen the one photo, and yet she was sure if he was there to be found, she would recognize him in an instant . . . and perhaps he would recognize *her* too, in some fashion. He was being hunted, driven from his home, and running for his life. He would be on high alert and possibly dazed with panicked exhaustion. She would know him by the way he sat, ready to spring from his chair, ready to scream. And he would know her simply because she was looking for him. It was an absurd notion, but also felt like it could be true.

She stepped across the dim galley to the other curtain, the one across the entrance to business, tugged it a little to one side for a look. The bald flight attendant was in the aisle, leaning over a passenger, possibly taking a dinner order, and no sooner had she touched the curtain than he lifted his head and caught her eye, as alert to her as if she had jangled a bell. She dropped the curtain. Frig. She sensed he was already moving toward her. In another moment he'd gently but firmly drive her back to her seat. She wondered about diving into the bathroom once more—a childish notion—and her gaze fell on the staircase. For the first time she noticed that the red carpet on those steps was stitched with copper dragons, unicorns, and lions. No doubt the entire British Airways fleet was subtly decorated with the impossible bestiary of the empire, the Welsh dragon, the Scottish unicorn, and the English lion . . . and yet in a glance Allie knew this was a tongue-in-cheek joke from King Sorrow to her and understood with a sudden surreal confidence that she would find Horation above.

Allie grasped the banister and ascended, the plane pitching her from side to side. She heard moans, back in economy, a sick lowing of unhappiness, and she felt like a wraith slipping loose from some region of the damned. She paused at the top step. Here was another little room for the flight crew, a sort of pantry with space for a coffee machine, a small fridge, a lavatory to port, an emergency door to starboard. The second-floor cabin was not large and only about half-full: a dozen rows, with a single aisle up the middle, two seats on either side. No one at all sat in the aftmost row. In the next row forward, a couple in their late fifties sat to port. A single man occupied the aisle seat to starboard, the window seat empty. This man, traveling alone, seemed to sense someone standing in the aisle behind him, and turned his head to stare blankly back at her.

Horation's eyes were puffy slits, the eyes of a former boxer, and his cheeks showed the corrosion of youthful acne. For all that, he was not unattractive. He projected a sleepy, surly masculinity, had the look of a man who didn't rattle as a point of principle. His gaze took her in, flicking down the length of her body, then up to her face, and he smiled, as if he had been waiting for her to turn up.

The cabin went dark. The screen, at the far end of the compartment, lit up with the Paramount Pictures opening credit, a whirl of stylized stars around snowcapped mountains. Time for the inflight movie; time for a little fun in the dark.

7:38 EST

4 hours and 22 minutes until dragonedy o'clock

She wasn't sure what to do but didn't think she ought to stand at the top of the stairs while she made up her mind. She started moving, touching seats to steady herself as she made her way forward. Allie had just made it alongside Horation Matthews when

8:39 Atlantic Time Zone (AST)

3 hours and 21 minutes until dragonedy o'clock

the 747 took a hard jolt and seemed to *drop*, to fall like a brick. Allie's feet lifted off the floor. She grabbed for something to steady herself and got a hand on Horation's shoulder. The airliner stabilized with a thump and Allie crashed into his lap. He had a drink in his hand, but he was graceful, lifted his plastic cup away without letting it spill. Not alcohol, Allie noticed, but milk.

"Make yourself at home," he said.

"I'm sorry," she said. "I'm so sorry."

She quickly slid out of his lap and into the empty seat between him and the window.

The plane found a patch of smooth air and settled into it. Allie found it hard to look at the killer beside her. She glanced past him, checking how many people had noticed her sudden appearance. The answer was: no one. Directly across the aisle, a slender, silver-haired woman in a tracksuit was asleep—or trying to sleep, anyway—with her head against one of those little white pads they euphemistically referred to as "pillows." Just beyond her, in the window seat, was an equally slender silver-haired man, watching the movie with a pair of headphones clapped to his ears.

"Allie," she said.

"I'm Randy."

"Are you?" she said. "I'd think the turbulence would've killed the mood."

He stared at her from beneath those drowsy, half-lowered eyelids, studying her like a virologist looking at a sample on a slide.

"Do you mind if I sit with you? I don't think I can sit alone. Too scared."

"Take a load off. I don't mind. You got to think that if we were bouncing over a backroad like this, no one would give it a second thought."

"I'm not worried about the turbulence."

He looked at her again, rotating his head on the thick stump of his neck. His barely there smile, his whole air of sleepy calm, offended her. The arrogance—the stupid certainty of it—was an affront to her sense of decency.

"Did you know," she said, "when you got on this plane, that you were putting all these people at risk, Horation? The King is coming for you."

She turned her face away from him, so she wouldn't have to face his inexplicably offensive, self-satisfied smile. She didn't see his right hand flash out, didn't know he was reaching for her until his hand clamped on her neck.

"What did you say?" he asked.

He squeezed so hard, so unexpectedly, she couldn't reply for a moment. She shoved herself back in her seat, kicking her heels, gasping. One shoe almost came off. Across the aisle, the older woman slept on. Her husband, in the window seat, stared raptly at the in-flight movie.

The plane rattled over rough air. The film flickered. Or maybe the flickering was in her head.

He relaxed his grip. Then his face was close to hers, and there was a frightening blandness to his expression, a look bordering on disinterest.

"Who are you?"

"He's after me too. The King," she said. It came to her all at once, just the right lie to tell. "You want to choke me out? Go ahead. You'll be doing me a favor. Better than being on this plane when he blasts it out of the sky."

He studied her mildly. He was so calm, it was hard to remember he had been strangling her a moment before. "You're safe with me.

He won't touch this plane. He'd *like* to. But he won't. Can't." After a moment he nodded to the window. "He's out there, you know. I can *feel* him. I feel him the way a rabbit feels the shadow of the owl. I feel him in my *blood*. Do you feel that too?"

"I guess I do," she said . . . and maybe she did. There was the mark they all wore, that tattoo they could only see in reflections—and even then, only sometimes—the wyvern that wound up her torso. She felt it on her skin, like the boning in a corset. She supposed she had been feeling it since she began to approach the airport, although in the rush and the panic she had not tuned into her own body, not paused to collect her breath and see what she was feeling.

He nodded to himself, looking her over. "You know my devotional name." It wasn't exactly a question.

"I had no idea you went by any other."

"How do you know about me at all? What are you doing on this plane?"

"I'm looking for you. What do you think I'm doing? I riddled with King Sorrow. I wanted to know if there was anyone else in . . . in my situation."

"Your situation?"

"Marked."

"For death."

She nodded. "I riddled with him and won and he told me about you. He said if I found you on this flight I might survive the night."

"He wasn't lying," Horation said, with some satisfaction. "What did you have to offer him if you lost?"

"My grandmother," she said. "He wanted my permission—I don't know why he even needs it—to tear her apart with his claws."

"Wickedness always requires an invitation: to one's house, to one's heart. And you were willing to gamble your grandmother's life?"

"Sure. She used to pull her false teeth out and snap them at me to scare me when I was little. Nasty yellow teeth. They smelled like she was already a corpse." This was all true enough, although her grandmother and her false teeth had gone into the grave almost a decade ago.

Horation laughed, a deep, low rumble. "And you were just as willing to risk the lives of these other passengers as I am, or you wouldn't be here."

"He said it was my only chance," she told him. "He said if I wanted to live, I needed to find you. Why is he after you?" Wanting to wipe the irritating half smile off his face, wanting him to remember the woman he had burned to death, the girl-child he had run off the road.

"For the same reason dragons rose up against knights in the Dark Ages. To stop the crusade. To stop me from sticking a knife in the heart of an evil power."

"What evil power?" Allie asked.

"The IRS. The FBI. The ATF. The Elders of Zion. Different heads on the same beast. We're moving against them now in our boldest stroke ever. That's what this is about."

"Oh," she said. "That's it then. It must be the goddamn Elders of Zion. That should've been my first guess." Thinking to herself that truly evil people were always too stupid, too lost in their own paranoid daydreams, to know they were evil.

He shot an appraising look at her, cold and speculative, and she wondered if she had put him on his guard again.

"You're talking Jews, right?" Allie said, feeling good now about being a little drunk. White wine was basically inspiration juice. "I was on a jury last year. Jewish judge. Jewish lawyers for the prosecution. They had some teenage boy on trial for burning down a synagogue. I was the lone vote to acquit. They had to declare a mistrial." Every word was a lie. She had read about the synagogue trial in the *Hartford Courant* on a weekend in Bristol with Van.

"Was the boy guilty?"

"Yes."

"So why didn't you convict?"

"Because I thought the kid was cute. He looked just like the actor in *Blue Lagoon*. Chris Atkins. He was too sexy to send to jail. Boy, those prosecutors were mad, though. It was worth it just to see how mad they got. They were just about tearing their Jew beards out. The judge too—I thought he was going to eat his yarmulke." Her father had heard exactly this kind of nasty stuff from his own supporters in his last couple years of office, at town hall meetings. Her father had one donor, a strapping fortysomething who owned a chain of twenty gyms in Ohio, who told him in complete seriousness that the Federal Reserve Board had engineered the recession of the 1980s on behalf of the Jewish Illuminati. Then there was a middle-aged woman in smart middle-aged clothes who braced him after a town hall to ask why he had voted to financially support a Holocaust museum when the Holocaust was a hoax. He had got out not long after that, didn't want to run anymore. There was more money in lobbying, and he didn't have to stand there with a big shit-eating grin on his face and nod while one of his voters told him fluoridated water was making people gay.

The plane rumbled continuously, like a big truck moving over grooved road.

"The Jews are a vindictive race," he said. "No doubt they put the dragon on you much as they put him on me."

"Why are you going to England?" she asked and waited for him to say he had found out about Arthur. Why Arthur, she wondered, and not the rest of them?

Only Arthur never came into it. Horation said, "There's some kind of stain on me—an invisible taint."

"A taint?" Allie asked, thinking of the dusky highway between nuts and asshole, and all at once she was fighting to hold down the giggles. She knew that was hysteria as much as hilarity working upon her. She knew too how dangerous it would be to laugh at this man, had not forgotten how efficiently he had closed her windpipe with one hand.

But he didn't clock her reaction. "I have been advised by the pastor of our church that there's a pool on the coast of England, in a place called Hastings. It's called St. Helen's Well. If I can find it, I can cleanse my evil taint."

Allie bent over, biting a knuckle to keep from screaming with laughter.

He began to stroke her back. "Are you all right?"

She nodded without looking up at him and took the knuckle out of her mouth long enough to gasp. "It's all the shaking around. It's giving me an upset stomach."

"And you've been drinking. I can smell it on you. How much have you had?"

"Too much." She took a deep breath, tried to exhale that wild, suicidal urge to howl with laughter. "St. Helen's Well?"

"A sacred font. A virgin child—a novice nun—was killed there by a troll when she wouldn't surrender her honor to him. I take 'troll' to mean a Black or a Jew. Though maybe there really are trolls. The existence of dragons would imply the possibility, wouldn't it? At any rate, some of her blood was preserved in a bottle, as a holy relic, and it is said a touch of it may heal the most desperate wounds. And the tears she shed, as she was dying, splashed to the ground and became a torrent of clear, blessed waters that have bubbled forth ever since. A man can wash off all evil marks there. A woman too." Looking at her meaningfully.

She thought about Ella Gresch, who had roasted to death screaming for water, screaming for help, and thought Horation Matthews would need a hell of a soak to wash that off him.

"And how does your pastor know about it?"

"He has made a study of miracles."

"But you'll never get there. To this well. In five hours it'll be Easter Sunday, and the King will blow this plane out of the air."

"Four hours," he said. "Possibly only three. I imagine we crossed into UTC-4—that's the Atlantic Time Zone—some while ago. We're rushing toward the hour of midnight as fast as it's rushing toward us." He didn't sound worried.

"We'll die. We'll all die."

"You must think not," he said, "or you wouldn't be on this plane with me. He said you might find safety with me . . . and you have. I am protected, for now. And so are you, as long as you're by my side."

"How are you protected?" she asked. He seemed so sure of himself.

"How much do you know about me?" he asked.

"I looked you up in the library—and on Yahoo. I know you're in a pretty intense church. I know the federal government doesn't like the things your pastor says on the radio. Jacob Weyland, is it?"

"They don't like that he goes on the radio and says there is a power higher than the US government. That there is a law higher than their law."

"Well, or that he says nurses and doctors who perform abortions ought to be beheaded."

"Do you spend a lot of time worrying about the rights of medical butchers who ram vacuums into women and suck babies out in pieces?" His tone never changed in pitch, never expressed anything in the way of feeling.

She ignored that and said, "And there was also a kerfuffle about plastic explosives? You were making your own and distributing the packages to militia groups?"

"Chemistry doesn't belong to the government, Miss . . . ?"

She hesitated, then said, "Alice Toklas," not sure why that name came to her. She had read it somewhere once, maybe in college. She said, "That's all I know."

"Not all. You also know about the dragon." He laced his fingers together. "If there was ever any doubt in my mind about the things I've had to do—about the life I've chosen to live—then it's behind me now. I knew there were bad people out there, people behind the whole rigged system, the banks and the courts, the abortion clinics and TV. People who want to keep us numb and passive while they spread sickness. People who . . ."

But she didn't care and found it hard to stay focused on what he was saying. He lectured her like someone reading from an old text, a religious tract from an earlier century. With his pale-eyed calm, and habit of speaking in the rhythms of one delivering a sermon, he was an impressive figure. But almost everything in his head was a cliché. Allie had been at the get-even game long enough to know that most really bad men thought entirely in clichés. You would expect a paranoid to have a rich fantasy life, but in fact, most of them brimmed with the stalest sort of rubbish, and in the next 120 seconds or so, he managed to touch on all of it, working through the whole trite checklist:

√ global banking conspiracies operated by the new world order
√ the coming race war
√ the secret agenda behind rap music, namely, encouraging America's daughters to engage in miscegenation
√ the secret agenda behind Madonna's music, namely, encouraging America's sons to try sucking the occasional dick
√ Vince Foster
√ Janet Reno
√ Hillary Clinton
√ Jews, Jews, and more Jews

He was like the flat-earther who believed the world was a vast game board resting on the top of a tower of turtles. To Horation Matthews, the entirety of American life was a morally bankrupt world, held up by a cabal of Jews. It was Jews all the way down. She didn't know how you could fix a person like that. She didn't know how one shook their maddening, serene certainty.

". . . again and again they have tried to turn their worldly forces against me: their courts, their tax collectors, their corrupt lawmen." He put a hand on her wrist, and she stirred herself to look at him with rapt admiration. "Every time, I made fools of them. There was nothing left but for our enemies to call upon powers unnatural. But if they believed their King of Sorrows would shatter my nerve or my belief in God's power, they misread me entirely. My faith has never been more certain than it is now. The devil has moved one of his pieces against me, which proves there is a game in play. And you can't play chess with just the black pieces. A white army must surely stand opposed. I have countered his move with a play of my own. My confederates are moving even now. Parker and Bridges. My own dragons."

She frowned at that, wondering who they were, then let it go. It was a problem for another night, if there ever was another night.

"None of this tells me why you think you're safe on this plane," she said.

He lifted a finger to signal for patience. "But you needed to understand why they hate me: it's the power of my beliefs, the power of my religion, which has held them at bay a thousand times already and will hold them at bay again tonight. Before I broke camp, I prayed with our pastor, Father Weyland. And then my brothers and I helped him onto a cross. He remains there even now, praying for my safety."

"Tied to a cross?"

He stared at her blandly. It took her a moment to understand, and when she did, she felt a throb of horror in the pit of her stomach.

"*Nailed?* You and your brothers *nailed* him to a cross?"

"Suffering is a crucible in which the raw ore of prayer is turned into an iron blade. Father Weyland's spirit holds the dragon at bay even now."

She laughed incredulously. "How old is he?"

"I don't know. Eighties."

"You left an eighty-year-old nailed to a cross? Are you sure he's still praying to save you? If I was in *his* holy loincloth, I'd be praying to die. He probably *is* dead by now!"

"I doubt it. He is strong in faith and body. My brothers will bring him water. My wives will wipe the blood from his wrists and the sweat from his brow."

Allie supposed it wasn't worth raising an eyebrow over *wives*, plural. When you were talking to a man who had nailed his religious guide to a cross, it seemed a bit trivial to argue the ethics of polygamy.

"We need to get off this plane. If King Sorrow is really out there—if he's really coming for us tonight—we need to make them land."

"How would we do that?"

"I could tell them I'm having a heart attack."

He placed two fingers on her wrist. "I don't think they'd believe you. Your pulse isn't even very fast."

"They wouldn't want to risk someone dying on the flight."

"People die on planes, same as anywhere else. They cover them with a blanket and pretend they're sleeping so as not to frighten the other passengers. Didn't you know that?"

She shivered.

"You could—I don't know—scream at me. Throw a punch. If we had a fight, a physical altercation—"

"—then we would be subdued and arrested when we land in London. And that won't do. I need to get to St. Helen's Well, and so do you. Therein lies our chance of salvation." He sat back in his seat and stared straight ahead. "We will be washed clean and then find the serpent in his lair and have off his head. In truth, King Sorrow is more afraid of us than we are of him."

"Wow," Allie said. "Speak for yourself, bro."

9:10 AST

2 hours and 50 minutes till dragonedy o'clock

Llewellyn Wren had loved his puzzle books, dainty mysteries by little old Englishwomen in which murder was an infuriating riddle. Allie had tried to read a Miss Marple once but gave up less than halfway through, couldn't get into it. Christie didn't address the sort of mysteries she cared about, like why Theo, who was fearless and kind, had died a virgin while she lived on, someone who got drunk and made out with women, someone who had to fake enjoying sex with her fiancé when she was sober. Her own heart was the most perplexing mystery she could imagine; her own impulses frightened and bewildered her.

But now she wished she had stuck with Dame Agatha. She had to solve a locked-room mystery between now and midnight, which was rushing at them at more than five hundred miles an hour. She had to figure out a way to kill Horation Matthews—a man significantly more imposing and physically powerful than her—in his first-class seat without being seen or connected to him.

He could believe whatever he wanted, but Allie doubted a scrawny, deluded old man nailed to a cross in central Iowa was going to help anyone. King Sorrow must've chortled at the idea. The dragon would view Jacob Weyland's slow, miserable crucifixion as an entertaining bonus. Maybe she was wrong. She wanted to be wrong. If belief could bring a dragon through from the Long Dark, maybe belief could keep one there, at least for a while.

But she didn't think she was wrong. The dragon had been hunting people off Colin's Enemies List since 1990, five years now, and all of them had prayed for intercession, had suffered, bled, feared, and bargained with Jesus, Allah, and the stars. It always ended in fire. Allie didn't know how hard it would be to penetrate the scales slabbing King Sorrow's body, but she was quite certain that devout prayer bounced right off them.

She was less certain about St. Helen's Well, where Horation hoped to scrub his evil taint. It didn't matter, though. He wasn't ever going to find out about St. Helen's Well. He wasn't even going to get to Heathrow. His life was going to end on this flight. The only real question was whether Allie could end it before King Sorrow did. Before King Sorrow blasted him, and all the rest of them, right out of the sky.

Horation was eighty pounds heavier than her, a foot taller, and looked as fit and healthy as an active-duty marine. She was not confident she could kill him even if she had a gun . . . he might well take it away from her and club her to death with it. She had one thing going for her, which was that he seemed to accept her as a possible confederate, rather than an adversary. Two things going for her, actually: he viewed women as helpless, hapless creatures, rated them not much higher than children. He might underestimate her.

She hadn't a clue how to go at him, though. She wished for another glass of wine, wished to be drunker. Inspiration lay somewhere just beyond a blood alcohol level of .12 percent. She was a little like a wine bottle herself now, every useful thought corked up in the bottleneck between conscious thought and unconscious possibility.

The corkscrew, she thought, and remembered that silver dragon embossed on its handle.

"You're drinking milk," she said.

"Alcohol makes you weak."

"Alcohol makes you drunk. Under the current circumstances, I say that's better than being sober. Look, what if your priest can't protect you? What if King Sorrow cuts this plane in half at the stroke of midnight? Have you considered that?"

He lowered his head and thought it over. Then he said, "I put it in God's hands. He is my sword and my shield."

And as if to punctuate this line of thought, there was a stroke of lightning so bright, Allie thought it had struck the plane. The cabin became a blinding capsule of light, a negative image of itself.

Someone screamed. The plane seemed to fall, to drop straight down, maybe ten feet, before arresting its plunge. Allie cast her gaze outside and there was a rent in the black thunderheads, and in the dying flare of lightning, King Sorrow was there. The sight was like being struck by lightning itself. It was a thunderclap of wonderment and terror.

She did not see the King himself. The lightning ignited a cloud from within and projected his shadow in sharp relief against a distant wall of churning pale vapor. It was impossible to guess his size. The shadow, though, was as big as the 747 itself. That flash of brightness pinned his shadow in place for one instant, his great, bat-like wings lifted above the colossal mass of his torso. Jaws of shadow gaped, as if he were screaming. Or laughing. His tail was a whip that went on forever, streaming behind him, disappearing into the larger darkness.

Black clouds whipped by and he was gone.

A sound rose around them. It was almost like a mournful, wordless song, a sustained, quavering note of despair, a mix of screams and moans, which was how Allie knew other people had seen the shadow too. The plane swam violently back and forth. Lights flickered. Allie found herself on her feet, without realizing she had stood.

Only Horation seemed undisturbed. He hadn't seen King Sorrow's shadow, and she doubted he'd care if he had. All up and down the cabin, passengers had thrown off their headphones and lifted their heads from pillows to gaze out in alarm. But Horation took only a cursory glance toward the window.

"You want to know what I'll do if the beast tears this plane in two?" he said quietly. "I'll die. That's all. I'll die, and a few hundred people—people who blindly paid taxes to a government that would disarm them to neutralize and sterilize the white race—will die with me. My brother is prepared to send a letter taking credit for the destruction of the plane. If the wreckage is ever found, I'm sure no one will be able to tell the difference between dragon's breath and high explosive." He let her take that in, then added, "But it won't come to that. Not if the prayers of a faithful man count for anything. And if my faith wasn't dangerous, the dragon never would've come after me in the first place." That maddening half smile was back on his face, and she thought whatever happened to the rest of them, it would almost be worth it to see King Sorrow plunge a claw through one of the portholes and rake that look off his kisser.

"I need a moment," Allie said.

She reeled past him into the aisle. He didn't stop her. No one saw her go. All the other passengers were gazing raptly into the simmering darkness beyond their windows. She might never have been there at all.

The waist of the plane was as dark as a basement, and at first Allie didn't see the gangly flight attendant, Albert Shook, or the little blond flight attendant standing next to him. They didn't see her, either, not at first. Mr. Shook had a phone clenched between shoulder and ear and was using both hands to direct his colleague back toward economy.

"Keep them calm," he was saying to her, "and make sure everyone has their shades down. Tell them the storm is keeping people from sleeping. Reach right over and lower the fucking shades yourself, while you thank them for their cooperation. And if anyone says they saw a—"

The blonde's gaze darted sidelong and fell upon Allie. She squeezed Shook's arm.

"Ma'am," Shook said, looking around and smiling in a way that made her think of a dog baring his teeth. "We can't have people roaming the cabin right now. Your seat, please!"

"I'll walk her back," Van said, ducking through the curtain from economy. "I was just coming to check on her. She's been fighting airsickness the whole last hour. Either that or the thought of getting married to me is making her physically ill."

Van offered the flight attendants a weak smile, gripped Allie's elbow, and propelled her through the curtain into economy. Twin strips of light ran down the aisle, casting a dim, golden glow about their ankles. The rest of the cabin was in gloom. The strongest source of illumination was the movie, playing on a fold-down screen against the forward cabin wall. Passengers stared toward the front of the plane with the terror of people who have been made to dig a pit and are now gazing up into rifle barrels. She was hit with a sour milk stink, the reek of fresh vomit.

Van was right behind her, but when he tried to lead her back to their seats she held him where he was, in the dim little entryway at the head of the cabin.

"He's here," she said, in a breathless hush. "Horation Matthews. Upstairs. I found him. We talked." She considered this fact with growing amazement. It seemed so astonishing, she had to repeat it: "We *talked*."

Van's features paled to the point of bloodlessness. "Why the fuck would you *talk* to him? We don't want to have anything to do with him! The safest thing for us to do is stay the hell away from him."

"No," Allie said. "No, we *can't* stay away from him. Oh, Van. We're in trouble. So much trouble. Colin was right."

Van shook his head. "The iguana has to protect us, that's one of the rules."

"He *doesn't*. He left a loophole big enough to fly a dragon through. King Sorrow only has to protect us from any *people* who come after us. Not from himself. Not from a burning plane."

"He told you if you were on the plane, no one but Horation needed to die."

"Yeah. And it's true. No one needs to die but Horation . . . as long as we kill him ourselves. Before midnight." *Not midnight. Before dragonedy o'clock*, she thought.

Van seemed dazed, his bright eyes struggling to focus. "With what? How?"

"You have to go to the cockpit. Tell them to land the plane. Right now. I can't do it. I smell like a wino."

"Where are we supposed to land? We're over the North Atlantic. I don't think there's anything down there except icebergs and water a mile deep."

She wished she had got Colin or Arthur on the phone. Colin was a deft strategist, would've known how to stop the plane from taking off without putting himself at risk. Logic puzzles didn't puzzle him. Finding his way to the surest solution—in a single, confident stroke—was Colin's primary personality trait. Arthur wasn't smart that way. He needed time to work things out; he got snarled up in the morality of things; he wanted to read a few books before he made up his mind. Arthur tripped himself up with his regret and his doubts, whereas Colin never let his conscience get in the way of making a decision. And yet for all that, Arthur had not just studied and written about English cathedrals. He had built one himself, in his head, a cathedral of fact and history, language and art. He had built it one block at a time, a stonemason of the mind. Arthur would've read something, heard something in a seminar, translated something from twelfth-century Coptic that would illuminate a way out of the corner they were in. No doubt the Copts had a lot of thoughts about preventing dragons from destroying jetliners.

But for herself, she had only ever been good at statistics and trying to make up for what her parents lost when they lost Theo. Van knew the lyrics to every song the Stones had ever recorded but was utterly baffled by conundrums. Arthur had tried that one about the goose, the fox, and the bag of beans on Van. Van wanted to know what kind of fox: "Redhead? Blond? I'm partial to blondes." His solution was to drown the goose, eat the beans, and sweetly lay the fox by the riverside.

The plane shimmied underfoot and Van lurched into her, then steadied himself.

"Let's sit down," he said. "I need to think. Christ, I might need to be sick. It was a bad idea to have so much wine."

Allie thought again of Robin's bottle of wine and that silver corkscrew. It was hard to believe security would let a passenger board a plane with something like that, something that could pop an eyeball out as easily as a cork. One of these days, someone was going to walk onto a jet with something like a corkscrew, and people were going to get hurt.

More and more she was thinking that day was today.

9:41 p.m. AST

2 hours and 19 minutes until dragonedy o'clock

The 747 shook steadily, a continuous, low-level rumble, which made walking back to their seats like crossing the surface of a trampoline. Robin saw them returning and her whole body seemed to sag with relief. She had been a professionally put-together forty-year-old when Allie first sat down next to her. Now she looked an exhausted, washed-out fifty, a woman in need of a comfortable bed and about nine hours' sleep.

Allie and Van had only just started down the aisle, hand in hand, when the little blond air hostess swatted through the curtain behind them. She followed close on their heels, pausing at each row to make sure the shade was down over the window. When it wasn't, she leaned across the seats to lower it herself, murmuring an explanation Allie didn't catch.

They were almost back to Robin when someone caught Allie's wrist. She let go of Van's hand and he kept going without her, didn't seem to know he had been released. She cast a look around and saw Frank Heck had leaned across the empty seat on his right to snag her arm. The great jet slewed sideways. Allie staggered, Heck gave her another tug, and she had to sit down in the seat beside him.

"Strap in, honey. Sit with your old buddy Frank Heck a minute. I could use the company, calm my nerves. It's a monster out there."

"You saw it?" she asked. She was surprised. He was in the center aisle, didn't have a window.

He surveyed her from the corners of his eyes. His hat was off to reveal a sad combover. "The storm is a monster. We're not done boogieing yet. I hope the wings are screwed on tight."

"I should go with my fiancé," she said, but when she tried to stand, Heck put a hand on her shoulder to hold her in place.

Van had already climbed over Robin Fellows to his own seat but now was looking back, trying to figure out where Allie had gone. His gaze found her and he stared at her with bewilderment, trying to work out why she had sat down with someone else. He began to shuffle toward the aisle again, as if he meant to come back for her. But the flight attendant was two rows in front of him, and when she saw he was trying to get back into the aisle, she straightened up and raised her voice.

"Sir, your seat, *please*."

"My fiancée—"

"You need to be buckled into your seat, sir. I don't want to have to ask you again."

Van shot Allie a helpless look and she made a patting gesture with one hand, *sit, sit*. He lowered himself uncertainly, looking as confused and helpless as she had ever seen him. And all the while Frank Heck was reaching across her waist to buckle her in, with the patience of a father securing his very small daughter. Allie should've resented it but felt a brief flash of fondness for him instead. Her father had buckled her in just so a thousand times.

"Stay with me, Allison," he said. "At least until we find clear air again. I was hopin' to have a word."

The flight attendant was in the aisle just behind them, alongside the father and son who were seated in front of Robin and Van. She reached over the two men to lower their shade. The older man shot her a calm, appraising look.

"What are you doing?" he asked.

"People are trying to sleep."

"In *this*?" asked his son.

The older man raised the shade. "No. I want to see it again."

"There's nothing out there," said the air hostess.

The older man laughed incredulously. "I waded onto Omaha

Beach into machine gun fire. My best friend, Chick Withers, got it through the teeth, right beside me. I didn't close my eyes then. If there's something out there, and it's coming after us, I'll be damned if I'll close my eyes now."

Frank Heck was suddenly on his feet, leaning over Allie, big belly in her face. "You misunderstood her, brother. She wasn't asking you to put the shade down. She was telling. You were a soldier on Omaha Beach? That's great. Then you understand the chain of command . . . and that a flight officer on this 747 has given you a direct order."

Allie heard him speaking, but she was looking at the butt of a small pistol in a shoulder holster, tucked inside his cheap sports coat. It seemed to her Frank Heck had told her he had some kind of business making novelty pajamas. That didn't seem so likely now.

The flight attendant glanced ever so briefly at Heck and nodded, then moved on, lowering shades as she went. Robin and Van didn't protest when it was their turn. Heck sat back down.

Heck shifted his gaze to her: that cool, assessing stare. "Did you know you parked your car in a slot reserved for professional drivers—chauffeurs—at the airport, Allison?" Had she ever told him her name? She didn't think she had.

"Are you here to give me a ticket?" she asked.

"And you left the keys in the ignition. Did you know you did that?"

She stared.

"Do you know what kind of people drive to an airport and leave the keys in their car? People who aren't planning to come back. Allison, I want to ask you something, and I'd appreciate if you'd shoot me straight. Where did you go when you left the cabin just now? You were gone a whiles."

She parted her lips but couldn't think what to say. She was saved by the PA snapping on. The pilot cleared his throat.

"Folks, this is Captain Vanhoenacker, checking in from the flight deck. We're passing through a stretch of extremely rough air, so I'm asking again that you stay in your seats until we're through it. For the last couple miles we've been flying in tandem with a Lockheed DC-10 out of Thule in Greenland"—he gave a warm, masculine chuckle—"and I guess a few people were startled to see 'em. There's no reason for alarm, they're up here testing some fancy new meteorological whiz-bangs and we're sharing a flight corridor with them."

"Who the hell does he think he's kidding?" someone said. Allie glanced at the father and son in the row ahead of Van and Robin. It was the son, curly-haired and raffishly disheveled in the way that always caught Donna's attention. He was shaking his head. "My ass that's a plane out there."

Vanhoenacker wasn't done yet, though. He said, "I'm also asking everyone to lower their shades so those passengers who want to sleep can. Rest assured there's calmer air ahead and we're making good progress. We still expect to land at Heathrow a few minutes ahead of schedule, about five fifty local time. Thanks much for . . ." his voice trailed off. He didn't seem to know what he was thanking them for. At last he said, ". . . putting up with a few bumps."

That, at least, was met with a scattering of laughter: high-pitched, weary, a little hysterical. The pilot's tone was so breezy, so disconnected from the animal terror of the last hour, one almost had to laugh.

"So," Heck said to her, hand on her arm. He wasn't holding her anymore, just lightly touching her. "What were you doing?"

"You have a gun," she said, "are you

10:54 Mid-Atlantic Time Zone (MST)
1 hour and 6 minutes until dragonedy o'clock

a police officer?"

"Something along those lines."

"Do you even have legal jurisdiction? We're not really in a country anymore." She thought to herself, *We're in King Sorrow's kingdom now.*

"Why do you ask about legal jurisdiction? You worried I'm going to arrest you for parking in the wrong area at the airport?"

She fought to get free of the briars in her head, but cleverness was beyond her. She was overmatched, and every mile they traveled brought them closer to midnight.

"We have to get off this plane," she said.

"Why's that, Allie?"

"It's going to be destroyed."

He leaned back in his seat, eyes narrowed. "Why would that happen?"

"What if I told you there's a bad man on this plane? A total David Koresh nutjob. Anti-government. Probably cuddles an M16 in bed."

"Depends. Is he a threat to the flight? Is there a chance he'll try to blow the plane up?"

"Let's just say if it blew up," she said, "it would be his fault."

"How do you know this total David Koresh–type dude, Allie?"

"He came up in some research I was part of," Allie said honestly. "And I recognize his kind of crazy. I spent a few months in a place for people with emotional problems, the year after my brother died."

"Poor Theo," he said. "Tell me about being institutionalized, Allie. Do you still suffer from paranoid ideation?"

Allie frowned. She was telling him she knew what a crazy person looked like, having spent a lot of time with them, and he was acting like maybe *she* was the crazy person.

"It was stupid. I started having loud conversations with God because I was angry with him for taking my brother. People who talk to God aloud outside of church tend to get funny looks." Which was true enough but left out the gay stuff that had made her mother breathless with panic and earned Allie a summer of conversion therapy at a pricey Bible camp. "Why are we talking about me? I'm not the problem. I went through a phase and I got better. I'm fine now. I've been sober of mind for years."

"Let's not get carried away there, kiddo. How much did you have to drink today?"

Allie said, "Not enough."

"Were you drinking before you left your car at the airport with the keys in it?"

Allie held her index finger and her thumb a fraction apart. "This much."

"How's your fiancé figure into this evening's merriment?"

"He doesn't. I didn't even know Van was going to be on the flight. He surprised me. He's a surprising guy. A week ago I wasn't even sure we were still a couple."

"Is that maybe one reason you took off for old Blighty all a sudden? Were you maybe operating in a state of emotional distress? Go someplace new, clear your head?"

"Maybe," she said, thinking that sounded more plausible than the truth. "Van likes to throw romantic gestures around, like cherry bombs, just to see what kind of bang they'll make."

"Here we are talking about bombs again." Heck snorted. "I'm almost done interrogatin' you, darlin'. Just a couple more things. Help ol' Frank out here now. So you have reason to think someone on this flight has both the intent and means to detonate a weapon. At what point did you realize we were in danger? Was it *after* you came on board? Or before? Is that why you got to the airport in such a rush and left your keys in your car? Were you distracted by bigger concerns?" He dropped his *g*'s and talked in a kind of prairie singsong, but then he would throw in a phrase like "intent and means" to remind her he was the law. The accent was just another kind of cowboy hat, a bit of costume dressing, she thought.

"I never said he had a weapon," she told him, and then wished she could take it back. Better if Heck thought Horation Matthews *did* have a weapon, that at least made sense.

Heck leaned his shoulder into hers, and said, confidentially, "Allie, do you know what the penalties are for making a false accusation to a federal officer? Or causing a plane to divert from its route by causing a crisis? You cause a panic on a loaded airplane, you can expect to do time."

"*You* aren't panicking."

He winked. "That's why they pay me the big bucks."

"You would if you knew what I know."

"Try me," he said. "What do you know?"

"What I know," Van said, "is that if you sit with this strange man for another minute, Allie Shiner, the wedding is off."

11:04 Mid-Atlantic Time Zone (MST)
56 minutes until dragonedy o'clock

The flight attendant was too far aft to interfere by then. Van was standing over her in the aisle, had a hand on her wrist, but he was looking at Frank Heck. Heck put a hand on her other arm, and for a moment Allie had the hilarious idea they were going to play tug-of-war with her.

"That's a good idea, Allison," Heck said. "You go sit with your man and think things over. Just don't vanish on me. I feel like we got more to talk about."

"I won't let her leave the state," Van said, and held her hand until she collapsed into the seat between Van and Robin. The two men in the row in front of her looked through the gap between their seats at her.

"You all right, darling?" asked Robin.

Allie nodded.

"What was that about?" Van asked.

Allie shook her head. "I got no spit."

"I can help with that," said the man who had stormed Omaha Beach. He handed her a plastic cup of what looked like soda water, a lime squished in between the blocks of ice. She drank off half his gin and tonic in two swallows. It was cold and sharp and good.

"Did you see it?" asked the older man.

"Dad," said his son.

"Don't 'Dad' me."

Allie nodded. "I saw it." She saw no reason to lie.

He extended a hand between the seats. "Raymond Pinet. This

is my boy, Gregg. It's Allison, yeah? Tell me this, Allison. *What* did you see?"

"He's hoping you can settle a disagreement," Gregg told her. He had a graying mess of brown hair, like he had just rolled out of bed. Donna would love him, loved men with untucked shirts, uncombed hair, three days of beard bristle. She was turned on by hapless, helpless men who let her boss them around. "My dad thinks he saw Smaug out there. You know Smaug? Kind of a sly dragon, sprawls around on piles of gold, eating hobbits and getting fat? And I'm, like, no frickin' way. This is the kind of thing you have to stick with a rational explanation."

Donna would like that too, the way he used the word *frickin'* instead of *fuckin'*. She liked innocents. She liked despoiling them.

"What's the rational explanation?" Robin asked.

"It had to be a UFO," Gregg told them. "They've been playing tag with our aircraft since we started putting planes in the air. All our modern technology was reverse engineered from the one that crashed in New Mexico in the late forties."

"Bullshit," his dad said. He found Allie's gaze again. "You know why my son and I are going to England? So I can look at old cathedrals. I love 'em. I fell in love with 'em when I was stationed over there, during the war. You know what old cathedrals are fulla? Monsters. Dragons and orcs and trolls hanging off every corner, vomiting water when it rains. People been carving monsters into waterspouts for as long as there have *been* waterspouts." Now he looked at his son. "If spacecraft have been visiting this world for centuries, you'd expect to see some of them carved into the chapel walls. But you don't. You get fire-breathing serpents instead. Why is that? How do we even know what a dragon looks like if no one's ever seen one? There isn't a lick of evidence for Roswell and little gray men, but dragons, kiddo, they get around. There's not a culture on earth that doesn't have stories about them."

"You'd love my friend Arthur," Allie said. "He wrote his dissipation on dragons." She didn't think *dissipation* was the word she wanted, and she downed the rest of the gin and tonic to clear her head.

"*Dad*," said graying Gregg. "*Satellites*. We've mapped every inch of the earth. I think if there were dragons lying around, we would've noticed."

"Who said they're of this earth?" Allie said. "Maybe they come from somewhere else."

Van gave her a warning glance. Gregg and Raymond Pinet didn't clock it, but Robin did. She let out an anxious sigh, folded her hands in her lap, then unfolded them again.

"Your friend Arthur, he's an academic?" Raymond said.

Allie nodded and then said, "You know what else is academic? Whether it's a dragon or a UFO. Totally the wrong question to ask."

"Mm," Raymond Pinet said. "You're right. Of course."

"What's the right question?" Robin asked.

Raymond Pinet looked from Allie to Robin and back. "The way I see it, there's two. The first thing you have to ask, is that thing out there going to swat this plane out of the sky?"

Robin pressed herself back into her seat. "Uh-huh. What's the second question?"

Raymond Pinet raised one eyebrow. "Are you right with Jesus? Because if you aren't, now might be the time to give him a holler."

11:23 Mid-Atlantic Time Zone (MST)
37 minutes until dragonedy o'clock

"It has to be me," Van whispered. "It has to be me, it has to be me."

Allie leaned into his chest, thought he was whispering to her, then realized he was talking to himself. His gaze was bright and fixed, pointed toward the waist of the plane. The dividing curtain was pulled to the side and buttoned out of the way. The gangly flight attendant, Albert Shook, was buckled into a fold-down seat, facing aft. His gaze was fastened on Allie and Van—he watched them steadily, with a combination of warning and loathing. His five-o'clock shadow was up to about eleven o'clock now, giving him the look of a man at the end of a three-day bender. The movie no one was watching cast a wan and sputtering light down the length of the cabin.

"It *doesn't* have to be you," Allie whispered. "It can be *us*."

He grudgingly pulled his stare away from the galley and met her gaze. The way he looked at her, Allie had never felt so loved—or ached so. Because he was staring at her with an apology, and a kind of regret too. The regret she understood, the apology she didn't. He had nothing to apologize for. It wasn't his fault she was so fucked up, so confused, so pathological. It wasn't his fault that when she drank or when she was sad, she slipped back into the person she was before she went to conversion therapy, before she learned that the things she wanted were a kind of self-hate, a kind of poison of the soul. It wasn't Van's fault that she always thought of Donna when she came, a thing she had prayed to God to forgive her for. He had tried to be exactly what she wanted. He went down on her a lot and he always had the world's best Bloody Mary ready next to her coffee in the morning. He tried to make a game out of it, encouraging her to check out chicks with him, but that just made her feel dirty. She had no resentment toward gay people at all, had loved old Mr. Wren, but she didn't want to be one, any more than she wanted to be blind, or in a wheelchair. When Theo died, her father had almost died with him, and her mother had come unhinged, and after all that despair, she couldn't bear to be the cause of more pain.

At least Van *could* look at her again. Could look at her with love and the helpless anguish that was like love's shadow. He had not been able to look at her at all as he was loaded into the ambulance, the night he nearly fell to his death.

After he overheard her on the phone with Mona, Allie thought they would talk about it. She was prepared to tell him everything. *Almost* everything. She could not tell him about going to dyke bars when she was new to New York City, didn't think it was necessary. That had been early in their relationship, and all she had done was look and blush and run home and masturbate and then pray for an hour or two. Those few trips to gay bars didn't count, not the way Mona counted, because the making out with Mona happened after Van offered her a ring and she put it on.

Allie waited in the bedroom, crying and trying not to cry and crying some more, but he didn't come in and didn't come in, and finally she went looking for him in the other half of his Park Slope apartment, and he was gone. No note. She spent a sleepless night shaky and ill. She hoped he was out fucking someone better looking than her. She hoped he'd walk in at two and begin shoving her stuff into a garbage bag while telling her what a shitty lay she was. Because then she could beg, she could plead with him not to hate her. She could tell him the gay thing was just this weird impulse, that she had worked through it before, she could work through it again. Only he didn't come in at two, or three, or at all.

She called in sick in the morning, but he still didn't come back, and finally she made up her face and left at lunch to put in a few afternoon hours. He wasn't in the apartment that evening either, and a dizzying fantasy began to roll over her, of him climbing on top of the fencing to leap off the Brooklyn Bridge, that he was dead, would be found bloated and chewed by minnows.

But he was asleep on the couch when she came home from work the next day, dried blood crusted around one nostril, dried blood on his shirt, a small baggy of cocaine in his shirt pocket. He smelled bad, like he had slept in a puddle of beer, and maybe he had. When he woke, there was no possibility of talking about what he had overheard. She had to look after him with ice water and pain medication and bland food. They watched TV, sitting on the floor, until 1:00 a.m., and finally she asked if he still wanted to marry her, and he said, "My dad would fucking strangle me if we canceled now. He's already laid out twenty-five thousand dollars on the reception. Marrying you is the first choice I've ever made in my life that didn't make my father want to throw me through a window."

"I'm sorry. I'm so sorry. I will never ever—*ever*—I don't even know why—"

"Shh. Stop. Listen." He was smiling at her, his eyes bloodshot and watering, and when he touched her face, she twitched, as if he had given her a jolt of static electricity. "I've kind of known for a while. I just didn't want to know. I need you to hear this: it's okay. You like girls and it's okay. You don't need fixing. You never did. I think it's a mistake to marry me—"

"I want to marry you, I love you, I love you so darn much—"

"—but I understand why you feel like you *have* to. I know your parents don't want you to be gay, and for some fucked-up reason you're determined not to disappoint them. As someone who disappoints his parents *every day of his life*, I can tell you, they'd get over it, people do. But if you have to be a certain way for them, then I will be your cover story. I will be your shield so you can sleep with other women and your parents won't have to know. I would stand in front of a tank for you, the least I can do is stand in front of your parents and pretend we have a normal marriage. I don't know what kind of life we will have together. I know I will prefer it to a life without you."

She kissed him to make him stop talking, kissed his face all over, even though he smelled like a dumpster after a summer rain, and then did her very best to fuck him like a rock star so he'd stop talking about how she was gay and see that she wasn't. The second time she came, it wasn't even pretend.

And she thought they'd get through it, she really did, except in March they went out to see Suede—Van had to write two thousand words about the influence of American country on Britpop for *Spin*—and Donna invited herself along. Donna was determined to see the show because she thought they were the sexy English guys who had done the song "Supersonic." Van saw no reason to correct her.

So Donna turned up in a denim skirt that was so short it barely covered her crotch and a black halter top with a Union Jack on it that left her belly button bare to show her taut navel, and what really struck Allie was how her lips were shiny with gloss, like hard candies. By sheer accident Donna had a pageboy haircut almost identical to Van's own short cut, and in the pulsing discothèque lights, they looked like twin sisters, not twin brothers.

They had watched the show in the crush, right up front against the metal barricade, and for a while Donna was right behind Allie, hips pressed into Allie's ass, leaning over Allie's shoulder to cheer, the two of them swaying together, Donna's candy-gloss lips close to Allie's cheek, her arms around Allie's waist, like they were sisters, the best sisters ever. Van had looked so happy, staring up at the stage, the light show making his eyes flicker and dance with a kind of fay brightness: it was like the reflection of an aurora borealis, which once, long ago, Allie had confused with the ouroboros. They screamed themselves hoarse and Allie had Van's hand in hers, and sometimes she let go to run her hand down his spine, thoughtlessly rocking her hips back again and again. It was the best she had felt in weeks, the freest, the easiest—feelings she only really associated with church, with hitting just the right high note in choir, her voice joined perfectly with a dozen others, feeling loved by God, feeling loved for who she was.

She had gone clubbing with Donna after the show, while Van slipped backstage to talk with Brett Anderson, Suede's lead singer. She promised Van she would be at his apartment in Park Slope by the time he got home, but actually Donna and Allie were out until almost two, drinking and dancing together, screaming along to Madonna, bellowing out the words to Boys II Men's "I'll Make Love to You," while they held one another and reeled drunkenly across the floor, laughing at the gloppy sentimental sexiness of it. "Half the guys in this room are going to go home and whack off thinking about us tonight," Donna whispered once, and Allie had shivered and was glad she had Donna to hold her, felt protected from pervy skeeves by Donna's sure embrace.

When she finally got to Park Slope, Van was lying still and stiff in bed already, pretending to be asleep. Her blood was wild in her ears. She felt like she was still being spun across the floor, felt the music pumping inside her. She couldn't remember the last time she had been so horny, so wet. She climbed over him, had her panties down and her skirt pushed up, and he tried to roll away, said, "I'm wiped, let's tomorrow," but she was insistent, pushing up his shirt, working her mouth down to his crotch, bucking against his thighs, saying his name in a kind of trance state, over and over, only then he took her shoulders in both hands and shoved her back and said, "Fuck's sake, stop it. Just. *No.*"

He got up. He pulled on his jeans. He went out. Her heart thrummed and the room wheeled slowly around her. She couldn't figure out what had gone wrong. She heard the door to the stairwell slam, a sound that panicked her slightly, thinking he was going to leave again, that he would be gone for days this time. She pulled on his T-shirt and went after him.

He was in the stairwell, in his bare feet, with a pack of cigarettes. They were on the fifth floor, a well of concrete steps, with a waist-high black metal banister looking over the drop. He couldn't meet her stare. When he tried to shake a smoke out of the pack, cigarettes spilled onto the floor.

"Go back to bed," he said.

"What is it?" she asked. "What did I do?"

"Nothing. I just need a smoke. Go to bed now." His voice was dull and unfamiliar.

"Please," she said, and reached for his free hand, the hand with the lighter in it. "Please tell me if I did something wrong. Donna, please, I love you so much, just talk to me."

He shot her a look then, a look that seemed to express some wild grief. "Jesus, you're doing it again. This is so fucked. I'm so fucked. Go to bed."

"I don't know what I did!" she cried, and he pointed that miserable, grieving stare at her once more, and said, "What's my name, Allie?"—a question she didn't even understand.

She reached for his hand again and this time he shoved her back, only when he shoved her, he tipped off balance himself, and his hips hit the banister and he tilted over it and in her mind she saw him fall five stories and his head smash open like a dropped watermelon, and she cried out and grabbed his hands. She pulled him back so hard he lost his footing, a leg wobbled, and he fell, slid down a flight of steps, flipped and cracked his head. He was unconscious for almost ten minutes, coming around as the EMTs were strapping him into the gurney to carry him out of the stairwell. When she learned she couldn't ride along, she told Van she would follow him to the hospital in his car. He said, "Don't, don't worry, go back to bed." She said she would call Donna and they would go to the hospital together and he laughed an ugly laugh and said, "You should've let me go over the banister." She didn't understand it then and didn't understand it now.

He was in the hospital for thirty-six hours, and by the time he got out, Allie had moved back to her rarely visited two-bedroom rental in New Rochelle to hide from her life. She wasn't sure which of them told their friends first the marriage was off. She wasn't sure either of them ever did. Somehow it seemed like something everyone knew without anyone talking about it. Donna and Gwen and Colin and Arthur knew from what they didn't say, what they didn't discuss anymore. They knew because she was in New Rochelle instead of Park Slope.

"There *is* an us, you know," she said now, thirty thousand feet over the Atlantic Ocean. "That *us* is one of the best things in my life. That *us* is a fucking dangerous weapon, Van." And it was true, as true as any of the empirical statistical laws, as true as any of the words of "Amazing Grace." He would always love her, would never ever quit caring about her, and that was fact. She would always want his happiness, and that was fact too. There were some other facts she didn't care to think about, facts that made her scalp crawl with unease, with worry, but this at least was a good truth, a truth that could be held like a single note in a hymn, a note that was sweet and clear.

"Allison Shiner," he said, beginning to smile. "Did you just say the F-word? I'm going to get a bar of soap and wash out your mouth." His eyes came unfocused slightly. "There's a bar of soap in my bag. I could put that in a sock and—but the bottle is better." He looked across her then, with sudden decision, and caught Robin's eye. "Let's have a last splash of that white, huh?"

Robin craned her neck to stare back at him. She reached for the bottle and swished it out of her purse, the cork forced back into it to save the last bit, the corkscrew hanging from an emerald ribbon around the neck. Van had crushed his plastic cup out of nervousness, but Allie's empty was still intact. Allie poured a last frothy inch into it and handed it to him. He threw it back like a shot and gasped and exhaled. Put the cup down, then eased the bottle out of Allie's hands and gave it a considering look.

"I bet Arthur would like a bottle of this," Van said. "I bet the whole gang would like a bottle. Maybe for Christmas. If we see another Christmas. I guess I should find out if they have a recycling bin for something like this?" He unbuckled his belt.

"Van," Allie said.

"I'll just put it in my bag," Robin said. "For God's sake, don't get up again, not while the plane is shaking like this. You want to break your neck?"

"It's nothing, besides, I have to wee," he said, already up, climbing awkwardly out over them. The plane jolted and he put most of his rear into Robin's face.

"Sorry about my fiancé's ass," Allie said.

"I'm an editor, love. Writers expect me to kiss their arses all day long. I'm an old hand."

Van made his way up the aisle, swaying from side to side, the bottle hanging loosely from his right hand. Frank Heck turned his head to watch him pass by with great interest. When he was nearly to the galley, Albert Shook unbuckled his belt and propelled himself up, into Van's path. Van said something Allie couldn't hear. The senior flight officer jabbed a finger toward Van's seat. Van didn't move, gestured with his free hand, and tried to get past the tall man. Shook sidestepped, stopping him again, getting his forearm up and pressing Van gently backward, speaking calmly but firmly, his expression an icy blank.

"I better do something before Van gets arrested," Allie murmured, unbuckling herself.

But when she was past Robin, in the aisle, she turned in the other direction. She walked swiftly to the rear of the plane, looking back only once, to see that the little blond flight attendant had joined Albert Shook, creating a bottleneck in the starboard lane.

There was a small dark nook at the rear of the plane, two more bathrooms back here. Allie crossed to the other side of the plane. She was about to start up the aisle along the port side when Robin Fellows caught her arm.

"What are you doing?" Robin asked.

"I thought I'd look for another stewardess back here," Allie said. "Someone who could help de-escalate the situation."

"Is that why you're holding my corkscrew? To de-escalate things?"

They both looked at the corkscrew in Allie's left hand, the silver curl of the screw protruding between her index and middle finger. She had been careful to remove it before handing the bottle to Donovan.

"What the hell is going on here, Allison?" Robin asked her. "What the hell do you and Van know about this flight that you aren't saying?"

Allie was going to reply, opened her mouth, closed it, then opened it again and said, "How did you have the courage to—be a woman?"

Whatever Robin was expecting, it wasn't that. She drew her head back slightly and then laughed. "I wonder the exact same thing about every woman I meet. Every day." Her smile faded slightly. "What are you doing? Can you please try to explain?"

"I can't, but maybe Van can, one of these days. Sit back down, Robin. Sit down and, I don't know, maybe Van can write you a book about all of this. God knows it would take a whole book to make sense of tonight. All I can tell you is that I'm trying to be brave. I can't be as brave as you, but I don't need to be. I only need to be brave enough to hang in there until we land."

She tugged her wrist free, took two steps down the open and empty aisle on the port side of the plane, looked back, and saw Robin still standing there. "Go on. Shoo." Whisking her off with one hand but smiling at the same time. She was glad she had met Robin at what was probably the end of her own life. Envied her a little. She had the courage to be who she was when Allie didn't, and never had. She would rather be married to Van for the rest of their unhappy and unsatisfied lives than be who she was.

Allie walked swiftly up the aisle, to the waist of the plane, her gaze fixed straight ahead the whole way. She felt somehow that to glance around would be to attract stares, and that as long as she didn't look at anyone directly, they couldn't see her either: a notion related to an infant's conception of object permanence.

She heard Van arguing with the senior flight attendant as she reached the forward part of economy.

"Ah, man, don't make me sit down, I gotta take a piss so bad my eyeballs are floating," Van said.

"You've got an empty bottle," Albert Shook told him. "Use that."

Then Allie was into the dark space of the galley, and across it, and climbing the stairs. She paused at the top of the steps. The old couple in the row across from Horation seemed, at first, to be hugging one another. When she narrowed her eyes, though, she could see they were both holding a rosary, whispering to one another while they counted the beads together. On the movie screen, at the far end of the cabin, the credits were rolling. The end had come at last.

Horation had moved to the window seat and had raised the

shade partway. He was staring into the night, but his eyes shifted to her reflection as she sat down. That was the moment. If she had any sense at all, she would've jammed the corkscrew in his ear right then. Done. Four hundred lives saved and she would take the consequences.

But when she sat down next to him, aware of the corkscrew in her left hand, her insides went watery and weak. Allie got it, then, the whole *Hamlet* thing. It was hard to stick someone with a knife. It was hard to imagine doing it with enough force to puncture an eardrum, to drive the thing into his brain. It was no trouble to kill from a distance. The gang of them did that every year. As long as it happened offscreen, you could almost not think about it at all.

He turned in his seat, so their knees were almost touching, and the moment was gone.

"I saw him in a flicker of lightning," he said. "Just now."

"I didn't hear anyone scream. Last time they all screamed."

"I think a lot of them are keeping their shades down. Most people *want* to do as they're told. They're eager to show how well they can obey. What about you, Allie? Do you like to get a gold star from teacher?"

"Depends on the teacher," she said.

"The first time King Sorrow spoke to me, he was in the little room under the stairs where I keep the mops. But I knew he wasn't really there. He was in my mind, not under the stairs. It was an *idea* of King Sorrow . . . not the beast himself. It's satisfying to *see* him, to see him and know he's really there. To see the immensity of him."

"Do you think it would've worked?" Allie wanted to know.

"What?"

"This holy well in England? Do you think, if you'd got there in time, you could've cleansed your taint?"

"I'm not out of time. It *will* work."

"I have a friend, Arthur. I think he'd love to hear your ideas about dragons. He thinks about dragons a lot himself. He teaches a course on them. He's a professor of medieval literature. He has an interesting theory about fiction. He says all the good stories are secretly instruction manuals for slaying dragons. He says that's why we write them."

Horation's eyes narrowed, and she wondered if she had said too much, if Arthur's study of dragons risked giving the game away.

"Did you ask *him* what to do about your dragon problem?" Horation asked.

"Oh, yeah."

"What'd he say?"

"He said to find myself a knight," she said, "who can defend me. Why do you think we're on a plane together?"

Horation cracked a smile at that. So she wasn't ready when he said, "I don't believe you. Not a word. I have daughters and lots of practice catching them out in lies. One of them, her ears turn pink when she tries to get one over on me. Another gets angry when she's telling lies to cover her fear of being found out. My first wife was a habitual liar until I trained her out of it. If I had time, I could train you out of it too."

"Allison, you wanna introduce me?" said Frank Heck, three feet away, at the top of the stairs, the gun already in his hands, but pointed at the floor.

"Who the hell is that?" Horation asked.

"It's not hell," Allie said. "It's Heck."

11:51 Mid-Atlantic Time Zone (MST)
9 minutes until dragonedy o'clock

"And you must be our hypothetical Koresh," Heck said. "You gon' put your hands in the air now, both of you."

Horation was still staring over the seat at Heck when Allie hit him in the neck with the corkscrew. It was like driving it into a tree trunk. He flinched and backhanded her with his right hand. There was a clap of blackness behind her eyes, and when her vision cleared she was on all fours in the aisle. Horation was on his feet, stepping around her.

"Do you see what she did to me?" Horation said, and pointed to the corkscrew, still planted in the side of his neck. He had modulated his voice, reaching for a higher register, and in that moment sounded nothing like the commanding white nationalist. He sounded like a suburban father, someone with a middle-management job in sales, who has never been so frightened in his life. "This bitch is crazy! She just stabbed me in the neck! I don't even know her."

Frank Heck kept the gun pointed at the floor and took a step toward both of them. For the first time that evening, Allie thought he looked unsure of himself. Allie tried to tell him Horation was lying, he was dangerous, but when she spoke, all that came out was the hoarse bark of a seal.

Passengers were looking around, making unhappy noises that were not quite sobs and not quite screams.

"Could well be, pard," Heck said, "but I reckon you're gon' need to get face down on the floor anyway while we sort things out."

"I'm the goddamn victim here!" Horation cried. "I've been hurt! Jesus, I think I need a doctor. I'm bleeding everywhere!"

"Don't," Allie managed, her voice a strangled cough, "trust him."

"Get on the floor and we'll sort this out," Heck said, and at that moment the plane lurched drunkenly, sinking like a bobber when a fish hits the line, and Heck tottered forward.

His shins struck Allie on the floor and he stumbled into Horation. The true believer moved fast, catching Heck's wrist and twisting it, pointing the gun down and to one side. He drove his other hand into Heck's throat. Heck's eyes bulged.

"Lie on the floor," Horation said. "So a G-man can put his boot on my neck? I don't think so." He reached with the left hand and clenched Heck's throat, began to choke him out one-handed. The cabin was filled with cries, with shouts, and Allie began to crawl. She crawled right between Frank Heck's feet for the stairwell.

"Where you think you're going, bitch?" Horation asked her. "There's nowhere to run to and no heroes left."

Heck flailed. Horation choked him with the one hand while twisting his arm out to one side with the other, wrenching it downward and plucking the gun out of his sweaty hand.

Heck opened his mouth, and a sound rose and rose, a high-pitched, warbling, unearthly scream, and it took Allie a moment to realize the sound was coming from outside the plane. An instant later the scream rose to a howling thunderclap. Allie's own thoughts were pitched at a scream to match it: HIM IT'S HIM IT'S *THE KING!*

11:59 Mid-Atlantic Time Zone (MST)
1 minute until dragonedy o'clock

The 747 banked violently to the left. Horation and Heck went down, crashing into the empty seats beside them and then disappearing into the footwell. Their legs thrashed. Horation's right arm rose and fell, pistoning up and down with the gun in it, clubbing Heck with the gun.

Allie reeled herself, first one way, then the other, into the emergency exit at the top of the stairs. Her forehead bonked the smeary little porthole in the exit hatch. She steadied herself against the door and stared out into the night.

An attack jet—an F-16, Allie thought—yawed away through the cloud, dragging that terrible scream behind it, the scream not of a dragon but of its massive turbofan engine. It tilted up on one wing to show the Vulcan cannon slung beneath it and flash its Sidewinder missiles, and then it fell away out of sight and into smoke.

The 747 leveled out. Allie staggered back from the emergency exit and looked up the aisle. Heck was face down, Horation on top of him, both of them on the floor in Horation's row. Heck kicked and made dry choking sounds, trying to thrash free of the man with a knee in the small of his back. The gun was over there somewhere, and in the movie version of her life Allie would've thrown herself into the scrum, come up with it after a desperate struggle, and put the barrel under Horation's jaw.

She ran instead. She fled past the blond flight attendant, who was crouched low on the top step like a soldier peering over the rim of a foxhole. She went down the stairs three at a time. Even then, her thoughts were not hysterical. They were *fast*, which was not the same at all. She thought she should dart for the cockpit and tell those pilots, really, no more fucking around, time to land. But when she hit the bottom of the stairs the plane angled steeply to port, so steeply it toppled her. She sprawled on the floor and stayed there for a moment, long enough to determine they were descending. She could feel their rapid descent in the roots of her hair. They were already landing, and if they had any sense they'd have the cockpit door locked.

No sooner had she found her feet than the deck pitched under her feet again. She let the momentum carry her to the exit hatch on this level. She needed to see what was happening out there. She peered into the dark boil of clouds, searching for the F-16 again.

Lightning pulsed deep in a thunderhead. King Sorrow flashed through skeins of vapor, a vast, monstrous shape, and Allie wanted to cry out at the sight, although whether from horror or exultation, she could not have said. Even from a distance, his enormity was breathtaking in a literal sense—it was like someone had stamped on her chest and driven the air from her lungs.

An F-16 flashed after him—she didn't know if it was the same plane or another—with a rending shriek and let go a Sidewinder. She saw the rocket strike King Sorrow and detonate with a clap of thunder and a great jet of flame. For a moment the dragon was illuminated in silhouette in all his terrible vastness, with his bat-like wings and his hundred feet of serpentine tail and his proud head with its open scaly fan like the crown of an emperor. The gout of flame brightened, flickered, and faded . . . but in its last guttering, smoky glow Allie saw King Sorrow drop, corkscrewing toward the earth. *Felled* was the word that came to mind.

Dragonedy o'clock

She shoved through the curtain into economy and walked right into Albert Shook. Her head rapped against his. He shouted and grabbed her by both shoulders.

"Will you *please* sit the fuck down?" he cried, which Allie thought was pretty restrained, given the circumstances.

Allie weaved around him, using the backs of chairs to steady herself. Van had been sent back to his window seat and watched her approach with his lips pinched tightly together. He half got up as she fell over Robin and into her seat.

"Where did you go? What did you do, you dim gobdaw? It's world war fecking three out there," Robin asked. She had reclaimed the empty wine bottle from Van McBride and cradled it to her chest like an infant.

"Goddamn it," Van said, catching hold of Allie, half lowering her into her seat. "You were supposed to stay here. It was *my* turn to do something stupid and heroic."

"I didn't do anything heroic. Only stupid."

The PA crackled and the pilot began to speak. His voice was still youthful and there was a tremor of emotion in it—but he had discovered a new, deeper tone that was both urgent and assured, the voice of a man who had reached for his courage and found it. "Folks, this is Captain Vanhoenacker on the flight deck. I'm going to be very simple and direct with you. Twenty-five minutes ago the USS *Nimitz*, an American aircraft carrier, put up a pair of F-16 Falcons to investigate a bogey of unknown origin making a threatening approach toward this aircraft. Some of you saw what happened next. They engaged and destroyed a hostile off our left wing. We have had to make some pretty jarring maneuvers to clear the airspace for them, and I want to apologize for that. I hope everyone is all right back there. We are now making an emergency landing at Narsarsuaq Airport, on the southern tip of Greenland. Carrier Air Wing Nine has been kind enough to escort us the rest of the way in, so if you see jets flying alongside us, don't be alarmed. Those are the good guys." The PA hissed for a while. At last, he added, "I don't know what they blew up out there, but whatever you all saw? We saw it too. So keep your belts buckled and do not leave your seat for *any reason* whatsoever. We are bringing this bird down in a hurry."

"What's happening?" Raymond Pinet asked, the old soldier looking at Allie through the gap between seats.

"You know as much as I do," Allie said.

"I'm not talking about the announcement, and I'm not talking about what's going on out there. Where do you keep going, darling? And where did the other guy go—the country-soundin' fella?"

"He's upstairs," Allie said. "I think he might be dead."

"Oh, God!" cried Gregg Pinet. "What happened?"

"He did," Allie said, nodding at the curtain as Horation came through it.

Horation's collar was bloodstained and the gouge in the side of his neck was an ugly, glistening red hole. There was a long red scratch down his face, running from his forehead and across his left cheek, skipping his eye socket. He scanned the cabin for only a moment before he saw her and gave a bloody smile and began to walk toward them, the pistol in one sticky red fist.

Allie gripped Van's hand. She didn't want to cry and thought she might. "You deserved better than you got with me, Donovan. I would've been a lucky girl to be your McBride."

"There's no such thing as better," he said.

Horation reached their seats, looked at Robin, lifted one lip in a disgusted sneer. He shot a disbelieving look at Allie. "You see this? You see why a man would want to build a world away from this? To keep his children away from this sort of perversion?" He turned his bright, inspired gaze back on Robin. "You're sitting in my fucking seat."

There were hectic red blotches in Robin's cheeks. She stood stiffly and said, "You're bleeding."

"It isn't fatal," he told her.

"Shame," Robin said. She took her carry-on purse and empty wine bottle and sat directly across the aisle.

Van rose unsteadily to his heels. It didn't seem possible he could get any paler; all the blood had drained from his face so he looked like a ghost of himself.

"You want to get shot?" Horation asked him.

"If you were a man, you'd beat me to death with your fists, the honorable way," Van said.

Horation grinned crookedly at that. "You got balls. You want me to feed them to you? Get lost."

"You'll have to shoot me," Van said.

"No, you won't," Allie cried.

Horation rolled the hammer back on the gun. People in the cabin cried out. Some of them had already unbelted and fled for business class.

"The way I see it," Van said, "there's only six bullets in that gun, pardner, and about four hundred of us back here."

"I'll be sure to put the first in your girlfriend's face," Horation said, and he stuck the gun into Allie's temple and pressed, so she had to bend her neck, put her right ear against her shoulder, and even then the barrel was digging into her.

"Don't," Van said. "Don't don't don't." Lifting his hands and shooting Allie a frantic look. He bent quickly and kissed her right eyebrow and then shuffled out of their row, his hands raised, palms out.

Horation stepped back to make room for him, and Van found a seat across the aisle with Robin, both of them tensed for their chance to make a move. Then the white supremacist lowered himself into Robin's vacated seat, put himself shoulder to shoulder with Allie. He didn't bother buckling himself in.

Although some had gone running, most of economy had remained in their seats. Some craned their necks to see what was happening, their faces ashen and fearful. Allie turned her head and stared through the window and was surprised to glimpse a string of lights far below. It was there, then it flickered out of sight, disappearing amid an archipelago of cloud. What was down there? she wondered. A highway, perhaps, some road following a bit of Greenland's coastline.

The F-16 on their starboard side was close, a black cutout against the paler darkness of the night. In outline it looked like a raptor, like a weapon, with its back-slung wings and sleek profile.

"What are you going to do when we land, Hoary?" she asked.

"Who said I'm getting off? I'm staying right here and you're staying with me. The dragon is dead. I don't need to go to England anymore. We could force them to take us to Afghanistan on this jet. I've read about the Taliban. I don't share their faith, but I admire their morality." He looked at her slyly. "Tell me about the dragon."

"You know what I know."

"Oh, I doubt that very much. We used to talk, King Sorrow and I. When I asked him why I had been chosen for death, he told me he served three daughters of Lilith and three sons of Cain, and they had picked me special. He offered to tell me their names if I could beat him in a riddling contest. If I lost, though, he said I'd spend the last days of my life blind. I didn't want to chance it. I reckoned it'd be best to keep my eyes in my head, so I could watch for the ones who wanted me killed. Are you one of them, Alice Toklas? Are you a daughter of Lilith?"

"'Fraid I'm just another child of MTV, champ."

He gripped her face with his right hand and forced her face against the porthole window, *thunk*.

"You wanted to stop me from getting to England. To the well. You were afraid I'd get rid of the dragon and then I'd find my way back to you. Admit it."

He kept her face smashed against the porthole. She saw a delicate web of lights glittering brightly in the darkness, saw something flicker between her and that distant city, something with enough mass to blot out the lights for a moment.

"I wasn't afraid of your well," Allie told him. "Because I don't think what's on you can be washed off."

The F-16 tried, suddenly, to break right, rotating up on its side and dropping away, but it was too late. It happened so fast. King Sorrow hit it from beneath and sliced straight through. Flame erupted in a blinding sheet and King Sorrow screamed in triumph. His shriek shook the whole plane and made the roar of the navy's jets sound shrill by comparison.

A piece of the F-16 rattled off the 747, which dropped suddenly, falling hard to port. Allie didn't know if people were screaming. She knew *she* was, but she couldn't hear herself over the ringing echo of King Sorrow's cry.

Several things happened in the moments that followed, the handful of seconds that stretched like taffy, assuming the depth and complexity of whole minutes, of hours. Bags flew. People were thrown from their seats. The pistol in Horation's left fist wavered, pointing up for an instant, long enough for an old soldier to move. Raymond Pinet's hand shot between the seats and caught Horation's wrist, forcing the gun away, to point at the ceiling.

The gun went off. Somehow Allie thought it would be louder. Through the ringing in her ears, it sounded like a kid popping a paper bag full of air in the next room over. The slug hit the luggage compartment above them. There followed a flat bang and oxygen masks dropped throughout the cabin. Wails and sobs rose in a horrified chorus of fear.

The 747 banked the other way, leveling out. Allie's head remained pinned to the window—she doubted Horation was even aware he was still holding her there—and she could see straight up, could see another F-16 maybe half a mile above them.

King Sorrow dropped on it, grabbing it by the tail in one claw and flipping it over his shoulder. The F-16 spun around and around, whirring like the blades of a fan. Allie didn't see it explode, that happened out of sight, but she saw the bright throb of light and heard the deep, reverberating *wham!* as it tore itself apart.

Allie twisted halfway around and was able to see into the aisle, past Horation. Robin was on her feet, the big green wine bottle in one hand. In that movie version of Allie's life, Robin brought the bottle down on Horation's head in a single glassy smash, coldcocking the man. But the plane lurched, dropped, and then rose just as suddenly. On Robin's first wild swing, she missed Horation entirely and bashed it into Raymond Pinet's brow. His head snapped to one side and he grunted, but he didn't let go of Horation's wrist. On Robin's second try, the bottle thudded dully off Horation's left shoulder with a meaty thump. Her third swing missed everyone entirely and carried her off balance, and she fell on her side in the aisle.

Van leapt up with a great war cry, launching himself across the aisle. But his feet caught and he fell, chinned himself on an armrest, and collapsed on the floor. The plane heaved and Van and Robin were flipped into the air, like small children on a trampoline, and fell out of her sight again.

Raymond Pinet blinked away blood, dripping from one battered eyebrow, and struggled with Horation's wrist. The barrel of the gun swung into Allie's face and she stared into its darkness. It swung away. It swung back. Allie had a wild sidelong look out the porthole and was surprised to see a corridor of jade lights, less than a thousand feet below: a runway.

She jerked her head to the side and the gun went off by her ear. The window exploded. There was a great grasping suction, as if God himself were inhaling, and the pistol was snatched from Horation's hand and disappeared. The wine bottle, which had been rolling around on the floor, flung itself at the window, banged off the back of Horation's head, and was vacuumed into the night. Loose belongings of every description whirled in the wind tunnel of the cabin.

Allie was belted into her seat. Horation was not. The window was a black hole into some terrible alternate dimension of darkness and uncaring stars, and it yanked Horation into it. His head disappeared into the night, then his shoulders caught on the wall of the cabin and he plugged the porthole like a cork. His collarbone popped. A shoulder cracked and splintered. The night was pulling at him, trying to turn him into toothpaste and squeeze him through the little hole of the window.

He had, in all this time, maintained a grip on Allie's face with his right hand. Now, though, his fingers slipped. He grasped wildly, reaching back, and caught the front of her blouse, tearing it open, buttons flying. Another bone shattered and he was squished a few more inches through the porthole.

Allie looked down the length of her body and saw the red-and-black tattoo of the serpent winding around her torso, its spade-shaped head resting above her left breast. She found it with two fingers of her left hand.

"King Sorrow!" She howled over the roar of air. She felt the tattoo flex and squirm, as if there was a living snake right under her skin. She felt the serpent tighten around her ribs, driving much of the breath out of her. Not all, though. She had enough air to shout, "Eat this evil motherfucker!"

Something struck the side of the plane. There was an anguished shriek of tortured metal and a dry snap, like someone breaking a handful of branches over their knee. Horation's right hand became a claw, gouging deep into Allie's chest. Then his body sagged, fell heavily upon her. Allie was pinned beneath him, face pressed to his abdomen, most of his upper body grotesquely mashed to fill the porthole window. The landing gear hit the ground with a tap and a soft, shrill whine.

AFTER: ONE

Flight Officer Albert Shook opened a door in the rear of economy and called for passengers to leave the plane single file, leaving their possessions and removing their shoes before they slid down the yellow rubber ramp. Allie led the way, Robin right behind her, half carrying Van, who couldn't seem to attach his dazed stare to anything. The Pinets followed, the son holding his father up, both arms around him. Raymond Pinet's eyes were blurry, and he had a gory streak of blood running from one eyebrow down the left side of his face. He was never clear on what had hit him in the face, and no one told him it was Robin with the bottle.

Allie took off her cork heels and sat on the top of the inflatable ramp and slid down it like a child at the county fair. The night was a slap of wet, briny cold. Greenland smelled like a mix of diesel and fresh herring. Allie wobbled away from the inflatable ramp and turned for a look back at the 747.

Three ragged slashes ran along the starboard side for perhaps eighteen feet, shearing deep into the stainless steel. They crossed from the upper part of the fuselage to the bottom, angling across the smashed window.

The porthole itself was filled with what looked like a burnt black mass of wadding. A spray of what might've been motor oil had been splattered back from Horation Matthews's decapitated corpse.

Van and Robin stood behind her, staring at the side of the plane.

"What in God's name—" Robin began.

"Don't bring him into it," said Raymond Pinet. "He didn't have anything to do with what happened up there." He and Gregg waited a few feet away.

Van blinked, looked at Allie . . . and then smiled crookedly. His lower lip was fat and gleaming with blood. He leaned in close to her ear.

"You know what this means?" Van asked.

"What?"

"You're going to have to marry me," he said, and planted a red kiss on her lips.

AFTER: TWO

Van and Allie had a room together, in the Hotel Narsarsuaq, with British Airways picking up the tab. They had more privacy than most. The hotel had just eighty rooms and needed to find beds for close to three hundred passengers—quite a few people were sleeping on cots in the hotel ballroom. Another hundred survivors were bedding down in the gymnasium of a secondary school on the far side of the fjord.

Allie couldn't sleep. In the months that followed, she was often only able to sleep in two- or three-hour snatches, twitching awake all of a sudden with a feeling like someone's hand was on her throat.

That first night, though, there was no tiredness in her, and not much thought either. She felt raw inside. She thought it would help if she could cry, but she couldn't cry and she couldn't sleep and she felt unclean. She felt tacky with blood and sweat and the diesel stink of jet fuel. She left Van snoring and tried to wash in the bathroom, scouring herself with hot water and scrubbing until her skin was pink. They had good hot water at the Hotel Narsarsuaq. But even shampooed and rinsed, she felt contaminated by the night, by the murder of the pilots flying the F-16s, by the death of Frank Heck (who had been removed from BA 238 in a body bag), by Horation Matthews's implacable madness.

"I hope his well is real," she whispered. "I wouldn't mind a dip myself."

"What well?" Van asked.

She hadn't known he was awake. When she had gone for the

shower, he had been snoring strenuously. She lay beside him in a towel, cooling off, above the blankets.

"He thought there was a holy well in England. Horation did. He thought he could take a plunge and wash King Sorrow right off him. I could use that. I'd like to get some evil off me too. Look at what we did."

"I'll tell you what *you* did, Allie. You saved four hundred people. You saved *me*. It's not about who died, it's about who lived. King Sorrow killed the bad guy and the good guys live to fight another day. The end."

Allie sighed. "I guess it could've been so much worse."

AFTER: THREE

Worse happened three days later, when Timothy McVeigh detonated thirteen barrels of ammonium nitrate, loaded into a Ryder truck, in front of the Alfred P. Murrah Federal Building in Oklahoma City. The truck was in the loading zone directly beneath the day care center on the second floor. The front of the tower was sheared away, as if it were a toy office building that someone had opened to show the interior cross-section. McVeigh murdered 168 people, 19 of them children.

Allison and Van and Allison's parents sat together on the foot of the bed, unable to pull themselves from the live coverage. Allison's parents had flown to Greenland to join them, the ex-cheerleader and former congressman, sitting with their daughter trapped between them. They were with her every minute except when she needed to sleep or attend another interview with the FBI. Her father hardly let go of her hand.

The street in front of the Murrah building had been obliterated, parked cars flipped over or cooked down to the iron frames. Allison thought it looked as if the Murrah building had been visited by King Sorrow. Even then, Allie knew this was somehow part of it, that somehow this was on her too.

She couldn't talk to Van about it until they went to bed, her parents finally gone. Allie and Van were under the covers, Van spooning her from behind, when she said, "We have to talk to Colin. He'll know what we need to do about Oklahoma."

"What the hell do you think we're going to do about Oklahoma? We aren't going to do anything except watch TV and feel fuckin' sick, same as everyone." After a few moments of silence, he added, "I need to get high."

"But, Van," Allie said. "The guy who did this, he's the exact same kind of creep as Horation Matthews. He wanted to get at the ATF, at the FBI. He wanted to water the tree of liberty with the blood of a couple hundred government employees. Don't you think the two things are connected? Oklahoma and BA 238? Matthews and McVeigh?" The TV had just started talking about McVeigh by name, said he was in custody, considered a person of interest.

Even as she said it, she recalled something Matthews had said to her: *You can't play chess with just the black pieces. A white army must surely stand opposed. My confederates are moving even now.* He had mentioned names. Timothy McVeigh hadn't been one of them, she was sure of that—which calmed her nerves when she couldn't sleep. No matter how she strained at it, she couldn't dredge up the names Matthews had mentioned. It was months before they came back to her—Bridges and Parker—and then only because she saw them in print. They had been favorite aliases of McVeigh and his compadre, Terry Nichols.

"What are you asking me, Allie?" Van asked her. "If they were all friends? That's your area, not mine. I think sometimes it's better not to know the odds."

In a while he was snoring in her ear, a light, soft, gentle buzz. His hand was around her waist and she held it in hers, and was more in love with him than she had ever been. When he slept, he reminded her of a stuffed doll at a yard sale, a skinny rabbit maybe, with a missing eye and some stitches going in one arm and dirt in his fur. It was impossible not to want to squeeze him close and wish to mend him.

She never knew what sort of aid and comfort Horation Matthews offered McVeigh and Nichols: weapons, or a stolen car, or faked-up driver's licenses, or money, or the offer of shelter, or simply encouragement. It seemed likely he would've offered his assistance, even if he wasn't under King Sorrow's shadow. But the dragon *had* been coming for him. Blotting out the moon at night over his compound and taunting him from the shadows. She thought a part of Horation had gloried in King Sorrow's attention. It made his struggle mythic, as move was met with countermove. It had thrilled him—was a form of validation.

It was late, well past dragonedy o'clock, and Allie had almost drifted off when she saw the golden flash of flames around the edges of the curtain. Adrenaline punched into her bloodstream in a cold rush and she sprang awake, thinking, *He's back, the dragon is back, and he's going to burn this whole village to the ground*. For a moment she was too afraid to move.

But the flare of brightness shifted and rippled and took on a new hue, a sort of glow-stick green, which began to shade back into gold. Allie pushed Van's hand away and herself free of the blankets and walked to the window in bare feet. She lifted the curtains and stared into the evening's last darkness, an atlas of stars spread across the night. A whip of emerald brilliance uncoiled across the sky and faded. Then a gold belt rose over the ocean, like a line of bronze spears, which fell in turn, collapsed like the Murrah building, and bright red wings unfurled and opened wide, a dragon as big as the night itself falling upon the shoreline below. Allison had never seen the northern aurora before—*the ouroboros!*, she thought—and the air caught in her lungs at the wonder of it.

She watched until the night burned itself down to the gray ash of dawn.

AFTER: FOUR

Her parents had arrived in Greenland to look after her, but Allie felt it was much the opposite: that she needed to look after them. They seemed so old and bewildered, so helpless. Her father was a big, rangy man with the look of a 1950s movie star, the kind of star who usually showed up on the screen in crossed gun belts. Her mother had been an honest-to-God cheerleader for the Dallas Cowboys, and looked it, even at sixty. Her hair was a glossy honey blond. It came out of a bottle now.

But her mother showed up in Greenland with a pair of granny glasses perched on the end of her nose and a tremble in her hands. Archibald Shiner looked too thin and shouted because he had left his hearing aids in America. When her folks saw her, in the lobby of the hotel, they pulled her into their arms and cried and shook, while she promised them it was all right, she was all right, comforting them instead of the other way around.

Her father wanted to sit in on her interviews with the FBI. He wanted a lawyer present.

"Don't dick around with me, amigo," he hollered at the agents conducting her interviews. "You think I don't know how you people work? I served in Congress for ten years. Go ahead and try something with me. You'll be making photocopies in the Chattanooga office the rest of your career."

Allie was starting her day with a Bloody Mary and drinking her coffee with Baileys in it, and although she was interviewed several times by the same agents, she was never quite clear on their names. She had the slightly hilarious idea that they were named Simmons and Garfunkel, but that might've been wrong. Simon and

Garfingle? Lennon and McCafferty? Paul and Oates? She was too sozzled most of the time to worry about it.

"We know who you are, Congressman Shiner," said the agent she thought of as Simon, a brisk, slender Black man with the quick hands of a professional pianist. When one hand flicked out to smooth his tie, it was like watching a hummingbird dip its beak for nectar from a flower. Allie thought it was nice of Simon to refer to her father as Congressman Shiner. Her dad hadn't been in Congress since 1986. "I want to assure you, your daughter is being spoken to as an eyewitness only and is in no legal jeopardy. We're working with a team of psychologists to reconstruct the events that took place during the flight of BA 238, and I am told it would undermine their work to crowd the room with family. Your daughter would naturally not want to upset you. You've been upset enough. But if she feels constrained by your presence, it will undermine our fact-finding mission." Looking at Allie as he spoke, telling her with his calm stare that he expected her to agree with him.

"He's right, Dad," Allie said. "Promise you'll have a bottle of wine ready when I'm done?"

"A bottle or three," her mother said.

"A lawyer," her father insisted.

"I'd like to get this done and send you all home," the agent said. "Of course, if you want a lawyer present, we can work on that. But we're in Danish territory, plopped down in the middle of an international investigation involving six agencies and four nations. If we can begin the interviews today, we might get you out of here on Friday morning. If you require a lawyer, we'll have to clear his presence with all of those agencies and countries, and I can tell you, he'll have to be a Dane. A US license to practice law means bubkes here."

"*Dad*," Allie said, which in the end was the only argument required, more effective than anything Simon said.

In the interviews, Simon took the lead and his partner, Garfingle, took the notes. He didn't in any way resemble Art Garfunkel: he had a pocked, round, bored face, a bristle cut, and pale belligerent eyes set too close together. The way he looked at her, Allie had the idea she disgusted him, which was fair enough. She disgusted herself: drunk before lunch.

And sometimes there was a third man in the room: a wide-body with a big drooping mustache like an Old West gunslinger, legs thicker than fire hydrants. He wore a bad sports coat and khakis straight from the Big & Tall Outlet and he stood against the back wall with his arms crossed, watching her without expression. Sometimes he stayed for ten minutes. Sometimes he stayed for the entire session.

The third time she saw him, Allison waited until he slipped out of the room, then asked Simon, "Who's the spare dude?"

"Who?"

"Fat guy with the Burt Reynolds mustache?"

"I don't know who you mean."

"He just left the room. Literally just walked out the door."

Simon looked at his partner Garfingle. "Did someone just leave the room?"

"Didn't notice," Garfingle said, without looking up.

"No. I didn't notice either," Simon said. "And if you want my frank opinion, Miss Shiner, it might be better if you didn't notice anyone yourself. Some things it's better not to see."

Yes, Allison thought. That was, in fact, the whole point of these daily interviews. That had become clear after just a couple of sessions.

In her first interview, she told the story she and Van had agreed upon . . . a story that had the advantage of being at least partly true. They were old college mates and on-again off-again lovers who had been circling marriage for years. They had even gone as far as booking a venue, paying for the invitations, before they both got cold feet and had an awkward, miserable falling-out. Allie was in a state of distress about her life and her future, and when she ran to the airport and bought a ticket to London, she was operating in a state of panic, struggling with scary, depressive thoughts about how she had destroyed her own life. She had wanted to see Arthur Oakes, one of her best friends in the world—one of Van's best friends too!—because whenever she found herself drowning,

Arthur had always been able to pull her out of the deep water. Only Van learned her plans from his sister and ambushed her on the plane and asked her to marry him, right away, no more waiting, and she said yes. It was one of the best and happiest moments of her life—she felt that with all her heart. It was to be followed by the most terrifying hours she had ever experienced.

They'd been toasting their elopement with Robin before the plane took off and they were pretty well potted when Donovan mentioned he had seen someone boarding who looked just like Horation Matthews, a notorious far-right separatist. Donovan wrote for *Rolling Stone* and *Spin* and read widely; he had learned about Matthews in an article about white nationalism that had run in *The Atlantic* months before. Donovan hadn't thought much of it, but Allie got a bee in her bonnet about it and wandered upstairs to interrogate the guy. Horation had initially denied his identity but seemed shaken. Allison had returned to Van, and both he and her new friend Robin had begged her not to trouble him again. But she couldn't let it go, and when she confronted him again, he lost it, attacked her physically. Frank Heck—who Allie learned was an agent with the Department of Justice, recently detailed to Interpol Paris—had intervened and in the scrap that followed, lost his pistol to the militiaman, who pursued Allison downstairs, into economy. In the fracas that followed, the gun went off, and Matthews was partially sucked out the window.

Simon and Garfingle (those hitmakers behind "Tell Us Again" and "We Just Want to Understand What Happened") didn't merely accept this part of the story. They seemed grateful for it, almost relieved.

Allison only got into trouble when she talked about the dragon.

"After the pistol went off," Simon said, "the cabin experienced explosive decompression and a brief electrical failure. At that time, there was an escort of two American fighter jets, F-16s, that had been tasked with seeing your flight to the ground. Did you have a sense, at that time, that BA 238 was out of control and might've swiped one or both of the jets?"

"And made them both go boom?" Allie said. "No, I'm pretty sure that was the big frickin' dragon. That's the one part of the evening I can't figure out. Do you think Horation was friends with a dragon?"

Neither Simon nor Garfingle showed the slightest reaction, playing another one of their hits, "Did You Hear Her Say Something? No, I Didn't Either."

"So you don't know what happened to your fighter escort," Simon tried again.

"I know all right. I saw a dragon as big as the plane cut through one like—I hate saying a knife through butter, that's really trite. My friend Arthur can't stand clichéd language. He'd take a whole grade off my report for that."

"No," Simon said, trying a third time. "It wasn't a question. It was a statement. You *didn't* see what happened to your escort."

"Okay," Allie said. "Uh. Sure."

"It's been a long afternoon," Simon said—another crowd-pleasing classic. "Let's pick this up tomorrow."

But they got stuck on the dragon again the following day.

"When were you aware that your plane had an escort?" Simon asked her.

"Are you talking about the jets? Or the dragon?"

The big man with the mustache happened to be in the room, and at this he barked with laughter . . . the first time she had ever heard a sound out of him.

"Are you familiar with the phenomenon of St. Elmo's fire?" Simon asked, smoothing his tie, then flashing out one of his pianist's hands to draw an invisible line in the air between them.

"That's, like, swamp gas, right?"

"Something like. When there's a strong electrical field in the atmosphere, it can surround iron objects in a kind of membrane of hot plasma. The effect has often been compared to dragon's breath. What you—and some other passengers—saw out the window was the F-16s, flying in tandem, collecting an electrical charge from the storm and tossing lightning bolts back and forth. It would've looked very frightening."

Allie said, "No, c'mon. The dragon was out there for a good half hour before anyone saw the F-16s."

Simon cast a knowing look at his partner, then leaned toward her. "Miss Shiner? I'm authorized to tell you that the F-16s were accompanying your jet almost from the time it left JFK. Frank Heck had alerted the ground that Horation Matthews was a passenger and there was concern he might attempt to seize control of the plane. The FBI was on the lookout for just such a possibility. We had been tracking increased chatter among the anti-government separatist militias for several months. All the signs indicated they were preparing to act. We stopped them here—*you* stopped them, Miss Shiner. Unfortunately, they got by us in Oklahoma." He let that sink in, then pushed a photo toward her. It showed a blob of light against a stormy sky. It looked oddly like a bent, greenish-tinted claw reaching out of a cloud, impossibly huge. At the center of it was a small T-shaped black dot. When Allie squinted, the T-shaped dot resolved into a jet.

"Did what you see look anything like this?" Simon asked.

Allie smiled and sat back. "Ah. I get it now. Do you *want* me to say this is what I saw?"

"We don't want you to say anything. We want you to clarify what you saw, for the record and for your own well-being. You've been through a deeply traumatic experience. You nearly died. No one would be surprised if you had a breakdown, especially given your history."

Suddenly the interview wasn't fun anymore. She felt the tattoo no one could see but her, scrawled around her torso, prickling and cold and tight.

"What about my history?" she asked, although she already knew what Simon was referring to.

He smiled apologetically. "We've had to hospitalize three passengers for their own safety. We don't know for how long. It's scary and very sad, for them and their families."

Allison was not confused about what she was being told. She leaned across the table toward the agents, found Simon's gaze, and held it. "It *is* scary and sad, when you won't say what people want you to say, and they have to lock you up. Reminds me of what John McCain went through in North Vietnam. You know John McCain's story, don't you? My dad loves the guy. We spend a little time with his family in Arizona every summer."

"Your father is a good man," Simon said. "That guy was a rock for Dallas. He had some great years for them. I have a picture of him in my head when he was twenty-four and unstoppable. It's a little jarring to see him now. What is he, seventysomething? He looks older. I guess losing your brother took a lot out of him. And the heart attacks. He was lucky to survive the last one, I heard. It's important to be strong for him, isn't it, Allie? Not to put him through even more. Your teenage episodes already put them through plenty, didn't they?"

Suddenly Allison wanted to lie down. She wanted a dark room and a cold washcloth across her eyes. "I think we should pick this up tomorrow," she said.

"Let's do that," Simon said, flapping a folder shut. "These sessions can be exhausting. It's healthy to have some time to collect your thoughts."

And at that, the big man in the cruddy sports coat laughed again.

AFTER: FIVE

"I've been thinking about what I saw," Allie told Simon and Garfingle the next day, "when we were coming in for a landing. Everything was flying around the cabin and I was pinned against the window, so I can't be sure. But I think our plane might've swept sideways and just brushed one of the F-16s."

The big man with the Burt Reynolds 'stache made a small nod—the tiniest gesture of approval.

Simon nodded encouragingly. "Or—would you say—is it possible the F-16s *collided*, trying to avoid your plane?"

"Yes. Actually, I'm pretty sure that's what happened."

"Do you think you could sign a statement to that effect?"

"Put one in front of me," she said.

Simon nodded again. "Yesterday you told me you saw something out the window, some sort of atmospheric phenomenon, perhaps. Say you were invited on *Good Morning America* and they asked you about your ordeal. What would you tell them?"

"First I'd tell Joan Lunden she has great hair. Then I'd say it was pretty scary out there. A lot of lightning flashing around. Big black clouds. Then a little kid started screaming there was a monster out there. We were all freaked out. But, of course, the only monster was the one on the plane with us. Horation Matthews."

The big man in the bad coat winked at her, pushed himself off the wall, and left the room. It was quiet after the door clicked shut behind him. Simon considered some papers in front of him.

"That's great," he said finally. "We'll work on a statement, and we should have it ready for your signature by this afternoon. I don't mind saying, Miss Shiner, that what you did on BA 238 was incredibly brave. There are four hundred people who owe you their—"

"Do you really think this is going to work?" she cut him off.

Simon lifted his chin and gave her a bland stare. "Is what going to work?"

"Do you really think you can get another four hundred people to tell this same story? After what we all saw?"

Simon cocked his head to one side, seemed to give it his genuine consideration. At last he said, "Why wouldn't they? It's the truth, after all. And people who can't tell the difference between truth and make-believe, Miss Shiner, are seriously ill. People like that wind up in hospitals pumped full of dope. It's sad. You hate to see it. But you figure it's best for them." He straightened up. "It helps that most people kept their shades down and were afraid to look." Which was the closest he ever came to admitting there had been something out there besides the F-16s. "I think we're done here. And please, I do hope I can offer my congratulations."

She frowned, had no idea what he was talking about.

"On your impending nuptials," Simon said. "I understand your pastor is flying in from Vermont? We're all so glad for you. I think one of our PR folks is hoping to touch base with you later this afternoon. *People* magazine would like to take some photos of the ceremony. Everyone loves a happy ending."

AFTER: SIX

They married in a beautiful pagan spot, in the hills above the fjord, at sunrise. It had to be done early—Allie and Van were flying back to the States with Allie's parents before lunch. BA had offered them first-class tickets, but they had declined. George Bush Sr. had sent the Gulfstream, was happy to lend his plane for a day. He and Allie's father were old friends, had golfed and prayed together, shot ducks with Dick Cheney, talked legislation and football over T-bones.

Donna and Colin and Gwen and Arthur, and Arthur's mother, the Reverend Dr. Erin Oakes, would be on the plane with them. They were all in Greenland by then, for the wedding, for the friends they had almost lost. They meant to see Allie and Van marry, and then the bunch of them would pile onto the private jet for a hop back to the coast of Maine. Allie and Van had decided to do some driving for their honeymoon, spend a night in Bar Harbor, another up on Prince Edward Island. After a week in Greenland, Allie had a taste for the cold, salty sting of sea air, for austere rocks and the cry of seagulls.

Allie was taken unawares by her own emotions when she saw a serious man walking out of the spring rain and into the lobby of the hotel on the day before the wedding. He wore a camel-colored wool overcoat that fell past his knees and an old gray sweatshirt beneath, the hood up. When the automatic door thrummed open for him, he had his hands in his sleeves, and his sleeves pressed together, and Allie had the wild idea that a monk had wandered in from the twelfth century. This man of the cloth would take her hand, would take her confession, would pray with her and dry the tears from her face.

But then the man smiled and took his hands out of his sleeves and pushed his hood down and she saw it was Arthur. He had shaved his head but grown out a thick, springy black beard to compensate. He crossed the floor to her, watching her with his dark, grave eyes.

He took her in his arms and squeezed her, and suddenly she thought she was going to cry. She couldn't help being emotional maybe. He smelled so good—like a library, of course—and held her so fiercely and looked so stricken.

"I'm sorry," she whispered to him. "I know I was stupid, it was all so stupid. I know I wasn't thinking clearly, but I was trying to fix it, Arthur, I swear. Don't be mad at me."

"As if that was even possible," he said. "Just promise me you didn't get on that plane hoping you could die with Horation. That would just about kill me, Allie. It would kill me if you left the rest of us behind."

The idea shocked her. It left her so stunned, she couldn't reply. Of course she hadn't wanted to die. She had been on the plane—well, because she *had* to be on it. Only in the days after BA set down in Greenland, with its fuselage half peeled open, it had become increasingly hard to believe that she had ever let King Sorrow talk her into the air in the first place.

When she boarded the plane in New York, her logic had the certainty of simple arithmetic, seemed unassailable. Now she couldn't see any logic in it at all, only desperation and fear. Grief, even. She had known, from the moment King Sorrow made his false promise, that she could die on that plane. That the passengers of BA 238 were going to die because of her. And under those conditions, she could not quite bear to go on living herself. The only way to make it right was to be there with them. Arthur saw this straightaway, the thing she had tried not to see. And why had Van climbed on the plane with her? Because he didn't want her to fly alone, no matter where the plane landed—in Heathrow, or in a rain of fiery scrap over the Atlantic.

The other reason to marry at dawn was the church, which Allie and Van had found on a hike together, a cool, wet tramp in the steep hills over the fjord. It was a fifteenth-century stone pile, the roof long gone, the walls mossy, uneven, knocked half away in places. The floor of the chapel was a tumble of mossy boulders and old slates. The rough, gaping doorway faced east, and when the sun kissed the edge of the hills, it would fill the old stone chamber with light. The idea excited Allie. She yearned for it: to be clothed entirely in the brightness of a fresh day, to kiss her husband in that bold, innocent light, to say their vows before the world had a chance to wake up. She felt sure it was the right new beginning for both of them. He would quit doing coke and she would stop thinking gay thoughts and they would get their drinking under control and they'd have polite, eco-conscious children.

Donna had been up all night, with staff from the hotel, carrying in benches, putting baskets of wildflowers up and down the aisle. She had arranged the dress too somehow, a sleek and modern white wedding dress, like a sheath of silk for a blade, no train at all, arms bare, but with the most extraordinary tulle veil that spilled all the way to the floor and uncoiled across the rocks behind her. It might've been too cold for such a dress before dawn in Greenland, but Donna & Co. had produced a generator and space heaters. When Allie stepped into the ruin, before dawn, arm in arm with her father, Donna was waiting with a crown of white snowberries, which she set gently on the hair Allie had been braiding since 3:00 a.m.

"You look so gentle and so pure," Donna said, "I want to throw you down and deflower you myself, right here on the moss."

"Too late," Allie said cheerfully. "By about ten years. Mick Dolliver, junior year. His braces actually gave me a bloody lip."

"Jesus," her father said. "Thank God I left my hearing aids in the States and can hear none of this."

Allie's mother was right behind her, looking pinched and resigned, as if required to attend a funeral for someone she hardly knew. Well, it was a wedding for someone she hardly knew, so not far off. The former cheerleader said, "I'm damn glad you aren't running for reelection again, Shiner. Goddamn female priest who murdered a cop. I guess you'd lock up the Black Panther vote, but I don't know who else would back you. In the church I attend,

Allison, women bow their heads and listen to what the *man* of God has to say."

"Oh, hush, you," Allie's father said to her. But then his brow creased with worry and he whispered to Allie, "Really, we should probably stay out of the photos."

"Yes, Daddy," she said, and then she kissed her mother on the cheek. "Just having you both here means everything to me." And it really did.

Van waited for her at the far end of the ruined chapel, looking good in a hot-pink suit jacket that might have come straight from an episode of *Miami Vice*. His red hair was a handsome, tousled mess: he looked delicious, like Molly Ringwald in drag, a strange thought. Arthur and Colin stood at his elbow; the Reverend Dr. Oakes watched her approach from behind the simple podium heisted from the hotel. The chapel was open to the last of the stars and a green dragon's-tail shimmer of aurora and smelled richly of the dew-soaked moss. People turned their heads to watch the bride approach, walked up the aisle by her best friend and her father.

"BA gave us a hundred and fifty airline-size bottles of Johnnie Walker for the guests," Donna whispered. "And a hundred and fifty air sickness bags to put them in."

"That's so nice," Allie said. "If you have enough of one you'll definitely be glad to have the other."

"Oh, oh! And silver British Airways pens. And Concorde silk ties for the men, ascots for the women. And those tasty shortbread cookies they give you with tea. They were very generous. Gregg and I were out here packing gift bags for hours last night," Donna said.

"Gregg?"

Donna nodded to Gregg Pinet, who sat at the end of one bench, looking at Donna with a simple, slightly stupid happiness, as alert as a trained dog waiting for a treat.

"This might be a cute spot for a wedding," Donna said, her breath smoking. "But it's ideal for a spot of pagan fuckery. I got grass stains on my knees."

Robin Fellows and Gwen Underfoot waited to the left of the podium, Allie's other bridesmaids. Robin was the best-dressed woman in the whole ruin. She wore a cream-colored gown stitched all over with butter-colored silk roses, as if she had somehow dressed herself in the wildness around them. Robin and Gwen wore crowns of flowers, dryads at a ceremony for the faery folk. Gwen threw Allie a wink.

"Ain't you fetchin'," she whispered, sounding for all the world like she had just stepped off a Maine lobster boat.

"I came this close to getting married in a pair of jeans," Allie said. "God knows where Donna found a dress like this with five days' notice, here at the end of the world."

Robin said, "The only thing you really had to put on today is a ring, darling. The rest of the wardrobe is optional."

"I like where she says your wardrobe is optional," Van said. "I feel the same way."

Colin Wren, looking smooth in a black suit with a skinny black tie, said, "I'm more worried about how she's going to feel when you take your clothes off, Van. But she survived the flight here, I suppose she has plenty of practice dealing with traumatic experiences."

"Is everyone here? Are we ready?" said the pastor, looking from Van to Allie and back and smiling in her kindly way.

"Almost," Van said, holding up two fingers and looking back through the uneven stone maw that served as the door to the ruin. He glanced at his watch, then turned his gaze to the doorway again. "Just waiting on one more."

Beyond the door: green hills, wearing white wedding silks of dew. A flock of small birds darted across the plum-colored sky. People shifted on their benches.

A blade of red flame appeared on the rim of the highest hill, and that white gown of dew became a rippling sheet of brightest gold. A spear of sunlight angled through the opening and fell upon Allie's bare shoulders and bare face.

"Ah," Van said. "There he is. Right on time to kiss the bride. Lucky bastard."

BA provided an airplane-shaped cake for them too for the reception afterward, but one wing fell off as the chef was rolling it across the dining room. Everyone laughed.

Second Interlude

GWEN, UNDER ARREST

1997

2.

Over breakfast, word went around that one of the born-agains, Deirdre Flannagan, skinny-ass bitch who slept with her Bible and cried while she prayed, had killed herself overnight in her cell. She had left a note saying it was a smaller sin to take her own life than to go on living the way she had been living.

"That's right, Daphne," *crowed Shanelle Emerson from across the cafeteria table.* "She actually preferred death to one more night of gobbling your nasty snatch."

"I bet it tastes hunnert times better than these aigs," *opined Jess Bloch, a woman with a swastika tattooed next to her left eye. She used her fork to push some gray reconstituted eggs around a puddle of dishwater on her tray.*

"You wanna give it a try, you'll have to take a number and wait your turn," *Daphne Nighswander said, and winked, but her insides were gripped cold and tight, and when she returned to her cell, she was not surprised to find two guards and Senior Officer Humbersome waiting for her.*

Humbersome, who was built wide, with tree-trunk thighs, and who had dull silver eyes under drooping eyelids, already had her baton out. "Convict 51-696, stand against the wall. We're conducting a search of your cell. Would you like to alert us to any potential contraband?"

"You find anything, it was fuckin' planted," Daphne said. One of the guards gestured with his own nightstick for her to stand against the wall, and he murmured, "Hands on your head," without looking at her.

"Convict 51-696," Humbersome drawled in a bored, declamatory tone, "will I find anything in your cell that could accidentally injure me?"

"I am the one being injured here. I am the one who don't have any civil rights. I am the one people conspire against and plant evidence against," Daphne said. "Been this way my whole life."

One guard stayed between Daphne and her cell. Another went in and Humbersome followed. They went straight to the toilet. They already knew where to look. The male guard, a tall, lanky guy with a lot of Adam's apple—the prisoners called him Jughead because he looked like the hungry, skinny kid in the comic—snapped on a glove and reached down into the steel bowl. He found the wire inside the trap and pulled up a foot of line and then another foot of line and then the plastic bag containing twelve ounces of black tar heroin. He held it up, keeping his arm away from his body, water dripping off it.

"What's this, Convict 51-696?" Humbersome drawled.

"What's it look like?" Daphne said. "My last shit. It's all yours. Consider it a souvenir."

"It'll have to be a souvenir to remember you by," Humbersome said. "If this is what it looks like, you'll be enjoying your last days here in Black Cricket, Nighswander."

"If I could get that Baptist bitch who tolt," Daphne said, "I'd kill her all over again."

2.

Gwen saw trouble coming long before it finally caught up to them at the roller rink in Gogan. What she didn't expect was that she herself would take the first punch . . . or that for one glorious minute, Arthur would hold off an army on his own.

By eight in the evening, Donna was drunk and Donna was loud. The one usually led to the other.

Gwen thought there was a chance Donna had been drunk since the mimosas at brunch in the handsome, clubby lounge of the Captain Lord Mansion. Allie probably spent the day drunk too, although it was harder to tell with Allison. She was the rare specimen who became quieter as she drank, settling into a cocoon of happiness, a warm, friendly stupor. It was a shame, Gwen thought, that Allie was almost certainly an alcoholic of the most severe type, because she wasn't a *nasty* drunk in the slightest. Instead the booze let her be as loving and carefree as she wanted to be. The only one she ever hurt was herself.

Gwen had a mimosa with them but switched to coffee afterward. Even then, at ten thirty in the morning, with light streaming through the French windows and dazzling off the deep blue of the ocean, she thought she should pace herself. One of them had to keep a clear head and look after the rest, and that role had always come naturally to Gwen.

They split up after lunch, the boys for a stag day, the girls out for their hen do. Colin had planned the festivities for the boys, so Gwen knew they were off for a whiskey tasting, followed by a haunted hayride.

"Boy, I hope it's not too scary," said Gregg. "True fact: I threw up after watching that horror movie where Jeff Goldblum's you-know-what fell off."

"They *don't* know what," Donna said. "You're going to have to say it, love."

"His, you know, boy parts."

"His *cock*. Jeff Goldblum's cock fell off in *The Fly*. Say it. It'll be good for you. Say 'Jeff Goldblum's big cock fell off in *The Fly*.' *Cock*. It feels good to say it. When you say it, your mouth makes the perfect shape for sucking one. Cock." As she said it, she was twisting a silver chain around her neck, a key bobbing on the end.

"Cock," he said, and she took his carefully groomed beard and wagged his head gently back and forth, and said, "That's my boy."

Gwen wasn't sure about the politics of five straight women going to a gay bar, but Donna hadn't put it up to a vote. It was the weekend before Halloween, and by the time they arrived at the gay bar they were all in costume. They had agreed upon a theme ahead of time: *Dungeons & Dragons*, the cartoon. Donna was dressed as Bobby the Barbarian, in a horned Viking helmet, a pair of crisscrossed leather straps over her tits, and a thick furry pair of panties. She fit right in at the gay bar, where most of the men were in black caps and black chaps, motorcycle boots and jingling spurs. Allie was dressed just right for the gay bar herself: she had come as Uni the Unicorn, and wore a tail, a white leotard, and a horn on her head. She even had hooves where her hands belonged, a clever pair of gloves. She positively twinkled.

Donna wasn't the only one in a fur bikini. Gwen, as Diana the Acrobat, was dressed the same, although she had thrown an ankle-length cloak over her shoulders out of modesty.

Gregg Pinet's sisters were along too, but they hadn't got the memo about the evening theme and had worn nun costumes. The sisters were named Lulu and Gigi.

"I been meaning to ask," Donna said. "What the hell is up with the names in your family? Does your mother have a stammer? Lu-lu-luh. G-g-gi-gi. Greg-*guh-guh*."

Gwen didn't think Lulu was exactly in love with Donna. She had the hint of a smile on her plain, unremarkable face, but her eyes remained dismissive, bordering on hostile.

"I think it's weird you're a Donna and your brother is a Donovan," said Lulu. "Does your mother not have an imagination?"

Gregg's sisters hadn't known they were going to a leather bar either, not until they were in the car. Gwen thought they'd balk at the door, but Lulu led them in, airy and undisturbed. Gigi twitched when a young man walked by her in a thong, the leather mask of a dog over his face. Gigi was breathless and nervous and skinny, a woman prone to tittering instead of laughing.

"There's a Halloween costume I've never seen before!" she exclaimed. She tended not to say things but exclaim them. "I'm not sure if he's going as a Doberman pinscher or a disturbing sexual hang-up! But I don't judge!"

The music pounded "One Night in Bangkok" and "I'm Too Sexy." Colored lights stammered and flashed furiously. Gwen was glad to see men so intent about the business of being happy, demanding the right to be joyful. She knew some of them. The old man at the end of the bar, in leathers, had raised his pint glass to her when she came in. He visited his lover every Sunday at the hospice where she volunteered on Sundays. He had it too—she knew the signs well, could recognize Kaposi's at a glance now—but it was not seriously advanced, and the AZT was beating it back in some men.

All the same, this wasn't really her scene, her music. Arthur had sent her a vinyl record by Lord Pretender in a battered cardboard sleeve. He had not bothered to include a letter. He didn't always. With its big dreamy horn sections and steel drums, listening to it was like taking a vacation in a black-and-white photograph of Tobago, like anchoring in some gentle harbor of the past. Gwen liked to be alone when she listened to music, where she could miss Arthur in peace. Lord Pretender's calypso was an outstretched hand that could not and never would reach far enough to take hers. There was too much ocean and too much sadness between them.

"A therapist would probably tell Gregg it's a mistake to get married so quickly," said Lulu. Lulu had to yell to be heard over Depeche Mode. "But I think it's great. You've been the ground under his feet ever since Greenland." That was how they referred to BA 238, it was always Greenland.

"If someone's going to be under someone's foot," Donna yelled back, "it's him. Right under my heel, where he likes it."

"If someone's going to be underfoot," Gwen said, "it's definitely me." But no one heard her.

A flash of irritation passed across Lulu's plain features. "What I'm saying is, you keep him grounded. He needs that steadiness. Greenland messed him up, you know? I was worried, at first, that he wasn't in the right place to make a lifetime commitment to someone. I even told him, I said, Gregg, maybe you ought to put this off for a while. Do you really think someone with obvious PTSD ought to be plunging into marriage? But he said, well, you know—"

"I hope he told you to mind your own fucking business," Donna told her. "Maybe worry about your own love life instead of trying to undermine his."

"Is she always so easy to talk to?" Lulu asked, looking around with a kind of desperate annoyance.

"*Nnnneigh*," said Allie, pawing at the edge of the table. She couldn't drink her own martini, not with her hooves on, and needed Donna to hold the glass to her lips. "Sometimes she's sober and then you can't get a single civil word out of her."

"What's the key for?" Gigi yelled across the table. Gigi didn't know where to look. A shirtless fat man, belly matted with hair, was wiggling only a few feet from their table, working his hips like a stripper while he lip-synched to "Vogue." Gigi had pinned her gaze on Donna's face and Donna was chewing the tip of that key she wore around her neck. Gigi was nervous, maybe even scared, but trying her hardest to be part of the fun. "Is it the key to my brother's heart?"

Donna let the key drop from her teeth. "No. It's the key to his cock cage. I lock it up so he can't get a stiffy without my permission. He loves it. He—"

"Enough," Gwen said. "You're embarrassing me and you're embarrassing Gregg's sisters. This might be your special weekend, but it doesn't give you license to treat people like shit, Donna."

Donna flushed, and Gwen wondered if they were going to have a knock-down-drag-out. Then Donna looked out across the floor.

"I'm sorry," Donna mumbled.

From the outside, it almost didn't make sense that Gwen and Donna could be friends. But you grew close to the people you killed with. And Gwen knew Donna would fight wild dogs for any of them, bare-handed. When someone loved you that fiercely, you could forgive a lot.

"They didn't hear you," Gwen said—but kindly.

Donna closed her eyes. "I'm sorry. S'key to the cottage on Martha's Vineyard. The summer place he bought for us that I'm not supposed to know about yet. I just—I know you disapprove of me and I've spent the last five months scared you're going to take him away from me. I keep worrying he'll come to his senses. Christ, where is my next drink?"

Lulu put her hand on Donna's.

"I don't disapprove!" Gigi cried. "Lock his dick right up! Fine by me! It's the nineties! I think more men should have penis cages. Is there a term for that?"

"Sure," Gwen said. "The penal code."

And they all laughed. Even Donna, although she was glaring at Gwen with a kind of bruised resentment. *Why would you make me apologize to the nuns?* her gaze seemed to ask. *Why would you make me apologize to people who want to sabotage me?* Gwen gave a half shrug with one shoulder. Two nights before, Gwen had not been able to save a man who had been half gutted with a broken bottle in a drunken scuffle with a mentally disturbed relative. After you had seen a few bloodlettings you lost your taste for them . . . even metaphorical bloodlettings.

3.

Donna was done with the nuns, but she wasn't done with the night. They had all agreed to meet at another bar, at eleven thirty,

the boys and the girls together at the famous Extra Life Pub on the outskirts of Gogan, where two walls were lined with pinball machines and classic arcade games. But no one had checked ahead, and it turned out Extra Life was closed, a plywood sheet nailed over the door and a hand-lettered sign tacked up to it: EXTRA LIFE IS POWERING UP WITH RENOVATIONS SEE YOU IN JANUARY. The limo idled in an otherwise empty parking lot, the boys not there yet. Donna climbed the steps and tore the note off the plywood and stared at it as if it might read differently on closer inspection.

"Well, that's fucking bullshit," Donna said. "I was going to play Joust."

She lifted her chin and looked around forlornly. Beneath the twenty-foot-high sodium-vapor lights, the parking lot was as bright as day, although everything had acquired a faintly orange-yellow tint, the color of unhealthy pee. The acres of asphalt also offered parking for a Dairy Queen (closed at this hour) and an all-night liquor store called Marty's. Donna crumpled up the sheet of paper and started walking toward the booze stand.

There were a few cars parked in front of Marty's, including a Chrysler LeBaron with about four hundred bumper stickers pasted across the rear end. One in particular, a dark yellow sticker, stood out on the bumper: NO FREE RIDES—GAS, GRASS, OR ASS. Gwen saw Donna glance at the LeBaron on her way to the front doors, but if she noticed that particular sticker, she gave no sign. Not then.

It was busy at nearly midnight on a Friday evening. Gwen stood just inside the doors while Donna picked up a bottle of pink champagne. The festive mood seemed to have petered out. Donna looked sweaty and bad-tempered, her eyes dull and unfocused. It came to Gwen, then, that it was probably time to stop the drinking. But she had shamed Donna once and didn't want to do it again, couldn't tell her to put the bottle back. She wished Donna could have some fun on her hen do, but Donna wasn't good at having fun, she was good at being angry.

Some kids from the college were horsing around in the back

of the liquor store, six stringy, pimply dudes wearing lacrosse jerseys under their coats. One of them had even come in with his lacrosse stick. It was the one sport Rackham College really dominated, lacrosse. Gwen had asked her father once how you won at lacrosse.

You play lacrosse because you've already won, he told her. *The goal is to have a bigger trust fund than anyone else on the field.*

Donna swaggered out onto the blacktop, champagne in a brown paper bag.

"Should we take that back to the hotel and get silly?" asked Gigi in her piping, overly enthusiastic voice.

"*Nee-e-eigh,*" replied Allie, pawing at the air.

"We can drink here," Donna said. "Until the guys show up."

The champagne bottle went off like a .38, cork flying into the night and foam spuming over Donna's hand. She licked it off, held out the bottle. Gwen had spent her entire life in Maine and was well acquainted with drinking in parking lots. She helped herself first, then held the bottle to Allie's mouth so she could have a sip.

While they were passing the bottle, Donna drifted over to stand behind that Chrysler LeBaron. She studied the bumper stickers, made a face—and then dug at the NO FREE RIDES label with her fingernails, trying to pick it off.

"This thing," she said. "This fucking thing. That's a rapist bumper sticker."

"Should she be doing that?" Lulu asked.

"*Ne-e-eigh,*" Allie said.

Donna found a piece of broken glass on the blacktop and tried to scratch the bumper sticker off. She even got a piece of it—it came off in a thin ribbon. So did some of the chrome. She scratched ugly lines in the steel of the bumper, working at it in a sullen fury. The other girls stood watching, unwilling to get between Donna and the object of her rage.

"Nine-year-old girl in Goshen, New York, last month," Donna said. "Asked her mom if she could walk down the street. A friend just put up a new birdhouse. She never got there. They found her in a dumpster with her head bashed in. We covered that story every night for two weeks, and I'll tell you something: it was the uncle. We can't *prove* he did it, but he's a known sex offender, and he's got a bumper sticker on the back of his Buick, it says NEVER TRUST ANYTHING THAT BLEEDS FIVE DAYS A MONTH AND DOESN'T DIE. They tell you who they are. They always tell."

She gave up trying to scratch the sticker off and wandered away—then came back with a piece of brick. She began to whack the bumper.

"Come on, darlin'," Gwen said. "Let's go sit in the limo and finish your champagne."

Donna ignored her. The brick went clang. Gwen saw a spark fly. Donna lifted it high and brought it down again and the whole bumper fell off the back of the car with a smash.

"Wow!" cried Gigi.

Donna straightened up, tossed the chunk of brick, and swatted her hands on the ass of her fur bikini to get the dust off them. It came to Gwen that she should've tried harder to keep Donna from getting so drunk.

They were still standing around the LeBaron when Colin Wren's '49 Caddy wheeled into the parking lot. The canvas top was up, but the windows were down, and their men were hanging out of them. Gregg was in the front passenger seat, his whole upper body stretched into the night. Colin was next to him, one hand on the wheel and the other on Gregg's belt to keep him from falling out. Van's head and one arm hung out a rear window.

"Look at that sweet furry ass!" Gregg cried. "I'm going to marry that!"

Van was screaming too, while the car did donuts. "Allie! Allie baby! Have you ever seen me roller-skate?"

"*NE-E-E-E-IGH!*" Allie cried, jogging after the Caddy and waving her hooves in celebration.

"Oh, man!" Van yelled. "Let's go, lover! Wait'll you see me carve up the goddamn floor! I'm a goddamn angel on wheels! A goddamn angel!"

Gwen looked past the Caddy, which was whirling around and around in tight circles, tires throwing smoke. Because of course there was *one* other place open on the strip on a Friday night: Merlin's Cave Roller Rink, on the far side of the highway. The neon sign showed a bearded man in a wizard's hat, holding up the sagging hem of his wizard robe and dashing along on a pair of roller skates. Gwen hadn't been there since a friend's birthday party when she was twelve.

The car stopped. Doors flew open, and Donna was the first one there, tumbling half over Gregg's lap, legs hanging out. He clapped one hand on her raised bottom.

"We got what we came for," he shouted, as drunk as her. "Let's go, birdman." His name for Wren.

The girls piled in. Allie sat in Van's lap. Gwen squeezed in between Van and Arthur and then Gigi plopped down in *her* lap. Colin got out long enough to let Lulu climb into the front. It was all a lot of work to drive two hundred feet across the road.

"She hasn't hurt anyone, has she?" Arthur asked Gwen, softly, his mouth close to her ear.

"Only emotionally," Gwen said, remembering how nasty Donna had been to Lulu.

As the Caddy pulled out, Gwen looked out the rear window.

The lacrosse squad was just leaving the liquor store, two of them carrying big brown paper bags that likely contained cases of beer.

The rink was a couple of acres of mirror-glossy concrete, pitted and scratched with age. There was a geometric arrangement of pulsing neon bars arranged across the black ceiling, and skaters whirled through a haze of color. This late in the evening, the kids out on the rink weren't really kids anymore, and Gwen wondered why they came here. Didn't they know it was for children?

She took her time tying on her rented skates. Arthur sat next to her, tying on a pair of his own. He wore a burly gray turtleneck and crisp jeans and a pair of horn-rimmed spectacles. He was as bald as Colin now, had shaved it all off, and wore a Nepalese smoking hat clapped onto his dome. She had never seen a hat like that before and wouldn't see one like it again until she saw one on Dumbledore in the *Harry Potter* films.

They didn't speak at first, had not been alone together the whole wedding weekend. They watched the floor instead.

Donna was too drunk to stand. She had sat down in one corner of the rink. Gregg had her by the hands and was jogging in place in his skates, trying to pull her back up. Sometimes he could get her ass off the floor and take them both on a laughing little pirouette before she sat down again.

Van skated with his unicorn, the two of them gliding as if gravity and friction didn't apply to them. He really was a hell of a skater, Gwen thought. He soared along without fear, raising his arms like a ballet dancer, then dropping to a squat to roar along like a bowling ball. Allie wobbled and scampered after him and once jumped on his back and let him carry her.

Gregg's sisters tottered along awkwardly, hand in hand, looking hopefully at Colin every time he skated past them. He skated alone, his hands behind his back and his upper body leaning forward, like a ship's figurehead. He seemed completely content, drawing great looping circles around the outer edge of the rink by himself—pleased by his own sure, unrelenting momentum. It was funny how even the way a person skated told you something about who they were. He was dressed as Venger from the *Dungeons & Dragons* cartoon: red cowl, black cape, fangs, and a single horn. He wore a glossy black orb around his neck, like a smooth piece of volcanic glass. The third time he skated past, Gwen was able to determine that the amulet was, in fact, a webcam. That made sense. He was the Sauron of the World Wide

Web, a shadowy wizard who cast spells in HTML, and no doubt the webcam was a justly deserved symbol of his arcane office.

Van had gone as Eric the Cavalier, in a gold tunic that looked suspiciously like a girl's miniskirt. He had the shield strapped to his back, a gold wheel of plastic. Arthur was supposed to be Hank the Ranger; Colin had special-ordered the costume, but it was too small, so at the last minute Arthur had bought a Gandalf robe with the texture of burlap at Spencer Gifts. Only it didn't make him look like a wizard. With his shaved head and beard and dark eyes he looked like a monk, up past his bedtime to ink an illuminated manuscript.

"I like your beard," Gwen said at last, and then wished she hadn't, it was such a dumb remark. *I miss you,* was what she meant to say. *I'm not allowed to say I love you,* was what she wanted to tell him. *To say that I will always love you.*

"I'm trying to become the person everyone hoped I'd be. The kind of professor people adore because you can sneak a nap in his class."

"I don't believe it, old buddy," she said. "Your mom says your classes are standing room only."

"You talk to my mother?"

"She was down to the coast just this summer. They had her over at St. Anne's in Kennebunkport as a guest pastor. We had tea and caught up."

She was too polite to ask why we aren't together anymore, Gwen didn't say. *When everyone knew we were supposed to be together.*

"Be good to see her again. This'll be the second McBride she's married in two years," Gwen said, nodding at Donna and Gregg. Gregg was sprawled on the rink with Donna spraddled on top of him, legs to either side of his chest. He wasn't trying too hard to get up. "I like Gregg. He seems like a sweetheart—openhearted and innocent and corn-fed. The kind of guy who never forgets an anniversary and scatters rose petals on the bed on Valentine's Day."

"And yet we're just letting him march off to his doom," Arthur said. Gwen laughed. Arthur smiled—but it wasn't much of a smile.

"It might be good for her," Gwen said. "To be with someone so trusting, someone who believes people are basically good."

"I think that might be part of the appeal," Arthur said, staring out across the rink. "She crept out of Colin's bedroom at five a.m. two days ago."

Gwen's insides went a little sick. *Oh, Donna*, she thought, and exhaled a deep breath to dispel the bad feeling in her tummy. "Well. Maybe it was one last time for old times' sake. Get it out of their system and be done? Something like that?"

Arthur didn't reply.

"At least Van and Allie are happy," Gwen said.

"They'd have the perfect marriage if she wasn't gay and he wasn't a drug addict," Arthur said.

"I see why your class is so popular," Gwen said. "Who could resist your relentlessly sunny outlook?"

"Come on," he said, and offered her his hand. "Let's skate."

5.

They circled the outer edge of the rink while Kurt Cobain screamed hoarsely over a screeching guitar and sang about being trapped in a heart-shaped box. For a while it was too loud to talk, so they just held hands. They were skating for almost a full minute before Gwen realized she was filled to brimming with an unfamiliar sensation, a deep sensation of warmth that had to be contentment. Arthur was better than the first cup of tea in the morning, better than a last glass of wine after a good meal.

The song cross-faded into Oasis, "Live Forever," Liam Gallagher making promises no one could really keep. The volume had dropped slightly and it seemed possible to speak.

"What does a professor in medieval studies do when he's not grading papers?" Gwen asked. "Polish battle-axes?"

"Lately? Mostly I read about trolls. There's some good writing in Elder Futhark—"

"I think I got an album by Elder Futhark," Gwen said. "Didn't they record 'We're an American Band'?"

"—from the ninth century," Arthur went on. "Part of a broken tablet in an abbey that was rebuilt about eight times in the last two thousand years. It documents a named troll in the southwest of England. Svangur the Sly." They skated a full loop before Arthur added, "I think he's still there. Svangur. I'd like to have a word with him."

Gwen glanced sharply at him. "Are you serious? A troll named— what's he named?"

"Svangur. It means hunger. He was probably the real-world basis for Grendel, actually; the name's not too dissimilar. Grendel, Svangur, Svangdel."

"You really believe in trolls?"

Arthur said, "You really doubt them, old buddy?"

"Why would you want to talk to a troll? You want to start a fairy tale zoo or something?"

"He's got a weapon hoard," Arthur said. "Collected over a couple thousand years now, usually from hapless paladins who thought they could make a name for themselves by taking him on. He has a blade, the Sword of Strange Hangings, that figures heavily in the Grail quest. It's held in a sheath of white silk and can only be drawn by one ready to make a sacrifice of himself for the greater good—someone humble of spirit. I think it could cut through the plating on a dragon. I'd like to get my hands on it. It's in Svangur's caverns, along with his other treasures. A vial of some saint's blood that can make wounds vanish and suspend the aging process. Riches beyond compare. Colin's very interested in riches beyond compare. He made me promise I won't go troll-hunting without him."

Gwen squeezed his wrist, hard. "I wish you hadn't told me any of this. The iguana can *see* us, you know. From the Long Dark. Even now."

"If his eyes are open," Arthur said, mildly. "And maybe King Sorrow can see us, but he *can't* hear us. He has to come closer to hear us—close enough for us to hear *him*." Arthur thought a moment, then added, "If I had anything I absolutely *had* to keep secret, I'd tell you on consecrated ground. You know how Superman can't use his X-ray vision to see through lead? I have an idea churches and synagogues and temples might frustrate King Sorrow the same way."

"Do you really think there's a living, breathing troll somewhere in England? Just going unnoticed?"

"He'll be protected by a glam of some sort. He probably looks like a man at first. Although I doubt the glam can hold up to any close inspection. Children almost certainly can see him as he is. Children and cats and—"

There was a commotion over by the exits. People were running to see what was going on, some of them still in their skates. Gwen took it in—saw grins, flushed faces, heard yells—and thought there was a fight getting underway out in the parking lot. Oh, well. It was her night off. If someone needed first aid, they could call an ambulance like anyone else. Arthur, though, was peering speculatively across the rink. She tried to bring him back to the conversation.

"And you think . . . you might be able to find him?"

"Sure. There's only so many bridges in the southwest of England. It shouldn't take more than ten years to look under all of them."

She laughed, because she thought he was joking, but he wasn't paying her any mind. "Live Forever" ended and there was an instant of silence between songs. He cocked his head.

"Do you hear that?" Arthur said.

"Hear what?" Gwen said. After Oasis and Nirvana her ears were numb.

"That's Donna," Arthur said. "I think she's screaming."

6.

Even as he said it, he was moving, skating out of the rink and onto the varnished wooden floor of the seating area. Gwen went after him, but he had a head start. He reached the crowd around the door and went right through them, as effortlessly as a slip of paper pushed under a door. Whereas somehow she got caught behind the mass of people and had to fight her way through. She was shorter than most of them, of course—no one saw her until she was shoving past them. It was one indignity after another, to be a hobbit underfoot in a world of men.

Colin's cherry '49 Caddy was parked under a towering lamp-post, in the middle of the parking lot. The lacrosse kids were scattered around it, and a few of them had brought their sticks. Someone had ripped open the canvas roof so it hung in flaps and knocked off the passenger-side mirror. One of the lacrosse boys had jammed his stick down between the trunk and the rear bumper and was using it as a lever to try and pop the bumper right off. He was a gangly, freckled boy, sweating and flushed, his upper lip curled in a sneer of rage.

"Come *off*. Mother. *Fucker*." He grunted.

Another lacrosse kid—a broad-shouldered dude, with a jutting, caveman forehead that threw his eyes into shadow—stood next to him, pointing his stick at the crowd, warning people back. Some of the other lacrosse boys were standing around with their sticks, looking anxious and defiant.

Colin and Gregg had their arms around Donna, who was

snarling, spitting, trying to get free and throw herself at the lacrosse squad. Colin watched them work on his car with an air of weary acceptance.

"*I'll take that stick,*" Donna screamed at the blockhead, who was pointing said stick into her face. "*And jam it up your ass! You fucking wannabe rapists! I'll put your wannabe rapist faces on the news and fucking destroy you! Poking your sticks in his car cause you can't poke a woman! I'll ruin you!*"

"Leave it, Donna," Colin said. "It's just a car."

Gregg looked drunk, scared, and confused. He had an arm around his fiancée's waist and watched the lacrosse boys demolish the Caddy in a state of dumb shock.

"Jeezum, boys," Gregg said. "That's a classic. What are you doing?" They didn't listen, probably didn't hear him.

Maybe twenty people had emerged from inside the rink to watch. They lingered a few yards back, laughing and shouting. Arthur, Van, and Allie stood at one edge of the audience, unsure what to do. Gwen skated past them, thinking she would get over to Donna, lead her back to the limo, calm her down. Donna always listened to her.

Only Gwen wasn't steady on her skates. She missed Donna, Gregg, and Colin completely, rolled right by them without meaning to, and sailed straight at the blockhead with the Cro-Magnon forehead.

His eyes widened in surprise as she elbowed his stick aside and kept going right into him. He startled, thought he was being tackled by some crazy bitch—she saw it in his face, right before he came around with his left hand closed into a fist. She didn't feel him hit her. She was just suddenly on the ground, both hands on the cold blacktop, her mouth full of blood.

"GWEN!" Allie screamed.

She still had her unicorn mask on, and it came out in a muffled whinny. Suddenly Allie was tearing at her costume and pounding one rubber hoof into her breastbone.

"*You're going to die!*" Allie began to scream at the boys in the lacrosse uniforms. "*You're all going to die!*"

Gwen had been struck so hard, it was difficult to think thoughts. She could still feel, though, and the sight of Allie trying to touch something on her chest filled her with a cold whoosh of dread.

Only Allie couldn't get to it. She needed hands to touch and had hooves instead. Her costume zipped up in the back and she couldn't get to her bare chest. And Van scooped her up—her roller skates came right off the ground—pinning her arms to her sides.

"No, Allie," Van said. "They're just kids. They're just stupid kids."

King Sorrow, Gwen thought. Allie wanted to pull King Sorrow out of the Long Dark to fry a few stupid children for vandalizing a car. *Neigh*, Gwen thought, and almost laughed. *Neigh*.

The Cro-Magnon was staring dumbly at her, stick at his side.

"You made me do that," he said. "You shouldn't a jumped in my face, bitch."

He was looking down at her, so he didn't see Arthur coming. Arthur was already up to full speed when he sailed into him, driving his shoulder into the Cro-Magnon's breadbasket. The kid *woofed*, doubling over, and Arthur snatched the stick out of his hands. He continued past on his skates and used the lacrosse stick to clothesline the freckly boy trying to pry off Colin's bumper.

"*Uck!*" Freckles flailed at the night and went down.

Arthur came around in an arc, wheels scraping and grinding on the blacktop. Freckles and the caveman had both dropped to the ground. Freckles clutched his throat. Caveman had his arms wrapped around his stomach and was groaning.

The other lacrosse kids tried to approach. One of them was shouting, "Hey! Hey, not cool, man!" Another kid yelled, "Beat his ass!" Another said, "Guys—hey—hey, guys, stop!"

Arthur was almost on top of Gwen when he began to spin. He kicked with one foot and began to revolve, like a figure in a music box. He came around with the lacrosse stick, *whoop, whoop, whoop*, in great whistling arcs, and the lacrosse squad fell back. One of them retreated so quickly he fell on his rear end. Another backpedaled into Donna, who lashed out with one foot and kicked him in the ass. A third boy fell back a few feet, ducked, came up with a stone, and threw it. Arthur came around and smashed it right back at him with the stick, a batter connecting with a hard slider. It struck the boy in the upper thigh, close to his groin, and the kid squealed.

Gwen felt faint, dizzy. The night pulsed strangely around her, spasming with lights. Arthur spun around and around, lashing his lacrosse stick over his head, looking for all the world like a druid with his staff, laying about him with his war club on the battlefield. The sight of him was thrilling—inspiring, almost. She had never seen him look so happy.

One of the teenage turds was trying to sneak in from behind, around one corner of the Caddy, to get Arthur when he was facing the other way. Only as he emerged Van soared in, squatting low, gliding the way he had on the rink, rumbling like a bowling ball, and he came up with his plastic shield and punched it into the kid's face. The kid went straight back over his heels and then Van was circling too, the rings around Arthur's Saturn, brandishing the shield with one arm and waving his free hand, *C'mon, fuckers, come and get it.* He was laughing hysterically. Gwen looked around and saw Allie had stopped trying to touch the tattoo hidden under her costume and was instead pawing at the air with her hooves, chanting Van's name.

"Van, Van, Van the Man," she cried, "if he can't do it, no one can!"

Arthur rotated slowly at the center of the universe, whiplashing his stolen lacrosse stick, Friar Tuck teaching Robin Hood a lesson in humility. Van swooped and dived about him, hummingbird near the flower, shield held up to the night in triumph.

Someone found her elbow: Colin. He had left Donna with Gregg and moved in to help Gwen up. Her legs were weak and her skates went this way and that beneath her, but he stabilized her, kept her from falling again. Colin was smiling. She had not realized until then how much Colin loved Arthur and Van—

maybe even hero-worshipped them. Colin stroked his webcam amulet and Gwen had a sudden thought, that somehow he was filming all of it, although that was impossible, webcams only worked when they were plugged into a computer.

He saw her looking and said, "Oh, yeah. Getting every beautiful minute. This right here? This moment is forever."

Arthur spun and spun, slowing steadily, winding down . . . until finally he was facing her and Colin. His eyes were bright with merriment, the night strobing around him. She didn't realize those flashing lights weren't just in her head until the police cruiser let out a little squawk with the alarm, telling the crowd to break up, let 'em through. The fun was done.

7.

Tana Nighswander was there to collect them when they were sprung loose at seven in the morning. Tana had been working as a bus driver the last couple of years—third graders were better company than pizzas and pot, she said—and when they shuffled out of the Cumberland County Detention Center into the gray, overcast cool of the morning, the bus was idling at an angle in one corner of the parking lot. The Pinets had parked right behind it and were standing next to their rented white Chevy Lumina. Raymond, the old soldier who had stormed Omaha Beach, had his head down, chewing on a toothpick, and didn't look at them as they approached. Sasha, his wife, in a gray crepey blouse and silver scarves, shifted from foot to foot and squeezed her fingers. The sisters—who had not been arrested—were sitting in the back of the car. Gigi had the soft, puffy, too-white look of a drowned corpse. Lulu was ramrod straight, watching them approach with the slightest hint of a smile at the corners of her lips—a nasty smile. One look at her face, and Gwen thought it was highly unlikely that Gregg Pinet would be walking to the altar with Donna McBride come Sunday morning. Or ever.

They were a sorry party of adventurers, creeping along in their socks, shamefaced, sweaty, and hungover. The manager at Merlin's Cave had demanded his roller skates back before they were loaded into the police cars, and no one had returned their shoes. At least there would be no charges. Gwen had answered calls with every cop in Gogan, and uniforms looked after each other.

Allie was especially pitiful, walking along with the full-head unicorn mask under one arm. Allie had always been the most beautiful girl Gwen had ever known, but in the raw light of the early morning, her face swollen, her hair drab, she looked twice her age and hard used.

Tana's son, Jett, seven years old, sat on the bottom step of the bus, clutching a toy fire truck to his chest, but he leapt to his feet in excitement when he saw them approaching, thrilled to see grown-ups dressed as idiots.

"Whadja get arrested for, Gwen?" Jett asked her.

"Crimes against fashion, most like," Tana said, glancing at Gwen's fur bikini. "Are you supposed to be a bear? Is that the bottom part of a bear costume?"

Donna's eyes were bright and blind, and she walked like she was balancing an invisible tray on her head, with a rolling gait but a curious rigidity of the body. She staggered, and Gwen had to catch her elbow to steady her.

"Is she still drunk?" Tana wanted to know.

Gregg had wrapped one arm around his head. "I think I'm going to be sick."

"I know I'm going to be sick," Allie said, shuffling to a stop, bending at the waist, and clutching her knees.

Donna didn't look back at him. "For Chrissake, don't do it on the bus. Neither of you. If I have to smell it, I'll puke too. Hork it up out here, why don't you?"

Sasha Pinet swooped in to intercept Gregg before he could follow Donna aboard. "Don't worry. He's coming with us. We'll look after him."

"Good," Donna said, without glancing at either of them. "Keep him. Fucker did nothing while my best friend got punched in the face."

"She doesn't mean that, man," Van said, following Gregg across the parking lot, looking past the groom to Sasha. "She doesn't mean that, Mrs. Pinet. None of us slept. There was an angry drunk in the lockup who screamed abuse all night long."

"I've no doubt," Sasha Pinet said. "I've met her."

Gwen couldn't figure out why Van was trying to fix things for his sister while his wife got sick. Force of habit, she supposed.

Allie was making little sounds in her throat, sounds something like the coo of a dove, something like a cough. Tana stroked Allie's back, and when she began to vomit, she held her hair back out of the spray.

"You get it all up, hon," Tana said. "Go on and cough up every bit of last night. Get it out your system and we'll take you somewhere and get some tea and warm toast in you."

"Oh, no," Allie moaned. "I got some on your shoes."

"I drive third graders to school," Tana said. "There isn't a week goes by some eight-year-old doesn't get sick all over them."

Only Colin looked well. Colin looked as bright-eyed and fresh as if he had spent a night at the Four Seasons. He had an arm over Arthur's shoulders. "Let no one ever say that Arthur Oakes is a bore again. The man has a PhD in kicking ass."

Then he turned his head to watch Sasha pile her son into the back of the Chevy Lumina with his sisters. Raymond Pinet lifted his head at last to toss his toothpick.

"You're a good boy, Donovan," Raymond said. "But you are damn bad luck. And one of these days you're going to be in a plane crash you can't walk away from. You and your sister both, maybe. Try and take better care of yourself, why don't you?"

And he walked around the front of the Chevy, got behind the wheel, and drove his family away. Van watched them go, rubbing the back of his neck.

"I think that's that," Arthur said, softly.

"Looks like it," Gwen said. "Too bad, huh?"

"Is it?" Arthur said.

Gwen thought about it and gave her head a little shake.

"None of us are having much luck at finding our way to 'happily ever after,' are we?" Gwen said.

Arthur smiled at her and bumped his shoulder against hers. "I don't think such a thing exists. Maybe there's only happy-for-a-little-while, old chum."

"Old buddy," Gwen said, and bumped him back.

Arthur and Gwen sat together in the back of the bus. She didn't mean to fall asleep with her head on his bicep. It just happened, before Tana even had a chance to pull out onto the road. At some point, Gwen was aware of Arthur rearranging her so her head was pillowed on one of his thighs and his arm was over her shoulders.

She never slept in his arms again, but while it lasted, it was good.

8.

They drove her south in an '84 Cadillac Brougham the color of infected piss. The guy behind the wheel, a US marshal of indeterminate age, closely resembled the Kingpin from Marvel Comics: big bald head disappearing into a fat neck, ham hock forearms and massive thighs. He had the look of a hard-ass but was soft-spoken and polite, and after three hours on the road, he pulled off the interstate and bought them KFC. Daphne ate in the back and wiped her fingers on her reading material. His partner was a woman of forty with the look of the prairie about her. Broad, pretty features, distant blue eyes, hair swept up. Their names were Winkler and Fromm.

"What's that you're reading?" Fromm asked, a half hour after Kentucky Fried. When Daphne had finished, she had discarded

the bones on the floor. They were scattered around her feet and sometimes when she moved, one would crunch under her heels.

"'Bout this plane nearly got blown out of the sky a couple years ago," Daphne said. "By a UFO. Right over Greenland."

"Oh, yeah," said Winkler. "British Airways. I didn't know it was UFOs. I thought it nearly got blown out of the sky by a white nationalist named Randy Mathers. You must have better information than I do. Where'd you get the inside dope? The National Enquirer?"

They were making fun of her. Daphne was acutely conscious of being condescended to, and always had been. She didn't mind, though.

"Inside View," she said placidly. "My daughter had friends on that flight. I woulda been heartbroke to lose 'em. I'd like to see 'em when I'm out, tell 'em how much it means to me, that they looked after my girl while I was stuck inside."

Fromm and Winkler exchanged another glance. Fromm said, "It's going to be three years longer after that stunt you pulled in Black Cricket. And I'll tell you what, lady, the days don't pass in West Virginia like they did in that summer camp you just left. You want my advice, you'll stay out of the heroin trade in FCI Hazelton. The Ecuadorians got that line locked up. Those bitches don't play."

"Yep," Daphne said. "Going to keep my nose clean, ma'am. Going to keep to scrapbooking." She shuffled through the little stack of newsprint she kept folded into a book stolen from the Black Cricket library, a book she had no interest in and had never bothered to read, *The Once and Future King*. There were three articles about BA 238, including a *People* feature covering the marriage of two passengers in the days shortly after the near disaster. There were articles snipped from *Spin* and *Rolling Stone*, all by the same journalist. There was a profile of a glamorous Fox New York news reporter. There was a news report about a Maine EMT who volunteered at a Podomaquassy hospice. There were a few academic articles by a professor in medieval literature. There was a piece from the *Wall Street*

Journal *about a young hedge fund manager from Podomaquassy who had staked out big positions in eBay and some other internet start-ups.* "I like to know what the kids I left are doing with their lives. I like to think about them. Makes me feel like I got something to look forward to."

Saying their names to herself, a recitation she had come to find comforting. The names never failed to lift her spirits. Saying them, she always felt like a bullet that had been fired into the future—no, somehow she was six bullets, fired into the next century. Fired at them.

Colin Wren.
Donna McBride.
Donovan McBride.
Allison Shiner.
Gwen Underfoot.
Arthur Oakes.

Book Three

DOUBLE FEATURE

2000

1.

Donovan McBride stood at his favorite window, sipping sweet coffee and thinking he and Allie were in terrible trouble—if they didn't get their drinking under control, one of them was going to die, punch out like John Bonham or Bon Scott—when something huge detonated around the corner, on Garfield Place. A blast of fire, twenty feet high, erupted through the gap between buildings. The explosion, a gas main maybe, made a deep, resonating *thud* that he felt more than heard, and drove a rippling shockwave down the avenue. Van saw it coming, the air going all wavy and distorted, like heat rising from blacktop, and had time to drop his mug and fall to the floor before the lovely, big, round window erupted. Glass showered around him in a bright drizzle of light.

"*Fuck!*" he shouted. "*Fuck! Fuck!*" He had long known that when he died, there would be no fine last words. It would just be *fuckshit fuckfuckFUUUUUCK* and then he'd be gone.

He rose to his knees and looked out the window and that's when it hit him. *Allie.* Allie was down there. Allie had gone to the Garfield Street convenience store for V8, had wanted a Bloody Mary with her eggs. He had encouraged her to go, didn't want her to see him starting his day with a couple of lines and a lonely wank.

Filthy smoke boiled from the brick canyon of the side street. A blackened confetti of debris fluttered in the air amid the sparks. The idea that Allie had just been blown off the face of the earth filled him with such shock, such horror, he could not compose a single clear thought. He was halfway down the concrete stairs when he realized he was still barefooted. He couldn't run shoeless all the way to Garfield Place. If nothing else, there was going to be a shit-ton of broken glass to cross.

He ran back to the apartment, ran around the kitchen hunting for his shoes. It looked as if the shockwave had scattered shit everywhere, though that was just the way their apartment looked: magazines and newspapers strewn on couch and floor, empty Chinese cartons on the kitchen island drawing flies. He found one of his Sperrys under the coffee table. He found one of his slippers in the master bedroom. They were both for his right foot. It was like a bad dream, scrambling about in his robe and pajamas, desperate for something to put on his left foot so he could go out and collect the pieces of his dead wife.

He was on all fours when the phone went off. He rose so quickly he slammed his head on the underside of the kitchen island, *hard*. A white flash went off behind his eyeballs. He shook his head to clear it and grabbed the cordless, sure it would be Donna. He had never been this scared and confused without Donna knowing it, even if they were miles apart . . . the one little part of their twin telepathy act that wasn't bullshit, wasn't a game to play on rubes.

Only it wasn't Donna. It was Allie.

"Van," she gasped. "Get out of the apartment."

"You aren't dead!" He was so relieved, he thought he was going to be sick.

"You have to go right now," she said. "There's men."

"Fucking Garfield Place just—and I thought fuck, *fuck*, I thought—"

"They're dressed like repairmen. They're with the fat man from Greenland, I never learned his name. I spotted him in a van, parked right in front of our apartment, but I didn't remember where I had seen him before until I was on Garfield—"

"Allie, I don't understand. You aren't making sense. Can you come home?"

"No. And you can't stay there. Get your wallet and go, Van. They're after us. One of them tried to stick me in the butt with a needle and I had to bring King Sorrow through from the Long Dark."

A snow of burning confetti fell outside the shattered window, a window he loved, his favorite thing about the apartment, the now-smashed panes composed in a pattern of petals that reminded him of a sand dollar.

"Someone tried to—*what*? Jesus. Are you sure? You weren't—you didn't—Allie, have you been drinking?"

"Have I been—oh. Oh, *Van*. Yes, sure, but I mean—not enough to be wrong about *this*. We can talk about it later, just please go. We'll meet at Washington Square. I can't talk anymore. I need to call Donna."

"Why do you need to call Donna?" Even through his disorientation and alarm he felt an itch of resentment. They couldn't have a life-or-death crisis in peace like other couples. Allie had to bring Donna into it.

"If they're after me and after you, they might be after all of us. Now get going."

"Okay," he said. "I just can't find my shoes."

She had already hung up. He was standing there in front of the blown-open window, holding the cordless in one hand and a Sperry in the other, when the needle slid into his neck. He cried out, a pitiful little squeak. He looked around, discovered two men behind him. The one with the syringe was a lithe little guy, with the dimples, the rosy complexion, and the tousled blond hair of a cherub in a Renaissance painting. The one grabbing Van's right bicep had black hair, slicked back, in the style of Bela Lugosi. It was a lucky thing he had Van's arm too, because Van's knees buckled suddenly, and the man behind him was the only thing holding him up.

"Don't worry about the other shoe," said a third man, standing just inside the open front door. He was a big guy, a wide-body with a Magnum PI mustache, and he was holding Van's other Sperry. "Found it."

Van opened his mouth to thank him, but couldn't seem to lift his tongue, or produce any sound at all beyond a slurred, miserable moan. The men standing behind him had him by the arms. They marched him forward, one step, and another, and then he walked right off an invisible ledge. He fell four stories—or maybe it was forty, who could really say—and struck the darkness waiting at the bottom with a resounding clap.

2.

Donna was crossing the concrete court to her office building when her sleek Nokia—Colin got her a new one for Christmas, year in, year out—went off. She stopped to answer it because it meant she could finish her cigarette. The after-breakfast cigarette was her favorite, better than the post-fuck cigarette even. Not that she really ate breakfast, just a juice smoothie, in the interest of holding her weight at 114 pounds for the cameras.

"Where are you?" Allie asked.

"Walking into the office."

"Get away. Right now. Don't go to work."

Donna heard sirens in the background of the call.

"What's going on, babe?"

"There were men. One of them tried to stick me in the bum with a syringe. I had to pull King Sorrow through from the Long Dark. They're all dead now. Please, Donna, *please*, walk away from the office."

Donna started walking, across the court, past the entrance to the tower. She strode swiftly up Sixth with her head down. Her pulse came in hard, jagged throbs. When she shut her eyes for a moment she saw water from a sprinkler, leaping through the sunlight, flashing like drops of mercury. She remembered the feel of a cold wet bathing suit against her skin, remembered shivering convulsively. Awful things to recall.

"These men," Donna said. "How many?"

"One in a pickup. Two on the sidewalk. At least two. King Sorrow wiped them out, but I know there's more. There was another team of three in a van in front of our apartment building. I recognized one of them. I didn't know him at first, but when I was almost to Garfield Place it came back to me. He was in Greenland. He was in the room when the FBI interviewed me. Not always, just sometimes, and I don't think he was an agent himself, I—"

"What about Donovan?"

"He's safe. I called him before I called you. He's already on the move."

"Why would they come after you? *Either* of you?" Donna asked.

"They must know something about King Sorrow. I think it was Van's gosh-darn book. He gave us away."

The book. Of course, the book. He had to write the fucking book. Colin had told him not to, but Van wanted it so much, wanted to be important, and Robin had promised she could get it on the bestseller lists. *Satanic Skies: The Impossible True Story of BA 238*. The book was huge with UFO nuts and people who believed in astral projections.

"Where are you now?" Donna asked.

"On a pay phone. Donovan and I were going to meet up at the Washington Square Arch. Can you meet us there?"

"I'm supposed to be at work."

"You can't go to work. I told you."

"Just because they want you and him doesn't mean they're after me. *I* wasn't on the flight with you."

"But you're in the book. And you're his twin. Donna, they could be following you now."

Donna fought back another wave of that shivery wet swimsuit feeling, the sensation she hated most in the world. She slowed, joining a gathering at the corner, all of them waiting for the WALK light, and had a careful look around. She scanned the crowd for anyone who might be following her. A young woman with glossy chestnut hair was picking a stone out of one of her sneakers. Had she also been on the subway with Donna that morning? A good-looking kid in his late teens, early twenties, was trying to scope her out without being noticed. Maybe a kidnapper, maybe a horny kid, maybe just someone who had recognized her from the local news. She couldn't keep track of all the people moving around her. Instead of crossing the street she turned right, just to keep moving.

"What about the others? Colin? Gwen?"

"Well, they weren't in the book, were they? It was just us. Van wanted to thank the rest of the gang, but Colin wouldn't let him, said it was 'ill-advised.' I don't know what to do, Donna. I just killed three men. At *least* three. And cars, a whole row of cars went up like someone hit them with a rocket launcher, like in a movie, Christ, he blew up half the block—"

"Stop talking and start walking," Donna said, having heard enough. "I'll see you soon." And flipped her phone shut with a clap.

A Black man, a few storefronts down from Donna, hailed a cab. The taxi started to slow for him, but Donna threw up her own hand and it put on a little jolt of speed to pull past him and alongside her. She leapt in, told the cabbie to roll. Middle Eastern driver, his radio babbling idiotically, smell of falafel thick in the air, fucking New York was getting more like Baghdad every day. When Donna glanced over her shoulder she saw the Black guy still on the curb, tucking one hand into the pocket of his gray slacks, a look of amused contempt on his face. She gave him an exaggerated shrug through the rear window. If he wanted better luck catching cabs, he should've been born with an ass like hers.

SHE DITCHED THE CAB at Fifty-Seventh Street, went underground to the subway, came up two minutes later on the opposite side of the street and caught the first taxi to come into sight. She hadn't seen anyone following her, but if there *was* someone back there, they were gone now. No way they had stuck with her through that. Her ride carried her downtown toward Washington Square Park.

Donna's thoughts were caffeinated, coming too fast. She had spent a lot of her life imagining what she would do if someone tried to grab her. It was her natural state. Unlike Allie, she had never touched the mark on her chest, had never brought King Sorrow through from the Long Dark. She'd never had to. But it brought her calm to know that if someone tried to stick her with a needle, she could blast them to cinders with a tap of her fingers.

She thought too, there were people dead in Brooklyn, and it was going to be a big story, and she wished she could have a piece of it. Which reminded her: they would start the day's editorial planning session in ten minutes, without her. She flipped open her phone to dial her producer, Morris Shanley, tell him there had been a big explosion near where her brother lived and she was worried about him, but her Nokia dropped the call after the third ring. It was hard to find a cell signal down in the shadowy canyons of brick and glass. Colin said that cell phones were more important than computers or laptops, but it was hard to imagine it, you couldn't use the fucking things anywhere.

Of course, Colin knew all about phones, and all about the future too, and he would know better than her. He had been living in the twenty-first century since at least 1990. His first company sold surveillance technology for hacking into cell phones to read people's texts and emails, for tracking their Web searches. His second start-up sold security software, to protect companies and government agencies from exactly the sort of hacking his first company specialized in. It entertained Colin Wren to peddle the virus and sell the cure. He had been highly involved in those first two outfits, had even written some early code for them, although he claimed he wasn't much of a programmer. He was mostly out of hands-on work now. He had started a venture capital fund (Smaugloot—he named all his companies after dumb Dungeons and Hobbits shit) and made his money investing in other people's clever ideas. *Forbes* said he was worth two hundred million dollars, but when Donna asked him, he twisted his mouth to one side in a little smile and said, "Hardly counts when you inherited the first twenty million."

The drive to Washington Square Park was stop-and-go. It was warm enough in the direct sunlight, but in the cool shadows of the cab that clammy wet swimsuit feeling came over her again. She hated it. She hated to feel weak and despised weakness in other women. Sometimes she despised it in Allie. The thought of men grabbing Allie made Donna shudder. Made her want to hurt someone. Gregg Pinet had liked it when Donna hurt him, or had learned to like it, anyway. He was married to an investment banker ten years older than him now—a chain-smoker with great legs, who made him sign a prenup. Maybe they had kids by now, a dreadful thought.

The arch loomed at the end of Fifth, dingy white marble against a blindingly blue sky. Donna flung herself out of her yellow cab and into the bright, bitter day. She found a bench under a bare tree. She had a signal here, but before she could call anyone, her phone hummed with an unknown number. After a moment's hesitation, she flipped her Nokia open and answered.

"Donna, it's me," Colin said. "Don't say my name. It's likely the people who are after you have already tapped your phone. I'm calling from a secure line, but you aren't, so assume they're listening. Your phone has a transponder in it. They can use it to find you. I want you to get rid of your Nokia as soon as we're done talking. They know about Allie—we just spoke—they know about Donovan, and I think it's a safe assumption they know about you. But that might be *all* they know."

"Because of that stupid book?"

"Because of the book. I thought it was a bad idea, but there's no use relitigating the past. If that's *all* they know, that's how I want to keep it. They're making their move—soon enough we'll make ours."

She was on her feet again. She felt like a loaded gun, ready to go off and kill some mother's son. Colin had that effect on her, made her feel like they couldn't lose.

"Get moving, Donna. I know where you are. You have to assume they do too. Allie knows not to meet you there now. We'll all meet up at the streetlamp that looks like a question mark. I'll look for you there every day at exactly six p.m. for a week. Don't call me—don't call any of us—unless you absolutely must, and then use a pay phone."

She began to walk, swift, long strides, heels clacking on the concrete.

"Anything else?" she asked.

"No. Hang up. Eject the SIM card—"

"What's a—"

"It's a memory card in a cartridge on the side of your phone. You can open it with a hairpin. Eject the SIM card and throw it away. Snap your phone in two and throw that away too. I'll see you at the question mark. Be safe. I love you."

"I love you too," she said, and it was true. She could've said it to any of them and it would've been true: Arthur, Gwen, Allie, Van. She would've died for any of them—although she'd far rather kill for them.

Donna dropped the SIM down a cistern. She struggled with the phone while she walked, finally snapped it in two at the hinge. She cast her gaze around her, scanning the other wanderers in the park, but if anyone was watching she couldn't spot them. She hastened down a cross street and emerged on Sixth at the Washington Square subway entrance. By the time she descended the steps into the roaring, steam-filled world below, she was running as fast as a woman in four-inch heels could run.

3.

She was in Penn Station, looking at a lukewarm piece of pizza she didn't want to eat, when a wisp of a man sat down and said, "Hey, Donna? Donna McBride from NY-25?"

He was beautiful, in a crisp white shirt and brand-new-looking jeans, with the sort of blue eyes that made her think of glaciers. His blond hair was so fine it was almost white, a crown of spun silver. He might've been an elfin prince.

She nodded. Although it gratified her to be recognized, it wasn't the best time.

"Hey, wow! Cool," he said. He clapped a hand to the counter. "I gotta show you something. You're a journalist." He dipped his head to peer in a slim leather satchel, a sort of soft briefcase, and came up with a manila folder. "Take a look—is this newsworthy?"

He flapped it open to show her a grainy photograph of her brother, in his jockey underwear and a canvas straitjacket, sprawled on his side on a padded bench somewhere. His bare, too-white legs were scrawny and pimpled. His eyes were shut.

Her stomach churned, and she was overcome once again by the old clammy swimsuit sensation. She braced her palms against the edge of the counter as if there were some danger she might slide off her stool. The elfin prince flapped the folder shut again.

"How'd you find me? I ditched my phone. There's no way anyone could've followed me."

"You called your boss from a pay phone when you got to Penn Station—Morris Shanley? We're up on his line too, and we traced your call to here." He tucked the manila folder back into his soft briefcase and went on: "I know there's an invisible mark on your chest, and I know if you touch it, you can bring an entity through into our reality to blast me right off this stool. I'll be honest. I don't love the idea. But I want you to know, if that does happen—"

"You'll kill Van."

"No!" he said, and smiled—a generous, lovely smile. "I don't have clearance for that! No, he's too valuable. You both are. We'll just lobotomize him. The team is pretty sure we can still use him to access the entity, even if we cauterize his frontal lobe. Speaking as someone who has read his writing, I think that would be a shame. He has such a lively, playful way of looking at the world. I'd regret it."

"No, you wouldn't. Because you'd be dead," she said.

"Good point. Donna, we could've tried to hit you with a needle, but this is an enclosed public place, and if it went wrong here . . . *well*. It could be a whole lot worse than what happened on Garfield Place this morning. Besides, I'd like to get off on the right foot with you, see if we can't establish a . . . productive working relationship. Come outside with me and I'll take you to your brother."

"And then what?"

"Then you give me a few weeks of your time. That's all. We can reach out to your office, tell them your brother was injured in the Garfield Place explosion. His injuries will require multiple surgeries, a lot of rehab, and you need some time off to help him out."

"A few weeks. To do what?"

"To help us understand what happened over Greenland five years ago. Something cut two F-16s in two, and we're pretty sure you can tell us what. Maybe we could also talk about Haruto Sagawa, who was killed at Easter the following year, in an explosion that destroyed a four-story building and killed nearly thirty other members of Aum Shinrikyo. Or Gilberto Herrera, the Columbian drug lord, who cooked to death along with two dozen heavily armed hard-asses in a mountain camp *last* Easter. Locals say he was destroyed by White Quetzalcóatl—the dragon the Aztecs worshipped." He gave her a sidelong, comradely smile. "We just want to understand, Donna. You can help us understand. Would you do that?"

"And then you'll just, what, let us go?"

"Yes. Absolutely. You'll sign an NDA with our outfit and we'll—"

"What a crock of shit."

"Don't make us lobotomize Donovan. Don't put us in a position where we might have to do the same to Allie."

Donna felt icy and sick. "You don't have Allison. She got away."

"We don't have her *yet*. But we will. She's in the wind for the moment, but I think you know she's a barely functioning alcoholic with no real gift for survival."

"You know who didn't have a gift for survival? The clowns you sent after her. You'll be scraping burnt pieces of them off the sidewalk for days." Her own hand had moved to the neck of her blouse. Her thumb touched the skin between her collarbones. She could feel it now, the silky tickle of the serpent wound around her torso.

He was watching. "How many do you think will die—besides me—if you bring him through now? *Here?*" He cast his glance around the pizza shop, as crowded as a subway car at rush hour. "That creature wiped out three of ours in Brooklyn, but you know what else it did? It put a mother of four through a plate-glass window. She's dead—broken neck. There are a dozen others in a burn ward. The entity, he's not exactly a precision weapon, is he? What do you think it would do if you unleashed him on Penn Station? A hundred casualties? Two hundred?" He put his hands together. "Let's go for a ride. There's so much I want to learn."

"Seems like you already know enough."

"Hardly! Does it have a name? I'd like to talk to it—is such a thing possible without being destroyed? With your help?"

She didn't reply. Her stomach hurt.

He slid off his stool. "Follow me or don't. If you come with me now, we don't have to take a hot drill to your brother's frontal lobe. Or you can stay right here. You've got a ticket for Boston, maybe we'll catch up with you there. Or maybe later. One way or another, you're coming with me, Donna. The only real question is if you love your brother enough to come with me now."

He waited, standing beside her. His eyes were so blue, they didn't look real. When she didn't move, he nodded reluctantly, as if they had agreed to disagree, and began to squeeze through the crowd to the concourse. He was almost to the marble-floored hall when he paused to look back. This time she stood up. She left her untouched pizza behind.

"At least tell me your name," she said.

"Valentine," he said. "Joe Valentine."

She shot him a sharp look. "That isn't your real name."

"No. In the old stories—in folk tales—it's important never to tell a faery your true name, lest she use it against you. I think there's only two ways you can turn the creature against me: if you touch the mark on your chest or if you have my name."

Men fell into step behind them. One of them, a big slab of a guy with a Tom Selleck mustache and legs as thick as telephone poles, lifted the lapel of his ill-fitting sports coat and murmured something into a mic clipped there. The other had the compact, muscly build of an Olympic swimmer and kept his black hair slicked back like Michael Corleone in the second *Godfather* film. As they strode along, this second man was always casting his gaze about, scanning the concourse for interference, for problems.

"Who are you with? CIA?" Donna asked. "NSA?"

"Oh, no! We're a private contractor, although we do quite a bit of work for Uncle Sam. In the federal budget, we're sometimes listed as technical support. Mr. Francis is with one of your national acronyms, but even I don't know which one." Nodding at fat Tom Selleck. Donna was surprised, had assumed he was just muscle.

"Which team do you play for?" she asked Mr. Francis. "The Democrats or the Republicans?"

"Neither," Francis said, looking bored. "I sell the peanuts. Democrats, Republicans, they both smile when they see me coming. Everyone likes a bag of hot peanuts."

"Not everyone," Donna said. "I'm allergic, so you might wanna keep your nuts well out of reach."

Mr. Francis laughed, a low rumble of amusement. "Noted."

Then they were on the street and she thought, *Now, NOW,* but Valentine took her right hand in his, while Mr. Francis put his arm through her left.

"Think about your brother, Donna," said Joe Valentine. "Maybe you don't care if a couple dozen people die on Seventh Avenue today, but you can't destroy me without destroying Van."

A single hard fleck of snow whirled down out of the impossibly blue sky and caught in one of Donna's eyelashes. She glanced around, couldn't figure out where it had come from. There wasn't a cloud in the sky. When she looked back, a nondescript battered green van pulled to the curb, a few yards ahead of them, and suddenly it was hard for her to breathe. Something pinched in her chest and her knees went weak. This was worse than the clammy swimsuit sensation, this was like a hand on her throat, applying pressure to her windpipe. She stopped moving for a moment, actually pushed her heels into the ground, and the elf-prince glanced around in surprise. She made a little sound, not quite the word *no*.

The van, she thought, *it's THE VAN*. She had promised herself she would never willingly get in THE VAN. She had kept that promise for nearly two decades—a wordless promise, an oath that went deeper than words. She couldn't move forward.

"Do you have something to knock me out?" she asked. She could barely make a sound.

Francis looked at her with what she thought was genuine sympathy. "Do you need something?"

"Yes, please," she heard herself say. Even as she said it, she was trying to push back with her heels. Not even for Van could she get in THE VAN.

Francis looked past Donna to Valentine, and the elfin prince nodded. Valentine said, "You're going to feel a pinch in your neck," as a cold needle pierced the side of her throat, a sharp twinge of cold and pain.

"Breathe," Francis said. "Just breathe."

He let go of her arm and she found she couldn't lift it. It was like her left sleeve was empty, like the arm had been amputated. Valentine tugged a BlackBerry out of his pocket and began to type on it.

"New world record," Francis said to him, speaking across her.

"What?" Valentine asked.

"Longest I've ever seen you go without using that thing."

"There's a reason they call them CrackBerries," Valentine said, both of them talking as if she wasn't there. "You don't know how great it is to get emails sent right to your pocket. I love the future. And you know the best thing about it? There's always more ahead of you. I mean, maybe not for her, but for us."

"Hey," Francis said. "Can that, doc. She's still conscious."

"Nah," Valentine said. "Look at her. She can't even keep her head up."

It was true. Her head kept sinking on her neck and it took a conscious effort to jerk it upright.

The rear doors to the battered, unmarked green van opened onto an awful darkness. A big twentysomething in a polo shirt and dad jeans reached out for her with both arms. Donna tried to push herself away and found her feet were dragging across the concrete.

Valentine and Francis lifted her over the bumper. Francis said, "Up you go," as if he were lifting a small girl, his own daughter perhaps, into the seat of a swing. And then they were pressing her into THE VAN, right there on Seventh Avenue, people walking every which way but no one paying the slightest attention. The twentysomething in the polo shirt took her by the arms. The doors slammed behind her and the darkness slammed in around her.

4.

They wanted the sprinkler.

"What you need the sprinkler for, wait ten minutes, is going to rain," Leticia told them.

But Cady Lewis had come over in a pair of shorts and her swimsuit because Donna had promised her the sprinkler, not a rain shower. They jumped on the couch and yelled while Van tried to watch *Laff-A-Lympics*.

"Jesus H. Christ!" Van shouted. "The Really Rottens are cheating again and I can't even watch the end of my show!"

"I don' need to hear about Jesus H. Christ from you, young man," Leticia said. "When I want to hear about Jesus H. Christ I go to mass."

But Leticia knew when she was beat. She led the girls across the yard, unspooling about a mile of hose, to get them away from Mrs. McBride's bougainvillea. Their house was a three-story Florida McMansion with gables and balconies and a tiled porch that went around two sides, set in a few green acres of professionally landscaped lawn. Nice—but not as nice as the estate they moved to the following autumn, after Donna's father inherited the family business from *his* father and took over the operation of five local newspapers and two local television stations.

Leticia set the sprinkler on the grass and rolled out the yellow banana, a rubber mat twenty feet long. They could make all the noise they wanted out here, down by the hip-high stone wall, the pretty, narrow, residential street just beyond.

It was a stormy-looking day, the tops of the palms thrashing in a wet-warm wind. Once in a while a warm spritz of water would fall—just a few drops of rain to bring out the spicy smell of wet concrete. The sprinkler flashed back and forth, *tittch!tittch!tittch!*, and when Donna cocked her head just right she could see a prismatic dance of colors in the flying drops.

Leticia brought the laundry out in a hamper to fold it on the porch, where she could keep an eye on them. The girls took turns jumping through the swaying sheet of water. Donna thought if you jumped fast enough and then looked back, you would see a girl-shaped hole in the spray, just like the coyote-shaped hole Wile E. made when he ran through a wall. They jumped and looked, jumped and looked. Both agreed they saw it, saw the girl-shaped hole in the world, but Donna was lying, and maybe Cady was lying too.

"I told my dad I want a swimming pool for Christmas," Cady said.

"It isn't Christmas for months."

Cady shrugged. "I just wanted to give him the idea. Last year I told him I wanted an Irish setter in October, so he'd have time to find one, and that's how I got Maisy. You have to give them time to do their Christmas homework. Besides, if he was going to have one done by December, they'd need to start digging soon. Anyway, after I get the pool, we can still play with your sprinkler. For old times' sake."

"We might get a swimming pool too," Donna announced. They had a tennis court, and a fountain with a stone baby in the center—water trickled from his little pee-pee, which was *so. Gross.*—but no pool. The beach was only a short walk, and when they wanted to swim, Leticia always took them there.

Cady shrugged, to show how little she rated that possibility.

Donna added, "Even if we don't, I'll still have the yellow banana. You love the yellow banana."

Cady looked at her pityingly. "But we'll have a slide at one end of our pool."

That deflated her, though she didn't let it show.

"You can't go fast on those little slides," Donna said. "Not like this."

She took a run at the yellow banana, threw herself at it, *hard*, and slid. She slid so fast and so hard, she shot right off the end, and her knee found a stone. She cried out, rolled away holding her leg.

"*Leticia!*" Cady called.

Leticia came to look at her knee. "It okay."

It didn't look okay to Donna. There was a big red scrape on it and blood. She rolled this way and that, gritting her teeth.

"I'm get you some rubbing alcohol and a Band-Aid."

Donna hopped a few steps across the slippery wet grass. She wanted to slide on the yellow banana again and prove she wasn't hurt and didn't need the rubbing alcohol. Rubbing alcohol was the worst. But Leticia caught her hand and began to lead her back to the house.

"You can stay off the bananya until after we clean up your knee."

Van appeared in the front door. "Jesus H. Christ! Leticia! It's Mom! On the phone! Right during the ending of my show!"

Leticia let go of Donna's hand at the bottom of the steps to the porch. "Sit here. I don' want you on the bananya, getting blood on it."

Donna sat on the bottom step. Cady called from the far side of the yard.

"Watch, Donna! Just watch! I'm about to make a girl-shaped hole in the world!" She leapt through the sprinkler and for one heartbeat Donna saw it: a dancing wall of glittering spray and the girl-shaped spot where Cady had jumped through to the other side.

"I saw it, Cady!" Donna yelled. "I saw it!"

Someone else yelled Cady's name, a moment later. There was a van on the far side of the road, on the other side of the low stucco wall. Donna didn't know how long it had been there. She thought it was blue, although sometimes she remembered it was green. It was filthy with road dust and it had bubble windows in the back that were tinted black, or maybe no windows. It was a Ford Econoline or maybe a Chevy. The driver's-side window was rolled down and a man's arm hung out. He was brown, like a Mexican, or maybe just tanned. Donna saw his profile, his big beak of a nose and shaggy gray eyebrows. Or maybe she didn't see his profile. Sometimes she thought she *wanted* to see his profile so much she had imagined it.

"Cady?" shouted the man in the driver's seat.

Cady took a step toward the wall. "Yes?"

"Hey, girl. I work with your daddy. Cady—Maisy got hurt. Your mom backed the car into her. Your parents took her to the emergency vet."

"What?" Cady cried.

He waved a hand at her. "Come on. We'll get you over there." He said *we*, which was maybe why, later, Donna came to believe there had been a second man in the van.

Cady looked back at Donna. Cady was already crying, her eyes bright with shock.

"I have to go!" she cried in a pinched voice. "Will you come with me, Donna?" She spun back on her heel and shouted at the van. "Can Donna come?"

"Yes," he said, with a Spanish accent, or maybe not. "Bring Donna."

Donna got up. She felt sick to her stomach. Maisy was always poking her cold wet nose in people's butts, but she was a happy, inexhaustible dog, a dog who would chase a tennis ball for an hour and then throw her head in your lap and drool on you while she snored. Donna thought she should go with Cady, only when she thought of seeing Maisy, her fur shampooed with blood and dirt, she felt dizzy and weak. Also, Donna's knee stung when she stood up, and when she looked, she had watery blood down her shin, and she thought she should get a Band-Aid before she went anywhere.

"Let me ask Leticia. I'll go in and get her."

"We better go, Cady," said the driver. "Maisy might not last long. Anyone comin' better come. We got to roll." He clapped his hand against the side of the door, and later Donna wondered if he talked Black, if there was something Black in the way he said *we got to roll*. She sometimes remembered actually his arm had been a Black man's arm, a creamy shade of brown.

"Okay!" Cady cried. She tossed a frantic look at Donna. "Are you coming?"

Donna wondered if Maisy had *literally* been run over, if a tire had thumped over her midsection and split her stomach open, and all her guts had squished out. A bubble of nausea expanded in her throat.

"I better wait till Leticia fixes my leg," Donna said.

"Jesus H. Christ," Cady said. "Just stay here then."

Cady ran across the road to the far side of the van in her bare feet, left her sneakers behind. A door slammed. The van hiccupped away from the curb in a couple of jerky leaps and something thudded inside. Later, Donna thought that was the sound Cady Lewis's head made as someone smashed it in with a wrench. The van jerked away from the curb, hitched to a sudden stop, then rolled sedately away and out of sight.

Donna sat on the bottom step while the sprinkler went *tittch! tittch!*

Thunder grumbled. Donna's swimsuit was cold and clammy on her skin. She felt sick about Maisy and rotten about letting Cady go alone and glad she hadn't gone with her. She hated to think of something small and helpless in pain, something that had been irreparably mauled by the world.

Leticia emerged with the first aid kit.

"Where's Cady?"

"She had to go. Her mother backed over poor Maisy."

Leticia put a hand to her mouth. "Oh, my God!" She sat on the top step and squeezed Donna's head to her bosom. "Is Maisy going to be all right?"

"She's at the vet," Donna said.

"Good. When I was little, we had a cat with three legs, but he could still jump on the kitchen table. He always jump on the kitchen table at breakfast. We set him his own place an' he eat with us."

Donna felt so ill, she hardly noticed when Leticia put the alcohol swab to her scraped knee. Cady had left her shoes at the bottom of the steps, and in a different version of her life, Donna pointed to them and asked Leticia if they could drive them to the emergency vet and check on Maisy. In that version of Donna's life, Leticia said *Yes, all right, we go now,* and she went inside to call the Lewis house, to find out which emergency vet they had gone to. In that other version of Donna's life, Leticia heard Maisy barking cheerfully in the background when Cady's mother answered the phone. In that other version of Donna's life, there were police cruisers on the interstate in minutes, police cruisers swarming the neighborhood. The van was pulled over ten blocks away, and two scuzzy Mexicans were pulled out, thrown against the side. A policewoman applied a cold compress to Cady's bloody head. An ambulance siren shredded the overcast afternoon. *You're going to be all right*, the policewoman said to Cady. *Your parents are on the way*. In that other version of Donna's life, Cady's parents rode to the hospital in the back of the ambulance with their daughter, and she got the swimming pool she wanted, and the slide too.

But in Donna's real life, no one realized Cady Lewis was missing until nearly seven in the evening, when her mother called to see if Cady was going to sleep over with Donna. In Donna's actual life, Cady Lewis was never seen alive again.

5.

Before he was aware of his surroundings, he was aware of his nauseating migraine. It felt like a steel rod had been pushed through his head. His hands were balled into fists, and when he tried to open his fingers, he found he couldn't.

He opened his eyes on a hotel room, dimly lit by the sunlight glimmering around cheap nylon shades. One corner of his queen bed was lower than the others, which made Van feel seasick. Cheap-shit clock-radio by the bed and a phone the color of Dijon mustard. He couldn't remember how he had wound up here, but he had an idea it was a shitty Days Inn, located midway along the road between nowhere and nothing.

He looked down and got his first surprise. He was wearing a mitten. It was a black leather mitten, so small he had to keep his hand in a fist. A wide, flat steel ring had been cinched around the wrist and was held shut with a padlock. He had a matching mitten on the other hand. *What fucking fetish bullshit is this?* He wore a T-shirt and loose white jockeys and was alone in his tangle of sheets: no dead girl next to him, no live boy.

He wanted something to drink, badly, and made his way into the little motel bathroom. He expected to find drugs, but the speckled Formica was as clean as if housekeeping had only just spritzed some Windex around and left. He knew there had been heavy drugs in his recent past from the quality of his migraine. His head was thumping as if it contained a second heart. He wished for a line of cocaine, had a day of crippling decompression sickness ahead of him if he was going to have to face it without chemical assistance. He shoved at the faucet, got a blast of warm water going, and drank. He hoped the girl who had buckled him into these leather mittens would come back before he needed to pee—it was going to be hard to aim his prick with his hands in bondage gloves—but for the moment he felt no desire to urinate at all.

It came to him that he was a married man who loved his wife, and if he was in a motel playing bondage games with some girl, then he had made some poor life choices in the last forty-eight hours. He wished he could look himself in the mirror and say it was the first time. Whoever he was here with had to come back soon. He would get the gloves off, give her a kiss and a friendly swat on the bum, send her on her way, and then call Allie and make up a lie. What lie, he didn't know yet. Not that it mattered. Allie didn't want to know if he was cheating. Maybe she was even glad if he cheated. She liked to be held and liked to hold even more, but when he screwed her, she shut her eyes and smiled a tiny, enigmatic smile, and hurried him to the end with the brisk cheer of a nurse changing a patient's catheter. And after, she would do some of his coke, her cookie for being a good girl. He wished she'd cheat on him too, but she had put that behind her, was fiercely loyal, would rather put a cigarette out on herself than screw someone else. By the clear light of day, he could admit to himself that Allie had always wanted to punish herself for being a sick, terrible person . . . and the punishment she had chosen for herself was life with him. But generally he didn't allow himself to stay sober long enough to think about it.

But the real question was not if he was at a motel with a girl (what motel? what girl?) but when she was getting back. He assumed she had gone for coffees and thought it would be quirky and fun to leave him in his bondage gloves. He was going to be in a hell of a fix if she had been hit by a car (*or*, he thought, *if a gas main exploded*, an oddly specific notion that gave him a tickle of unease. His next thought—*didn't Allie go for V8?*—was so terrible, he shoved it away).

He went to the picture window next to the hotel room door. He twitched the edge of the curtain aside for a peek into the parking lot—and was overcome by a shock so intense it almost put him on his ass.

There was no parking lot out there. There was, instead, a wide, brilliantly lit white corridor. White lino floor, white drop ceiling, an open door on the far side of the hall. Van didn't have a good angle to see into the room opposite, but he thought he could see part of a conference room, a whiteboard on one wall. A woman walked by, Black, older, handsomely dressed in tweeds. She was typing on a BlackBerry with one hand. The other tugged at a pair of librarian glasses, hanging around her neck by a silver chain.

"What the fuck is this shit?" Van cried and pounded on the window with one mittened hand, but she had already moved on.

He shoved the curtain all the way back. It shrieked on the rod. It was like peering into the hallway of a research-and-development lab for 3M. He looked at the door again and saw there was no chain on the inside to lock it, no bolt.

Van fumbled at the knob, but it only turned uselessly, wouldn't open. A big guy, built like a weightlifter, in a tight pink polo shirt, walked by pushing what looked like a library cart. Van hit the glass again with one fist. The guy glanced at him without much interest and went on.

He staggered on weak legs to the bed and sat down. He fumbled with the receiver, got it between shoulder and ear—then realized there was no dial, no number pad.

"Guest services," said a voice on the other end of the line, female and friendly. "How can I help you?"

"What the fuck is this?" Van asked. "*Can* you help? I'm in a room in a, I don't know, a hospital? And I can't open my door."

"Yes, Mr. McBride. Someone will be along with your breakfast and your pills very soon. Do you need help in the bathroom?"

"Do I—what? No. Who are you?"

"This is guest services."

"I can't use my hands."

"Well, how did you pick up the phone then?" She sounded very amused.

"I mean, I've got these, I don't know, leather bags on my hands. I can't get them off. They're fastened with padlocks."

"Yes, Mr. McBride. That's a safety measure."

"What are you keeping me safe from? Jerking off?"

"It's not to keep *you* safe, Mr. McBride. Mr. Valentine will explain everything. He's in a meeting now, but I'm sure he'll be glad to hear you're awake and suffering no ill effects."

"Suffering no ill effects from what?" he asked.

Only it was coming back to him now. His heart had been beating exactly this way when the shockwave blew in his favorite window, the one that always made him think of a sand dollar, and he thought Allie had been killed by an explosion. A gas main, that was his first thought. Only it wasn't a gas main and Allie wasn't dead. Because she had called him. She had called him and told him to run and he would've if only he could've found his shoes.

"You can't just hold me here."

"Try to remain calm, Mr. McBride. Mr. Valentine will be along after you have breakfast, and he can explain everything." There was a click as she disconnected.

He slammed the receiver down so hard, it bounced out of the cradle. People were walking by in the hall and he didn't want them to see him. He ran across the room, snared the curtain between his leather mittens, and yanked with so much force, he accidentally pulled the rod down. He sobbed with unhappiness and tried to put the rod back in its brackets, but it couldn't be done, not with his hands in the bondage mittens. Now everyone who went by could see his pimply legs and scrawny ass in his white jockeys. It wasn't to be borne. He staggered back to the bed, scooped up the bedspread, and wrapped it around him like a kind of robe. He sat, suddenly exhausted. He could not remember the last time he had needed a drink or a line so badly.

He stared at his reflection in the surface of the Zenith television. A television. If he could find a local news station, maybe he could figure out where he was, what time of day it was. Van got back up and fumbled with the on/off until the screen lit from the center, the brightness spreading out to the edges of the glass. There was no sound.

Donna was on the screen, in a T-shirt and a pair of white panties, her hands in bondage gloves and her hair mussed up. She was on her side, curled into a fetal position on top of her sheets, her eyes closed. Her bedroom was identical to his, down to the cheap watercolor of a seaside boardwalk in a sweeping blue rain. The sight of her took the last scrap of life and hope out of him. It was like being unplugged.

There was a dial to change the channels. He fumbled through the glove and turned it with a clunk. The picture shifted to a different angle on the same room. He clicked listlessly, numbly, through five views of Donna's room before coming back to the first . . . which was when he realized there were cameras in his room too, sealed in sleek glass balls on the ceiling. No doubt she would find him on her own television if she turned it on.

Five channels of Donna McBride, all day long: well, that had always been her daydream.

6.

He was still wrapped in the blanket when Valentine turned up with a nurse and a spare thug.

Valentine's eyes were so blue, they were a little shocking. They looked like a special effect. His hair looked like a special effect too, a mess of golden-white curls.

"Joe Valentine," Mr. Valentine said. "I'd offer to shake, but my mother taught me no one loves a tease."

The nurse pushed a rolling cart with Van's breakfast on it. She had a pert snub nose and the sunny attitude of a young preschool teacher.

"I bet you're thirsty!" she announced, poking a straw through the tinfoil lid on a cup of orange juice. "Let's wet your whistle, Mr. McBride." She pushed the straw toward his mouth and—resentfully—he drank. It was cold and sweet and good.

"You want to watch out for my sister," Van told the nurse. "She'll let you put a straw in her mouth and then she'll spit in your eye."

"Oh, no!" said the pert nurse. "I'm sure she wouldn't."

The thug positioned himself just inside the room. He was almost as wide as the door, with a Freddie Mercury mustache. That mustache was familiar somehow. Van looked again and remembered. He had been in the apartment when they came to get him, had been holding one of Van's sneakers while someone stuck a needle in his neck.

The nurse chirped, "We have some oatmeal and we have some yogurt. What would you like?"

"What I'd like," Van said, "is to feed myself. What I'd like is for you to take off these fucking gloves. Help me out, lady, and when this goes to court I'll tell them you tried to do the right thing."

She went on as if he had said nothing. "We want to stay with soft white foods for the next twelve hours. You've been under heavy sedation, and we don't want to make your tummy work too hard."

"I'm not recovering from an operation. I'm recovering from a kidnapping. *You* are one of my kidnappers. You get that, right? That you're a criminal? That when this is over, you're going to go to jail?"

She cast a fretful look at Valentine. It was getting harder for her to maintain the smile. "Let's try some oatmeal."

"You try it. Go ahead and pack some up your ass."

Mr. Valentine took the only chair in the room—it went with the desk next to the TV—turned it around and straddled the straight back.

"If he doesn't want to eat," Valentine said to her, "you can do the rest of it, Nurse Dover. Maybe he'll be hungry come lunch."

She put down a white plastic spork, reached under the tray, and came up with a blood pressure cuff.

"Where am I?" Van asked.

"A secure facility," Mr. Valentine said.

Van said, "What state? Is this still New York?"

Valentine shook his head.

"So we can add human trafficking across state lines to the charge of false imprisonment." He looked at Nurse Dover while she pumped the black bulb, inflating the pressure cuff on his arm. "How old are you? Twenty-five? You'll be eligible for social security by the time they let you out."

She ripped the Velcro strip and tore the cuff off his arm.

"Your blood pressure is higher than I'd like," she said, "for a man coming out of sedation."

"That'll be the cocaine," said the thug with the Freddie Mercury mustache.

Van was surprised, hadn't expected the muscle to contribute to the conversation. The mustache was still nagging at him. He felt he should know that mustache.

Allie's voice on the phone, breathless, rushed: *They're with the fat man from Greenland, I never learned his name.* That was it. Recognition clicked into place.

"You were there—in Narsarsuaq. You sat in on the debriefings," Van said.

"I'm surprised you remember me," said the man with the mustache. "I would've bet a hundo you were stoned during your interview."

"Who do you work for?" Van asked.

Valentine cast a casual glance back at the big man with the mustache. The big man crossed his arms and declined to reply. Valentine turned to face Van once more.

"We don't have to hold you long. If you help us out, we can have you back in New York inside of two weeks."

Van laughed. Nurse Dover tried to poke a thermometer in his mouth and he turned his head away.

"Two weeks is thirteen days and twenty-three hours too long, old son," Van said. "But never mind that. How the fuck are you going to let me go? I write for *Rolling* goddamn *Stone* magazine. I smoked pot with Jesse Ventura before he was governor of Minnesota. I got a book been published in eight languages. How are you going to let me go, when I will spend the rest of my life having every one of you crucified in the court of law and public opinion?"

"No," Joe Valentine said. "I don't think so. You'll sign an NDA. You'll be glad to, glad to resume your life. In fact, by the time you pack your bags I predict we'll all be friends."

"You tried to snatch my wife right off the streets. You tried to stick her with a needle and kidnap her. *My wife.*"

Valentine drew back slightly and gave Van a woeful look, as if Van had struck a particularly low blow—although a smile remained at the corners of his mouth. "Yes, we *tried*. A second-year field agent got overexcited and was charbroiled for his error, along with the rest of his team. I think we can call it even. But let's talk about what happened in Brooklyn, Donnie."

"*Donovan.*"

"Let's talk about how five people died, forty-two people were injured, and your wife slipped away from us. For the moment, I should add—she will be joining us shortly, I think I can pretty well guarantee that. Now, I happen to know there's a mark on her chest. You have it too. So does your sister. We can't see it, although we're going to do some studies to see if it can be revealed by different wavelengths of light. She touched the mark and brought the entity *through*. I have a lot of questions, but let's start with an easy one. Does it have a name?"

"He has a face," Van said. "And you're going to see it, mister."

Valentine clapped a hand against the stiff back of the chair. "Okay! This is how we begin. There's so much I want to know. Where it comes from. How you control it. But this is where we begin. Help me out, Donnie. Help me help you. Give me a name and let me show you my appreciation. I can get you something for that headache, and I'm not talking about Tylenol either." And he tapped the side of his nose. "Steak for dinner and a Macallan twelve-year double-cask Scotch to wash it down. Let me know! Mr. Francis, we're all set here."

He rose from his chair and nodded at the big man. Mr. Francis moved to the door and rapped his knuckles against it. There was a clunk and a hiss—it looked like a motel door, but it was steel reinforced and someone on the outside had to press a button to pop the lock—and the door swung open. Nurse Dover trundled out, pushing her tray ahead of her. Van's head rang and the orange juice had left an unpleasant metallic aftertaste.

Valentine had one foot in the hall when Van called out.

"You should've left my sister alone. This is going to fuck her up so badly. Let her go and maybe we can talk. As long as you're holding her too, I'll never help you."

Valentine looked back from the doorway. "No, Donnie. You've got that exactly backward. As long as I'm holding her, I *know* you're going to help me."

7.

Donna sucked on the straw until her mouth was full and then spat orange juice into the nurse's face.

The nurse squawked and patted her face with the sleeve of her uniform. While the nurse was trying to recover her composure, Donna kicked the cart. It went over with a jingling crash and the glass bowl with the oatmeal in it smashed.

"Be good," said Joe Valentine.

"Make me," Donna said. She was almost enjoying herself.

Until Joe Valentine flipped on her TV and she saw Van. He was in bed, wrapped in a cheap quilt just like the one in her room, turned on his side. His skinny feet stuck out from the bottom of his cocoon.

"What's your point?" Donna said. She wanted to sound dismissive, untouchable, and didn't quite pull it off.

"Donnie didn't have breakfast, and because of you, now he's not going to have lunch. If you still can't control yourself, we'll pump sodium pentachlorophenate into his room."

"I don't know what that is."

"Neither do I, really. When it was applied to prisoners in North Vietnam, it caused chest pain, breathing distress, and a feeling that the arteries were filled with acid instead of blood. Convulsions, eventually, although I'd like to avoid that on the first day."

"You can't do that. We have rights. Even in a war, prisoners have rights. You can't just . . . set his blood on fire."

"What about Haruto Sagawa and the thirty or so followers who died with him? What about Horation Matthews? Were their deaths in the spirit of the Geneva Convention? I don't think so. To be clear, nor do I care—my sympathies for a man who offered aid and comfort to the Oklahoma City bombers are limited. The point I'm making is that there isn't going to be one set of rules for you and your friends and another for us. If you can burn up people who bother you, well, Donna, so can we!"

Donna looked at the TV. Her brother didn't move. It might almost have been a still picture.

"What do you want?" she asked.

"Good girl. Let's start small. What do you call it? The creature that obliterated three of my men, several bystanders, and half a dozen parked cars?"

She had decided to tell him something, until he called her a good girl. It turned out one didn't need to inhale sodium pentachlorophenate to feel their arteries were on fire.

"I'm not supposed to say," she said. "That's one of the rules."

A line appeared across his handsome brow. "There are rules?"

She nodded.

"Why can't you say his name?"

"It's like what you said in Penn Station. Names have power. And if you know *his* name," she said, "you can command him."

His eyes widened slightly. Donna looked at the nurse, and past him to the bored looking widebody with the Tom Selleck mustache who stood by the door. She nodded toward them meaningfully.

"They can't hear," she said. "The fewer people who know, the better. Can you send them out of the room?"

"No, but what if you whisper it to me?"

Donna considered, then nodded shyly.

Joe Valentine sat on the foot of the bed with her and leaned his head toward hers. She put her mouth close to his ear—then snapped her teeth together on it.

Valentine screamed. She chewed. She sank her teeth in as hard as she had ever sunk them into anything in her life, chewed and twisted, her mouth filling with the sweet salty burn of blood. He struggled to get away, shrieking, batting ineffectually at her. The widebody came alive, reached her side, and tried to pry them apart.

For a moment she opened her teeth, but only to get a better hold, taking half the ear into her mouth, snarling with delight. She gave a last violent wrench of the head and tore off nearly the entirety of his right ear. She spat it into Joe Valentine's face.

The big man gave her an elbow in the breastbone and she was driven back, fell across the tangle of sheets. Valentine screamed and screamed, clapping one hand to the side of his head, falling off the foot of the bed to his knees, the nurse grabbing for him. Donna sprawled on the bed, making desperate gasping noises, tears trickling from the corners of her eyes.

By the time the widebody and the nurse got Valentine to the door, Donna had her breath back, and her gasps had resolved into laughter.

8.

Someone had to come back for the ear.

In the struggle, most of the blankets and sheets had been kicked to the floor, and the ear wound up in the tangle. Two men held Donna against a wall while a different nurse, wearing latex gloves, came in to look for it. The nurse picked it out of the blood-spotted sheets and held it up to the light, like a philatelist inspecting a rare stamp. His nose wrinkled at the sight.

"Tell him I said thanks for breakfast," Donna called. "And I'd love to have him back for lunch sometime."

The big man with the Tom Selleck mustache—she had taken him for one of the guards, but he let the other men hold her, was standing in the open door—laughed. Donna took note. Once you amused a guy, you were in his thoughts. He would naturally wonder how else you might entertain him.

"You don't seem too worried about getting gassed," said the mustache.

Donna said, "If you're going to poison us, let's just get to it. Sooner or later you'll find a reason to do it anyway." Then she said, "But you might want to make this room airtight before you pump in the gas. There's a big crack under the door to the hall."

The big man stroked his Selleck mustache and smirked. "Aren't you a treat? You haven't even been here forty-eight hours and I'm already wondering who's holding who hostage." He rapped his knuckles on the door to be let out.

The TV continued to broadcast the Donovan McBride show on every channel, for the rest of the afternoon. There was nothing else to watch. At some point he got up to explore his bedroom in a desultory sort of way, and he found some clothes in a bottom drawer. He spent twenty minutes struggling into pajama bottoms. Donna had to laugh. It wasn't easy to dress while wearing tight leather mittens that forced your hands into fists. When he had finally wrestled on his PJs, he dragged out some more clothes and spent a while arranging them on the floor. When he was done, he had arranged two socks and a T-shirt into a heart shape. He stared forlornly at the TV. Donna looked up into the camera over the TV and rolled her eyes, then pretended she was vomiting. The tiniest of smiles crept onto his face—her second victory of the day. It turned out she was good at being a captive, and maybe that was no surprise. She had spent most of her life thinking about what she would've done if it had been her instead of Cady in the van.

A nurse brought her lunch. Another brought her dinner. She let the lunchtime nurse spoon her alphabet soup and clean Valentine's blood off her face. The dinner nurse, though, was the same girl who had been in the room when Donna bit off Valentine's ear.

"I'm Nurse Dover," she said. "And I hope you're not going to spit at me again."

Donna opened her mouth to receive a spoonful of creamy pasta and, when Nurse Dover's right hand got close, lunged and barked like a dog. The nurse screamed and dropped the spoon. Donna cackled while she fled.

A bit before five, she saw Van sitting at the foot of his bed, holding himself, and she realized he was shivering helplessly. Her first thought was that Valentine had begun to pump Van's room full of the sodium pentagramwhatsis and at any moment he was going to collapse onto his side, foam bubbling from his mouth.

But he just sat there trembling, didn't have a convulsion, didn't seem to be struggling for air. The next time he looked at his own TV, Donna clutched herself, shook in an exaggerated way, and then shrugged expressively. He tipped back his head and mimed drinking deeply from an invisible bottle. She nodded, feeling hollow in the pit of her stomach, and wondered when he had last gone so long without a drink. She wondered how bad it was going to get for him.

Someone monitoring their security cams must not have liked seeing them speak to each other in charades, because a few minutes later, the video feed of Van's room cut out. The screen filled with a blizzard of static, and the TV roared with white noise—a senseless, furious blast of sound. She turned the Zenith off. Donna hated to be bored, much preferred ruthless interrogation and the threat of torture. There was nothing to do except think about how hungry she was. She hugged a pillow and sucked on the corner of the pillowcase to reduce the pangs. After a while she pulled the straight-backed chair to the picture window, pulled the curtain aside, and watched the hallway. It was just a white hallway. People went by sometimes. Once, a lean Black woman in tweeds stood on the other side of the glass with a cup of coffee in a paper cup and watched her for a moment, as if she were an exhibit in a zoo. Donna glared—but the Black woman smiled as if she were adorable. Donna stuck out her tongue. The woman in tweeds stuck her tongue out in return and left her.

She thought they'd put Van back on the TV in the morning, but they didn't. The screen was still filled with static; the speakers still produced their idiotic roar of sound. A male nurse brought her breakfast, the same nurse who had come back for the ear. He was good-looking and fit, cleft chin like a comic book character, but there was something oddly unmemorable about his handsome features. It was a face without any of the irregularity that makes a face individual.

"Go ahead and bite if you have to bite," he said. "I've been bit before. I'll probably be bit again. But if you snap at me, the next thing you eat will be your own teeth. Do you want some oatmeal or do you want to be hungry today?"

She opened her mouth and let him spoon in oatmeal. When he leaned forward to wipe the corners of her mouth, she put her knee against the inside of his. The man with the Tom Selleck mustache stood in the open door, arms folded across what seemed like a yard of chest, watching intently. She was glad, wanted him to see, wanted him thinking about the possibilities.

"You're not really my type," the nurse said. "Sorry, I like dicks.

Now, if your brother starts humping my leg, it'll be a whole different story."

"How long am I going to be here?" she asked.

"Dunno."

"Where is here?"

"There's people who are paid to talk to you. I'm paid not to."

"What's your name?"

"Nurse Lansing."

She thought about it. "That's a state capital. That nurse yesterday, she was Dover. They're all state capitals. What's with the fake names?"

"You'd have to ask Mr. Valentine."

"Christ, this isn't a prison. It's a fucking holiday special. I want coffee. *I'd* suck a dick for a coffee."

"Everything is negotiable," said the nurse. "Use what you got to get what you want, you know what I mean?"

"Tell you what. Bring me a coffee and my brother will suck your dick. He's good for it."

The nurse smiled at her. "You want a coffee, I can bring you one hell of a Colombian grind. But we need information. You ready to work with us?"

"After yesterday, Valentine wants another date with me?"

"If you're ready to talk," the nurse said, "I'm sure he'll be all ears."

"Send him in," Donna said. "I can fix that."

Tom Selleck rumbled with laughter.

"Too easy," he muttered, before he slipped away, pulling the door shut behind him.

9.

Van saw it on the Zenith, when she bit Valentine's ear off. A few minutes later, Valentine staggered past the picture window, surrounded by nurses in white, trailed by security men in khakis and polo shirts. Valentine was screaming, a hand clapped to his ear and blood threading between his fingers. Van felt a surge of something, some powerful emotion, close to rage, but happier; close to pride, but uglier. He had never loved his sister more.

The lack of windows and natural light gave him the sense of being underground. When he inhaled deeply, it seemed to him the air had the dusty, stagnant quality common to basements. In such a place, one felt removed from ordinary time. The clock beside the bed said it was one twenty. It might've been one twenty in the afternoon or one twenty in the morning. He decided it was early afternoon. A little before three, he began to sweat. It was a bad sweat, with a chemical odor, a whiff of biology lab. He thought of dead frogs, unzipped from throat to crotch to show the jellied organs, for a sixth-grade anatomy class. His intestines cramped and then cramped harder.

Van fumbled with the phone. The voice from earlier was there again, chipper and sunny.

"I'm going to shit myself!" he cried.

"Someone will be there shortly to assist you, Mr. McBride," she half sang.

"Hurry!"

A male nurse arrived, a young man with the bland good looks of a plastic action figure. He was accompanied by one of the security goons, the fit man with slicked-back hair, his biceps swelling the short sleeves of his polo. He had a tattoo on his forearm showing what looked like a Spartan's helmet. The nurse and the goon manhandled Van into the small, unremarkable bathroom.

"Oh, God!" Van cried, his guts boiling, the pressure in them doubling every few seconds.

They got him turned around and the nurse lowered his pants just in time. His stool was almost liquid, a hot spray. He made a pitiful little sound as he was emptied. The nurse wiped him, once, twice, a third time, working carefully, while Van shut his eyes in shame.

By the time the clock said 9:27, he knew he was going through withdrawal, and he knew it was going to be bad. He stretched out on his bed to try and sleep, but his muscles twitched helplessly as soon as he was still for too long. Spells of diarrhea swept over him with sudden, unexpected force, sending him lunging for the phone. With his hands in leather sacks, he was clumsy, and often dropped it with little shouts of frustration and fright. He desperately hoped not to shit himself.

He never had the DTs, not once in the five days that followed . . . but he passed in and out of consciousness, sleeping for hours at a stretch, on no particular schedule, and the same dream was always waiting for him, as intense and convincing as hallucination. He was climbing a concrete stairwell, from darkness into darkness. He was running up the stairs or trying to run up them. His legs were rubbery from exhaustion and his heart kept losing its rhythm, firing unsteadily, in random bursts. His breath screamed in his throat and echoed in the cold concrete silo. Other voices rang out from below him, some he recognized and some he didn't. Jayne Nighswander was down there.

"What are you going to do when you get to the top?" Jayne called out. "Where you going to go? There's no way out! There's no way out and there's no free rides, bitch. Gas, grass, or ass!" She laughed, and others laughed with her, and he knew everyone they had ever killed was down there in the (long) dark, a thought that made him sick with fear.

When he was awake, there were times when he wanted a drink so badly, he could hardly bear it. He felt his craving in his skin, which seemed to want to climb right off his body. Other times, his perspiration would smell of vomit, and the thought of alcohol made him tremble with nausea. His head thumped.

Nurses brought him meals, listened to his heart, took his blood pressure, helped him to the bathroom, and showered him. At first it was humiliating to have someone else wiping his ass, then it was just how he went to the bathroom. There were at least half a dozen nurses on duty, but two of them were senior: a sunny, lively girl named Dover who acted like a young mother hosting a birthday party for five-year-olds and the bland action figure named Lansing. Once Dover and Lansing came together to draw six vials of blood. He was too sick to talk to them. His migraine threw dazzling halos around the lights. Van had seen halos like that around the morning sun in Greenland, sparkling hoops of color and brilliance created by ice flecks high in the air. He remembered Greenland with reverence, remembered how the sharp air had made him feel sanctified. Had made him feel he almost deserved Allie.

In those first days he was too ill to hold a conversation with *anyone*—he was as ill as he could ever remember being in his life. Not that anyone was conducting interrogations. Van had the sense nothing could happen while Joe Valentine was recovering, and it was four days before Van saw him again, striding down the hall past the picture window. His head was swaddled in bandages. A great lump of gauze smothered the right ear. Van supposed they had sewn it back on. A shame—he wished Donna had had the good sense to swallow it.

On the fifth day—or maybe it was the sixth, things had got a little fuzzy while he went through the throes of withdrawal—Nurse Dover turned up in what he took to be early morning, to give him his usual brief physical. The security officer with the Bela Lugosi hair stood inside the closed door, arms crossed over his chest.

"'S'your name?" Van asked him, out of curiosity. His voice was a dry croak.

"Salem," the guard told him.

"Two questions," Van said. "First, did they let you pick it or was it just assigned to you?"

"I hope the second question is better than the first," Salem said.

"Is Joe Valentine free? Why don't you find out, and tell him I'm ready to talk. I'll tell him whatever he wants to know, in exchange for a coffee with a splash of Irish cream in it."

Salem nodded, smiling ever so slightly in a way that made Van hate him and hate himself for begging. "I'll pass it up the line. If you're ready to work with us, I'm sure all requests will be given reasonable consideration. You may have to buckle up and hold on a while longer, though. Valentine was pulled away this morning and isn't expected back for a day or two. Who knows, you might not be missing your wife for much longer." And he winked broadly.

Van's insides bunched up and there was a dull ache, a kind of physical memory of earlier cramps. His heart did an erratic giddy-up—there had been a lot of that lately too—and made him short of breath. His first, shameful thought was that he hoped they got her, because he wanted to see her, to be near her, more than anything. To put his head against her chest, even for a moment, would be better than any drink, any bump of cocaine. He recoiled from himself, wished he could unthink such an evil notion. If they got her too, who knew what they might do to her, to force him to talk. The thought made him weak.

But they didn't get her.

Late in the afternoon, Nurse Dover fled down the hall, a hand clapped over her mouth, tears streaming from her reddened eyes. She was pursued by Nurse Lansing and the Black woman in the tweed skirt, who wasn't smiling for once. Lansing caught up to her and got an arm around her, began to murmur comfortingly, although Van couldn't guess what he was saying. The window was all but soundproof. The Black woman in the tweeds ushered them both out of sight. Nurse Dover wasn't the only person in tears that Van saw that day. All afternoon, people were going up and down the hall, everyone in a hurry. Once, a chubby clerk came chugging down the hall in something close to a run, and crashed into the guard named Salem, who was coming the other way, head down, speaking into a walkie-talkie. The clerk was holding a manila folder. Papers flew, and the chubby little clerk bounced off Salem as if he had run into a lamppost. Salem glared, looked for an instant like he was going to use the walkie-talkie as a club, then gave his head an irritated shake and stalked on. The clerk got down on all fours to pick paper off the floor. Van stood at the window and had a look, saw a grainy faxed photograph of a burning tree with a car in it.

Lansing turned up with dinner, later than usual: a pile of limp green beans and a slice of rubbery turkey. He fed Van precisely cut pieces of white meat, chased with sips of cool skim milk.

When Van was about halfway done, he said, "How many died this time?"

Lansing shot him a sidelong look. "You're here to answer our questions, babe, not the other way around."

"I *was* going to answer questions. This morning, I would've prostituted my own mother for an Irish coffee." But that was eight hours ago. Now he had a dull, sullen headache and a dry mouth... but for the first time since arriving in Motel Hell, he did not feel he was dying, nor did he wish for his own death. "I was expecting Valentine."

"He's been held up. He might be back tomorrow. He might be back the day after."

"So he survived, then. Sorry to hear it."

Lansing flashed him a sharp, penetrating look, but only said, "How about some green beans?"

It was Nurse Dover the next morning. Her color was bad and there were lines bracketing her mouth Van had never noticed before. She bent to cut up a pancake for him. He watched her work without speaking, regarding her red-rimmed eyes and faraway stare.

When she lifted the fork to feed him a piece of pancake he said, "Did Allie wipe out someone you knew?" and she squeaked and dropped the cutlery.

"That's not—" she began and bent and snatched the fork up and wiped her sleeve at her eyes. "I've got nothing to say to you about—" She fought down a fresh wave of emotion. "You don't think it could happen to someone you know. But that's the work we're in."

Van nodded, slowly, with a show of gentle understanding, making sympathetic eye contact. "I know, right? Who would've thought anyone was going to get hurt? In the middle of a violent abduction attempt?"

Feelings worked their way across her face: a spasm of hurt, lips puckered in outrage, a twitch of disgust. She put the fork back down on the tray and wheeled the trolley to the door.

"Can I at least have my coffee?" he asked.

She rolled the cart out without replying, and for days after he only got Nurse Lansing. There was no sign of Joe Valentine either, who, between getting his face eaten and walking his team into another massacre, was having a tough few weeks. Van's heart went out. He didn't see Valentine, Nurse Dover, or Mr. Francis again until the night of the Christmas party. People walked by the picture window in twos and threes, dressed in Hawaiian shirts with Christmas patterns on them. Some of them carried piles of presents in shiny wrapping. Others carried red plastic cups. Francis went by in a Hawaiian shirt with a print of reindeer fucking on it. That interested Van, who had been a journalist for nearly ten years and could spot a telling detail. Hawaiian shirts, not Christmas sweaters. Wherever he was, it was somewhere people could go around in shirtsleeves.

He sighted Joe Valentine wandering down the hall, poking at his BlackBerry. The Black woman with the librarian glasses strutted beside him, swinging a tinsel boa and gabbing at him in a cheerful way. No one paid Van any attention, standing at the glass, like a broke urchin staring at pastries through a bakery window. Nurse Dover went by the window, wearing a little red Christmas elf's skirt, a pair of felt reindeer horns on her head, and Van's heart ached for Allie. Allie in her unicorn outfit, pawing at the air, offering him her rubber hooves so he could swing her around the skating rink again. No one else got it. How he loved the way she could plunge into foolishness with all her heart, giving herself over to pretend, to absurdity. For most of his adult life, he had been hung up on intoxicants, but Allie's foolishness was the only one that didn't come with a hangover. Plus, she was an alcoholic too, and would never say those four terrible words, "Maybe we've had enough."

He stood in the dark of his room, watching them come and go in twos and threes, drinking gin fizzes, flushed with happiness and companionship. Late in the night, Nurse Dover staggered by in her green heels with a couple of the security thugs, and one of them said something that set her off, and she got laughing so hard she tottered into the wall, then slid down it and sat on the floor, with her legs apart, and Van could see a black triangular flash of her panties. She was so drunk. The sight didn't turn him on—it repelled him. He could not have been more repelled if she had pissed herself. He thought, *I hope I never swallow another mouthful of booze in my life*. The sight of her happiness enraged him. Everyone who went by, drinking, chattering, making merry, wearing their cheerful fucking shirts, stoked his fury. He wished King Sorrow had got more of them. He wished for their obliteration. It felt good—to hate so purely, so simply, without the diluting effects of alcohol.

After they were gone and he was in his bed, he had another thought. If it was Christmas this week, then it was New Year's next week. Soon it would be time for Colin to give King Sorrow a name or two. It was his turn this year.

10.

"Donnie!" cried the Black woman in the tweed pencil skirt as she came into his little room in Motel Hell. She spoke with the good cheer of one greeting an old friend at the airport. "We haven't been introduced yet! I'm Dr. Patrick. How are you feeling today?"

The security guard was someone different today, a freckly boy, mid-twenties, built like a stack of bricks, curly yellow hair and widely spaced, pale blue eyes that suggested an IQ hovering in the mid-eighties and a fondness for *Archie* comics. Dr. Patrick tugged out the straight-backed chair at the desk and turned it to face Van, who sat on the foot of the bed. She settled and clapped her hands to her thighs and beamed at him, as if Van had promised her a surprise and she was just waiting for it to be revealed.

"Well, Dr. Patrick," Van said, clearing his throat. "When I want to take a shit, I have to call the desk for help, because I can't wipe my own ass. I spend at least sixteen hours a day in bondage gloves, which leaves my hands in terrific pain. When I go to bed, they come off, but only so my wrists can be cuffed to some kind of plastic belt around my waist, which means I can't scratch or blow my nose. Last night I sneezed and wound up licking my own snot off my face. But I detoxed without a convulsion and I've been clean and sober for at least three weeks now, and I'm surprisingly happy about that. Do I get a thirty-day chip when it's been a month?"

"Do you want a thirty-day chip?" Patrick asked. "Or do you want a cold, very dry martini? The executive kitchen makes a mean one. If you want to help us out, we can probably start bringing you a Bloody Mary with breakfast. You like that, don't you?"

It was an evil thing to dangle in front of him—as evil as one of King Sorrow's suggestions. He waited to be overcome by desperate, humiliating need. Only the need didn't come. He didn't know until he slowly exhaled that he had been holding his breath.

"That's more my wife's drink. I always preferred an orange juice and a couple lines of cocaine."

"Cocaine is on the table too, Donnie. I can make that happen. Medical grade."

At that, his nerve endings throbbed with a prickling thrill of anticipated pleasure. This was followed by a clear, simple thought, one he heard not in his own voice, but in Arthur's: *If you give in even once—if you take her coke, Van—they'll own you forever, and Donna will be at their mercy.*

But it wasn't Arthur's voice that made up his mind. It was his memory of Nurse Dover sitting on the floor of the hall, legs hanging apart, laughing so hard that spit flew, her whole face turning a grotesque shade of red.

"Donovan," he corrected, speaking with a firmness that surprised him—and surprised her. "It's not Donnie. I hate that. Donovan or Van, thanks. And: no. I want my sister back on the TV. I want to go outside for a walk, and I want Donna to join me."

Dr. Patrick considered this, then whipped her BlackBerry out of the pocket of her tweed coat and made a note, typing furiously with her thumbs.

"Van, that's very reasonable. I think—"

"Hang on, I'm not done."

"When she's talking, you listen, bro," said the kid with the wide-spaced eyes.

Van glanced at him. "Who are you?"

"Little Rock," the kid said, and Van couldn't help it, he laughed. A little dimple appeared between the kid's eyebrows, suggesting that a difficult and unpleasant thought was meandering through whatever passed for his mind.

"Salem," Van said. "Little Rock. Lansing. The plebs are state capitals. The upper echelon are all saints. Francis. Valentine. You know the thing about saints, Dr. Patrick? Most of 'em got eaten by lions. If I was in your shoes, I might be worried about running into something bigger than you. Something with an appetite."

She didn't look threatened. She looked delighted. "That something bigger is exactly what I want to talk to you about. I am quite curious about the big fellow's care and feeding."

"Seems like you're getting some firsthand experience with his feeding habits. How much of a mess did Allie make when you took your second run at her, anyway? It was worse than Brooklyn, I know that, because Joe Valentine was gone for two weeks doing damage control."

"I'm not sure what you're referring to," Dr. Patrick said. "But we'd like very much to talk to you about Allison. We're worried about her."

"Okay," Van said, "this conversation is over, then, thanks very much, and let's play again sometime. I'll see about answering your questions when you feel like you can answer a few of mine."

Dr. Patrick studied him. He wondered if the glasses hanging around her neck were just for effect. Her stare struck him as sharp and perceptive.

"Twelve men," she said suddenly. "We don't know how she made our people. She was approached with an exquisite level of care this time. Three of them were in a Jeep Grand Cherokee, and your girl blew it right off the road and into a tree. Like it was hit with a shoulder-mounted rocket launcher. It was burning upside down in a willow when the police got there. Quite a thing."

"I wish I could say I'm sorry, but truth is, I'm only sorry Allie didn't get more. Course she will get more, before this is done." And then, without any transition, he said, "I want a CD player and some music. Anything the Stones recorded between '68 and '74 will do. And anything off Rod Stewart's first four solo albums, but nothing from his career after that. I've been made to suffer enough in this place."

Dr. Patrick leaned back. Her legs were crossed. She watched him with satisfaction.

"And what do *we* get?"

"Well. We could start with what we call the thing that swatted a car into a willow tree. The thing that killed twelve of your men a few days ago and charbroiled three of your agents in Brooklyn at the end of November."

She sat a little straighter, her eyes bright with expectation.

"King Sorrow," Van said. "That's his name. And God help you if he ever learns yours . . . whatever it really is, Dr. Patrick."

11.

Three men rolled a gurney into Donna's room and forced her down onto it. She thrashed. She spat on one of them. She kicked another in the thigh and made him grunt. Didn't matter. They were all big, implacable men, twice her size. They wore khakis and polo shirts, as if they were planning on an afternoon of golf. After they had pushed her flat on the gurney, one of them—Mr. Salem, his close-cropped black hair always gleaming as if he had just come from the shower—pressed a clear plastic mask down over her face, hard enough to squash her nose. She threw her head from side to side, tried to keep him from buckling it into place, and he grabbed her hair close to the scalp to hold her still. She wanted to bite him. She wanted to scream. She couldn't do the first and wouldn't allow herself to do the second.

They rolled her along wide white hallways, beneath fluorescent lights, and she tried not to think about gang rape. On a rational level, she did not think she would be raped beneath clinical fluorescent lights, in a facility with as many women as men. But rational thought didn't reach to her racing heart.

No one even copped a feel. Instead, she was wheeled into a white room with a great, luminescent ring in the wall. A hole in the center of the ring looked into a chamber filled with an aquatic, rippling green light. She was not reassured by the sight of it.

"What's that?"

"It's an MRI, girlfriend," said Mr. Valentine, coming forward out of a dark corner with a clipboard in one hand. Her heart began to do a ragged, uncertain trot in her chest.

"I'm not your fucking girlfriend," she told him.

His right hand drifted absently up to touch the ear that had been crookedly stitched back into place. "No, I suppose not. More like your idea of lunch." And he smiled his old, innocent child's smile.

"Why do I need an MRI? Do you think I have cancer?"

"I think you are one," he said. "Put her in."

Salem moved to the bottom of the gurney. More than anything, she didn't want to be pushed into that little hole in the wall, so like the drawer in which they placed corpses in a morgue.

"Where's Mr. Francis?" Donna said. "I want to speak to Mr. Francis."

"Away for the afternoon, I'm afraid."

"I don't need an MRI," she said. Salem began to push her into that narrow glass tube. "I can't get enough air in this mask."

"You seem to be getting enough air to bitch at us," Valentine said.

"I don't like small spaces," she said.

"This will be over soon," Valentine told her. "Forty-five minutes at most."

She was thrust deep into the tunnel, wrists locked to the hard plastic bars on either side of her gurney. The lights went off. It was like being zipped into a body bag. The world around her began to whir and slam and thrum. She couldn't seem to draw enough breath, no matter how desperately she gasped for air. She counted to sixty. One minute. She counted to sixty again. She counted to sixty over a hundred times before she began to scream. She couldn't help herself. It was like being buried alive, being under a thousand pounds of dirt. She screamed until her throat was sore and her voice mostly gone. The pounding sounds continued, inside her own head, long after the machine stopped.

Then, abruptly, the aquamarine light fluttered back on around her. She was eased out.

Joe Valentine stood by her gurney, loomed over her. They were alone in the little room, although Nurse Dover and Salem stood together on the other side of a glass window, at a control panel.

"Did I say you were only going to be in there for forty-five minutes? Sorry, I lost track of time. That was almost two hours," he said. "I guess it's pretty scary in there for someone who suffers from acute claustrophobia? That's in your file—the claustrophobic fear."

"You don't know anything about fear. But you will." She hated that she could feel tears drying on her face, hated that he knew she had been crying.

He stepped away to a wide flat-panel screen displaying a scan of her chest. It was like looking at a work of ghost photography, her lungs and spine etched in light against the glassy, obsidian darkness behind. She had to look twice before she saw the wyrm: a serpent coiling twice around her chest and resting its spade-shaped head on her heart. It was a different shade from her bones and organs. The arched chambers of her rib cage were traced in brilliance, while the snake worming through her chest was the hazy color of a poison gas.

"There it is," he said. "Turns out he's something of a cancer after all, isn't he?"

"He?"

"King Sorrow."

Her arms prickled with gooseflesh. "Van told you his name."

"He told us more than that."

She felt a brief spasm of resentment—that little pussy, of course he told—but couldn't hang on to it. Very likely he had thought by cooperating, he could protect her in some way, could prevent them from doing the sort of thing they had just done. She flashed to a sudden memory of sitting in Arthur Oakes's bedroom, after Jayne Nighswander and Ronnie Volpe had kicked the stuffing out of them, remembered Colin saying they should just pay them off. *You can't horse-trade with these people*, Gwen had warned them. You could no more strike a bargain with them than Cady Lewis could've struck a bargain with the men who kidnapped and assaulted her. They would take what they wanted and anything you gave them was just extra, a little sauce for the goose.

Valentine was looking at that glowing serpent painted across her ribs again. "And all you have to do is touch it and—then what?"

"Take these gloves off and I'll show you."

He turned back to her—as he pivoted, she had a good look at his mangled ear, the awful stretched white scarring where it had been stitched together—and showed her his angelic smile. He came to her side and she thought if he touched her tit she would begin to scream again, she would scream until what was left of her voice was gone. He didn't fondle her, though. Instead he tapped one finger, hard, against the plastic mask over her face. Each time he tapped, she flinched.

"You should know I put in a formal request to amputate your hands," he said, "as a simple safety measure. I was voted down. But you know the great thing about democracy, Donna? There's always another vote."

12.

But when she saw Valentine the next day, something had changed. He didn't look at her when he came in the room. He seemed distracted, staring at his BlackBerry, tapping the keys in a disconsolate way.

He was joined that morning by Mr. Salem, Nurse Lansing, and Mr. Francis, back from wherever he had gone the day before. She didn't want to be glad to see him, was determined to resist any weak-ass hint of Stockholm Syndrome, and was embarrassed by the intensity of the relief she felt to have him there. It had gradually become clear to her that Valentine was the gas pedal and Francis was the brake, and that it was no accident Valentine had waited until Francis was gone for an afternoon to slam her into the MRI and leave her there.

The room was quiet while the male nurse, Lansing, went through the usual daily physical, checking her blood pressure, pulse, and temperature, listening to her heart. It was easy to check her pulse because she didn't have the bondage gloves on today. Instead, her hands had been cuffed to a nylon strap around her waist.

Valentine typed on his handheld. Francis and Salem flanked the door to the hallway. At last—just as Lansing finished and began stowing his gear back on his trolley—Valentine wrote a sentence with his thumbs, pressed a button, and she heard the whoosh of an email sending.

He looked up at her and blinked. It seemed to take him a moment to recognize her. "Donna, your brother is answering our questions. We're going to ask you the same things we're asking him. If you answer differently, he's the one we'll hurt. Unless we think it would be better to hurt you, on camera. On the other hand, if you can be a good girl, *well*. We've promised Van that if we get cooperation from you *both*, maybe the two of you can have a walk together, outside, at the end of the week. Do you think you'd like—"

Nurse Lansing had just wheeled his trolley into the hall and Salem closed the door behind him. It clapped shut with a flat bang and Valentine jumped halfway up with a cry, his BlackBerry clattering to the floor. His chair almost turned over, but he caught it, righted it.

"Something been eating you?" she asked, then licked her lips. "Besides me?"

Valentine didn't smile. He stared at her with a chilly fascination.

"I didn't sleep well," he said, and sat down.

She kicked his BlackBerry to him and he bent and picked it up.

"Who knows about this place? Do you report to the head of the CIA? Senators? The president? I wonder who you're sending those emails to. Whoever it is, I hope they're careful with 'em. I hope they don't accidentally click the forward button to share with Brit Hume."

"I remind you again that we're a private contractor. I make no comment on who might or might not be underwriting the valuable work we're doing here with you and Donovan. I will tell you that I'm not too worried about Brit Hume reading my emails. Messages from this system can't be forwarded." Valentine held up his BlackBerry. "They can't be printed out. They can only be read on a limited number of devices. End-to-end encryption. We're safe from Fox News, CNN, and *Good Morning America* . . . not to mention Mossad, the FSB, and the Chinese. In a humorous coincidence, the tech outfit that designed it calls it Dragonware."

She made a strangled noise in her throat.

"I want to start in the earliest days," Valentine said, settling himself back in his chair. "You were in college. Your brother tells me you used to entertain your friends by pretending you had twin telepathy, and your—"

She made the strangled sound again and stamped her foot. She lowered her head, clenched her jaws together.

"Are you all right?" he asked her.

She gasped and blinked tears away and made the sound a third time. It really sounded, even to her, like a sob.

"I'm just so alone," she said, in a roughened voice.

Valentine was quiet while her shoulders shook and a tear or two fell. At last, he spoke, in a softened voice that at least attempted kindness: "If you work with us, you *will* get to spend time with your brother again. That's a promise, Donna, from me to you."

Donna nodded and, when she had recovered her composure, forced herself to sit back up.

She darted a brief sidelong look at Mr. Francis, over by the door, but his face was a bored, stony blank. If he knew she had only barely staved off a laughing fit, he gave no sign of it.

13.

Van knew his lies and Donna's lies couldn't match up, so he tried to say as little as possible and tell as much of the truth as he thought he could afford.

"A woman named Jayne Nighswander," Donovan said. "And her thug of a boyfriend, Ronnie Volpe. We killed them first. They died in Southern California, in the spring of 1990, in an abandoned drive-in. They tried to run, you see. You can't run. Not from the King."

"Why did they have to die?" Dr. Patrick asked him.

It was the second or third week of January—he couldn't be sure of the exact date—and Dr. Patrick was still full of pep and vigor. If anything, she was fizzier than ever, like the first drink was just hitting her bloodstream and she was ready for the dance floor. She could hardly sit still and often fumbled her BlackBerry or backed into lamps. Maybe he should've guessed something was up sooner than he did.

"I owed them money for drugs," Van said. He was fairly sure they didn't know about Arthur or Gwen or Colin, and he intended to keep it that way for as long as he could. "I couldn't pay and I was scared. It was really Donna's idea. Donna wanted to save me. Donna has a thing for rescuing people from scumbags."

"WHY DID YOU PICK HER? The Nighswander woman?" Mr. Valentine asked Donna.

"She has a sister, a little sister, Tana? At the time Tana was only eighteen, nineteen. Jayne was prostituting her. Jayne had run up big debts with drug dealers, so she pimped her sister out for every cent she could get. She even offered her to Van once. Jayne Nighswander was a disgusting person. You can't fix a person like that. They're like those flesh-eating bacteria, you just have to hit something like that with a blast of flame, before it can make too many people sick."

Donna watched Valentine tap some notes on his BlackBerry and smiled.

"SO YOU WANTED to kill Jayne Nighswander," Dr. Patrick said. "To protect yourself. Why not run her down with your car one night? Or buy a gun?"

Van was always grateful when he didn't have to think up a lie. Coming up with a convincing line of bullshit was too much work. The early detox days of icy sweats and hallucinatory dreams were behind him, but he was still prone to grinding migraines, and now and then his heart fluttered in a way that left him breathless and scared. Atrial ventricular contractions, Nurse Lansing said—nothing to worry about. He worried anyway.

"No, I didn't want to kill her. I wanted her to be dead. Do you see the difference?"

"You didn't want to do it yourself."

He nodded his aching head. "Also, you have to remember—back then, I was heavily into 'shrooms and Willie Nelson. I wanted to get in touch with some cosmic forces. I wanted to throw open the doors of perception, like Jim Morrison, and maybe have an erotic encounter with an alien or an angel. You know all the paranormal stuff they used to talk about on *Unsolved Mysteries*? Haven't you ever wanted to see a UFO or the thing supposedly swimming around in Loch Ness? Haven't you ever wanted to see a giant monster?"

Dr. Patrick laughed—a little shrilly.

"Well," she said. "Obviously."

There were sweat patches on her silk blouse, under her armpits.

"TELL ME ABOUT THE DRAGON," Mr. Valentine said.

Sometimes his right foot would jiggle up and down, until he noticed and made himself stop. It was a new habit, something that had started in the last couple of days.

"That's what I've been doing," she said. "For weeks now. When do I get to see my brother? You promised we could go for a walk together. Outside. You said if we cooperated. You *said* we could trust you."

"Tell me how he predates on his victims." He put a hand on his knee to halt his idiot jackhammering leg. "What does he do to them?"

"You know what he does."

"I know how it ends," he said. "But you told me Jayne Nighswander and Ronnie Volpe ran. What were they running from?"

"They began to see him. They'd go for a drive at night and glance up into the sky and see him flying above them, blotting out stars. Or Jayne would get up in the middle of the night because she heard a sound, and he'd reach for her from under her bed."

"How can he be large enough to blot out stars, but small enough to fit under her bed?"

"Because . . . he wasn't really curled up under the bed at all. He was curled up in Jayne's mind. He wasn't in the sky, he was in her imagination. I think it's easier for him to leave the Long Dark and slip into his target's mind than it is to take a physical form . . . The border between a person's thoughts and the Long Dark is . . . softer. More permeable. Porous enough so he can whisper through it."

"What else did they experience? Phantom smells?"

"Yeah. He smells like charred wood in the rain."

Valentine's right knee started going again.

"Let's talk about how you pick targets. You aren't the first to summon King Sorrow to our world. We know he was over Dresden in the Second World War. Wolf Messing wrote about him in his journals. He called him 'Imperator Slez,' which might translate as the Emperor of Tears. A study of his journals, and of the larger historical record, indicates that you would need someone's true name to choose them for death. One is safe from King Sorrow—from you—if you don't have their true identity."

"That's right. Unless we bring him through in our own immediate defense."

Mr. Valentine lifted his chin, studied the blank white ceiling. "Do you know *my* name, Donna?"

Donna began to smile.

"Joe Valentine."

"That's a good name. That's who I am in this room. Did someone—Mr. Francis perhaps—slip and give you a different name? Just by accident?" He clapped not one, but both hands on his right knee to stop it from moving again.

"Why do you ask?" she said. But she thought she already knew. "How are you sleeping these days, Joe?"

He filled his chest with air, exhaled slowly. Donna thought he was making a conscious effort to be impassive.

"If you know my name," Valentine said, "my *other* name, my *outside* name—you need to be honest about it, Donna. You need to tell. You *will* tell . . . if not now, then later. But I'd be grateful if I didn't have to go to a lot of bother to get an honest answer out of you."

"Are you worried *I* know your name?" Donna asked him. "Or are you worried someone else knows it? Someone who smells like charred wood in the rain?"

The tip of his pale tongue appeared to touch his lips. He got up suddenly, so suddenly his chair almost fell over, *would've* fallen over if he didn't reach out to catch and steady it. She was sure by then . . . so sure she wanted to laugh.

He must've seen her amusement on her face because he nodded, his gaze distant. "All right. You had your chance to come clean. I'll let it go for now. We'll take it up again—next time we talk."

She thought they'd talk again tomorrow morning, same as always. But next time came sooner than that.

14.

It was forty minutes after lights-out, but Donna wasn't yet asleep when her TV switched itself on.

The screen cast a watery light across the ceiling. It was as if a ghost had entered the room and was standing at the foot of her bed. She lifted herself up on her elbows to peer at the Zenith. Her hands were cuffed to her belt, at her hips.

The picture showed a small garage, the floor cleared except for a steel keg filled with ice and water, sitting on top of a wooden crate. There was a folding table with some monitors and hard drives and keyboards on it. A couple of golf carts had been parked to one side. Joe Valentine stood next to the steel keg. The camera was on the ceiling, and he had to lift his head to look into it.

"Good evening, Donna," Valentine said.

Donna wasn't the sort of person who yelped, and she almost yelped anyway. She had never heard any sound out of the Zenith at all, except for the hiss and roar of white noise, which was all she could get when they shut off her feed of Van's room.

"I know you're awake," Valentine said. He gestured to one of the monitors on the folding table, to establish he could see her. "That's good. We need to talk. You've been holding out on us. You and your brother both. I don't believe you figured out how to bring King Sorrow over from the Long Dark, just you and Donovan and Allie. No. You have *confederates*. *Allies*. Agents working against us."

"No," Donna said. "It's just us."

"That's a lie, and I'm losing patience."

Somewhere in the garage, a door shut with an echoing bang. A pair of guards hauled Donovan into the picture: Mr. Salem and the guard who called himself Little Rock, a freckly kid with the lean build of a middleweight boxer and the vacant stare of one who has taken too many shots to the head. Van was naked, his scrawny thighs trembling. He put his heels down, making it necessary for Salem and Little Rock to drag him, each of them gripping his arm just above the elbow.

"Don't do this," Van said. "Please."

Joe Valentine gave a nod. Salem and Little Rock hauled him to the edge of the steel keg, bent him over it, and forced his head into the water. He struggled, spraying both of them, dampening their tight polo shirts.

"There *is* no one else," Donna said.

"We know this is a lie," Valentine said. "And they're going to hold him under until you give us a name."

"You'll kill him."

"Fortunately, we have two of you. Which makes one of you expendable."

"Do you want me to make a name up?" Donna cried.

Valentine didn't reply. He only stared blandly into the camera while they held Van's head under.

"There *is* no one else," Donna shouted.

"Mr. Salem," Valentine said. "Mr. Little Rock?"

They pulled Donovan up out of the water. He coughed, choked, and spat, trembling convulsively. Joe Valentine turned to him.

"Donnie," Valentine said. "That was only a minute and a half. Next time you go in for three. I'm going to ask you a question. You need to answer me truthfully." Joe Valentine reached over to the folding table and tapped a key on one of the keyboards, and suddenly the feed was muted.

She could see Valentine speaking. Donovan replied. But the picture quality wasn't good enough to read lips, even if she knew how to. Valentine nodded slowly, thoughtfully, then gestured with his chin. Donovan was shoved back into the water. His feet skidded and slipped on the slick floor. His gaunt butt cheeks flexed convulsively. Joe Valentine casually tapped a key on his keyboard. The sound returned.

"Donnie was very helpful," he said. "I hope you can be helpful too. He just gave me two names. If you give me the same names, this ends now. If you don't, we're going to hold him in there for the full three minutes. After that it will be four and a half. Do you think he can hold his breath for six? I don't."

Donna had wanted twin telepathy her whole life, but never more than she did right then. She felt as if she couldn't breathe herself.

"Elwood Hondo," she cried. "And Philip Aylesford. Take him out, you motherfucker. I'll kill you. I'll kill all of you."

Valentine said, "Interesting. Van said Stephen Earle and Jeffrey Tweedy. I don't think there's any real person with the name Jeff Tweedy—that isn't even a good lie. Although not as ridiculous as someone named Hondo. You're going to tell me, Donna. Who's working with you? Who else has the power to contact King Sorrow?"

"He's coming, isn't he?" Donna said, with a sudden, desperate savagery. "He knows your fucking name and he's coming for you. For all of you. I don't need to kill you. Because he will."

"You're going to fucking tell!" Valentine shrieked.

"Joe," Salem said, glancing over his shoulder. The water bubbled furiously around Van's head. "That's three minutes, I don't think—"

"Keep him under!" Valentine stabbed a finger at the camera, at *Donna*. "You're going to watch your fucking brother *drown*. He's going to *die* because you let him, and then we're going to do the same to—"

She heard the echoing bang of the door closing somewhere off camera. A shadow appeared, a big one, stretching across the concrete floor, and for an instant Donna thought, *It's King Sorrow, you motherfucker, and he's going to skin you like a deer*. It wasn't, though. It was Mr. Francis, moving swiftly across the floor, two more men with him. Little Rock and Salem looked around . . . although they still held Van's head in the water. Salem looked like a kid who has been caught writing dirty words on the side of the school without realizing a teacher has been standing behind him the whole time. Little Rock just stared, jaw slack, eyes empty.

"Let him up," Donna hissed. "Let him up."

Valentine touched that key on his keyboard and the picture went silent. She saw him adjust his glasses and say something to Francis. Francis replied. Over at the keg, Van had stopped kicking.

At last, with a show of great reluctance, Valentine gestured toward the keg. Little Rock jerked Donovan out of the water. His head lolled, and when they lowered him to the floor, he wasn't moving. Francis said something else and Valentine casually touched a button on his computer. The picture on Donna's screen jumped to a blizzard of white static and the TV roared with white noise, the sound of annihilation, of madness.

15.

No one came the next day. She turned on the TV but saw only static, heard only the maddening roar of a dead signal. Donna felt carbonated, bubbling inside with fury, with wild ideas, ready to erupt, to foam over with emotion. She paced desperately, eight steps down the length of the room, eight steps back. Once she saw Salem walking past her window and she smashed her mitten against the glass and screamed, *What about my brother, what about Van*, but he didn't even look at her. At two in the afternoon she did something she hated. She picked up the phone to speak to the operator in a hideous personal display of weakness.

"Yes, Ms. McBride, how can I help you?" asked the cheery female voice on the other end.

"I want to know if my fucking brother is alive."

"Mr. McBride is resting comfortably."

"I want to *see* him, you dumb twat. I want to see he's all right."

"Is there anything else I can help you with?" she asked.

"Does King Sorrow have your name?" Donna yelled into the receiver. "Because if he doesn't, he will. Someday he will."

The phone hissed for the count of ten, and then, in a low voice, curdled with hate, the woman on the other end said, "Don't threaten me, you high-toned bitch. Not unless you want your brother to go for another ice-water dip." Then, suddenly, her perky tone returned. "Is there anything else? We've got hot espresso!"

Donna crashed the phone back into the cradle, collapsed on the edge of her bed, and sobbed—sobbed with dry eyes. It was a sensation closer to the dry heaves after a long run in the heat, than to grief. If she was standing over the operator with the bright, manically cheerful voice, she would've strangled her with the phone cord. It wasn't a wishful notion. Donna knew she could actually do it. Choke her until her face went black.

No one came the next day either. Not Joe Valentine, not his second-in-command, the infernally sunny Dr. Patrick, not Mr. Francis. She wondered if her brother had been underwater long enough to suffer brain damage.

On the third day, Nurse Lansing entered her room in the midmorning with Salem. She was sitting on the edge of the bed.

"Ready to go, hun?" Lansing asked, taking her by the upper arm. Salem took the other arm.

"I want to see my brother," she said.

"That's the plan," Lansing told her.

They walked her into the wide, brightly lit hallway and marched her to an elevator, one on either side of her. Donna didn't remember the elevator, but supposed she had been in it at least once, when they brought her down. There were four floors: L-2, L-1, 1, and 2. A person needed a physical key to access L-2 and L-1. Lansing wore his around his neck on a lanyard. A bronze plaque on the wall read:

2: BSL-2, Computer Center

1: Lobby, Conference Rooms, BSL-1

L-1: BSL-3 Restricted Access

L-2: BSL-4 Restricted Access, Red Pass Only

"BSL?" Donna asked.

"Biological Safety Level," Lansing said.

Salem said, "Level Two is where we keep everything really dangerous. Ebola, smallpox, and you."

"You don't know the half of it, bitch," she said to him. "There's gonna come a day you wish you drowned both of us when you had the chance."

Salem laughed.

The elevator opened on a wide hallway with a glossy marble floor the color of graham cracker. The lobby was to the left and faced a two-story wall of windows. Donna's eyes were unprepared for daylight, and all that brightness hurt. She flinched from it.

They turned her away from the lobby, walked her through the back of the building and outside. Outside for the first time in months.

Seagulls screamed. The air was briny and cold and sharp, stung her cheeks, filled her chest with an icy ache, and she thought she had never smelled anything so good in her life.

She was in a sprawling parking lot, among Quonset huts. The tarmac was old, faded and patched. Beyond the huts she could see bare trees and high yellow dune grass but not the ocean. The facility had an air of abandonment. There were no cars here except for a pair of idling jeeps. The drivers were already in them, men in fishermen sweaters and hunting jackets and wool watch caps. Maybe they were supposed to look casual, but it didn't really work, not with the walkie-talkies and the rubber truncheons on their belts. Joe Valentine sat in one of the jeeps, with Donovan perched right behind him, staring at the back of his head.

"Van," Donna called, but her brother didn't look around or acknowledge her at all. She didn't like the look on his face, which was a stunned blank, as if Valentine had gone through with the lobotomy he had promised at the beginning. She thought again of brain damage.

Dr. Patrick waited by the other jeep, dressed in a quilted winter jacket, ankle length, buttoned to her throat, hands plunged into the pockets. As always, she had her face set in a wide, enthusiastic smile. Donna thought that grin made her look deranged today—like one of the Joker's victims.

"How about that sea air? Who needs coffee this morning! That breeze will wake you right up." Dr. Patrick stepped toward Donna and hung a loop of wire around her neck, a microphone hanging from it. She fiddled with it, adjusting it, patting it to make it rest smooth against Donna's sweater. "I've been arguing to let you out of the facility for weeks. A person would go *crazy* stuck in that basement for two months. I've been telling them, we need to reframe the conversation. It's all been too adversarial. We need to let you know we aren't the enemy here. We want to *help*. We want to understand this—*thing*—you've had to live with for years. We want to know how it all works. How you bring him to our world and, also, how you make him go away." She had stopped playing with the wire and began patting Donna's shoulder in a very peculiar way. "I can't imagine what it's been like, carrying this secret around. The psychological weight of it must be awful."

"It's not all bad," Donna said. "But—Dr. Patrick—if you do want to help me out—maybe you could tell me something. What day is it?"

Patrick looked into Donna's eyes and looked away. She was scared too.

"March third."

"Wow," Donna said, nodding. "So you'll be dead in six weeks. All of you. Huh. Now you want to talk about carrying around a psychological weight . . . that's gotta be a burden."

Patrick took a step away from her. She wasn't smiling anymore.

"No one has to die," she said.

"Everyone dies," Donna said. "It's just a question of when and how ugly."

"Help her into the jeep," Patrick told Salem and Lansing, then she turned her back and climbed into the jeep herself.

WHEN THE JEEP WAS MOVING, the wind roared, and had an especially icy bite. Donna didn't mind, liked the sharpness of it, the way it tore at her hair. As they raced across the vast expanses of blacktop, she saw that the compound was not quite desolate after all. There was an airfield with Apache attack helicopters—two of them—behind a line of hangars. In another open hangar she glimpsed a Humvee, with a big machine gun mounted on a turret in the back.

She sat in back between Salem and Lansing, Dr. Patrick up front with the driver. Lansing's eyes were bloodshot and he rocked with the jeep, staring straight ahead. She didn't see him blink once. He had a faint smile on his face, but after a while, Donna decided it was the kind of automatic smile a person produced out of habit.

She spotted a gray cold sore, glistening with pus, at the corner of his mouth, and decided King Sorrow was after Lansing too. Fear started a person rotting before they were even dead.

If the dragon was coming for Salem, Salem wasn't troubled by it. He held his chin up, face turned into the wind, enjoying the blast of air the way a dog would. If he wasn't her kidnapper, he'd be an ideal fuck. A little rough, a little thoughtless, thoughtless enough to hurt her the way she liked and be hurt the way she liked even more.

"What is this place?" she asked Salem.

"Fuck's it matter?"

"Right. Because I'm never leaving."

He glanced at her sidelong, with a little humor. "Cherokee Island."

"Where's that?"

"North Carolina. Not really an island at all. It's connected to the mainland by a causeway. There's a bird sanctuary out here—the bird people need a special permit to visit the north side of the island, where it's marshy. I guess there's a heron that only nests here and the bird people get real excited to see it. Down this side, that's where we've got the Cherokee Island Federal Virology Research and Response Center. Only they haven't studied viruses here for years. Our people got it for a song."

"Did the government throw in the helicopters, or was that extra?"

"We already had the helicopters. They threw in the tank."

She nodded and said, "It won't be enough."

He laughed again.

THEY LET THEM OUT of the jeeps at the top of a sandy path between the dunes, leading down to the water. Joe Valentine hopped out of his jeep and addressed them with his hands clasped in front of him and his face blank. The yellow-haired punk named Little Rock stood a step behind him at parade rest.

"Your hands will stay in your gloves," Valentine said. "Mr. Little Rock and Mr. Salem will follow behind you at a discreet distance.

You're miked, and we'll hear everything you say. If one of you tries to run, the other will be shot."

"You expect me to believe you're going to kill one of us?" Donna said. "You need us. Isn't that exactly what you found out two days ago, when Mr. Francis wouldn't let you drown my brother?"

"They don't have to shoot to kill, Donna," Valentine said. He had lost weight, and his eyes glittered at the bottom of dark hollows. "If we have to maim one of you, I promise you'll get excellent treatment from Nurse Lansing and Nurse Dover. Be aware that the current is strong here and your wrists are cuffed together. If you run into the ocean I'm not sure anyone will be able to pull you out before you drown."

"Be honest, I'd rather not try," Salem said to her. "The water is cold as fuck."

Donna waited for Van to say something witty and rude, but he didn't make a sound. He kept his head down, his coppery hair in his eyes.

No one gave them permission to start walking. No one said a word to them. After a moment Donna bumped Van with her shoulder and started down to the wide strip of dingy sand. She was out of the dunes before she noticed her brother hadn't moved. She had to call to him before he turned and came after her, swaying, head down, hands cuffed before him.

Van scuffed through the sand in his old Sperrys and shivered. Gulls screamed and wheeled down the beach. When Donna looked back, Little Rock and Salem were there, maybe twenty feet away, strolling side by side in matching insulated hunting vests.

For the first time in their lives, Donna and Van didn't know how to talk to each other. She wasn't sure how to begin, and he didn't look like he wanted to talk at all.

"How they hanging?" she asked at last. She was unused to tenderness, didn't know how to do it. Allie was good at caring for people. Gwen was even better, in her own brisk, efficient, good-natured way.

"Same as always. Down to my knees," he said, and there was the ghost of a smile on his face. He glanced at the ocean. "Funny

Valentine felt it was necessary to tell us not to try and swim for it. I'll never go in the water again. I screamed for them to stop. I was screaming underwater. I know they heard me."

Donna felt something hardening behind her breastbone, like a petrified organ. She had heard cancers could be as hard as slate, as hard as bone. The rage in her chest was harder.

"They're going to die," Donna said. "All of them. King Sorrow has their names. And they know it."

He nodded, then said, "But we won't live to see it. They're going to drown one of us and make the other watch. Then they'll shoot whoever is left. They're close to panic now. Pretty soon they'll lose their last shreds of restraint. Right now they're following some rules, laid down by someone with power over them. They have a protocol to follow. Mr. Francis is enforcing it. But eventually even that will go out the window. They'll do anything to us to save themselves. And if they can't save themselves, there's always revenge."

"How much have you told them?"

"That we brought King Sorrow out of the Long Dark to kill Jayne Nighswander and Ronnie Volpe. Because of the money I owed them. That we didn't really think it would work. That we didn't know the deal was for life and we'd have to pick someone for King Sorrow to destroy every year. Some of it they already knew—they knew at least half of the people we chose to die before I started giving them names. Did they tell you they recovered a scale from Greenland, big as a dinner plate, black as a meteorite? Has a melting point higher than tungsten steel. When they hit King Sorrow with a Sidewinder missile over Greenland, it must've been like taking a lukewarm bath for him. They know so much."

"They're going to learn more. They're going to get themselves some close-up firsthand experience."

Combers creaming with foam raced at the beach. The sky was a pale, cold blue and unbearably lovely.

Donna said, "What are those birds? Are those wrens?"

Van looked out over the dunes at a rising whirl of small black birds. "I wouldn't know a wren if it laid an egg in my hair."

So. He hadn't told them about Colin. That was maybe the only thing that mattered. It was true that when they pretended to have their own secret twin language, it was only a bit of half-remembered Creole they had learned from Leticia Delva, their old nanny. But it was also true they could share information obliquely, saying things without saying them. Van could communicate more to her in one veiled, sidelong glance than most men could manage with a half hour to chew her ear off.

Van said, "Well, I've walked far enough." He sank down into a squat, then rocked back onto his bottom and sat on the beach, with his legs spread, facing the ocean.

Donna turned to face the water and the wind snatched at her hair and blew it back from her face. She didn't want to sit down, didn't want to get her bottom sandy and damp. It was like Van not to care.

"Sooner or later I'll tell them everything there is to tell," Van said. "Everything they want to know about you and me and Allie."

Which was his way of adding that Gwen and Arthur were safe too.

"Fuck that. Why tell them anything when you know they'll kill us anyway?"

"I'll do it for a few minutes of mercy. I'm not tough like you. I've never been tough like you." He paused, then glanced up at her. "You know they asked me to choose? They said they would drown one of us and make the other watch. I said I'd go. And if they ask again, I'll go again. I can do that. It's the only thing I'm proud of."

She grinned. "Thank you, Van. For what it's worth, I'm also willing to let you die for me."

They looked at the water. Salem and Little Rock stood watching from twenty feet away.

Van scrabbled in the sand between his legs with his mittens, digging with a sudden intentness. After an instant he held up his mittened hands with a sand dollar cupped between them. He pursed his lips and blew the sand off it. It was a disc of bone with an impression stamped in the center like a five petaled flower. A child could not have looked any happier than Van did at his discovery.

"Isn't that something," Van said. "Funny you can be in a place like this and still see something so beautiful it knocks you off your feet."

"You aren't on your feet." Then she said, "What are you going to do with that, anyway? With those bags on your hands, you can't even put it in your pocket."

"I don't need to keep it to see it's lovely. Besides. It's better if I don't keep it." He laughed, without humor then. "Boy, I learned that one too late, didn't I?"

She said, "I don't give a fuck about seashells."

He nodded. "Well, you weren't the one almost drowned the other day. But then you couldn't afford to love things, even before we came here. If you loved something, someone might throw it in a van and take it away from you. It's easier to be outraged all the time. It's easier to be a dragon than it is to be in love."

"I wish *I* wasn't wearing these mittens," she said. "Then I could write down some of these pearls of wisdom."

"Writing down my pearls of wisdom is what got us into this mess. I can't believe you haven't used this opportunity to tell me I shouldn't have written that stupid book."

"I told you already. I said it fifty fucking times while you were writing it."

Donna knew that Gregg Pinet and his father had argued about whether the thing out the window was a UFO or a dragon. In the book, Donovan had slyly gone with Gregg's interpretation, that the plane had been harried by visitors from another world. Or at least he thought he was being sly.

In the book, he turned the dragon into a biological spacecraft, an alien vessel made out of scaly green tissue. It had battled the scrambled fighter jets with a death ray. Van interviewed several passengers (although very few were willing to go on record), and Donna knew he had carefully primed them to say what he needed them to. Even so, some had tried to tell him they saw a dragon. He simply left those quotes out of the book. In Van's version of events Horation Matthews was a religious wacko who lost it at the sight of the UFO, which he believed was "Satan's Chariot," come to drag them all to hell. He decided if he could kill Robin Fellows, a transgender woman and obvious sinner, he could save them all. Robin published the book, knowing not a word of it was true. The whole thing was written in Van's very best Hunter Thompson, full of GONZO CAPITALIZATIONS AND ITALICS, breathless run-on sentences, and lurid caricatures. The subtitle of the book was, after all: *Spaceships and White Supremacy at 30,000 Feet—The Impossible but True Story of BA 238 as Told by the Admittedly Drug-Addled Journalist Who Was There*. With a subtitle like that, no wonder it hit the bestseller list and Johnny Depp was attached to the movie.

Now, watching the tide bash the shore, her brother said, "I'm a Van too. Cady was taken away to a horrible fate by one van—Allison Shiner was taken away by another. It wasn't my job to marry her. It wasn't my job to try and keep her. She needed me to tell her she was perfect and beautiful as she was, not as I wanted her to be."

"You didn't murder and rape her."

"I hoped I could murder something in her. She had to get drunk to fuck me, and she never once really enjoyed it. I guess I don't think it was rape—but it wasn't right neither."

"Stop it. You aren't the bad guy in this story. They are. Those two standing over there, and the people paying them."

He rolled onto his knees and then, with a pant of exertion, climbed to his feet. He stared at the water a moment longer, then twisted at the waist and flicked the sand dollar into the sea.

"That sand dollar will have to go on being beautiful without me," Van said. He stood blinking, the wintry sun in his face. "If I never walk out of this place, it might not be the worst thing that ever happened to Allie Shiner."

"I said stop it and I meant it. She loves you. So do I." Her chest felt very full and tight, and it was hard to breathe. "If I didn't have you, I would've been in jail or an institution by the time I was eighteen. I wouldn't have gone to college if you hadn't gone to college with me. I was too scared to go anywhere you weren't. I've spent my whole life saying terrible things to people and you've spent your whole life apologizing for me. You're a good man, Donovan. Your politics suck, you're married to a girl way too good for you,

you're the laziest person I ever met in my life, and you've smoked half of Mexico and snorted half of Colombia ... but you care about people who aren't worth a shit. People like me. And you try to do the right thing. Some days I wish you ate me in the womb. But you didn't. So I'm here to tell you: you don't get to quit. We're going to walk out of here together. Believe it. All hail the King."

He looked at her out of the corner of his eye. He was pale and hunched and cold looking, but the sky and the sea brought out the blue in his eyes, and when he smiled it was real.

"All hail the King," he said.

16.

Two weeks after Cady Lewis climbed into a van and was never seen again, a third grader named Gerry Lean crept up behind Donna during recess, screamed, "Imma kidnapper!" and grabbed her arm. Donna twitched and suddenly a great dark stain spread across the front of her Wranglers, down the inside of her left leg. There followed a stunned, dreadful stillness. Kids froze and stared. A small girl keened with hysterical laughter. Donna later said they were all laughing at her, but that wasn't true. Van saw it all. Most of the other kids looked as if they wanted to be sick, or cry, or run and throw their arms around Donna to shield her from any more embarrassment.

A scream began in Donna's chest. It rose and rose. It sounded like an eagle in a nature documentary. She whirled, and in the next instant Gerry Lean was down and she was sinking her teeth into his face, under his left eye. She bit a fat piece of cheek off and spit it out.

Donovan got to her first and hoisted her off the sobbing Gerry Lean while she fought him and teachers ran toward them and children shrieked in terror and scattered like ants after someone has delivered a swift kick to the anthill. A cosmetic surgeon spent six hours working on it, but Gerry Lean's face never looked right again.

GERRY LEAN'S DESK was next to Donovan's in history. Gerry had always been too big for his age, his head too big for his neck, and he had the staring eyes of a witless poodle. Even before Donna tore part of his face off, he spent most of history class staring wistfully into the playground rather than paying attention. Donovan began doing his in-class work for him. He colored in the part of America that had been snapped up in the Louisiana Purchase; he slipped Gerry's worksheets off his desk and filled them out as soon as he was done working on his own. Gerry hardly seemed to notice. Once or twice Mrs. Hamilton spotted Van putting Gerry's worksheets back on his desk, but she never commented.

Gerry didn't come back after Christmas break. His parents had decided to make a fresh start in Miami, while the legal suit played out.

LETICIA STAYED ON after Cady Lewis was taken away to her death. No one blamed her, not even the Lewis family. But she was different after the abduction, less talkative and more serious. She didn't let Van and Donna play in the front yard anymore, which was fine by both of them. For the first couple of months after Cady was taken, Donna wouldn't go out at all unless someone made her, and even then she wanted to hold an adult's hand. Van had always preferred sitting in front of the TV anyway.

Everything Leticia did, as both nanny and housekeeper, was quiet and careful. She even loaded the dishwasher with great care, as if clinking a dish might wake a sleeping infant. She took to nervously brushing Donna's hair while they all watched cartoons, brushing and brushing until it shone like new-minted copper filaments.

One Easter Sunday, when Donna and Van were in fourth grade, Leticia borrowed them for a family brunch at her mémère's house: shrimp and eggs, jalapeño cornbread, and sangria at eleven in the morning. Her family had come from all over the panhandle, and the islands, and New Orleans, even two cousins from East Texas, two of the blackest Black men Van had ever seen, Emmanuel and Simon. Shafts of warm, golden light hung in the smoke from the barbecue outside Mémère's big old nineteenth-century house, half concealed by oaks hung with Spanish moss. Van couldn't remember a morning that smelled so good, of ocean air and crawfish and spicy tomato sauces. Emmanuel and Simon had a van just like B. A. Baracus's in *The A-Team* and a soccer ball that they took turns bouncing on their feet and knees, seeing how long they could keep it from touching the ground, while Jimmy Cliff played on the van's stereo. Van had five good bounces and Emmanuel and Simon yelled with happiness for him. Simon smoked big hand-rolled cigarettes that smelled good and that later Van knew were pot. Donna stood on the grass, twenty feet away, and watched, and said nothing.

When she went home, she told her father she had seen the van again, and that Simon was the man who had been driving it the day Cady was taken. Donna had recognized the van right away, and a tattoo of a blue anchor on Simon's inner arm, although she had not mentioned the anchor in her statement. Van's mother looked as if she had been punched in the stomach: June McBride was a thin, wiry woman who had suffered from migraines since the kidnapping and often spent afternoons in her bedroom, in the dark, with the shades pulled. June and Lenny, Van's father, stayed up late that night, talking in low, grave voices. Early the next morning, Lenny called Leticia and asked her not to come to work. Then he called the police. By then, June and Lenny had pretty well talked themselves into believing Leticia was part of it, had given her cousins the nod when it was safe to grab the Lewis girl.

In the investigation that followed, it turned out that neither Emmanuel nor Simon could've kidnapped Cady Lewis for the simple reason that they had come to the country illegally only four months before the Easter brunch. They were expelled back to Haiti. Leticia's husband, Martin, was arrested for possession of marijuana with intent to sell, although he insisted he was not a drug dealer, and that the stash was being held for a friend's bachelor party. He ultimately served five years. Before Leticia was cleared of any wrongdoing, someone in the neighborhood threw a rock through the windshield of her car. Her pastor asked her to stop coming to her church.

Donna was unapologetic. The investigation had proved Leticia and Martin were drug dealers. In her opinion, Leticia was probably high as a kite when Cady was kidnapped. Maybe if she hadn't been, Cady would still be alive. And if her cousins weren't kidnappers, they were illegals, and who knew what else they had done while living among real Americans?

Six months after their family let Leticia go, Donovan saw her outside an ice cream shop, down by the ocean, and ran across the street to throw his arms around her waist in a hug. She had bent and kissed his forehead and begun to cry. She was still crying when Donovan's mother caught up and pulled him free by the wrist.

"Stay away from us," June said. "Stay away from my children."

DONNA THOUGHT SHE SAW the van again, in 1985. Some Mexican landscapers in flannel shirts and work pants were unloading their equipment from the open back doors of a black Econoline. When she called the police, she did not say it was the van that had taken Cady Lewis. She said she had seen pot.

They all had their green cards and there was no weed in the van, but one of the men was arrested anyway, because his name—José Garcia—matched the name of a man who had committed multiple rapes just across the state line, in Georgia. He spent five days in a Florida jail before he was driven to Macon . . . where he was able to prove he was a different José Garcia entirely.

That was April. The landscapers had contracts for a few houses in the large, gated community where the McBrides had moved after Lenny took over operation of the family newspapers and TV stations. One afternoon at the end of May, Donovan saw their landscaping van parked in front of a house down the road, where the street began to curve south. He walked home, went into the basement, found two cases of cold Coronas, and walked them back. The rear of the van was unlocked. No one saw him put the cases in the van, gently shut the door, and stroll away. It wasn't going to make up for five days in a Florida jail, but Donovan was only fourteen and it was the best he could do.

His father thought Van and his friends had helped themselves to his Coronas. His parents pulled him out of an upcoming trip to Puerto Rico, part of a cultural exchange organized by his school. When Donna heard Van wasn't going, she withdrew herself.

"I hope you feel good about ruining this for your sister," their father told Van.

Donna said, "I *never* wanted to go. Puerto Rico is the AIDS capital of the world. Fuck that."

"This is really better for both of us," Van told him. "Also better for Puerto Rico."

SOMETIMES DONNA HAD NIGHTMARES and would wake in the grip of a shaking fit, a trembling spell that was almost convulsive in force. When she had control of herself again, she would let herself unsteadily into Van's room and ask if she could sleep on his floor.

He always made her take the bed. He slept on the floor instead, in his sleeping bag.

They held hands. She'd hang an arm over the side of the bed and he'd take it. They would lie awake listening to country music on the radio, volume turned low.

"Why don't you hate me?" she asked. "I'm an awful person. Why did I say that about Puerto Rico?"

"I guess 'cause you're kinda racist," he said.

She giggled, as if he had made a dirty joke, and squeezed his fingers. "No, I'm *not*. I don't even see color." She was quiet a while and then whispered, "I can't go to Puerto Rico if you're not going. I can't. I won't sleep. I'll be sick all the time. There's something sick in me, Van. The people who took Cady—they took something from *me* too. I'm scared of everything. I know I don't seem it. But I'm the most scared person you know."

"You should try smoking pot sometime. It would help with your nerves."

She laughed, then made a disgusted sound. "Emmy Davis smokes pot, like, all the time. Have you ever noticed how she smells like burnt cat hair?"

Van knew *exactly* how Em Davis smelled, and it wasn't anything like burnt cat hair. Her natty-white-girl dreads smelled sweetly of coffee, cigarettes, and wildflowers baking in the sun. Van knew because they had made out, after passing a joint a few times, outside the roller rink last Saturday. Van loved skating—he was the fucking

John Travolta of the roller rink—but he loved his tongue in Em Davis's mouth even more

"It ought to be legal," he told Donna. "Weed. Wouldn't that be cool?"

But Donna didn't answer. She was only holding his hand with one finger, had dozed off in his bed. Van, on the other hand, was wide awake. There was a pretty good college station out of Georgia, and at this time of night he could just about pull it in. They played a kind of music called cowpunk, hillbillies thrashing it out over banjos and fiddle, and he loved it. He slipped his hand out of Donna's and tugged a ziplock bag from under his mattress. There were two skinny pre-rolled joints inside, all he could afford to buy off Em, who was two years older than him and well known around school as the one dealer who would never sell you crap.

He reached under the mattress again and tugged out a copy of *High Times* magazine. Em had loaned it to him, said him there was a cool article about evil things the US government was doing with pesticides.

"Yo, old son," Em had told him. "The feds want to put this shit on *all* your veg, man, not just pot. This is some shit they talking about here—paraquat will make your *dink* shrink. You got to inform yourself."

He lit up, folded the magazine open to the article, and began to read by the light of his alarm-clock radio. Donna lived too much in her own imagination, and look where it got her: jangled, scared, and angry. One of them had to live in the real world. One of them had to have the facts. He took a tight, careful hit—a sweet, spicy, lovely, golden hit—and started to inform himself.

17.

They were back for him five days later: Lansing, Salem, and Little Rock. At the sight of them entering his room, Van's kidneys turned to cold jelly. *They're back to finish what they started last week*, he thought. *Get ready to go for one last swim.*

Van was sitting on the end of the bed in his pajama bottoms. The Zenith was on, but the screen showed a flurry of digital snow, and the only sound was the insensate roar of the white noise. He had been watching DTV—Donna Television—until about an hour ago, when the power in the whole complex stuttered and went out. In the hallway, beyond his picture window, a strip of emergency lighting had blinked on, producing a dingy, jaundiced glow. His bedroom had become a box of discolored shadows, filled with a sepia-tinted gloom. A few minutes later there was a powerful whir and thrum, somewhere far away, and the lights came stammering back on. The TV came on too, but by then Donna was gone, replaced by that flurry of white pixels. Van watched it anyway. He thought it looked like his future—disintegration and violent emptiness.

"Field trip!" Salem called. Nothing ever seemed to get Salem down.

Little Rock hauled Van up by the arm. The kid was massive and slow, and Van would've bet anything he still watched cartoons over his breakfast.

"Hey, Little Rock," Van said, as the kid marched him to the door. "Of all the capitals in this country, why do you think they picked that one for you?"

Little Rock gave him a vaguely hostile look. "Why do *you* think they picked that one?"

"I was just wondering if it was supposed to refer to your physique," Van said, "or those things rattling around in your skull."

Little Rock slammed him into the doorway on their way through. "Are you getting smart?"

Van stood straight, let them walk him into the hall. "Naw, old son. I wouldn't want you to feel left out of the conversation."

They walked one on either side of him, Salem to the left, Little Rock to the right, Nurse Lansing following behind and studying a clipboard. They passed an open door onto a break room. The single round folding table was strewn with papers and empty cups. A stack of folders had been dropped on one of the molded-plastic chairs. Several had slid off and scattered across the linoleum. It looked like no one had been in to clean for weeks. A man sat on the floor, under the cork notice board, his knees pulled to his chest and his arms wrapped around them. He watched Van go by with watery, hateful eyes.

"So morale is good, huh?" Van said.

They walked past a picture window looking into a space that resembled a dentist's examining room. Donna was on a reclining tan leather couch, her mittens locked to the armrests. A black microphone dangled directly above her, mounted on an articulated steel arm. An IV bag had been wheeled alongside the chair. Joe Valentine stood over her, dabbing the inside of her arm with an alcohol swab.

Van's escort led him into the examination theater. Mr. Francis was there, at a desk in the corner, in a revolving chair twisted halfway around so he could watch the rest of the room. Dr. Patrick was there too, her arm across the back of another reclining exam couch, showing all her teeth in a ferocious grin that Van thought looked less like an expression of enthusiasm and more like a manifestation of madness.

"*Good morning, good mornnnning,*" she sang, swaying a little. Van looked, and then looked again. She had missed a button on her silk blouse and it gaped to show the bridge between the pink cups of her bra. The buttons above the gap were lined up wrong. Panic was like an open wound, everyone saw you bleeding.

"What's this?" Van asked.

"They're going to poison us," Donna said.

"Would we do that?" Dr. Patrick cried, still half singing. "Sit down, sit down!" As if Van had a choice. His guards manhandled him onto a second couch. There were steel rings on the armrests. They tightened them on his wrists and buckled them in place with brass padlocks. He and Donna had matching microphones, dangling above their recliners. It struck Van that autopsy rooms were designed along much the same lines, with a microphone hung above the corpse, so the medical examiner could narrate his findings as he sliced and diced.

Donna's chair was turned so he could see her in profile. She struggled and squirmed while Joe Valentine pushed a needle into the exposed vein on her right arm and used some white tape to hold it down. A few weeks ago Valentine would've had a nurse to do that for him. Apparently good help was getting hard to find.

Valentine didn't look so good. His chewed right ear was bent at the wrong angle, sticking out from the side of his head. His shirt was wrinkled, his tie was too loose, and his silvery-blond hair was a mess, as if he had rolled out of bed and walked into work without giving it a comb.

"This'd be the way to do it," Valentine told Donna, while he fixed strips of tape in place. "One part saline and three parts bleach. I wonder how long it would take you to die."

"I know how long it would take *you* to die," Francis said, from the desk. "As long as it took me to unholster my weapon. There's a priceless military asset in this room, Valentine, and it's not you."

"What are you sticking her with?" Van asked.

"Sodium thiopental—Sodium Pentathol, under its brand name. Truth serums are out of fashion in first-world countries. Doctors are squeamish about pumping prisoners full of barbiturates. But elsewhere it remains a trusted method of extracting intel from difficult subjects."

"Let's prep Donnie, Nurse," Valentine said, turning to Van's chair. He pushed Van's sleeve up and dabbed the inside of his arm with alcohol.

Nurse Lansing widened the opening at the top of Donovan's

Henley and slipped the cold stethoscope in against his chest. Van's heart was thumping along in a series of sketchy, galloping jags. It happened so frequently, he hardly noticed anymore. Lansing listened for a while, then frowned and gave Van an accusatory look.

Van said, "I know, I know. It's been doing that all day."

"Doing what?" Valentine asked. He had brought the needle of a syringe close to Van's inner arm, but hesitated now, fixing Lansing with a sharp, cold stare.

"He's arrhythmic," Nurse Lansing said.

Valentine's thin lips whitened. "You're telling me this now? Why didn't you take his vitals back in his room?"

Lansing said, "Why didn't you tell the thuds not to haul him out of the room right away? Was I supposed to examine him while they dragged him down the hall, kicking and screaming? You are aware I don't have any help down here."

"Wait, wait. I feel grossly misrepresented here. There was no kicking and only a little squealing." Van played back in his mind what Lansing had just said, and added, "What do you mean, you don't have any help down here? Where's Nurse Dover?"

"Bitch fucking ran for it," Lansing said. "Just fucking—"

"All right, Lansing," Francis said, from the other side of the room, and Lansing bit down on his lower lip.

Valentine turned his back on Donovan and Nurse Lansing both. His movements were jerky, uncoordinated. Donovan wondered how he was sleeping.

"Get him some orange juice, for fuck's sake," Valentine said. "And we'll see if his heart has calmed down in ten minutes."

"I'll get it!" Dr. Patrick cried, as if Valentine had said it was time to bring out birthday cake. Patrick leapt to her feet and sashayed to a mini fridge in the back of the room, dancing to music only she could hear. She returned with a cup of orange juice, a straw pushed through the tinfoil top. She held the straw to Van's lips and Van sipped a mouthful of cold sweetness.

He felt so grateful to her he murmured, "Your blouse."

She looked down and trilled with nervous laughter. "My apologies! I didn't mean to give everyone a free show."

"I'm sorry," he said. "That it's so scary. I wish that wasn't part of it. It's bad enough that he's after you, I don't know why he has to terrorize you first."

Dr. Patrick blinked, her eyes suddenly bright with wetness. She jerked the straw away from his mouth. She fought for a grin and didn't win.

"Don't try and pretend you're a nice guy," she said, in a shaking voice. "And don't imagine you can manipulate me. I have a PhD in psychology. I know every trick in the book."

"If you think empathy is a trick," Van said, "then I'm even more sorry for you."

"Dr. Patrick," Valentine said, without looking at her. "I'll be handling this interview."

The lights gave another flicker, stammering like Donovan's unsteady pulse. No one paid it any mind except Mr. Francis, who lifted his chin and considered the lights on the ceiling.

"Nurse Dover, your maintenance men," Van said. "Seems like anyone with any sense is hoofing it. Looks like they're more afraid of King Sorrow than you, Mr. Francis."

"The difference between me and your dragon," Francis said, "is that I don't wait till Easter to deal with people who make problems." And gave Van a flat look.

"Breathe deeply and steadily, Donna," Joe Valentine told Donna. He had rolled a stool to the side of her bed. "Just like you're filling your lungs before diving under water."

"Fuck you," she said, but there was a dreamy quality to her voice now.

"Maybe later," Valentine said, and Donovan thought he sounded almost his old chipper self. "Deep, slow, calming breaths. We're getting ready to dive down now. We're going to dive down into thought, you and I. You don't have to be afraid. I'll be with you the whole way. I'm going to ask you some questions, and every time you give me an honest answer, you're going to feel better about yourself. Lighter and easier. You don't have to keep any secrets anymore. You can be free of them. Light and free and easy. Are you ready to tell me the truth, Donna?"

"All right," she sighed. "I guess it doesn't matter what I tell you. You're going to die soon."

There were spots of color in Joe Valentine's very white cheeks, the only sign this last statement had got to him. He had a clipboard on one knee and a pen ready to take notes, though Van was sure the microphone would get everything. Dr. Patrick offered him the straw once more and he sipped, watching Donna with fascination.

"This is all light and easy stuff, Donna," Joe Valentine said. "What's your name?"

"Donna Mehitabel McBride," she said. "Allie says my middle name is my secret eighteenth-century lesbian spinster name. Allie is gay for me, isn't that sweet? The one time we did it as roommates I was just experimenting, but she's still hung up on me."

Van coughed orange juice up his nose, choked, coughed again. Nurse Lansing came over with a cloth to pat his face dry.

"And where were you born?" Valentine said, and the lights stammered again—and blinked out.

A strip of emergency lighting along one wall came on, casting a dull, golden glow that lit faces and hands, and left most of the rest of the room in suffocating darkness. The distant steady throb of the generator—it was less a sound than a kind of constant vibration—trailed off into stillness.

"Goddamn it," Valentine cried. "Can nothing go right? I lose my power now?"

"Your mistake," King Sorrow said from Donna's mouth, his voice a good-humored, reverberating rumble, "was believing you had any power to begin with, Norman Barclay. You want to know where I was born? I hatched in the cauldron of Mount Hekla, five thousand years before Christ. Upon my birth, the volcano erupted and choked the world with so much darkness and ash your ancestors, a gang of pitiful and incestuous monkeys, believed the time of judgment was at hand. And they were right, mate. It's been a time of judgment ever since . . . and I am the judge."

18.

Donna exhaled slowly and deeply, just as she had been instructed—and curls of gray smoke drifted from her nostrils. Dr. Patrick mewled in the darkness. Little Rock lunged for the door, yanked at the handle. It wouldn't open.

"Where are you going?" Mr. Francis asked.

"Get help!"

"For chrissake, resume your post," Mr. Francis said. "No one is going anywhere till we get the power back. Those locks are electric."

Joe Valentine hugged his clipboard to his chest, staring over it with wide, fascinated eyes. Only of course that wasn't his true name. His true name was Norman Barclay, and somehow Colin had found it out and whispered it to King Sorrow. His name and forty-two others.

"Your Grace," Norman Barclay gasped. "Your Majesty. I'm honored."

"Is that how you'd describe it? I would've said you were pissing yourself," King Sorrow said through Donna.

"Mother of God," whined Little Rock. "I gotta get out of here."

"Shut him up," Francis ordered Salem.

Salem slipped his nightstick out of the loop on his belt and came around with it, driving it into the stomach of the pale-eyed boy. Little Rock said *oof*, doubled over, and sank to his knees.

Valentine paid no mind. He was watching Donna. They were all watching Donna. Her eyes were shut. Smoke trickled from her lips and nostrils.

"You have pledged to kill forty-three members of our staff on

Easter morning. Is that right? Why were some chosen and others spared?"

"No one will be spared. Those who see me and survive will dream of me the rest of their lives. We will meet again, often, in the Long Dark, where they will scream and grovel before me and weep and be torn apart. You see, those I slay in the weak light of actuality only have to die once . . . which makes you one of the lucky ones, *Norm*."

Little Rock, who was still kneeling on the floor, opened his mouth, took a deep breath as if to offer an opinion, and vomited a thick stream of brownish slime.

"Jesus Christ," Lansing whispered, and he gripped Van's forearm. It took Van a moment to realize he had clasped his arm for comfort.

"This is the wealthiest and most powerful country the world has ever known," Barclay said. "Whatever you're getting now, to serve Shiner and the McBrides, we can give you so much more. Whatever you want, to spare our lives—we can give it to you. I have been delegated to speak for several multinational corporations, companies with billions in assets, and the federal government of the United States. They have indicated they are ready to pay a tribute for your services. Anything within reason."

"How about Nebraska?" King Sorrow asked.

Van didn't think he had ever seen Valentine recoil. He had been young, bright, agile, and sunny three months ago. Now, in the gloom of the emergency lights, Van could see how he would look when he was old. Then Van remembered he was never going to grow old.

"Give me Nebraska. Your army will fence it in. If anyone tries to leave, they will be shot—no exceptions. I will have the electrical grid shut off. I will blight the fields to create mass starvation. I will keep fires burning, so the sky remains black with soot and the sun is never seen. I will ask for ninety-nine virgins a year and I will insist their deaths be broadcast on national TV in prime time. We will have our own Major League Baseball team, but they will only play home games, and at the end of every match the losing pitcher will be beheaded on the mound. I will poison the waters with my tears and allow only two beverages to the citizenry: Diet Dr Pepper and Schlitz."

"I don't think we can give you Nebraska," Valentine said, and he shot a questioning glance at Francis.

Francis gave his head a little shake. "Yeah, Nebraska is off the table."

"And you said I could have anything. Kiss me, you big tease." And Donna puckered her lips and made smacking noises.

"Is there some other way we can . . . serve you?" Valentine asked.

"Your nation already serves me. It was serving me in My Lai, where American soldiers shot old women and raped children. It was serving me when your people butchered the village of No Gun Ri in North Korea. You served me every day you offered your money and your intelligence to Augusto Pinochet while he disappeared his enemies—seizing them and taking them to places much like this, to force information out of them, and then dispose of them. You offer me your allegiance, but I already have it."

"Let me live," said Valentine. "Please. Let me offer someone in my place. I can offer a whole bunch of someones if necessary. I'm not ready to die. I'm doing important work!"

"How many someones? Five?"

Valentine nodded.

"Five then," King Sorrow said from Donna's mouth. "But their names must remain between the two of us. I don't want your Mr. Francis to hear. Or the microphone. Come close and I'll whisper them to you."

Valentine rose like one in a trance, swaying a little, and Van thought, *You dumb ass, don't do that,* but suddenly he couldn't find his voice. Valentine took a step next to Donna's reclining seat and began to lean forward.

"The fuck you doing?" Francis asked, getting up himself. "Grab him! Stop him!"

Salem began to move forward, but he had to make his way around the recliner, and by then Valentine was leaning toward Donna's lips. He had turned his good ear to her mouth.

Van saw her eyes snap open and they were yellow, stained with poisonous, jagged bands of red, and her pupils slit like a snake's. Her jaw fell open. They somehow seemed to come *unhinged*, her chin dropping too far, almost falling to her breastbone, and King Sorrow's great green claw leapt out of her open mouth and peeled Valentine's good left ear off the side of his head, and some of his cheek too. He raked off half of Valentine's face in one swipe. Valentine howled. His knees buckled. He dropped his clipboard. The ear was still impaled on the claw when it was yanked back down Donna's throat. Her mouth snapped shut . . . but only for an instant.

"Johnny," she muttered, in King Sorrow's voice. "John Leonard Boone. If *you* want to live, get off your knees and kill Valentine. Beat him to death with that club on your belt. Do it now and I will spare your sorry, pointless life. Kill him for me and you'll live to see your fiancée again."

Boone—the big boy Van had always known as Little Rock—lifted his head and stared across the room at Valentine.

"Don't listen to him," Francis told him. "He's lying to you."

Valentine collapsed. He writhed on the floor, screaming. Dr. Patrick dropped to one knee beside him, got a hand under his head.

"Sweet Jesus," she said. "He's bleeding like a stuck cow. I need something to put pressure on this. Lansing? Lansing!"

Lansing had stiffened, a thin whining sound coming out of his pursed lips, his fingernails digging into Van's arm.

Boone gazed at Valentine like a man in a trance, his face slack.

"In the name of Christ," Mr. Francis said. "Don't do it, Boone."

Boone unholstered his nightstick. His eyes were wide and unseeing. He came heavily to his feet and began to stagger toward Valentine, stepping around Van's recliner.

"Shoot him!" Mr. Francis shouted.

Boone made it three steps before Salem began firing from the far side of the room. In the enclosed space of the examination room, the gun stunned Van's eardrums into near deafness. Salem's first shots missed Little Rock entirely and whapped into the picture window facing the hallway. The glass fissured into a thousand blue pebbles with an audible crackling. The window collapsed a moment later, raining to the floor in a loud clatter. Nurse Lansing threw himself across Van's body, getting low.

"Don't shoot me, don't shoot me, you assholes, I'm a valuable US asset!" Van screamed. He could hardly hear his own voice over the ringing in his ears.

A bullet struck the boy John Boone in the neck and tore it open. He kept coming. Another bullet hit him in the shoulder and half spun him. He went on. He was lifting his nightstick to club Valentine in the skull when Valentine himself lashed out with one foot, kicking Boone's leg from under him. Boone went down on one knee and a bullet struck him in the center of the forehead, snapped his head back.

"Hold your fire!" Mr. Francis yelled. Salem was walking forward, lowering his gun to point it at the body on the floor, the muzzle flashing as it went off again and again. "Stop shooting! Stop *stop* STOP!"

Salem stopped and stood over Little Rock's body, studying it impassively. The air was hazy with propellant, the smell of gunfire, and the coppery zing of blood. Nurse Lansing stayed where he was, lying across Van's chest, his arms around him.

"Thank you, man," Van said. "Thank you. You can get up now."

Nurse Lansing didn't move. Van's chest was wet, and he wondered if Nurse Lansing was having himself a little cry.

Valentine kicked and twisted on the floor, screeching hysterically, one hand clapped over an ear that was still very much there. Of course it was still there. It wasn't Easter yet. They had all seen King Sorrow yank the ear off the side of his face, but only in a kind of shared dream, one of King Sorrow's powerful suggestions . . . a preview of coming attractions.

"Hey," Van said, in a louder voice. "Nurse Lansing. Valentine is okay. He's still got his ears on. More or less."

Nurse Lansing still didn't reply. Van was conscious of something sticky drooling down his left arm. He began to get a bad feeling.

Donna rolled her head on her neck. Her eyes were still those of a serpent. Her voice was still his voice.

"Oops," King Sorrow said.

The lights spasmed and flickered back on as the generator roared to life. Donna blinked and her eyes were her own again. Under the glare of the fluorescents, it was easier to see the wet red mess of Nurse Lansing's hair. The electric bolts slammed open and the door crashed in. Men in polo shirts spilled through. Donovan fixed his gaze on the ceiling, didn't look while men lifted Nurse Lansing off him.

"If someone could get a washcloth," Van said, "I think I've got brains running down my arm."

19.

Van couldn't sleep, so he sat in the straight-backed chair in front of his picture window, staring into the corridor, which is how he happened to be awake the night Nurse Dover came back.

There was a nighttime setting for the lights in the corridor. Only one in every three fluorescents was on, creating little blocks of brightness between long stretches of darkness, a bit like a document that has been heavily redacted by some government agency, black bars covering all but a word here and there.

At some point a procession began to approach, appearing in flashes, approaching through those scattered cubes of lit hallway. Men in polo shirts pushed gurneys past the window, without looking at Van. Van had the impression that not only had they not observed him, but that he wasn't there at all. He was asleep in bed and the version of him that sat at the window was an astral projection.

There were corpses under the sheets. One, two, three, a fourth. The maintenance crew. The last was imperfectly covered. A swollen, soggy foot protruded, blue from cold, the toenails painted a cheery red. Some straggly blond hair, still dripping from the sea, spilled out from beneath the sheet at the other end of the gurney. A crab, hardly bigger than a half-dollar, crawled along some of her locks, then fell suddenly to the floor.

When the parade of security men and their dead were gone, he watched the almost translucent crab. For a long time, it remained as still as Van himself. Then it crept slyly sideways, into the darkness, and was gone.

20.

Some number of days later, Mr. Francis opened the door of Donna's room and let himself in, pushing a trolley ahead of him. He was alone. Donna could not remember receiving a lone visitor in months, not in all the time since she had torn off Joe Valentine's—check that, Norman Barclay's—ear.

"I already had dinner," she said. "Is that dessert?"

"Yes," he said, and she saw there was a bottle of Scotch on the trolley, and two glasses.

"When did you start delivering refreshments?" she asked.

"When most of our nursing staff contrived to get themselves dead," he said. "Hope you didn't want ice in that Scotch. The machine is broken and the maintenance team is long gone."

"I haven't had a Scotch in months. I'm not about to spoil it with a bunch of ice."

"Good girl," he said.

"Don't ever say that ever again. I'm not your good girl."

"Noted."

He poured an inch, looked at her, poured another half inch. She took the glass between her mittens, put her nose over it, and inhaled. It smelled like Christmas, like The Briars.

"So you're shorthanded all around?" she asked.

"In every department except security," he said. "We're up to a half company of soldiers now, and more coming in every day. Thermopylae is pulling resources from all over—Yugoslavia, East Timor, Chechnya. Anywhere there's a squalid little fight going on over oil or emeralds. The best way to keep your black site detention center off the books is to outsource it to the professionals."

"Don't leave war crimes to the amateurs," Donna said.

Francis saluted her with his glass.

"Thermopylae," Donna said, trying the word out to see how it felt in her mouth.

Francis nodded. "Thermopylae Security Worldwide. Second only to Blackwater among private military contractors."

"Private military contractors? That's a nice euphemism for mercenaries. And you work with them," Donna said, curling her upper lip.

"They still would've taken you," Francis said, "even if the people I represent weren't involved. Better to have them on a leash."

"And that's who you are? The man holding the leash?"

"No, Donna," Francis said. "I *am* the leash."

She tasted her Scotch. It was a smoky lick of flame.

She exhaled softly and met his gaze and said, "You can get me drunk, but I still won't tell you where to find Allison."

"I wasn't planning to ask. You can't tell me what you don't know."

"Here's what I *do* know. In nine days, my pet iguana is going to murder a whole slew of you, but it's not my fault. I didn't paint a target on your backs."

Francis gave her a considering look. "But somehow King Sorrow knew forty-three members of the team by name anyway. Their real names. How do you think that happened?"

"Allie has her resources."

"What a crock of shit," he said, without any hostility at all. "The only contacts Allison Shiner has are the people who work at her local liquor store."

"Her daddy was a congressman. He's got friends all over the federal government, in the military, with Central Intelligence."

Francis nodded his big, ugly, English mastiff head. "That's certainly what Valentine thinks . . . that Allison was able to work her daddy for confidential intel somehow. I don't see it myself. We know she called him once, forty-eight hours after Park Slope. Told the old man she and Donovan were checking into a clinic to sober up. That they'd be out of touch and not to worry about them. We were listening to the old man's phone calls, of course. We've had men on him ever since Allison slipped away. She hasn't called him since, hasn't approached him . . . she's just gone. Don't you think it's interesting that she made up a story to explain a long-term disappearance? That she didn't try and tell him the truth? 'Daddy, some men tried to stick a needle in me and take me away. I think they got Donovan. Please help.'"

"She was just doing what she always does," Donna said. "Giving them a story they can live with, because the truth would scare them too much."

"A truth, like if she told them she'd rather be fucking girls?"

"Not just any girls," Donna said, exhaling Scotch fumes. "Classy girls."

"Imagine that. Marrying a guy to make your parents happy when you don't even like dick?" He tasted his Scotch, paused to enjoy it. "Naw, it wasn't Allison. One of the others told King Sorrow who to kill."

"What others?" Donna asked. A tingle of alarm shot down her nerve endings, right into the tips of her fingers, a prickling electrical charge.

"Your other friends, the ones who helped you bring King Sorrow through from the Long Dark. Arthur Oakes, for one. What are the odds you all would've gone to school with the world's foremost expert on dragons in medieval literature and he doesn't know about King Sorrow? Problem is, he's a UK citizen and it would be hard to extradite him, even if we did know where he is. Which we don't. Allison must've called him right after she called you. He told Oxford University he was going to Indonesia to study the dragon in traditional temple architecture, but he never left the UK. We've got CCTV footage of him with a backpack, walking across the parking lot of a Tesco in a Welsh village called Penmaenpool—no idea if I'm pronouncing that right—wearing a backpack so big it's hard to believe he could lift it. He walked into the woods there, left his car behind, and no one has seen him since. There's a lot of woods out there. A lot of mountain."

"He doesn't know anything about—about King Sorrow," she

said, but her uncharacteristic stammer gave her away. Mr. Francis laughed.

"We don't got to talk about Arthur," Francis said. "Or any of the others who are in on it with you. It's almost nine and I'm drinking Scotch with a good-looking woman. We don't got to talk shop, do we?"

"So what do we talk about?"

"How about Cady Lewis?"

She felt like he had put ice in her drink after all and a lump of it was caught in her windpipe, behind her breastbone. She had thought of Norman Barclay as the torturer and Mr. Francis as a possible ally. But they were both torturers, of course, both in the business of forcing her to talk about things she didn't want to talk about. It was the good cop, bad cop game, and she had let herself be taken in by it. In her vanity, she wanted to believe Francis had a little bit of a yen for her. But she was the only one having fantasies.

"You already know about Cady. I bet you read a whole file on her."

"I don't know what you know. Only what I read in newspaper clippings."

"She was a friend of mine who got into a van with strangers and they fucked her and killed her. She was eight. What else is there to tell?"

"You were there when it happened, weren't you? You watched her get into the van. You think about it much?"

"No, never crosses my mind at all."

He made a little sound, halfway to a laugh, and had another taste of his whiskey.

"You ever think, what if you got in the van with her? Or *instead* of her?"

"If it was me instead of her no one would've died. I would've bit a son of a bitch in the pecker."

"No. You would've got your head bashed in like her. You would've been raped and killed just the same."

She held the whiskey glass between her mittened hands and

calculated whether she could smash him in the head with it. He smiled, as if he could see her working through the thought. "They wouldn't have got away with it. I would've screamed so loud."

"Maybe they didn't get away with it," he said. He rolled his glass back and forth between his big hands. It nettled her that she couldn't see his angle, couldn't figure out what he wanted out of this conversation.

"What do you mean?"

"Guys like that, they don't do it once, and their issues never stop at grabbing little girls. For all you know, one of them is doing life in East Texas right now for strangling his girlfriend in a domestic incident. And his partner got knifed in the kidneys during a thirty-day stint in the county jail for exposing himself to a child. He's on dialysis now. He's never going to be off it."

"Is that true?" she asked, her breath roughening with emotion.

"Dunno," he said, and the tension went out of her. "I just made all that up on the spot. Point is, it's over."

"You don't know that. You don't know how many other kids they hurt. For all you know they're still at it."

"I doubt it." His certainty pissed her off. He had no right to dismiss Cady that way. "The piece of shit that killed her, something will have caught up to him, or if it hasn't yet, it will. A cop will make a routine traffic stop and find his child porn. He'll meet someone worse than him and get a shovel in the brains. Or he died with a needle in his arm. These guys, they don't die peacefully at eighty with their loved ones around them."

"Are you trying to make me feel better? Because you're about as comforting as a rash."

"I guess if no one's caught up to them yet," Francis said, "King Sorrow might, one of these days. If you could only learn their names. And in the meantime, there are so many other men like them. So many other Cadys."

"Thanks for the amateur psychoanalysis. Only one quick session to sort out all my personal issues and completely solve me as a person. How much do you charge?"

"That's how you make peace with it. You get the bad guys no one else can. You're the one driving the murder van now."

That touched her off, was more than she could allow. "The fuck I am. King Sorrow is waste disposal. All he's done the last ten years is incinerate trash. Don't twist this. Don't try and make me out to be anything like the people who killed Cady."

"What about Tokyo? An apartment building full of members of Aum Shinrikyo burned to the ground. That was one of yours. They were a bad bunch, no argument about that. Only thing, one of the worshippers was in the building with her nine-month-old."

She felt her thighs beginning to tremble. "We didn't know there'd be kids there, and anyway, that wasn't my pick, that was C—"

She caught herself before she could say his name . . . but even before she did she saw Francis put a finger across his lips and casually saw it back and forth. If she didn't know better, he was telling her to *shhh*. It confused her, why he would try to shut her up just when she was about to give up a name. His eyes had darkened ever so slightly.

"All I was saying," Francis said, "is that you were after one of them in particular, probably Haruto Sagawa, the mastermind. It's too bad you didn't have more help, a support team. He could've been lured out of the building on Easter. Maybe so many people didn't need to die." He finished his own whiskey and exhaled heavily. "The thing about cults like Aum Shinrikyo—or the Scripture of the Kingdom Church in Iowa—is that people join their shelters, their compounds, *expecting* to die. They go there to wait on the end of the world. I wouldn't feel too bad about giving it to them. At least they didn't die disappointed." He looked around the room, considered the cameras mounted on the ceiling. "This place is also a bit like a cult compound now. The people here wanted to learn about King Sorrow, and soon they will."

"You too, buddy," she said.

He got up. "I was content with what I already knew about him. Once a year, King Sorrow comes out of the Long Dark to destroy bad people and bad places. And in less than two weeks, he's going to do it again. Same as always. Same as ever. He's going to wipe out a private corporation that runs torture sites and the world is going to be a better place for it. I'll leave you with the bottle?"

He didn't wait for her answer, just rapped his knuckles on the door and slipped out when the guard on the other side unlocked it.

21.

The reinforcements were there.

Van watched them walk past his window. They began piling in the week before Easter, passing down the hall in teams of three and four: young, sturdy, and tanned, with close haircuts and bored eyes. They had carbine rifles over their shoulders—Van was pretty sure from the banana clips they were M4s—and pistols strapped to their thighs.

The cannon fodder had been milling in the hallways for three days when Van came awake one night, suddenly knowing someone was in the room with him. As his eyes adjusted to the dark, he spied Mr. Francis leaning against the inside of his door. It was dark in the evil little motel room, and the brightest thing in it was the coal burning at the end of his cigar.

The men looked at each other. Francis had a zip-up windbreaker on.

"I always loved fireworks," Francis said. He studied the glowing tip of his cigar. "The rockets' red glare. The smell of them. One way or another, this Easter is going to be a hell of a show. They've got shoulder-mounted RPGs, you know. Two assault helicopters. A tank."

"They've got shit," Van said. "Do any of them have any idea what they're up against?"

"The foot soldiers have no idea. They believe you and your sister are Serbian nationals, loyal to Milorad Luković. Ever heard of him? No? Doesn't matter. Bad fuckin' Yugoslavian. They've been warned that Luković wants you free or dead and has activated a paramilitary team here in the States, a kind of sleeper cell, with access to military-grade weaponry. There are a few men here with a higher level of security clearance, who know the truth. They've seen the video of King Sorrow from Greenland. They're operating under no illusions about what's coming."

"If they really understood what was coming, they wouldn't be sticking around. Why did you come in to watch me sleep? I hope to God you haven't made a regular habit out of it. If I have to have a stalker, I want her to look more like Glenn Close."

"I came to tell you that whatever Barclay asks for in the next few days, give it to him," Francis said. "Tell him whatever he wants to know. It doesn't matter now. This is almost over. You just need to get through these last few days. But you need to know I can't protect you. I'm being pulled out. If they bring back the bucket of ice water, this time you're going to drown."

"Protect me?" Van asked, angry now at the fucker with his shitty mustache and stinking cigar. "My sister has been tortured. I've been tortured. We've been held for four months in a secret prison on American soil."

"You've also killed again and again for ten years with a weapon that blows anything our nation has right off the battlefield. So don't give me the puppy dog face about how you've been treated. You tell me some kids got a dirty bomb in their possession, I'll do what I have to to get my hands on it and sweat the Bill of Rights later. Besides, the Bill of Rights is for American citizens."

"I *am* an American citizen."

"Are you? I think you belong to the Long Dark, Van. I think you pledged your allegiance to a king, not a constitution. Still." Francis looked at his cigar tip again. "This country has made deals with kings before. I told them what would happen if they tried it Barclay's way, and after Sunday . . . well. They'll have to do it my way. Try and stay alive until then?"

He rapped on the door and was gone.

22.

The power was out again when they came for him.

He was in his underwear, but it didn't matter. He didn't care about his dignity anymore. It had never mattered much to him, and now it meant even less.

Van knew they had come to kill him. He knew it when they came through the door. Valentine came first, Salem, and one of the new arrivals, a short, powerfully built woman with black hair in a bristle cut. She was dressed as one of the boys, in a black Lacoste with the alligator over her left breast, and she lumbered along like a bear, head down, shoulders rounded, her mostly bare arms heavily but slackly muscled. She could probably tear a New York City phone book in two, arms like that.

It was the fifth time they had lost the juice today. The only illumination came from the emergency lighting running down the length of the hallway. That lighting was Halloween colored, like candlelight burning inside a pumpkin, and turned his visitors into orange-faced ghouls. Van flashed back to Jayne and Ronnie on Arthur's porch, wearing troll masks. No matter how many trolls you wiped out, Mordor always had more.

He was sitting on the edge of his bed, eating cold toast smeared with jam off the breakfast tray. It wasn't much of a breakfast, and it was pitiful as last meals went, but he closed his eyes and made himself taste it, really taste it: the sweetness of the strawberry jam, the creamy salt of the butter beneath, the chewy, slightly burnt texture of the toast. It hadn't been much of a life, but there had been coffee with Allie, the smell of Allie's hair in the morning, the light on her face.

"You guys mind if I pull on some—" he began, and the woman yanked him to his feet by the arm. "No? Okay, never mind."

Salem caught the other arm, and the two enforcers buckled the bondage mittens together, his hands at the small of his back. It was funny to think his salvation was right inside those gloves, that he could blow everyone in this room out of this world if he could only touch two fingers to his chest. They had Glocks on their thighs, but he had a scaly nuclear weapon that talked like a London cabbie, and all he needed to do to light it up was get those infernal mittens off.

Valentine pushed a hand back through his pale hair and Van saw a great wispy tuft of it come right out of his scalp and drift away. Van almost laughed.

Salem and the big woman hauled him toward the door. Van said, "Does this one got a name?"

"Juneau," Salem said.

"Never been there. Somehow I don't think I'm ever going to get there now," Van said.

Van thought Salem's sidelong glance—his slight smile, his cocked eyebrow—was actually sympathetic.

"There's still a way to turn King Sorrow aside," Valentine said. "I'm almost sure one of you can choose to die for us. It's in all the literature. We can still be saved. So here's what's going to happen now. You're going to offer to die in my place, Van. Otherwise, we're going to beat your sister to death, slowly, in front of you. It's the classic prisoner's dilemma."

Van got his feet under him—his knees gave out—he was dragged—found his feet once more. They led him past the open door of a break room just as the fluorescents came buzzing and flickering back on overhead. Van had a glimpse of a dripping brown splash against the wall, which at first he thought was coffee. Then he saw the spatter of tissue and hair on the drop ceiling and wondered who had shot himself. When they dragged him past the open door to an office, he caught a glimpse of a digital clock on the desk and he saw it was only 10:47 a.m. He felt himself wilt with despair. He might've had a chance if it was later in the day. If it was ten in the evening, instead of ten in the morning, he thought he could hold out—shut his eyes and mind, deafen himself with his own screams—until King Sorrow came. But thirteen hours and change was too long.

They hauled him past a picture window, and he had a glimpse into a conference room crowded with the soldiers in their khakis. They were gathered around a map of the compound, spread on a table and held down with battery-operated lanterns. The lamps threw a harsh blue-white light and gave the people in the room the cast of zombies, purple lipped and dead eyed. Many of the warriors had M4s over their shoulders. At least one had what looked like a machete strapped to his thigh. Van fought down a wave of laughter. A machete. A fucking *machete*. What was he going to do with that? Van supposed in an emergency he might be able to jump on it before King Sorrow ripped him apart. It amazed him, the way arrogance multiplied exponentially when men gathered in groups. Arrogance was a kind of stupor, like drunkenness.

He was glad he was sober. He was sure the time that remained to him would be easier if he was drunk or comfortably stoned. He wouldn't be so aware of his own bad breath or the tremble in his legs. But he didn't want to miss the last moments of his life, didn't want them to blur by him. He wished he could go back and have another bite of toast, wanted to examine the flavor of it, consider it the way a scientist would consider it.

Salem yanked the door open and led them into a concrete well five stories high. He hit the light switch out of habit, but the stairwell remained a silo of darkness. The only light came from a couple of narrow window slits, five floors above them, the gray gleam of an April morning on the Atlantic coast.

The concrete steps were chilly and rough under his bare feet. The staircase was narrow and required them to walk two abreast. Salem took the inside of the stairwell so that Van had the banister on his right. Juneau went behind them, while Valentine was in front, leading the whole sorry parade. Juneau's breath was heavy and harsh, echoing in the stone silo. She was powerful, but she wasn't fast, didn't like climbing stairs.

"Being here hasn't been all bad," Van said. "I'm glad I kicked the booze and the rest of it. This wouldn't have been my first choice of rehabs, but it did the trick. I think I only stayed drunk so I wouldn't feel so bad about making Allie marry me. We have that in common, Valentine: we're both wardens of secret prisons. You trapped me, but I trapped her. She's free now, though. I'm surprised how happy the thought makes me. That, and thinking how many of your boys she fried like eggs."

"We'll get her," Valentine said.

"No, you won't," Van told him, and this time he did laugh. It felt good. "She cooked a whole bunch of you, and the barbecue ain't done yet. It'll be your turn next."

They reached the first concrete landing. Van leaned, looked over the railing at the drop, then straightened up and walked on.

"Tell me again about the prisoner's dilemma," Van said. "How's that one work?"

"Do you know anything about game theory? It's a numbers thing."

"The only numbers I know about are the ones I've rolled," Van said, and he smiled at the memory of smoking pot with Colin Wren, blue haze and sweet spice. Colin's good CIA-sourced pot always made Van feel like it was Christmas afternoon, gave him a sense of snowed-in, childlike contentment, all the presents open and waiting to be played with. Weed had never been that good again. It wasn't just that he couldn't find the same quality of ganja in New York. The experience hadn't improved with time. Mostly the drugs had taken things away from him: had stopped him from seeing his own life, from seeing his own wife. Sober and clearheaded, he kept picturing Allison in the bright clear light of early May, that strong, bold, innocent light. He could almost imagine her with someone else—a woman—her head resting on the other's shoulder, both of them enjoying a morning together, coffee and silent companionship. He wished she hadn't been taught to hate the one thing that might make her happy.

"In the simplest version, you've arrested two outlaws. They've both committed a killing, but you can only prove it by getting them to rat on each other," Valentine said. "There's no physical evidence. There's one thing you can prove: you can send them to jail for stealing a car together . . . they were arrested while driving it. So that's one year in jail each. But you separate these two murdering scumbags—let's call 'em Donna and Donnie—and you offer them each a deal. If Donnie will tell the truth about Donna's part in the murder, he won't be charged and she'll go to jail for life. If he won't play ball, and *Donna* tells the truth, he'll go to jail for life, and *she'll* get off scot-free. If they're both willing to testify against each other, the DA will only ask the judge for twenty-year sentences for each."

"I don't see how it applies," Van said.

Valentine looked back with undisguised disgust. "How do you not—*look*, you fucking hillbilly stoner. They're obviously both going to tell on each other. They'd rather do twenty years, or none, than risk jail for life. Self-interest always trumps loyalty."

They went on. The stairwell echoed with the scuff of their shoes. When they reached the next landing they would be on the ground floor. That's where they'd leave the stairwell and head to the garage, Van thought. They had half drowned him there the last time; this time it would be Donna's turn, and there would be no going halfway about anything. He looked thoughtfully over the railing again and walked on.

"Obviously, with you and your sister," Valentine said, panting, "it isn't quite the same. But the deal you have with King Sorrow—he's going to kill all of us, unless one of you offers yourself as a substitute. You'll ask King Sorrow to take you instead of us, to make us stop. Stop what we're doing to you, sure, but more important, stop what we're doing to *her*."

There was a window on the ground-floor landing and another on the floor above. Van found himself climbing steadily into a pearlescent and forgiving light.

He clicked his tongue, gave his head a little shake. "Nope. It don't work, my son. The logic don't hold."

"How do you figure?"

"So Donna, we'd play Monopoly or something, and if she was about to go bankrupt, bitch would get so pissed she'd toss the board so *no one* could win. And that's the problem with your little game theory."

"That your sister is a sore loser?" Valentine said.

"No," Van said. "That we both are. Trouble with your dilemma is, it only works if you still have both of us."

Van stopped dead, just as Juneau was climbing the step behind him. He snapped his head back into her face and heard her nose break with a dry, brittle crunch. She yelled, tottered, and Salem turned to grab her before she could go crashing back down the stairs, and that was Van's moment to move. He leapt forward, body-checking Valentine into the black metal railing. Valentine's eyes flew wide, and for one delicious second it seemed he might go over the railing. But he grabbed the banister to steady himself and Van went straight by him, no time to stop.

He hit the third landing and wheeled around, climbing the steps toward the fourth and final floor. All of them were yelling behind him. He began to laugh, a kid running from his mother across the yard. He felt lightheaded, the stairwell above him seeming to rotate like the lens of a kaleidoscope, and he remembered his roller skates grinding across asphalt, remembered whirling in a hoop around and around Arthur Oakes, the two of them making their stand in the fall night. It seemed all his adult life he had been flying around and around in manic, pointless circles, while Arthur stood fast, the one secure thing in the world he could reach for when he was almost too dizzy to remain on his feet. How he had loved the big, quiet man and his steadiness, his unshowy decency. How he had wished he could've been more like him.

Donovan jumped up the steps three at a time, like a man racing to his beloved, a man who has been apart from his wife for far too long. He dashed up the last flight of stairs into the morning brightness. There was a fire door to the roof on the landing, but he didn't bother with it. It might be locked. He glanced back into the stairwell. Salem was six steps away, huffing as he heaved himself up the stairs. Juneau was a full flight behind him, gasping for breath.

Van had time to look out the narrow slot of the window. He shoved his face to the embrasure and saw the ocean a quarter of a mile away, beyond the hangar roofs, out past a band of sun-bleached seagrass. The grass rippled and flowed, an ocean of rippling yellow itself. The sky boiled with gray, cold-looking storm clouds, but they were rent in places, and the sun cast a rippling light across the water. He was surprised to find himself grinning. He was grateful for it, to have been allowed this last look at the sea.

Salem was two steps away when Van put his waist against the black metal banister, tilted forward, and let himself drop. The floor, four stories below, rushed up at him out of the darkness. He felt like he was falling into bed, like he was falling into Allie's arms.

What a thing, to fall and be caught by love at the end.

23.

Donna expected them in the morning, but they didn't come. She couldn't imagine what kept them. They were almost out of time to break her—it had to be today. There was no tomorrow . . . not for most of the men here.

The power came and went. It was off in the late morning when a thud shook the whole building, as if someone had dropped a sack of flour from a great height. She heard cries and slamming doors. One of the last remaining nurses ran by her window, rolling a gurney ahead of her. Donna supposed another one had killed themselves.

A little while later the lights flickered back on. The stillness and boredom oppressed her—she had never been good with either. Loneliness had always frightened her. Made her feel like a child again, trapped in the haunted house of her mind, and she couldn't bear to walk there alone. She needed someone she could argue with, tease, mock, someone who wanted to fuck or fight. She shut her eyes. Maybe if she rested for a while. It was better to sleep than to be awake and alone, and her dreams were always interesting. She met famous people in them and found herself in absurd but entertaining sexual situations, and occasionally she had to shoot looters.

The power was still off when she heard the door and opened her eyes. Valentine let himself into her room. Salem was with him, though he stayed by the door, leaning against the wall. For the first time she could remember, Salem looked uncomfortable, didn't seem to know what to do with his hands. First he crossed his arms, then he dropped them, then he tried hooking his thumbs in his pockets. Valentine seemed so tired he could hardly lift his feet. He slumped into the straight-backed chair.

"I'm hungry. I want lunch," Donna told him. She felt it was always best to begin a discussion with a list of her demands.

"I'm surprised you have any appetite," Valentine said, and laughed humorlessly. "God knows you made a meal out of me." One hand fluttered to his ear and then fell away again. "Your brother is dead."

"Mind games don't work on me when I've got an empty stomach. Try again after I've had an egg salad sandwich. Make it fresh, for fuck's sake. Whatever I had the other day spent at least twelve hours in Saran Wrap."

"No kitchen staff. They all ran. No lunch for you. Do you even care about your brother? I told you, he's dead. He killed himself."

"That's a lie. I don't believe you."

"You want me to wheel his corpse past your window? I'll be honest. I don't think you'd want to look at him. He got away from us in a stairwell and jumped headfirst over the banister. His skull split open like a melon. Most awful thing I've ever seen. Made me sick, actually. I can't get the taste out of my mouth."

"No. If he fell down a stairwell, it's because one of you threw him. And he isn't dead. You just want to fuck with my mind."

Valentine gave her a hopeless look. "You think your brother is any good to me dead? I was going to drown you in front of him. I was going to hold you underwater until Van offered to die in our place. Until Van offered to be King Sorrow's meal. I know that's one of the rules. I know one of you can offer to die for us. But he can't die for us if he's already dead. I had the game all set up and he—he tossed the whole board."

Donna felt as if she were falling herself. As if she had been pushed off a high ledge and might never hit bottom.

"No," she said. "*No*. If he was dead, I'd know it. We have, like, twin telepathy. When he cuts himself, I feel it. When I can't sleep, neither can he. You're lying."

"I'm not. Van is gone." It was Van now, Van at last, after months of calling him Donnie, and that was how she knew it was true. When Valentine spoke again, there was a certain cruel satisfaction in his voice. "He *left* you. He went and *left you behind*. But not for long. I'm going to bring the two of you together again soon enough, Donna."

She couldn't think. She didn't want to think. Nothing good would come from thinking. Donovan was one of the central facts of her life, as fundamental as the air in her lungs. She wasn't sure she could breathe without him.

"Why couldn't you just give me what I wanted? We would've offered you anything," Valentine said. His eyes lit up slightly at a sudden inspiration. "It's not too late, you know. Offer your friend Allison Shiner to King Sorrow instead of me—*us*. You want your own Gulfstream jet? It's yours. Twenty-five million dollars a year, for life? Done. There's nothing you could want that isn't in my power to give."

"I want my brother back. Can you get me that?"

The light went back out of Valentine's eyes, and his hand slid into a pocket.

"No. Of course you can't just *help*. *Of course* you can't be a decent person. It makes me sick. I have a goddamn master's degree. I have a lot to offer people. I read more books in a year than you and your brother probably read in your whole lives, both of you put together. What did you have to offer the world, besides a look at your tits on the evening news?" His hand slipped out of his pocket holding a gun. Salem, over by the exit, stiffened, stood away from the wall.

"Mr. Valentine," Salem said. "I'm not sure—"

"I am. Now shut up." He pointed the gun her way, but not too seriously, and sort of shook it at her. "You know I haven't slept in five days? I can *smell* him on my sheets. That fucking snake. He was in my glove box yesterday morning. I'm so tired I can't think, and the worst is the idea that tomorrow I might be dead and you might be alive. That will not fucking stand."

The lights came back on in a sudden stammering series of flashes, and a great roar of hate and madness came from directly behind Valentine. He twisted to look over his shoulder, his mouth opening to scream, only it wasn't King Sorrow, it was the TV, blasting static. He had tipped his chair up on its back legs, and when Donna hit him it was easy to drive him straight back into the Zenith. His head went through the tube of the television, smashed it in with a glassy crack. The gun went off. His chair collapsed and he fell, shrieking, his head sliding back out of the Zenith's smashed-in screen.

If she was shot, Donna didn't notice. She went down on top of him and the chair and felt the gun trapped between his chest and hers, in his right hand. He was barely holding on to it. She clapped her mittens around it and pried it away from him. He didn't fight, didn't even seem to realize she was taking it from him.

At the sound of the gunshot, Salem had ducked low and frozen in place. She pointed the barrel at him. Even with her hands swaddled in the leather mitts, she was able to force a finger under the trigger guard. She wasn't sure she could actually fire the gun, but he didn't need to know that. The fluorescents brightened and dimmed, brightened and dimmed. Either that or her vision was pulsing.

She meant to say something menacing, but what came out was, "Did he shoot me?"

Salem scanned her from about four paces away. "I don't think so."

Valentine shrieked again. The heel of his left foot kicked and dug into the carpet and he screamed through clenched teeth, a sound that went beyond pain and into a kind of hysteria. She could smell blood. When she looked down, Donna saw a smear of it on her thigh, but she still didn't feel any pain.

"Get the fuck out," she said.

Salem drove an elbow hard against the door and it opened the tiniest bit. A big woman in a polo shirt was in the hall. She had a piece of white tape across her turnip of a nose and a pair of black eyes.

"The fuck is—" she began, but Salem was already shoving her back into the hall, slamming the door behind him.

Donna scrambled behind the bed, the gun clapped between her mittened hands. She felt as if she had been punched in the chest, felt as if she had a bruise on her overworked heart. Valentine shrieked, paused to get his breath, and shrieked again. A crooked artery bulged in his forehead. His hands were clapped to his groin, but Donna could see his crotch was a sopping red ruin. When she had knocked him back into the TV, the gun had gone off into his crotch. She cast her gaze over the bed to the picture window. At first glance she thought the hallway was empty. Then she saw Salem peeking around one corner of the window frame, from over by the door.

She crawled out from behind the bed and got an arm around Valentine's throat.

"*No!*" the man who was really Norman Barclay screamed. "*No! Don't! Move me! For the sake of CHRIST, I need medical attention!*"

Donna dragged him back toward the bathroom, keeping him in a headlock, holding the gun under her left armpit. It dropped again, but this time it didn't fire, just clunked on the floor. She got Valentine into the bathroom before she went back for it, then retreated into the john and collapsed against the wall.

"*I'm dying!*" Barclay screamed. "*Oh, God! Oh Jesus Christ, I'm dying here!*"

"Shut up," she told him.

He held his obliterated crotch while blood oozed around his clenched, white-knuckled fingers. He was on his side on the floor, smearing blood all over the dingy white tile. His face was a hideous color, a hectic purple, with waxy white blotches. His eyes were wide but unseeing.

"*I'm dying, I KNOW it! For God's sake! Get a doctor!*"

"Stop it!" She couldn't think with him screaming at her that way. She kicked him in the face, once, twice, and he shut up. Maybe he fainted. It was hard to tell, his eyes were still open.

For a time there was silence from the other room. She heard a soft click as the door was unlatched ever so slightly. She stuck her head out far enough to peer into the room. Salem was still out in the hall, the door open only a sliver.

"Donna," Salem said. "Don't make us come in there. Throw us the gun and come out of there."

"Here's a better idea!" she shouted. "Come in and get me! First bullet goes into Valentine. Second one is all yours, Salem!"

"You don't want to do that."

"You bet I do. I can shoot you. Can you shoot me? I'm still a million-dollar asset. What are *you* worth, Salem?"

There was a long silence.

"Donna, sweetheart. Darlin'. Let us send someone in there for Mr. Valentine."

"*Help me!*" Valentine cried. He was still screaming, but not as loudly as before, and he was almost singing it, like a child. "*Help me! Help mmmmee!*"

"Shut the fuck up or I'll kick you again," Donna said.

"Darlin', you're holding one of our standard-issue nine-millimeters," Salem called out. "If we come in there wearing full body armor, them bullets will bounce right off. But I'll be honest, that armor is heavy, it's hot, and I don't want to bother with it. I guess I will if I have to. Can you do me a favor and just come on out of there?"

"Anyone enters the room, Valentine dies," she said. "That simple."

He didn't reply for a bit. When he did, his voice was weary. "Goddamn it, girl. He's probably going to die anyway. Let us send a medic in to get a compress on that wound. You can keep a gun on the guy the whole time."

"Don't waste medical supplies on him. Keep the Band-Aids for you. You're going to need them. What time is it?"

"Seven p.m."

"Tick tick tick. Midnight in five hours. Can you really afford to spend them dickering with me?"

He went silent. Donna watched the door from her position just inside the bathroom. It was open only an inch.

"Hey, Salem," she said.

"Yeah?"

"Is my brother really dead?"

He didn't want to answer that. When he did, his tone was reluctant. "Yeah."

Donna hated crying more than anything, even more than being alone. She blinked at hot tears, hating them while they welled up and fell, hating the sting of them, hating the way each choked sob seemed to scoop her insides out.

"Sorry," Salem said, after a while.

Donna wiped at her face. Her mouth was full of the taste of tears.

"Salem," she said.

"Yeah?"

"You need to run."

"Me and these boys out here, we don't run. People run from *us*."

"You listen to me, Salem. King Sorrow had, what, forty-three names? How many of them are left on this base to see him tonight?"

"Eighteen. Counting Valentine. There are a few others in the wind."

"Eighteen. You aren't one of them, but if you get in his way, you'll join them. And even if you don't, even if you get lucky and the dragon passes you by? Next year, someone will give King Sorrow *your* name. They'll remember what you did to me here. To my brother. And King Sorrow won't just have your name. He'll come after your wife. Your children. Your parents. You need to understand that. Your men need to understand that. If you don't run for yourself, run for your loved ones. Throw down your weapons and leave now and our business with you is done. I promise you won't be hunted down. But stay here and tangle with our pet lizard, and I can't protect you from the consequences. You need to ask yourself—all of you need to ask yourselves—what you'll really do to protect those you love most in the world."

Salem didn't reply to that, and after a while the door clicked shut.

24.

She watched Valentine bleed to death.

She found some hand towels and threw them at him. He balled them up and jammed them against his crotch. Pretty soon they were soaked through, and she didn't think they were doing much to stanch the bleeding.

"I'm thirsty," he sobbed.

"Get used to it. I've heard people in hell want ice water, but I guess you'll find out for sure pretty soon."

The fluorescents went out without warning, and darkness fell upon them. Donna shifted to sit in the bathroom doorway. The door to her bedroom remained firmly shut. The curtain was pulled back on the picture window, and the hallway beyond was only dimly illuminated by the emergency strip lighting. No one seemed to be watching, and she judged that if there wasn't power for lights, there wasn't power for security cameras. She bolted back into the room, the Glock clamped under her left arm, against her side. Fangs of glass bristled from the frame of the television set, curving toward the hole in the center, like the toothy mouth of a flukeworm. Donna pried one large blade free and scrambled back to the bathroom.

She sat under the sink, let the gun clatter to the tiles beside her hip. She began to poke and saw with the glass spear at one leather mitten.

"You can't watch me die," Valentine whispered.

"Good thing the lights went out," Donna said. "Now I don't have to."

"You're a monster," he said.

"Oh, now," said King Sorrow from somewhere deep in the blackness of the bathroom. "That's not fair to monsters, is it? I would've bit you in two by now, put you out of your misery, if it was up to the likes of me. You want some real cruelty done, you need a human, mate."

She had thought Valentine was all screamed out, but he let loose the most terrific shriek she had heard yet and kicked and squirmed toward her, to get away from that voice in the darkness.

"*No! It's not time! Stay away!*" Valentine screamed. "*I have until midnight! Stay away!*"

An eye opened behind the semitransparent shower curtain. It was the size of a headlight and had a cat's-eye pupil, and the iris was a shade of dark yellow, stained with threads of blood. It regarded Valentine humorously for a moment, then closed itself and disappeared.

Valentine's head bumped her hip. He was shaking. He didn't look at her.

"It's not time," he whispered. "It's not time."

She poked and stabbed and slashed. Sometimes she poked her own fingertips, right through the leather, a delicate shock of pain. She could feel blood on her fingers, trickling into her palm.

"Do you feel sorry?" Valentine croaked. "For any of it?"

"No. The people who have met King Sorrow had it coming. They wrote the invitation themselves. They spent their whole lives writing it. You too." She felt the tears close again. She punched the spoke of glass into her right mitten and gouged herself, a necessary, clarifying pain. "People like you think you can make other people disappear. You can put them in a van and drive them away and no one will care and it won't cost you anything. But this is where the van is going. This is where the ride always ends."

The dragon's eye opened behind the shower curtain again. He stared hungrily down at Joe Valentine.

"No! It's not time. I still have time!" Valentine cried at the dragon's eye. "You can't have me!"

"No," Donna said. "He can't." She had sliced her right-hand mitten open across the top and now she pushed it down to her wrist, forcing the hand all the way through a four-inch slash. She transferred the spear of glass to her right hand. "I've got dibs."

She didn't know how to cut a throat, so she straddled him—straddled his sopping, bloody crotch, in a gory parody of the sexual act, pinning his arms to his sides with her knees—and began to poke the blade of glass into his neck, while he thrashed and shouted.

She had reported on murder victims who had been stabbed dozens of times. She had always assumed the attacker must've been in the grip of a homicidal rage, carried away by some frantic need to pierce and pierce again. But it turned out it was *really* hard to stab someone to death. She put the knife in his neck at least twenty times—it looked like the side of his throat had been bitten by a wild animal—before the motherfucker shut up and stopped moving. By then her right hand was slick and red with blood. His. Hers. She wiped her palm on her chest, then shoved her hand under her shirt.

They were all of them waiting on midnight, but the thing about midnight, Donna thought, it was like happy hour. It's always happy hour somewhere.

At 8:47 p.m., EST, Donna McBride's right hand found the tattoo of the coiled serpent on her chest. She could *feel* it, could feel the snake wound around her ribs, as if it were a cold leather belt, and when she put her fingers to its spade-shaped head, the belt tightened, driving the air out of her. The snake under her skin seemed to *squirm* and rearrange itself. She blinked and for a moment there was a film over her eyes, the nictating membrane of a reptile, and all the world looked as if it was made out of a sooty mist. She blinked again and her vision cleared. Her hands were so cold she could hardly feel them. She looked at the mirror over the sink and could see the dragon's eye, watching from behind the shower curtain.

"Burn this fucking place to the ground," Donna said.

"Darling," King Sorrow told her, "I was just waiting for you to say the word."

The eye of the dragon sealed itself shut and was gone.

It wasn't long before the gunfire—and the screams—began.

25.

She heard the first distant burst of fully automatic fire while she was searching Valentine's pockets. It didn't sound like much: a flat and steely banging that brought to mind that wind-up toy that looked like a pair of chattering teeth. She found the key to the bondage gloves, undid them from her wrists, and threw them under the sink. She felt lightheaded, with a mix of exhaustion and hypervigilance, had the twitchy, overcaffeinated sensation she remembered from college all-nighters. She stuck her head out of the bathroom.

"Hey, Salem," she called. "Don't you hate when the guests arrive early?"

There was nothing from the hallway. Somewhere men were yelling. There was another steely, mechanical clattering of a machine gun—and then, very close, there was a great thud, and the building shook.

Donna remembered the thud from earlier in the day, the thud that had been the sound of her brother falling down a stairwell to smash his head open. This was less like a falling body, more like a falling truck. The picture window rattled in its frame. She waited, tense with anticipation. Something boomed and the building shook again. She could feel the shudder of it in her teeth.

When she heard King Sorrow scream, it was a long way off, and still a great shock of sound that seemed to go through the whole structure.

That was followed an instant later by a bottle rocket whistle, then another, then a series of rippling detonations. Shoulder-mounted rocket launchers, perhaps. The fluorescent lights flickered, held—and went out again, this time for good.

Donna fumbled around on the tiles and found the gun. Something several floors above her came apart in a series of tinny crunching sounds, as if a tornado had struck one of the Quonset huts and was peeling it apart.

She heard a choked, raggedy scream, and a pair of polo shirt soldiers stumbled past in the hall. One of them had an arm around the waist of the other, was helping him to stagger along. Only he lost his grip: his comrade went down with a cry, striking the window and leaving an ocher smear across the glass. His buddy kept going, reeled a yard down the hallway, then half turned and looked back at the injured man.

"I'll come back for you, bro!" he shouted, and ran on.

He never came back.

Donna crossed the bedroom as dust trickled from the white drop ceiling, as if people were jumping up and down above her, having a house party. She reached the picture window and looked out into the hallway, not trying to be secretive about it, not taking cover in any way. By the pumpkin-orange glow of the emergency lights, she could see the polo shirt soldier on the floor. His left leg had been torn off at the upper thigh. Strings of black, blood-soaked khaki hid the worst of the injury. She didn't see anyone else out there. She tried the door, but the bolt was secure and it wouldn't open.

Donna stepped back and pointed the gun at the glass. The 9-millimeter jumped in her hands and the flat *wham* of it half deafened her. The slug slammed into the glass and produced a fractal spiderweb of slivered cracks. She fired again and a third time, planting the other bullets close to the first, watching jagged lines leap through the glass. Then she dropped the gun on the bed, picked up the toppled chair, and threw it at the window.

The glass exploded and sound rushed in. She heard men screaming, yelling, heard the idiotic stammering of machine gun fire. There came another whistling shriek and the *CRUMP* of detonation. She inhaled the dizzying stink of burning chemicals: it smelled like a bonfire made out of old tires. She smelled burnt hair too, as if someone had tried to incinerate a cat. Donna got the gun and clambered through the broken window, carefully stepping around the dying man on the floor. She thought he was unconscious, but when she tried to walk away, he reached out and grabbed her ankle.

"Help me!" he said. "Help me, lady! I don't want to die down here in the dark!"

She ripped her ankle free and left him behind.

There was smoke in the hall. She didn't know what was on fire and didn't intend to stick around and find out. She had a sense of where the elevator was and the stairwell beside it.

In the gloom and the haze, she didn't see the men running toward her until they were almost on top of her. One of them was some kind of mechanic in oil-stained overalls, his face slick with sweat. There were two polo shirt soldiers right behind him, running for all they were worth. The mechanic hit Donna dead-on, spinning her on one heel and dropping her to the floor. Someone stepped on her wrist. Someone else stepped on her back, going right over her.

"Guys!" one of them was screaming in a thin, boyish voice. "Guys, don't leave me! I got a cramp!"

Donna crawled a few feet, her ears ringing, feeling a wetness right under her hairline. She thought she had smacked herself in the face with the gun when she was knocked down. The gun. She didn't realize she had dropped it until she was all the way down the hall, and she didn't trust herself to find it if she went back.

She went around a corner and saw the elevator through the acrid pall of smoke. The dragon screamed—the closest he had been yet, the sound so piercing she instinctively shrank low to the floor, sticking in place for an instant. Then she was moving again, pushing herself off the wall and zigging toward the door into the stairwell.

Only in the haze and the darkness she had got herself turned around. She opened the door to a deep custodial closet, took one step forward, and bumped into Dr. Patrick. Dr. Patrick swayed backward and then swung forward, to draw Donna in an embrace. Her hands were cold. She had hanged herself with an electrical cord, tied off to an exposed pipe, part of the sprinkler system. The cable was sunk so deeply into her wiry neck, it had almost disappeared into bruised flesh. Her tongue was a fat sausage sticking out of her open mouth, and there was a white froth down the silky front of her blouse. Donna screamed as the doctor's dead hand swished across one of her breasts. She had pinned a note to her short tweed coat. JESUS FORGIVE ME.

"Maybe he will," Donna said. "I won't."

She backed out of the closet and pushed the door shut. The stairwell was on the other side of the hall. It was dark in there. She glanced to her right at the bottom of the steps, couldn't stop herself, looking for some sign of the impact her brother had made when he struck the floor, but if there was anything to see, she couldn't make it out in the poor light. Two floors above her, guns blatted, sometimes in great flurries, and went silent. Men hollered to one another. There was a great *THWAM* as if the roof had dropped on one of those Quonset huts. She took the railing and began to climb toward the sounds of war.

26.

She tugged open the door to ground level and stepped out into the last minutes of a firefight. She looked to the right, away from the lobby, toward the rear of the building. She saw four polo shirt soldiers gathered around the doors to the rear parking lot. There was a fifth man, but he was dead, stretched out on his back behind them. It looked like he had been raked with a claw the size of a loader's bucket. One talon had carved him open from his right shoulder, down across his chest, to his left rib cage. A second had split his gut. Wet loops of intestine spilled back between his feet, dangling like loose suspenders. The dead man's head was twisted toward her so he seemed to be staring down the hallway, and his mouth was open as if to scream for help.

The rest of the polo shirts were very much alive, crouched to either side of the Plexiglas doors. She saw flat-top haircuts, M4s, khaki vests, khaki trousers, and panicked expressions. Beyond them, through the doors, she could see what King Sorrow had done to their friends.

There was a half-track out there, or what was left of one. It was burning as if it had been struck with a missile. The whole top half had been peeled off. A couple of men had got out but had made it only a few yards before falling over—their corpses were still on fire. The line of Quonset huts had been destroyed. One was ablaze. One had been crushed in on itself. One looked as if it had been swept entirely away, cleared off the board by a swipe of God's own hand. As Donna watched, she heard someone scream outside—and then saw a man fall out of the night, dropped from a height of perhaps two hundred feet. He split apart like a rotten fruit when he hit the ground: a human body compressing on itself, striking with enough force to become jellylike. She flinched back a few steps.

One of the polo shirt warriors looked back over her shoulder. It was the big woman with the meaty biceps, a white piece of tape across the bridge of a recently broken nose. At first, in the dimness and drifting ash, she didn't seem to recognize Donna. Then she did.

"Bitch," she said, an angry crease appearing between her eyebrows. "You fuckin' bitch. You did this. You did this to us. You—" But a sound was rising, drowning the big woman out.

It was a mechanical whirring that built and built, a noise like a great iron weight being swung around WHUP—*whup*—WHUP—*whup*—WHUP and Donna began to back toward the lobby while the big woman rose from a squat, lifting her M4, putting the stock against her shoulder, WHUP-*whup*-WHUP-*whup*, and Donna stumbled, almost went down, steadied herself against the wall, and that terrible sound built and built, speeding up as it came closer, and the big woman sighted down the barrel and WHUP*whup*WHUP-*whu*WHU*whu*

At the last instant, Donna turned and tried to run. She took three strides toward the lobby, waiting for bullets to stitch across her back. She didn't see the chopper plow into the side of the building behind her, but the shockwave lifted her off the ground. For a moment her legs pedaled uselessly beneath her—she ran on air like a cartoon character—and then she dropped and there was a shattering blast behind her. Glass and steel flew down the hallway in a burst of dazzling, razor-edged confetti. Flame gushed behind it. It didn't reach her, but she could feel its heat on the back of her thighs. A clap of pressure went off in her ears and then all she could hear was a high-pitched whining sound.

It was a few moments before she could turn over. She was covered in broken glass. She could see it falling off her in a sparkling haze but could not hear it tinkling against the floor. When she looked back where the polo shirt soldiers had been, she saw the tail end of an Apache helicopter, the rotor still spinning, jutting down the hallway behind her. The whole chopper had been spiraling around and around when it came down, struck the building, and liquefied the squad who had been sheltering to either side of the exit. The front end of the Apache was on fire, rotor blades deformed and folded upward. The tail had sliced through several walls, torn through the whole back half of the building, shredding drywall, tearing open the ceiling so it was possible to see the bundles of wires and PVC piping in the space between floors. The still-spinning tail rotor pumped a steady stream of hot air and sparks down the hall.

She got up. One leg of her pajamas was open from ankle to hip and her left knee was bloody, glass stuck in it. She had blood on the side of her face too. From her ear, maybe? She didn't know. She tried to walk straight but her balance was wonky. She staggered into a wall, bounced off, kept going.

Her unsteady route took her into a grand lobby, two stories high, with a brushed-chrome reception desk and a corpse in a polo shirt hanging from a chandelier. The full-wall windows were blown in, glass glinting everywhere. Outside, she could see a trio of burning jeeps. One of them appeared to have been picked up and dropped on its front end: the rear bumper pointed into the night. It was hard to take it all in. Some details caught her attention and stayed in her mind, while her gaze passed right over others (a black combat boot with a foot still in it and a bone jutting out, a smoldering office chair inexplicably tossed out in the parking lot, a burning palm tree) without registering them.

There was a two-story building on the far side of the parking lot, a nondescript office made out of tan brick, the windows dark, smashed in. Someone was firing from one of the shattered second-floor windows. Donna could distantly hear the pop-pop-pop of the gun, but it was like hearing something through noise-canceling headphones. She could see the white flash of the muzzle but not what it was shooting at. Something out of sight. Something in the air.

A Sheridan tank, modified for the desert, rumbled swiftly into view, treads frantically clanking, moving from left to right. It made it about halfway across Donna's field of view before a deluge of flame erupted from above and billowed over it. Donna had never seen such a jet of flame. It was a blinding rope of fire twenty feet wide. The air quavered from the heat of it, turned the outside world into a rippling desert mirage. The jet of fire poured down on the tank for a count of three before it was suddenly cut off and King Sorrow screamed again, the sound cutting right through the damage to her ears and making her nerve endings hum.

The light tank trundled another thirty feet, but it was drifting off course and slowing all the while. It was still on fire, a bonfire on iron treads. Bullets went off inside it, a sound like a string of firecrackers erupting on Independence Day. The tank finally ground to a relieved stop and a moment later something exploded inside it, lifting it off the ground and dropping it again. An iron hatch fell with a clang fifty feet away, embedding itself a foot deep into the blacktop.

The man in the building across the street opened fire again. Donna had the dazed impression he was the last one fighting. She couldn't hear any other guns.

"Come on, you son-of-a-bitch!" Salem shouted from his position in the office building. *"Come on and get a mouthful a this!"* He loosed a fresh burst from his assault rifle.

A streetlight, thirty feet long, a great lance of chrome, was thrown like a spear from the night into that open second-floor window. It impaled the whole building with a jarring slam, and the gunfire abruptly stopped.

The silence that followed was so deep, so intense, it stunned; another explosion would've been far less stunning.

King Sorrow gave a grinding, ugly shriek of satisfaction. Sparks whirled in the smoky night. By the time Donna made it to the far side of the lobby to look outside, he was gone.

She climbed through a broken window and onto the asphalt. She stepped on a dead body and almost fell over, got her balance back, and went on without looking back.

The night stank of burning kerosene and scorched metal. A hot wind whipped at her hair. Beyond the central laboratory—the secret prison in which she had been held for over four months—Donna saw a curving wall of sandbags, about chest high. The wall was on fire in places, smashed in at others. Dead men hung over it or lay together in mounds. Another Apache helicopter had been tossed into the side of a different two-story building made of beige bricks—the tail protruded into the night.

Out beyond the curving wall of sandbags was the nearly twenty-foot-high chain-link fence, with coils of barbed wire on top. It had been flattened here and there, including the gate and a thirty-foot-wide section of fence on rails that could be opened from a sentry booth. A motorboat had been dropped on the booth itself, flattening it entirely.

Beyond the smashed-down gate was a wide two-lane dirt causeway to the mainland, with seagrass and sand on either side, and as she approached it, Donna caught a mouthful of fresh air: the cold, briny breeze running in off the Atlantic. *I will live where I can see the ocean*, she thought to herself. *I will live the rest of my life where I can smell this smell.*

As she walked toward the fence she saw headlights approaching. She was out in the open, halfway between the fence and the wall of sandbags, and had nowhere to go, nowhere to hide. She was too tired for hiding anyway. She could hardly stay on her feet but had one hand ready to reach for the King, if she needed to. She swayed, nearly overcome by lightheadedness, but Van steadied her. She rested her head on his shoulder, even shut her eyes for a moment. Then she remembered Van was dead and jerked her head upright, came out of her waking doze.

The headlights brightened and came closer, and through her injured eardrums she could hear music. A couple of guitar-slingers were dueling with one another while Geddy Lee produced a dragon shriek of his own over a jaunty seventies beat. Or at least she thought it was Rush—it might've been Boston. They all sounded the same to her. Van would've known. She felt herself relaxing, going almost boneless as she limped on toward the gates. The approaching vehicle passed under a streetlamp and then she knew who it was for sure. She had been in that car often enough, buckled into the passenger seat of Llewellyn's cherry Caddy convertible.

It drove rattling over the collapsed gate and right up to her, and before her knees could give out, Colin was out from behind the steering wheel to catch her. Firelight reflected off the polished-looking surface of his bald dome. He put his arms around her and she rested her head on his chest, limp as a raincoat.

"It's all right," Colin promised her. "It's all right now. Are you ready to go home?"

"Van—" she choked.

"I know. I've been reading their emails. I know all about it. We're going home now. To The Briars. No one can touch you there. No one is going to touch you ever again, my love."

The causeway was just over a mile long, and she was almost asleep in the passenger seat when they reached the mainland . . . but she lifted herself up when Colin slowed and then stopped the Caddy and rolled down his window.

There was a black Porsche 911 pulled over on the side of the road, pointed back toward the compound. Beyond the Porsche was a sign: CHEROKEE ISLAND FEDERAL VIROLOGY RESEARCH AND RESPONSE CENTER—AUTHORIZED PERSONNEL ONLY.

Mr. Francis climbed out from behind the wheel of his 911 and stood in the open driver's door, wearing a bomber jacket. He looked toward Colin, clocked Donna in the passenger seat.

"That car suits you, Donna," Francis said. "So does freedom. What happened to Valentine in there?"

"Me," Donna said. Francis nodded and then stared toward the red haze of sparks and smoke where the lab had been.

"Paul," Colin said. "Paul Follett."

Mr. Francis slowly turned his head once more and looked impassively back at him. "You know my name then?"

"For a few months now, yes. I'm Colin Wren—so now you know mine. If you didn't already. Give me a call sometime?" He put his thumb and pinkie finger to the side of his face, miming a telephone. "We've got a lot to talk about. How this is going to work from here on out. Who's going to report to who. What will be done to make amends for this—this—foolish and destructive waste of my time and my friend's life."

Mr. Francis nodded again, as if all this struck him as perfectly reasonable.

"One more thing," Colin said. "We want the body back. Donovan's body. So we can put him in the ground properly. I expect the coffin to arrive at the Portland Jetport in Maine by Monday night. Let us bury our boy . . . or you're going to wind up burying a whole bunch more of yours." And at that he stopped smiling.

27.

They rolled north from the slaughter, and for a while Donna dozed with her head on her brother's shoulder and his arm around her. In the months to come, she found that Van was often there, close beside her, when she was nodding off. He waited for her at the edge of sleep, standing on the lonely strand between wakefulness and dreams, his jeans rolled up and his feet in the surf of an ocean big enough to make the Atlantic look like a child's wading pool. He wore a necklace of sand dollars.

She woke once and glanced into the rearview mirror and saw Van looking back, eyes narrowed in amusement beneath his slender eyebrows. That was the other place she could find him, in the months after his funeral, after Erin Oakes delivered the eulogy at his graveside. If Donna looked at her own reflection and focused only on her eyes and narrowed them ever so slightly; or if she entered a darkened bathroom and saw the shape of herself in the mirror, just the outline, if she stood a certain way, with her head cocked just so.

Donovan had looked back at her from inside a cracked mirror, the night they called King Sorrow forth from the Long Dark. They had passed that cracked mirror around the table (although Allie insisted it was a big conch shell, like out of *Lord of the Flies*, and Arthur seemed to believe they had passed a World War II–era Russian helmet filled with tap water). The door to the hallway kept flying open and then slamming shut. Each time it slammed, it frightened her all over again. Donna wanted to believe it was a prank, it was Colin playing a stupid, mean prank, that he was controlling the door with a button under the card table. Only she knew he wasn't, and not just because Colin kept his hands firmly in sight the whole time.

She knew because once she looked at the door when it flew open and saw a sky full of strange, wheeling constellations where the hallway should've been. She knew because another time she looked through that open door and an eye as big as a tractor tire was staring back.

At some point Allie got up to play piano. Not long after that Arthur went outside through the French windows into the snow. The mirror was passed to her and Van was squeezed in on her left, so they could both look into it at the same time. A crack ran down the center of the glass, dividing it into two sections, and when Donna stared at her half of the mirror, she saw Van, and when he stared at his half, he saw her. The version of Van in the mirror smiled at her (the Van beside her was not smiling at all) and held up a card: the dragon of hearts. The version of her in the mirror showed Van a dragon of spades. And she understood what they were being asked to do. They both did, knew without discussing it.

Van found two decks of cards and shuffled them together. They sat on the floor, across from one another, and they began to play War. Their oldest game, and one they had never really grown out of. They had been at War with each other since the beginning. Allie pounded out the melody to "Puff the Magic Dragon" over and over on the player piano. Colin sat away from them, at the French doors, blowing smoke rings. Van took her ten of hearts with a queen of hearts. She took his king of clubs with an ace of spades.

"If dragons are real, then what else is?" Van asked.

"What do you mean? Like maybe Santa is real?"

"Or giants and shit. We ought to summon a giant instead of a dragon. Tall women turn me on."

"How the hell would that work? You aren't going to have sex with a giant. I guess you could go spelunking in her pussy, but it ain't going to be sex, old son," she said.

She played a three of clubs, he played a two of diamonds, and she won the trick. He played a king of clubs and she played an ace of clubs and won the trick.

"Fuck you," he said.

"Incest is best," she said.

Outside, in the snow, Arthur Oakes was pursuing someone in a slow-motion chase. Donna had watched them both go by a couple of times, a hundred feet apart. The stranger fled across the snow and Arthur followed. Colin blew a smoke ring that widened until it was the size of a manhole cover.

"You and Colin got a thing going?" Van asked.

"No," Donna said. "Just fucking."

The next card Donovan played was a star from the Zener deck, but she beat him with three wiggly lines. She played a plus sign and he beat her with a circle. They did not discuss which card was higher, they just knew. In fact they did not discuss anything at all. It came to Donna then that they hadn't opened their mouths once the whole time they were playing War, had been carrying on their conversation in their minds.

"Oh, shit," she said without opening her mouth. "Oh, shit, oh, shit."

"You're just noticing now?" he asked without opening his mouth, and gave her that smile, the one that made her brother one of the handsomest men in the world. "Twin telepathy, baby. Twin telepathy for real."

And she played the dragon of spades and he played the dragon of hearts. They held the cards up to show each other, both of them beaming, exhausted, and happy. They kept holding them, even when the cards began to burn. Donna's burned from the inside out, a red lace of flame widening and spreading toward the edges. Van's smoldered and ignited at the left corner, began to burn down.

"Who won?" she asked her brother, but she had to say it aloud, the connection broken.

"Game suspended on account of dragons," Donovan told her.

Third Interlude

GWEN, UNDER THE SHADOW

2001

1.

They got a twenty-year-old Rackham student to Podomaquassy Hospital in the midmorning. She had gone over the front of her skateboard, trying to grind the rail on the bike path, and smashed her skull in. Gwen didn't think Amanda French was going to graduate from Rackham College now. If Amanda was lucky, she might graduate from soft foods to solids someday, assuming she could figure out how to use a fork and knife again, but Gwen wouldn't have bet on it.

Gwen held her hand in the back of the ambulance while it ran reds, forced traffic out of its way, and swerved around potholes. Amanda had a mask clapped to her face to keep her blood oxygen rich and reduce the danger of hypoxia. The big neck brace buckled around her throat was literally keeping her head screwed on straight. That head was capped in bandages, although her pretty brown curls hung out from beneath the gauze. They were lathered with a creamy red shampoo of her own blood, dripping onto the floor.

Amanda's eyes found hers. The pupil in one eye was a pinprick. The pupil in the other was an enormous tunnel looking into darkness . . . into the Long Dark, maybe.

"Hold—hold—hold—hold—" she said, over and over again, unable to find the next word in the sentence.

"I got you, darlin'," Gwen said. "I'm right here. Gave yourself a little bump on the head, but we're going to take care of you."

She had always known she would be good at this part of it, and she was. She could meet the eyes of the maimed and the dying and find her smile for them. She spoke to them like a school nurse putting the Band-Aid on the scrape, letting them know from the warmth in her voice and the kindness in her eyes that all would be well, they would be ready to climb on the monkey bars again tomorrow.

Amanda said, "Hold—hole—hole—" and then she stiffened and went silent, and Gwen looked at the heart monitor to see if they were about to lose her.

When Gwen looked back into Amanda's face, the young woman was staring at her with an unnerving calm. "It's not a hole. It's a trap. One of them isn't coming out. I can't see which one because it's dark in the hole, it's so dark. The human carcass is a sheath and every soul a sword. You already have the blade you need." Her mouth went slack and she began to shudder in the grip of a seizure, heels kicking against the slippery plastic of the gurney's thin mattress.

But by then they were at the hospital. They got her out at speed and passed her off to a pair of male nurses who had come out to meet them. Gwen had a hard time letting go of Amanda's hand. She felt that as long as she could hold on to Amanda's hand, she could keep her breathing. Gwen yelled information at the nurses, told them to stick her with adrenaline, that they would lose her if they didn't get the pressure off the brain in the next few minutes, all things they already knew. Then Amanda was gone, wheeled away into the depths of the ER.

There was nothing for them to do after that, and Gwen was

tired. The others were too: Ben Hammermill, who had been in the back with her, and Julius Roth, who had been behind the wheel. It took something out of you, trying to keep a dying person alive. They made their way to the break room together. Ben had blood up to his wrists and wanted to wash. Julius propped open the door to the parking lot and sat in it to smoke a cigarette. Gwen wanted a cup of tea and to sit alone for a bit. Maybe if they stuck around, they'd hear if Amanda made it.

She dropped onto one end of a sofa upholstered in leatherette, patched with strips of duct tape. A nurse sat at the other end with her shoes off, painting her toenails. The smell of the varnish—astringent, chemical—made Gwen lightheaded.

"Well," Julius said, from his position in the open door. The cigarette wobbled off his lower lip, still unlit. "Look at it this way. The worst part of the day is behind us."

Gwen nodded wearily.

On CNN they cut to New York City, where a passenger plane had smashed into one of the Twin Towers.

2.

Colin patted a hand against his chest and said, "That one was on me, guys. I have to own it."

Snow fell outside in fat heavy flakes. Silence seemed to fall with it, hushing the world.

It was the first time they had been together since they had stood around Van's grave, holding hands. They had collected in the study at The Briars, just fourteen hours into the new year: Colin and Arthur, Donna and Allie, and Gwen herself.

Arthur wore a peacoat and a Nepalese smoking hat and looked like he had never laughed in his life. He had a well-kept beard, thicker than ever, to compensate for the lack of hair on his head, and gold-framed spectacles. They were all wearing coats except for Colin. He was just back from the West Coast, had landed the afternoon before in his personal Gulfstream, and the heat was only just coming up in the house. Still, Colin didn't seem to mind the chill, had on gray denims and a white waffle-knit cashmere Henley. Gwen had read an article about him in *Fast Company*, and apparently he had a closet full of white Henleys and iceberg-colored skinny jeans. It was all he ever wore now. He said it was one less decision to make and that it was important to avoid decision fatigue. Gwen didn't get it. How tired did it make you to pick out a sweater? Did he wear the waffle-knits to the beach? To weddings? What about if you were eating spaghetti? It was shit, trying to get red sauce out of white cashmere.

"What are you talking about?" Arthur said.

"Nine Eleven," Colin said. "Bin Laden's been on our Enemies List for years, but he never got to the top. I never took him seriously. He took a pass at the World Trade Center a few years ago, with a bomb in a truck, and to be honest, I thought it was laughable. We all did. Like trying to burn down the White House with a pocket lighter. I figured when Clinton went after him in '98, it was only to make people look away from the whole Monica Lewinsky thing—"

"Fucker," Donna spat. "Sleazy fucker. Not that *she* didn't want it. Monica. She couldn't wait to get down on her knees and suck his dick. At least he didn't have her bumped off. Like some of the others."

Everyone went silent for a moment. It came to Gwen that they were waiting for Van to reply—no one had been better than Van at responding to Donna's mouth and Donna's rage. But the days of Van fencing with his sister were behind them now, and Donna had grown accustomed to sharing her angriest thoughts with a receptive audience. She recorded an AM radio show out of Portland now, three days a week. It had been picked up all over the country. A lot of stations ran her right after Rush Limbaugh, and some days she did better numbers than him. She was even, Gwen had learned, coming out of satellites somehow. People listened to her on something called XM radio that was broadcast all over the world. The thought was faintly alarming: Donna McBride's hate being fired down upon the earth from outer space, like a sci-fi death ray.

"No one is to blame for 9/11," Allie said, "except for the men with box cutters who were on the planes."

Colin shook his head, but he didn't seem distressed. He spoke of the whole matter as if he had gone to the supermarket to get eggs and had somehow come home without them.

"It won't bring a single person back to get him now. But it might prevent us from getting mired down in Afghanistan. After we finish him, we'll want to turn our focus to Iraq. We can't undo 9/11, but maybe we can stop it from happening again. Saddam is working to get enriched uranium from Nigeria . . . he may already have enough to build seven bombs. The intel on that is unshakable. So we'll do Osama this year—an unfortunate but necessary makeup call—and next year we can send the iguana after key members of Saddam's—"

"No," Donna said.

They all stopped again. Colin smiled at her in a puzzled sort of way.

"Donna, why wouldn't we go straight after Bin Laden?" Colin asked her, his voice gentle. "After what he did? Innocent people leapt from the towers to escape the flames behind them. Innocent people held hands to jump together."

"I don't know how innocent they were," Donna said. "They elected a sexual predator. Clinton won New York by how many points? They all voted for him."

Gwen couldn't take it. "I love you, girl, I do, but I never heard such a pile of trash. That creepy Bin Laden motherfucker burned a few thousand people alive. Now it's his turn. I never felt less guilty about sending King Sorrow after anyone. Let's cook his ass and call it a good day's work."

"It's not a vote. It's my turn to pick. You didn't take a vote when you decided to kill Colin's grandfather, Gwen."

Gwen felt her stomach knot, as if she had gulped down her whiskey all at once. It was a cheap shot, and like a lot of cheap shots, it struck hard. Allie stroked Donna's hand, as if she were the one who had just absorbed a blow.

"I think Donna needs to feel what she needs to feel," Allie said.

"Arthur? Want to jump in here? Any thoughts?"

Arthur held his tumbler in one hand. The whiskey had caught some of the wan afternoon sunshine, and as he rocked the glass back and forth, the light dashed this way and that. "Yeah. I think I miss Van."

Donna's chin wrinkled as she struggled down a convulsion of emotion. Her eyes brightened but didn't spill. Arthur didn't look at her but went on studying his glass.

"Yes," Colin said. Gwen thought he sounded almost irritable. Had she ever heard Colin irritable about anything? "So do I. Every day. But I was asking about the question before us. We have to choose who dies next. I'm of the mind we need to act together, *now*, to wipe out a monstrous evil."

"Thank God," Arthur said. "It's about time. So what's your plan to get rid of King Sorrow? I'm all ears."

Colin shook his head. "Did someone call a family therapy session and forget to tell me?" He tossed back the last of his whiskey and grinned, moving a cube of ice around in the pocket of his right cheek, and Gwen was struck with a sudden realization: he was *pissed*. She had never seen him angry before, and he was *seething*.

Arthur was unperturbed. "My own view is that you can't cure evil with more evil. I was wrong to ever think we could—but in my defense, I was desperate and scared and didn't really understand the stakes of the game. What I think these days is that we should deal with our own sins first and worry about someone else's later. The world is full of dangerous people doing terrible things. Including us. You want to reduce the sum total of suffering and slaughter in the world? We can start with our own dragon."

"Did you ever consider that, by crossing names off the Enemies List, we might've already prevented half a dozen *other* 9/11s? I mean, it's impossible to prove a counterfactual, but almost everyone we've eliminated has had Bin Laden's potential to perpetrate a mass atrocity."

"Potential is another word for something that hasn't happened. Most civilized nations don't execute people for what they *might* do. And have you ever turned it around? How much have we *raised* the potential for a mass atrocity by hounding our targets to the edge of sanity before striking them down? Horation Matthews might be dead, but the church to which he belonged is more popular than ever. One adherent of his fucked-up version of Christianity walked into a Sikh temple three weeks ago with an assault rifle—I guess he couldn't tell the difference between Sikhs and Muslims—and would've butchered everyone there if his gun hadn't jammed."

Colin said, "On the subject of Osama bin Laden, we've moved past the question of his *potential* for violence. His potential has been realized in full. Are you saying you want to let him off?"

"If it's up for debate, then sure, make it him," Arthur said. "Better him than anyone else. Though it'll backfire on us somehow. Because it always does. You sow dragon's teeth, all you get is more dragons."

"But it's *not* up for debate," Donna said. "I already told you. It's *my* turn, and I'm not taking requests. It would've been Van's turn, but he's dead, so it's mine. And King Sorrow already came to me, and I already told him who's the lucky girl this year. It's done."

"The lucky . . . girl?" Gwen said. It really seemed to her she had heard wrong.

"Don't worry about Osama, Colin," Donna said. "The New World Order will sort him out when he's not useful to them anymore. In the meantime, I've got other . . . fish to fry." And for some reason, at the word *fish*, a dirty little smile twitched at the corners of her lips.

3.

Wednesday night, they had three cardiac cases (one fatal), a drunk who had put his fist through a plate-glass window and nearly bled out, a woman who had washed down so many sleeping pills with booze she almost stopped breathing, and a five-year-old who had swallowed the contents of a glow stick because his older brother said it would make him glow in the dark. A stroke, a car accident, a man who slipped on some ice and fired a nail gun into his own foot. Another day of people who were tired, angry, stupid, wasted, or sad, maiming themselves and others. Another day of the American diet delivering the bill.

Gwen had nearly nine hours in the meat wagon and was as efficient and steady as ever . . . but felt oddly at a remove from herself. Her thoughts drifted to Donna's smug, dirty smile. *I've got other fish to fry*, with an emphasis on the word *fish* that Gwen didn't like. She found herself considering the way Colin sat behind the card table, looking at each of them in turn, as unruffled as ever, smiling even, but with that glare in his eyes she didn't think she had ever seen before. He wasn't used to being undermined and he didn't like it.

They each had their turn, deciding who would die, but when she thought about it now, it seemed to her they mostly picked King Sorrow's meal off a menu Colin had meticulously prepared on his own . . . which really made every choice Colin's choice. There had been just two exceptions: when Gwen had decided on Llewellyn and when Donna had surprised them yesterday. When Gwen picked at it, even the idea that they were choosing something from a menu was a bit of an illusion. Each year,

Colin had a way of steering things toward one name or another. There was no standing against his sensible calm and his carefully gathered intelligence. It was good of him—noble, even—to do their homework for them, Gwen supposed. She wondered why it didn't quite *feel* good.

Above all, she considered Arthur. She had known how to read him once. She had known how to fit her head just so against his shoulder. Now, though, he was as far away as England, even when he was sitting next to her at the card table. She knew that monks took a vow of silence, and sometimes it seemed he had taken one too, even though he still spoke as he liked, offered his thoughts when asked for them. He had retreated to a kind of inner silence, a place of watchful stillness, like a cleric in his cell with a book of prayer.

There was more of himself in what he wrote. She had tracked down and read many of his essays. They had been written for other medieval scholars like himself, and they weren't exactly *fun*, not the sort of thing Gwen usually read for pleasure (she read Oprah books, mostly, and Patricia Cornwell, and sometimes, when she was feeling lonely and blue, a smutty romance with smoldering men in kilts). But she liked the way he wrote a sentence. "Dragons are not hatched from eggs, of course, but from imaginations, from rotten dreams, from night terrors." That was one she remembered. And "We long for dragons—if only everything we hate could be made to wear scales and be pierced through the heart with a silver sword." And "Courage can be found in the humblest of places: a cup of tea, a woman's warm laughter, a homemade chicken salad sandwich on soft brown bread." She thought, when he spoke of the tea and the laughter and the homemade sandwiches, he was speaking of her, and her love for him swelled so much it hurt, made an ache behind the breastbone. Of course, there was a lot of other stuff in there, mostly about Jung, and early Catholic scholars, and the Saxons and whatnot. But she liked when he wrote about courage and chicken salad sandwiches.

She was with Arthur in her mind all through work and after. It was full dark, no stars, when she drove back to Gogan, although it was barely after 5:00 p.m. She was going to see him in Brunswick later, for drinks with the others, at a bar called Shepherds and Sheep—Colin said they had the deepest wine list on the whole coast, a fact that mattered only to Colin. She meant to run home first and wash off the smell of the ambulance. She had a black dress with golden flowers on it that she had bought in October and hadn't worn and hadn't consciously admitted she was saving for Arthur.

The thought of the dress, of wearing it for him, so distracted her, she almost drove by him, almost didn't see Arthur Oakes at all. Her route home took her past the old factory where once, in the sixties and seventies, they had made canoes. The long hill behind it had been the sledding place in Gogan for as long as there had been a Gogan.

Her headlights swept across the scrubby gravel parking lot, behind the abandoned brick factory buildings, as she made the turn onto North Hill Road. And there he was, standing behind the Ford Explorer he had rented for the week. He had the back open and was pulling something out—a spare tire, Gwen thought. He was changing a flat, then.

She reversed back up the road and into the lot. His rental was still running, and he waited in the red glare of the taillights, wreathed by exhaust. He stood behind a fat inner tube that had to be five feet across. It must've been a squeeze to get it in the back of the Explorer.

Gwen met him in the space between her car and his. The cold stung her bare face.

"What are you doing out here, professor?" she asked. "Studying on ways to break a kneecap?"

He adjusted his colorful Nepalese cap. "Does that happen much here? Do you get a lot of calls out to this hill?"

"Last winter a kid named Timmy Reynolds went into some half-buried chain-link fence down there and got a steel wire right through the cheek. We had to use bolt clippers to cut him free."

"Good thing I've got a trained medical professional handy

then." He considered the hill. "If you really want to be sure I get to the bottom safely, we could go together. You can sit in front and be my human shield. What do you say, old chum?"

She took the tube away from him and bounced it a time or two. "Where did you find this thing?"

"I was driving back to the hotel and—you know that inlet, about a mile from The Briars? There's an old windmill near it, like something out of a Dutch painting? This inner tube was just out on the ice, no one anywhere around. I don't know why someone would've just left it. I thought maybe it was a sign."

"Do you spend a lot of your time looking for signs?" Gwen asked.

She was joking, but he only nodded, yes, gave no sign he knew he was being teased.

She shook her head at him, as if to say there was no helping some people. Then she turned and crunched through the snow, carrying the tube to the edge of the drop. They had the hill to themselves—it was too cold for sledding, really, the sort of cold that hurt to breathe. He held the tube while she sat down on the front and then he pushed it along and as it began to slide under its own power he leapt on, landing so that her body was between his legs and her head against his chest. They dropped off the face of the world into the rushing cold darkness, falling faster, then faster still, the tears burning in Gwen's eyes, whipping down her cheeks and freezing against her skin. At some point they raised their arms and whooped together, cheering for the magic of acceleration.

The tire turned halfway around at the bottom, squeaking gently, and came to rest against a tangle of brush caked in ice. She felt easy and relaxed, her head on his breastbone and his arms around her. They sat in the darkness, their breath misting around them.

"You need a girl who will do more than go sledding with you. Found one of those yet?" she asked, promising herself she wouldn't care about the answer.

"What, and drag her into my horror show?" He laughed. "Or, worse, try and keep the King a secret? She'd be like that woman who married Ted Bundy. Sooner or later she'd find out I was killing people."

She didn't correct him, say it was King Sorrow doing the killing. She didn't want to argue terms and definitions. She wanted to know if someone else had what she wanted and could never have.

"Has there been *anyone*?" she asked.

"I fall in love at least once a year. I like to look, you know? I like to hear a girl laugh. I like to be challenged, to argue the meaning of a story with some well-meaning teaching assistant who gets more and more prettily flushed in the heat of battle. I like girls in glasses—I like to imagine taking them off. But I don't need to take them to bed. I enjoy watching a young woman hunt a man down and ensnare her prey. I cheer them on. I like the chase, but I don't need to be chased or chase myself. It's enough to be a spectator."

"Humph," she humphed.

"Did you just say the word *humph*, like a character in a comic book?"

"Humph. Flushed teaching assistants. I don't like the sound of that. You're a father figure to them, you pervert. Try and have some goddamn respect. I thought you were a feminist."

He cocked his head to one side and said, "Wherever I might sometimes wander in my imagination, I assure you my hands know better. I've only ever played the letch once, when I skeeved on an eighteen-year-old high school girl, too naïve to defend herself from my unwholesome designs."

Gwen had to laugh at that.

He nodded. "You? There must've been someone."

"No one who hung in there."

She almost said, *I don't have time*, which was true enough, but when she considered it, it seemed that she had made *sure* she wouldn't have time for a relationship, that she had constructed a life around fifty-hour workweeks. What meager spare time remained was reserved to help Jett Nighswander with schoolwork or, in the summer, to coach his Little League team. She volunteered at the hospice; she looked after her parents. She had been determined not to be the fourth generation of Underhills caring for Wrens . . . and yet somehow still took a paycheck to keep The Briars plowed out in the winter and landscaped in the summer. Her life, she thought, was carefully engineered to avoid having one.

They began the slow struggle up the long incline. Gwen tottered once and reached in the dark and found Arthur's shoulder and steadied herself. It felt good, to find him in the gloom, to have him close enough to grab.

"So is Allie with Donna now?" he asked.

Gwen laughed. "Is she—? No! Not like that. They'll *never* be together like that, especially now. Even if they both wanted it, it would be a betrayal of Van."

He cocked one eyebrow. "You say so?"

"I do. He died for Donna. She's not going to fuck his widow. And Allie will always hate herself for failing Van by not being sufficiently heterosexual. No, Allie just likes to . . . be close to Donna. To look after her. All she ever really wanted was to look after Donna."

"I guess no one gets a happy ending in this story," Arthur said. "Not Allie. Not Donna. Sure as shit not Van." He thought for a while, then added, "Not you and me."

"Maybe Colin has his happy ending," Gwen mused.

"Maybe not. Did you see the way he looked when Donna said she wasn't going to use King Sorrow the way he wanted?"

"Oh," Gwen said. "You spotted that too?"

"Colin needs his systems and his spreadsheets. That's how he deals with life. He's as trapped and desperate as the rest of us, but he can use data analysis to hold King Sorrow at a distance. It gives him a sense of control. As long as we follow his carefully worked-out programs, he can pretend it's all fantasy baseball instead of a sickening nightmare."

Gwen nodded . . . but was not sure she entirely agreed. Colin didn't fall into traps. He designed them.

"I'd ask how *you* deal with it, but I already know," she said. "I've read your essays."

"And?"

"Not exactly John Grisham, but I can see why everyone thinks you're such a smart guy."

"To be fair, I also look damn good in tweeds. You'd be surprised how much of my reputation as a first-rate literary mind rests on my wardrobe."

"I don't believe it." They paused, catching their breath on the steepest part of the hill. "So. Do you know how to kill him yet?"

He considered the starless sky. It smelled like snow.

"I met a giant," he said slowly, "in Wales. After Van and Donna were kidnapped and we all went into hiding. I hunted for eight weeks before I found him pretending to be a stony hill. Moss right in his ass crack."

She laughed—then looked again and realized he wasn't joking.

"A real giant?"

"I thought I should use my time in hiding productively. In one of the stories, the giant in question killed a clutch of baby dragons by sitting on them, then strangled their mother when she expressed her irritation. I figured he might know something. It wasn't easy to talk to him. My Welsh sucks. I've always been good at languages, but Welsh is a pisser. I feel like I'm trying to swallow gravel. Whereas Trig didn't have any English at all, he—"

"His name was Trig?"

"His old name, his *true* name, is something in old Welsh that sounds like a dog choking on a bone, and which translates roughly into Big Stone Dick. But the Royal Geographical Society planted a geodesic plaque on his left shoulder in 1892, a trigonometrical point, which led him to believe he had been renamed Trig by Queen Victoria."

She laughed.

"Anyway, conversation was slow. He hadn't talked to anyone in about sixty years, and as a rule, giants need an hour or so to think a new thought. I asked him what to do about King Sorrow and he told me I should wait. He said in another few years, forty or fifty at most, I'd be dead, and then I'd have no more trouble with him. The fears and regrets of men baffle him. None of the things we worry about seem of any great importance when you live in geological time. He admitted that while I seemed a pleasant enough chap, it was his feeling the era of man couldn't end soon enough. He took an especially sour view of cell phone towers. He was afraid one would be planted in his bunghole the next time he took a nap."

"Are you fucking with me, Arthur? Is this a real conversation we're really having? You found a giant and asked him for advice? If there are giants wandering around Wales, how come people haven't seen them?"

"They have. The stories are full of them."

"*Old* stories. What about now? How come no one has seen them in the modern day?"

Arthur's hand had slipped into his pocket, and now he took it out and flipped a disc of smooth, clear glass. "Maybe they just don't know how to look."

"What's that?"

"The Surrealist's Glass," Arthur said. "It belonged to Salvador Dalí for a while, but it was already at least four hundred years old by the time he got his hands on it. I found it at an estate auction and bought it for six pounds. Which is a bit like finding the Holy Grail in a charity shop or the martyr's robe in a heap of nightgowns at a yard sale."

"The martyr's robe?"

He shrugged. "A sacred garment. Does the usual sacred garment stuff. Keeps one from the flames of hell, hides a person from the eyes of the wicked." He considered the lens in his hand. "The martyr's robe might hide you from evil eyes, but it wouldn't hide you from this. The Surrealist's Glass shows the secret truth of things, sees through enchantments. It'll show you ghosts, giants . . . trolls. There's a troll in the southwest of England who might be more use to us than Trig. If I can find him. Svangur the Sly. I mentioned him to you once before. Like most trolls, he has a hoard of treasure he's accumulated over the centuries. I think he's got the Sword of Strange Hangings in his possession."

"Oh, right. I was wondering where that was."

He smiled at her. "It's a sword that can cut through dragon mail. A blade forged from a human soul instead of iron. The Sword of Strange Hangings is clasped in a sheath of brightest silk and can only be drawn by someone who has rid himself of wicked intentions." He gave her a good up-and-down ogling and did a Groucho Marx waggle with his eyebrows. "Which probably rules me out, *schweetheart*."

She laughed again and looked away, felt a pleasant heat in her face.

"Anyway: if I ever come across Svangur, I'll know him. As long as I see him through this." Flipping the Surrealist's Glass and catching it once again.

"Trolls and giants and magic robes and swords made out of souls. All this fairy tale talk makes my head feel funny."

"Fairy tales make sense . . . which is more than I can say for everyday life. They're how I cope. I keep thinking if I study fairy tales long enough, maybe one of these days I'll write a happily ever after for the one that's got hold of us." He narrowed his eyes. "I don't have to ask how you cope. How many lives is it now? Do you keep track?"

"Nope," she said.

"Is it possible you've saved as many as a thousand lives, Gwen?"

"If it wasn't me in the ambalance, it would've been someone else."

"But it *was* you."

She made a face. "Speaking of Ted Bundy . . . did you know Bundy worked on a suicide hotline for a few months? Say he talked a hundred people out of topping themselves. How many murders does that make up for?"

They stood with the inner tube between them at the top of the hill. He looked down the slope. "Take another run?"

"Skip it. We aren't kids anymore. We keep testing our luck, it's liable to fail us. Any idea who Donna's going after?"

"No," he said. "Maybe Allie knows." He tightened his jaw. "Do you know Donna only drinks bottled water now? She's worried the government will put a sedative in the tap water, knock her out and take her away again."

"Who can blame her? Someone really did come for her once. They might again. They could come for any of us."

"No. That's over. Colin made sure of it. Got them off our back somehow."

She squinted at Arthur in the dark. "Yeah. I guess. You ever wonder *how*, though?"

Arthur shrugged. "He's a security consultant for half a dozen agencies and half a dozen senators. They all use his software. They *depend* on him. Colin is the most dependable person I know. Before I had a dragon, I had him. He saved my ass from Jayne Nighswander. He saved all of us."

"Is that what we are, Arthur?" Gwen asked. "Saved?"

In the space between his car and hers, Arthur leaned in and brushed his lips against her cheek, and she leapt back as if he had come for her with a knife, her heart thrumming in her chest.

"No," she said, and he retreated, a wounded look in his eyes.

Your kiss, Gwendolyn, will condemn your beloved to death, she remembered King Sorrow telling her, and she was thinking *Oh, God, oh, God, too late, I just murdered him, I just murdered my best friend in the whole world, and it was always going to end this way*—but then she caught her breath. *Your kiss, Gwendolyn. YOUR kiss.* The exact phrasing always mattered to King Sorrow . . . if they had learned anything by now they had learned that. Arthur Oakes was safe. Still.

She expected anger—resentment—but instead Arthur looked

away, very calmly. "For what it's worth, I don't forgive me either. Not for Tana and not for pulling you into this mess." He squeezed her arm. "See you for drinks in a while? With the rest of the gang?"

"In a while," she promised, her heart still beating too quickly. She could still feel his mouth on her cheek.

She drove away first. Before she turned into the road, she looked into her rearview mirror and had a glimpse of him in the glow of the taillights. He rolled the tube down the hill and stood there watching it as it leapt away into darkness.

5.

Gwen texted Allie a few days after Arthur flew back to England: We should talk about the iguana—wondering where it's going to spend Easter. How's Donna doing? I'm worried about her.

Her phone rang a few minutes later. It was Allie's number on the caller ID, but when Gwen answered, it was Donna.

"If you want to know how I'm doing, Gwen, why don't you call me?" Donna asked.

Gwen was sitting outside the hospital, on the loading dock, with a Styrofoam cup of weak coffee. "I didn't like to trouble you, Donna."

"You mean you wanted information and decided to go behind my back to get it."

"I suppose that's the most paranoid way to put it. How exactly *did* I text Allie and wind up getting yelled at by you?"

"Because she brought her phone right to me. Because she isn't a fucking collaborator. I *won't* be spied on. Not by the US government, not by a foreign government, not by the UN Security Council, not by the G-7, not by the billionaires who get together at Davos every year to carve up the world, and not by *you*. You want to know what King Sorrow is going to do next? Buy a newspaper on Easter morning."

Donna hung up and that was that.

6.

But Allie *did* tell. A text came in the night before Easter morning, three words.

Francine Trout. Confession.

7.

Gwen fired her Dell up—the Dell was another of Colin's Christmas presents, he always made sure they all had the latest tech—and listened to the modem screech. She sat in her father's old blue terrycloth robe, hair sticking to the nape of her neck, navigated to Yahoo, and typed *francine trout confession* into the search box.

The story was in the *Boston Globe* and the *Miami Herald*, and on a message board called Have-A-Cold-One-On-Me. The *Globe* and *Herald* stories were only partially readable—you had to have an online subscription for the full articles—and dated to August 2001. The *Herald* story was titled "New Leads in Twenty-Year-Old Disappearance," while the *Globe* proclaimed, "A Confession Provokes Skepticism and Curiosity."

But she didn't need to read either article to get the gist, because it was all on Have-A-Cold-One, a true crime message board with threads on hundreds of unsolved cold cases . . . including one on the abduction, rape, and murder of little Cady Lewis, who was snatched from the front yard of a friend's house. A friend who would grow up to become talk radio firebrand Donna McBride.

As she read about Cady Lewis, Gwen was overcome with a feeling of sadness—and understanding. It was the first time her angry friend Donna had ever really made sense to her. Gwen was sorry for Cady Lewis, who had a bad end before her life had even begun. But one way or another Cady's sorrows were over. It was Donna who Gwen pitied most. Donna, who would never get even with a world that kept taking good people away from her, destroying them before her eyes. Donna was not furious because she hated but because she loved.

Cady had been abducted in the early summer of 1977, during a visit to Donna's house. A man had told Cady Lewis that her dog had been hit by a car and that he had been sent to pick her up. The only living eyewitness, Donna herself, was sure there had been someone in the passenger seat as well, although she was at the wrong angle to see a passenger. In fact, Donna's description of the man in the driver's seat had wavered across the years, which opened her to quite a bit of ridicule among the posters on the Cady Lewis thread. As a child, Donna said she had seen the driver's left arm, hanging out the open window of his vehicle, and described a dark tan. Later she would revise her statement to suggest the driver might've been Black; still later, she suggested it was possible he had been Latino.

I swear to God this bitch was looking through some kind of racism kaleidoscope when Cady Lewis got snatched, one woman had posted on the thread.

Cady's profoundly decomposed body was found months later, in a drainage ditch overgrown with weeds. A sexual assault could not be proved after so much rot, but her pelvis had been shattered in two places, which suggested blunt force trauma to her sexual organs.

The amateur crime-solvers on Have-A-Cold-One had identified over a dozen possible suspects without coming to any consensus. It didn't help that the only eyewitness had been eight at the time and could not even give the color of the van for certain. Had it been black? Or a dark evergreen? Or even navy blue? Was it even a van at all??? It might have been a truck with a hatchback on the flatbed! Men had been arrested, investigated, and released for lack of evidence. No one was any closer to finding out who had killed Cady Lewis today than they had been on the day she was abducted. The posters on the Have-A-Cold-One message board were in a constant state of trench warfare with one another, defending their pet theories while launching merciless assaults on the favored hypotheses of others. And the latest lines of battle had been drawn up around the claim that Francine Trout had been present during Cady's last hours.

Trout was serving life in a maximum-security prison in Tennessee. She had, with her husband, Ezekiel Trout, fostered seven children over seven years, offering them a clean, spacious farm, a kindly but stern Christian upbringing, and intense homeschooling. They were making almost a hundred thousand dollars a year to look after the children and had even been profiled in a local paper in a glowing article titled "School of Trout: Loving Locals Offer Foster Children Faith, Fellowship, and a Future."

They were both arrested for murdering one of the kids and burying the body in the cellar so they could continue cashing checks from the state. After the arrest, the other children described a life of terror and abuse. Zeke routinely sexually abused boys and girls alike. He punished children by chaining them in the unheated basement, sometimes for days, leaving them to sleep in their own filth. He escaped a life sentence by hanging himself while awaiting trial. His wife and accomplice wouldn't meet with her parole board until she was seventy-one.

Francine had come forward in early 2001 to confess to her part in the Cady Lewis killing. Cady had been snatched years before she and Zeke got into the foster parent game. At the time of Cady's abduction, the Trouts were living in Pensacola, not ten miles from the McBride house. Zeke was a television technician who did house calls, and Francine often accompanied him in his black van. They had gone out on a house call, but Zeke had written the wrong address down, wound up miles from where he was supposed to be. They had stopped to look at a map, and while they were parked, Zeke had seen two girls playing in the sprinkler in their front yard. He lured one of them over to the van. Francine knew her duty, and when the girl came around to the passenger side, she smashed the child's head against the open door and dragged the stunned girl inside. Ezekiel found an empty gravel lot at the end of a dirt road and raped Cady Lewis in the back of his van. Francine held Cady down while he strangled her.

Francine had traded this story (and others), for a transfer to Black Cricket Women's House of Correction in Vermont. Her (much) younger sister lived in Vermont, and it would be easier for them to visit with one another. It was also an upgrade from the supermax in which Francine had been held before. In Black Cricket, a prisoner could work with horses; she could earn field trips; there was a chorus club, a knitting group, a club for doing puzzles. Her transfer was granted because some of Francine's stories had been true. Some of Francine's other tales, though, were . . . well, not lies, but perhaps fantasies. Francine claimed Zeke had been in Aspen, Colorado, to perpetrate the well-known rape-murder of a pair of college students in 1975. Only it was impossible: Ezekiel Trout had been in the South Pacific at the time, had spent all of 1975 employed on a container ship. It was true Zeke and Francine had lived in Pensacola the year Cady Lewis had been abducted. But records from the Bureau of Motor Vehicles revealed that Ezekiel hadn't bought his black van until the following year. In 1978 he was driving a Pinto cruising wagon.

As one poster on Have-A-Cold-One pointed out, *Do you know how many people have confessed to killing Cady Lewis? FOURTEEN. Fourteen known CONFESSIONS. How crowded was it in that fucking van? Shit . . . just imagine if ALL of them were telling the truth. They wouldn't have been driving a van when they snatched her, they would have been driving a fucking SCHOOL BUS.*

The sad, stomach-churning story of Francine and Ezekiel

Trout absorbed Gwen fully. It was hard to stop scrolling through the thread. The internet did that to you, a thing she had just begun to discover. It was as compelling as the hypnotist's watch and just as hard to tear one's gaze away. Colin viewed this as a feature, but Gwen was quite sure it was a bug. When she blinked her sore, tired eyes, she discovered with a little frisson of terror that it was after one in the morning. Easter. The hour of the dragon had come and gone. Gwen feared that Francine Trout had come and gone with it.

But as it turned out, it was much worse than that.

8.

When she put on the TV she thought, for a few bleary, half-awake moments, that it was video from 9/11. Some great building had been smashed to rubble. She saw the scorched yellow stone remains of a wall. The structure behind it had fallen in on itself. It was an acre of toxic smoke and blackened ruin, sown with a thousand chunks of broken glass.

But, of course, it wasn't New York and it wasn't September. It was Easter morning, and that was the Black Cricket prison. The chyron read: GAS EXPLOSION AT WOMEN'S PENITENTIARY—HUNDREDS FEARED DEAD. The phone rang before she could turn up the volume.

"You seeing this?" Tana Nighswander asked.

"Your mother—" Gwen said.

Tana said, "Bad news: she's still alive. They transferred her out of Black Cricket dog's years ago. She was so badly behaved, they sent her to a supermax down south. Figures. She's too evil to die. Think about it, though. If she wasn't such a savage bitch, she woulda been there to burn with the rest. She woulda wound up just like Jayne!"

"Just like Jayne," Gwen repeated, numbly.

"Jesus, look at it," Tana said, as if they were both in Gwen's living room, watching the TV together. "If I didn't know better, I'd think something came down out of the sky to attack this country all over again."

They said goodbye, but the phone rang again, almost the moment Gwen set it back in the cradle. It was Julius Roth, her wheelman.

"You still sore about missing out on New York?" Julius asked.

Gwen had wanted to go to NYC after the towers fell—they all did. But their employer, Cumberland County Emergency Rescue, spent days talking with officials, trying to find out what they could do to help . . . and in the end, it turned out the most helpful thing they could do was stay home. By 9/14, Ground Zero was overwhelmed with rescue teams. Squads had come from Alaska, from Italy, from Japan. They needed bottled water more than spare bodies. And meanwhile, people in Maine kept having strokes and car accidents.

"Was I sore?"

"*I* was," Julius said. "Kid I went to summer camp with was in one of those fucking towers. How would you feel about a makeup call? I talked to the office, they already signed off on it. And Vermont is asking for experienced hands to help with the rescue. What do you say?"

"I say I'm in," Gwen said. And then, after a moment, added, "But Julius, do you really think there'll be anyone to rescue?"

Julius didn't seem to know how to answer that one.

9.

She got there with Ben and Julius in the ambulance just after sundown. The dusk-light had a weird smoky orange tint to it, as if they stood in the light of some great, glowering, sooty furnace. The rescue teams had set up floodlights on fifty-foot poles, casting a silvery brilliance across the acres of seething bombed-out wreckage. A massive five-story chimney remained untouched, a silo of red brick. The whole face had been sheared off one wing so the prison stood open like a dollhouse. Each open cell was a charred cubbyhole. Rebar jutted from the concrete between floors, while water spurted from severed pipes, making pools in the wreckage below.

The parking lot—what was left of it—was thick with fire trucks, police cruisers, ambulances, military jeeps, cranes, and loaders. The Vermont National Guard had set up sprawling tents, strung with bare lightbulbs. One was a bustling headquarters. Tables had been arranged beneath those pitiless lights, with blueprints of Black Cricket spread across them. Folding chairs had been arranged in rows before a pair of whiteboards covered in scrawl. Another pavilion served as an open-all-hours cafeteria and place to sack out if you were too tired to drive to the Best Western a few miles away.

They had enough construction equipment to build the on-ramp for a superhighway, but most of the work was being done by hand. Squads in hard hats worked in the rubble, shifting bricks and blackened stones. They passed rocks from hand to hand, into piles at the edge of the ruin. Sometimes someone would pick something up—a child's drawing in crayon, a singed pair of women's pajama bottoms—and carefully store it in a clear plastic bag. The bags were handed out of the wreckage along a different line of volunteers, to be sorted at a line of folding tables.

Julius parked the ambulance well back from the site, and the three of them walked in through the RVs and pickups together. They paused at the outer limit of the ruin to take it all in before reporting to the duty tent. They hadn't put on their N95s yet, and the hazed air was sharp with the scent of crushed stone and burnt plastics. Someone had a saw going, Gwen could hear the buzz and whine of the blade cutting into stone. And there was the pumping hiss of hydraulics, as a man in a bucket was lifted to one of those torn-open cells so he could shine a powerful hand light into the interior. But hardly anyone spoke, and when they did, they said as little as possible. Walkie-talkies went off in crackling bursts, then cut out just as abruptly.

The quiet was so somber and widespread that Gwen's ears soon picked out the only continuous voice. She peered into the gathering dusk and saw a circle of men taking the knee to pray together. A preacher knelt with them in the robes of her office. Gwen could not make out her words, but her tone was kind and steady and comforting, the voice of a mother reading a bedtime story to her brave, tired boys. A few phrases swam out of the darkness:

"Help us to know when we can't do any more, when we need to *accept* help instead of offering it . . . Remember everyone you find is *someone* saved, whether you got them out alive or dead. If we couldn't save them, know you saved someone from the anguish of not knowing what happened to someone they loved."

Gwen knew the voice, although she had not heard Erin Oakes since she presided over Van's memorial service, in the Rackham chapel, half a year before. She waited until the men said *Amen* together and came to their feet. The reverend stood with them and seemed to see Gwen as she rose.

They met each other in the bright strobes of the emergency vehicles, and Erin took Gwen into a mother's embrace.

"They found any living?" Gwen asked, without preamble.

"Eleven in the first hour. Three more since then. None since two this afternoon." She drew back but went on holding Gwen's arms. "Forty bodies recovered so far. Three hundred and seventy we don't know about." And she looked away into the darkness.

Gwen saw them, then. The body bags had been stacked neatly in the back of a dump truck, parked beyond the lights, well to one side of the lot.

"Do you have a hotel room yet?" Erin asked her. "I've got only one bed in mine, but I'm little, and it's a queen. There's room in it for you. Wait'll I tell Arthur who I have in the sack with me. He'll be so jealous."

Gwen had to laugh again. It felt good to laugh—even with the smoke from smoldering chemicals burning the back of her throat.

"Just remember you're a woman of God," Gwen said. "I expect you to leave space for Jesus between us at all times."

Erin put her head to Gwen's shoulder and they laughed together, and when Gwen wiped her eyes, she could pretend it was the chemical smoke.

10.

They found no one alive for the next two days, but on the third, Gwen heard someone banging a pipe.

Gwen was toiling in Zone Four, although no one called it that. On site, it was commonly referred to as the Swamp. It was under the eastern wing, the one part of the prison that still stood, raggedly torn open to show that dollhouse cross-section. There were pits amid the rubble, filled with chilly water and slicked with oils. The air fumed with the cloying odor of chemicals.

She was passing rocks up out of a depression when she paused and cocked her head. She thought she had heard a sound, a distant *clank-clank* of steel striking steel. Her first thought was that a workman had to be hammering on something nearby. She looked up at Julius, standing at the rim of the crater, his face dirty, the lenses of his spectacles filmed with ash.

"You hear that?" Gwen asked.

"Hear what?" Julius asked her.

The clanking tailed off. For a while—almost a minute—she heard nothing. Then it started again. A construction worker began to run a jackhammer fifty yards away, the heavy machine gun sound of it drowning out everything else.

"Hey!" Gwen shouted at Julius suddenly. "Get that meathead to knock it off! *Now!*"

Julius twitched in surprise but leapt into unsteady action, hurrying off in the direction of the deafening roar.

Gwen stretched out on the tumble of rocks and dusty rebar, putting her ear first to one dark cavity and then another. The jackhammer abruptly cut out. A ringing silence rushed into the stillness.

She listened with all the attention she had. *Yes. There.* She moved her ear to another dark cavity, so small she could have only slid two fingers into it. The sound was louder, a desultory, hopeless *clank, clank*.

"I got a clank here!" she cried. She looked around wildly, saw Ben Hammermill sitting on the edge of the depression, staring at her as if she was out of her mind. "There's someone down there! Get a dog! Get a live dog over here!"

There were two kinds of dogs working the disaster scene, live dogs and dead dogs. In fact, both kinds of dogs were very much alive. But "dead dogs" responded to corpses, while "live dogs" liked to find someone still sucking oxygen. Ben clambered to his feet—gangly, long-limbed, dusky, and ethnically uncertain Ben—and loped away.

Gwen put her mouth to the hole where she could best hear the clanking and screamed, *"I hear you! We hear you! We're coming! Help is coming!"*

But the clanking went on, slowly, wearily, and Gwen doubted she had been heard. There were three clanks, a pause, and three more.

Gwen cast her gaze around, found a piece of stone, and began to bash it against a spear of dusty rebar. She banged it three times—waited—and banged three times again.

For the space of a breath there was no sound at all. Then, from a long way off, Gwen heard steel on steel, two clanks. She responded in kind, banging stone against rebar, two blows. A moment later, from somewhere twenty, thirty feet down, Gwen heard a flurry of excited banging: she pictured the steel leg of a chair striking the steel pipe of a bedframe. She wanted to laugh. She wanted to jump into the air, jump like a child full of sugar giving their mattress a workout. When she looked around, she saw Ben and Julius had returned with almost a dozen men in tow. Among them was a French boy, olive complexioned and handsome, with a dog—lean and powerful and as colorless as ash. It looked for all the world like the ghost of a German shepherd. It bounded into the depression, past Gwen, stuck its wet nose into the little hole where she had been listening . . . and after one intent moment of study, it began to bark.

22.

Gwen was still there just before midnight when they heard the survivor's voice for the first time.

They worked under the spotlights and they worked by hand. Bringing in a loader, even a small one, would be too much weight on the shifting debris and could crush whoever was down there. They labored on beneath the looming, gutted face of the east wing. Steel braces had been brought in to support the walls, but now and then something would fall anyway. Once a cinder block dropped with a crash and people over twenty feet away jumped for cover. It made Gwen dizzy to look at the ruin looming above her. It seemed at any moment it might pancake down on top of them.

"'Ello!" called the French boy, suddenly. He was on his knees in the declivity and he bent forward, ass in the air, to listen to the pile of rubble beneath him. His dog was wandering the rocks above, duty done, but the kid had stuck around to work. He had flown all the way from Paris, where he worked in rescue services, to assist with the effort at Black Cricket. A whole team of boys with dogs had come from Europe. "'Ello? I 'ear your voice! Can you 'ear my voice?"

"I'm here! I'm down here!"

Gwen lowered herself to her knees next to the French boy and placed her mouth close to one of the gaps in the rubble.

"We're coming, darlin'! We're coming! What's your name?"

"I'm cold!"

"Oh, darlin'. I know it. We're coming as fast as we can."

"I'm in water, it's cold!"

"What's your name?"

"Arthur!" she cried, and a dreadful chill spread in Gwen's chest. *Arthur's in the hole*, she thought. *Arthur's down in the hole and I'll never get him out.* The girl shouted again: "Wendy Arthur! Cell C-13."

"Wendy," Gwen said, willing herself to bring her thoughts back to *here*, to *now*. "I'm Gwen Underfoot. We're going to get you out. What can you tell me about your situation?"

"It sucks!"

Gwen laughed. So did the French kid.

"I know it, but what else can you tell me?"

"I'm in water. It's cold!"

"How high is the water?" She was yelling herself hoarse, but when someone held a megaphone to her, she waved it away. You couldn't use a megaphone to project a voice through rubble, all you'd do was create a blast of distorted sound.

"My, uh, belly button. It smells bad. I keep getting dizzy. I keep going in and out."

"Wendy, I don't want you to drown. You need to keep your head high. Can you make sure if you need to rest, you don't go under?"

"Yes! My bed frame is on its side and I've got one arm through the rail. Even if I fade out, I can't slide any lower."

"Good. What else can you tell me?"

"I'm under, uh, a wall. It's on my leg. I think my leg is messed up real bad, Gwen."

"Don't you worry about your leg. You're alive and we're going to get you out. Wendy?"

But it was a while before Wendy could reply. Gwen thought she needed a cry before she could go on. Gwen thought the leg was likely very bad indeed.

Despair was as dangerous as the water and the fumes. She wanted Wendy to think about daylight and tomorrow, not darkness and fumes and amputation.

"Wendy! Wendy, girl. Do you have any family?"

"Ah. Ah. My mom?"

"Okay, great. What's her name, darlin'? We can get her here."

"No!" Wendy cried, a little hysterically. "I hate that bitch! Please! No!"

Gwen laughed again. "Okay, scratch that. Anyone else?"

"I have a little boy. He's only three."

Gwen rested her head against the stones.

"Don't bring him either, Gwen," Wendy Arthur said.

"No, love," Gwen said. "Of course not."

"He doesn't know me anyway. I don't want him to know me. He lives with my ex and his girlfriend. She's better for him than I ever coulda been."

"Don't you believe it, Wendy. You're going to climb out of there and see your son, you hear me?" Gwen thought a moment, then said, "Are you religious, Wendy?"

"I'm trying to be."

"Would you like someone to pray with you?"

"Yes, please."

"Okay," Gwen said. "I know just who."

When she looked around for the French boy he was already on the move, jogging off to find Erin Oakes.

12.

They worked their way down another eight feet before they hit a big slab of cement. They dug for the edges but couldn't find them. A rivulet of stinking, polluted water trickled across it from somewhere. Who knew where it was coming from. A little after five in the morning Mark Ruffner, field marshal for the Green

Mountain Search and Rescue services and head of operations, said they were going to have to cut.

Ruffner was a sinewy little man, with a black mustache and black decisive eyes, and Gwen both liked and trusted him. His voice was purposefully quiet—it forced people to listen carefully. He was the best kind of authority figure, the sort who had no desire to throw his weight around, who attended to the people who served him with interest and focus. There was a team from the governor's office that wanted to have a press conference about finding a survivor, but Ruffner had shut them down.

"The work you guys have done these last few days is extraordinary, and a survivor is a big feel-good story," the press secretary from the governor's office told him. "I don't see what's wrong with giving yourself a little pat on the back, Mark."

"I need both hands free for shifting rock," he told her, "but thanks. When we got something to celebrate, I'll be there with a party hat on, but she's still down there."

Erin Oakes told Wendy to hang on, that they wouldn't be able to talk for a while. Conversation would be impossible once the stone cutter started going. Erin had been in the declivity all night, talking to Wendy, praying with her sometimes, joking more often. Listening, mostly. When Wendy was nineteen she had killed a man, driving drunk. At the time of the accident, Wendy's ten-week-old was in the back of the car. He had survived unharmed, aside from some scratches from flying glass. In the aftermath, even before she was sentenced to nine years, child services had swept in to transfer custody of the infant to his father, an estranged ex-boyfriend. Wendy told Erin losing her baby boy was the best thing that ever happened to her—because now she wouldn't be able to ruin him.

Erin told her it was a lie. Erin said she was going to hold her boy again. Erin said her son was going to find out how strong his mother was someday . . . strong enough to try and do some good in the world after making a terrible, stupid mistake. Erin told Wendy she had been imprisoned in jail herself once, right here, in Black Cricket. Erin said she killed a man too. Erin said for a while she had also believed she was unworthy of her son's love but had found out no one was unworthy. Either that, or maybe everyone was unworthy and we had to love and be loved anyway.

Gwen came to get her, and Erin climbed out of the pit, dusty and swaying a little with tiredness. But her eyes were bright and she gave Gwen's hand a quick squeeze.

"She's a trouper," Erin said. "Forget getting a hug from her son. He's going to have to wait in line behind me."

A big, three-hundred-pound Pole with a face like a ham lit up his stone cutter and bent to the concrete. Sparks flew.

"Hey! Hey!" Gwen cried, pushing Erin aside. "The hell you doing, hoss? Shut it down! *Shut! It! Down!*"

He couldn't hear her over the grinding roar of the spinning blade, and she had to catch his attention by waving her arms. Mark Ruffner spied her agitation and closed in, joining her at the edge of the pit. The Pole lifted his saw—it was so big it had to be held with two hands—and switched it off. He looked befuddled behind his goggles.

"What's up, Gwen?" Mark said.

"That saw isn't water cooled," Gwen said. "That kid down there is up to her chest in who knows what and that saw is throwing sparks."

"That kid down there is almost out of time and that's the best saw we've got on hand. The water-cooled saw got mangled yesterday, over in Zone One."

"Get another one."

"We're working on it. Maybe by tomorrow night. Do you want to wait that long?" He waited for her to reply, and when she didn't, he waved a hand for the Pole to continue.

The saw whined, hit the stone, began to flay the air with sparks. Mark leaned to Gwen to shout in her ear.

"She's got a mashed leg and she's in rotten water. She's in and out. And, Gwen, the water is still rising."

"How? How the hell is it rising? Ain't we got it shut off?"

"Everywhere. But the kid we're trying to save, she's down in the basement now. Below the ruptured boiler tanks." He clapped a hand on Gwen's shoulder. "She's been lucky this far. Have a little faith."

Gwen did have faith—but not in anyone's luck. Her faith was in King Sorrow . . . and the grief that trailed behind him, miles longer than his tail.

23.

About an hour later, the Pole took a break and Erin and Gwen got back down into the pit. Erin stretched out on the concrete—it was hot now in the direct sunlight, and the rivulet of water had dried to a greasy chemical slick—and called down to Wendy.

"What do you want to eat when we get you out?"

"Ugh. I got no appetite." Her voice was closer now. It was like listening to someone shout from the next room. "The smell down here, it makes my head swim. What I'd really like is ice water."

Gwen thought, *People in hell want ice water,* and felt ill at heart.

"How about an ice water with a slice of lemon in it?" Erin called.

"How about an ice water with a lemon and a shot of gin, hold the water," Wendy said, and laughed. "Kidding. I got a hundred and twenty-four days sober. You'd be surprised how easy it is to get drunk even in jail."

"No, I wouldn't. I had a cellmate who kept mashed grapes and Wonder Bread in a plastic shower cap for a couple weeks to make some kinda hooch. That stuff was like the punch they served in Jonestown."

"How are you doing up there?"

Gwen shouted, "We're almost to you, girl. We'll have you out by dark."

"That doesn't tell me anything. It's always dark down here." She laughed again, a weak, confused laugh. "You hear creaking up there, Gwen? Like, metal creaking?"

"No. What are you hearing?"

"I don't know. Sometimes things creak. I guess this mess is still settling. I get crazy ideas like it's getting smaller in here. It's not getting smaller, is it?"

Erin said, "No, Wendy. I'm sure it isn't."

Maybe Erin was sure, but Gwen wasn't. She said, "Wendy? Where's the water now?"

For a few moments, Wendy didn't reply—Gwen wondered if she had heard her. But before Gwen could shout again, Wendy squeaked: "Oh, shit."

"Wendy, we're almost to you. We're going to get you out soon."

"Oh, shit. Gwen? It's almost over my boobs. It was only up to my navel before. It *is* getting smaller in here, isn't it? Like when you squeeze a paper cup full of water and it runs over the sides."

If Gwen had doubts about running a hot stone cutter before, she dismissed them now. They would save her with what they had or they wouldn't save her at all.

"You listen to me, kiddo. We aren't going to let you drown. You copy that?"

"You promise?"

"I promise," Gwen said, carefully avoiding Erin's eyes.

"I knew I might not get out. You ever think luck is like money? What I'm thinking, I used up most of my luck the night I had my car accident and my baby didn't get killed. I used up the rest not getting smooshed when the building fell. There's nothing left now. I'm busted, Gwen!"

"You don't need luck. You got me."

"Wendy?" Erin called. "He's going to begin cutting again in a minute."

"Ugh. Okay. You wouldn't believe the noise it makes down here—the roar of it. I was fading out last time, when he started cutting, and the sound scared me awake. For a minute I thought that *thing* was back."

Gwen felt a cold prickle across her back, between her shoulder blades, down her spine.

"What thing?" Erin asked.

"The thing that fell on the penitentiary. It hit us with a scream. I thought it was a bomb, like artillery, only it screamed again and again, after the first hit. It was *in* the building. You guys must know about it. I could hear people shooting at it. And some crazy Spanish bitch—'scuse my language, Reverend—was howling, 'el diablo esta aqui!' You know what that means?"

Gwen had picked up a little Spanish in her years riding in the ambulance jump seat . . . but that one required almost no familiarity with the language at all. *The devil is here.*

"What a nightmare you've been through," Erin said, giving Gwen a mystified look.

"Does anyone know what happened to us?"

"A gas main ruptured," Erin said. "If you heard gunfire, it might've been ammunition exploding in the heat." But she didn't sound like she believed it.

"No. No way. They were fighting that thing for almost fifteen minutes. You could hear them yelling for backup. You could hear the guards screaming for their lives. Is that what they're telling you, it was a gas main? They're lying, Erin. *Someone* is lying. I don't know what hit this place, but I think that Spanish lady was closer to it than you are. 'El infierno no tiene gobernante ahora porque el diablo está aquí.'" Wendy laughed and said, "You wouldn't believe it, a bozo like me, but I got As in Spanish. I was great at languages. My teacher used to say, Arthur, you've got a gift. If you work hard, you could have a real future. Well. He wasn't wrong. Everyone has a future. Mine was to die here. In a hole."

"You're not dying here," Gwen said, but she had no spit. She didn't like hearing Wendy call herself Arthur. She didn't like knowing Wendy Arthur was good at languages, like her oldest chum.

"Wendy?" Erin said. "Would you like to pray with me again? We've only got another minute."

"Yes, please. Can we pray for my son? I want to pray he'll know love . . . that the people who look after him will be better at it than I was."

"We can pray for your son. We can pray for the day you hold him again," Erin said.

The two of them began, and Gwen got up and walked away—reeled away, really. Her legs felt shaky. The sun had been beating down on her hard hat and she was lightheaded and woozy, half-stunned by the heat. She found Mark Ruffner talking with one of the structural engineers, a narrow-faced, sharp-nosed man in a pair of square-rimmed glasses.

"Mark," she said.

He held up a hand, palm out—*hang on a minute*—and said to the engineer, "We keep cutting."

The engineer pointed at the torn-open dollhouse looming above. "You're destabilizing what's left of the east wing. You need to back off. We can find another way. Let's dig in Zone Three. Get forty feet down and then burrow—"

"What's your time frame on that? Two weeks? Wendy Arthur doesn't have two more *days*. We cut."

The engineer put his hands on his hips. "And maybe lose six people instead of one?"

"I won't ask anyone to work in the pit without understanding the risks," Ruffner said. "If it comes to it, I'll cut myself. We're getting that girl out tonight. Right, Gwen?"

Gwen nodded. "You said it, boss."

But they weren't.

24.

When it happened, it happened fast.

They had cut a triangle out of the concrete slab, three feet wide along each side, and winched it free. Beneath was a bent girder, with more rubble beneath. But the girl was close now, her voice only feet away. The Pole bent to the girder and the saw hit the steel with a tortured whine. A brassy Catherine wheel of sparks flew from the spinning blade.

He was at it for most of a minute before Gwen saw the first thread of smoke. The slanted concrete platform now had a split running through it, a jagged crack running from one corner of the triangular opening. The Pole stood with his feet spread wide, his boots on either side of the fissure. The deeper the saw bit, the more it sounded like a hysterical scream. Gwen looked, and then looked again. A silky ribbon of smoke was coming from that crack. The chemical slick on the cement was fuming.

"Hey! Hey, we've got smoke!" Gwen cried from the rim of the crater. Erin saw it in the same moment and began to yell with her. They both stood on the edge of the concavity, waving their arms.

The big Pole didn't—couldn't—hear, but Ruffner was in the hole with him, and *he* heard. Heard, and looked around, and saw the smoke rising beneath him and grabbed the Pole. The saw cut out . . . but the scream continued for a few moments longer, a choked, panicked, wordless cry. Smoke boiled up out of the rubble beneath the girder. Wendy was down there at the heart of it, banging her pipe on the bed frame.

"Oh no," Erin said. "Oh, God. What's happening?"

"The sparks musta lit something up, lower down. A mattress. Some shitty insulation. I don't know, I—" Gwen said, but Erin wasn't listening. She had leapt into the hole, pushing through the other rescuers, and dropped to one knee.

"Wendy, we hear you. Hang on! Hang on, dear!"

Steel groaned. Something fell between Gwen and Erin, a chunk of rock, which raised a cloud of dust. When Gwen threw her head back and looked at the east wing, it seemed the whole rotten edifice was *swaying*, ever so slightly.

"Get out!" Gwen screamed, and leapt into the pit.

She began to push at the men gathered around the saw. She shoved the Pole and made him stagger. She shoved at Mark Ruffner, shoved at Ben and Julius, who had been moving debris by hand. "Get out!" she screamed again, and they looked up at the torn-open remains of the east wing and fled.

Gwen whirled to face Arthur's mother. Instead of running, Erin had flattened onto her stomach across the concrete. She had her face in the smoke coming up out of the triangular hole. Her face was slicked with sweat and ash, and she was coughing and yelling to the girl below.

"Wendy!" Erin Oakes yelled. "I'm here. I'm right here."

"We have to go!" Gwen screamed and got the woman by her arm and wrenched her up to her knees, then to her feet.

A concrete block fell and smashed, two feet to their right. A steel bed frame slid out of one of the open cells above them, dropped like a missile, and crashed to the rocks. There was a splitting sound, followed by one crack, and another. One of the steel braces that had been brought in to hold the structure up folded in the middle with a squeal. Gwen had Erin Oakes by the arm and hauled her back, to the edge of the concavity, spun her as if she were a child, and shoved her in the ass, drove her up the side of the hole, pushing her on whenever she tried to turn back. Erin stopped again at the edge of the crater and Gwen got an arm around her waist and almost lifted her, staggered three more steps, and the east wing fell behind them.

It didn't topple so much as *dissolve*. There was a last shudder and the constituent parts suddenly crumbled and thundered down in a smoking blizzard of granite, Sheetrock, rebar, and cement. Rubble buried the hole and everything around the hole. It was roaring for most of a minute, this once solid four-story building, coming apart like a glacier dropping into the sea. A flying brick hit Gwen in the small of her back, and she collapsed.

Erin and Gwen were engulfed in a rolling cloud of white chalk, of pulverized building. It whirled so thickly about them that Gwen was blinded for a time. The bitter, stale taste of rock and plaster filled her mouth. She couldn't see Erin anymore, but she had a hand on her hip and could hear her sobbing. Alive. Still alive.

Gwen turned on her side. Pain detonated in the small of her back, again and again. Bruised kidney, she thought, and she was right, bled for the next week like it was her period. She squinted into the gritty, ashy glare. A thousand sparks spun up from the collapse, flaring and disappearing: a whirlwind of burning butterflies. The sun was dim, white, distant, and cold. The cloud of debris eddied around her and for a moment, a black and serpentine shape seemed to rise with it, uncoiling its neck and opening its wings. It was perhaps only a trick of the eyes and a ringing head, but it looked for all the world as if a dragon of shadow had lifted itself up from the ruin and was opening its jaws ... not in a scream of victory but in a laugh of delight.

Almost got you, Gwen, that King of Shadow seemed to be saying. *Almost got you both.*

25.

They were in the bed together, Gwen and Arthur's mother, neither of them sleeping, when Erin started to speak.

"Did Arthur ever tell you why I went to jail?"

"Someone told me. I don't remember who." She remembered exactly who, remembered Van and Donna and Colin talking about it in a matter-of-fact sort of way, hanging out in the kitchen while Gwen washed their dishes.

The digital clock on the end table said it was 2:43 a.m. They had been lying there, both of them thinking about Wendy Arthur, for hours.

"There were six of us," Erin said. "Harold Mitchell, who was a philosophy professor at the university, was a self-taught electrician. He got us over the electrified fence, did something with jumper cables to divert the charge without tripping the alarm. We went in with hammers, garden shears, paint cans, and stencils. This was the navy yard in Portsmouth, New Hampshire. They had brought in the *Henry Jackson*—that's a US submarine—to arm it with the new Trident One missile, eight warheads on each, each warhead carrying the explosive force of over a million tons of TNT. A single missile with twenty-five times the power of the bomb that leveled Hiroshima. They said one would be enough to kill every man, woman, and child in Moscow, and they said it like it was something to be proud of. Like it was something to celebrate—that now we had a gun pointed at every child in Moscow. If someone pointed a gun at a child—if someone pointed a gun at ten children—wouldn't you do anything you could to make them put it down? So we brought in stencils to spray peace signs on the submarine. And hammers to dent the tail fins on the missiles. That was how we were going to stop World War III. With red spray paint and tools from Ace Hardware.

"We got down to the docks, but we never made it to the sub. We got close enough to see it, but a few navy boys spotted us and came after us. They thought it was a scream. You should've heard 'em. Like little boys playing tag in the schoolyard. Right up until someone died, it was funny. Even *we* were laughing, running from them. I remember thinking about how I would tell Arthur the story later, my night of true-blue real-life adventure. Harold and I hid from the navy kids and doubled back. I was determined to do some damage. I was out of breath and laughing, but I was deadly serious too. I wanted them to know I was a mother. I wanted to let them know what I thought of threatening to turn children to ash. Harry and I worked our way back around to this concrete wharf and the sub was right there, right alongside it. We were still a couple hundred feet away, in a sort of side parking lot, stretched out flat under a pickup truck. That's where we were when this retired police officer came up on us. His name was Jason Einaudi, sixty-one years old. Three children. Two grandchildren. A Patriots tattoo on his arm. He grabbed Harold by the foot and dragged him out from under the truck, and when Harry tried to get up, Einaudi dropped onto the small of his back with one knee. So hard Harold screamed. Jason Einaudi was almost two hundred and fifty pounds, and Harold was built like a skinny eleven-year-old. As I got out from under the truck, Harry tried to lift his head, and Einaudi bounced his face off the sidewalk. Einaudi had his teeth gritted—he looked out of his mind. I thought he was going to kill my friend in front of me . . . so I sprayed red paint in his face. I didn't shove him. I didn't hit him. I just wanted to distract him. It wasn't even going to blind him ... Einaudi had a big pair of glasses on, so the paint couldn't get in his eyes.

"But it scared him. He fell back into the next car with a scream. I think he thought it was Mace or pepper spray. Maybe he thought I threw blood on him. He grabbed his gun, even though he couldn't see, and both of us took off. We made it four steps before the gun went off. I don't know if he meant to shoot. Harold staggered and I thought he had been shot. I screamed and stopped, but Harry righted himself and kept going. If I hadn't stopped, I wouldn't have looked back. I wouldn't have seen Jason Einaudi with his throat torn open. The bullet ricocheted off a nearby forklift, bounced back, and took a piece out of Einaudi's neck. You could've fired that gun three hundred times and never got that result again.

"I ran back. I thought Harry would come back too. I thought he was right next to me. We were both pacifists. You don't leave someone dying if you're a pacifist. I got my shirt off and wadded it up to stop the bleeding. I called for help, but there was a klaxon going off by then. No one heard me. No one saw us hunched down between the cars. It wasn't the blood loss that killed Jason Einaudi. It was a heart attack. He'd already had one, a few years before, which was what forced his retirement from the police. He was gone a long time before anyone saw us there. So was Harold. Harold got back to the others and over the fence and still teaches to this day. I walked out from between the cars with blood all over me, crying my eyes out, and hardly even noticed when they put handcuffs on me. I was found guilty of murder on federal property—a man had died while I was in the act of felony trespass, which is not only considered homicide under the law, but carries the death penalty. Only I had provided medical aid to the dying man and I was a person of faith. I could've avoided jail altogether if I had been willing to name the people who entered the navy base with me. I wouldn't do that, so I was sentenced to twelve years, with a three-year minimum. After my sentence was announced, someone called my name, and I turned, and Jason

Einaudi's daughter, Heather, leaned over the rail and spat in my face. I can't say I blame her. I wouldn't have blamed my own son if he'd spat on me."

Erin was quiet for a while. A tractor trailer roared past out on the highway. She said, "I think I forgot whose life we were trying to save today, Gwen. We set out to save Wendy, but I think by the end I thought we were saving mine. I was going to give her back her kid . . . and then maybe I could have back mine."

"You never lost Arthur," Gwen said.

Erin smiled in the dark. "I don't suppose you notice he ran for England just about three seconds after I was paroled."

Gwen didn't have a reply to that.

"Do you think you can ever save enough lives to make up for even one killing?" Erin asked.

Not even one, Gwen thought of saying, *and believe me, I've tried, Reverend.*

Instead, Gwen told her, "I think Officer Einaudi should've left his damn gun in his damn holster. I think it was one kind of travesty that the court found you guilty. And it's another that you think they were right."

Erin took Gwen's hand in the dark. "God bless you, Gwen Underfoot, but I don't think you can really understand what it's like—to think you're going to save a life and end one instead."

Gwen's throat hurt, it was so constricted with emotion, but she didn't utter a sound. If she did—if she lost her grip on her emotions—she wasn't sure if she would laugh or sob.

16.

A little after 5:00 a.m., the reverend let herself out to walk across the street to the all-night gas mart and get them some coffees and cheap breakfast pastries. Gwen hadn't slept and still couldn't, so she sat on the edge of the bed and she called Donna.

"It's early, Gwen," Donna said, in a voice crabbed with sleep.

"No, darlin'," Gwen said. "It's not early. It's late. We got things to talk about, and we should've talked about 'em a long time ago. There's four hundred women dead because you wanted to wipe out one of 'em, and she probably didn't even do what you think she done."

"Doesn't matter if she did or not. She helped bury a murdered foster child."

"She was as much a victim as any of those children."

"She still knew it was wrong to bury a child in a cellar. A nine-year-old—"

"Oh, give it a rest. I didn't call to argue about Francine Trout, and I'm not going to play the moral version of rock-paper-scissors with you. There's forty-eight guards, six night nurses, and a half dozen other staff members burned up with all the prisoners in Black Cricket. You want to claim you have a right to judge any of the women in that prison, when you just killed four hundred plus yourself? Erin Oakes was down on her knees yesterday, praying with a woman trapped in the rubble, when a wall fell. It almost crushed her. It almost crushed *me*. Do you remember Erin Oakes? Woman who officiated at your brother's wedding? Spoke at his funeral? *Arthur's mother?* Do you vaguely remember how we all sold our souls to King Sorrow to keep *her* from being hurt? Don't you fucking get it yet? We gave away something precious—we gave away our happiness, our peace—to protect the people we love. Only the people we love *will be lost anyway*. King Sorrow will take everything we give him and he'll take everything we wanted to save. He's already started! Look at what happened to Van."

When Donna replied, she sounded almost businesslike. "You're hysterical, Gwen. I can't do hysteria before my first cup of coffee. The difference between you and me is you want to live in a world where we all pay to look after murderers and rapists and child abusers, and I think a world without those people would be a fucking Eden. You run around in that ambulance of yours, resuscitating drug addicts, so they can get stoned again and maybe run someone down when they're behind the wheel of a car. Whereas King Sorrow burns the wicked right off the face of the earth before they can hurt anyone else. You want to ask me who I think does more good? I say all hail the King."

Gwen sat with the phone in her hand for a long time after Donna hung up, while the little hotel room slowly filled with a gray morning glow.

27.

The following September, Amos Finch, a retired phys ed teacher in Florida, fifty-five and Caucasian, was arrested in a sting; he had started up a conversation with whom he thought was a thirteen-year-old in a chat room, and agreed to meet her in Sarasota, only to find the vice squad waiting for him. He made bail and the following evening shot himself with an unregistered gun.

A careful investigation of his house revealed a hole in the wall behind the washing machine and a bundle of photographs and little girls' underwear, several prurient videotapes of girls changing into swimming suits . . . and a friendship bracelet identified as belonging to the late Cady Lewis. Finch had briefly been a suspect in the Lewis abduction—he coached her swim team and owned a black van—but had been cleared back in the day, on the testimony of his now ex-wife who claimed he was home and napping at the time of Cady's disappearance. When the police went to interview the ex about her former testimony, they discovered she had fled the country as soon as she heard of Finch's death.

In the weeks that followed, one of Francine Trout's former court-appointed attorneys wrote an opinion piece for the *Miami*

Herald, claiming that Francine had been highly suggestible and would gladly have admitted to almost anything if she thought it might mean a better prison, a better cell, and a chance to be close to horses. He used the piece to call for reform in the way confessions were extracted. He said Francine had been a victim all her life and only a society wild for payback could have been blind to it.

On her talk show, Donna McBride was entirely unsympathetic and reminded her viewers that Francine Trout had participated in the abuse and murder of a foster child.

"That child was buried in a basement and Francine was buried in rubble," Donna said. "Don't tell me God doesn't have a sense of fair play."

Gwen, back in Maine by then, was going to call Arthur, had to talk to him, wanted, maybe, to cry a little to someone who cared. But at the last moment she remembered it was something like two in the morning in Oxford. So instead she sat in her open window, staring up into the star-littered night. Now and then a plane would cross the darkness, big as a dragon, climbing into the sky from the Portland International Jetport, lights blinking at the ends of its wings. She wished she were up there on one of them, flying away, instead of down here, in Gogan. At some point she got down a steel thermos of dragon tears, holding all Llewellyn Wren had not swallowed. She swished them back and forth, inside the thermos, and wondered if they tasted as sweet as Llewellyn had said.

28.

Bitches were crying from one end of the block to the other. Word had come after lights out, passed along by one of the guards: Black Cricket prison, in Vermont, had been destroyed in a massive gas explosion. They were already talking three or four hundred dead, a disaster on an enormous scale, women crushed, women burned to blackened bones. When Daphne Nighswander thought about it, she just had to laugh.

She should've been there. She should've died with them. Only a scrawny, addicted born-again had killed herself, and in her suicide note had blabbed about Daphne's heroin supply. The powers that be had shipped Daphne off to the supermax in West Virginia. They wanted to punish her for being a bad girl, but they had saved her life instead. Seemed like God was watching out for someone, and it wasn't emaciated born-agains who committed suicide because they felt guilty about licking a little pussy and being addicted to black tar.

"And you know what day it is," said the woman sitting at the foot of Daphne's bed. Her occasional cellmate.

"Sure do, babe," Daphne whispered. "The day they took you from me."

There was a doctor who said Daphne had done damage to the white matter in her brain, probably through the habitual use of methamphetamines in her younger days. She said Daphne might experience issues with her balance and could struggle to retain new information. She might even hallucinate. Daphne didn't say that she had been seeing Jayne off and on for over a year. They might prescribe a pill to make her go away. Daphne didn't want that—Jayne was good company. And on lonesome nights like this, when the cellblock was full of people whispering and sobbing and carrying on, it felt good to have someone close.

Jayne stretched out behind her, spooning her from behind and putting one blackened, withered arm around her mother's stomach. She was good company, but Daphne couldn't quite get used to looking at her face, where the skin had blistered off to show the charred muscle and cooked skull beneath.

"Easter," Jayne said.

"The day of the resurrection," Daphne said to the dead girl holding her from behind.

"The day of the return," Jayne promised. "Your return is

coming, Momma. The stone will roll back and you'll walk out of this place where the world tried to bury you and you will pass judgment upon the quick and the dead."

"I plan on being the quick," Daphne said. "There's some others are going to be the dead."

"Shut up in there," a guard said, and banged the barred window of her cell.

Daphne squeezed her lips shut to clamp down on fresh laughter and burrowed back into her daughter's embrace.

1.

The Gulfstream kissed the runway at Heathrow without a bounce or a squeak and Colin Wren took off his headset, pleased with how he had set her down, aglow from six hours above the Atlantic, no one but him and his cute little copilot, Ron, a twenty-nine-year-old with bubblegum-pink lipstick and a mess of curly brown hair. Ronnie, he knew, was debating with a couple of friends whether or not Colin was down to F. He knew because he had read the last six weeks of her text messages that morning. Colin didn't go anywhere with anyone without reviewing their emails and messages and call history, even if he had known them for years.

I could pretend I dropped something on the floor of the cockpit and then blow him at 30,000 feet what do you think y/y? was one message.

Y! I still think he's gay but he can shut his eyes and pretend you're a dude, replied her friend. He probably loves you have a boy's name and no tits.

Colin had to laugh at that. Ronnie's friends were as spunky as she was. As for finding out whether or not he was gay, Ron would have to wait a few days while he took care of some business in the southwest of England.

They had a Mercedes with black-tinted windows waiting for him on the runway. It drove him six hundred feet to a VIP entrance. That was all it did, drove people like him from their private planes to their private entrance. He felt a little sad for it, a hundred thousand dollars of brand-new CL-Class Benz, with black leather seats and a massive twelve-cylinder under the hood, condemned to ferry wealthy fat-asses across a distance they could've walked. A young man used a scanner on his passport in the small room where people like him passed through border control without waiting in line.

"What are you going to do in London for three days, Ron?" Colin asked her, while they rolled their baggage down a sterile white hallway that would lead them to the main lobby in Terminal 5. He was being polite, he already knew her plans. High Tea at Fortnum & Mason with a friend; an afternoon shopping at Harrods; shopping for lingerie at Agent Provocateur that she hoped but was not sure she would get to use before the weekend was out.

"I've got a hotel room at the Savoy," she said, "with a view of Big Ben. Do I have to do anything? Can't I stay in bed and have men with sexy English accents bring me mimosas?"

He noted how she made sure he knew where she was staying. Not that he didn't already know. He didn't need spyware on her phone for that . . . it was right on the company credit card.

"You should stop by if you get a chance," she said. "They have an amazing bar. They imported a bartender from Scandinavia to make special Scandi drinks you can only get there."

"What's in a special Scandi drink? Ground-up, fermented gnomes?"

"You'll have to stop by and find out, d-doll," she said, and blushed. "Damn it, I can't believe I tried to call you 'doll.' I'm so bad at this. Guys usually make passes at *me*. Did you hear me stammer just now? I used to stammer as a kid—I was a hopeless case until sixth grade." She gave him an affectionate, embarrassed look—her cheeks were flaming—and he grinned and touched her elbow.

"You're talking to a man who is allergic to his own hair," Colin said. "No apology required. Let's see how things look when I'm back in London."

When they passed through the door and into the reception area on the other side of customs, she was swinging her overnight bag and looking like she wanted to whistle.

Arthur sat at a table for two in Café Nero, beardy and professorial in a woolly Fair Isle cardigan and shabby corduroys, his smooth head capped by his brightly colored Nepalese smoking hat. He rose and took Colin into a hug, both of them as physically comfortable with the other as brothers.

When Arthur loosened his embrace, though, his brow was furrowed with worry. "Are you ready for this? Where we're going—it's dangerous. I've taken every precaution, but it could all go sideways very quickly."

Colin patted Arthur's stomach. "You haven't taken *every* precaution or you wouldn't have let your gym membership lapse. What's this, Paddington? Can't resist the donuts in the teacher's lounge?"

Arthur stepped back, considered his podge, lifted his chin proudly, and said, "A certain girth is only natural for a man of wisdom and education. History is littered with rotund fellows that contributed greatly to the world's store of knowledge. Think of Chesterton. Orson Welles. Jonathan Belushi, PhD of brewskis. I could go on."

"You know why history is littered with 'em? Cause they fell dead on their fat asses." They turned toward the exits, Colin rolling his carbon-steel suitcase behind him. "Besides, I don't recall you had the option of leaving me out. I don't want to brag, but I only needed six weeks to solve a problem you've been working on for most of a decade. You knew what it was going to cost you."

"I do. It's what it might cost *you*—that's what I'm worried about."

Arthur led him out into a concrete courtyard and a spitting rain. He flipped up the hood of his parka and stuck his hands together so they disappeared into the sleeves.

He looked more than ever, Colin thought, like a grave and friendless monk. It was impossible to imagine him throwing back popcorn and laughing in a movie with a girl—even with Gwen—but easy to imagine him lighting candles for vespers and looking forward to a nice private scourging in a cold cell later.

"You can sleep on the ride if you like," Arthur said. "Personally I think it's mad to go south tonight."

"I'm not tired. I'm energized. I've never seen a troll before. I've dealt with hundreds of them online, but this is the first one I'll be meeting in person."

"Trolls online," Arthur mused. "What a thought."

"It's the second age of the trolls. They've returned from a ten-thousand-year sleep in Mirkwood to post dick pics on the internet."

"You think you're being funny, but some of them probably *are* trolls . . . and I'm not speaking euphemistically. I have reliable information that the Russians are farming them. They grow trolls like potatoes in the permafrost of Siberia," said Arthur.

They had stopped at a car, a vile Austin Mini Metro, mustard yellow, a little cube of a thing sitting on comically small tires. Going from the Gulfstream to Arthur's Mini was like stepping from a bullet train onto someone's toboggan.

"Arthur, are you fucking with me? Because that would be very out of character for you."

Arthur had a tiny smile playing at the corners of his mouth, but only threw open the driver's-side door and told him to stow his stuff in the back.

2.

It rained, a cold steady drizzle, and the rubber strip had come loose from one wiper so it was just slapping water around. The headlights cast a dim yellow glow as they made their way along the Great West Road out of London, past flooded soccer pitches, sooty chest-high stone walls, and brick rows of flats. Colin's knees bumped the dashboard, and every time they struck a pothole the glove compartment popped open.

"I love your car," Colin said. "It's so you."

"Cramped, out of shape, and rusting? What are you driving these days?"

"Depends where I'm at. I've got a prototype Tesla Roadster at the Malibu place. Elon let me have it for a song because I was an early investor. He's only made about ten of them so far. You've never driven anything like it. The closest I'll ever come to flying an X-Wing fighter."

"What's an Elon?"

"It's a South African emerald mine that dates hot models and has far too many opinions. What are we listening to? Is that a *cassette* player? That's so charming. I didn't know they still put those in cars."

"I just started buying CDs," Arthur said.

"Well, stop. Wait two years and you'll be able to download any song you want."

"To what?"

"To your phone. Oh, shit, I forgot. I gave you a cell phone and you never use it."

"I have a landline. Will I be able to download songs to that? No, never mind. I wouldn't want to even if I could. It would be too much like being on hold."

The cockpit swam with calypso horns and an insouciant West Indian voice. Colin thought it was probably an old recording—it had that flattened hiss he associated with the era before compressed digital sound.

"My people made this music," Arthur said. "My father's people, anyway. The Windrush folk. They came to London after the war. They rebuilt the skyline by day and they rebuilt the English libido by night."

"That's interesting, because the melodies and lyrics are cheerful, but the effect is melancholy. It really drives home that you *could* be some place with palm trees, beaches, rum, and minimally dressed women—but instead you're in England."

"Your scorn for England is misplaced, Colin. You owe this nation everything. Turing dreamt up the computer—if not for him, you'd still be whacking off to magazines. Arthur C. Clarke, Anthony Burgess, H. G. Wells. Orwell. Englishmen single-handedly invented the future."

"That's understandable. Anything to escape their present."

"Who am I kidding? You never did whack off to porn. Be honest with me, Colin. Have you ever looked at a bar code and got a boner?"

"I love you, Arthur. I hated it when you left. Hated it. I'll never understand it. You've lived here—eating their crap food, shivering in their badly heated flats—for fifteen years, *by choice*. Bad enough you left me. But you left Gwen. How could you?"

Arthur considered for a time, then said, "I let her down, and she had the good sense to hold me accountable instead of making excuses for me. Once I knew we weren't going to be together, there was no reason to come back. It was easier to do the work here. When it comes to dragons, only the Chinese surpass England's body of study, and unfortunately, I could never pick up Mandarin. I tried. It kicked my ass."

"Ah, well. Give it another fifteen years and you'll be able to translate any language in real time, probably with your cell phone. If you ever buy one. No one will need to study languages again."

"I hope you're wrong."

Colin laughed. "Of course you do. You never want to do anything the easy way."

"When you're translating yourself—reading medieval French, say—you aren't just taking one word and mentally transposing it to English. You're able to think and feel things you *can't* think and feel in modern American. Things only a French yeoman might've thought and felt about his place in a cosmos ruled by a God at war with a beast—the beast in the human soul."

Colin was quiet for a moment, letting it roll over him. Then he said, "That's a lovely line of thought. Is that from one of your lectures?"

"Intro to Medieval French Poetry. I usually deliver that one in the first class. How'd it land?"

"Aces, man. You gave me a shiver."

"That's why they pay me the big bucks."

They hit a pothole. The glove compartment popped open.

"Euphemistically," Arthur said.

"You should really let me put a word in with Elon for you," Colin told him.

3.

"No, seriously, how come you don't sleep?"

Black trees rushed by in the wet darkness. They were approaching a place called Basingstoke, which sounded like the name for a fearless vampire hunter.

"I never have," Colin said. "I do my best work after everyone else is asleep. I can check on the Nikkei index, write my most important emails, then hit the treadmill. I usually only sleep from about one to five a.m., out like a light. Donna says I don't move, don't snore. It's like I'm petrified."

Arthur nodded in the dark. "I read somewhere that sociopaths also suffer from insomnia."

"Well, and I take Adderall, mixed with an MAOI and the very occasional microdose of DMT. That keeps me perky."

"I understood at least half a dozen words in that sentence. Are you and Donna together now?"

"Not in any old-fashioned sense. Not in the sense you probably mean. I think you're aware I'm polyamorous. You know, *Homo sapiens* are literally the only ape that shows an inclination toward monogamy. I view the institution of marriage a bit like . . . well, like medieval French. There's a reason it went away."

"To complain that I could only be married once was like complaining I could only be born once," Arthur told him.

Colin frowned. "You're quoting someone."

"Chesterton."

"Ah," Colin said. "And I *thought* it sounded like John Belushi. Tell me, do you ever get your dick wet? It's fine to be married, but you aren't, except maybe in your imagination."

"You, of all people, Colin, should know not to underestimate the imagination. What's King Sorrow, if not a weaponized act of the imagination? He's a bad dream with teeth. For a few years, I wondered if we'd ever wake up from him."

Colin lifted an eyebrow. "So you think there's a way to be rid of him?"

"I'm glad we're doing this a week after Easter. King Sorrow wouldn't admit it—he doesn't care to admit weakness—but it tires him to pull himself through into our reality. After his Easter feast he slithers back into the Long Dark and sleeps for a few months. If we're going to move against him, this is the best time. He isn't watching. And yes, I may have found a way. By the way, how did Easter go this year? I didn't see anything on the news or in the papers."

"You wouldn't, would you? We blasted a few dozen soldiers for AQI out of the slums of Ramadi. There wasn't much coverage. The Department of Defense keeps a tight lid. You know AQI? Al-Qaeda in Iraq?"

"Oh? Al-Qaeda is in Iraq now? That's new. Because they weren't when we invaded."

Colin smiled indulgently. They had reached the outskirts of an old tension. The shock and awe campaign of April 2003 that had obliterated Baghdad—sheets of fire raining from the sky, temples caving in, vehicles blown off the roads, and civilians buried in rubble—had mostly been King Sorrow. It had been Arthur's turn to choose, and he had attended to Colin, read his research, listened when he warned that if Saddam Hussein survived the spring, he might have a nuclear weapon by fall. Colin had the intel to prove it. Only it turned out the intel was a pile of lies. By some accounts six thousand people had died in a week, and although King Sorrow could not have been personally responsible for more than 20 percent of the fatalities, Arthur had felt the weight of them all.

After the last day of Hilary in Oxford—that was what they called their spring term, because they were too ancient and erudite to call it second fucking semester like any other college—Arthur had collected some things in a sturdy mountaineer's backpack, caught a train to Scotland, and disappeared. Really disappeared, beyond even Colin's formidable powers to track and trace. Colin had feared Arthur had decided to join Donovan in the Long Dark, but in the end he had come back, reemerging with his beard thicker than ever. He'd missed Trinity but returned in time to teach the Michaelmas term.

"Where'd you go?" Colin had asked.

"I found a ruined abbey," Arthur had replied, "and stayed to pray. After a while some of the monks joined me."

"There were monks living in the ruin?"

"These monks weren't living at all," Arthur said, and offered no more. Colin didn't doubt that Arthur had spent weeks praying with ghosts only he could see. Colin had, himself, acquired something very close to telepathy, because when you could see everyone's texts and emails, and read their search history, you could know everything relevant about them. But Arthur had a search engine of his own—a head full of fairy tales and the Surrealist's Glass that showed him the secret truth of things. It fascinated Colin, the way Arthur seemed to live in a separate, heightened reality, full of Jungian symbolism and metaphors made real.

"What about getting Osama?" Arthur asked now. "We've got a dragon. Why haven't we used it? He's the one person in the entire world I'm sure actually deserves to meet King Sorrow."

"I'm more interested in stopping the *next* Osama, not in punishing an insane old man who lives in a state of terror, always fearing this is the day someone from Seal Team Six will send him back to Allah. He's the one trapped in the tower now, with the fire at his back. No way out, no hope for him. He can jump if he wants, if he has the courage, which he doesn't. Or he can wait for the fire to reach him at last. And it will."

"So did you kill the next Osama in Iraq this Easter? Or did you give birth to him by burning his family alive?"

Arthur's doubts and challenges didn't distress Colin but didn't terribly interest him either. They had been having the same conversation for fifteen years, when Colin thought it had been all talked out in fifteen minutes. He wasn't even terribly upset that, in the end, Saddam had been too incompetent and lazy to build a weapons program that could threaten the Western world. It was enough that he *might've* and was crushed entirely, his country smashed, everyone who supported him slaughtered or humiliated. Game theory suggested it was helpful to send the message that the United States might overreact at any time, obliterate a nation just because it could. Other countries would have to fear what America might do on a whim; they would learn it was a mistake to pull a dragon's tail.

"I don't know if Iraq will produce the next Osama in twenty years. But I do know some of *our* soldiers will live because many of *theirs* didn't. That's the simple arithmetic of a war, and I like to see the equations come out in our favor. The First Armored are going into Ramadi in a month—you didn't hear that from me—and King Sorrow just made sure a bunch of our boys will come back out."

"You know a lot about what's going on. They keep you close, the intelligence people, don't they?"

"I prefer to think that I keep *them* close."

They had come to an arrangement after North Carolina. The week after Colin brought Donna home to The Briars, he reached out to Paul Follett . . . the man Donna referred to, even now, as Mr. Francis. In late May, Paul and Colin had gone for a walk together on Boston Common and hammered out their agreement. The national security apparatus would keep its distance and they'd make sure other interested parties, public and private, kept theirs. They had to; their cooperation was no longer optional. Colin had emails, PowerPoints, reports, and images that would make Abu Ghraib look like Disney World. He had a record of every nasty snatch-torture-and-kill Thermopylae had done while on the payroll of the federal government, and he assured Follett that it was all on a dead man's switch. It would be released if Colin went missing for even thirty-six hours.

But Follett didn't walk away with nothing. Colin would be supplied with a monthly intelligence report and recommendations, which he could distribute to the rest of the Get-Even Gang; Paul made sure that Colin received the Pentagon's "Shopping List" every fall, the names of the men they most wanted to put in cold storage. It was a thoughtful gesture . . . although Colin's firm was already in the business of handling most of the government's web services, and his own information was broader and deeper than anything Paul could offer him.

In the end, Follett had even offered Colin and company a "consultancy fee." Colin had turned it down, couldn't say yes, not unless he wanted to wake up some morning, his crotch throbbing and wet, and Donna holding his scrotum in one hand and a pair of garden shears in the other.

"They killed her brother," Arthur said. "I don't understand why Donna would accept your having an agreement with them at all."

"Everyone who killed her brother is dead, and they were all in the employ of a now-defunct private security company. Only Paul Follett, the NSA man, walked away from Cherokee Island, and Donna seems to think he's half the reason she walked away herself. Also: we've been able to demand our share of concessions. Key appointments. Key firings. That kind of thing. I can't tell you how good it's been for her to exert control, to know they're afraid of her instead of the other way around. John McCain is going to run in 2008, but I'll tell you what—I'm pretty sure I can fix it so Donna can pick his VP for him. I was thinking that would be a cute birthday present."

"Not if we wipe out King Sorrow. Then we won't have anything left to trade."

"But we'll also be free," Colin said. "And I know we all want that."

4.

Arthur had booked them rooms at a public house that had been serving pints since the American colonies had broken away from the empire: a sprawling, timber-framed place with gables and a slate roof. The front door was flanked by stone corbels, a glowering face carved into each—a lumpish nose and eyes staring out from beneath a jutting brow, a couple of monstrous hooked teeth—they were almost tusks—protruding from beneath their lower lips. Colin did a double take at the sight, then looked meaningfully at Arthur, who nodded slightly.

"That's our boy," Arthur said. "He's been operating in these parts for eight, nine hundred years at least."

"How could anyone carve an image of him? I thought men can't see him for what he is."

Arthur tipped his head to one side, thinking this over. At last, he said, "I'll explain tomorrow. Let's get out of the rain and get some shut-eye."

Colin's room was the best in the house. Two rooms, really, a study connected to a bedroom. An uneven floor, doorways he had to duck under, a clutter of eighteenth- and nineteenth-century furniture. None of it was really to Colin's taste. He preferred Pacific coast modern, clean lines, big windows, minimalist décor. It was as cold inside as it was out, despite the blazing radiator tucked into one corner of his rooms. He slept three hours, then got up just before dawn to go for his run. He took the Castle Road through town, past bakeries and tourist shops, past an ancient post office with a swaybacked and mossy roof. He plunged down a steep and narrow road while the sun set fire to the world behind him, lighting the tops of the trees. At the bottom of the lane, he took a sharp left and drove himself up the steep coastal path, no more than a ribbon of dirt winding through knee-high straw. He found himself atop a monumental cliff. The wind blasted across the ledge, a cold and briny gust that stung his cheeks. Below, where cliffs met the blue crash of the Atlantic, the rock faces were pitted with vast yawning caverns. Arthur had told him the whole coast was Swiss-cheesed with such caverns.

A tower of rock rose on the far side of a dizzying chasm, and the ruins of Tintagel were scattered across the top of it. It looked like a green chessboard for giants, with great crude blocks of stone for pieces. There was no way to get over there, to reach those barbaric ruins, except by descending to the beach below and then climbing a jagged and precarious staircase cut into the side of the granite. One half expected to see a band of shivering, desperate hobbits making their way up those steps.

The serfs had broken their backs building Tintagel for some unwashed, flea-bitten lord, and now it was just a dramatic pile of rock, something to show the kids before you bought them wooden swords in the gift shop. The thought amused Colin—all that labor, and it was ultimately so pointless. The Romans had deployed their efforts more productively, creating a modern system of currency, knowing full well that finance was more effective than the sword when it came to subjugating a people. And of course, when it came to one's own defense, a castle was nothing next to money.

He was back in the pub, working on his second coffee, and had just finished reading yesterday's *Wall Street Journal* when Arthur joined him. In his burly fisherman's sweater and baggy khakis, he looked thoroughly English, all the American rubbed right off him by fifteen years in Oxford. Arthur settled at the corner table with him and ordered himself the sort of breakfast Colin associated with heart disease. Colin himself had worked out a diet optimized for performance, most of which he could consume either as a shake or in tablet form. It always pleased him when he could make it through the day without touching a fork.

"You were going to tell me about the troll," Colin said.

Arthur was distracted, didn't seem to hear him right away. He kept looking out toward the little reception area.

"You know some of it already," Arthur said.

"You told me grown-ups can't see Svangur for what he is, and yet he's carved into the posts to either side of the front door of this very inn. I assume those carvings weren't made by children."

Arthur peered into the lobby for a moment longer, then swiveled his head around to take Colin in. "You can't consciously see him if he doesn't want you to. But the unconscious mind registers a lot that we miss in the everyday rush of our lives. It's a little like when one's wife is having an affair . . . you don't know for the longest time and then one day all is revealed. And yet later, it seems to you, some part of you *did* know, all along."

"As Rummy says," Colin told him, "there's what you *know* you know, there's what you know you *don't* know, and then there's what you *don't* know you don't *know* . . . the unknown unknowns."

"Rummy?"

"Rumsfeld. Donald." Colin and Rummy spoke on the phone a few times a year and had dinner now and then, when Colin was in Washington.

Arthur winced slightly, as if his back was stiff. "Yes, well—this really belongs to a fourth category, one that . . . *Rummy* . . . missed: what you don't know you already know. The unknown *knowns*. Artists may be particularly in touch with that. Sometimes I think the whole act of painting or writing a poem is to try and access that reservoir of things that are known unconsciously. Children, of course, *always* see a troll for what he is. You can't get anything by them. Adults, on the other hand, are mostly hopeless. They live too much in the world to see beyond it."

"But *we'll* be able to see him as he is. Svangur. The troll."

Arthur put his hand in the pocket of his trousers. "Yes." And he set a monocle on the table between them, a thin, scratched lens set in a dull silver hoop.

"The Surrealist's Glass," Colin said. "May I?"

"Yes. I only ask that you don't look at *me* through it."

Colin cocked his head at that. "No?"

"I don't want to be seen through the glass, and I wouldn't look at a friend through it either. I don't even look at myself. Not anymore. I did once, and it made me sick."

The idea fascinated Colin. "What did you see?"

"My own true face. No one should have to see that."

Colin lifted the lens and scanned the room. At first he saw only the room, through a foggy haze of scratches. The barkeep had his back turned to them and was indolently cleaning a glass with a rag while he watched football highlights on a muted TV. A cat slept under a table. Colin was about to put the lens down . . . when he saw a dark eyeball in the lintel of the back door. It looked as if it was carved there, until it blinked. Colin cried out.

He lowered the Surrealist's Glass and pushed it back to Arthur. "There's an eyeball in that door."

Arthur nodded. "Dryad. A lot of these old buildings have butchered dryads in the beams. Tree spirits."

"I love that," Colin said.

"You wouldn't if you saw a gaping mouth, open in a scream," Arthur said. "It can take a dryad that's been hacked into pieces a few hundred years to die."

Colin thought he would still love it even then.

"Remind me: How many bridges have you searched under for this troll?" Colin asked.

"Three or four hundred. And I might've looked under three or four hundred more without your clever little—what did you call it? Algorithm?"

"Well. You told me the troll needed to eat. You said he likes lamb and fat children. You said he'd have a crypt—a cave system—to keep his hoard and that he'd stay there come hell or high water . . . not that high water would bother him since he has a certain amphibian quality. And you said it would be a place where blood had been spilled . . . that your troll—Svangur—would like the smell of it. Once you've outlined the parameters of the search, it's just a matter of pouring the information in and letting the software connect the dots. The UK has several impressive national organizations that do work to find missing children, and almost all of them use our software. Some of them have already uploaded a truly stupendous quantity of data about lost kids. Knowing Svangur likes 'em buttery and fat was the key. Five of the fattest kids to go missing in England in the last hundred and fifty years disappeared in the area around Slaughterbridge. To be honest, the name of the bridge itself was sort of a red flag, don't you think?"

"You would. Only 'slaughter' is an Old English word for a swamp, not a battle."

"In other linguistic trivia, you can't spell 'slaughter' without 'laughter.'"

"Only five children," Arthur said. "Somehow I thought he'd take more than that. But of course, I was thinking on a human time scale. After making a meal of someone's chubby daughter he probably needs to sleep it off for a while. And he can make do with goat, sheep. Fish. Children are a pleasure, not a necessity. Some of the reading suggests trolls may even be a bit like cicadas, emerging cyclically, every nine years or so. He shows up, munches on some livestock, goes back to bed. Maybe every second or third time he's awake, he'll devour a boy or a girl as a special treat."

"I was perplexed by the lack of any evidence for a historical massacre at Slaughterbridge, though. Nothing in World War II. Nothing in World War I. No great bloody labor clash. I went back hundreds of years. Nothing."

"Hundreds of years wasn't far enough. Geoffrey of Monmouth named it as the location of Arthur's final battle, where he slew his son, Mordred, and was mortally wounded himself. That may have been the massacre we were looking for."

"As I said, I'm surprised you didn't already check Slaughterbridge out."

"This country is full of rivers, and every one of them has been choked with corpses at one time or another—verifiably, not just mythically. Every bridge in this country has seen tragedy—a battle, a suicide, a collapse, a flash flood. And Cornwall is chock to the brim—the absolute brim—with gift shops selling King Arthur T-shirts just because some old book mentioned that Lancelot shagged a barmaid behind a nearby haystack."

"Arthur, I *have* been meaning to ask. The trolls I remember in the stories, they seem to be disagreeable sorts. Tell me again why you think this one is going to cooperate? I mean, are we sure he won't just tear off my arm and beat you to death with it?"

"I'm not sure about that at all. I told you I have one . . . well, call it a talisman . . . that might protect us, but I can't be positive it will work without trying it." Even as he spoke, he was rising from his chair and raising an arm. "Robin!"

Which was when Colin Wren got his first surprise of the day. A woman in jeans and a moss-colored corded sweater was swaggering across the lobby and into the bar, a wool cap pulled over her blond hair. Colin had first met Robin Fellows at Van and Allie's wedding; he had last seen her at Van's funeral. In between those two events, she had published the book that had led to Van's death in a cement stairwell. It had been brainlessly reckless to write the book in the first place; she had aided and abetted Donovan in his criminal stupidity. Aiding the Get-Even Gang in acts of criminal stupidity seemed to be something of a habit with her. How else to explain her presence this morning?

He put on a smile that he didn't feel. Out of the corner of his mouth, he said, "What do you call this, Arthur?"

"I call it backup," Arthur said.

5.

Robin Fellows didn't know all of it. Not even most of it.

They had an afternoon to kill—Svangur wouldn't be found now, couldn't expose himself to daylight—so they piled into Robin's Land Rover and she drove them out to see St. Nectan's waterfall and hermitage. They hiked the length of a cool green gorge toward the roar of running water. Colin checked a time or two, but there was no cell coverage at all out here. He tried not to let it irritate him. The British were so in love with their own past, they were apparently happy to let the future slip away. Some people couldn't be helped.

Robin was eager to see some birds called dippers that apparently liked to dive into the water and shoot around like little black torpedoes. Colin was behind her on the narrow path and admired her round, swinging can. He found himself wondering about her anatomy—and if doing it with a trans woman put one on the spectrum of homosexuality. The possibility intrigued him. He had always viewed sex as a kind of sport. He enjoyed the challenge of a new partner and relished a good encounter. The other parts of relationships bored him. He liked that Donna didn't need a lot of pillow talk after a good fuck. She tended to fall asleep and snore with her mouth open.

What really turned him on was knowing secrets. Discovering the things people didn't want you to know about them—that was the best sort of penetration.

"And this guy you're meeting later—Stuart Finger? He's, what, homeless?" Robin asked.

"I don't know if he has a permanent residence," Arthur said.

"But he knows the local cave systems. He's led other people down into the Camelford Crypts, to Arthur's Steps. There's a Celtic inscription I'd like to see there, and I don't trust myself to locate it. I called you because, if Colin and Finger and I are going to wiggle into a hole in the ground, I thought it would be nice to have someone topside to call emergency services if we don't come back."

"But you're not going to go at night? Not really? You'll just meet him tonight and make arrangements."

"It's always midnight underground. Tonight is as good as tomorrow."

Robin glanced back at Colin. "And you flew all the way over here to jump in a bottomless grave with him? Midlife crisis?"

"Arthur and I have a well-established relationship," Colin said. "He falls into a hole, and then I fall in trying to pull him out. It's too late to change now."

"And how do you even know about this Stu Finger?" Robin asked, leading the way as they crossed a narrow, slippery bridge of two-by-fours over the stream.

"Oh," Arthur said, without any trace of humor at all, "he's a legend."

6.

Even Colin had to admit, St. Nectan's was worth the walk. They paid an entry fee at a tiny hermitage and then descended through a winding tunnel of greenery. A series of slick stepping stones led across pools of water to the secluded waterfall. The cold tumble of water spouted down between colossal walls of moss-fuzzed granite. The air smelled deliciously of new-forged steel. Colin took half a dozen really excellent photos on his top-of-the-line Ericsson K800i.

Arthur stood next to him on a stone shelf at the bottom of the gorge, the waterfall booming down before them. Colin bowed his head over the screen, clicking through the pictures, considering the blurred misty light, the foaming cascade of water. Any one of them would be a lovely wallpaper for his computer desktop.

"I'll send them to your email," Colin promised. "As soon as I get a cell connection."

"No need," Arthur said. "I was here. I saw it."

Colin nodded. As they were walking back, it crossed Colin's mind that he had forgotten to look himself, had only seen the waterfall through the image on his phone's screen. But then, he reflected, it was more interesting on the screen. The light on his Ericsson was brighter and sharper than the light of the natural world—much like peering through the Surrealist's Glass, reality became more vivid and interesting viewed through the intermediary of the cell phone. Also, for Arthur, the moment was already over; but for Colin, the moment was now his forever. Captured like one of his grandfather's butterflies, held to the velvet by a silver pin and lovingly embalmed. It did not matter a butterfly had to be dead to be kept that way. In a sense, when they were preserved and mounted and displayed behind glass, they had really been made eternal. Life was no way to live. It was always over far too soon.

7.

The road to Slaughterbridge was a strip of blacktop dropping down the side of a steep hill, between ten-foot-high stone walls and looming screens of dense hedge. There was a dotted line painted down the middle of the road, although it was barely wide enough for a single car. Twenty-five yards up the hill from the stone piers of the bridge, Robin slowed her Land Rover and turned clattering across a cattle grid and into a Cornish meadow, soggy from a late-afternoon shower. Colin thought her total self-assurance behind the leather steering wheel of the big four-by-four was a reminder Robin hadn't grown up with a dollhouse and books about ponies. He found he didn't much care for that—one of the things he liked best about women, even someone like Donna, was the way they contentedly allowed their gender to be their destiny. Men drove, especially if the vehicle in question was a big truck; women wrote thank-you notes with hearts dotting the i's. But Robin Fellows might expertly apply a pair of false eyelashes and then hit a fleeing purse snatcher in a flying tackle like a former cornerback. Colin preferred people who lived their limits, people who knew what they could and couldn't do and took it to heart. People like Arthur—there was a man who let himself be ruled by his natural shortcomings.

They climbed out into the meadow, the soaked grass an almost hallucinatory green in the dying light.

Arthur eased himself into his old hiking backpack with the steel frame, and then tested his flashlight, a big Cree hi-thrower. Arthur had picked up one for Colin and another for Robin. He had instructed them both, if they felt threatened, to flick the torches on to their highest setting, but hadn't said why—to blind an attacker, perhaps, or signal the others that they were in trouble, Colin guessed.

"You haven't even met him," Robin said. "You really think this Finger is going to want to go down into this crypt tonight?"

"I think if we find him, he will show it to us now or not at all. He either likes you or he doesn't, is what I heard."

"Do you think he'll like you?" Robin asked.

"Can you imagine anyone *not* liking me?"

"Yes," she said, but they began walking down the road—single file, ready to dive out of the way of passing cars—toward the lively music of the River Camel.

"So," Robin began, after a few moments of padding along silently, "you aren't going to tell me what this is *really* about?"

Arthur bowed his head in thought. At last, he said, "I haven't told you anything that isn't true. We really are meeting someone who can lead us to a crypt of great historical importance, a place I very much want to see. And in any caving expedition there's some risk, which is why it's important to have a friend who knows your plan, where you're going, and when you'll be back."

"But I *don't* know where you're going. Not really. And you've asked me to stay by the bridge while you and Colin talk to him . . . which makes me think you aren't worried about the cave at all. You're worried about your guide." Robin had come prepared for the wait with a folding chair—she had it strapped to her back—waterproof boots, and a thermos of tea.

"Whatever risk there might be," Arthur said, "it's ours to face, not yours."

Robin nodded slowly at that. The bridge was in sight now: an arch of gray stone, with ancient retaining walls, sitting on rough-hewn granite piers. The river beneath was wide and shallow and black, rushing over smooth stone and through scatterings of brush.

"Can you tell me one thing, Arthur?" Robin asked. "Does this have something to do with Van? Does it have something to do with whatever was in the sky the night we landed in Greenland?"

Arthur had stepped off the road. He was looking at the embankment beneath the bridge, his eyes narrowed. Then he turned and beamed, like a man walking into a pub and seeing all his closest friends bellied up to the bar.

He took Robin's hand in both of his and squeezed it warmly. "He's there. I hoped he would be. We leave each other here. Don't cross the bridge alone, Robin, and if we aren't back by one a.m., get help."

She looked pale, her mouth pursed in a dark bow, her dark green eyes clouded with worry. He squeezed her hand again.

"I'm sorry," Arthur said. "I can't tell you more, and I can't bring you with us. Van and Allie would never forgive me if anything happened to you. It doesn't matter Van is dead. I still owe him your safety."

"And do you think Van and Allie could ever forgive *me* if anything happened to you two?"

"Sure they would," Colin told her, and winked. "They know what ungovernable pricks we are."

8.

Colin had seen him too. He was a gangly derelict, sprawled on the dirt, half under the bridge amid his clutter, one leg sticking out into the dusk. His clothes were piled on, a tattered olive coat over a moth-eaten cardigan over a stained T-shirt. The T-shirt showed a black knight in a bucket helmet, with blood spouting from a severed arm. A slogan in Gothic print read, 'TIS BUT A SCRATCH. His worldly belongings were heaped in a rusting shopping cart. He even had a TV, flipped on. It was about the size of a walkie-talkie and had an antenna like a walkie-talkie too. The picture was black-and-white and showed some young women in thongs walking on a beach.

"You sure it's him?" Colin whispered.

"Absolutely," Arthur said, and then added, "He's watching *Love Island*," as if this was determinative in some way.

They started down and across the embankment, but as they angled their way toward the darkness beneath the bridge, some dirt gave way, and Colin got his next surprise of the day. Colin put in a minimum of twenty-six miles a week on the treadmill and attended private Pilates classes. He aspired to agility, to move fast and break things. But he slithered in the mud, doing a comical soft-shoe to try and stay up, then went down anyway, wrenching his left knee and banging his hip. Arthur had to grab him to keep him from sliding into the river. Colin leapt back to his feet but winced at the sharp stab of pain in the knee. He was unused to being clumsy. His carbon-fiber hiking sneakers, with their deep-tread outsoles and Gore-Tex lining, squeegeed right over the ground, while Arthur had on a pair of battered Timberlands that sank into the soft earth like concrete blocks.

"You okay?" Arthur asked.

"Peachy, boss," Colin said . . . but he wasn't. He felt the knee with every step he took. He'd be limping soon. It was a bad start.

Svangur had stringy blond hair to his shoulders, badly combed over a pink bald spot, a patchy yellow beard, chapped lips, a cold sore at the corner of his mouth. He was like syphilis with a human face. His watery blue eyes drifted to them and away, back to his TV.

"One's black as an old dog shit, other's slick as a moneylender," he said to his TV, and chuckled to himself. "Slick has money, you'n smell it on him. Farts through silk that one. Getcher coin for a little suck, little coin'll getcher a pint, one swaller pays for the next and all thirsts are answered, heh heh." He didn't laugh—"heh heh" was a pair of distinct words.

"Finger, is it?" Arthur said.

"They has fingered me rightly on the first try."

Arthur said, "I've heard you know the path to a particular hole in the ground."

Svangur chewed one dirty fingernail. "There's a hole'n the ground waits for all men. 'Tisn't so hard to find."

"This one leads to a crypt."

"I am sure you shall have a crypt if you wants one."

"And below the crypt is a natural formation sometimes called Arthur's Stairs? My friend and I would like to see it. I'd pay you to show us the way."

Svangur looked at his TV and said, "Better he pays to see Arthur's Stairs than Finger's Fundament, though both holes is just as dark and just as tight. How much, though? Slick, he smells of pound notes. His man has a wealth of words which makes him almost as poor as poor Stu Finger. You can have a head full of silver-dollar words, but take 'em to the bank, they won't give you a penny for them, heh heh."

"Ten quid now," Arthur said. "Ten more when we get back."

"Ach, and miss the rest of me *Love Island*? I hate to miss my show." He grinned to reveal black teeth and said in an aside, "The nig-nog is the rich man's butler, mark me now. He speaks for the money as if money can't speak loud enough for itself."

If Arthur was bothered by *nig-nog* he gave no sign of it.

"Forty then," Arthur told him. "Twenty now, twenty later. Or my friend and I can go back to the pub and spend our money on the beer you won't be drinking tonight."

"Heh heh, he'll fuck you if you *doesn't* take his money, Finger, not a wery good bargain for you, no sir. He'll have one pint after another and probably leave them half-drunk without a thought, and there's a thought to drive you mad. Wasted beer, an evil notion!" He scrambled to his feet, dusted off the bottom of his sweats. "A spring walk is just the thing to work up a proper thirst. I sees you is ready for a difficult scramble. Just as well, heh heh, I has no worries you will keep up. I sees you is men born for the briars." Colin thought one corner of his mouth twitched up in a nasty grin at that. Arthur gave Colin a nod and Colin produced a twenty-pound note.

Finger snatched it away and held it up to the dim dusk light, examining the queen.

"Her maj!" he cried. "Her glorious maj! Long live her cobwerbbed quim!" He planted a kiss on her before he crushed the bill up and stuck it in the breast pocket of his army jacket. He switched off his TV and pushed it down amid his other belongings in the shopping cart, and then, without a word, began to lurch away into the dusk.

"Come on. He might be satisfied with that twenty. It's not just money to him," Arthur said. "It's also pornography. He might slip away to be alone with it. Best to keep up."

They went after him.

9.

They went upstream with the river on their right. For a little while there was a path, a hard dirt track that wandered through hummocks of close-cropped grass. Then they were climbing for higher ground and there was hardly any path at all. They worked their way up through a curious stand of ancient gnarled trees, like passing through a bewitched forest. The gathering night smelled strongly of leaf mold and wet earth, and they emerged from the trees into a clearing, a sort of landing on the side of the hill. In the center of the clearing was a jagged tooth of granite, spotted with lichens and moss. As they approached it, in the dimness, Colin could see it was inscribed: someone had chiseled Pictish lettering into it a thousand years ago, little whirlpool symbols and dashes with lines through them.

"Ogham inscriptions," Arthur said. "The written language of the Celtic holy men."

"Follow Finger round," Stu Finger said. "And round again. 'Tis an old tradition what does no harm to no one. It throws off any ghosts'd follow you." Their guide touched one dirty fingertip to the leaning stone and began to circle it. He cast a knowing look over one shoulder, eyes glimmering to either side of his bony nose. "Now where we go, you may hear sounds like voices, heh heh, but they are the red-throated divers down south, toward the Crowdy Reservoir. The sound carries out here. It's a funny thing, yes. Wery funny! Pay it no mind. And when we go down the hole, you may see shapes in the dark, like the shadows of men, but if they disturb you, look away and think of 'em no more. Watch the tussocks ahead, gennlemen. The briars out here, they grabbet you. They grabbet and they like to keeps what they grab."

Colin did as Arthur had already done, touched a fingertip to the stone and began to circle it, his knee sore, throbbing whenever he put weight on his left foot. He went around once and again and as he circled it that second time he felt a wave of lightheadedness roll over him. The world seemed to *bulge*, like a soap bubble expanding from a bubble wand as it filled with a child's breath. It was such a queer sensation, he almost needed to sit down. On his third circuit, he dropped his hand at the sight of a gate. There was an old leaning wooden frame and a white stone lintel set across the path; the original gate was long rotted away and had been replaced by a rusting blue car door, with loops of copper wire for hinges. But the gate hadn't been there the first time he went around the stone, or the second, he was almost sure of it. Finger was already shuffling across that pale stone lintel, without a look back.

Arthur had paused, and before Colin could follow Finger through the open gate, Arthur grabbed his arm.

"Now," he whispered, and offered Colin the Surrealist's Glass.

Colin lifted it to one eye, and what he saw so shocked him he almost cried out.

Through the Surrealist's Glass he saw not a dilapidated wooden gate with a car door for an entrance, but a twelve-foot-high arch of alabaster stone, with ogham inscriptions scratched into it. It looked as new as the day it had been planted in the earth, perhaps a millennium ago. The tunnel of briars on the other side was a dark and thorny passageway, as much of a cave as anything Finger had promised to lead them to.

But it was Stu Finger himself who startled Colin most. Seen through the glass, he was almost seven feet tall, his right shoulder higher than the other, his features grotesque and malformed. He was hairless, his skull a bumpy, bulging ridge. He wore a tunic, not an army jacket, and the much-patched canvas pants of a court jester. He had a great gaping slot for a mouth, and a pair of curved, yellowing tusks, half a foot long each, rose from among his lower teeth. His hands, big as hubcaps, were knuckly, callused, with horny fingernails that looked sharp enough to carve a person open. Worst of all, though, was his skin: the kind of purply-gray skin one associated with millipedes and other things found under rocks. Finger cast a look back over his raised shoulder, to see if they were following, and Colin lowered the glass.

He panted. And swallowed. And gave Arthur an uncertain grin as he handed back the monocle. He was suddenly conscious of having no spit. He wondered, not for the first time, what talisman Arthur kept that he believed would keep Finger under their power—a ring that could call down a lightning bolt, perhaps, or some splinter of Christ's cross, worn on a loop of twine, hidden inside his shirt. He wished now he had compelled Arthur to tell him what he had brought for their protection. The not-knowing was almost as frightening as what he had just glimpsed through the Surrealist's Glass.

"Does he know we know?" Colin asked quietly.

Arthur gave his head a little shake and proceeded through the dilapidated gate. Colin hustled after him, ducking through that narrow opening in the thorns.

The roof of the tunnel through the briars seemed low, so low Colin kept ducking, although he knew it had to be higher than it seemed—Finger made his way through with no trouble at all and had been *huge* when seen through the glass. Colin stayed close to Arthur, was aware that with each step they moved deeper into the landscape of fairy tale. In fairy tales, it was unwise to be separated from your companions in the deep, dark forest.

Something began screaming, and Colin stopped. That scream—a high-pitched wail—broke off, started again, broke off once more, then disintegrated into a nasty chuckle. A bird, maybe. The red-throated divers in the Crowdy Reservoir, perhaps. But it had sounded for all the world like an insane child, wailing in delight.

The tunnel widened as the briars thinned away, then ended completely. They had reached flat ground, scattered with boulders. One boulder in particular loomed over all: a black dragon's egg of a stone, the ground crumbling away under one curve, leaving a dark space beneath. Finger was already on his back, wiggling into the gap. The narrow black Cheshire Cat's grin opening under the boulder could not have been more than a foot high.

"We're going in *there*?" Colin asked.

"This is a bad moment to tell me you're claustrophobic," Arthur said, slipping off his backpack. They would have to pull their gear behind them.

Colin tucked his flashlight into his backpack, while Arthur kept his firmly in his right hand. Arthur knelt and slid into the gap feet-first, wiggling through, dragging his backpack behind him. He had to tip his head back to get under the rock—Colin thought of a man baring his throat for the knife. Then he was gone. His backpack went after him, sucked through the hole with a whisper and slap of nylon.

Colin did as Arthur and Finger had done. As he wiggled his stomach under the boulder, he wondered how much it weighed. Two, three tons? More than a pickup truck. He imagined a grinding of earth and the stone suddenly shifting, dropping on his midsection and squeezing his guts out of his own mouth and asshole like toothpaste. The thought made him breathless with exhilaration.

He dropped. Not far. His feet scraped smooth, damp stone as he hung by the one hand gripping his backpack, now stuck in the crevasse above. His left arm was stretched high over his head, the toes of his sneakers barely touching the floor.

Arthur clicked on his flashlight and a disc of brightness slid up an earthen wall, thick worms of roots poking from it, and, amid the dirt, a bit of ancient fresco, a faded painted medieval face peering out from the filth. Colin could see Arthur but not Finger and was wondering where their guide had gone when there was a scrape in the dirt behind him, and a snort of laughter, and Colin was whopped from behind, a blow across the kidneys that sent him swinging like a piñata. The backpack above abruptly slipped free and he dropped to the ground on his bad knee. Pain lanced up the thigh and he cried out—a shameful moment of weakness.

Arthur spun, and as he did he punched the button on the side of his flashlight, cycling the bulb up to the highest setting. A beam of pure sunshine stabbed into Colin's face, blinding him for an instant. The light bobbed past him, and Finger screamed.

"Oh, *the bastard*! The pestilent *bastard*, he brought a bad light to hurt us! Who made such a bad light as this and how does it come to be in Stu Finger's hole, to blind and hurt and punish? Who fashioned this nasty lance of light to sting poor Stu Finger?"

"I couldn't tell you who made it or by what sorcery. I bought it in a Homebase," Arthur said, keeping the beam of light between them and Finger. "This is a Cree hi-thrower, a high-intensity discharge lamp. The hippies use them to grow pot in their basements because it so closely mimics sunlight. You don't like sunlight, do you, Finger?"

"This lying nig-nog! There's no electric torch can throw a light like that," Finger said to himself. "His black mouth tells blacker lies."

Colin touched his back and felt blood. He saw Finger cowering against a back wall . . . with a shillelagh in one hand, a deformed club bigger than a baseball bat, with what looked like nails and bits of broken glass superglued to the business end. Finger must have whacked Colin with it, and he thought Finger had been stepping forward to sink it into his head when Arthur came around with the light.

"The *fuck*?" he snapped at the troll.

"*Are* they lies?" Arthur said calmly. "Let's find out." And he flicked the spot of light toward Finger's face.

Finger reeled backward with a howl, retreating from the light instinctively, and Colin looked past the man at the wall of the cave and went breathless. Finger's shadow was that of the troll, not the man. Colin could see, quite clearly, the enormous, lumpish shape of the head, the hooks of the tusks, and the great blunt hands, printed on the stone in darkness. The Finger that threw the shadow was still a scrawny man with pale hair . . . although to Colin's eyes his gaunt, filthy face was suddenly *less* convincing. It was less a man's face, more an artful rubber mask of a man's face, starting to come loose around the eyes and mouth.

Some perverse streak of curiosity must've got the better of the old troll. Having instinctively dodged the hi-thrower beam, he hesitantly lifted one hand and reached toward the glare. Finger's hand slipped into the light . . . and Colin saw the tips of the fingers suddenly shift from pink human flesh to a cancer-bruise purple to gray. Skin crackled, and what looked like a powdery ash started to spill from his hand, floating in the air. Finger screamed in pain and fear and yanked his hand back and clutched it to his chest.

"Stone!" Finger screamed. "He mean to make a stone of us! He lured us down here to make it our grave and Stu Finger to be his own headstone!"

"Enough!" Arthur cried, with a sharpness that Colin had not imagined he possessed. It was not the voice of the frightened and hopeless boy who had suffered at Jayne Nighswander's hands, but of an old schoolmaster who has seen enough foolishness to last a lifetime, and it came to Colin that he hardly knew this Arthur at all. "If I wanted to make a rock out of you, I'd've done it by now. The only one who meant to make this a grave was *you*, Svangur the Sly. I ought to cook your hands to stone right now for taking that club to Colin. But you might need them to lead us to your hoard. You have things that I want. Give them to me and you'll live out the night."

"*This* was your talisman?" Colin asked. Pain pulsed in his back, and the left knee was stiffening up on him. His aches were bad—but the breathless thrill of fear in his chest was worse because it was so unfamiliar to him. "A *flashlight*? I thought you had, I don't know, a cloak of invisibility or something."

"I do have a cloak of invisibility," Arthur murmured. "It's called academia."

Finger moaned. "He wants the goodies! He'll take all our favorite things and leave us with nothing! Our favorite thigh bone. Our best piece of rope. The Jenna Jameson videos. He doesn't even *want* them, he just doesn't want us to have them!" He sounded close to angry tears. "He'll take it and make a big stupid rock of us anyway."

"No. I will deal fairly with you. Not that you deserve it. You've killed children, Finger, and left their mothers ruined with grief. You've stolen everything you own, and you murdered to take it."

"Mr. Finger hasn't killed anyone in a really, *really* long time!" Stu Finger cried.

"What's a long time?" Colin asked.

The troll held up seven fingers. "Nine years! Nine big fat ones!"

Arthur laughed without humor.

Stu Finger sucked the gray, cracked tips of his fingers. Colin thought they were already beginning to deepen in color, returning to flesh.

"What does he want? The blood of a saint, to heal his sick black heart? The hairy monk's robe that will let him walk through fire?"

That seemed to check Arthur, cause him to consider for a moment. Colin thought Finger had admitted to possessing a few items Arthur had not at all expected to find down here.

"I came for a sword. One that will cut through a dragon's hide and is made of something more than steel. The Sword of Strange Hangings it was known as once."

Finger's eyes widened with fascination. "Take it and kill Stu Finger with it?"

"I don't need a sword to kill you. I aim to sink it into something quite a bit larger than you."

"If you want a blade to cut through a dreadful wurm, then you have problems bigger than poor Svangur, heh heh. If you've got problems with an ancient wurm, you best take that sword and fall on it. End your suffering. You have no chance of getting it into a great snake."

"You let me worry about that. Do we have a deal?"

Finger chewed the yellow shiv of his thumbnail and muttered to himself. "Turn down your light? So it won't accidentally shine on poor Stu Finger and turn his cock harder than it's ever been, heh heh? Come along, gennlemen. Don't dawdle. Don't fall behind. Stay close to me and Finger will show you how deep this old hole goes."

10.

Colin lifted his backpack, pulled the flashlight out, and waited for Finger to shuffle past him before he drew the straps over his shoulders. Finger had the shillelagh in one hand, but Arthur twitched his flashlight toward the wall.

"Leave that here."

"As you like, as you like," Finger said, in a joyously groveling tone. "Finger shall leave one club but bring the larger for our general security." And he squeezed his crotch and leered. He let the shillelagh thump the wall and slunk past Arthur, and only then did Arthur dim his light to an ordinary yellow glow.

Colin threw his own flashlight on—the regular setting, not full spectrum—and cast it at the shillelagh to see what had almost been buried in his head. Behind it was a faded fresco of the Virgin Mother in her blue and white gown, raising her hand in a blessing over a pile of shrouds.

"The Black Death," Arthur told him. "This was a plague cave."

"How it stank," Finger said with a certain satisfaction. "The full-grown died quietly. But not the babies. The babies sounded like little bleating goats. There were a thousand men, women, babies died down here the first time the plague touched these shores. They brought them in, then rolled the boulder over the entrance because the flies came in the millions. Many were still alive when they did it, but only the children screamed. The adults were grateful for the dark, so they wouldn't have to see the blackness consuming them. Blacker even'n you, young gennleman, heh heh!"

It was not, at first, the sort of cave Colin expected, neither a nasty, dirty, wet hole nor a dry, bare, sandy hole, but a series of carefully hollowed-out rooms connected by a series of low, vaulted doorways. There were carvings above these openings: fourteenth-century Gothic skulls framed by wings, Celtic crosses, and runic symbols. Places to sit—like long pews of stone—had been carved into the walls.

"It would've been a religious retreat, before it was a mass grave," Arthur told him. "Cells for monks to fast and listen for God."

"A place for them to bugger one another in privacy," Finger said. "If any called for God in them days, it was only when he made a hot little squirt up a fundament. There are no atheists in foxholes or buried balls deep neither. And no God in holes like this."

"Light can find its way into the darkest of places, Svangur," Arthur told him. "As you've learned to your dismay. Carry on."

The troll's shadow led them from one vault to the next.

"God," Colin grunted. He was feeling the knee with every step. "I've thought a lot about God over the years, Arthur. I had an idea about him."

"I didn't know you were a believer. What's your idea?"

"He's an egregore. A Philip. The greatest Philip of all, perhaps. It would explain so much. Did you know people have better health outcomes when they pray?"

"Yes."

"And they have better health outcomes when someone prays *for* them . . . even if they don't *know* someone is praying for them? Which somewhat undermines any argument based on the placebo effect. Mass Christian belief could be powerful enough to throw the occasional shimmy in reality. What do you think?"

"I think you're halfway there, Colin. God isn't our egregore. We're His. He doesn't exist because we believe in Him. We exist because He believes in us."

Colin smiled. "You should've followed your mother into her line of work. You have a knack for that—giving a phrase an inspirational twist. Do you really think a loving and independent God would've let Black Cricket penitentiary collapse on four hundred women?"

"Did God let that happen? Or did we? I think if you refer to the record, Colin, you'll find it was us."

Finger ducked into a round tunnel at the far side of the latest crypt. The big man almost filled it . . . if he was still a man at all. It seemed to Colin that Finger's right shoulder was hiked up, and that he was broader through the chest than he had been when he first squirmed under the boulder to enter the caves.

As Colin climbed into the narrow passageway, he saw that the walls were heavily frescoed here. Some artist of the twelfth or thirteenth century had painted black spiders on it, sitting in nests of artful, geometric spiderwebs. Life-size pale candles had been painted between the spiderwebs, golden rings of light spreading out between them in broad, even discs of brightness. It was all so faded, they were less paintings than the memory of paintings. Finger was ten feet ahead, and as he walked, the big troll ran his fingertips across the walls, arms stretched out to either side.

"Be honest, Arthur. Doesn't the problem of pain shake your faith?" Pain was very much on Colin's mind and his breath came in short spurts. His kidneys felt sick. "Think about the children who died down here. The people who watched the stone roll over the entrance, leaving them to their fevers and the darkness. Why forgive God for that suffering? You wouldn't forgive yourself, if you caused it."

"You take the same view of sorrow as our pet iguana. I don't. Sorrow and love are a single coin—the one we pay as the price of our humanity. Take it away and we'd be the worst kind of poor. And it's a mistake to believe the value of a life is erased by anguish at the end. If there's one thing atheists and the devout can agree on, Colin, death is where you leave your suffering behind."

Colin felt ill from the throbbing in his back and knee . . . ill and woozy. His ears were not exactly ringing, but there was a kind of susurration in them, as if he was listening to a seashell—an Aztec conch perhaps. The tunnel seemed to be whispering around him, a disturbing notion.

"I'm telling you," Colin went on, irritated now—that hushed, felty fluttering in his ears was grating on his nerves—"you could've made a lot more money preaching on the internet. I could've custom-designed a website for you to stream your ministry. You could've been the first big televangelist of the new—eesh!" Something brushed his hand and he shook it in reflex. A spider dropped to the floor. A fat one: black and fulsome.

Only when it hit the floor, it fell amid other spiders. Colin half turned, glancing around him, and a rush of cold blood surged toward his heart. Colin had not known, until that moment, that he had a phobia of spiders. Not until he saw that the paintings of them were peeling themselves off the walls and scuttling toward them. There were so many he could *hear* them . . . that was the faint, whispery, scrabbling sound his ears had been detecting for the last few moments. One dropped from a transparent line onto his head. When he opened his mouth to scream, another climbed into his mouth.

He tried to run and went down on one knee. There was webbing spun around his shins. It was only a few threads, but it wouldn't break, tight and tough as nylon. He tried to yank it free and his hand stuck to it. Stu Finger was already at the end of the tunnel, looking back at them and huffing with laughter.

"You never know what pests will come crawling into these holes," Finger said, "but fortunately they keep the spiders fed."

Colin struggled to loosen his right hand from the tacky webs around his shins, and as he fought to free himself a spider crawled up the back of his hand and around his wrist, paused, and then sank its fangs into his flesh. Another was biting his ear—it felt like being burned with a cigarette. He could feel spiders crawling under his shirt, a sensation so awful, it brought him to the edge of panic, a thing he could not ever remember experiencing before. It was a fear so sharp it made thought impossible.

Arthur was down too, sitting on the floor, a gray and sticky binding of webs around his shins and upper thighs. There were spiders rooting in his beard, spiders on his cheeks. Arthur's right arm was already bound to his chest by more webbing—several spiders worked in a determined fashion, scrambling in circuits around his torso. Soon enough they would both be cocooned.

But Arthur's left arm was free, and he lifted the Surrealist's Glass to one eye, searching the walls for something. Colin saw a fat, fuzzy spider burrowing into the side of Arthur's neck like it was hoping to wiggle all the way in.

"The candles," Arthur gasped.

Arthur lunged and fell on his side, across the curving, narrow floor of the passage, shaking a few spiders off. Arthur clawed at the wall with his free hand and his fingers found one of the painted candles—so faded it was almost colorless. Arthur shut his eyes. His lips, Colin thought, were moving in prayer.

"What are you doing?" Colin cried, although his mouth was full, and his words came out in a choked muffle. He spat out a wet, bitter wad of spider.

"Trying to believe in candles," Arthur said, with his eyes shut, as he peeled the candle right off the wall. Only as he pulled it free it was somehow a *real* candle, a four-inch taper of smooth ivory wax in a little gold dish, the flame dancing and wavering.

Arthur brushed the candle at his own neck and the spider that had been trying to burrow in emitted a tiny shriek. It was a whistle of pain, almost too high-pitched to hear, but an instant later the spider fell away. Arthur tried to lower the candle to the webbing that pinned his right arm to his chest, only a spider bit the back of his hand. He cried out, dropped the taper, and it rolled away from him. When Arthur reached for it a trio of spiders crisscrossed his forearm and briskly, efficiently pinned it to the stone with cobwebs. The candle was a few agonizing inches away from his outstretched fingertips.

Colin had a folding carbon steel knife with a Teflon grip in his backpack, but he would choke to death on a throat full of spiders before he ever got to it. They were all over him, on his face, on his chest. He slapped the wall above him, put his hand on one of those painted candles. *There's nothing there*, he thought, *but paint and stone, nothing, nothing*—the panic fizzing up on him. Holding that panic back was like trying to hold a door closed with someone bigger than him pushing against the other side.

Only an idea *wasn't* nothing. King Sorrow had only been an idea once and had still uncoiled himself from the Long Dark of the unconscious mind to come through into their world, to burn and bite. The idea of a candle was real enough, in the mind. And his *desperation* was real. His need for a candle made a few neurons fire, and a candle lit itself in his imagination. Thought had a *physical* reality—neuroscience insisted on it—so he reached for the candle in his imagination and when he opened his eyes it was in his hand, throwing a clear, bold, golden light.

He burned the spider sinking its mandibles into his wrist and was rewarded with another of those pathetic shrieks and the stink of burning hair. It fell free. He touched the thickening straps of spiderweb around his shins and ankles and the webs ignited like straw, turning to hot copper, wilting and shriveling and falling away. Colin lashed out with one foot and kicked the candle Arthur had dropped back to his friend's fingertips. Arthur spun it, so the flame licked at the webs across his forearms, and in another instant he was free. They both were.

They clasped hands and heaved each other up, and then stood back-to-back, stabbing this way and that with their candle flames. Spiders squealed and smoked and fell, curling up on themselves. Arthur and Colin turned in a slow ambit, forcing the spiders away from them. The spiders retreated up the walls . . . and settled back onto them, flattening, joining the stone again to escape the flames. Colin never quite saw it happen, but one moment there would be a black, fleshy spider on a wall and the candlelight would flicker and then, when the light wavered back, what had been alive a moment before was only a painting. The two men continued to rotate in a circle, shoulders pressed to shoulders, until Colin realized the corridor was empty and they were no longer holding candles anymore but clutching their flashlights instead. He was never clear when the candles had rejoined the wall.

The excitement had seeped out of Stuart Finger. In the gloom, he was more the troll than ever as he stood at the end of the tunnel, his long apelike arms dangling at his sides. Most of his wispy yellow hair was gone, and Colin didn't like the look of his mouth. His lips had a rubbery quality, and the mouth seemed more and more like the gaping mouth of some cold-blooded fish, a pike maybe. His glee had vanished and his eyelids sagged with disappointment.

Colin's skin was still crawling and he couldn't stop checking himself over, looking to see if he had any spiders left on him. He hated the hairy feel of them. He had never liked hair. He wanted the whole world to be like his phone or his computer: smooth and glassy and perfect. At the same time, he was breathless with an excitement that was very close to exaltation. It had always delighted him to be in the presence of the impossible, to see reality dribble and run like candle wax. Even when it bit him.

"We should turn him into a rock," Colin said. He hardly recognized his own voice. His breath came fast and harsh. "How badly do we really need him, Arthur?"

Arthur put a cautioning hand on Colin's bicep. "He had to try. I was expecting something like—well, not that. But something more than his club."

"Of course they need us," Finger said to himself. "Maybe not to find the hoard, but to find the way out for sure. No good leaving a trail of breadcrumbs. It's too late now and the rats would eat 'em anyway. They come out with us or they don't come out at all."

It crossed Colin's mind that he really *didn't* know the way back . . . and that every room they had passed through no doubt had multiple exits that he had failed to observe in the dark. And any one of them could contain more spiders . . . or worse.

"Shit," Colin said. "How come we didn't think of that?"

Arthur lifted one eyebrow. "You mean you didn't? We turn him to a rock now, Colin, he won't just be his own headstone. He'll be ours too."

11.

They made a descent along what seemed to be a naturally formed staircase of white stone . . . and in the beam of the hi-thrower, the walls flashed and gleamed, as if speckled with gems or silver. The ceiling was a vault of pink quartz, a profusion of luminescent ruby spears.

"These might be Arthur's Stairs," Arthur said. "A local legend. They say after Arthur cut down Mordred—his own son—he carried him here. Mordred's blood didn't fall, but dripped upward, staining the ceiling to make this blaze of quartz."

"How he cried," Finger said. "Boo-hoo. The great king wept so hard for the little murderer, you can sometimes still hear the echo of it. He should've wept for himself. He didn't survive his wounds. He suffered oh so much from them. They stank and blackened until even his woman couldn't approach him without gagging."

Colin's ear stung where it had been bitten. His wrist throbbed, his knee was swollen and stiffening up, and his back felt ragged and sore. The battering of the last hour had soured his mood, threatened to undermine what had mostly been, up to now, a great lark with an old friend. Arthur had been bitten just as badly, but it didn't seem to have shaken him at all, and a moment later he picked up their conversational thread as if nothing had happened.

"See how Svangur dwells on disgust and human failure?" Arthur observed. "That's always his trump card. That peril, suffering, and fear prove life is a squalid struggle with no point, since it always ends in loss. He thinks—and you've said so too, Colin—that it proves if there is a God, he's a sadistic war criminal, a bystander who watches while children drown. But that's not what it proves.

What it proves is that acts of love and sacrifice have real value—that they're the only currency that matters."

It might've been the spider bites, but Colin wasn't in the mood to fence with Arthur about theology anymore.

"Love, Arthur, is just evolution's way of making sure we look after the carriers of our DNA. That's all. You should read Richard Dawkins. Could be real eye-opening for you."

"I've read him and I know the type. The evangelical atheists. The way they obsess over a God that doesn't exist, endlessly returning to His many failings, again and again, is itself, of course, a kind of devotion. Like the man who can't stop talking about a woman he claims to despise . . . at a certain point, one begins to suspect the issue is really quite the opposite."

"Word games," Colin said. "Why am I playing word games with you? Down here, in this hole? You always dance around in circles."

"You love it," Arthur said. "Music to your ears."

"Music to our ears! Hah hah!" Finger said. "You'll make some pretty music soon if you don't step lively now. There is the most astoniching echo in this next chamber, and if you slip on the ledge, we will still hear you screaming long after you're dead. Choose where you put your feet most wery careful here."

They had reached the bottom of the steps. The tunnel opened and widened . . . to reveal a great drop into darkness. It was a well, of sorts, beneath a vast unlit chandelier of rose quartz. The chasm was ten feet wide, ten yards long, and roughly ten thousand miles deep. A stone lip wrapped around either side, but each was rarely more than two feet wide, often much less. Water trickled down the wall in glistening runnels that made the white, rounded stone slick. Finger wasn't concerned in the slightest. He traipsed along the ledge to the right, humming to himself and leaping along without seeming to pay any attention to where he placed his boots.

"It was dark, dark, dark," Finger sang and his voice rang back at them from the depths of the hole. The well repeated *dark, dark, dark* at least a dozen times. "In da park, park, park . . ."

Colin leaned over the well and shone his light down into the chasm. When he glanced up at Arthur, he saw the other man had closed his eyes and was rubbing two fingers against the center of his forehead.

"You all right?"

"Heights make me dizzy. *Of course* there was going to be an endless drop. You don't understand. You fly jets. I get woozy when I climb a ladder to clean out the gutters. Which side do you want?"

"I don't care," Colin said, "but you're taking the other one. If you get wobbly, the worst thing you could do is grab me to steady yourself. If you're wobbly on your own, you'll naturally flatten against the wall, or sink to a knee. Whereas if we're together you could pull us both over the edge."

"Any tips?"

"Don't fall."

Colin played his light along one ledge, then the other. There was more of that frescoing above the ledges, at eye level, a series of Gothic skeletons holding hands, boogieing in a line with people in shrouds. The danse macabre, Colin thought.

He stepped onto the right-hand ledge. Arthur took the left. Colin turned inward to face the wall and spread out his arms, flattening himself against the rock. He began to shuffle forward, with the well at his back. After a few steps, he was aware of his heels sticking out over the edge. He looked over his shoulder and saw Arthur advancing toe to heel—a terrible way to cross the ledge—with his eyes shut—even worse. Colin wanted to call instructions to him but didn't want to add to his disorientation, and the chamber was echoey enough as it was.

Finger was almost to the end of the ledge and the broad avenue that waited on the other side, a great downward sloping passage. Colin thought he saw a dim, aqueous glow somewhere farther down that passageway. The troll sang on:

"When I heard a talk, an' a creepin' walk, an' I look around frightfully, I seen I was in da center of a cemetery."

His voice was somehow amplified by the chasm, returned to them with a new aural shimmer, a jangle and rattle that almost brought to mind percussion. Or maybe that was the bars of quartz above, resonating to his voice. Or—*no*—Colin caught himself, listening. Those *were* marimbas, he was almost sure of it. And, a thousand miles away, the sudden blat of a horn.

"*I nearly bus' my head*," Colin heard Arthur singing across the chasm, his voice low, breathless with fear. "*Ah running from the dead.*"

A *song* was playing down there . . . a jazzy calypso, steel drums and upright bass, so far below, it could only barely be heard over the echo of their breath. Colin had started to shuffle on, but now he realized, with a stroke of giddy fear, that his whole body was beginning to *sway*, to ripple along to the music. He almost laughed. Instead he whirled, spun suddenly around on the tiny ledge, throwing his arms up over his head and rolling his hips. It was involuntary movement, as uncontrollable as a convulsion. His bad knee almost folded up on him and he only stayed upright through a furious act of will. He swayed, sickeningly, and opened his mouth to cry out—

And instead found himself singing, "*I fall down inside the tomb, an' get up with a zoom-zoom-zoom*, Arthur, what the fuck is happening?" Colin had never heard the song they were singing, didn't recognize the melody echoing up from the well, yet the lyrics were *there*, pushing their way out of him, demanding to be sung.

"St. Vitus's dance," Arthur panted. "It's a *compulsion*. I'm not going to fall. I'm going to jump to my death. The song is going to make me."

"No. That's not happening."

"It is, it will, I—" And as he spoke, his voice unsteady with alarm, Arthur hopped, spun, landed, and pinwheeled his arms desperately. "I can't stay still!"

"If you have to fall," Colin shouted, "fall toward me, okay?"

"But I thought you said *don't*—"

"Never mind what I said," Colin cried. He had a thought, wild, irrational, and almost exuberant: it was a dance (or was that *danse*?) and you couldn't dance without a partner. If he didn't dance with

Arthur, he would go for a waltz with death instead, would do a merry pirouette in the arms of the laughing skeleton, down into the pit, screaming all the way.

Arthur nodded, but he was singing again . . . and as he sang, Colin heard, quite distinctly, the uncanny echo of horns, answering his lyrics with a cheerful blast of trumpets. *"And what has me sad—even really mad—is I was jus' about to start—a romance with meh sweet'art!"*

And Arthur leapt again, threw his hands in the air, and then *dived*, throwing himself straight toward the hole. Colin was directly across from him, and he pitched toward Arthur at the same moment. He threw his arms out and Arthur's hands struck his, as if they had decided to slap one another ten over the hole. The force of their palms smacking together drove them both back and upright, safely onto their ledges.

Colin jumped, skipped, and took two ridiculous steps *backward*, was *impelled* backward by the steps of the dance. He felt an urge coming over him to dip sideways over the hole.

"Arthur!" he shouted.

Colin dropped sideways into the hole, one hand stuck straight out. Arthur fell toward him at the same time. Their hands met again with a fleshy whack, and for one instant their fingers enlaced. Arthur nodded. They shoved off one another and came upright again, Colin feeling something twang in his bruised lower back.

"Finger!" Colin roared. "Do something, you motherfucker!" He was furious. He was giddy. The line between rage and delight could be very fine sometimes.

Finger stood at the far end of the hole, clapping his hands—they were much larger than a man's hands now—along to the song, and laughing with his wet, malformed mouth open. Yes: there were a pair of bony tusks rising from his jaw now, protruding over his upper lip. "We are, we are! We are keeping time!"

Arthur dropped to a squat, popped upright, jumped, landed on the ledge. Water was trickling over the stone and his heels smacked down and threw spray, like Gene Kelly in *Singin' in the Rain*. One foot shot out and Arthur fell and flailed with both hands. Colin didn't think. He reached over the hole, caught him, twisted, and flung him toward the far end of the chasm, only a few yards off now. Arthur hit the stone rim on his stomach, his legs hanging over the side. His colorful Nepalese smoking cap whirled off and disappeared into the darkness below.

Colin tottered, overbalanced, and threw himself across the well in desperation. His bad knee wobbled and this time he couldn't stay upright, couldn't keep it from collapsing on him. He lunged as he dropped off the side of the ledge and caught the waist of Arthur's cargo pants. A button flew and the pants were yanked straight down to his ankles. Colin dropped like a stone clutching the bunched-up rope of Arthur's trousers in both hands. His insides did a slow, lazy roll and his head went deliciously light.

"Arthur!" he cried, his voice thin, hardly recognizable as his own.

The danse macabre had followed them from one end of the chasm to the other, but here at the far side of the hole, they had suddenly left it behind. The song ended with a last flatulent squall of a trumpet and an outburst of distant, dirty laughter and applause. Perhaps if he let go, he'd fall all the way down to some nightclub located in the outer precincts of Hell, where you knew they had to have a heck of a band. Kurt Cobain would be performing with Michael Hutchence all evening.

Above them, Stu Finger moved forward. He wasn't chortling now. Colin saw his shadow fall across them and knew in the next moment Finger was going to plant the heel of one boot in Arthur's face and shove him off—shove them both off.

But Arthur had the Cree hi-thrower, hanging from his wrist by the strap. He flicked his hand and it leapt into his fist. He stabbed the button and shone the disc of light into the troll's face. Finger was no more. He was entirely Svangur now: Colin glimpsed the dark, smooth, almost glossy head, the color of a deep bruise, the bulbous nose, and the great misshapen cavern of a mouth, bristling with lumpish teeth, each like a Stone Age arrowhead.

"You're going to pull both of us up now, Stu," Arthur said. It amazed Colin, the steadiness with which Arthur spoke, hardly a tremor in it. It was inspirational. "Or you're going to spend the next ten thousand years as a column of rock standing over this pit. All I have to do is poke the button again, to switch it to the highest setting, the *daylight* setting. Don't think of it as saving us. Think of it as saving yourself."

Colin felt a wave of faintness roll over him and forced it aside. If he blacked out—even for an instant—it would be the end of him. He felt a hysterical impulse to shout with laughter. He had done lines of nearly pure cocaine, had taken enough ecstasy to feel he was walking weightless on the moon, and it was all nothing compared to the exhilaration he felt now.

Svangur grunted, bent, and gripped Arthur's left hand. He took three steps back and reeled them in, as easily as a man pulling a hooked sunfish out of a pond. Colin collapsed across Arthur's bare brown legs, his head on the inside of his friend's thigh.

"Arthur," Colin panted. "I have sometimes accused you of having your head up your own ass. I want to take a moment to apologize in full. If anyone has come close to putting his head up your ass, it's me, and I couldn't be happier about it."

"I'm glad for both of us I put on clean underwear this morning," Arthur said.

12.

They needed a while to get their breath back. Svangur stood a couple of yards away, slouched in the darkness, all seven and a half feet of him, arms as thick as telephone poles, elbows jutting, lumpish head sunk between his shoulders.

"How does that work?" Colin asked. "How come you don't look like a man anymore?"

"'S'like anythin' else. You gets your eye in," Svangur told him.

"His little glam is effective but also like the reflection on a window. With a little concentration you can see right past it," Arthur said, rising at last and tightening his belt. He had lost the button at the top of his pants. His bare brown head shone with a damp gleam in the subterranean gloom. "We must be almost there."

Svangur sulked. "You see it now, Finger. They will have whatever they likes and if you don't let 'em, they'll make you into a stalackamite. They will have all your old issues of *Score*, and all your copies of *Penthouse*. They will break your Slade *Greatest Hits* for spite."

"Spare us your sob song," Arthur said. "We've heard enough music for tonight."

Svangur led them down a tunnel as wide as a road, with a sloping roof. There were sources of illumination below, a kind of greenish flicker like sunlight seen through shallow tropical waters. Colin was acutely aware of his pulse thrumming in his wrists and throat as they approached the chamber below.

When they reached the edge of the room, he thought, for one dizzying moment, they had emerged into night. A sky of hallucinatory bluish stars glimmered in the velvety darkness above, strewn in unfamiliar constellations. But in another moment his vision sharpened, and he could see it was a spattering of some luminescent substance on rock.

"What is that?" Colin said.

"A kind of glowworm, I think, though I've never heard of them in England."

Water dripped and plinked in the cathedral-like vault before them: an animal den filled with chewed, dirty bones. Colin played his flashlight around the space, drifting the ray across the skull and rib cage of a horse, over tibias and collarbones and teeth. It was mostly bones, drifts of bones knee deep. But there was also an old white refrigerator—it had to date from the 1940s—thrown open and filled with magazines. Most of them were porn, although Colin saw a stack of gun magazines as well. There were several broken TV sets, an office chair, a bloodstained mattress, and an inflatable sex doll. The sex doll had been deflated through heavy use and was crusted with what looked like white sea foam. There were panties—lots of pairs of panties, cast here and there, hanging over bones, two hundred years of panties, from tiny purple Victoria's Secret creations to puffy yellowing grammy bloomers. It looked like he had chewed the crotch out of most of them.

"Crap!" Colin said. "It's all crap! I thought it would be, like, piles of gold coins."

"Treasure is in the eye of the beholder," Arthur said. He cast a desultory glance toward Finger. "The sword. Let's have it."

"Don't know where we might a left it," Finger said.

Arthur turned the Cree hi-thrower to the most powerful setting and Finger squealed, even though the light was pointed away from him.

"There!" Finger screamed. "There! In our cabineck of curiossitease!"

Arthur's flashlight found, at the far end of the chamber, an elevated white stone box. A Celtic cross had been carved into a lid speckled with those phantom lights cast by the glowworm. A tomb, Colin reckoned. They waded through the bones toward it.

"Did he kill all of these?" Colin asked.

"No. This was the plague. The tomb will have belonged to someone who could afford to die in style. A knight, or the wife of a lord. Svangur probably moved the bones in here to make it more homey." The troll followed them halfway across the room and then Arthur waved the light close to his feet. "Stay there, Finger. You've made it this far by being good. Don't spoil things now. Colin?"

Colin took one edge of the stone lid. Arthur took the other and looked at him across the top.

"What if this is another trap?" Colin asked. "What if it's full of, I don't know, soul-eating centipedes?"

Arthur traced his fingers across the Celtic cross, shook his head. "No. They couldn't bear it. Not if this cross means anything. Come on. Lift."

They heaved. Stone ground against stone. As the lid was tipped back, a smell billowed out . . . a surprisingly sweet and grassy odor, as if they had opened a door to a meadow on a cool spring morning.

The sword was in a loose sheath of silk, so white, so clean, it almost seemed to radiate a light of its own. It lay in the bottom of the granite box, on top of a neatly folded brown-and-gray robe made of human hair. A simple glass phial, corked and sealed with wax the color of vanilla frosting, sat on a stone ledge at one end of the coffin.

But mostly, the eye was drawn to and held by the sword. The hilt was another cross, this of dull gold. The silk was so clean, so lovely, it made Colin unhappily aware of his own dirty hands.

"So here's where we find out," Colin said. "Here's where we find out if only a good man can draw the sword from its sheath."

"Or to put it another way," Arthur said, "here's where we find out if I'm a good man."

"Oh, Arthur. I don't have any doubt of it. I've never had any doubt of it. If anyone has tried to be good, it's you."

Arthur smiled at him suddenly and put a hand on his shoulder and squeezed, gently. "I wish I was half as good as my friends believe I am." He looked into the box again. "It might be enough that I know in my heart what I want to do with this blade. That's how it judges, you know? Not what you've done before, but what you choose to do now. Maybe knowing my intentions will be sufficient. If not—then we've come a long way and risked our lives without much to show for it."

Arthur bent and reached for the hilt of the sword. If there was an enchantment on that loose sheath of silk, Colin saw no sign of it. The blade—as bright as a mirror—slipped from its shroud with a soft ringing sound, as if someone had stroked a finger across a wind chime. It flashed an eerie aqueous green in that chamber of mystic lights. Arthur exhaled heavily and seemed to sag slightly.

"Oh, Colin," Arthur said. "I thought it would fight me. But when I put my hand on it—it felt like the whole world was saying *yes*. It was like a first kiss." His eyes were as bright as the Sword of Strange Hangings. He turned it this way and that.

"Can I see?" Colin asked.

"Yes," Arthur told him, and turned it around, and offered him the hilt.

Colin took the hilt in his hand—and felt an ache in his teeth and joints, a kind of nasty thrill of pain. It was like biting a sheet of tinfoil or licking a battery. There was an almost electric sense of repulsion.

"Do you feel it?" Arthur asked, softly. "Do you feel how good it is? Like hearing women laugh on a summer night? Like being called home for dinner?"

Colin nodded. "I do. And it will cut through anything? Even a dragon?"

Arthur nodded and turned and looked back into the stone coffin. "Yes. And the robe will protect whoever wears it against dragon flame. The vial of saint's blood might be enough to restore one of us if we're struck down in the attempt. I think we want all of it. What we'll do, we'll gather the others for a conference at The Briars and—"

He frowned, as if struck by a troubling notion, and lowered his gaze, and looked down, at the sword Colin had pushed through his abdomen. Colin kept pushing, driving it in almost to the hilt. It wasn't hard work. The blade was quite keen, and there must've been something, some magic in it, because it slid through human tissue like it was passing through water.

Arthur stared at it, his hands still gripping the edge of the stone coffin. His knees softened and he sank down, as if to pray. He made a sound in his throat, a kind of *hunh*, and finally his confused gaze found Colin.

"I couldn't have drawn it from that sheath," Colin said. "I know that for sure."

"Why?" Arthur said. His voice was weak and breathless. "We could've stopped him, Colin. We could've stopped the King."

"Why would we *want* to stop him? He's doing so much that needs doing. *You're* the one who had to be stopped, Arthur."

Colin let go of the hilt. Arthur had lifted his hands to grip the blade, but they held it only very loosely. Colin felt a little embarrassed by the look on his face, like a boy who has dropped his ice cream on a hot day and is watching it melt on the sidewalk.

"Oh, hell, Arthur," Colin said. "I'm sorry. I mean that. But did you *really* think you were the hero of this story?"

He took Arthur's shoulder and gently helped him to sprawl on his side. There was a lot of blood. He was already lying in a lake of it. Colin put his head against Arthur's, his mouth close to Arthur's ear.

"You aren't the hero here," Colin whispered. "*I* am."

13.

He put the sword back into its shimmering silks—and then, experimentally, tried to draw it again. It wouldn't move. It might've been sealed fast in cement. He laughed. It was a wonderful trick.

When next he looked for Stu Finger, the troll had moved closer and lifted a splintered thigh bone.

"Do you wants old Finger to hit him a stroke or two?" Finger asked. "Mr. Wren? To be sure he dodn't make any more fuss?"

"No, Stu, thank you. What I would've liked is not to have had spiders crawling all over me."

"Finger took you the way was easiest."

"Finger hoped we'd both fall into that hole so he wouldn't have to hold up his end of the deal."

"Never in life! Finger knew a bit of dance and a bit of sport wouldn't perturb the likes of two bold gennlemen such as yourselves. And the nig-nog—"

"Call him that again and you'll see my ugly side. But not for long, because you'll be a pile of stone."

"Oh, yes, yes, of course, sorry, sorry, wery sorry, my deepest apologies," Stu Finger said, and his crude, gaping mouth convulsed in a parody of a grin. "Svangur forgets what bosom buddies you both were. Like brothers, really. Well, like Cain and Abel, anyway." Colin's brow creased. It vexed him, to think he was being teased by a thing that lived under a rock. The troll went on: "Finger only meant to say, he was a clever cove, now, wannit he? I couldn't have spared you our little pranks. He would've been on to us in a flash if it had been hard on him and easy on you."

Arthur sprawled on his side. His eyes were open and staring.

At the very end, he had muttered Gwen's name and then recited a bit of Psalm 23. It made Colin sad. There would be no green pastures for Arthur, no still waters, and no house of the Lord. For all his plans and precautions, he would never leave this hole in the ground. But then, no man was promised anything better. The idea of burial had never suited Colin. Which reminded him. He reached into the casket and picked up the little vial. A few mouthfuls of what looked like merlot slopped around inside.

"Over a thousand years old," Colin said. "And it looks like it was only just spilled."

"There is the blood of a woman who seen the gates to parydise opening before her, the blood of a woman who forgave him who kilt her, even as he twisted the knife. If you splashed suma that on the nig—on your best-loved friend, even now, you might bring him back. Even now, it might not be too late for him. There is no wound it cannot heal, except for wounds of the soul, which may only be cured by a penitent life, such as is unsuitable to fellows like us."

"And a single swallow will make a man younger?"

"A taste of her life's blood would turn the clock back ten years and give you the stiff pecker of your randiest youth."

"Good. Dying might be fine for people eager for the next life. But I find this life perfectly adequate to my needs."

"Finger was promised trade for trade, like for like," the troll said, his black tongue falling out of his mouth to lick wetly at his chops.

"Yes," Colin said, and it was his turn to tease now. "You can take the Surrealist's Glass out of Arthur's pocket if you like. He won't stop you."

The troll's shoulders sagged in dismay. "What am I supposed to look at with that? I live alone in a hole. You promised Finger—you swore to bring him such power—"

"Yes, all right. Don't snivel. It makes you even more unattractive than you already are." Colin sank to one knee and opened his backpack to remove a Sony Vaio laptop, matte black, brand-new. The little antenna, which could use a cell signal to access the internet, was already plugged in, the red LED blinking to show it had no signal down here. "Here you go. Top-of-the-line, as promised."

"And we can play Doom on it?" Stu Finger asked, drumming his fingers on his chest and looking at it anxiously.

"It does so much more than that. You can watch internet videos with it, no lag," Colin said. "Wait till you discover cam girls, Finger."

Svangur took the laptop in both arms with a sigh of ecstasy.

14.

Arthur had spent most of six years looking for a troll. He drove to dusty local parishes and spoke to their priests about disappearances and tragedies and local bogeymen. He plundered little local libraries for stories of unsolved deaths, tales of massacred goats and sheep. Spent who knew how many hours in the basements of historical societies, brushing aside cobwebs to get at water-stained cardboard boxes full of diaries and regional legends. He poked around and got his feet cold and wet under ancient bridges, leading to at least one case of pneumonia. Six years without finding his troll.

Colin's custom search engine only needed six weeks. And it didn't stop when it produced an 87.3 percent likelihood of a troll working in the area of Camelford, down by the river. It read emails and text messages and examined social media posts made from IP addresses in the area and soon concluded the troll was online. Svangur had his favorite searches: "goat butthole," "proof the holocaust was faked," "lickable fat children," "do vaccines make people fags." He had some rudimentary HTML skills and liked to deface message boards for synagogues, replacing pictures of the happy congregations with photos of uncircumcised penises. He liked to hang out on message boards to argue that racial integration had been a mistake, that Columbine was a false-flag operation to eliminate gun rights, and that George Soros was head of a cabal of Jewish bankers trying to create a one-world nation. Anything to get a reaction. Colin could not help but notice a certain overlap between the things Finger posted to spread panic and confusion, and some of what Donna McBride actually believed. She had never heard a single awful thing about George Soros that she didn't suspect was true.

Svangur wasn't even the first troll Colin had found. It surprised Colin when Arthur told him the Russians farmed trolls on the steppes... because, in fact, Colin already knew this to be true. They harvested at least a few hundred a year. Maybe a few thousand, if they had puzzled out how to grow them hydroponically. They were teaching them to fire rocket launchers—trolls loved rocket launchers—and how to code.

Arthur had known so much, just none of the things that mattered. In October, Colin sent Stu Finger an email. By late November, they had a deal. Finger didn't give a damn about enchanted swords or vials of holy blood, but he was sick to death of slow web page loading times.

Colin took the rough brown robe—it was itchy and unpleasant, but then it would be, it was woven from human hair—and folded it around the vial. He zipped the bundle into his pack. Colin left the sword. He could imagine circumstances in which he might want a robe that could protect him from both a dragon's gaze and a dragon's flame, but he didn't need a magic sword. He had a dragon.

Besides. The sword hadn't liked him. He knew it the moment he touched it.

He patted Arthur's pockets and found the Glass. He liked to think Arthur would've wanted him to have it, would've been hurt if he left it with the troll. Then Colin took Arthur by the hands and Svangur gripped him by the ankles, and they heaved him into the stone coffin. Colin arranged him carefully. He lifted the hood of Arthur's parka up and his old friend was once again the learned monk of loneliness. He took another pass at Arthur's pockets and was not entirely surprised to discover, among his spare change, a Welsh pound with a dragon passant stamped into it. Another had a Celtic cross on the obverse side, almost identical to the cross engraved on the coffin lid. He placed them on Arthur's eyes... and then flinched. The effect was far from soothing. Arthur had the blind silver eyes of an angel now and seemed to be gazing back at Colin with a sort of impassive judgment.

Svangur lifted the limestone lid alone, though it had to weigh nearly three hundred pounds, and set it down with a clank.

"Want to say a few words over the dearly departed?" Svangur said.

"May God bless my friend Arthur Oakes," Colin said. "He had good intentions."

"We know where those gets you." Svangur leered and waggled his tongue. His breath was terrible.

15.

Finger led Colin out, carrying the laptop under one arm. There was no music in the chasm, the frescoes stayed on the walls, and Finger effortlessly hoisted Colin up through the crevasse beneath that great dragon's egg of a boulder. Colin wasn't worried about being torn in two. He still had the Cree hi-thrower.

Finger did not follow him above but peered through the crack under the rock. When Colin looked back he was the homeless derelict again, with the stringy blond hair and patchy beard.

"Finger will tell you a secret, Colin Wren, if you would like to know it."

"What's that?"

"You didn't need that vial. You could've collected the blood leakin' out of your dear friend as he lie dying. That was the blood of a blessed man. We could smell it on him. And do you know why he wept at the very end? It wasn't for himself and it wasn't for his beloved on a far coast neither."

Colin waited for it.

"He wept for you," Finger said, and laughed. "For *you*, Colin Wren."

Colin felt cold and tired. The small of his back was sore and wet with blood. His knee felt as if it had swollen to twice its previous size. He was all talked out. "Goodbye, Finger."

"You'll be seeing lots like Stu Finger online soon," Finger said. "The world you're making—that world of thought that exists on the computer screens—that world belongs to us. To the trolls. And we thank ye for it, Colin Wren! We thank ye wery much!"

He was still laughing as Colin made his way across the clearing and back into the thorns and twisted whips of the briars.

16.

He had brought some Visine, and when he was in sight of the bridge he dripped it into his eyes, let it spill down his cheeks, and threw the bottle into the undergrowth.

"Colin?" Robin cried. She had heard him coming, was already halfway down the embankment, peering under the bridge.

He reeled toward her out of the darkness, into the moonlight, blinking, face scratched and bleeding from where he had run the last hundred yards through the briars. He let himself slip in the mud, go down hard on his hurt knee. His cry of pain was not faked.

"Colin!" Robin cried. "What happened! Where's Finger? Where's Arthur?"

She caught his hands, helped him struggle to his feet.

"Robin!" Colin cried. "We need emergency services. We need cave rescue. It all went wrong! I tried—I tried so hard—but I couldn't save him." He put his face in her presumably surgically crafted bosom. "It's all my fault, Robin. If he's dead, it's my fault."

"Oh, Colin," Robin said, beginning to cry herself, taking him deeply into her arms. "No, no. Whatever happened, you mustn't blame yourself."

17.

He knew exactly what he was going to see when he looked into Wolf Messing's helmet, brimming with cold water. Colin knew when he looked into the water he wouldn't see his reflection at all, and he was right.

The face that stared back at him was thin and long, a little horsey, with mussed hair the color of straw and a shimmer of black scratches where his eyes belonged. It was the face of a sly shit-kicker, a face he had never seen before and knew at once belonged to Corporal Elwood Hondo. The sight thrilled and exalted Colin, drove the breath right out of him. Hondo leered, lifted a cigarette to his mouth, inhaled—the tip of his butt was a bright orange eye flashing in the water—and blew a series of three smoke rings.

Music crashed from the piano. The doors to the patio slammed shut. Colin looked away in time to see Arthur padding out into the snow. The twins sat across from each other on the floor, Donovan dealing them each a pile of cards for a game of War.

When he looked back to the card table, the helmet was gone and he found himself holding a silver hand mirror that had belonged to a murdered Russian princess. A Y-shaped crack, a bright silver fracture, ran up the middle of the glass. There was a different image on either side of the crack. On the left, he saw Donovan McBride scramble up a flight of concrete steps to a high landing in a cement stairwell. Van shot a last wild look out a small window . . . then turned to the banister and tipped himself over it, fell into darkness. On the right-hand side of the crack, Arthur twitched and quivered as someone—Colin couldn't see who, they were beyond the mirror's edge—pushed a three-foot blade through his torso.

Colin flinched, looked away. When he had recovered enough to look again, there was a new future-movie playing in the two halves of the mirror. To the left, Donna was limp and broken in a pile of rock and books, face powdered palest white with concrete dust. Allison was under a scarred wooden table, just beyond her, and as Colin watched, the table was buried in a great collapse of enormous stone blocks. On the other side of that jagged silver fracture line, Gwen was coughing blood and lying in an inch of it. As he watched, a great forked tongue, as long as a man's arm, lapped across her cheek, delicately tasting her life's blood. The tip of a green tail spilled in from the other side of the image to offer her a gentle caress.

"No," Colin said, watching Gwen Underfoot die, watching that serpent's tongue lick the blood off her. He shut his eyes again, counted to three before he opened them.

Now, on one side of the Y-shaped crack, he saw his own face on the cover of *Forbes* magazine. He was dramatically lit in close-up, half his face in darkness. The headline read: SACRIFICE AND ADVERSITY—HOW COLIN WREN TURNED GRIEF INTO STRENGTH AND BUILT THE FUTURE. In the right-hand side of the broken mirror, Colin saw himself on a stage in a nineteenth-century theater. He wore black robes and humbly bowed his head as an elderly woman draped a medal around his neck. The face on the medal appeared to be the calm, bearded visage of Alfred Nobel.

A wave of wooziness rolled over Colin, and he had to put the mirror down and grip the edge of the card table. Allie was bashing out "Puff the Magic Dragon" for the fifteenth time. Gwen had climbed up onto a chair and was taking down Llewellyn's framed and matted butterflies. Donna was winning at cards. Outside, the moon turned the pitted field of snow into a lunar landscape. A dark man fled across it and Arthur followed.

A telephone burred, and when Colin looked down at his hand, clapped to the table, it no longer contained a mirror at all. The Russian hand mirror had been replaced by the bleached Aztec conch from his grandfather's collection, the one that had famously been featured in acts of human sacrifice. The conch rang again with a call from the Long Dark. Slowly, hesitantly, Colin lifted it to his ear.

"We don't have long to talk," Elwood Hondo told him.

"I don't want my friends to get hurt," Colin said.

"Everyone gon' die, boy," Hondo said. "But some people get to die for something beautiful. Don' you dare take that away from them."

"I didn't see how *I'd* die," Colin said.

"When that gloomsome day finally comes, a long time off, someone who loves you will be holding you close, as you take your last breath. Now that's a promise."

"What's so beautiful it's worth all of them being killed?"

"When they go—and don't go buryin' 'em just yet, Colin, good buddy, they got a whiles—they'll be dying for *you*. For you and thousands of others. Ruling beside King Sorrow, you can make sure no one ever hurts you again, the way your momma hurt you by being weak, and your daddy hurt you by killing her, and your granddaddy hurt you by getting some evil fuckin' *diz*-ease. You can stop the wicked and the cruel and the undeserving before they can hurt *anyone*. Think on all the lives you'll save and all the people you'll help. Think of what you can build when ain't no one can step on you or stop you or say no to you anymore. It's up to you, boy, but if you ask me, I think your friends would be glad to give their lives for all the good we both know you'll do."

A dimness surged at the edge of his vision, accompanied by a feeling of lightheadedness so strong, he had to grip the edge of the card table with his free hand to steady himself. Even then, he heard things in Elwood Hondo's offer that he knew were unwholesome. It was all well and good to talk about stopping the wicked, but what was that about stopping the undeserving? Undeserving of what? It was noble (Nobel?) to imagine his friends dying so thousands of others might live. It was another to expect them to die so that no one could ever say no to Colin Wren. But it was hard to think. He had smoked a lot of pot and swallowed a fair bit of Scotch, and every time he closed his eyes he saw the blade going through Arthur again, saw it so clearly—the mirrored edge was wet and red as it came out of his guts—he might've been pushing it through his friend himself.

"How do I know you're not blowing smoke up my ass?" Colin said.

"I'm not the one blowin' smoke," said the voice in his ear, the voice of the dead hillbilly who had killed over a dozen men in the 1950s. "That's gotta be you, son. You need to send up a few smoke signals, show King Sorrow where to find you. Go on now. Get some of that good weed of yours and get puffin'. Make a path in the sky and he'll follow it back to you, Colin. I promise it, as his envoy and ambassador. You kneel to him, and the world will kneel to you. He may be the King, but in every way that matters, you'll be the one wearing the crown."

There was a click and a dial tone. Colin lowered the conch. Allie began "Puff the Magic Dragon" again. She had been smashing the keys so hard, she was getting blood on the ivory. Gwen was on the floor, pulling silver pins out of dead butterflies. Outside, Arthur stalked past again, no closer to the dark figure he pursued. Donna and Van played on. Van never seemed to win a single trick and never seemed to run out of cards to play.

Colin went around the couch and found the glass bong. He opened the French doors and sat cross-legged on the stone, facing the night. The air was bitterly cold and cleared his head, while he packed fresh blue ganja into the bowl. The stars flashed in the deep and velvety dark, like little shattered flecks of mirror. Colin held a lighter to the bowl, put his lips to the glass, and inhaled. His chest filled with smoke, and he was lit up with the sweet, intoxicating sense of burning inside. He supposed it felt much the same to be a dragon.

Colin exhaled and the first rings of smoke rose into the night, reaching toward the Long Dark and the future that waited just beyond.

18.

The British Cave Rescue Council was eight days plumbing the caverns around Camelford, concentrating on the path that led to what was locally known as Arthur's Stairs. Colin joined them several times and realized these stairs—a wide series of shelves descending into a dry, roomy hole—were nowhere near the steps they had walked with Svangur. In fact the BCRC never came anywhere near the hole under the boulder or even the trail through the briars.

Gwen came. She told him she had always wanted to visit England, then melted into tears and had to stand with her head on Colin's chest and his arms around her until she stopped shaking. He kissed her forehead and held her loosely and enjoyed the warm feel of her against his chest.

There was an HQ pavilion set up on the downs, above the River Camel and the forest, which drew a thick green serpentine through the bottom of the valley. Colin and Gwen left the rescue crew behind and went for a walk along the ridge, beneath a bright spring sky, with the wind blowing and doing pretty things to Gwen's hair. He took Gwen's hand. She squeezed, gently, grateful for him.

"So what really happened down there? He didn't slip, didn't fall into a crevasse. Is there any hope of finding him alive at all?"

He told her how the spiders had come off the walls. He said they were both soon engulfed in shrouds of webbing. He said Finger had dragged Arthur away by the feet . . . and that later he had heard muffled screams from deep in the cavern. He said he had given up all hope, had shut his eyes and waited for the troll to return, when he had seen light through his eyelids, and realized the candles on the wall were emitting a gentle brassy glow. He told her he was able to lift one of the candles right out of the fresco and burn his way out of the webbing. He told her he searched for Arthur for hours but in the end, had only found his way out, and he had run, he had run and shouted for help until his voice failed him.

"So he's gone," Gwen said, flatly.

"We don't know that. And he'd never give up on us. We have to give these rescue guys more time to do what they do best."

"Find trolls?" Gwen laughed, harshly, and stood, and looked out across the valley. She blinked back tears, struggling to keep her emotions under control. "Did he say anything? Before he was dragged off? Anything at all?"

It was in Colin's mind to tell her, *He said your name, Gwen, and it was just about the last thing he ever said*. That would've been the truth.

But he thought it too painful a truth to share, so instead he told her, "No. Nothing. I'm sorry. There was no time."

She nodded and shut her eyes, and he took her into his arms and held her the way she needed to be held, the way Arthur would've wanted her to be held.

19.

He'd told Gwen that they shouldn't give up on Arthur because Arthur would never give up on them. But it was tricky to define "giving up." Colin stayed three more days, then offered to fly Gwen back to the States on the Gulfstream. She said she was going to stay awhile longer. He had pushed his stay in the United Kingdom as long as he safely felt he could. Dragonware was pitching a suite of services to the Department of Homeland Security in another week, and he had several venture capital offers to give his consideration. A driver in a black Mercedes—the same model as the one they had at Heathrow for VIPs—picked him up in Tintagel and rushed him back to London and the Savoy hotel.

Pilot Ronnie had been there the whole time, on hold, and she met him in the lobby, wearing a bubblegum-pink miniskirt and enormous pink heels. Colin loved it! It was so sleazy and desperate. She gave him an unasked-for hug.

"I can't imagine what you've been through," she said. "Let me look after you tonight? No arguments."

He nodded obediently. He had read her latest text messages to her friends on the ride to London. No man in grief turns down a comfort fuck, Ronnie had texted her best friend, and he really had to agree.

He told her he'd meet her in the bar and went up to his suite to shower and change. It was while he was naked, in the big, brightly lit bathroom, that he picked his sweats off the floor and found the Surrealist's Glass. Curious, he placed it to his eye and looked into the mirror.

And there was no Colin at all. There was, where his face belonged, a whirling black hole of nothing. He was a void—a darkness punched into the world. *The Long Dark!* he thought, with a giddy thrill. It wasn't a place that existed somewhere outside their universe after all, but a zone that existed within them. Within *him*, anyway. It went on forever and ever, a place no light had ever touched.

He put the Glass down and padded naked into the cool dark of his room. He found the little phial, peeled away the wax, popped the cork, braced himself with a deep breath, and had a sip of a saint's blood. It was a mouthful of salts, a taste of brine—a swallow from some vast ocean Colin had never seen and never intended to visit, that sea that encompassed all grief. He popped the cork back in, and by the time he returned to the bathroom, the ache had gone from his back, the black bruise there had almost faded away, there was no twinge of pain in his knee, and he was as fit and trim as he remembered being at twenty-five. A pulse of heat and weight throbbed in his crotch and he remembered what Finger had said, that it would give him the stiff dick of his randiest youth. He didn't know if that was true, but he thought Ronnie was about to find out.

Fourth Interlude

GWEN, UNDER ATTACK

2015

1.

Robin Fellows took a pull off her e-cig, filled her lungs with a dizzying hit of sweet vapor—she thought it tasted a little like a Wispa bar—and said, "You must be right out of your head, bitch," then got out of the car, into the rain.

It was coming down at a slant, falling in white needles through the headlamps, a freezing November shower that tore leaves from the wych elms and the yews. She checked her phone for a signal, there in the desolate pasture, standing next to her positively ancient Land Rover. She had two bars—enough to pull up Twitter if she so desired. At some point in the last two months she had realized she no longer read newspapers. There was no point. Every story they published was already hours old, and hours felt like weeks now—whatever the breaking news, she had already read about it, and the backlash, and the backlash to the backlash, on social media, in real time.

Twitter was where she had come across the video of the man devouring the goat. Twitter had a weird app—it was a dumb novelty really—called Vine, where users could share six-second loops of video. Vine produced an endless stream of irresistibly stupid clips: here was a dude in a wet suit, snorkeling in his bathtub; here was a guy swallowing a cigarette, then coughing it up, still lit; here was a teenage cheerleader doing her baton-throwing routine with a raw turkey. Part of Robin thought those videos were the end of the human attention span, that soon no one would want to think about anything that required more than six seconds of focus. She hated them. She watched about forty a day.

The clip had turned up a few days ago and swiftly racked up a couple hundred thousand views. It had been filmed by a Camelford teenager who went by the handle @onepurrfection and whose Twitter bio read: Saving It For Marriage Or Harry Styles, STAY AWAY FROM MY MAN Taylor. Or at least that had been the information in her profile right up until she deleted her account, earlier that morning.

@onepurrfection had gone down through the reeds to the river at dusk for a sneaky smoke. Only there had been a man on the far side of the River Camel, in a black tracksuit and a white bucket hat—@onepurrfection described him as a "Liam Gallagher looking weirdo"—petting a goat with one hand while he drank a can of Newcastle. He had seen her looking, offered a little wave, called out cheers. She asked the name of his goat, and he said Second Breakfast, and then he said he'd show her a magic trick if she'd get her tits out. She said go on then, let's see the trick first, holding her phone low to film through the reeds.

In the six-second clip the derelict was a little out of focus—the air had a fine mist in it and water drops had caught on the lens of @onepurrfection's camera. The sun was down but the sky was still a lurid shade of crimson; the phrase "blood-dimmed tide" occurred to Robin's literature-tuned mind. He was a lanky guy, stringy black hair, cheeks corroded by old acne scars, filthy high-top sneakers unlaced. He didn't look anything like the man Robin had seen from a distance under Slaughterbridge, almost ten years before. That guy had been blond, and anyway, would be in his fifties by now. This guy looked thirty.

The bloke in the bucket cap stroked his goat's ears . . . and then bent forward and his jaw distended, came unhooked, opening more, and then more still, stretching grotesquely, impossibly wide, and he swallowed the goat's head. It tried to kick its way back and away, to escape, its hooves tearing strips out of the soft earth, but the derelict had it by the nape of the neck, and then he was forcing its whole upper body into a mouth as wide as a laundry chute. His upper body deformed, mushrooming and swelling like an image in a fun house mirror. His head cocked back, eyes staring at the sky, mouth open like a manhole. The goat's back legs kicked and it disappeared into that impossible hole in the man's face and then the clip was over, leapt back to the beginning.

Responses varied, but generally fell into one of three essential categories:

@scoresesescores: whooooo look who just got Adobe After-Effects for her birthday and thinks she's George Lucas. Note: leaving key elements of the image out of focus is what really marks this as amateur hour stuff. You might not be ready to send your CV to ILM just yet, LOL LOL 😂.

@foreverreall: this goat has been disbudded to remove his horns do you have any idea how fucking cruel that is they scream while theyre horns are burned off. Their not pets, their not food, and their NOT PROPS, you c**t. #animalcruelty #getthefacts #PETA #vegan

@svangur_bro: so *did* you get your tits out? Make that your next video, my luv. Or I could pop by your house on 63 Lankersham Lane & see em for realsies.

@onepurrfection hung in there for about twenty-four hours before posting a last distraught thread of her own.

@onepurrfection: The vine I shared yesterday was 100% real, but in the last 24 hrs I have been doxed, accused of lying, teased, bullied, and creeped on.

@onepurrfection: I gave the raw video file to Cornwall law enforcement & was told I could be charged for wasting police resources. My mother slapped my face because I won't admit it's fake.

@onepurrfection: Fck this site, my life, and every troll here who got off on harassing me. Goodbye thx.

Six hours later her account was gone, although her video lived on, mirrored by other accounts, and often digitally reedited and reinvented. A popular version showed Hillary Clinton bloating and swelling to eat corporate money. In another, minor presidential candidate and reality show host Donald Trump distorted to devour Hillary, gulped her down with a belch, and wiped his mouth with a silk napkin. The trolls had to have their fun. It seemed there were more and more of them online every day.

Robin had watched the original Vine probably sixty times. Half the time she hardly looked at what was happening to the goat. What captured her attention was the derelict's T-shirt, visible when the unzipped top of his tracksuit bulged open. It showed a black knight standing on one leg, his arms and the other leg lying in a pile of severed limbs beneath him. A slogan in Gothic print read, 'TIS BUT A SCRATCH. The last time she had seen that shirt, Stuart Finger had been wearing it and Arthur Oakes had still been alive.

She pulled up the hood of her slicker and started toward the bridge, her wellies splashing in the puddles. Wellies and a slicker always made her feel she was sixteen again, walking home from school in Orpington. Even now, her definition of happiness remained a rainy day, an Ursula Le Guin, a strong cup of black tea, followed by a nap. A sweet, dreamless nap, with the rain tapping on the roof tiles.

There hadn't been much in the way of sweet, dreamless sleep in the years after BA 238 made its emergency landing at Narsarsuaq Airport. For a long time, no sooner had Robin closed her eyes than she found herself on the plane again, the aircraft rattling with turbulence, the lights stammering furiously overhead. These dreams always played out the same, with only the tiniest variations. Papers flew as the 747 dropped. Passengers wailed. Some of them were craning their heads to see out the windows, and Robin herself leaned across Van in an attempt to glimpse whatever was out there. Rain streamed across the glass and black clouds churned. Van took her hands in his, his slender freckled face gone almost bloodless.

"Allie," he whispered. "Why did I let Allie get out of her seat? She isn't safe. She should be with us."

"I'll find her. I won't let anything happen to her," Robin promised.

She unbuckled her belt and came to her feet. The 747 lurched. She fell across the aisle, grabbed a seat back to steady herself, and Frank Heck, sitting in the next row, turned his head to look at her. His face was swollen and black in death, the blood vessels burst in one eye so one cornea had turned a milky scarlet.

"What part of remain in your seat don't you understand, babe?" he asked her.

Robin reeled up the aisle, her heart thudding high in her throat. The thought that Allie might be hurt—small, lovely, foolish, kind Allie—was so terrible it overpowered all other notions. But the girl was nearby, Robin could sense it, and if she could get a hand on her, it was still possible to save her life. Allie was just on the other side of the curtain drawn across the waist of the plane, Robin knew it. But when Robin ripped aside the curtain, there was no front of the plane at all. The 747 had been sheared in two. Beyond the curtain was only the roaring black night, the pelting rain, the shriek of the wind. Everything in front of the wings was gone.

Robin opened her mouth to scream and the dragon screamed first. The dragon erupted from the clouds, great golden jaws open in a nerve-freezing howl, a sound terribly like steel grinding on steel. That hideous, awful cry always shocked her awake and became the sound of steel wheels keening on iron rails. The tracks out of Waterloo East curved past her apartment, not forty feet from the windows, and in those days, the scream of the last train often drew her shouting from sleep.

It wasn't so bad, waking at 1:00 a.m. from a dream like that. Allie, at least, was still awake, on the East Coast, where it was only eight in the evening. In the dream, Robin was trying to rescue Allie, but after she woke, in the early hours of the morning, Allison was Robin's parachute, letting her gently down from terror to calmness.

Robin would send a text: Welp, the plane crashed again. If I was getting air miles for all the time I've spent flying that plane in my dreams, I could get us round trip tix to Tahiti, doll.

A minute or two later, Allie would write back: Oh, Robin. Are you okay?

And Robin would text: At least I got to see Van again. That part of the dream is all right.

Allie would text back a few hearts. And once she wrote: Sometimes I think that's 50% of why we dream. To see the people we lost. I see him every few nights, you know. He still has the best smile. I can carry that smile inside me all day long.

If dealing with grief is 50% of why we dream, what's the other 50%? Robin wanted to know.

So we can have sex with famous people, obvzly.

She used the flashlight on her phone to light the wet blacktop and found her way to the old stone bridge, the Slaughterbridge, an arch of ancient rock sitting on colossal piers. She had spent the whole drive west talking to herself and shaking her head. Twice she hit her blinker to take an off-ramp, turn around, go back to London. And twice she had let the exit ramp slide by, kept driving. There was no reason to believe she would find the derelict from the Vine here in Camelford (the video had, in fact, been shot at least a mile down the river, the bridge nowhere in sight), and even if she did, he wasn't Stu Finger, didn't look anything like Stu Finger.

Except. Except there was something else tugging at her consciousness, something she had overheard and never forgotten.

The last time she had been to Tintagel, Arthur had asked her to meet him at the King's Bestiary, the seventeenth-century inn where he had rooms with his friend Colin Wren. Robin had arrived early and let herself into a handsome, empty lobby with walnut wainscoting and a lot of old scuffed brass. She heard Arthur in the next room, his voice rising and falling in the pub at the rear of the inn. She crossed to poke her head through the doorway and wave hi . . . then slowed and dropped her head, listening intently.

After making a meal of someone's chubby daughter he probably needs to sleep it off for a while, Arthur said. *And he can make do with goat, sheep. Fish. Children are a pleasure, not a necessity. Some of the reading suggests trolls may even be a bit like cicadas, emerging cyclically, every nine years or so. He shows up, munches on some livestock, goes back to bed. Maybe every second or third time he's awake, he'll devour a boy or a girl as a special treat.*

Some tickle of unease had made her withdraw, return to the front door, and enter again, making more noise this time, so Arthur would be sure to hear her coming. Robin had almost wished that she could unhear what she had heard. It made her think of the flight again, of Allie and Van's secrets, and of the thing she had seen in the clouds that had torn two F-16s apart like they were paper airplanes. That monstrous animal—the dragon—that they had all seen and never discussed. Robin Fellows had swiftly come to love Allie and Van and to enjoy their friends. She also believed that Allie and Van and the others kept a secret, that they knew more about the thing that had nearly destroyed BA 238 than they dared admit. The thing that had chased BA 238 through the skies had been pursuing them all for years. The six of them had a way of laughing all together that made her think of captured soldiers sharing a raunchy last joke before they faced the firing squad. They lived curious, haunted lives, as close to each other as lovers, and at a slight remove from the rest of the world, communicating in a mix of coded references that was almost their own language. They talked about *pulling a Nighswander*, and *inviting a Philip to the party*, and *borrowing Sheldon's lighter*, phrases that they all instantly understood, and seemed to have no interest in explaining. Not that Robin asked for explanations. She only listened. And remembered.

And what had Arthur told Colin, before he knew she was there? *Some of the reading suggests trolls may even be a bit like cicadas, emerging cyclically, every nine years or so. He shows up, munches on some livestock, goes back to bed.*

Nine years. It had been just over nine years since Arthur Oakes had walked under the bridge and out of Robin Fellows's life forever. The man in the video didn't look like Stuart Finger, but he was tromping around in Fingers's backyard, wearing Fingers's shirt, and he had chowed down on some livestock for his elevenses. There was no rational reason to believe the grotesque derelict from @onepurrfection's Vine would be found under the Slaughterbridge . . . but there *was* a kind of dream logic to the idea, which was the only kind of logic creatures of the impossible obeyed. And as Robin began to edge down the slippery embankment, she heard someone whistling. A tune echoed from the stone vaults beneath the bridge, cutting through the crackle of rain in the trees and the melodic rumble of the river. She knew it right away—it was the *Love Island* theme.

She caught herself halfway down the steep slide to the water and peered into the darkness. A homeless man sat under the bridge, surrounded by Tesco bags full of junk. He had a battered black Sony laptop folded open across his thighs and was watching a Nigel Farage speech while eating Wotsits.

"Hello?" she called, shuffling sideways. The footing was all slick mud, and she felt at any moment she might go down on her silly arse.

He didn't look at her but remained fixated on his screen. "That's right, mate—England for the English, not the fucking Pakis. Not the fucking wogs. Getting so there's parts of this country look more like Islamabad."

It wasn't Stu Finger—and it wasn't the man from the Vine either. This man was old, a few dark streaks in his long gray hair and scraggy beard, and he wore a pair of square-framed glasses with thick lenses, taped at the bridge of his nose. She was relieved, she supposed. She hadn't really wanted to find the man from the Vine here. She wanted even less to see Finger. Yet her blood seemed to fizz and she was jumpy all the same. Finger had been under the bridge just so, nine years ago.

"Hello," she called again, and he glanced her way, without any interest.

"Who's this?" he called out.

"I'm Robin Fellows," she said, stopping in the rain, ten feet away.

"You're a fellow all right," he said. "Fellow in a dress." And he roared with laughter and orange bits of Wotsit flew.

She smiled indulgently. She had heard that one before.

"What'd you want then?" he asked. "You want a little suckee-fuckee, you ought to know Glen Schrödinger is straight and Glen Schrödinger won't go queer for anything less than twenty pounds."

"No, that's all right, but thank you!" she cried. "What about twenty pounds for a little talk?" Reaching into her great beaded purse and leaving her hand on what she had in there for Glen Schrödinger. "I'm looking for someone."

She would've liked to duck under the bridge, out of the wet, but if she went any closer, she'd be close enough for him to leap and get her by the wrist, a thought that made her woozy. He set his laptop down, although it continued to light his face from beneath, giving him a pasty, greenish, corpse-like cast.

"Who'sat?" he asked, sliding toward her on his bottom but staying under cover. And when he rotated toward her, she saw it. His coat fell open to show the Monty Python shirt beneath, crusted with old stains. 'TIS BUT A SCRATCH. "Glen Schrödinger knows anyone who's anyone around these parts . . . but better than that, he knows anyone who's *no one*, and it's them who are no one who are hardest to find."

She was going to say, *I'm looking for Stu Finger*, but her mouth was suddenly dry, and when she spoke at last, her voice was a low croak. "I used to have a friend named Arthur Oakes. Gone now. I guess you could say *he's* no one now, although he'll always be *someone* to me. Ever heard of him, Glen Schrödinger?"

He tapped one dirty finger against his jutting lower lip. "Arthur, Arthur. There was an Arthur got knifed in these parts, most 'orrible. Died of his wounds very near here, he did. Don't recall his last name was Oakes, though. Pendragon as I remember it, and he called 'imself king of these parts. Is that who you might be thinking of, my darling?"

"No," she said. "This was a Black man. A professor of medieval literature. He came looking for a man named Stu Finger."

"Stuart Finger! Now there is a name Glen Schrödinger hasn't heard in years, though once upon a time, we knew him as well as we know our very own self, heh heh." He leaned forward as he spoke. The rain was on his face now, running down his cheeks. Robin didn't care for the effect. It gave her the dizzying sense that his face was beginning to soften and run. "Did Arthur Oakes find him? This Stu Finger? Did they run away to claim their happily ever after together?"

"I don't know. You tell me."

"There aren't many tales end happily ever after, you know. Very few are allowed a noble end. The first Arthur impaled his own son, stuck him through the stomach and watched him die squealing like a piglet. Then he staggered away to die himself, knowing all he had fought for in his life was laid a-waste. I imagine it was much the same for *your* Arthur. They both found the one kingdom promised all men: a hole in the ground and eternity to rule it. What did he want of Stu Finger?"

"Arthur? Arthur was looking for a sword."

"No doubt he found it."

"A friend went with him," Robin said.

"No," said Glen Schrödinger. "I'm sure not."

"Yes. He was with a man named Colin Wren."

"No *friend* went with Arthur Oakes into the ground," the derelict said. "He may have gone with this Colin Wren and that Stu

Finger, but he still went friendless. Is there a penis under that skirt, my love?"

"That's none of your business."

His face appalled her. It sagged like a loose rubber mask now . . . especially around his gray eyes. There was something dull and weary and ancient in those eyes.

"No, it isn't!" he agreed. "'Tisn't Schrödinger's business at all, is it? But isn't it interestin' how many go costumed in this world? You cloak yourself in the garment of womanhood, and it suits you, no doubt. You might ask yourself who else goes cloaked and in what garb. Maybe our ownself! Maybe others. There is a cat with our name, a wery famous cat, what is somehow alive but also dead at the same time. What a peculiar world, with cats that are alive but also dead, people on the innernet who are men but also trolls, videos that are as viral as plague, women who tweet more than birds, hawks pretending to be wrens, snakes pretending to be kings . . . and you standing there holding *our* twenty quid as if it's still *your* twenty quid."

His tongue fell from his mouth and licked his lips, and when it withdrew she had a glimpse of his teeth. They didn't quite fit in his mouth anymore. Two of his canine teeth were enormous and hooked upward, curling almost over his upper lip. Boars had teeth like that.

"Whatever you're thinking," Robin said, "please don't do it." She tried to keep the tremor out of her voice and failed.

She took a step to the left, thinking it was time to go, but the ground gave way and she wobbled, went down on one knee. Her hand was still stuck in her purse. She couldn't seem to get it free.

"Glen Schrödinger doesn't *think*," he hissed, the flesh of that false face drooping horribly off whatever was beneath. "Glen Schrödinger *does*. We has that in common with Stuart Finger, who did not need to think a minute about leading your Arthur Oakes deep into the earth to see him slaughtered by that slick cove who was with him. Oakes wanted to find a knife and he did—when his friend Mr. Colin pushed one right through his black guts."

"Stay back," Robin said. He was out from under the bridge now, coming at her across the mud on all fours, apelike, knuckles in the muck. His mask of skin hung so loose, she could now see the real face behind it, lumpish and obscene. "Stay back, man."

"I think we both knows by now," said Schrödinger, "ain't neither of us truly men."

He lunged, his mouth yawning wide, wide enough to swallow a watermelon in one gulp, and it was *him*, it was the thing from the video, and it was also Stu Finger, she knew that now, could see it in his eyes. As he bounded from under the bridge and across the embankment, he seemed to get bigger, to bulge and deform, his shoulders splitting the seams of his coat. She fumbled in her purse—it took a moment to get a firm grip on the shaft of the Cree hi-thrower. For one terrible moment, the lens caught on the edge of her purse and she couldn't pull it out. Then it came free. It was a long, stainless steel light, and she meant to smash it in Glen Schrödinger's melting, grotesque face. But her thumb found the switch instead and punched it on, straight to the highest setting, which was, after all, what Arthur had told her to do, should she ever find herself in danger here by the bridge. In that moment, Arthur might almost have been behind her, his hand over hers, his thumb pushing hers down to light up the Cree.

Schrödinger was one leap from her when he threw himself into the beam. His mouth was open in a scream of lunatic hunger and joy when his face turned to a gray mask. Instantly it split and fissured, hairline cracks running through an ill-sculpted stone bust. His hair—every fine strand of it—stiffened into a thread of what looked like concrete. He made a last whistling sound as he petrified in the sunbeam of the Cree hi-thrower, a sound like gases escaping as someone removed the stone lid on an ancient tomb.

His momentum carried him on, up off the ground and into the air, but by then he was already falling to his left. The hands sticking out of his sleeves were the gaunt, bent claws of an old man, but Robin swung the beam around to follow him as he tumbled, and the light passed over those too. By the time Glen

Schrödinger—or whatever Glen Schrödinger was—hit the River Camel, those hands were bent claws of stone. He was a crouched and leering granite gargoyle, like something fallen off the side of a Gothic church, when he struck the water and tumbled away in the roar and froth of the flood.

2.

A little after seven, Gwen's laptop began to chime with the FaceTime alert. When she saw who was calling, she hesitated, doing the math in her head. It had to be almost one in the morning, Greenwich Mean Time. Robin Fellows had never rung her so late, not in all the years they had known each other. Gwen settled in front of her computer and clicked the green button to accept the call.

Robin appeared in a room lit only by a desk lamp. Rain slashed across a window behind her. In the last two decades of climbing in and out of ambulances, Gwen had conservatively treated seven thousand women for assault, and her first thought, in a moment's glance, was that Robin was calling to say she had been raped. Robin usually applied her makeup with the greatest of care and always kept her honey-blond hair carefully sculpted in the style of late-seventies Farrah Fawcett. Now her mascara had run down her cheeks in crooked black veins, she had an eyelash missing, her hair was a wet tangle. She was wrapped in a blanket, pulled off the bed behind her. Gwen didn't FaceTime Robin often enough to know the inside of her flat, but she didn't think this was it. It looked like an attic room under the eaves of some grand old house, and Gwen was sure Robin lived in a brick open-plan place that had been converted from a Victorian warehouse into condos.

"What happened?" Gwen asked.

"Gwen," Robin said, shaking furiously. She lowered her head, clenched her jaws, couldn't go on. She was too powerfully overtaken by the shivers.

"You ought to be in an emergency room."

"Can't. Can't go."

"Were you attacked?"

Robin said, "You could say I went looking for it."

"Bullshit. No woman goes looking for it. I want you to hang up and call the police. Do it now."

"But I *did* go looking. I'm not in London. I'm in Tintagel, at an inn. And I can't tell the police about any of it."

No obscenity in the entire language made Gwen quite so ill as the word *Tintagel*.

"Why are you in Tintagel, Robin?"

"I was looking for Stuart Finger. And I found him. He doesn't look anything like the Stu Finger I saw nine years ago, but it was him, the same man, I know it was. Gwen, he didn't hurt me. *I* hurt him. I think I killed him. But not before he talked to me. Not before he told me about going underground with Arthur and Colin. Not before he said what happened."

Gwen felt as if she stood at the edge of a hole herself, the ground beginning to give way under her feet.

"What . . . what happened?" Gwen asked, and waited while thousands of miles away, the wind screamed and the rain dashed against the glass.

3.

"It was Colin," Robin said, and Colin hit the space bar to pause the video playback.

He took the headphones off, got up, and did a lap around the bedroom. He waited to see what he felt. A sense of alarm would've been appropriate—alarm that he was found out, that Gwen knew who he was now, what he had done.

But as was so often the case, he could not find it in himself to feel the things he was supposed to feel. Instead of anxiety, he felt nearly overcome by hilarity. He wanted to laugh. He twitched aside a heavy curtain for a peek at the bright morning. The trees were lit up in the sunshine, their branches powdered with a half inch of fresh snow. The cold white brilliance of the grounds corresponded to his own feelings of glinting excitement. To be discovered was, it turned out, a physical thrill, like leaping into bed with a new lover.

In the dark behind him, Donna groaned and turned over under the sheets.

The video was three days old. Gwen and Robin had sat there whispering, like little girls telling each other ghost stories at a sleepover, as if somehow Colin might overhear them. And all the while they were videoconferencing with one another on Gwen's computer, the one he had given her, the one that recorded every stroke of the keys, every search term, every mail she sent.

He kept an eye on all their communications with one another: Gwen and Allie and Donna. He had for years. He had always wanted to read minds, had longed for the power to see into another's thoughts, to possess their secrets. And now he could and did. He knew Allie would begin searching for hot girls and lesbian videos after a glass or two of wine—and that the next morning she would hit the Christian self-help sites *hard*. He knew Donna searched *Donna McBride Sexy* and *Donna McBride Awesome* every day to see what people were saying about her online. He could find out where in the world Gwen Underfoot was at any one moment because he could geolocate the phone he had given her.

He lowered himself back into his seat at the desk on the far end of the bedroom and composed himself. He was almost too wound up to sit. Headphones on and he hit play.

But he had to stop again only a minute later, as energized as if he had downed a double shot of espresso.

"I need to think," Gwen had told Robin, while her hand drifted unconsciously to her throat, to her own collarbone, stroking a spot only inches from the mark that was upon them all. "This is . . . a lot to take in. And, Robin, it might not be true. It probably isn't. This *thing*. What you saw. It isn't much interested in what's true, only what hurts."

Robin said, "Sometimes the truth *does* hurt."

Gwen nodded, distracted, her fingers moving in little circles near her collarbone. "If it was true, then—"

"Then?"

"Colin could never be punished for it. Nothing could ever be proved against him. But there are other ways to deal with him. I get scared thinking about what it would take to make sure he can't hurt anyone else. If I had to, though. If I was sure." The thought had trailed off there.

"Gwen," Robin had said, "you don't want to do anything stupid. You don't want to, you know, attack him and get yourself arrested."

"No." Gwen had shook her head. "Trust me. I wouldn't attack him."

Her finger close to the mark. *I* wouldn't attack him. No. She wouldn't need to, would she?

He circled his bedroom again and paused at the floor-to-ceiling windows for another peek outside, and yes, there she was. He had been expecting her. Gwen herself was out there, in her daddy's old pickup, plowing out his driveway. She had taken over the care of the grounds not long after old Mr. Underfoot dropped dead of a colossal stroke. The plow came grinding up the drive, throwing a prow-wave of bright white snow, then paused, halfway around the circle. She had seen him looking.

She lowered the driver's-side window and waved, a half-smile on her face and her gaze studiously blank. He waved back . . . and then turned away, dissolving into laughter. Three days now, she had known, and here she was to plow his drive. He walked back to his laptop and sat down.

Donna groaned again. Her eyes were squeezed shut. She had a

finger looped around the dull chain around her neck, an old key hanging off one end. She had worn it ever since Colin draped it around her throat.

"Did Gwen really have to plow us out at the crack of dawn?"

"It's ten," Colin said.

Donna pulled a pillow over her head. Colin put his headphones back on and resumed watching the video. He thought it was best to review everything Gwen and Robin knew before he spoke to Donna. He was already working out what to tell her, how to shape the narrative, so when she expressed her opinion, it would be one that suited him. He was good at molding her reactions to things. He had been doing it for years. Not that her opinion mattered.

In the end, she'd leave it up to him—she always did—and he had already decided what to do.

Gwen stopped the truck when she saw Colin watching her from upstairs. She rolled down her window and stuck her arm out and waved to him, this friend of twenty-five years who had murdered Arthur in a grubby hole in the ground. Ran a sword through him and watched him bleed to death and then lied about it. She forced a smile onto her face.

"He might not be guilty of anything," Arthur said, leaning across her to peer out the driver's-side window.

"He's guilty of plenty. We all are."

"But you don't *know* he stabbed me in the back."

"Well, *did* he? Why don't you just tell me?" she asked, but only in her mind, without opening her mouth, and Arthur didn't reply because he wasn't really there, on account of being dead.

Arthur often joined her when she was out on a drive. They

talked as much now as they ever had. More, really. It was always a relief to be alone with him and to know she could tell him anything. That was one thing about the dead: they were naturally great listeners.

She was in no sense delusional, knew the Arthur who kept her company existed only in her mind. And yet it was somehow wrong to insist he was imaginary when she knew that ghosts were as real as sound waves, as real as ice on the moon. Once upon a time, Donna and Van had pretended they shared a secret twin language. It turned out, in the end, that they had. Love was the secret language of twins. It was the private code of a husband and a wife. It was the telegraph system of best friends. When you had it, a glance could suffice for ten minutes of talk. When you loved someone enough, you did not simply remember them. Some part of them was copied into you forever and so when they were gone they weren't gone. She did not need him physically there to hear his voice, to take his advice, to smile at his jokes. And that was a ghost, as much as any Philip. Like a Philip, the Arthur in her head couldn't know anything she didn't know herself. He could still surprise her, though. He wasn't an invention, wasn't an imaginary friend. He was more like the deep-buried roots of a tree after the trunk has been cut down. She could feel them still, grown deep into the soil of her own being, her everyday experience of the world.

She was another twenty minutes plowing the driveway, and in all that time she was alone. But when she got out and began to push the snowblower, Arthur joined her again, yelling to be heard over its clatter and roar.

"What do we know about Stu Finger? He's a troll! What do trolls do?"

"Trolls gonna troll," Gwen said.

"That's right!" Arthur pounded his mittened hands together. "What the hell is a Black man doing this far north? Ninety-eight percent of the Black people on this planet are too sensible to live somewhere this cold."

"What are you complaining about? You're dead."

"Yeah, well, ninety-eight percent of Black people are too sensible to *haunt* somewhere this cold."

"What's with the statistics? You're sounding like Allie. Don't be Allie. I need you to be you."

By the time she rounded the corner to the patio, the snowblower roaring, she had lost him. It was always a mistake to remind a ghost he was dead. It startled them off.

Not that it mattered. He had made his point. Just because Finger had said it didn't mean it was true. In fact, the opposite held. Something was even *less* likely to be true if Finger insisted on it. She needed to know for sure before she could take the next step. Not that she knew what the next step was.

She went on, pushing the snowblower ahead of her, circling the problem of Colin in her mind. Then it struck her the problem might not be Colin alone, because there was Donna too. Would Donna have gone along with it, even encouraged Colin to strike Arthur down? Gwen didn't want to think so and couldn't quite rule it out. Arthur wanted to take King Sorrow away, wanted to strip them of their power to punish the wicked, and what had Donna told her after Black Cricket? *I say all hail the King.*

Their relationship with the dragon did not trouble Donna, and of course Colin *loved* it. He relished drafting his yearly menu of enemies and selecting one to sacrifice to their pet iguana each year. He had *always* loved it, although he performed regret and reluctance, because regret and reluctance made him more acceptable to his friends. Perhaps he told himself that what they did was necessary, had moral value. They only killed people who had it coming.

Didn't they?

Gwen's insides crawled, a sensation like a bellyful of live ants. Of all the questions she had asked herself in the last three days, this was the one she was least eager to examine. Because, in truth, she had long since stopped caring who Colin fed to King Sorrow. It had ceased to seem relevant to her, in the years after Arthur descended into the earth with Stu Finger and didn't return. She chose for herself, when it was her turn, and that was enough. She volunteered Sunday afternoons at St. Daniel's Hospice, which was just a short walk from the campus of Rackham College, in sight of both Rackham's chapel and library. Twice in the last ten years, she had eased someone's passage, as she had eased Llewellyn's, using the tears she had won by stumping King Sorrow with a single stupid joke. It took only a sip to kill, and even after Llewellyn was gone she had nearly eight ounces of the stuff.

In 2009 Gwen had assisted Rose Ellroy, a former English professor at the college—her specialty had been the Romantic poets—suffering from the rapid onset of Alzheimer's. Rose had wanted to die before she forgot Shelley. She drank the tears from Gwen's thermos with a small smile on her lips.

"*My heart aches, and a drowsy numbness pains,*" she said, with a certain satisfaction, sparks flying from her lips, "*my sense, as though of hemlock I had drunk,*" clutching Gwen's hand as her bright eyes slowly dimmed.

In 2013, Gwen had offered the thermos to a broad-shouldered, long-haired Native American named Eddie Knockwood, dying of emphysema and diabetes, who wanted to find the exit before they amputated his legs. In 1989, he had placed twenty-third in the Boston Marathon. At some point in the nineties, he had actually won the Lidingöloppshelgen in Scandinavia. He wanted to run into the afterlife on his own two legs, wanted to run to his wife, who had died thirty years before. He had never remarried.

Gwen asked him what he felt, when Eddie sipped the tears and began to breathe smoke, and like Llewellyn he said, *I think my soul just caught fire.*

That doesn't seem good, she said.

He gave his head a shake and showed her a sly, confident smile. *Feels good.* Then he lifted his shaggy eyebrows and said, *It could burn a hundred thousand years and not even come close to burning out. Maybe that's all a sun is. A single soul, burning itself up, bright enough to light worlds.*

As for the others King Sorrow had taken? Colin chose for himself . . . but he also chose when it came around to what would've been Arthur's turn. That had been acceptable to all of them. Arthur had always examined every new Enemies List with care and attention. He wouldn't have been himself if he shirked the homework. But in the end, he always signed off on Colin's recommendation anyway.

And when they came around to what would've been Van's turn—well, Colin chose in Van's place as well. It should've been Donna's choice, but Donna didn't care anymore. Something had gone out of her after Black Cricket; after the man who murdered Cady Lewis killed himself. She often seemed distracted, listening for some faraway sound only she could hear. She wasn't any less angry, though these days she mostly saved her fury for her podcast. Gwen had read somewhere it was one of the ten most downloaded podcasts in the world. She was angry about new things now. She raged about her usual bugbears, the globalists and the elites . . . but she had also come out hard against the incarceration of Black men for the personal possession of marijuana, boiled with disgust about pesticides on crops and GMO foods, was vituperative about the domestic surveillance program begun under George W. and continued under Barack Obama. When she talked about legalizing weed and outlawing genetically altered strains of produce, Gwen thought she sounded like Donovan, although Van never would've expressed himself with such malice. Maybe that faraway sound Donna sometimes seemed to be listening for was Van's voice. Gwen supposed she wasn't the only one who trafficked with the ghosts of those she loved.

As for Allie, she had never wanted to choose, had been glad to let others decide for her. So Colin made her selections as well. Allison had come back to Podomaquassy at last, like all of them, had accepted a teaching position at Rackham College in the Department of Statistics. As the survivor of a famous air disaster, her course "Plane Crashes, Shark Attacks, and Falling Coconuts: The Odds of an Interesting Death" was the single most popular class on campus. It didn't hurt that she was beautiful, that most of her male students and probably a quarter of her female students had crushes on her. She had rejoined the campus choir, as well, and sang in the chapel every Sunday morning, attended every service . . . when she wasn't too hungover, anyway.

Now that Gwen thought about it, Colin chose for all of them, except her. She didn't know whose turn it would've been that year, but it didn't matter. It wasn't hers, so it was his.

"They were bad people, weren't they?" she asked, and then realized she had spoken aloud and was glad for the roar of the snowblower. "The people we offered to King Sorrow?"

"You could find out," Arthur said. He had returned to her, was blowing on his mittened hands. "Easier than finding out if he stabbed me."

It jellied her insides, to think of going back over the dead. Of taking another look at the kill list. Of what she might learn.

"How *do* I find out what Colin did when he was down in that hole with you?"

"Look for proof."

"What proof? You think he kept notes? You think he kept evidence against himself?"

Arthur rolled his shoulders in a shrug. "You won't know if you don't look."

She slowed the snowblower at the French windows, wondering where Colin kept the things that mattered most to him in the world. Then she turned her head and stared through the glass, past her reflection, at the Cabinet of Curiosities, behind Llewellyn's old desk.

And for the first time noticed there was a new lock on the doors.

5.

Gwen parked on campus in the student lot adjacent to Arundel Hall. It still didn't feel right to her. In the old days—in the years when she picked up summer work at Rackham, in the employ of her father—she had only ever parked in the lots for custodians, cafeteria workers, and groundskeepers. She always half expected to be asked if she was lost. It took a conscious act of will to shoulder her messenger bag and leave her pickup parked where it was. She had, after all, as much right to be there as any student.

She had, at forty-two, enrolled in Rackham College at last. She had gone back because Arthur had wanted her to, had wanted it badly enough to pay for it himself.

They had declared him dead two years ago. Seven years after he went to Tintagel. Although he did not have so very much to give, what there was he had left to her: twelve thousand dollars in savings, fifty thousand from the insurance, and three file boxes of notebooks. The boxes were shoved under her bed. She had tried to look at them—she had really tried. He had seven chapters and some unfinished bits and pieces for a book titled *Toolkit for the Well-Prepared Dragonslayer*. It was, she thought, an attempt to present some of his ideas about Arthurian legends and folktales to popular readers. But the margins were littered with notes written directly to her. The first she saw was, "G., is this too academic?" The second was, "G., be honest: Does this make me sound like a pretentious jackass?" The third was, "G., I hope you will tell me when I'm being boring, you can't be afraid to hurt my feelings," and that was enough, she couldn't read anymore, her vision was blurring, and she could taste tears in the back of her throat. There were thousands of comments like that in his notebooks, and each one was like losing him all over again.

The day the check cleared, she had called admissions at Rackham and told them she had been accepted to the college as a freshman in 1990. She was wondering if her acceptance still held. It was three weeks before they replied by email to say it was the opinion of the entire admissions department that yes, as the offer had never been withdrawn, her original acceptance remained valid. Twenty-two years was an uncommonly long deferment but not disqualifying. Gwen thought Allie had done some work behind the scenes to ease things along. Colin too. Colin had a lot of pull at Rackham College. He was one of its biggest donors, was building the college a computer center.

In A. A. Milne's stories about Winnie-the-Pooh, the titular bear liked to retreat to what he called his "Thotful Spot" when it was time to do some serious pondering. Gwen had a Thotful Spot of her own: the Brooks Library, with its towering stone halls and stained-glass windows, its stillness and calm, its smell of books. She was grateful for it every time she stepped through the doors, grateful for the glow of the desk lamps in their glass shades, the worn and nicked walnut tables. It always made her think of Arthur, who had been all stillness and calm himself, who seemed happiest when he had an eighteenth-century book open in front of him, paper flaking from the browned and hand-cut edges. It pained her to think he had been forced to steal from a place he loved. She was never closer to him than when she was here and they could talk without being shushed, since the conversation was in her head.

It was just beginning to snow—white flower petals, thrown at a wedding. Her path took her past the glass box of the new computer center, all but finished now. Rows of computer monitors—a phalanx of blind obsidian mirrors—waited on glass tables that seemed to float. The official opening was in a few months; Colin would be coming by to cut the ribbon himself. She had never told him she hated it, this building that looked like an Apple store, which appeared to have been dropped by accident among the nineteenth-century halls with their arrow-slit windows. The old buildings were places to think, to read, and to remember. Colin's glass tomb of a computer center made her think of a jar, something a brainy child would use to trap bugs.

She left the future behind, in the gathering gloom, and went on into the Brooks Library, where the past was as near as the closest bookshelf. She sat at a long table in the western hall, laptop open, probably looking to the other kids less like another student, more like a professor here to do personal research. Her mousy brown hair had a big streak of gray in it. Age had drawn a pale brush across it in one swoop, falling from her brow.

Gwen began to work her way through the names on the Enemies List . . . the names they had crossed out over the years. A colonel in Boko Haram who locked children into suicide vests and then pointed them at military checkpoints and crowded marketplaces. A Naxalite-Maoist judge in India who kidnapped bureaucrats and their families and sentenced them to slow deaths by impalement. She despised them and felt grimy reading about them—there was a reason she had not wanted to look too closely at any of Colin's selections.

When she couldn't stomach anymore, she took a break to be with Arthur. Not the version she carried around in her head, but the one on her laptop. She put on her headphones and pulled up the video Colin had sent her by way of a Christmas present, the year Arthur had died. In two clicks, Arthur appeared on the screen against a backdrop of an improbably warm October evening.

He whirled around and around on roller skates, laying about him with a lacrosse stick, fending off the barbaric hordes with a look of peace and even amusement on his face. Colin's voice floated in from off camera to say, "This right here, this moment is forever," and it was. In the final seconds of the video, Arthur spun to a slow stop and seemed to look into the camera, holding his stick out almost as an offering. His face breaking into a slow, sure smile. His lips moved but it was impossible to discern the words coming out of his mouth. *Let's split? Beat feet? Crazy shit?* Something like that.

"What the hell were you saying?" Gwen wanted to know.

"Dead men tell no tales," said the Arthur in her head. "Although they can roller-skate, so. You take the good with the bad, I guess."

She went back to her Google search results, continued working through the names they had plucked off the Enemies List. A serial rapist in California. A Middle Eastern poisoner. She was at it another forty-five minutes when she came across something that made her straighten unconsciously in her chair.

In 2010 they had sent King Sorrow to get a lawyer in the

Congo with ties to a terrorist outfit called the Nyatura Militia. The attorney served militia leaders in a legal and business capacity, ensuring money flowed in to arm and train their child soldiers. Colin had intelligence that suggested his renumeration included nights with fresh twelve-year-old recruits. That was all Donna needed to hear, never mind stories of villages burned or Hutus buried alive in mass graves. Gwen had agreed easily enough herself after considering Colin's bullet points, spreadsheet, and biographical file, which included intercepted emails and photos of the lawyer lunching with war criminals.

But three pages into her Google search results, Gwen saw the lawyer mentioned in quite a different capacity. He had also represented an international charity looking to expose and *end* child labor. They had gone after half a dozen cobalt mines in the west of Congo, where children as young as eight often worked ten-hour shifts in the hole. Several had died there, buried by collapses in caverns that skirted basic safety practices. What troubled her was the list of tech companies that had used Congolese cobalt in their devices: Apple, Tesla . . . and Dragontooth, a subsidiary of Colin Wren's very own Dragonware.

"Why's this lawyer guy care about children working in cobalt mines?" Gwen asked Arthur. "He defends men who employ child soldiers for genocide. And he assaults the kids."

"According to Colin's intercepted intelligence," Arthur said.

She didn't like the way he said that, didn't like the suggestion beneath Arthur's blasé tone. He could be a goddamn smug conversational partner for a dead man.

Gwen said, "Colin has access to intelligence gathered by the State Department, the CIA, all those guys. They give him reports . . . but he also sees the stuff that *isn't* in their reports. They use his software. He reads their emails. He sees their text messages. Satellite images. Social media profiles. He sees it all."

"*He* sees it. You don't."

"What's that supposed to mean?"

"So Colin shows you an email he says was written by a CIA field agent in Congo. This field agent has sources that *swear* the lawyer takes his payment in children. But do we know—do we know *for sure*—that Colin didn't write that email himself? How would you know? All of Colin's sources are filtered through Colin himself."

"He wouldn't do that," she said—actually said it out loud, whispering it to herself in the library.

"Hey, girl, are you okay?" Allison Shiner asked, and Gwen blinked and looked up. Her friend of twenty-five years stood on the other side of the table, holding a stack of books. At some point dusk had crept over the campus, and now the brightest source of light was the lamp with the emerald shade, on the table between them.

"Yes? Yes," Gwen said, her voice uncommonly small. "What are you doing here?"

"Had a study session with my seniors. You don't *look* okay," Allie said. "You look like you just saw a ghost."

Arthur Oakes shook his head. "Can't get anything by her."

6.

On the second day of the new year, Gwen parked her daddy's old pickup in the drive of The Briars. The front door opened before she got to it, Colin standing in the entrance in one of his white waffle-knits and his concrete-colored skinny jeans. He smiled as if she had arrived for a holiday party: good Scotch, little sausages on toothpicks, and Trivial Pursuit. But it wasn't a party. It was time to pick someone to die.

Allie and Donna were already there. Gwen sat down beside them, at the old card table, Colin behind it, prepared to symbolically deal them a new hand. The empty stools, where Van and Arthur belonged, seemed to take up far more space than the occupied ones. Odd to sit that way, Gwen thought, the three girls lumped together over to one side, to leave room for their dead.

Allie, who had always been thin, looked half-starved. Her sweater hung off bony shoulders. She had the sort of frail, waifish look that had made Kate Moss one of the most famous models in the world, and Allie was no less stunning. The last person Gwen had met who had looked so wasted, though, was an oxycodone addict who OD'd. He didn't make it to the hospital. There was a reason they called it heroin chic.

The booze wasn't helping, and Allie always drank when she was with Donna. Donna insisted on it. It was morning, but there was already only a splash of Scotch left in Allie's glass.

While Allie had become gaunt, Donna had coarsened. She still had a hell of a figure and she dressed well, emerald silk blouse falling off one shoulder to show the nice line of her collarbone. But her face had thickened, and her features were flushed and blunt in a way that made Gwen think of a man in a bar, sick of waiting for the bartender to refill his drink and about to make some ugly noise.

Gwen had read somewhere that at fifty you had the face you finally deserved. Was that Orwell? They were all creeping up on fifty and could no longer disguise who they were or what they had made of themselves.

It's not age, Gwen thought. *This is what killing does to you. You harden to it, like Donna, and it shows in a hard and unkind face, the face of someone who steps over a beggar without a glance. Or you spend your life trying to find an escape from it, and you wind up with the bright scared eyes of a junkie, the shaky hands of an addict.*

And what about you, Gwen? What has nearly thirty years of this done to you?

Only Colin seemed unchanged, unlined, unworn. He might still have been twenty. He had the pink, scrubbed, healthy look of a college athlete, captain of the swim team maybe.

She glanced at him and wondered if he had been smiling when he sank the knife into Arthur's kidneys. She had to look away. He mustn't know she was afraid of him now. He mustn't guess what was in her mind.

He loved Arthur, she thought. *You really think he could do that to him?* But of course he could kill him. When it came to murder, they all had plenty of practice.

Colin gave them each a folder. Gwen dreaded opening it. Instead, she looked idly around the room. She tried not to let her gaze rest on the locked cabinet for too long.

"Good luck with the new semester, college kid," Donna said. She raised her glass in a toast. "Try and get some studying done in between the all-night raves."

"I went to a rave just a couple months ago," Gwen said.

Donna blinked. "No shit?"

"Yeah, I went in the ambulance. A kid had a convulsion after he popped some molly laced with fentanyl."

Allie finished her Scotch and Donna reached for the bottle to pour her a refill. Allie shook her head. "No more, please."

"Drink it," Donna said, and spilled another finger in her glass. "You know you can't do this sober."

"You don't have to drink it," Gwen said.

"She does and she will."

"It's all right, Gwen. I really did want another glass."

Gwen turned her face away from both of them.

"I know things didn't work out with you and Arthur," Colin said. "But I'm sure it would've made him happy to know you went to Rackham and were just as brilliant as he always thought you could be."

"She's never had a single semester when she hasn't been on the dean's list," Allie piped up suddenly.

"Funny," Donna said, "Van never had a single semester when he wasn't on academic probation." Her breath caught and she looked at one of the empty stools. "I used to hassle him about it, but he knew better than I did. Why kill himself to make A's? He was going to be dead in ten years anyway. Did you know mayflies are born without mouths? No point in eating. They die too quickly." She drained the rest of her own Scotch.

"He was a good writer," Allie said. "A *fun* writer. His book has been reprinted *forty* times. Robin suggested maybe I could write an afterword for the twenty-fifth-anniversary edition—"

"Have you talked to Robin lately?" Gwen asked.

Allie opened her mouth, but Donna spoke first. "Allie had to tell Robin to stop bothering her. Well. I told her she needed to draw a line, and if she couldn't do it, I would. It was getting weird, Robin always asking about her love life, her drinking, prying at things, telling her we don't have a healthy friendship."

"I'm sure Robin wasn't trying to say that," Gwen said, although, in fact, she was sure Robin had been trying to tell Allie exactly that.

And why hadn't Robin told Allie about the troll? For the same reason Gwen hadn't told her. Allie couldn't keep anything from Donna, and once Donna knew, Colin would know too. If he had murdered Arthur, Gwen only had one edge: Colin's certainty that he had got away with it. If he found out what she knew, she was doomed. Robin too, probably.

"Are *you* in touch with Robin?" Colin asked, gazing at Gwen with bright, amused eyes. He looked like he had a very clever joke to tell.

Gwen said, "We talk now and then."

"What about?"

"Arthur."

"Yes," Colin said, nodding. "It broke her heart when he was finally declared dead. But it was time. We all needed to move on."

"Was that what you needed?" Gwen asked. "You needed him to be dead so you could move on?"

"Sorry, say again?"

"Was it a relief for you—when he was declared dead?"

"I was surprised at how much it lightened my heart. I didn't know that a part of me was still holding on to him. And I was glad for you. Because you finally had the money to go to school. Honestly, I always thought it was going to be you and him forever."

"It *is* you and me forever," Arthur said to her, there on the stool that had always been his. "Even when you find someone else. I'll be cheering you on."

No one else, she promised herself.

"I hope that's a promise you break, Gwen," Arthur said, but she pushed the thought back, didn't want this sweet, hope-affirming, fake Arthur-ghost in her brain, this Arthur-ghost who always said just what she needed to hear, whether she deserved to hear it or not.

"Come on already," Donna said. "Tell us who we're going to kill."

"We have five good options this year," Colin began.

"Fuck all that. Just tell us who you chose. It's your year to choose, and even if it wasn't, you always get your pick."

Colin smiled bravely—Gwen knew he loved the day they decided, knew he loved it more than Christmas, prepared for it all year. He hated any suggestion they might cut things short. He lifted the decanter. "Anyone want another splash before we start?" Shaking the decanter. "No?"

7.

She had a shift in the ambulance from five to eleven: an OD, a stroke, a fall down the stairs, a woman who had been punched by her husband and who said she fell into a kitchen table.

"You should get a new table," Gwen told her. "One that won't kick you in the side once you're on the floor."

When she got back to the little house in Gogan where she had lived her entire life, it was beginning to snow and she still had fifty pages of reading to do, Eliade's *The Sacred and the Profane* for Advanced Topics in Religious Movements. She read at her desk in her bedroom under the eaves, book on her left, a steno pad on the right for taking notes. The old pipes clanked and the iron heater steamed. She thought maybe some fresh air would liven her up, so she turned to the window over the bed. It was old and swollen, the brown paint around the frame chipped with age, and she struggled to push it up, reaching across the mattress without leverage. It moved one quarter inch, and then another, the window squeaking and bumping in the frame as it rose.

"Come on, you hoor," Gwen said.

"Let me help with that, love," King Sorrow said, and his claw came in out of the darkness, reaching under the window to pull it up half a foot with a shrill squall. His yellow talons gouged lines in the wood.

Gwen toppled back, missed her chair, sat on the floor.

His claw slid out from under the window and away into the darkness.

"What do you want?" she asked.

"See, it's about this year's selection," King Sorrow said.

"It's not up to me. Talk to Colin. It's his pick."

"That's the thing. I did talk to him," King Sorrow said. "And he picked you."

8.

The buzzer sounded—a grinding, mechanical sound—and the door opened. The old woman shuffled through as if she were wearing leg shackles, in little sliding steps. She kept her eyes averted and her head down, and Officer Augusta Plemons couldn't help but feel sorry for her. A lot of them were like this, after a long stretch like hers, nearly thirty years: frightened of what was waiting for them on the outside. All those years of being told what to do and when to do it, of hot meals made and delivered on a schedule, of free medical care, of not worrying about the bills. It was a lot to leave behind.

"Those clothes look like they fit all right," Plemons said to the poor dear, a small, scrawny woman with a disordered spray of

hair the color of steel wool. Sometimes her lips moved, as if she were reciting something to herself. "Do you like them?"

"Nn," said the old woman, nodding. She wore a pair of new Wranglers, clean white Keds, and a faded mustard-colored blouse, courtesy of Uncle Sam, who did most of his shopping for ex-convicts at Walmart.

Plemons was on one side of a white Formica counter, with this scrawny old felon's paperwork and her going-away package. She showed the old woman where to sign, turning pages on a clipboard for her and waiting while she scrawled her name.

"Now there's two hundred dollars here for you, darling," Plemons said, pushing the envelope containing her gate money across the counter. "And here's a check, this is for everything that was in your commissary account, plus your earnings for the work you done while incarcerated. That's forty-six hundred dollars!"

"Nn," the old woman said, nodding again.

"There's an Uber outside, that's paid for—"

The old woman's eyes darted toward Plemons with querulous alarm.

"It's like a taxi, kinda. You pay for the rides through an app. On your phone. This one is going to take you into Morgantown, to the Quality Inn. Do you have some family, going to come down and get you, take you back north?"

"Nn," the old woman said. This nn had a different quality than the others, seemed negative in nature. Plemons wondered if she had suffered a stroke at some point.

"Are you going north, though? Back to where you come from?"

The old woman looked again—and this time Augusta Plemons felt a little shiver of surprise. She had been working in the prison system for most of the new century and had dealt with plenty of hardcases—sweary, insolent bitches all marked up in scars and ugly tattoos—but she had never been stared at with a pair of eyes quite so dead, quite so empty.

"Count on it," the old woman said.

Plemons swallowed and swiftly looked away, down at the

paperwork. "What you going to do on your first night out? Anything fun? The place we got you checked into, it's just a short walk from the Sizzler. They've got a steak and shrimp combo for twelve dollars, might be the best thing you've eaten since you got locked up."

"Doubt it," the old woman said, and fixed her eyes on the cross around Plemons's neck. "I was in a cellblock with this teenager some years back and ate plenty of her nineteen-year-old pussy. Too bad she was a Baptist. She got feeling bad about all the sinning we were doing and hanged herself. I guess that's one way to defeat the temptations of the body."

Plemons tucked her cross back into her blouse, feeling a hectic flush rise into her cheeks. "You do have someplace to go, though? Somewhere you're aimed at?"

The old woman issued a grunting little laugh. "You could say that. I got some people I mean to drop in on. Some folks who were close to my eldest. The girl who burned to death while I was locked up in here."

"Ah. I hope catching up with your daughter's friends will bring you some comfort."

"I'm sure it will." She took the bills out of the envelope and folded them up and put them in her back pocket. She took the check and folded it and put it with the rest of the money.

"Do you know what you're going to do with all that cash money?" Plemons asked. "I know it looks like a lot, but it will go faster than you might expect. You want to be careful too. There are a lot of people out there will try to take advantage of a lady your age, to get whatever they can from you. You want to invest it wisely."

"It's not so much money," the old woman said. "But it's enough for a car and a gun, and once I've got those, making more ought to be no problem a'tall." She grinned then. "Just teasin'." And she winked.

Bill Hanscom, who worked prisoner processing and release with Plemons, stepped in from the parking lot and held the door open to the day. The afternoon behind him was so bright it was blinding.

"The Uber is here," Hanscom said.

"You take care of yourself and be safe," Plemons said, what she told all the convicts before they left, although her voice came out thin, and uncertain. "You don't ever want to come back here, Mrs. Nighswander."

"Nope," Daphne Nighswander said. "After thirty years inside, I can say I've learned my lesson: never let them take you alive."

And she turned and went out, pushing open the iron door and slipping around Hanscom, to be swallowed by the bright, blazing inferno of the day.

Augusta Plemons was unsettled and distracted for the rest of her shift, pouring coffee until it overflowed her mug because she had gone off into her thoughts and forgotten what she was doing. Nighswander's empty eyes and saw-toothed grin were bad enough. Her talk about getting a car and a gun weren't much better. But what rattled Plemons most was the way the old woman had stood there for a time, eyes downcast, lips moving as she spoke to herself without making a sound.

It had seemed to Plemons then that Daphne Nighswander had been reciting a list of names.

1.

There was a ribbon-cutting ceremony at ten thirty—a couple of dozen faculty members, some local press, a few students, Donna, Allie, and Colin himself—for the Llewellyn Wren Computer Center that Colin had paid for. (The *Portland Press Herald* reported a final price tag of $3.6 million.) Colin said a few words, standing in front of the glass doors to the brightly lit glass box behind him, and he snipped a black ribbon while a smattering of cameras flashed. The dean said he could keep the scissors.

There was a reception planned afterward, at the dean's house. The crowd began to push down the gravel path between snowbanks, out to the winding lane where the cars were parked: here a Benz, there a Benz, everywhere a Benz-Benz. All except for Colin's cherry Caddy, which looked the same as it had thirty years ago, except now it was all electric: there was a Tesla battery under the chassis, three hundred miles of range, motors on each tire so it could accelerate from zero to seventy in three seconds. Elon'd had his guys see to the conversion personally.

As he closed in on his ride, Colin spotted Gwen Underfoot's pickup truck parked right behind it. She got out when she saw him, climbed down, and stood there in her peacoat, rubbing her hands together against the cold. Her small, round face was solemn and pale, and he thought he knew what this was about but couldn't be sure. He was walking with Donna, his hand on her upper arm, and now he squeezed it and leaned in to whisper.

"Look who."

Donna's gaze leapt up. She saw Gwen and caught in place.

"I've got this. Get in the car with Allie." He looked back over his shoulder at Allie, who was a few steps behind them and hadn't seen Gwen yet.

"What if she's got a gun?" Donna murmured.

"What if?" he asked and tapped his chest. "He's faster than she is. If someone ever managed to shoot me, then I guess I'd have to admit I'm wrong about everything."

He released Donna's arm and she swiveled away, turning back to Allie. People streamed by them on the way to their cars, although most of the crowd remained behind Colin. He quickened his pace, walking past the Caddy to get within ten feet of Gwen.

"You missed the boring bit," he said. "But you're in time for mimosas and little quiches at the dean's. Want to join us? I'm sure it wouldn't be a problem to come with."

"Did you kill Arthur?" Gwen asked.

He glanced around to see who might be listening. No one. The scissors dangled from his right hand, the blades a foot long. But he had a better weapon on his chest. He unbuttoned his coat. If he called King Sorrow now, he figured only a half dozen or so would die, just the people standing closest to Gwen. But the optics would be rotten and it would ruin a good day.

He had been fighting a wave of bad noise lately. He had had to appear in front of Congress in May to explain why Dragonware had sold the personal data of 120 million users (hey, kids, if you didn't read the terms of service, you've got nothing to bitch about) to foreign powers. There had been a nasty little *Guardian* hit piece about the money he had banked in Monaco, Ireland, and other nations where the tax code hadn't been designed to create a Marxist welfare state. There was anger about his data mining software being used by the Chinese to spy on their own citizens (like Apple and Facebook weren't cutting exactly the same deals for access to the Chinese market). The heavy money invested in his VC fund was making unpleasant noises; he spent most of every morning now responding to emails that boiled with rage, accusations, and lightly veiled threats. He had a sense of humor about it . . . and he also knew how to create a good story to bury a bad one. Photographers loved to take his picture in front of glass buildings, surrounded by pink-cheeked kids. He looked like Lex Luthor's leaner, fitter, kinder twin brother, looked like he was probably dreaming up how to make low-cost jet packs or build a luxury hotel on the moon.

"I know *you* think I did. You and Robin."

Her eyes widened—then narrowed. "Oh. Of course. I'm so stupid. You're up on my computer, aren't you? What do they call it, spyware?"

"Gwen!" Allie called. Donna had her arm and had clearly tried to steer her toward the back of the Caddy, but Allie had seen her friend and was waving and looking a thousand times more cheerful. She was drunk, of course. How Colin tired of it sometimes, the stink of it on her. She had a smell like someone had squirted perfume on the dumpster behind a Hooters.

Donna opened the back door of the Caddy, but Allie—in a really shocking show of independence—pulled away and came toward Colin and Gwen. Not ideal.

"Do they know?" Gwen asked.

"Know what?" Allie asked, reaching Colin's side.

"Colin sicced King Sorrow on me," Gwen said. "I'm this year's sacrifice."

Allie shouted with laughter and put a mitten to her mouth. She gave Colin a jolly sidelong look, nudged him with her elbow, as if to say: *Good joke, huh?* Colin smiled back—but Allie saw something in his face. Her hand fell from her mouth and her very blue eyes muddled with confusion.

"What?"

Colin shifted his gaze back to Gwen. "What did you say to Robin? *I* wouldn't attack him . . . with your hand right here?" Brushing his fingers across his collarbone. "You would have used the mark and called King Sorrow down on me. Or waited until next year, when it's your turn to pick. I had to protect myself."

"You thought *that's* what I meant?" Gwen asked. Her jaw slackened slightly. She looked genuinely incredulous.

"Wait, what?" Allie asked. "*Gwen* was going to kill you? Am I going crazy here?"

"I had my hand on my heart," Gwen said, "because I just found out about Arthur. It's a gesture common to people with emotions, Colin."

"What did she find out about Arthur?" Allie cried.

Donna took her arm. "Come on. Let the grown-ups talk, Allie."

"And you heard what you were afraid to hear," Gwen said. "You got the emphasis wrong. I didn't say '*I* wouldn't attack him.' I said, 'I wouldn't attack *him*.' I was talking about going after King Sorrow. Not you. This all ends when we end him. I can't forgive you for what you did to Arthur, but I don't want to kill you—or anyone else, Colin. It's time for the killing to stop. Don't you get that? Don't you know by now that killing only sows more dragon's teeth?"

He turned this notion over in his mind, tried to calculate if he could've misunderstood her. Then he discarded the whole chain of thought. It didn't matter. She knew about Arthur, and that wasn't all. He had seen her Google searches.

Allie yanked her arm free. "Get your hand off me." Any trace of her loopy good humor was gone now.

"This is a terrible place for a conversation," Colin said, glancing around, hoping there wasn't any press nearby. The NECN news van was parked up the lane, already loading up. No one seemed to be loitering to listen in on them.

"Sorry I didn't pick a more private place to discuss my own death," Gwen said. "But I figured this would be the safest place to meet. You can only use the mark against me if I'm right in front of you, an active threat. But you won't reach for it here, not on your big day, not with all these people around." Three elementary school children went by tailing their mother, chattering loudly, and Gwen looked at Colin defiantly, as if to say *See what I mean?* "Two years ago, we used King Sorrow to kill a Middle Eastern financier who was privately funding jihad. The dragon took him at his granddaughter's wedding and killed forty other people. Forty *innocent* people. Oh, and that financier? Maybe he was funding jihad and maybe he wasn't, but his tech start-up won a contract with the French Department of Defense that you wanted for Dragonware, didn't it? Be honest, Colin. Did he have anything to do with terrorists at all? Does a guy who finances terrorism help French security services protect their people? Seems a bit contradictory. And then there was the Congolese lawyer. The engineer in Turkey. Is that all of them, or did I miss a few?"

"This isn't real. This isn't happening," Allie said.

"Tell me something, Gwen. Is it gone?" Colin asked, genuinely curious. "Your own mark?"

"Yes. That's the one good thing about being chosen to die, I guess. I'm finally out of it. I'm not one of his subjects anymore—I'm free of him. You're safe from me. But then, you always were, Colin."

"I know what I heard," Colin said, and, playing it back in his mind once again, he felt his certainty return in full. "You know how I'm sure you weren't talking about getting rid of King Sorrow, Gwen? Because that's like talking about getting rid of the sun. It can't be done."

"Stop it!" Allie cried. "You didn't. Tell me you didn't, Colin."

"Get in the car, Allie," Donna said.

Allie looked at her as if she didn't know her, then back to Colin. "Take it back."

"No takebacks," Colin said. Then he strode three feet closer to Gwen and said, "And I don't believe you. I think you'd kill me right now if you could. I think you'd kill us all." He raised his voice slightly. "Like you killed those helpless old folks." Gwen gave him another bewildered look—he might've just started speaking in a foreign language—and while she was trying to puzzle him out, he lifted the scissors and pushed the blades at her chest, forcing her back a step. "I'm saddened, though, that you think I'd touch the mark on my chest and summon King Sorrow before your time. I *want* you to have the weeks ahead. You deserve that—time to see the people you love. Time to make arrangements. Maybe you did some things that shock me . . . maybe you made some choices that just about break my heart. But you also did a lot of good for a lot of people. Some of them—most of them—probably weren't worth it. God knows how many lard-asses you brought back from heart attacks they paid for with a lifetime of cheeseburgers. You've spent a quarter century looking after Tana Nighswander, who doesn't even know the father of her own baby. But whether their lives are worth a damn or not, they're here because of you, and I'm sure their love means something to you. See 'em while you can. Get a good life insurance plan and you can set Tana and her kid up for decades. Make your peace with the world and your loved ones."

"You want to help me make peace? I know what you did to Arthur, but I want to hear you say it. You ran a blade through him down in that hole," Gwen said, "didn't you? Because if you hadn't, *he* would've struck down King Sorrow."

"No, Gwen," Colin told her. "I didn't kill Arthur. *You* did. The day you told him you didn't love him. Everything after that was just waiting. His life was functionally over. And I think he always knew, deep down in his heart, you rejected him because he was Black."

At that Gwen staggered back a step, her eyes suddenly bright. She looked winded, as if he had shoved the blades of those scissors into her breadbasket.

"You goddamn liar," she whispered, but she was fighting tears now.

He thought his work was done and started to turn away—which was when Allie leapt on him. She was screaming as she threw her bony fists at his chest. She had all the weight and mass of a twelve-year-old, but he wasn't ready for it, and the impact carried him to the ground. The scissors sank into his knee, piercing his iceberg-colored denims and pushing into the thigh.

"Take it back!" Allie screamed at him. "Take it BACK you take it BACK you take it *OFF HER!*"

She went on pelting him with her fists, even as Donna got her arms around Allie's waist and hoisted her kicking into the air. The door to the back of the Caddy was open, and Donna heaved Allie through it, stood in front of her when she tried to get back out. The day pulsed unsteadily around Colin, blood thrumming behind his eyes, the light dimming and brightening as if clouds were racing in front of the sun. He looked around. People had stopped walking to their cars, were staring his way in alarm.

Gwen dropped to one knee beside him. He tried to get an elbow up, drive her away before she could grab for him, and she pushed his arm aside. She had something in one hand, a white pad.

"You need to get something on that wound," she said. "If you stuck yourself in the femoral, you could bleed out in five minutes." She was pushing his trouser leg up.

That was a wadded-up rag soaked with dragon's tears in her hand. She meant to kill him right now, in front of everyone. Somehow she had planned this. He felt a certain calm admiration—it was exactly the sort of thing he might've done. He put his hand in Gwen's face and shoved her back onto her ass. At the periphery of his vision he saw some kid, a flushed, copper-haired college student, pointing a cell phone at him.

Donna slammed the car door, turned around, holding up her hands, getting between Colin and the crowd. "Sorry! We have an unwell family member. Crowded places sometimes set her off. We're all right here!"

Gwen sat in the lane, on her rear, holding a white handkerchief in her hand. A new thought occurred to him then, sudden and unexpected, that the cloth in her hand was just a cloth, that she genuinely meant to stanch his bleeding. He swiftly shoved the idea aside. He had sentenced her to death, and no real human being would attempt to provide first aid to their murderer. The thought was absurd—as absurd as her claim that she had not meant to revenge herself upon him for Arthur. Of course she had.

"Well, Colin," Gwen Underfoot said. Seven weeks to live and she was shaking her head and smiling as if *he* was the one who deserved pity. "Maybe I am going to die, but I can think of worse things. I could have to live another forty years as you, for starters."

Donna held out a hand and Colin caught it, came limping to his feet, forcing a smile. His pant leg was drenched with blood. People gaped at him the way they'd gawp at a horrific car crash.

"Maybe I should've built a new health center!" he joked. "I'll put that on the to-do list." Donna had his arm over her shoulder, and he hopped around the front of the car to the passenger seat. Forget the health center—he was going to need the Podomaquassy Urgent Care Clinic. So much for canapes at the dean's.

"Kid with a phone," Donna murmured.

"Fuck," he said. "Maybe I can slap it down."

"You just slapped down a woman trying to offer you emergency aid in front of a crowd," Donna said. "You've probably done enough slapping folks for one day, son."

He flinched, quashed the urge to push her aside too. He hated to hear the Florida panhandle in her voice, that lazy countrified drawl. It gave him a weird feeling, like he was cozied up to Van.

Allie was sobbing breathlessly in the back seat when they pulled out. Gwen sat on the curb, looking for all the world like she had nowhere to go and nothing better to do than sit there and enjoy the morning.

2.

A little after nine, Gwen let herself out of the kitchen and sat on the back step above her backyard. The snowy slope before her fell steeply away into brambles and a strew of rocks. Somewhere at the bottom of the drop, cold water gurgled in a brook. Gwen found she wanted to be outside most of the time now, wanted to taste the air. Wanted to put her hands in the snow, feel it burning her bare skin. She wanted to feel it all—touch it all—while she still could. Seven weeks to live.

She spent thirty minutes crafting three messages for Robin in her Notes app. Did Colin have her screen mirrored somehow, so he could see every single thing she did? Or did he only see her texts, her emails? It didn't really matter. She was writing them for his consumption as much as Robin's. She *wanted* him to see them.

Finally, she was done. She cut and pasted and sent.

> Robin. I took your suspicions to Donna McBride and she brought Colin and me together for a sit-down. I think now that the creature you met, the creature going by the name of Schrödinger, lied to you, hoping to turn Colin and me against each other. Schrödinger was what I guess you would call a troll, just like in the fairy tales. A thing like that delights in creating heartache and suspicion, in sowing division.
>
> You were right to bring your story to me, but I want you to put your concerns about Colin Wren out of your mind. Arthur and I had a private phrase, a cutsie pie thing we used to say to each other, to let each other know all was well. It was the last thing Arthur said to Colin down in the hole. He never would have shared that with his killer—and for me that settles the question.
>
> You've learned that my friends and I brought something terrible into this

world, years ago. It haunts us still. You've almost died twice because of your proximity to us . . . once in the skies over the North Atlantic, once by the River Camel. Enough. While I think the world of you, I'm going to ask you to stop communicating with me . . . and Allie . . . and Donna . . . and Colin. Please. If you keep sticking your nose in, the third time might be the charm, and I don't want that on my conscience. Go back to your life. I can't deal with any more of your questions—the answers would only endanger you. So leave off. Please respect my request for distance. I ask this out of love, not resentment . . . but if you don't abide my wishes, resentment will come. I will be muting your replies. Be well. Gwen.

She hit send and send and send again, then lowered the phone and held it against her leg. She turned her face to the sky just in time to be kissed by a falling snowflake.

Her phone pinged with a text. She had not yet muted Robin's replies and looked to see what she had said, surprised she would reply at this hour—it had to be the early a.m. in London.

Only the message wasn't from Robin, but Colin.

Well done. You just saved Robin Fellows's life.

Gwen put her phone down again. Later, when she looked back at the message from Colin, it was gone, as if she had imagined it. She didn't know he could do that—make a text disappear. King Sorrow was a dragon, but Colin was some sort of dark sorcerer, and she couldn't, for the life of her, say which of them was the more frightening.

3.

Daphne Nighswander went from the supermax to the Quality Inn in Morgantown. The motel was almost tucked under the on-ramp leading up to I-79 and set across the street from the biggest gas station Daphne had ever seen in her life, a Kroger that seemed to have a million pumps. Eighteen-wheelers blasted their air horns at all hours, while traffic boomed along the interstate. Drunks fucked in the other rooms, loud through the wafer-thin walls, going at it hard enough to jiggle the pictures on the walls. One night a car caught fire in the parking lot and the lot lizards came out of their rooms to watch it burn. They were like little girls at a campfire, only lacking sticks and marshmallows. It wasn't uncommon for ambulances to show up in the wee hours to zip one of the lizards into a body bag, needle stuck into one bruised arm. Daphne found the noise and the chaos comforting, easy to live with. It was like prison. Besides. She was not always alone. Some nights she woke and found Jayne sitting at the little table under the picture window, Jayne with her face black and crackling and split open like the skin of a burnt hot dog.

"What are you doin' there?" Daphne asked her.

"I just like to watch you sleep," Jayne said, and grinned. When she grinned, the splits in her skin bulged open to show the crispy muscles of her face.

"I felt the same way about you when you was a baby," Daphne said, although she could not remember if this was really true.

Daphne stayed there for somewhere between ten days and five weeks, she didn't know how long for sure. At some point, a decade into her sentence, time had begun to hop about in funny, random circles, like a small bird with a smashed wing. It went around and around without ever taking off or getting anywhere except closer to death.

She was in no hurry. She contented herself with luxuries like White Castle and Kentucky Fried, and she did her research. She had never been much of a student, had left school after eighth grade, but in her middle age had discovered at last a subject that fascinated her: the lives of those young folks she thought of as the Goodbye Six, the trust fund babies who had murdered *her* baby and who turned Tana against her. Daphne had followed their lives from the inside, using the limited resources available in the prison library and her occasional computer time, and she revisited her studies now, with visits to both the Morgantown library and to a local Books-A-Million.

The men and women who burned Jayne to death, they had lived interesting lives. Daphne had shot a postman while high and the state had taken most of her adult life. The Goodbye Six had butchered Jayne and Ronnie and wandered off to be well paid and happy . . . in between the occasional shocking scrape. Two of them had been on that plane that set down in Greenland after it was half torn open in the sky. Donovan McBride even wrote a book about it, said the whole air disaster had been the result of a UFO attacking with a death ray. Daphne read the book twice. The first time, it gripped her so completely, she forgot the author had a hand in slaughtering her daughter. The second time, she studied Van's account of terror in the air, as if she were preparing to give testimony on it. The book was where the idea began to form that there was something unnatural about the six of them.

Jayne's death, of course, had been unnatural in its own right, when you considered the way she had been cooked down to the bone, the way Ronnie had been found in pieces (pieces!). But at the time, Daphne's thought was simply: Colombians. The really rich one, Colin Wren, had probably hired Colombians. The Colombians were great ones for putting heads on sticks, burning people alive, taking pieces off a person with garden shears. But after Daphne read the McBride book, she began to wonder if the Goodbye Six were touched with something *else*. Contaminated. Fire followed them wherever they went. Fire and garish death.

The other McBride, hot little piece of ass who was a rising star on Fox News, suddenly abandoned her career and disappeared for a while. Her brother disappeared with her. Six months later, she reemerged alone. Van was gone, had succumbed to drug addiction. The family asked for privacy and understanding.

Maybe a year after that, Daphne had come across a thread on a message board that claimed Donna and Donovan McBride were secretly psychics who had been held by the government for a time, detained and studied, at a place in North Carolina called Cherokee Island. The island had been wiped out, burned as if it had been napalmed, destroyed in an apparent industrial accident. To be fair, the message board in question was dedicated to such outlandish conspiracy theories (its most popular thread claimed that Russia was attempting to farm trolls in their northern tundra), and the person posting the Cherokee Island theory went by the online handle of VisitorFromPlanetGor. VisitorFromPlanetGor claimed that in fact the McBrides had burned Cherokee Island with their MINDS, that they had the power of pyrokinesis. Van had been engulfed in a fire he himself started. The thread was written with frequent use of CAPITAL LETTERS and *whole paragraphs in hysterical italics* and generally had about as much credibility as the idea that the moon landing was a hoax or 9/11 an inside job (both highly popular topics on this board). And it didn't make a lot of sense—why hadn't the government simply recaptured Donna? Or had her assassinated? Would they really just let her go after she toasted their whole facility? Whatever the answer to those questions, it was impossible to miss the recurring theme. Where the Goodbye Six went, fire followed.

And Cherokee Island had been incinerated on Easter. Like Jayne.

Like the near air disaster that had ended when BA 238 set down in Greenland in 1995.

Like the destruction of Black Cricket penitentiary.

This last especially fascinated her, not least because she had spent the first leg of her sentence there. Daphne was in the Morgantown library, poking around on the internet, when she found an impassioned essay about one of the prisoners who had died there: Francine Trout, a fat feeb who had claimed, probably falsely, to have had a hand in the killing of a child named Cady Lewis. The name of the victim leapt out at her. Daphne Nighswander had been listening to Donna McBride's podcast for years and happened to know the Lewis girl's death was personal to her: the abduction had occurred in Donna's very own front yard. Suddenly there was a logic to the Black Cricket disaster. Bad things happened on Easter to people the Goodbye Six didn't like.

It felt like a cosmic makeup call that Daphne hadn't been buried in the Black Cricket collapse herself. If you were inclined to believe in the Lord, you might say that he took with one hand and gave with the other, ending Jayne but sparing Daphne. Personally, Daphne found it far easier to believe in the devil than the Lord. And the devil, Daphne thought, had made arrangements with the Goodbye Six.

Daphne was making arrangements of her own. The day before she cleared out of Morgantown, she paid a pair of junkies three hundred dollars for a Sig Sauer P365. The hopheads threw in a box of 124-grain hollow-point bullets as a gesture of friendly Southern hospitality. The Sig's magazine carried fifteen shells. With Arthur Oakes and Donovan McBride long dead, that meant she could shoot each of the others twice and still have a few left over for anyone dumb enough to get in the way.

4.

In the first bitterly cold days of the new month, Gwen dragged the three file boxes crammed with Arthur's Leuchtturm1917 notebooks from beneath her bed and began to read *Toolkit for the Well-Prepared Dragonslayer*. She had tried once before and quickly set his papers aside. She could hardly read a paragraph without her eyes starting to sting and blur, the words doubling themselves on the page. The notes in the margin were the worst. "G., I know I'm phrasing this badly, any ideas?" and "G., is the reader having fun here? Are YOU having fun?" The book was an immense crossword puzzle. He had meant for them to finish it together, a thought that had been, for a while, unbearable to her.

Now, though, she wanted his voice, longed for his company, before she ran out of time. It was bad enough that King Sorrow had not allowed them to be together, but it was worse—it was obscene—for Gwen to hold him at bay when she didn't have to anymore. So she turned the pages and read his book and, after a while, began to make notes in the margins herself, carrying on the conversation he had started there.

It was a good book, what there was of it. On the surface, it was about dragons and how they were defeated in the old stories. But beneath that, she thought he wanted readers to see how the qualities of the successful dragon fighter might be of use in everyday life. He felt there were still modern applications for a sense of personal honor, a desire to serve something bigger than the self, humility about the limits of one's own knowledge. He felt gallantry was a quality that never went out of fashion. He also recommended a good, leisurely breakfast before fighting evil, which she thought was sound advice. If she had two years left, and not two months, she might've finished the *Toolkit* for him, and Robin could've published it.

She was in her bedroom, at the desk, working her way through the second notebook, when she felt her cat, Old Ben, put his paws on her right leg, as he often did before he jumped into her lap. But he didn't jump up. He just left his paws there, and then she remembered she had buried Old Benjamin three years ago and looked down and it was King Sorrow's black claw resting on her thigh, almost in her crotch, his ancient yellow talons, long and thick as the teeth of a crocodile, tracing the inside of her leg, and she screamed and jerked away so fast she went over backward in her chair. By the time she rolled onto all fours, he was gone.

"That all you got, bitch?" Gwen asked. But her voice was shaking.

5.

She was climbing into her pickup two days later when he flickered across the full moon, hauling an endless length of tail behind him. The sight of him winded and awed her, the black jagged shape of him moving across a dark sky blazing with stars.

Gwen stood staring for a long time after he was gone, the frozen air burning in her chest, needling her lungs like steel shavings.

6.

Daphne Nighswander drove north in her ruin of a car: a 1970 Shelby Boss Snake. She had paid eight hundred dollars to buy it from a wrecking yard. It had been parked out front with a hissing serpent drawn on the windshield in soap, next to the words $1000 A CLASSIC RUNS GOOD. The hillbilly running the yard had got most of the soap off the glass, but a ghost of that coiled snake remained, flashing up out of the dark every time she passed under a streetlamp. Rust had eaten half a dozen holes in the roof, and when Daphne got it up to fifty, those perforations began to *scream*. They sounded like a chorus of lunatics shrieking in delighted harmony. Cold air whistled in, so she drove with a blanket across her lap . . . and her Sig under the blanket.

She liked traveling at night the best, liked chasing her headlights into the dark. The car was barely road legal: there was no hood, the rear bumper was held on by coils of barbed wire, and the radio didn't work, except when it did. Sometimes, when the Boss Snake struck a pothole, the face of that radio would light up a lurid, radioactive green, and for a minute or two she'd hear voices: a gospel preacher attesting that Jesus would return not to bring peace but the sword, a newscaster who said 80 percent of long-haul truckers reported hallucinating while behind the wheel. Then, slowly, the radio's fey green light would dim and fade and take the voices with it. But even then, she was not without company. Daphne Nighswander roared north in the Boss Snake, and in the wee hours, her daughter Jayne traveled with her.

"Listen to this old shit-box scream," Jayne said. "You know what would make me want to scream? It's not just that they burned up your oldest and best daughter. That's bad enough—and believe me, I took it personally. But the other thing, Gwen Underfoot? She helped herself to your own grandson. Took him away. Poisoned Tana and the boy against you and raised him like her own child while you spent the best years of your life in a West Virginia lockup."

It was drafty in the Boss Snake and Jayne's clothes were charred tatters blowing on her gaunt frame. Her face was a blackened, grinning mask.

"I think about it," Daphne said. "I heard him screechin' once, little Jett. I called Tana up not long after you died. Only time I ever heard his voice, screeching in the background. That's all I got of him. Tana wouldn't take my calls after that. Told me she'd never let me get close to the kid after what I did to her. She wouldn't have that child if not for me. I introduced her to the father, fuck's sake."

"Damn right," Jayne said.

To be fair, Daphne had set her daughter up with several men, beginning when Tana was thirteen.

"I've been thinking about how that gun of yours carries fifteen in the mag," Jayne said. "You're going to have some left over."

"For Tana?"

Jayne said, "I was thinking more about her brat. That'd teach her a thing or two about disrespect. That'd teach Tana and Gwen both. They took the boy away from you. You'll have plenty of shells. No reason not to take the boy away from *them*."

"Huh," Daphne said, a sound almost like a laugh. And the wind shrieking through the roof of the car—that sounded like laughter too. "Okay. Summin to do. But only after the others."

"Only after the others," Jayne affirmed.

The Boss Snake hit a metal bridge, the grooved iron grill humming under the tires, and when she bumped down off the other end, the radio came back on. Through a blast of static she heard a beloved song from her youth, the guitar and drums of an old Judas Priest number rumbling along like a line of Panzer tanks rolling over dead bodies.

"Allison Shiner," Daphne chanted to herself.

"Colin Wren. Donna McBride," Jayne said along with her. They were like two old ladies, counting the beads of their rosaries together.

"Gwen Underfoot," Daphne said. "And Jett Nighswander, if it's not too much trouble." She rocked back and forth in her seat. If she had looked in the rearview mirror and seen herself lit by the fading glow of the radio, she would've seen a face like a skull, eye sockets glittering with an elvish, unnatural light.

"If you think I'll ever let it go," Daphne whispered to the night, "you got another thing coming."

7.

Gwen thought the lizard would have a harder time fucking with her in front of witnesses, so she loaded a few of Arthur's notebooks into her messenger bag and went to the Brooks Library.

She still had her student ID, although she had withdrawn from her classes. There was no point in going on with them, and at the beginning of the month she had emailed the registrar to ask for another deferment. The registrar, Mrs. Howard, had signed off on her leave, mentioned the campus had mental health resources if she was struggling, and closed with a wry request not to wait another twenty-five years to finish her studies. Gwen was sorry she was going to have to disappoint her. It appeared she was not going to get her degree after all.

Gwen found a spot at her favorite table and read on. Her time with Arthur's *Toolkit* had quickly become the part of the day she looked forward to the most. She liked especially that Arthur had written everything longhand, enjoyed his flowing, almost calligraphic script. If she had been reading him on a screen, Colin would've been reading with her. That would've spoiled a little of her happiness.

What came through Arthur's writing most clearly was his excitement for the details he discovered in books. No one needed a magic wardrobe that opened into Narnia if they had a library card; if you had a library card, you had a thousand magic wardrobes to choose from, ten thousand. That was how Arthur saw it. A library card was as good as a sword drawn from a stone.

He had a lot to say about magic swords, weapons with names, quirks, even romantic attachments. They wanted to be looked after, wanted proof they were loved. They could be stubborn and haughty, or playful and tricksy. Arthur said the famous swords of antique myth had vivid personalities for good reason. Such weapons were best thought of as stand-ins for the human soul, which was itself a kind of blade, and a body only its sheath.

Next to this was an even more provocative thought, left in the margins for her eyes alone: "G.—I'd be more proud of this metaphor if it wasn't a metaphor. If an evil spirit can enter our world from the Long Dark, in the form of a dragon, then I've no doubt a righteous spirit can be drawn in the form of steel. I'd try drawing one myself, instead of going spelunking with a troll, but knowing my own history of moral stupidity, I worry the first thing such a sword would slice in two would be ME."

He had his findings too about the business of killing dragons. He believed they all had a weak spot, like Smaug's missing scale. Only the weak spot was not a flaw in their armor, but a flaw in their character: their insatiable, blinding greed for sorrow and blood. Though they were otherwise cunning creatures, their compulsion to taste their victim's grief often led them into mortal danger. In many fables, heroes found ways to get close to a dread wyrm by making themselves invisible to them (see the case of one Baggins, Bilbo). Stories were littered with magic rings and enchanted draughts that would do the job of disappearing someone who needed to vanish. This too was a reminder that evil had its blind spots. The wicked could hardly conceive of the motives that drove the kind and the compassionate, and it left them vulnerable. The truly cruel carried the seeds of their own destruction, which was why the ouroboros was the simplest and truest story ever told about dragons, because they could not help devouring themselves. The cheat cheated himself; the poisoner, in a careless moment, drank his own poison; the snake ate his own tail.

She was with Arthur in the library until after dark. At five, she piled the notebooks back into her bag and went out into the sharp cold. She had switched off her phone while she was in Brooks but reactivated it at the bottom of the granite steps and saw she had a voicemail from Allie, not six minutes old.

She hit play and heard traffic noises, the blast of a horn, someone cursing. Allie breathed wetly.

"Gwen, there's about a ninety-seven percent chance I'm lost," Allie said. She sounded like she was struggling not to sob. "I wanted to see you. I wanted to tell you I'm sorry. I didn't know. But I *should've* known, I should've, I should've asked questions, I *should've* been a better person, and I should probably not've tried to walk to your house, are you at exit nine or exit—"

"FUCK OUTTA THE MIDDLE THE INTERSTATE YOU MAD BITCH!" someone screamed, and a horn wailed and Gwen's heart seized. The interstate. Allie was on foot . . . on the interstate. Gwen had a sudden vision of Allie weaving along the right-hand lane while headlights rushed toward her from behind.

"—almost at exit eight I think I'll get off there an' ask for digressions," Allie was saying, but Gwen hung up.

Gwen was a ten-minute drive away but exit 8 in Gogan was just a quarter mile from the Market Basket where Tana Nighswander was general manager. Gwen dialed Tana and started to run.

8.

Gwen sped, swerved her pickup into the left lane to get around a Ford Escape, then had to cut back to get past an Infiniti. Both vehicles wailed their horns at her. The sound bounced right off her consciousness, hardly registered.

When she imagined Allie walking to Gogan, she pictured her in the southbound lane, walking *with* the flow of traffic. But as she approached exit 8, she saw Tana Nighswander's Elantra, off the road, down in the snow, the hazards flashing, on the far side of the *northbound* lane. Gwen knew, then, that Allie had been wandering into *oncoming* traffic, and that Tana had been too late to save her. Someone had struck Allie and simply kept going. Tana had found her mangled and dying in the snow, at the bottom of the embankment. Gwen got off the interstate and circled around to the northbound side. She rolled up the ramp, light-headed with dread. At the top, she eased off the turnpike and onto the dirt. As her headlights splashed up the back of the Elantra, she saw Tana sitting in the open hatchback, one arm around Allie's waist, a rough gray blanket over Allie's shoulders. Gwen was almost shaky with relief. She pulled in behind them and got out.

As she crossed through the headlights, Allie looked up, pale and wet-eyed.

"Are you going to yell at me?" Allie asked meekly.

"I ought to."

Gwen took her in her arms and Allie began to cry.

"You might wanna watch out," Tana said. "When I gave her a

squeeze, she threw up on my shoes. Which—do you remember the night you all got arrested?—is *not* the first time."

"I gotta stop doing that," Allie said.

THERE WAS A DUNKIN'—a cube of brown brick and glass—across from the Market Basket. The floor was filthy with dried slush. The few doughnuts remaining behind the counter had begun to petrify, like bits of troll in sunlight. Gwen had worked in this exact Dunkin' when she was a teenager. Tana had worked alongside her. Gwen used to hate coming home with the smell of Dunkin' Donuts in her hair, a perfume of coffee, creams, and (in those days) cigarettes. Her father told her to get used to it: that was the smell of working for a living.

Tana and Allie sat together on the other side of the booth from Gwen. Allie drank swallows of coffee and Tana tore pieces off a plain doughnut and handed them to her.

"I don't want that," Allie said. "It'll make me sick again."

"So this time aim for *her* shoes," Tana said, nodding at Gwen.

Allie barked with laughter and then looked startled—as if someone else had laughed and the sound had caught her off guard.

Gwen said, "You could've killed yourself." When Allie didn't reply, Gwen added, "I guess that was the point."

"Don't be mad at me," Allie said, in a small voice.

But Gwen *was* mad. The idea of Allie walking into traffic felt like an insult—it struck her as an act of staggering selfishness.

"Do you know what it's like, cleaning someone off the highway after they've been smeared across a half mile of blacktop? Because I do."

"Don't," Allie whispered. "Please." Her head sank and her fingers drifted up to squeeze her temples. "I just felt so bad. It's not fair."

"What's not fair?" Tana asked.

Gwen was relentless. "And never mind you almost killed *yourself*. You would've made someone *else* a killer in the process. Someone would have to spend the rest of their life reliving the thud it made when they drove over you."

"Stop," Allie moaned.

"After what we've been through, you'd put that on someone else? Make a murderer of someone?"

"What have you been through?" Tana asked.

Gwen ignored her. "That was your idea of saying sorry? Getting yourself smashed like a melon? Or did you want some attention? 'Never mind *your* problems, Gwen, think about *me* a little?' Are we in some kind of competition, see which one of us can die first?"

"*What?*" Tana asked. "What's this about a competition to see who's going to die first?"

Allie lifted her bloodshot, tearful gaze and gave Gwen a warning glare.

"Nothing. Forget it." Gwen reached across the table and took Allie's hands. "This isn't your fault. I *know* this isn't your fault. It's all right. It's just the way things turned out. Look at me." Allie looked. "*It's all right,*" Gwen told her, squeezing her hands, trying to say something for which there were no words.

Tana looked from one to the other and back, her pretty, freckled, impish face gone hard.

"I hear you two talking, but it doesn't make any sense. It's like that thing about twins, you know how twins are supposed to have their own private—"

"We know," Allie and Gwen said together.

After a moment of silence, Allie said, "Please, can I stay with you tonight? I don't want to go home and be alone. I'll drink if I do, and if I drink any more I'll pickle myself. And it's not like I can go to The Briars. Can't I sleep on your couch?"

"No."

"She can sleep on mine," Tana said.

"I'm out of here," Gwen said, getting up. She leaned across the booth, impulsively, cupped a hand behind Allie's head, and kissed her brow. "It's not your job to fix the world, Allie. It never was."

Allie's face shriveled. She lowered her chin and her hair fell in front of her features and she began to cry again.

Tana said, "I don't understand any of what you two are talking about!"

Gwen said, "Thank you, Tana. Take care of her."

She didn't look back as she walked away. Her hands were shaking.

9.

She was so tired her eyelids felt sandpapery. Her temples thudded from the mix of caffeine and adrenaline. Gwen thought she might not even bother undressing, would just fall face down into bed. And tomorrow Easter would be another day closer.

Only as she pulled into the driveway, her headlights slipped over a figure sitting on the front steps: a broad-shouldered woman with Farrah Fawcett hair, a suitcase to either side of her. As Gwen climbed down from the truck, Robin Fellows rose from the steps, brushing snow off her overcoat. She looked good, Gwen thought, and remembered that thing about how at fifty a person had the face they deserved. With her expertly applied eyeshadow and bright lip gloss, Robin looked like the pop singer Bonnie Tyler.

"You didn't expect me to buy that rubbish you texted?" Robin asked.

"Fuck's sake," Gwen said, but not because of Robin.

Because a battered white Elantra, filthy with road salt, was pulling in along the curb, and Tana was rolling down her window. Allie sat in the passenger seat looking miserable . . . though not entirely contrite.

"Allison tells me you're going to die soon," Tana said. "And the odds are she's right. Because if you don't explain what's going on, I'm going to kill someone, and you're handy."

10.

"Whatever you think you want to know, you don't," Gwen said. "So drink your tea and go."

"I been twenty years in AA. Whatever it is, I can hear it," Tana said. "I sponsored a girl who had a seizure from bad coke while she was suckin' a cock, bit it right off, and almost choked on it."

"Oh, I know her!" Gwen said, passing around steaming mugs of tea. "I was in the ambulance that responded to that call. She still sober?"

"Just got her five-year chip last month."

"Good for her. You still don't want to hear this."

"Is it about what you did to my sister and Ronnie Volpe?" Tana asked. "The six of you?"

They had gathered in her living room, Tana, Allie, and Robin squeezed together on the sagging tweed couch under the swordfish Gwen's father had caught on vacation in Cabo. He only ever took three vacations his whole life: Cabo, Jamaica, and Disneyland. He should've had more. There should've been more frozen drinks by the pool, more tropical sunlight, more of his goddamn life. He had dropped dead shoveling snow at Rackham, only a few yards from what was now Colin Wren's computer center. He was gone in minutes. If Gwen had been parked right there with her ambulance and all her gear, she could not have saved him.

"What happened to your sister was terrible," Gwen told her.

"Nothing happened to Jayne Nighswander she didn't have coming," Tana said. "Allie here isn't the only one with a suicidal streak. I tried it. More'n once. Tried to hang myself. Tried to drink myself to death. Jayne made me hate my life and hate the world, and if not for Jett and you, Gwen, I wouldn't be here. And I wouldn't of helped anyone else. And I think maybe I *have* helped a few people here and there . . . in AA and at Market Basket, where we sometimes throw folks a line when the SNAP benefits come up short. My older sister prostituted me to pay her debts. She threw me to Ronnie for fun. She made me a drug dealer and a drug user. I thank God every morning she never got a chance to hurt my baby. But in my heart I knew it was wrong to thank God. I should've been thanking you. You, Arthur, and the others."

"Jayne died in California," Gwen said. "I was right here, finishing my senior year of high school. It's a pretty good alibi, Tana."

"So you hired someone. Or, you know. Not *you*. But your rich friend. There was a story Colin's granddaddy was with the CIA. I figured he knew bad people. Come on, Gwen. I know you had a hand in it. I've always known. Did Colin or one of you others know some bad people? People worse'n Jayne?"

"It wasn't bad people," Gwen said, after a long and careful silence.

Robin said, "It wasn't people at all. It was a dragon."

Tana glanced at her and back at Gwen and laughed.

Robin didn't crack a smile. "I *saw* it. It was in the sky, outside the plane. I thought I was going to die." And she reached across Tana to take Allie's hand. "And was glad I was going to die in the company of a sweet couple like you and Van."

Tana narrowed her eyes. "I know Allie's wasted, but this one don't look drunk a'tall. Am I supposed to take this serious?"

"Every word is true. Allison, Van, and I were on a plane that was almost torn in two by a dragon. We all saw it, and by the time we landed I had a pretty good idea Van and Allie knew more about it than they were willing to admit."

"You saw something that *looked* like a dragon. But it wasn't. Not really. I'n believe Jayne was burned up by a psychopath with a can of gas and a lighter. Tellin' me she got et by Godzilla is a little tougher to swallow."

Allie looked down at her chest, undid one button of her blouse, then another, and opened her top to show the upper part of her chest. "Tana, he looked a little like this."

She brought her fingers close to her left breast, and as she did, ink rose to the surface of her very white skin to paint the twisting, serpentine figure of a dragon. Tana recoiled, fell back into Robin, crying out. Allie dropped her hand, and the tattoo faded as quickly as it had appeared.

"The fuck is that?"

"That's one of the ways we can call him," Gwen said.

"Him?" Tana asked.

"Does he have a name?" Robin asked.

At that, Gwen and Allie traded a look.

"You bet he does," Gwen said.

11.

Gwen put a frozen tray of Beecher's mac and cheese into the oven, pricey stuff, but better than Stouffer's. She had spent too much time hanging around trust fund kids, it had given her airs. She filled the kettle again, came back with more tea.

"I gave up the hard stuff twenty-five years too soon," Tana said when they were done telling about Jayne, and the people after Jayne, and BA 238, and Arthur's trip to Tintagel with Colin to find the Sword of Strange Hangings.

"Wait," Robin said. "It gets better. Let me tell you about what happened a couple months ago, when I went back to the Slaughterbridge to look for Stuart Finger."

THE MAC AND CHEESE was ready around the time Robin finished telling her part of it. Allie ate hers, then ate Tana's. She was looking better, although all the crying had sketched very white lines on her usually pink cheeks.

"So who's your dragon gonna wipe out this year? Who's the lucky guy?" Tana asked.

"Not lucky guy," Gwen said. "Lucky girl." She pointed her thumb at herself.

Robin's eyes flashed and her whole body tightened. "This is because I told you about that Schrödinger cat. Because I said it might've been Colin that killed Arthur. So he chose you as the next target."

"Colin *did* kill Arthur," Allie said. But then she leaned across the coffee table to take Gwen's hand. "But Donna wasn't part of that. Donna loved Arthur too, and when Colin says Arthur died in a cave collapse, she believes him. And she also believes him when he . . ." Allie's voice trailed off and she grimaced, let go of Gwen's fingers.

"What?" Gwen asked.

Allie made a face. "Colin has Donna mostly convinced that you used King Sorrow's tears to poison a few nice old people who didn't need to die. That you get off on it. Like one of those serial-killing nurses we used to watch about on *Unsolved Mysteries*."

Gwen couldn't help it. The notion was so outrageous, she barked with laughter. "No! What? *No.* And Donna . . . ? No!"

Allie regarded her with wide, grave eyes. "Donna can be very credulous about other people's motives. And I think she almost *needs* to believe it might be true. Because of Black Cricket. Because you told her the facts about herself and she couldn't bear it. She hated having a mirror held up to herself like that. Then Colin comes to her one day and says he's learned this awful secret about you, that you're dangerous, you're sick. Can't you see what a relief that was to her? She isn't the villain in the story anymore. You are."

Gwen weighed that up and then nodded, slowly. How it gladdened Donna's heart to have someone to despise.

"There *has* to be a way to turn King Sorrow aside," Robin said.

"There was," Gwen told them. "Down in Stu Finger's cave there was a weapon we coulda stuck right in his heart. But if Arthur didn't get it, I'm not going to. And I'm afraid Cumberland County is a bit short on dragon-fighting implements." Only maybe that wasn't quite true. A phrase of Arthur's wavered at the edge of her consciousness, gnat-like—*a righteous spirit can be drawn in the form of steel*—and was brushed aside so quickly she hardly registered it.

Allie set her tea down. "Mm. I'm not sure about that, Gwen. I might know about *something* you can use. This all started with the Cabinet of Curiosities, Llewellyn's collection of murder weapons and occult paraphernalia. Colin has kept it going, and there's other things in there now. A bottle of blood, a weird old monocle he says belonged to Arthur . . . and there's also this scratchy smelly blanket. It's made from human hair and it's huge, you could just about hide an elephant under it. Donna said it was so disgusting she was going to incinerate it, and Colin laughed and said she was welcome to try.

So she threw it in the fireplace, on top of a big blaze. It didn't even get warm. She squirted lighter fluid on it and it wouldn't catch. Colin used tongs to take it back out and said if he ever had dragon trouble, that would be the first thing he'd reach for. Donna said if it doesn't also deflect dragon *teeth* it wouldn't be much help, and he said it does better than that, but he didn't explain."

"The martyr's robe," Gwen said.

"What's that?" Robin asked.

Gwen shook her head, couldn't form a reply, not yet. What had Arthur said about the martyr's robe, that night on the hill, the inner tube between them and their breath coming in plumes of white smoke? That it would keep you from the fires of hell . . . and from the eyes of the wicked.

A righteous spirit can be drawn in the form of steel, she thought once more, and was conscious of her heart quickening with a sudden rush of blood, a rush of possibility.

She became aware of Robin watching her closely. Gwen offered her a weak smile.

"We want that robe, don't we?" Robin said. "If it would protect Colin, it will protect you."

"What's she going to do? Walk around in a smelly blanket made of hair for the rest of her life?" Tana asked. No one had an answer for that.

Allie said, "Thing is, we can't just walk into The Briars and grab it. A few years ago, Colin put a lock on the cabinet. And it's no ordinary lock, either. It was forged out of something, some kind of alloy that isn't on the traditional table of elements, and the lock makes you dizzy even to handle it. Real fairy tale stuff. You can't even mess with that lock unless you've already got the key."

"Jesus," Tana said. "I was just getting my head around dragons and trolls and you had to throw in a fuckin' Harry Potter lock. You gotta find a way around that."

"It won't make you dizzy if you have the key," Allie said.

"Where's the key?" Gwen asked, prying herself up out of her thoughts with some effort and glancing around.

Allie looked glum. "Donna has it."

12.

Gwen went out on the back step at two in the morning to clear her head and count the planes flying out of Portland. She was up to three when the door softly shut behind her.

"Okay if I join you? I'm *crackling*," Robin said.

Gwen nodded. Robin put her back to the wooden railing and found her glass e-cig.

It was just them. Allie and Tana had left a few minutes before in the Elantra. Allie was going to spend the night on Tana's couch. The following morning she would drive to The Briars, ashamed and contrite. She would apologize for things she had said to Donna. She would tell Donna that Gwen and Tana had rescued her from her wander down the interstate, but Gwen had been too disgusted and angry to speak to her: disgusted by her drunkenness, angry she wouldn't give up her friendship with Donna. Tana had been more forgiving, had taken Allie home, let her sober up, and then asked if she wanted to attend an AA meeting with her . . . which Allie was going to do. Allie would tell Donna that she had scared herself, could've been killed, and needed to try sobriety for a bit. It would sell.

And why does Allie gotta tell her all that? Tana asked.

Robin was first to the answer: *Because Colin Wren is up on Gwen's phone. He's already listened to the voicemail Allie left for Gwen . . . and knows Gwen called Tana straight after she got it. We can't allow any suspicion that Allie's allegiances have changed.*

They haven't *changed*, Allie said, with an unexpected fierceness. *I was for Gwen before and I'm still for Gwen now. I was for Donna before and I'm still for Donna now.*

And Colin? Robin asked.

Allie shook her head and said, *Darn it, don't get me crying again. I'm sick of being the one who cries.*

So no more texting, Tana said. *Ain't none of us can text each other anything about anything.*

Oh, I don't know about that, Gwen said. *I plan to text Allie tomorrow that I never want to see her again.*

Allie's eyebrows flew up at that, but Gwen held one palm out in a calming gesture.

I learned about disinformation ops from Colin, Gwen said. *There's no reason we can't run one of our own. It would be ideal for us to have a falling-out now, Allie. It'll give you your best shot at the key.*

At that, Allie had smiled shyly and said, *I don't even like to pretend I'm angry at my friends. But I'll try if that's our best chance to get the robe.*

The robe, Gwen said, *and something else.*

"Why a cracked mirror?" Robin asked now.

Gwen said, "It came in handy once before."

"Want to fill that out with any details, darling?"

"I can—but not tonight. I'm not trying to be mysterious. It's been a long day and I just need to think for a while. All right?"

Robin nodded and blew a rippling stream of vapor, which mingled with Gwen's own frozen breath.

"Look at the two of us," Gwen said. "Out here puffing like dragons ourselves."

"No knights in shining armor coming to save these princesses. Guess we're going to have to armor up ourselves."

"I don't know about '*we*,'" said Gwen. "*Me* maybe. When push comes to shove, I'd rather you girls look after yourselves. You're not on King Sorrow's kill list."

"Not yet. But sooner or later Colin is going to know I flew into Boston yesterday afternoon and rented a car to come see you. Sooner or later, he's going to know if Allie loots his Cabinet of Curiosities. Assuming he doesn't catch her in the act. If it was just a matter of courage, I think Allie could pull it off. But she's not the girl I met on that plane twenty years ago. It's like she's suffering from a wasting illness."

"I think the medical term for what she's got is 'grief.' For Van and for Donna too."

"It must be hard on her. To love someone she knows is no good. The booze is one hang-up. Donna is another. I think it's quite normal for a self-hating gay to get into a relationship with someone who doesn't treat them well, someone who will never, ever return their feelings, someone unobtainable—it's their way of punishing themselves. It's hard not to internalize it, you know? The idea that there's something basically abhorrent about yourself, because that's how others see you. I used to like being beaten up by men. I had a couple teeth broken once. It took me a while to decide I didn't actually need to be thrashed for the crime of being trans." She turned her head to blow out a last mouthful of smoke, clicked off her e-cig, and put it away. "So. Any requests for your funeral? Music you want played? Particular kind of service?"

"I'd say I want to be cremated," Gwen said, "but if things don't break my way, I think King Sorrow will see to that."

13.

Allie was fourteen days sober before she realized she was going to have to get Donna drunk—really, really drunk—if she wanted the key to the Cabinet of Curiosities . . . and the only way to do that would be to get drunk herself. It was, she saw, the next right thing. And in the last two weeks the notion of doing the next right thing had come to seem like a stick of driftwood she might grasp to keep her head above water.

Tana Nighswander had talked about the next right thing at an AA meeting, the third one Allie attended. Tana told her drunkalogue, how she used to deliver pizza and drugs, how sometimes when she showed up to make a delivery, it turned out the men waiting had paid for her as well. She used her tips to buy gin. She said she had her first blackout when she was fifteen. She was not frightened of brain damage—she hoped for it, wanted to lobotomize herself with gin, so she could just go along with the things her sister made her do without feeling bad. When she was seventeen, she lurched awake in the front seat of a friend's car, off the road, a tree branch through the windshield and broken glass in her lap, a six-inch gash along her hairline. She didn't remember where she had been driving, didn't remember anything from the day before. When she learned she was pregnant, she vowed not to drink anymore. Her sobriety lasted three days. She did PCP while she was pregnant too. Three months after Jett was born, she got home drunk, forgot he was strapped in the back seat of the car, and passed out on her couch. If her friend Gwen Underfoot hadn't come along twenty minutes later, Jett would've died from heat exposure. As it was he needed a day in the hospital on fluids. After Tana nearly killed him by leaving him strapped into a hot car, she had wanted to die. She had never wanted to die more. She wanted to be dead so Gwen would take the baby and give him a good life.

"But I guess Gwen really wanted to see me suffer, so she took me to meetings instead, and that's how I wound up sentenced to life in AA with alla you clowns instead," Tana said to reliable laughter.

Tana went to ninety meetings in ninety days, while Gwen was the mother to Jett that the baby needed. Tana said in those first days she was scared all the time. Scared she was going to drink. Scared to be alone. Scared the baby would cry and her resolve would crumble and she would start drinking again and wake up and the baby would be dead, blue and cold and stiff. She could not have been more terrified if she was in a car sliding out of control down a steep slope toward rocks. The meetings were her way of frantically pumping the brakes, trying to bring the vehicle to a stop before it was too late.

That was doing *the next right thing*, Tana learned—and although those first days of free-falling panic were behind her now, it was still how she tried to live her life. She went to a meeting. She went to work. If someone walked into the Market Basket with their toddlers and couldn't afford groceries, she helped them out. She wasn't a doctor or a professor or an airline pilot . . . she made forty-one thousand dollars a year managing the Basket. But no single mom, red-eyed from crying, ever went home hungry when they visited her supermarket. If an old fella came in using a walker, she went out to load his groceries herself, because that was the next right thing. She went to church on Sunday and prayed for the strength to get through the next day sober; it was the next right thing. Whenever she read a story in the paper about a baby who died because of negligence or shitty bad luck, she lit a candle in the chapel, thanked God for saving her child from her, and promised herself again she would do the next right thing and try to do the next thing right.

Allie believed, at first, that she was going to the meetings with Tana because it made it easy to meet Gwen and Robin afterward for a council of war. Twenty minutes over coffee, or just five in a parked car. But the morning she heard Tana talk about the next right thing, she was struck by two thoughts. The first was that for her, the next right thing she could do for herself was go back to her faculty housing and pour out the wine, one bottle of it after another. It pleased her to imagine doing that and being able to tell Tana she had done it. The second was that she had it the wrong way around. The AA meetings were not a pretext so the gang could meet in private to discuss Gwen's situation. Meeting Robin and Gwen was the pretext to go to the AA meetings.

Not only that: Allie was the *last* one to realize that the meetings were the part that mattered most, not their secret conversations afterward. What did they have to meet about? Until she got into the Cabinet, not much. Allie believed at first they had joined forces to save Gwen . . . only to discover they had joined forces to save *her*. And the other women had known it all along.

Allie knew other things too. The daughter of evangelical Christians and a lifelong churchgoer herself, she knew that Easter belonged in April . . . but in that year of 2016, the movable feast of the Resurrection fell at the end of *March*. They had seven weeks to send King Sorrow back to the Long Dark forever or Gwen was ash.

And she knew about the key that Donna wore everywhere, not on a rope of silver, but on a chain of dullest iron. Donna said it *whispered* and had once clutched Allie's head to her chest so Allie could hear it. At first Allie had only been aware of Donna's heartbeat beneath the swell of her breast. It had made her almost breathless to have her face pressed to Donna's chest (and she thought Donna knew it too, maybe even took a cynical pleasure in it).

But then, slowly, she thought she began to detect a susurration, not unlike the roar-and-hiss she had heard, once upon a time, in the Aztec conch. Only this sound stirred a profound feeling of unease rather than a sense of wonder. It was the sound of a madman whispering to himself in a dungeon. A madman sobbing under his breath with laughter. How iron might whisper and what secrets it had to share, Allie could not imagine.

Allie could think of only one set of circumstances that might allow her to slip the chain off Donna's neck. It might just about be possible if Donna got plastered, pissed, pass-out drunk. Allie had seen her that drunk a few times before, knocked out with her head on her arms, snoring the buzzing, labored snore, not of a petite middle-aged woman, but an asthmatic fat man. And the only way to make sure she got that drunk was to get that drunk with her.

Allie had learned from Tana and her AA meetings that she could live with herself as long as she did the next right thing, and by the end of February she knew the next right thing was to go back to drinking.

What surprised her was how ill she felt at the thought of losing her sobriety—the first fourteen days of bitter, refreshing clarity she had had in nearly thirty years. But beneath the guilty feeling was a rotten excitement, an eagerness to drink and drink until the booze hit her like a hammer between the eyes. To drink until she didn't feel so bad about Gwen, until she didn't feel like locking herself in the bathroom and crying herself sick, as she had done three or four times already. The eagerness to pick up a drink and be obliterated didn't surprise her, but the regret . . . the regret almost gave her hope for herself. You could only regret losing something if it was worth having.

In the second week of February, Colin had to pop down to New York City for a dinner with several of his largest financial backers the inner circle of billionaires who invested with his equity fund and who held the largest positions in Dragonware. Ostensibly, the conversation was about the firm's expansion into machine learning and artificial intelligence. In truth, though, Colin was being called on the carpet. CNN and MSNBC had both run with the shaky iPhone footage of Colin shoving Gwen Underfoot down at the opening of his Rackham College computer center. In the video, Colin's face was a dead blank, his eyes slitted, his mouth a thin line. He showed all the emotional warmth of a cobra striking from beneath a rock. Gwen—who was not identified by name, only described as an off-duty EMT—was clearly moving to apply a compress to his injured leg. It was almost impossible not to flinch when Colin put his hand over her face and shoved.

Colin had put out a brief statement saying he had just been attacked by an emotionally unwell friend and felt terrible about lashing out at a woman who was only trying to offer medical assistance. He had been in a defensive crouch, acting without thought, and wanted to offer his sincerest apology to the woman in question. This statement had not stopped shares in Dragonware dropping by almost 45 percent in two days. Between the video, the congressional investigations, and the ugly stories about Dragonware's handling of private data, the whole company had lost almost forty billion in market cap in the last eighteen months. There were men far richer than Colin—including a Middle Eastern princeling and a pair of Russian oligarchs who vacationed in Italy with Vladimir Putin—who wanted to know when he was going to stop setting fire to their money.

Allie was hardly in the video herself. The kid with the iPhone had only started filming as Donna peeled Allison off Colin's back, and Allie's hair was across her face, hiding her outraged features. But the school knew full well who had jumped on their biggest private donor. They were conducting their own investigation, and in the meantime, she was still teaching. But Allie had a pretty good idea that she would be looking for work again by the end of spring term. God knew who would hire her now. Come June, she'd have nothing but the shirt on her back, and the twenty-four million dollars her parents had left her when they died. And the house in Texas. And the other house in Cape Cod.

Colin drove to the jetport in Portland, Maine, to meet his Gulfstream, at nine in the morning, and left Donna to hold down the fort at The Briars. Donna had a house of her own, but Allison wasn't sure she spent any time there. They lived together now, Donna and Colin, in every sense that mattered. Allie waited until four in the afternoon before she texted her:

Okay, I've got this bottle of gin you gave me for Christmas three years ago, the one with the funny name, and I feel guilty pouring it down the drain. Do you want it?

> The Port of Dragons gin?

Yes.

> Come over here. You can pour it down my throat instead.

Okay. But I'm not staying. I think the one thing that would make me drink now is watching YOU drink. Two weeks today. Hard but good.

> You don't have to watch. Just come to the door and hand it to me.

Okay, Allie texted, thinking she would pretend to let her resolve crumble when she got there. Only when she reached The Briars, Donna answered the door in a red-and-black silk kimono, loosely belted, and a pair of red-soled Louboutin heels, and Allie didn't have to pretend. It was the kind of outfit designed to give her a twist in the pit of the stomach—Donna right there, naked except for the kimono, the heels, and her smirk.

And the chain with the key on it. She wore that too, of course.

14.

As they went upstairs together, Allie was conscious of a wobble in her legs. She felt like she was climbing the stairs toward moral disaster and personal disgrace. She didn't know what she wanted more: to pour some gin, or to see Donna's silky kimono fall around her feet. Donna glanced back at her and smiled a little contemptuously, and Allie felt a sudden flash of anger at her, and at herself. Van forgave Allie for wanting to kiss women, be held by a woman—he forgave her more easily than she had ever been able to forgive herself. But why did it have to be *this* woman?

(*Why do you think?* Allie thought in Tana's voice. *'Cause you can't have her. She's Van's sister. 'Cause it makes you feel terrible and it's important to feel terrible, isn't it? It's a good justification for drinkin'. Not that folks like us need a justification.*)

"I hate to do this to you. I'll even apologize to Tana for you if you want. But I think you're going to put off your new life of sobriety for one more day," Donna warned her. "The two of us need to pour one out for Spock."

"Leonard Nimoy? Didn't he pass away last year?"

"Yes," Donna said, solemnly, "but they're running a best-of-Spock marathon on TV to mark the one-year anniversary of his death and it's making me sad, and you know I hate to feel feelings when I'm sober."

"Oh," Allie said, in a weak voice. "I don't—I can't, really. I shouldn't, anyway."

"You can and you should. We're in mourning. *I'm* in mourning. I'm doing the very important mourning I neglected to do last year.

Don't make me do this alone. You've had fourteen days. It's not like you're wrecking five years of AA."

"Donna," Allie said. A whine in her voice.

"Tell you what. Pour two, one for you, one for me. We can toast him together and then I'll drink both. I can't toast him by myself, and a toast when one glass is full of ginger ale doesn't count. Not unless you're nine."

Allie made an uncomfortable sound that was not quite agreement and not quite argument.

They settled in the room under the exposed beams where, once, when they were six in number, they would gather to watch *Unsolved Mysteries* together. On the screen, a young Leonard Nimoy examined piles of Tribbles, standing next to an exasperated DeForest Kelley.

Allie's hands shook while she made the drinks, getting elderflower-infused tonic out of the mini fridge, only the good stuff for Colin and Donna. There was a window steps away, and once upon a time, Allie had looked through it and seen a dark figure walking in the snow, a man who turned out to be Enoch Crane. Maybe if the shade had been down, Arthur and Donovan would still be alive now, and wasn't that a thought?

She missed Van, suddenly, with a kind of painful happy-sadness. She had believed—had desperately wanted to believe—that if you loved Christ enough, and prayed hard enough, you could stop being gay. But it wasn't true. She had never been able to stop feeling breathless around a pretty woman with a dirty mouth. Dirty words—the words Allie never used herself, because her mother insisted that was how trash talked—made Allie weak with want, always had.

But Van, Van, sweetest Donovan—if only he hadn't been so determined to marry her. There had never been a better friend! They could've been the Lennon and McCartney of best friends. She thought maybe, finally, at the end, Van had regretted putting a ring on her finger, had wanted to let her go, to be who she was. Maybe they could've had that friendship anyway if they had been allowed the chance.

"How long do you think Van and I would've lasted?" Allie asked. She sat on the couch and handed Donna a G and T.

Donna shrugged. "I don't know why you married him in the first place. It was the shock of surviving the flight, I guess. Or maybe you just had something in you, Allie, something that made you seek out a lifetime with someone who could never make you happy."

Allie almost flinched at that. In Donna's mind, Allie's impulse to be with someone who couldn't bring her happiness was a thing of the past—but it came to Allie that old habits died hard and Donna was the proof.

"He *did* make me happy," Allie said after a moment. "He made me laugh. No one could make me laugh like Van."

"He just didn't make you cum."

That was a good word—*cum*—one that almost always gave her the shivers. Only tonight it didn't. She still hadn't touched the drink in front of her, although the smell was as lovely as always, an odor of lemons and mint, the very fragrance of ruin. Donna threw down half of hers, then noticed Allison looking into her own glass.

"Just drink it. You know you're going to. You wouldn't have come upstairs if you weren't. We can spend the next two hours arguing about it or we can skip over that and get to the part of the evening where you loosen up and start enjoying your life again."

"Fourteen days," Allie said.

"Not interested and not interesting," Donna said. "Fourteen days of people wallowing in their fuck-ups. Competing with each other to see who had the more awful life. Fourteen days of lousy coffee and worse doughnuts in church basements. *Boring*. If you plan to be boring, you can go do that somewhere else."

Allie's hand trembled when she lifted the glass to her lips. She meant to take just a sip, but Donna reached over, gripped the bottom of the glass, and gave it a deeper tilt as Allie brought it to her mouth. Allie had to take two icy swallows to keep from drowning.

"Remember when we all went as Scooby-Doo characters for Halloween and Van dressed up as Daphne? Fishnet tights, microminiskirt? I think he was hoping you'd confuse me for him and want to do him."

Allie felt herself shrivel inside with horror and shame. It was almost like Donna *knew* and enjoyed sticking the knife in. Then it occurred to Allison that of course Donna knew, she had *always* known that Allison wanted her. Donna knew . . . and it pleased her. Disgusted her but pleased her as well. It felt good to have so much power over another person.

"Are we going to talk about Gwen?" Allie said.

"Not when I'm this sober. And not when you're this sober either."

"I can fix that," Allie said. She finished her drink and got up to pour another.

"I'D LOVE TO TRY A STRAP-ON SOMETIME," Donna said. "Bend Colin over the back of the couch. He'd love that, you know. He's entirely free of inhibitions."

It was the kind of thing she said to get under Allie's skin, the sort of comment that usually made her pulse leap. Only for some reason now it disheartened her, struck her as a crude attempt to get a reaction. Allie wondered how many hours she might have to sit here before Donna passed out.

Donna said, "I would've liked having a cock. I *deserved* one. More than Van, anyway. How did *he* wind up the boy? I could throw a football. I could win a fight. I wanted to get on TV when I was a kid and I got on TV, goddamn it. He never *wanted* anything. Besides you, which was kind of pathetic."

"He wanted you to be okay. He wanted all of us to be okay."

"Shit." Donna looked away. "Don't fucking do that. You know I don't like to cry."

"Did you cry for Gwen? After Colin told you it was going to be her?"

Donna banged her G and T down on the coffee table hard enough to slop some over the rim and shifted on the couch to face her. Her cheeks were flushed and hectic. "Gwen was *going to kill us*, so we got to her first, and that's all there is to it. She was going to kill us like she whacked those old people in the old folks' home."

"It wasn't an old folks' home," Allie said. "It was a *hospice*. And they were acts of mercy. I think on some level you know that."

Donna ignored this. "She's been working up to lashing out at us—at me—ever since Black Cricket."

"You think she needed ten years to work up to it?"

"No. All she needed was a reason, and that motherfucking perv in a dress gave her one. Robin Fellows ought to go too, in my opinion, but Colin is satisfied he won't bother us again."

"She," Allie said, in a quiet voice.

"Oh, don't start with the pronoun shit. Thing is, even if Gwen *didn't* try to kill us—even if, like she said, she only wanted to destroy King Sorrow, and don't ask me how the fuck she was going to do that—she knows we'd wind up dead anyway. Without the dragon to protect us? There are people out there, the kind of people who took me and my brother and tortured us—tortured your husband, Allie! I know you loved his heart even if you didn't dig his prick. They'd come for us again if we ever let the iguana wriggle off the leash. Or we'd get a visit from friends of the people we destroyed. And you know what? I'm not sorry about anyone we wiped out. The world is a better place for it. Because of us, no one has set off a dirty nuke to annihilate Jerusalem. No one has wiped out San Francisco in a chemical weapons attack. We saved lives by getting *them* before they could get *us*. That's what we signed up for."

"I thought we signed up to help Arthur," Allie said, but Donna didn't seem to hear her. "Would you make Colin take it back—would you let Gwen off the hook—if I got on my knees and begged?"

"You'd love to do that anyway," Donna said, and snickered. "The idea probably gets you hot, you fuckin' perv. Put the thought out of your head. I'm a goddamn hestro—heterosecular woman. Your glass is empty. And so's mine."

Allie made them each another.

"DO YOU LIKE ME?" Donna asked her, without any warning at all.

"I love you," Allie said.

"But do you *like* me?"

"Not much."

"No," Donna said, satisfied. "I don't like me either. It was the best part of being Van's sister. I dinn't have to care about people. I knew he'd care about them for me. I'd break it and he'd fix it." She lowered her head and blinked and a fat tear fell. "I en't know why I'm horrible to you. Tell me one good thing about me."

"You're braver than anyone I know," Allie said.

Donna shook her head and looked at her with real sadness. "How can you be so wrong about everything?"

Donna's breath hitched and a tear caught in her eyelashes and for the first time in her life, Allie thought, *How did I wind up so fascinated by a boring drunk?* A notion that gave her a sudden, inexplicable, wild stab of joy. Maybe she could be free of her. Maybe she could meet another girl. Maybe she had *already* met another girl.

"*Shh,*" Allie heard herself saying, and she stroked Donna's head, and Donna put her cheek in Allie's lap.

"Want me to gobble your pussy?" Donna asked miserably, her voice clotted by tears. "I could, you know. If that's really a thing you need."

"No, thank you," Allie said. "That's all right, darling. Just rest and feel better."

"*Oh-*kay," Donna said, sounding for all the world like a weepy child up past her bedtime.

She made an unhappy sound, twisted this way and that to get comfortable, and produced a wet, chesty burp. Five minutes later, she began to snore. Allie had to reach carefully over her to set down her tonic water. It was after one in the morning, and she was fifteen days sober. Had not put so much as a drop of gin in her glass all night.

15.

Allie stroked Donna's hair, smoothing it out and away from the nape of her neck. There was the clasp of that odd, flat iron chain, lying between two knuckles of her spine. Allie squeezed the latch with her thumbnail and the necklace popped off, fell into her crotch, slithered half under her. That was the easy part.

The hard part was shifting Donna's head off her, squirming out from under. Allie raised her skull out of her lap and edged to the side, an inch at a time, her butt squeaking over the leather, and was there a more embarrassing sound in all the world? Every squeak sounded like a trumpet blat, and she expected Donna to twitch and wake and look blearily around. Allie contorted herself to slip out from under Donna and then set her head down and got up. The necklace—and the key—was now half buried under the couch cushion, and Allie had to lean across her friend and dig for it, her belly almost in Donna's face. She found it, collected the chain in her fingers, and stood up, key dangling from her fist.

She rose and looked down and found Donna staring back at her. Her very blue eyes seemed almost angry, her face blotchy. Allie felt as if all the breath had been driven from her lungs.

"I love you," Donna said, with unmistakable resentment, and shut her eyes again.

"I love you too," Allie said.

She turned off the light but left the TV on, the sound muted.

Allie went down the stairs in her bare feet, through the kitchen, and into the study.

She stood by the piano for a moment, letting her eyes adjust to the moonlit dimness. The French windows threw tiles of bone-colored light on the floor. The dead butterflies might have been stamped from silver foil. Allie's hand drifted to the piano, touching it lightly, as if warning it to remain quiet. It had been a long time since she had been able to trust that piano.

Allie circled the desk and stood before the Cabinet, tall and narrow as a coffin. The big iron hasp was across the two doors, that ancient lock decorated with ornate scrollwork, holding them shut.

She hesitated, then put the key aside and approached the door without it. To feel again, for herself, the sensation she had felt when Colin brought the lock home and challenged her to touch it.

I'll catch you if you fall, he promised her, a smile touching the corners of his lips.

I'll need a few more drinks before there's any chance of that, she told him, but in fact, the moment Allie put her hand on the lock, he had needed to grab her arm to keep her from going down.

Now she spread the fingers of her right hand and stretched them toward it and she *felt* it. It was a little like pushing two magnets toward each other, only her hand was one magnet and the lock the other, and the reverse polarity wanted to shove her arm down. As her fingers closed to within an inch of the dark iron, the blood rushed from her head and the world grayed out around the edges of her vision and she wobbled ... then she quickly retreated, placing a hand on the desk to steady herself. Well, then. That first experience with what Colin called the Distortion Lock had not been imagined, had not been the power of a pre-hypnotic suggestion. The hand on the edge of the desk felt around and found Donna's key.

This time she held the key out in front of her, brandishing it the way she might've brandished a pocketknife if menaced by a drunk in an alley. She waited for another rush of dizziness, but it didn't come. There was a sensation of pushing *through* something, almost like thrusting a hand through water, or something more viscous than water, and the key slid into the lock and turned, and abruptly the sense of fighting against something was gone. She thought of an electric fence; when she turned the key, it was as if someone had flipped a power main and cut off the juice.

She slipped the lock free from the hasp, weighed it in her palm. Allie had heard about an object in the ruins of Chernobyl, a lump of radioactive slag called the elephant's foot, which was considered the most lethal object on the planet. She could not help feeling the lock itself was made of far more dangerous stuff. She tossed it in the general direction of the desk, glad to let go, and opened the Cabinet.

A smell of sweetly seasoned wood spilled out, an odor of cedar and oak. Allie's hand flitted here and there, touching, as if for luck, old acquaintances. John Smith's gun, the ball-peen hammer from the Los Feliz murder house, the 8mm Elwood Hondo film. Her hand dropped two shelves and rested on the cloak, carefully tucked into a large square of silky white paper. Set atop it was a glass bulb filled with what looked very much like blood. The cork had been pulled more than once, but Colin had melted fresh wax each time to reseal it. Allie could see where different-colored waxes had bubbled down over the older wax.

She slipped the martyr's robe out of its envelope of pale paper and left the paper behind. Maybe Colin wouldn't even notice it was gone. She found the Russian mirror, the one with the Y-shaped crack across the face, and folded it inside the cloak.

It unnerved her, to be alone in the study at this hour of the night, in front of this cabinet full of murder weapons and objects with ghosts stuck to them. She put her bundle on the seat of the desk's chair, glanced about for the Distortion Lock—and couldn't find it. She remembered tossing it on the desk, but it wasn't there. It had slid all the way off and dropped almost soundlessly in the inch-thick carpet. She tried to pick it up by Donna's necklace, that loop of dull iron chain hanging from the key, and tugged the key right out of the lock.

A door closed somewhere deep in the house.

Her blood quickened, rushing to her heart. Donna was up, she was awake, and she was coming. Allie dropped the key on top of the folded robe and, in her haste, bent and grabbed for the lock, had forgotten what would happen.

Darkness rushed up behind her eyes. The floor tilted beneath her. She reeled and grabbed at the desk to keep from toppling. She could taste bile, sweetened ever so slightly by elderflower, in the back of her mouth. She sank to one knee and waited for her head to clear. A light came on in the hallway.

She took one breath, and another. Allie grabbed the key with one hand, snatched the lock with the other, and this time remained clearheaded. Footsteps approached. For the life of her, she didn't know what she'd tell Donna. At least Donna was drunk. Tomorrow, she might not even remember finding Allison here.

Allie shut the Cabinet, put the lock on it, and turned, just as Colin stepped into the doorway. He beamed at the sight of her.

"Did you get lost?" he asked her.

He was in the doorway, one arm resting against the doorframe, his whole body sagging to one side. She couldn't see his face in the dark, although the moonlight gleamed off his bare, shiny scalp. Her heart flew to her mouth, and for a moment she was too frightened to speak.

She was surprised when she finally found her voice and it was relatively normal. "Lost?"

"Did you get lost looking for the Excedrin?" he said. "And is it for you? Or Donna? How much did she drink?"

"For me," Allie said, and her gaze fell to the desk once again. There were plastic cubes to one side, a collection of paper clips in one, Sharpies in another. There had always been a third, full of the Excedrin that Colin ate like candies, but she couldn't spot it in the dark.

"I had to stop taking them," Colin said. "They were chewing up the lining of my stomach. I have a powder now, a mix of oxycodone and Adderall. I rub it into my gums. Do you want?" He began to pat his pockets, feeling around for it.

"That's all right," Allie said.

He nodded.

"You're back," she said. "I didn't think you'd be back tonight." To her own ears, this sounded like the beginning of a confession, a thief explaining why she thought she'd get away with her crime.

"I was in New York City for six hours, and that was five and a half hours too long." He tried to draw himself up to his full height, then gave it up as too much effort and slouched once more against the doorframe. He was drunk himself, then, or stoned, or both. "I spent most of my afternoon in a boardroom seventy-five floors up from Fifth Avenue, surrounded by money guys who wanted to nail my scrotum to the table. One of 'em said it was lucky for me the windows didn't open, or they'd chuck me out. I had to laugh at that, just thinking what would happen if they tried. Would've been a hell of a thing to see King Sorrow come through the glass and start playing Frisbee with billionaires."

"How much trouble are you in?" she asked.

"With them? None, really. Not in any way that matters. What are they going to do? They can't get their money back now. It's like that old saying: if you owe a bank a hundred thousand dollars and you can't pay, you've got a problem. If you owe a bank a hundred million dollars and you can't pay, *the bank* has a problem. Dragonware took some hits last year, and that shitty little video of our stupid altercation at Rackham, that was the icing on the cake. But if my investors pull their money now, they walk away losers. They can only walk away winners if they stick with me."

"They can't, I don't know, take your company from you? Vote you out as CEO?"

He stared at her blankly, and she felt her skin roughen with goose bumps. No. Of course they couldn't. He'd scour them off the face of the earth before he'd ever let that happen. He had a dragon, after all.

"I don't really care if the equity people like me," he said at last, which was no answer to her question. "But I do care whether you do. Are we cool, Allison Shiner? The last time I saw you, you were expressing a difference of opinion with your bony little fists."

Allison said, "I was drunk. And I didn't understand. Donna made me understand. I didn't want to believe it for a while. When I jumped on you, I was mad about you sending King Sorrow after Gwen, but I guess maybe I should've hit you for not doing something sooner." As she said this, she was painfully aware of the martyr's robe, folded up on the seat of his desk chair. All he needed to do was take a few steps forward and he'd be able to see it.

Colin bobbed his head in a slow nod. "It's one thing to wipe out people who are dangerous, people who mean to strike at the innocent. But harmless old folks . . . ? And I *do* feel partially responsible. Gwen didn't have our education, wasn't really equipped to deal with what we laid on her. She was a working-class kid who never had to wrestle with anything deeper than whether to buy Pabst or Schlitz on a Saturday night. She never should've been part of this. It's not a surprise the strain of it made her sick inside."

"Yes. I think that's right," Allie said. What a terrible person Colin was, with his money and his shitty intellectual superiority. What a terrible person *she* was, to have been his friend all these years. To have ever sought his approval or love.

"I'm glad you and Donna had a—what do we want to call it? A kiss-and-make-up session?" Allie felt a rough heat in her face. It had always been obvious to everyone how badly she wanted to belong to Donna. It was a running joke to everyone but her.

"We watched a *Remembering Leonard Nimoy* marathon and had a healing sisterly cry over ol' pointy-ears," she said, pretending his dirty little innuendo had sailed over her head.

"I tried to honor Spock's death by not getting emotional about it." Swaying from one side of the doorframe to the other, then pushing off and wandering into the room at last. He couldn't quite manage a straight line but was listing toward the bookshelves. "I probably drank too much before getting on the plane. Especially since I was the one flying it. If we're not still mad at each other, can we hug it out?"

Allie left the robe folded in the chair and crossed over to him. He took her in his arms. That was when she realized she still held Donna's key, on its heavy iron chain, in her right hand. She squeezed it into a fist to hide it. His chin rested on her shoulder. His lips slipped close to her ear as if to whisper some intimacy.

"I have to urinate *so* bad," he said.

He let go of her and swayed across the study. As he passed the desk he wobbled and put a hand down to steady himself, set his hand on the back of the chair. Allie expected him to turn his head, look down and see what was in the seat, his face befuddled—and then his eyes clearing, as understanding dawned upon him. But he didn't slow, just kept going, staggering into the darkened bedroom and out of sight. A toilet seat banged. Pee drizzled into the bowl.

Allie almost sprinted to the desk to get the folded cloak.

SHE LEFT THE MARTYR'S ROBE and the Russian mirror in the grand entrance hall, hidden under her snow parka, and hurried upstairs in her stocking feet. Donna was right where she had left her. She did not stir while Allie looped the necklace back around her throat. In sleep, Donna's features were bunched up in an expression of ugly, childish resentment. On impulse, Allie reached with one thumb to smooth her eyebrow, then leaned in to kiss her temple. It felt as if she were kissing her goodbye—and not just for the night. Donna's face relaxed, and she sighed and even smiled slightly. And in spite of herself, it pleased Allie to think she could bring Donna any relief at all, even if only in her sleep. It had to be exhausting work, being her all the time.

Colin appeared in the front door as she was pulling away from the house. She raised one hand in a wave, her heart drumming as if she had just escaped a psychopath, which, in a sense, she supposed she had.

When she pulled out of the gates, she turned left.

She didn't see the Shelby Boss Snake parked to the right, off the road, didn't see it turn on its headlights, wasn't aware of it following her at a distance of a quarter mile. But then she hadn't seen it when it followed her to The Briars either.

16.

When Gwen and Robin walked into the chapel on the campus of Rackham College, three days after Allie kissed Donna goodbye at The Briars, the 8:00 p.m. meeting was still going on downstairs. Gwen took a seat in the pews. The chapel was open all night long to students, but at this hour, only the accent lights were on, throwing brilliance onto the ornate stonework overhead. A century-old Bible, a book twice the size of Enoch Crane's journal, was open on the altar, and Robin wandered up to give it a glance. She had a smug look of satisfaction when she got back to her pew.

"Psalm forty-four, eighteen–nineteen," Robin said. "'Our hearts were never false and our feet never left your path, though thou hast sore broken us in the place of dragons, and covered us with the shadow of death.' I wouldn't have expected anything different."

They sat in a companionable silence, Robin leaning back, legs crossed, Gwen in her pea jacket, a messenger bag between her feet. Folding metal chairs clanged in the basement, and Gwen heard the shuffle and thump of the attendees gathering their things to go. Gwen watched some of the alcoholics, anonymous, as they appeared in the mudroom—the narthex, she remembered, great crossword fill, that word—and slipped out through the big double doors into the unseasonably warm night.

Allie and Tana were the last to arrive at the top of the steps, Tana lugging a giant stainless steel coffee urn, Allie clasping their coats to her chest. As Allie came into the dim glow of the church, Gwen thought she looked like a woman restored, her blond curls bouncing on her shoulders like she had just stepped out of a shampoo commercial. Tana had squeezed into a pair of jeans that looked as if they had been spray-painted on. Gwen wasn't sure it was entirely moral to wear a pair of jeans like that in a place of worship. Then again, not-entirely-moral pretty much covered Tana Nighswander's operating philosophy.

They took the pew in front of Robin and Gwen and twisted to face them.

"Are you ready to spill it, then?" Tana said. "You going to finally let us in on what you're thinking over?"

"*Can* you?" Allie asked. "Can't King Sorrow spy on you—on all of us?"

Gwen gave her head a little shake. "He can . . . but not here. Arthur told me once that he thought places of worship were, to dragons, a little like a lead apron is to radiation. If he came through into our world, he could smash the roof in on us, but while he's in the Long Dark, I doubt he can hear us through these walls." She did not add that Arthur had no proof for his theory. It had been little more than a wistful notion.

"Get on with it then," Robin said.

Gwen flipped back the flap on the messenger bag at her feet and began to remove items, one at a time, starting with the items Allie had procured a few days before. First the martyr's robe. She gently set the silver-handled mirror of the Russian princess atop it, the glass turned face down. She did not want to look into it until the time was right, had a not unjustified fear of what she might see there. Her hand dipped into the bag again and came up with a battered green thermos. Next to that she placed a stainless-steel cylinder, about the size of a soda can, painted matte black. Lastly, she produced five of Arthur's Leuchtturm1917 notebooks, bundled together with heavy red rubber bands. She did not really need the notebooks, knew them by heart, forward and back, but it felt good to put them next to her. *Arthur Oakes has entered the chat*, she thought, and almost laughed. She doubted Arthur had ever logged into a chat room in his life.

"When Arthur died, he left me some money, and he left me some notebooks. The money was precious. There was enough of it so I could reduce my hours to part-time and go back to school.

But I know now the notebooks were worth more. Arthur had an outline and about seven chapters of a book called *A Toolkit for the Well-Prepared Dragonslayer*. At first, I thought it was an attempt to present his ideas about fairy tale monsters to popular readers. But now I think it was also at least partly a very long letter he was writing, some things he wanted me to know, in case something happened to him. See, by the time Svangur led him into that hole in the ground, Arthur didn't just think he could kill King Sorrow. He *knew* he could."

Allie sat up straighter, her fists balled on her thighs in excitement. Gwen supposed she was overselling it—Arthur didn't deal in certainties, only luminous possibilities—but she thought the hope might be as useful as anything she had pulled out of her messenger bag.

"The easiest way to get rid of a dragon is to learn its true name, which gives you the power to banish him from the mortal realm, for at least as long as you live. King Sorrow's true name was almost certainly in the Crane journal, and if it hadn't burned up in the fire at Fleming's Antiquarian twenty years ago, we could've been out from under our pet iguana decades ago. Dragons can also be tricked into trying to eat things they shouldn't, like a sun, or their own tails, but unfortunately King Sorrow sticks to a limited menu. I guess you could say he's on the paleo diet. The crafty old snake only has a taste for blood seasoned by grief and hopelessness. They can be outfoxed in a good riddling contest, but that's another nonstarter for our guy. I got him once with a bad joke about lousy beer. I'll never get him again, not that way. He's got five thousand years of riddles in his head, and what I've got—what we've all got—wouldn't fill a bad jokebook. A person might also kill one dragon by summoning another."

"If that's why you wanted the mirror," Allie said, "to summon another dragon, then I'm going to put it right back where I found it."

"No worries there. One was enough for me. Finally, as anyone who's ever read even one story about Camelot knows, there's another way to take a dragon off the board, and that's to chop off its head. Bullets—and Sidewinder missiles—bounce right off something like King Sorrow, but stories of mythic adventure are full of magical blades, like Excalibur and the Sword of Strange Hangings, which are sharp enough to cleave through dragon scale. Arthur talked about swords like that almost as if they were people, with names, preferences, moral certainties. Excalibur, for example, could only be drawn by an idealist who would place the law above his own authority. The Sword of Strange Hangings—which Galahad took with him on the Grail quest—could only be drawn by someone who was ready to give his own life, with a light heart, for others.

"Only Arthur didn't just think these weapons had personalities . . . he thought they had *souls*. In fact, he said they *are* souls, pure spirits forged into blades. He wasn't being metaphorical either. He wrote that the human body is itself a kind of sheath for the blade within, and death is the moment the sword is finally drawn, another weapon in God's armory." Gwen's hand had come to rest on the notebooks. "That was almost the last thing he wrote before he went down into the cave with Colin and the troll. But there were also some notes in the margins that I didn't understand right away. He said it was too bad—he already had the sword he needed, but he couldn't draw it while he was alive, and he wouldn't be around to draw it after he was dead. He wrote that the thing he needed most he could never reach."

"Remember, I'm new to this," Tana said. "You have to talk real slow for the townie. You can pull someone's soul right out of their body and use it like a sword?"

"I don't know how you'd pull a soul out of someone's body," Gwen said. "But I know how you pull one out of the Long Dark." She tapped the mirror with one fingernail, *click, click, click*.

"You want to bring Arthur back," Allie said in a hush. "And use him to fight King Sorrow."

Robin was frowning, prettily, thoughtfully. Tana's features were bunched up into an expression of concentration, tinged ever so slightly by anger—she was a woman who hated uncertainty. Only Allie seemed to get it, nodding to herself as she thought it over.

Tana said, "You'd have, like—one of your séances? Like what you used to bring King Sorrow into the world at the beginning?"

"Yes. I'd find a place that was important to Arthur emotionally and call for him to return. Cast the spell, same as we cast a spell to bring King Sorrow through from the Long Dark." She moved her hand to the cylinder that resembled a black soda can—a Bluetooth-enabled projector for iPhone. "I've got a recording of Arthur from a few years back. I can project the video onto the wall, which will bring him right into the room with me. We know a bit of Elwood Hondo's ugly spirit got stuck to a piece of film. Maybe there's a bit of Arthur stuck to my video." She gestured at the mirror. "And there's the mirror. It was one of the instruments we used to summon King Sorrow. It operates as a kind of window into the Long Dark."

"I didn't use the mirror," Allie said. "I used the conch. I should've brought that too. I'm not sure the mirror will work for me, Gwen."

"Don't worry about that, Allie," Gwen said. "This isn't going to require the conch."

Allie frowned, didn't understand what that implied. Before she could follow up, though, Tana said, "So you repeat what you did to bring King Sorrow into this world—"

"Yes. Only for Arthur's spirit. Play the video and call for him to join us. There'd probably also be a task to complete, something that would bend reality ever so slightly. Last time I had to bring some dead butterflies back to life. I don't know what it'll be this time."

"And if everything works, Arthur's ghost shows up carrying a sword?"

"No," Robin said. "Arthur *is* the sword. Isn't that right? You draw him from the Long Dark, just as the other Arthur, the famous one, drew the sword from the stone."

"That's right," Gwen said.

"And that's why the robe changes everything. You can hide under the robe," Robin said, "so King Sorrow can't see you and he can't burn you up. He'll have to come close to find you . . . close enough you can stick the Arthur-sword into him."

"Yes. That's the idea."

"Okay. It sounds like a lot of foolishness, but at least it's consistent with the foolishness that got you into this situation in the first place. Where were we going to bring Arthur back? You said it has to be someplace important to him." Robin rubbed her hands together and shivered. "I'm excited. I haven't been to a séance since I was twelve and Brian Knab pulled out a Ouija board at a sleepover. Where and when do we go to work?"

"*Where* is the Brooks Library. Arthur loved that place. He hated stealing from there. It was like—I don't know. Being made to assault a lover at gunpoint. But . . . Robin . . . *we* aren't going to bring him back. I am. By myself."

This was met with a tense, startled silence, and blank looks. Allie was the first to break out of it. She began to shake her head.

"No. No way," Allie said. "You're not doing this alone."

"Of course I am. You've all already done your part. Robin, I wouldn't know about Colin if you hadn't found the troll."

Robin sat back, jaw set. "Yeah, I was fine help to you there. Got you right on the death list, I did."

Gwen ignored her, went on, "Allie, this wouldn't work without the martyr's robe and the mirror. You got me both."

"Not sure what the hell *I* done," Tana said.

"I am," Gwen said. "Without Allie, I'm nowhere. You picked her out of the road. You've looked after her for most of a month."

"You got me sober," Allie said, in a small voice. "The last three weeks have been the first sane weeks of my life in years."

"But I have to do this last part alone."

"No." Allie was shaking her head again, her eyes brimming.

Gwen put her hand over Allie's. "Yes. All you can do if you come with me is get killed. My conscience is already carrying all the weight it can stand. If I lost one of you it would shatter me."

"We can help bring Arthur through," Allie said, and then sat up, eyes widening. "We could bring Van too. One sword good, two swords better. Van would come back for me. I know he would."

"Yes," Gwen said. "I think he would too. But you're still not coming."

Allie said, "Wait. Stop. Think this through. If you face him alone, you have to wait until he comes for you at Easter, when he's at his full strength. But if we work together, we don't have to wait. Gwen,

I could touch my mark and bring him through *tonight*. He's weaker now. Smaller. Isn't that true? Isn't it true he grows in strength and size as Easter approaches, until he's finally big enough to break through into our reality?"

Gwen grudgingly nodded her head.

"So how big do you figure he'd be if you yanked him into our world right now?" Tana asked.

Gwen shrugged. "Size of a car? In another couple weeks, the size of a helicopter? But we're still not doing it that way, sorry."

"Why? Give me one good reason."

"Well, for starters, anyone who's with me probably winds up charbroiled."

Robin said, "But that isn't all of it. Or even most of it. Is it? There's another reason you don't want us along, isn't there, Gwen?"

Gwen nodded. "After his Easter feast, he slumps back to the Long Dark, weak and exhausted. He sleeps, and I guess he shrinks." What had King Sorrow told them? That he started as small as an evil thought, a worm in the brain. Gwen shuddered at the memory of it.

"So?" Allie said.

"So if Gwen can't kill him, we try her plan again, and we call Van through. And then *he's* the sword," Robin said.

"And Allie can use the mark to summon a version of King Sorrow as weak as a kitten," Tana said.

"I don't know if he's ever as weak as that," Gwen said. "But you'd at least have a fighting chance."

"I want *you* to have a fighting chance, Gwen," Allie said. "Let's do it together. Tonight. *Please*."

"I do have a fighting chance. It's right here," Gwen said, and touched the robe and the mirror.

"You haven't said what this was." Robin pointed at the green thermos.

"Dragon tears," Gwen said. "Someone who swallows them can breathe fire . . . a fire hot enough to burn even a dragon. I could blind him with these. Or at least enrage him, so he's not thinking too clearly when he comes for me."

"Thought that stuff also kills," Robin said.

This time Gwen did not reply.

"Gwen doesn't care," Allie said, and one of her eyes overspilled. "She isn't planning to survive."

"I was planning to drink the tears one way or another," Gwen said. "This way, at least, I have a chance to take a dragon with me. Besides, I won't swallow them if I don't have to. Think of it as an emergency escape hatch. Whatever happens Easter morning, at the very least, I can cheat him out of killing me. I know he'll hate that."

"Everyone good dies," Allie said. "Everyone bad lives. I hate it. I hate it so much."

"Not everyone good dies," Gwen said. "Why do you think I'm leaving you and Robin and Tana out of it, Allie?"

"I don't agree to this plan," Robin said. "Not yet. I need to think about it. Will you give me time to mull it over, Gwen? Time to convince myself that letting you face him alone really is the right thing? It doesn't *feel* right, but what feels right and what *is* right aren't always the same."

Gwen shrugged. "Nothing happens until Easter. I guess there's time for us all to sit and think on it."

But about that, Gwen was wrong.

17.

They made their way out, Gwen with the messenger bag over one shoulder, her personal kit for the well-prepared dragon slayer packed into it once again. Robin opened one leaf of the tall wooden doors and held it while the others marched through.

It was late, and cool, and there was some damp in the air, but for all that it was warmer than it had been, and the snow had shrunk to filthy piles under the trees. At the bottom of the stone steps, Tana hugged Allie goodbye—she was headed to the cafeteria to return the coffee urn, while the rest of them made for their cars. Gwen thought Allie shut her eyes and let herself be held a trifle longer than was necessary. She glanced at Robin, and Robin met her gaze with a raised eyebrow. Allie watched Tana go, then turned and saw Gwen and Robin watching her.

"What?" she cried. Her cheeks began to burn. "*What?*"

"Tana and Allie, sitting in a tree," Robin sang.

"Oh, stop it," Allie said, and began to stalk swiftly away.

They followed at a leisurely pace. Somewhere, a pack of college kids laughed, a sound of hearty pleasure and ease. It was as splendid an evening as Gwen could remember, the air fresh and sweet with the smell of wet pines, and she wondered if it was her last good winter night.

She heard music coming from a white Shelby, old and battered, the tinted windows rolled down. The wheel wells were lacy with rust. It was parked right behind Gwen's pickup, and she frowned at it. It was out of place on campus, wasn't the sort of thing that might belong to a parent or a professor. A student, maybe, who wanted to own something shabby and retro. As Gwen approached, she could see a bumper sticker under the road filth. She squinted to read it, but it was too far away.

"You think the conversation is over," Allie said. She had slowed to let Gwen catch up, and now she affectionately bumped a shoulder against hers. "But it isn't, and I'm not letting you do this alone. I'll change your mind. I can be very persuasive, especially once I start crying."

"I'll give you something to cry about, bitch," Donna said, putting her foot into the back of Allie's knee and shoving, so Allie's leg folded and she went down, hard, with a shout.

Gwen turned as Donna stepped out of the dark, onto the path. She saw Donna cocking her foot back to kick Allie again—and then Robin hit her with one shoulder in the small of the back in a rugby tackle and Donna stumbled over Allie. Gwen caught Donna's shoulders with both hands before she could sprawl face-first on the concrete.

"Let go of me," Donna snarled.

"Okay," Gwen said and dropped her. Donna went down onto her chin with an audible crack.

Robin was behind Donna, looked ready to drop onto her back with both knees. But Colin moved in first.

"Everyone take it easy," he said, appearing out of the dark from beneath a big oak. He looked good, in his gray jeans and his trademark white Henley, the buttons undone to show the hollow of his throat. Two fingers rubbed at a spot between his collarbones. "Or we're going to see the dragon tonight. I know you're eager to arrange a visit, based on what I overheard in the chapel. But since you haven't had time to prepare for him, I'm guessing you'd rather avoid that. So let's all cool down."

Robin was panting hard, her hair mussed. She looked from Gwen to Colin and back.

"Can he just—"

"Bring King Sorrow through from the Long Dark and kill us?" Gwen said. "Ayuh."

"I wouldn't like to," Colin said. "Not here on campus. There's kids around. Not to mention Allie! Someone could be hurt. I mean someone besides you, Gwen. I'm not a monster, you know."

He reached out with one hand. Donna took it and got to her feet. She had scraped her chin.

Gwen said, "You should let me look at that. I've got an alcohol swab in the car and—"

"*Stop it*," Donna said. "Stop playacting Mother Teresa. No one is buying it anymore. And I've heard all about the kind of medical treatment you give. Hard pass."

Donna offered her hand to Allie.

"Get up and get in the car," she said. "I'll deal with you later."

Allie stared at her. Donna tightened her jaw and reached and grabbed Allie's wrist.

"I said get up, goddamn it," Donna said.

"Donna?" Allie asked.

"Yes?"

"Go fuck yourself." And she pulled her hand free.

Donna looked as if she had been struck. Gwen herself twitched as if Allie had spat in Donna's face. Gwen tried to think if she had ever heard Allie swear before—this pretty girl raised in Texas who said *frack* instead of *fuck* and *shoot* instead of *shit*. She didn't think she had.

Donna squeezed her lips together so tightly, all the color bled out of them. "I'll drag you up by the hair."

"The hell you will," Robin said, and it was Robin who reached down and found Allie's upper arm and helped her to her feet.

"This your thing now?" Donna asked. "You're okay with dick as long as it's jammed into a pair of panties?"

"What a horrible person you are, Donna," Allie said, and took Robin's hand in hers. Allie's cheeks were blotchy, and she was struggling not to cry.

Donna opened her mouth and closed it again.

Gwen said, "So what now, Colin?"

"Let's go to The Briars," Colin said. "It'll be easier to talk there."

"Easier to kill me there, you mean," Gwen said.

Colin looked at her with something like fondness. "There's about sixty acres of backyard. We've had plenty of bonfires out there. One more won't bother anyone . . . and there wouldn't be any casualties but you."

"What if I won't go?"

"If you don't go," Colin said, and two fingers caressed the space between his collarbones again, "we do it right *now* and maybe Robin and Allie die with you." He took a step closer and said, gently, "It doesn't have to be awful. You've got the thermos. It could be like with Llewellyn. We could have a nice old Scotch, break out the good stuff. You could drink some tears and float away. Isn't it a nice night for it? To float away? Like rings of smoke?" He breathed deeply and looked around.

Gwen took a breath herself—of that sweet air, redolent with damp soil and blue spruce—and felt something go out of her. It was like a cramped, clenched fist opening at last.

"Okay," she said and she meant it. She was tired. Confronted with Colin's cool logic, all their plans seemed like a lot of ridiculous effort, and she was glad to be spared it. Maybe she *would* have a mouthful of tears and close her eyes. Maybe when she opened them, Arthur would be there to make things right.

They began to walk, the five of them, along a narrow path, under the spreading oaks, through the lovely night. A new song started playing on the radio in that parked Shelby.

"Do you think it would've worked?" Gwen asked, strolling shoulder to shoulder with Colin, the others following behind.

"Pulling Arthur back from death in the form of a sword? Concealing yourself in the martyr's robe to bring King Sorrow close? Maybe. We'll never know now."

"Did you kill him? Did you kill my Arthur?"

"I guess I did."

Her vision darkened for a moment, as if she had stood up too quickly. She had not known that hatred could make one lightheaded.

"For what it's worth," Colin said, "it didn't hurt. Not much."

"That thought brings me a real sense of peace, Colin." He didn't seem to hear the disgust in her voice.

"Personally, I think the easiest way to get rid of the dragon would've been to speak his true name, if you could figure out how to pronounce it. It was about fifty damn syllables long, one of these words only Arthur could figure out how to say. I almost remember the first bit of it. I should have written it down. It's the only thing I regret about torching Bridget Fleming's town house and the Crane journal with it."

"You—!" She stopped walking. "*No.* You . . . that was the day of the memorial for your grandfather. You were at the reception."

They had stopped a few paces from the curb. An old woman in a man's flannel shirt got out of the Shelby, slammed the door, hitched up her jeans, began to walk toward them.

He smiled and stopped walking with her. "You forget. I left early. Remember? That loon, Sheldon Westerberg, the guy obsessed with John Norman's Gor novels . . . he saw me, you know. I stopped in that same café, for an espresso. Right after I lit the fire. And he was there. I told him if he went around the corner, he'd see something that would make him glad. I'm not sure why he never mentioned me to the cops. I'm still grateful to him for that . . . and even more grateful he was in the neighborhood to take the fall for me."

Donna, behind them, said, "Fuck sake, let's go. My chin is killing me. I need to get iodine or some shit on it."

The old woman stopped a foot shy of the curb, less than three yards from them, and reached behind her as if the small of her back ached. She had a hard, bony face and the glittering eyes of a magpie.

"Colin Wren?" the old woman asked.

"Yes?" he said, putting on the smile he saved for photographers.

"Jayne Nighswander says goodbye," Daphne Nighswander told him, and came around with the gun.

The Glock barked and a small black hole appeared in Colin Wren's throat. His head snapped back. His hand flew up in a defensive gesture—or perhaps to touch his tattoo. He didn't reach it in time. The next bullet took off his right middle finger, continued on into his right shoulder. Flame leapt from the barrel. The next two bullets went into his chest and stomach, popping like firecrackers. His legs gave out and he collapsed.

Gwen turned and collided with Donna and they both fell as Daphne fired at them both. It was her only wild shot. The bullet struck the blacktop path, somehow missing Gwen entirely, ricocheting to strike Donna in the foot. Donna roared, twisting away and coming down on her stomach. Gwen spread herself on top of her, thinking she could cover Donna long enough for her to get a hand on her tattoo. *Waste this crazy bitch, Donna*, Gwen thought. Only Donna's arms were trapped beneath her and she couldn't get them to the mark on her chest—either that, or she had forgotten she had it, had, in the shock of the moment, forgotten King Sorrow was only a touch away.

Daphne Nighswander stood over them and put three bullets into Gwen's back. Gwen coughed. It felt as if someone was stomping on her. She felt the impacts more than any sense of pain.

Robin Fellows had her arms around Allie and carried her right off the path. Daphne swiveled, the gun outstretched in one hand, and squeezed off another shot. A bullet blew a chunk of wood off the side of a king oak as Robin fell behind it, dragging Allie with her. Gwen wanted to tell her to let Allie go; she had Allie's arms trapped to her sides. Allie could end this bitch in an instant, she just needed a free hand. Gwen drew in a rattling breath to call out, and when she exhaled, blew bubbles of blood instead of shouting, which was how she knew one of the bullets had perforated a lung. She had blood in her nose, making it hard to breathe.

Daphne stepped over Gwen and Donna and closed in on the tree to the left of the path, meaning to come around it and shoot Robin and Allie. She was looking toward them . . . and so she didn't see Tana coming out of the dark from the other side of the path, the lid off that tall steel urn of hot coffee.

"Hey, Momma."

Daphne turned toward the sound of her voice.

Tana said, "Drink up, you thirsty bitch," and threw a few liters of hot coffee into her face.

Daphne screamed, turned her face away, and blindly pointed the gun toward Tana. Did she mean to shoot her own daughter? Gwen never found out. Tana swung the urn down on the old woman's arm. The gun flew. Daphne's withered old face was already blistering where it had been scalded by coffee.

The old woman growled and bent, clawing for the gun with her left hand, and Tana Nighswander brought the urn down again. This time it connected with the back of her mother's head. The urn made a low metal bong—a musical, almost playful sound that covered the crunch of the old woman's skull caving in. Daphne went down, her head turned so Gwen could see her face, which looked like a half-melted rubber mask, covered in grotesque bubbles. Steam boiled off it.

From a great distance Gwen heard people shouting, screaming for help. She wasn't in any pain, she was just wet, her clothes sopping with blood. Donna shuddered beneath her, producing a series of hoarse, rough coughs that gradually resolved into sobs. Gwen became aware that she was gently stroking Donna's hair to soothe her.

"You're all right," Gwen said. "You're all right now, Donna."

Donna reached up blindly and found Gwen's hand and squeezed it. Somehow, though, she didn't seem comforted—if anything, Donna was crying harder than ever.

Gwen didn't want to look at the horror-movie mask of Daphne Nighswander's face anymore. She struggled to lift her head and was at last able to turn it away. She had fallen in such a way that she could see the rear bumper of the Shelby Boss Snake now, was close enough to make out the bumper sticker. NO FREE RIDES, it said. GAS, GRASS, OR ASS.

"No free rides," Gwen said to herself, and nodded. *Truer words were never spoken*, she thought, and closed her eyes.

18.

The light was blinding. They had her in the operating theater, a mask cupping her nose and mouth to give her oxygen. A doctor in latex gloves and a surgical mask stood on her right. He was splashed up to the wrists in blood. Gwen was aware of nurses hurrying about at the periphery of her vision. There was a blue curtain behind the doctor and a great brown smear of gore across it. A stack of monitors to the side of the bed captured her vitals: her pulse, her temperature, her oxygen levels.

"Where am I hit?" she asked or tried to. She wasn't sure if the sounds she made were words.

The doctor turned his head to meet her gaze and she saw it was King Sorrow. Behind the mask, his skin was a sheath of black scales. His golden eyes, shot through with those threads of crimson, glittered with good humor.

"Looks like that old bitch shot you right in your only chance to beat me, love," he said. "But don't worry. You've got one in the lung, one in the rectouterine pouch—my, *that* sounds dirty—and one in the hip. It's bad. But it's not fatal. I'm *sure* we can keep you alive until Easter. You ought to be on the slow, painful road to recovery when I hit this hospital like a cruise missile. The ICU is right below the maternity ward, and there is nothing quite so sweet as the smell of roasted newborns."

Something was moving behind the paper mask covering his mouth, as if there was a great slug in there, where his lips belonged.

"I'll kill myself first," she whispered. "I'll go right out the window."

"You won't be strong enough, Gwennie, darling. It'll be months and a hip operation before you can walk again. And you don't *have* months, Gwen. You have *weeks*."

"Doctor," a nurse said, "the patient is articulating."

He twitched his head slightly and when he spoke again, it wasn't King Sorrow's voice, but a nasally American accent. "I hear her. You're with the nursing school? They won't have talked about this in your classes. It isn't uncommon, when the patient's blood pressure is this low, for a certain amount of anesthesia awareness. It isn't *true* consciousness. It will pass as we continue the infusion."

The doctor, who still had King Sorrow's face, looked back at Gwen and winked.

"Not that I'll let *you* burn to death. Just everyone around you." It was King Sorrow's voice again, and she understood no one could hear him but her. "*You*, Gwen—I've been dreaming of you for years. How sweet it'll be to tear you apart and watch your guts slop out, while you're still alive. And how sweet it'll taste to lap at a lake of your blood. How often have I told you that regret and failure and grief season one's juices? And after all *your* failures, all your regrets, after everything you've lost—and you've lost so much, Gwen, it's almost *funny*—I get dizzy just thinking about it. In fact, how would you feel if I had myself a little aperitif right now? The blood will have to wait, but I know something *almost* as good."

A black, impossibly long, forked tongue slipped out from behind the mask and flicked at the tears running from her right eye. She hadn't known until then that she was crying.

"*Irresistible*," he said.

19.

Donna couldn't stand hospitals, so in the morning she slid to the edge of her cot, hung her legs over the side, and reached for the aluminum crutch leaning against the wall.

She got it under her left armpit and lowered herself carefully down. She put her bare right foot on the floor. The left foot she kept raised. It was wrapped in gauze from toes to mid-shin and encased in some kind of black bionic boot with Velcro straps, like a snowboarder's boot. The heel throbbed hella bad and she clenched her teeth. Her johnny flapped open at the back to show her bare ass to the morning. She didn't give a fuck. If she had to breathe hospital air for another minute, she was going to gag—that odor of iodine and blood was suffocating. She hopped-shuffled-skipped her way to the swinging door and pushed through it and continued out onto the beach on Cherokee Island.

The cold sand felt good under her bare right foot. Thin clouds unraveled across a chilly sky. Gulls wheeled over the dark water, crinkling with whitecaps. Van waited for her, down by the edge of the sea, one hand in the pocket of his jeans and the breeze playing with his red hair. His pant legs were rolled up almost to the knee and his bare feet were sandy. She thought he had never looked so handsome. He waved, then bent to look for seashells. A wave broke and foam rushed up the beach to hiss around his toes.

She made her slow, awkward way across the drifts of sand to him, no easy thing to do on a crutch. As she neared him, he discovered a perfect sand dollar and held it to the sky. His other hand came out of his pocket and she saw, as she approached, that he had already collected half a dozen of them.

"There's a sight," Donna said. "Van McBride with more than five dollars in his hand. First time ever. Pro tip: don't try and buy weed with it. Your dealer will laugh you into next Monday."

He smiled at her with a heartbreaking fondness. "This is the only wealth that really means anything, you know: the time to collect sand dollars and lungs to breathe the ocean air."

"Fuckin' hippie."

The corners of his eyes wrinkled with happiness.

They turned and fell into step together, walking side by side. It was easier, down here, close to the water, where the ocean had pounded the sand into a hard, wet, flat surface.

"I miss you so much," she said, and then wished she could take it back, because she hated to cry.

His hand rested on her back. "That's still no excuse."

She lowered her face. "Goddamn it. If you're just going to scold me, you can go back to being dead."

"It's no excuse for the way you've lived. What you've done to yourself and what you've done to the people who love you. What you did to a few hundred women who lived lives of abuse and grief. Every one of them a Cady Lewis."

"They were *nothing* like Cady," Donna said, jerking away from him so violently, the crutch slipped and she tumbled, fell with a shout to the sand.

"They were all Cady," he said, looking down at her benevolently, but doing nothing to help her up. "Even the person who killed Cady Lewis was a Cady Lewis himself once."

"It doesn't matter *what* got done to you," she snarled, from the sand. "I don't care how much abuse you soaked up. I don't give a fuck about what you didn't have and what got taken from you. It doesn't matter! It doesn't matter how much hurt anyone feels, it doesn't give them the right to destroy other lives."

"Yes. This is my point exactly," he said. "I think we agree on something for the first time in our lives."

The sun was behind him, and his red hair burned like a crown of gold.

"You want to scold someone, go haunt Gwen!" Donna cried.

"She's as bad as me! Do you know what she was doing in that hospice?"

"Yes. And so do you. Giving people their dignity back. Gwen almost died trying to claw a sad, fucked-up kid out of the rubble in New Hampshire. Is that the kind of person who offs old people for kicks? You never believed that, not for an instant. You can bullshit others, but you can't bullshit me. Or yourself."

"I can't fix it," she said, and covered her face. He was too beautiful to look at, and she was crying again. "I'd give every dime I have to fix it, Van, but I can't. Not with all the money in the world."

"No. Not with all the money in the world. But there are other kinds of wealth."

And he crouched and took her hand and put a sand dollar in her palm and folded her fingers over it.

"This isn't real," she said. "This is a dream."

"It's more than that," he said. "When you wake up, and see this sand dollar in your hand, you'll know it's not too late to make things right." He bent forward and she closed her eyes and her brother kissed her cheek.

She opened her eyes and found herself in her hospital bed, staring at the drab drop ceiling. Her foot was elevated by a stainless steel gantry and a collection of rubber straps. Her right fist was squeezed tight. Donna thought she could feel a sand dollar pressed into her palm, and for the longest time she didn't want to look, because when she opened her hand and saw it was empty, she would know for sure it was too late to fix anything, and she was afraid to start crying, afraid if she got going, she might never be able to stop.

20.

They took it in shifts to sit with Gwen during visiting hours. On Monday it was Tana in the morning and Allie in the afternoon. In between, Tana and Allie had lunch together in the hospital cafeteria. When they separated—Allie to walk to the elevators, Tana to head to the parking lot—Tana reached to squeeze Allie's hand and Allie turned to air kiss her cheek and they clonked heads. Allie laughed, rubbed Tana's head, kissed her skull, and then without thinking, lightly kissed her mouth. It was no big deal at all, Tana didn't even seem to notice, but when Allie was in the elevator her heart was racing and a chant had started up in her skull, *Stupid, stupid, NEEDY, stupid.* She wrote and erased a text—Sorry! Accidental kiss!—six times, lacked the courage to hit send every time.

They had put Gwen in a peaceful private corner suite on the third floor. *Mostly* peaceful. The maternity ward was directly overhead, and sometimes it was possible to hear a baby producing a goatlike bleat from somewhere above. It hardly registered with Allie.

Gwen was rarely conscious. She had lost part of her left lung and more than a gallon of blood. They had reinflated the lung. The tracheostomy hole in her throat was sealed again, under a thick pad of gauze, held in place by a white plastic bracelet like a zip tie. A bullet had dinged off her pelvis and cracked her hip. It would have to be replaced, but that was for later. Another had passed through her abdomen and nicked some kind of pouch—in Allie's mind, it was like the pocket mama kangaroos carried their babies in—before spinning out of her body. This last injury had seemed most inconsequential and turned out to be the one that might kill her yet. They had her on intravenous antibiotics to fight the infection that had taken root in the rectouterine pouch and spread to her blood. Her skin was always cold, but she sweated as if she had just finished a run on a warm morning. Allie spent a lot of time next to the bed, patting her mouth and brow with a wet cloth. Sometimes Gwen opened her eyes and stared at her without recognition. Other times, her eyes were blank with fear.

Once Gwen whispered, in a cracked, whistling voice, ". . . babies. Oh. Oh. Oh . . . baby."

"Yeah," Allie said. "Oh, baby. It's been a hell of a month, huh?"

Gwen shut her eyes and began to cry then, which made Allie feel awful, as if she had misunderstood something. Soon Gwen was dozing again, even though a couple of newborns were wailing above them.

Whenever Allie visited, she planted herself in the chair by the cot and caught Gwen up on current events, whether she was conscious or not.

"I guess Colin is talking," Allie said one day. "But he might not live. He got clipped in one chamber of the heart. I thought that would kill a person for sure, but I guess not. They've got him on machines. Of course, they've got him on machines. They're probably going to open his skull and wire him for internet."

Another day, she said, "The police asked Tana if she would sign for the release of her mother's body, and she told 'em they could dump her with the rest of the medical waste, far as she was concerned. She's tough. She's as tough as Donna, I think, only, you know, she looks *after* people instead of looks *down* on them."

There was the day she filled Gwen in on Donna. "They released her yesterday. I haven't seen her. She calls, I don't answer. She texts, I keep her muted. Don't care. She wanted me drunk all the time because she liked me helpless. If I ever see her again, there's an eighty percent chance I'll just start throwing things. A fifty percent chance. A ten percent chance. Okay, there's a one hundred percent chance I'll just start crying, but I will *not* let her talk to me."

"The police had Robin give her statement three times," Allie told Gwen one afternoon, "not because they had problems with her story, but because they like the way she says things in British. Every time she told it, there were more cops to listen to her. I guess having a British accent is kind of a superpower. It makes you sound smarter than other people. I was worried Maine cops would be gross because she's trans, but you never know how folks are going to be. They're just charmed."

And another time she whispered, "I like Tana," and then blushed so hard her face hurt. Gwen was the one person she felt comfortable telling, and even then, only when Allie was sure she was asleep.

But mostly Allie talked about the plan, about Easter, about King Sorrow.

"I don't know what to do," Allie said. "*None* of us know what to do. The police kept everything as evidence. The robe. The mirror. It's all gone. You need to tell us what to do. You need to get better so you can figure something out. So we can stop Easter from coming."

But Gwen slept on.

Following her awkward, unintended kiss with Tana, Allie did not offer Gwen her usual summary of recent events. That afternoon she merely sat next to the bed and touched the damp cloth to Gwen's forehead, while she worried about what she had done. She wanted to throw up. Tana was probably straight and definitely her sponsor and there was a 110 percent chance she had crossed an ethical line. Then she thought, *What the fuck does it matter? Gwen will die and I will use her death as my excuse to start drinking again and Tana will give up on me and life will be awful and it will be what I've got coming for everything I've done.*

That idea was so terrible, Allie had to hurry to the bathroom and gasp over the sink for a few moments while her stomach heaved. Her lunch—beef chop suey—stayed down.

When she lifted her head and looked at her own reflection in the mirror, she could see into Gwen's bedroom behind her, could see King Sorrow's tail slithering out from under the bed to wrap itself around her.

"No!" she screamed, spinning from the sink.

His tail, a ten-foot coil as thick as an elephant's leg, had wrapped around Gwen's abdomen. His claw had emerged from the other side of the bed to clasp her throat.

"No!" Allie screamed again, running across the room, grabbing the tail, and trying to pull it loose. "Go away! You can't have her yet!"

The tail loosed itself and began to retreat under the bed. But his claw—that humanlike hand with scaly fingers and yellow talons—remained. One talon caressed Gwen's cheek, traced her lips, while the rest of the hand clutched her throat.

"What do you mean *yet*, love," King Sorrow said. "She's been mine from the beginning. *All* of you have. I'll have her this year, and you *next* year, Allie. Donna will choose you next year—unless you choose her first. What do you say, Allie? Want to make next year's pick right now?"

"No," Allie whispered. "I wouldn't. Not now. Not ever. And Donna wouldn't either."

"She doesn't love you. She never did. She only wanted to control you. You know that, don't you? You know what! I just had a thought. Maybe Donna will use her pick to take *Tana* next year. To punish you for your faithless heart."

Allie's eyes stung. "Let go of my friend."

"I can release her throat. But I'll never let go of *any* of you. And she won't be drinking tears to get away from me now. Too late. All gone. You can't save her, love. You can only try to save yourself."

"No. I'm not worth saving. Not after the things I've done."

"True enough. Glad you know it."

The talon lifted from Gwen's throat. King Sorrow patted the dying woman's cheek and his claw slipped away.

"See you soon, Allie," King Sorrow said. "Count on it."

It was twenty-seven days until Easter.

21.

Colin had guys on the door of his room, private security: big men in polo shirts. Donna loathed them immediately, the one on the right with his shaved head and stupid mustache, the one on the left with a fucking goatee. Her thought, absolutely insane, was that Colin had hired the same freelance soldiers who had held her on Cherokee Island. But, of course, there had been nothing left of Thermopylae Security by the time King Sorrow was done with them. Colin's goons had to come from a different outfit.

Although. When she looked at the bald one, at his hairy forearm, she thought she saw a shiny lump of scar tissue where a tattoo had been removed.

One checked her driver's license to make sure Donna was who she said she was. That bugged her too—she expected to be recognized, if not actively lusted for, especially by middle-aged white guys. That was her target demographic. He unlatched the door and pushed it open.

It was late and most of the lights were off, although the room was partially illuminated by some fluorescent underlighting along the cabinets. Colin's bed was elevated so he could sit up. His throat was swaddled in bandage. The first hit had taken a fist-size chunk out of the side of his neck. A second bullet had struck his rib, and a splinter of bone had punched through the lower right ventricle of his heart. It was a nine-hour surgery to remove it, and the wall of his heart had been permanently damaged. His hands were bloated from edema, looked like the Pillsbury Doughboy's hands. A third bullet had caught him in the bladder. If he survived, he'd be pissing in a bag strapped to his leg for the rest of his life.

His hands were swollen and fat, but his face was starved. His eyes glittered in deep hollows. His face had never looked more skull-like. He patted the edge of the cot with a few sausage-plump fingers.

"Sit," he said, giving orders like she was a dog.

She leaned her crutch against the wall and planted herself in a metal chair by the bed.

"Why do you need security? You've already got all the security you could ever want. It's stamped on your chest."

"Lot of good it did me. That was always a weak spot in King Sorrow's protection, wasn't it?" His voice was weak, raspy. "If you're asleep, or too slow, or unaware . . ." His voice drifted off. So did his gaze. He seemed to be having trouble focusing. Finally, he said, "Why didn't you come sooner?"

"I was shot myself, remember?" she said, and lifted her foot in its bionic black boot.

"In the heel," he said, dismissively. "You've been out of the hospital for days. No. Don't bother explaining. I know. You were drunk, am I right? We should do something about that when I'm back to a hundred percent. Allie might be onto something with AA . . . and if you start going to meetings together you can get her back on our side before it's too late."

"You're never going to be a hundred percent again, Colin," Donna said. "Nothing can fix your damaged heart." She did not say she thought now it had always been damaged.

He said, "No. You're wrong. I need you to listen to me carefully. There's a glass flask in the Cabinet. It's half-full of blood—you'll know it when you see it. I think I'll need all of it, but if I don't, we can dab what's left on your heel and maybe get rid of your limp. Bring it to me. I'll have to drink some, and we'll pour the last of it into my wounds. It doesn't work immediately, but it *does* work fast. I could be well enough to come home in a week. I might be fully recovered by June . . . and I do mean fully. Like I was never shot at all. I hate to use it all up—it could've kept me fit and healthy for another sixty years—but we must adapt to the situation."

She opened her mouth and closed it, her mind going back over what he had just told her. *It could've kept me fit and healthy for another sixty years.* Yes. She had known that Colin wasn't aging like she was, like any of them were. That the years went on, but his face remained unlined, his eyes lively with youth, his body as fit and trim as a professional diver's. He had not thought to mention what he had found to her—to any of them.

"There's something else," he said. "Something we must do before I douse myself with what's in the flask, with the blood of St. Helen. King Sorrow will finish Gwen, but we've got other problems beyond her. There's the Fellows woman and there's Tana Nighswander. There's Allie too, but I'm hoping it's not too late for her. We might yet bring her back to herself, make her our old dependable Allie again. But the other two, they'll move against us. They know it's their lives or ours. And we can't wait for King Sorrow to get around to them in a year. Give them time and there won't be any more King Sorrow. They know how to kill him now, and they know when to strike—right after Easter, when he's at his weakest. I think it's long odds they could pull it off . . . but long odds are not the same as impossible."

"So are you going to have a couple guys drop in on 'em?" Donna asked. "Does your security service cover that kind of thing too? Where'd you get 'em, anyway?"

"Who cares where I got them? No, we're not going to use them. When we deal with Fellows and Nighswander, I don't want it boomeranging back on me, or on the company. There's another way. There's *always* been another way. King Sorrow isn't our only Philip. I want to bring Elwood Hondo back. Just you and me. It'll be easy because I'm close to death. Right here, right now, I'm on the bridge over the Styx. Elwood will hear my voice quickly enough if we call to him. We know he'll be willing. He likes to kill. He prefers to strangle young men, but a couple middle-aged women will do in a pinch. Boggarts can't be choosers."

"You want to make a deal with something *else* from the Long Dark? Because the deal with King Sorrow has worked out *so* great for us."

"Didn't it?"

"My brother jumped to his death so they wouldn't torture us for information about the iguana anymore. And look what it did to Gwen. Drove her out of her mind, made her the kind of person who gets off on killing sick old people." Donna paused, then added, "Kinda funny how that one snuck up on us. The woman we overheard in church sounded like the same decent old Gwen. You wouldn't think a serial killer who preys on old folks would be so determined to protect the lives of her friends." What had Allie said? *Donna can be very credulous about other people's motives.* That one had stung almost as badly as Allie telling her to go fuck herself.

Colin shrugged. "I'm sure even when she euthanized her patients, she believed she was rescuing them in some manner. As you know, she has a complex about rescuing people—if she was a man, we'd say she suffers from white knight syndrome. As for Van, what happened to that kid broke my heart. We got high together, Van and me. He was my brother too." It sounded good, but his eyes, under their pink, sore eyelids, were dull and empty.

"What about Arthur? Was he like a brother too?"

"Arthur was my hero. What happened down in the cave killed me."

"Metaphorically," Donna said. "But in reality, what happened in the cave killed *Arthur*."

"King Sorrow has cost us more than we ever imagined. But I think about the women you wiped out at Black Cricket and I know it was worth it. Psychopaths. Pedophiles. How many kids will grow up healthy and well because you took that house full of monsters off the board?"

"Arthur's mother was in Black Cricket once. Was she one of those monsters?"

"Oh, come on. Stop that." He squeezed her hand. "We're the good guys in this story."

She slipped her hand out of his. "You really think you can reach Elwood Hondo?"

"Bring the conch and Wolf Messing's helmet and we'll try. Hondo is so close, I can almost see him standing in the corner."

She looked in the corner. It was dark there, a pocket of shadows.

She felt a bad crawly sensation up the back of her neck and swiftly returned her gaze to Colin.

"Tell me something. The guys on the door. Do you think there's any chance either of them worked with the same outfit that held me 'n' Van back on Cherokee Island?"

His eyelids sank shut. "I haven't been in a state to examine their employment records. If they work for us now, does it even matter?"

"You should rest. And I should go."

"You'll get the blood? And the rest of it? Conch and helmet?"

"Yes. Absolutely. As soon as I get back to Podomaquassy."

He was breathing weakly when she let herself out.

She paused after she shut the door, glanced at the soldier with the pink shaved scalp and the old-fashioned handlebar mustache.

"You guys take care of him, okay?" she said.

"It's what we do," he said.

"How long has he had your company on contract? He told me the name of your outfit, but I already forgot."

"It's Rohan Security," said the dude with the goatee. "Used to be something else, I forget what."

The bald security guard carefully placed one hand over his forearm, to cover the shiny patch where it looked like a tattoo had been removed.

Goatee jerked his head toward the doors and Colin on the other side. "You could ask him. I think he's had the company on payroll since the beginning. Twenty years?"

"No kidding," Donna said.

The bald guy said, "Will you be back to see him tomorrow?"

"Not for a million fucking dollars," she said, and got out of there, as swiftly as her crutch would carry her.

It was twenty-three days until Easter.

22.

The three of them—Robin, Tana, and Allie—were waiting in the family lounge down the corridor from Gwen's room when Donna appeared in the hall. Even though she was prepared to see her, Allie felt all the breath shoot out of her at the first sight. She was so rattled, it took her a moment to notice Donna was walking normally, had lost the crutch.

Robin tossed down the *Good Housekeeping* she had been browsing and got off the couch. Allie was already on her feet, too jittery to sit still. Tana had planted herself on the wide windowsill with the sunlight at her back. In her jeans and cowboy boots she looked like a country musician who had done a few decades of drinking and breaking hearts and was ready to sing about it.

"You wanted us here," Robin said. "Say what you have to say and go."

"Your plan," Donna said, "to wipe King Sorrow out. Colin thought it might work, but I'll be honest, it sounded like desperate bullshit to me."

Tana said, "I'll have you know that desperate bullshit is the specialty of the house."

Donna twitched—then laughed.

"You're off the crutch," Robin said. "And you're in heels. How are you in heels after getting shot in the foot?"

Donna turned a watery glare upon her. "I want to see Gwen."

"No," Allie said. "And if you try to come to her funeral, Donna, I'll fight you. I'll fight you right there next to the grave, with my fists and everything."

Something, some gentle emotion, passed across Donna's face,

and Allie felt it like a physical blow. It was so rare to see anything gentle in her face.

"With your fists and everything," Donna said.

"She won't have to do that," Tana said, and she slid off the windowsill to stand next to Allie. When she took Allie's hand, Allie almost jumped. It was as if Tana had placed a wire with live current running through it into her palm. "Because you get anywhere near her, I'll get you by the scruff of the neck and haul your scrawny ass to the curb."

Donna struggled with a smile. She nodded and said to Allie, "Good. It's about time you found someone who'd stand up for you. I never did. Not once. Why you cared for me, I'll never know. You were like Van. Something good that just fell in my path. I saw him, you know. Van. Last week. We went to the beach. He gave me a sand dollar." Donna held out one fist, then slowly opened it and looked into it. Her palm was empty. "In a dream, anyway. It wasn't real. Just an idea. But then I was thinking, in a way, King Sorrow is also just an idea, and look at all he's done. If King Sorrow can be imaginary but real, so can Van's sand dollar."

"Have you been drinking?" Robin asked and arched an eyebrow.

"Oh yeah. You'd never guess what," Donna said. She dropped her hand. "There isn't going to be any funeral. Not for Gwen. Not if you let me see her." She dug in her Michael Kors purse and produced a dusty glass bottle. It had been sealed with wax, but the wax had split and crumbled when someone had yanked the cork. Allie recalled it from the last time she opened the Cabinet. "Colin took this from the troll's cave." Glancing now at Robin Fellows. "He's used it for years to keep himself young and fit. It's the blood of a saint."

"Thousand-year-old blood would be dry as clay," Robin said.

"It should be, but it isn't. Colin has a terror of being ill, of being weak, of being old. He was planning to live to be a hundred and twenty. All the tech bros are planning to be a hundred and twenty, but Colin is the only one who might've pulled it off. If he didn't get shot first."

"I don't believe you. That's poison. Same as dragon tears," Allie said.

"Why would I poison her, Allie? She's going to die in three weeks anyway."

"Because you hate her. You hate her because she's a good person and you aren't."

Donna sat on the coffee table and unstrapped her right heel and stuck her leg out. "Where was I shot? Show me where I was shot, Allie."

Allie didn't want to look at Donna's leg, at the line of white thigh disappearing into her skirt. She didn't trust herself to touch her ankle. It was Robin who lowered herself to one knee, took the foot in both hands, and considered it, moving it this way and that.

"I don't even see a scar."

"I applied blood to the wound, three days ago. And had a small sip. At the time, my ankle was shattered and there were eight stitches sealing the bullet hole. Forty-eight hours ago, the bone was healed, and the wound was an angry red scar, shaped like a comma. By then I could put weight on it without pain. That scar was still there last night, when I went to bed, but it looked at least twenty years old. It was gone this morning."

"She's lying," Allie said. "Messing with us. I don't know how or why, but I know what she's like. That's a bottle of some evil magical strychnine."

Tana gave Allie a sidelong look that was almost pleading. "I don't think she's lying, babe. Her foot *is* better."

Donna stared into Allie's face for a moment, then popped the cork. She held her thumb to the mouth of the bottle and turned it upside down for an instant, then right side up again. When she lifted her thumb away, it was stamped with a red circle of blood.

Donna licked it clean with one swipe of her tongue. "Satisfied?"

Allie squeezed herself, said nothing.

"Go on, Allie," Donna held out the flask. "Take it. If you don't want me to see Gwen, *you* give it to her. Splash it on the wounds and make her drink the rest."

"That doesn't seem very hygienic," Robin said.

"You know what's really unhygienic?" Donna asked. "The inside of a dragon's mouth. Go on. Take it and make Gwen better. Let's see if her plan is as good as Colin thinks."

When Allie didn't take it, Tana did.

Allie stared at the woman she had loved for twenty-five years, looked at her the way a woman might stare at a passing bus that had nearly flattened her. "Why? Why would you help us now?"

"Because King Sorrow has killed a thousand people in our names," Donna said, "and the world is still the world. Because no matter how many people he kills, Cady Lewis goes right on being dead. Because we made three new killers with every person we struck down. Because I read Gwen's notes and I understand that we killed some people just so they wouldn't make financial or legal trouble for Colin. Because that bald-headed motherfucker has been working with the same people who tortured me, who killed Van, for twenty years, because he admires their work. Because I'm sorry. Mostly because Van gave me a sand dollar in a dream."

"You read Gwen's notes?" Robin asked.

"Yes. They were in her messenger bag. Remember? I took it off her shoulder outside the chapel? The police returned it two days ago. They thought it was mine."

Robin and Allie traded a look. Robin said, "The robe? The mirror?"

Donna nodded. "Got 'em. And her Bluetooth iPhone projector."

"And the thermos," Robin said.

"What thermos?" Donna asked.

"There was a green thermos in the bag," Robin said.

Donna shook her head. "No."

"It's full of dragon tears," Robin said. "Gwen thought she could use them to spit fire. It would only have cost her her life."

Another shake of the head. "I don't know what to tell you. The robe, the mirror, Arthur's notes, that shitty little projector from Sharper Image. That's it. I didn't see a thermos."

"Christ," Tana said. "You think it rolled out of the bag? I hope some kid doesn't find it and *drink* it."

Robin said, "I doubt it. The police will have gone over the whole crime scene. It must've rolled free and been collected separately."

"I can ask," Donna said. "Colin has contacts with the local PD. He bought them a couple SUVs. They love him."

Robin hesitated and then said, "No, it's better if it's gone. Gwen was a little too in love with the idea of drinking some. We're not bringing her back from the edge of death just so she can kill herself at the end of the month."

"Come on," Tana said, and shook the bottle. "Let's splash a little eau de holy gore on Gwen and see what happens."

Allie quivered, still staring at Donna. She felt as if she had swallowed dragon tears herself, her insides incendiary.

"You are *not* forgiven," Allie said. "Because you are unforgivable."

Donna's eyes met hers. They were clear and frank and untroubled. "You think I don't know that? I'm not asking to be forgiven."

"What *are* you asking for?" Robin asked.

"When it's time to kill the fucking iguana?" Donna said. "*I want in.*"

23.

The three of them permitted Donna to enter the room with them, but she did not join them at Gwen's bedside. Donna stayed by the door, her back against it, to keep anyone from coming in at a bad moment.

The other three women gathered around the dying patient. Robin lowered the sheets. Allie stripped off Gwen's johnny. Donna was not prepared for the sight of Gwen's bandaged torso and sweat-slicked, collapsed stomach. She had lost enough weight to look childlike . . . no longer a woman of forty-five but the skinny kid she had been as a teenager. It pained her to see Gwen so frail, so weak that she could be moved this way and that like a doll. Robin turned her on her side. Tana hunted in a cabinet and returned with Q-tips as long as chopsticks. She handed the Q-tips and the dusty bottle to Robin.

Allie looked faint and Tana put a hand on her back, between Allie's shoulder blades, and stroked in small circles. *Good*, Donna thought again. This was followed by another idea. Whatever they had done wrong—all the blood they had spread around, all the sorrow—they had at least saved Tana Nighswander for this moment. They had saved her so she could be here now to care for Allie. Donna had taken hundreds of lives and never saved a single one, but this was the next best thing, she thought. She could save what was left of Allie's life by letting her go.

Robin brought a dripping Q-tip out of the bottle. Tana and Allie held Gwen on her right side while Robin worked the Q-tip under the bandage to find the bullet hole that had perforated the lung. She dipped and painted, dipped and painted, three times in all, before moving on to the bullet wound in the lower abdomen with a fresh Q-tip. They were fifteen minutes slathering the bullet wounds in ancient and sanctified liquid, finishing with the one that had struck Gwen in the hip.

"There's no way," Robin said. "No way in hell this works."

"You saw a hobo turn into a rock," Allie said, "but you draw the line at holy superblood?"

"When you put it that way, love." The Q-tip dipped under the bandage over Gwen's throat to touch her tracheostomy. Robin shook the bottle. An eighth of an inch splashed in the bottom.

"Now she drinks it," Donna said. "All of it. That's what Colin was going to do." She didn't add that Colin had not anticipated a full recovery until June. "Don't skimp."

"Right," Robin said. "Bottoms up, darling."

She tipped the bottle to Gwen's lips and blood gurgled out in a thick syrup. Gwen made a little sound—a kind of grunt—and her throat worked as she drank reflexively. A single sticky drop plopped onto her chin.

Allie choked and ran to the bathroom.

Donna was hardly aware she herself was moving, had crossed the room before she realized her own intentions. Tana glanced around and saw Donna approach and looked briefly alarmed. Donna had an idea she was ready to get an arm up between her and Gwen, ready to tackle her if she tried anything. In the end, though, she didn't block Donna when she reached for Gwen's hand. Donna held Gwen's fingers in hers. Colin's hand had been damp and hot, but Gwen's fingers were so cold and stiff, it was as if she was already dead.

"When this is over," Donna said, "everyone is going to remember *I* saved *you*. You didn't save me—*I saved you*. How do you like that, Saint Underfoot?"

She let go and turned away. When Donna McBride walked out the door, it was three weeks until Easter.

24.

Robin had started knitting when she was forty and at forty-three had made a lateral shift to crochet. She was quite good at making wooly Ewoks and Yodas. She had crocheted several large vaginas that could be used as pocket purses, for friends who liked that kind of thing. She was crocheting a knight's helmet now, one that could be pulled on like a hat, with a slitted visor to cover the eyes. She had an idea to crochet one for all her dragon-fighting ladies. She was making Gwen's first, so Gwen could enjoy it before King Sorrow killed her.

Such was her focus, it was several minutes before she happened to glance up to find Gwen awake and watching her.

"What's that? Looks like a condom for King Kong," Gwen rasped.

Robin lowered the big wooden crochet hook and leaned forward. "How are you, Gwen?"

Gwen's tongue traversed the length of her upper lip. "Thirsty. Inside of my mouth tastes like I've been chewing on copper wire."

Robin clamped down on a shiver. "I'll get the nurse. You had a fever, but it broke in the night." After a moment, she added, "Donna came to see you yesterday."

Robin thought Gwen might tense at that. The last time she had been with Donna, the other woman had been marching Gwen to her death. But Gwen closed her eyes and seemed to wiggle deeper into her pillow.

"Is she okay? I thought maybe she had been hit."

"It was . . . nothing," Robin said, her scalp crawling at the thought of Donna's smooth, youthful, undamaged foot. "You'd have a hard time believing she was hurt at all."

"Ha," Gwen said. "No one who meets Donna McBride would have a hard time believing she was hurt. But I take your meaning." She thought for a moment and then wearily shook her head. "Don't I have the worst luck?"

Robin said, "It's not as bad as it might be. At least you're alive."

"Yes," Gwen said. "That's what I mean."

Robin was still trying to think of a reply when she realized Gwen was asleep once again.

25.

Tana was in the room when the nurse lifted the bandage to look at Gwen's tracheostomy—and screamed.

No: not a scream. More of a high-pitched shriek.

"That bad, huh?" Gwen asked, sleepily. Tana hadn't been sure she was awake. Her eyes had opened and closed a few times, but never seemed to focus on anything.

"No, I—it's not bad. Not bad! It's—no, it's fine! I just want to have—someone—someone look—" The nurse backed into a bedside cart on wheels, which banged and clattered and startled her all over again. She turned and hurried out of the room.

Gwen shifted her gaze to Tana. "Hey, Nighswander. What do you think she saw under the bandage? I've heard about spiders laying eggs in open wounds. Think there's a spider's nest under there?"

"Jesus," Tana said. "Spiders? You oughta write horra novels, the stuff you think."

Tana had been sitting on the windowsill. She liked to position herself close to a window if she could, liked to have a view of sky and trees. In her years with Jayne they kept the shades down throughout the house in case they were under surveillance. Tana was forbidden even to raise the blinds in her bedroom, which made sense. They often stored drugs under her bed, or money. Jayne figured if someone had to take a fall, it ought to be Tana. The law was notoriously lenient on teens. Also, when Jayne traded Tana to men for more time to pay off a debt, the action always went down in there. A few years of that had largely ruined men for Tana. Men and dark rooms both.

In the years since Jayne died, Tana couldn't stand to be in a room with the curtains drawn. She needed the sky. The sight of trees tossed by the wind sometimes stirred in her an almost childlike excitement. A windy day made her thank God for her life: that she had outlived Jayne, that she had raised her son and known his sturdy kindness, that she had made friends and had at least some sex that wasn't terrible. She was looking forward to some not-terrible sex with Allie someday, although for the time being Allison Shiner needed a friend more than a lover. It had been the most important thing in the world to pretend she had hardly noticed when Allie impulsively kissed her. After she had a year of sobriety under her belt—a year of building up her confidence and sense of well-being—then, maybe, *maybe*, she would be able to make a reasoned choice about who she wanted in her bed.

Gwen was watching her carefully. "What do you think is wrong with my throat?"

"Maybe nothing is wrong. Maybe something is right."

Gwen narrowed her eyes. "You know something, don't you? What do you know, Tana Nighswander?"

"I know Tom Brady is the best quarterback ever played the game. I know you don't want to buy the fish once we stick the manager's-special sticker on it down at the Basket. I know I've bought almost five thousand Megabucks tickets and never won once. Though now I think it, I did win the lottery once—the day you decided to be my friend. I know I'm not a doctor, but that nurse went to get one, and I'm as interested to hear what he has to say as you are. And that's about all I know."

The door opened and the doctor entered, a skinny woman in Buddy Holly glasses. Her name was Lee. It still surprised Tana when a doctor turned out to be a lady. When you grew up in Gogan, you didn't need to be a man to be a chauvinist. The nurse was right behind her but stayed a few steps back from the bed and stared at Gwen with a mix of suspicion and anxiety, as if there really had been spiders under her bandage.

"Let's have a look at how the tracheostomy is healing up, yes?" Dr. Lee said, and began to loosen the bandage.

Dr. Lee came in smooth, but once she had a peek under that bandage, she staggered back into the rolling bedside table too.

It was nineteen days until Easter.

26.

On the night of the nineteenth, Garrett arrived back in Boston from The Briars, with everything Colin had asked for in a cardboard box.

It was late, well past visiting hours, but when you were rich enough to buy the hospital a new pediatric cancer wing, people made exceptions.

Garrett was a veteran of Afghanistan, a big man, head shaved, all except for a low, bristly mohawk. The tattoo of a Spartan's helmet had come off his arm years ago. When he entered the hospital room, Colin saw him about to flip the light switches on with his elbow.

"Don't," Colin told him, and Garrett stopped himself just in time.

Colin couldn't bear the light anymore. Even the overhead fluorescents hurt, felt like being stabbed through the eye sockets. The cardiologist had him on digoxin for now, to ease the strain on his punctured heart, and photophobia was one of the more common side effects. Colin could only just bear the monochrome monitors stacked to the side of the bed, with their green digital readouts.

"The Cabinet was open?" Colin asked.

"Yeah. Lock sitting on the desk, key in it."

"And Donna?"

"I didn't see her around. You want, we can go get her." He mentioned this possibility—abducting a well-known podcaster with two and a half million followers on Twitter—as if offering to pick up a bag of groceries.

Colin smiled at that. "You could try. Put the box next to the bed, please? And close the door behind you when you go?"

Garrett did as he was told. Colin called to him again when he was about to step back into the hallway.

"Garrett? I don't want to be disturbed. No doctors. No nurses. If you hear me talking with someone, don't give it a thought. I have to make a few calls. I have to speak to an old friend. If I want you, I'll call for you by name. Otherwise, best not to open that door, no matter what you hear."

Garrett's brow furrowed at that . . . but after a moment he nodded. He shut the door gently behind him.

Colin reached for the bedside table—his hand moving past the cardboard box to grasp his phone. Even extending one arm produced a trembling feeling of weakness, a *soreness* at the core of him. He could put on a good face for Garrett, but he had never, in all his life, felt so overcome with a single emotion . . . and that emotion was dread. He woke from every doze covered in flop sweat. Sometimes, as he started to fall asleep, a sensation would come over him like he was tipping backward off a high ledge, and he'd lurch awake with his heart fluttering weakly and desperately in his chest.

He had thought his heart would be on the mend by now. He had thought to see Donna, with St. Helen's blood. When she did not return the day after her visit, he texted to ask if there had been a holdup. She did not reply. He figured she was drunk—an irritation, but she would sober up eventually. He tried her again the next morning, and again in the afternoon.

Where is the blood, Donna?

She didn't get around to answering his question until the third day.

I poured it down the fucking drain.

A reply that had made him dizzy with fear again. Fear! Of all things! It turned out fear of a significant intensity had symptoms not unlike flu. When he calmed himself, he sent her a laughing emoji and asked when she was bringing it to the hospital.

I'm not. It's gone. But you're right, I didn't pour it down the drain. I tried some on my foot to see if it worked. My ankle is good as new. I was so happy with the results I drank the rest and now my tits look like they did when I was twenty.

Donna, with apologies, I'm not finding this witty or clever. I could still die. Without St. Helen's blood, I'll never be myself again.

But that would be a good thing, Colin. If you were never yourself again. If you didn't have the strength to be you anymore. You want to know what I really did with it?

I gave it to Gwen.

He had gone short of breath at that, had needed to wait for his heart to stop slamming erratically in his chest before he could reply.

That's another joke and it isn't funny.

The joke, Colin, is that I ever believed you when you said Gwen meant to use King Sorrow against us. If she wanted me dead, Colin, tell me this? Why did she cover me with her own body when the shooting started? Even if she DIDN'T want me dead . . . why would she try and protect me? After everything I've done. After the life I've lived. There's a riddle even King Sorrow couldn't answer. Neither can I. If I knew the answer, maybe I'd be more like her and less like you.

I can't be your person anymore, Colin. If you want a friend and a confidant, try Elwood Hondo. He's more your speed anyway. I think you two are cut from the same cloth exactly.

His thoughts raced. His thoughts stood still. It was another ten hours before he could articulate a plan to himself. It frightened him, how hard it was to work out a single line of reasoning. It was like trying to catch a handful of spiders—a notion that reminded him horribly of the spiders crawling all over him down in Finger's cave.

Colin had summoned Garrett, who oversaw his security team, and told him to go to The Briars. He said there were things he wanted from his Cabinet of Curiosities. He told him what. Then he said he was probably going to need Donna's help—that the Cabinet would only open with the key she wore around her neck.

"Or two swift kicks," Garrett had said.

"Without the key, that Cabinet is more likely to kick *you*."

"Some kind of booby trap?"

"Just do it my way," Colin had said.

"You bet, boss," Garrett told him. "You're writing the checks."

In the end, though, Donna hadn't come into it, and he had what he wanted, the conch and Wolf Messing's helmet. He would've liked the cracked mirror too, but the police or Donna or Gwen had it now. Not that it mattered. He had learned the night they summoned King Sorrow that if you had even one of the divination tools, you had them all.

He was a few minutes preparing himself. He set the helmet on the bedside table, upside down, and emptied a bottle of Poland Spring into it. He placed the conch on the bed by his side. He unlocked his phone and pulled up his private videos. Colin had long ago transferred the Elwood Hondo movie to a digital file. He placed a slim hospital pillow in his lap, rested the phone against it, and played his grandfather's old film with the sound down low.

When Llewellyn and the others began to cheer Elwood Hondo on, Colin cheered with them.

"Come on, Elwood," Colin said. "Talk to me. Go ahead and call collect from the Long Dark. I'll accept all charges." As he said it, he was listening to the Aztec conch, hoping for a whisper, hoping for a voice.

But his arm was weak and trembling. It was hard for him to hold the conch to his ear. There was a grinding ache in his chest. He used his free hand to flick the trigger on his morphine feed, give himself a blast of relief. He was running the video full screen . . . but had not expected the brightness of the image to hurt his eyes so. He turned his face away, shut his eyes, and when his arm started wobbling, he put the conch down. He gasped, his heartbeat stammering, felt the warm trickle of fresh piss into the bag against his leg. It was awful to be so weak, to feel so helpless, and the easiest thing in the world was to slide away from it, into sleep.

THE CRASH OF FOLDING METAL CHAIRS brought him awake again with a jerk. He had nodded off in his seat to Llewellyn's left. They were singing, the whole crowd of them at the long folding card table, under the map of Cuba. They sang, *Nooooo time for looooosers!*

Llewellyn sat on Colin's right, looking trim and well in his burgundy turtleneck. He was almost Colin's own age precisely. His face shone with sweat, as if he were trying to lift some immense weight, but he was grinning. His teeth were yellow and crooked under his fey mustache. He had always had bad teeth.

Across the room, a 16mm camera whirred away on a wooden tripod, recording everything, while folding metal chairs jumped from one wall and fell *crash-crash-CRASH*. One of those chairs opened and closed, opened and closed, doing an ecstatic, palsied jig across the floor. A reel-to-reel recorder stood on a shelf almost directly behind Colin, the spools turning with a plasticky rasp, and Colin understood that he had not just come awake inside the film, but that he had *always* been in the film, had always been one of the out-of-focus figures sitting at the table with Llewellyn.

Colin looked to his left, where a broad-shouldered, middle-aged lady with Mary Tyler Moore hair was rising to her feet. An instant later, Colin found himself rising with her. He had to. The table was pulling itself off the floor, and all of them had to stand to keep their fingers pressed to it. Colin laughed, breathlessly, humorlessly; it was either laugh or shout in alarm.

The table thudded down an instant later. One of the other women screamed. Colin's heart leapt like a deer. All his life, he had longed to be here with his grandfather when they brought Elwood

Hondo into the world, but now that he was, he couldn't enjoy it. A heart wasn't supposed to do what his heart was doing, bounding in his chest the way it was. Llewellyn laughed hysterically.

"What's so funny?" Colin asked him.

"I was just thinking," Llewellyn said, "that everyone around this table is dead now. We're not bringing Elwood to us—he brought *us* to *him*." And when Colin looked at his grandfather again, he saw black scribbles covering his eyes, scratches clawed impossibly right into the air.

Colin felt a scream rising in his chest. He had never screamed in terror in his life, but that terrible cry was building up inside him, a ragged, aching pressure behind his breastbone. Something slammed behind him. He twisted his head around and saw that one of the big chunky buttons had clunked down on the reel-to-reel tape recorder. Another button slammed. The reels screamed, running in reverse. A third button went bang. The reels began to play.

Warbling voices rose in harmony: *BA-A-A-A-A-AD MISTAKES!*

It was like hearing music while drowning—distorted and terrible. The tape stopped, rewound, began to play again.

BAAA-A-A-A-AAAD MISTAKES!

Colin looked wildly along the length of the table. The others were staring at him . . . or they would've been staring at him if their eyes weren't covered by those awful black scribbles. A dozen men and women, blinded by death.

I'VE DONE MY SENTENCE, the voices on the reel-to-reel shrieked.

Colin wondered if he was having a heart attack. It felt like he was being knifed. It felt like someone had pushed a broadsword right through the center of his chest from behind. He hunched over the table, shut his eyes, wishing it all away, and when he looked up, he stood alone behind the séance table.

I'VE COME THROUGH, sang the voices on the tape recorder. The tripod beneath the camera suddenly snapped shut and the 16mm tilted over and crashed to the floor.

Then it was very still. The overhead lights had shut off while his eyes were closed. There was a single door, to Colin's right, with a pane of pebbled glass set in it. A figure moved on the other side, a dark and shifting shape, turning to face the door. Colin knew who was out there, and suddenly he didn't want to see him anymore, or, far worse, be seen by him. The thought that the door might be about to open made Colin want to scream, but he couldn't fight a breath down into his lungs. The doorknob began to turn and he squeezed his eyes shut again, wishing with all his ruined heart, *Please, PLEASE, stop this, stop this right now RIGHT N—*

HE LURCHED AWAKE, flung an arm out. His elbow struck the bedside tray and Wolf Messing's helmet fell, clanged to the floor. Water sprayed.

His phone had slipped face down in his lap. He didn't know what had happened to the pillow it had been propped against. The Aztec conch had dropped back to his side, was turned so he could look into its slick, vaginal interior. His hospital monitors blipped softly.

Colin lifted his hand to wipe drool from his mouth. His pulse was still galloping. It was the morphine—the morphine had whacked him good and hard, had put him to sleep, and even then, had not entirely ameliorated his pain. It felt as if a corkscrew were twisting slowly in the center of his chest. It outraged him, that Donna could've brought him St. Helen's blood, that he could be healing now . . . healing instead of dying.

Colin had found the darkness of his room comforting, easier on his eyes, but now it frightened him. The room was plunged into darkness in every direction. The depth of the shadows made it hard to breathe, made him wish for all the light in the world. Even when he looked at the monitors, the one source of brightness in the whole room, black spots darted and drifted in front of his vision. He had a thought then, so terrible he wanted to cry out, that there were black scribbles in front of his eyes, that he had already joined the dead. He clawed for his phone, found the camera app. He needed to look into his own eyes, know he was still breathing.

He was not reassured by the sight of himself on the screen. What he saw wasn't something to share with Instagram. He felt he was staring into a dead man's face, the features of someone who had died of hunger and thirst in one of the plague caves Arthur had talked about. Although at least his eyes, feverish and bright, were still his own. No scribbles yet.

He felt a sudden fierce pulse of missing Arthur's steadiness, Arthur's boring, banal courage. Colin had a sudden notion that the darkness around him would not be so dark if Arthur were still in the world. He had an idea—wild, imprecise, and worrisome—that Arthur had been equipped with something Colin had lacked. Colin remembered how Arthur had brought the Cree hi-throwers along for their underground walk, so they would carry daylight with them even underground. But then Arthur had brought daylight with him wherever he went. Colin wished with all his injured heart for a Cree hi-thrower in his hand and Arthur by his side.

But it wasn't Arthur by his side. Colin heard a boot step into the puddle on the floor with a wet smack. Colin studied the screen of his iPhone once more and saw for the first time the man standing to one side of the bed and a little behind him. His companion had been far enough back in the shadows that Colin had missed him at first: a skinny young fellow, with hair the color of straw, and thin lips twisted in an unpleasant smile. Colin couldn't see his eyes. Those were just hollows of darkness . . . bottomless wells of shadow, a thousand times deeper than a troll's cave.

"Elwood?" Colin whispered. "Elwood Hondo?"

The young man bent and found Wolf Messing's helmet. He turned it over in his rawboned hands. "What's this now? I like it!"

"It belonged to a figure infamous in occult circles," Colin gasped. "A disturbed and dangerous man."

Hondo set it on his own head. "Why, it's a perfect fit for me!"

Colin's ears were playing tricks on him. He thought he could hear, from a great distance, the sound of "We Are the Champions," slow and distorted. At first, he thought it was coming from his own phone, but when he glanced around, he realized it was trickling from the conch. *Bad mistakes. I've made a few.* Colin nodded absently. Him too.

A bead of sweat crawled down his throat. It was important to stay focused. This was what he had hoped for. He had *wanted* to bring Elwood Hondo through to deal with Gwen's accomplices.

"I need you to kill someone," Colin told him.

"Hey, good buddy! You don't gotta ask me twice," Elwood said, and lifted the pillow he had taken from Colin's lap while Colin slept.

Elwood clamped it down on Colin's face with both hands. Colin screamed a scream that made no sound. He gasped and inhaled a deep wad of cotton. He grabbed for Elwood's arms. Elwood's forearms were cold and hard, like frozen legs of mutton, and Colin couldn't shift them. That corkscrew in Colin's chest twisted harder and harder still. Lights flashed behind his eyes, faraway sparks in the distance, at the bottom of a long hole. *Arthur!* Colin thought. It was Arthur down there, holding a light, a painted candle peeled right off a wall and made real. *Arthur, help me!* Colin thought again.

He pedaled his feet, thrashed with both legs. The conch fell off the bed with a glassy crack. In his mind, he was racing, he was sprinting with all he had, toward that spark of light. But the small gleam of brightness was moving away faster than he could run. It dimmed. He gasped but had no air and his legs began to grow tired. *Arthur, wait for me!* he wanted to scream. *I'm scared of the dark! Arthur!*

The light shriveled and winked out and Colin plunged on, blindly, screaming without words, without making a sound, screaming with no one to hear, because in that darkness that seemed to last forever, he was alone.

27.

Allie was braiding Gwen's hair when Gwen opened her eyes, and closed them, and opened them again, very slowly.

Allie curled the braid and set it on the top of her head. She was making a crown of braids for Gwen. She thought Gwen looked very regal, a lovely if beleaguered queen—one preparing to sip a magic draught and sleep for a thousand years.

"Hey," Allie said. "You back with me?"

Gwen said, "Is Colin dead?"

Allie's knees knocked the side of the cot and she smoothed her hands on her gray corduroys.

"Why do you say that?" she answered, at last.

Gwen shut her eyes again. "I dreamt I was home and the phone rang. Only when I picked up the receiver, it wasn't a phone at all. It was that Aztec shell. You remember the conch? I held it up to my ear and I could hear Colin in there. He said it was dark. I could hardly hear him and I kept asking him to speak up but then he told me he had to whisper because there was someone else in the cave with him. I asked who and he said it was Elwood. That he could hear Elwood Hondo coming for him. That he had to go before Elwood got any closer. Then he hung up. He sounded . . . afraid. I've never heard Colin sound afraid before."

"His heart gave out," Allie said. "At three this morning. There was a glitch in the software at the nurses' station and their equipment was rebooting when he passed away. By the time the alert came through, it was too late to save him. He had been dead at least ten minutes."

"Do you wish you saved some of that holy go-juice for him?" Gwen asked. "Do you think it would've fixed his heart?"

Allie shook her head. "I think you'd both be dead." She did not say that it hardly mattered. Anyone could see Gwen wasn't recovering fast enough. Easter was now only fifteen days away. If they had saved her life, they had only saved it for King Sorrow. She patted Gwen's hand. "What was wrong with his heart was beyond even magic to fix."

"I don't think his heart got him," Gwen said. "I think Elwood Hondo did."

28.

Gwen had a view of some maples and the birds springing about in the red-tipped branches: little birds with soft white breasts and dove-gray backs. She wasn't sure what sort. Arthur might've known. Birds belonged to his half of the crossword. She was studying them intently when there was a light rap at the door.

She glanced around as Robin opened the door and Donna took a step into the room. Robin stood in the doorway, frowning in a worried sort of way—ready to grab Donna by the arm and haul her back out at a word, and never mind that Gwen had asked for this meeting herself.

"Robin," Gwen said, "would you give Donna and me a moment? We've got to say some things, and it might be easier if it's just us."

Robin didn't look happy about it. But she nodded and said, "I won't be far," and eased the door shut behind Donna.

Donna stood on the far side of the room.

"Well?"

"Sit down. Rest your foot."

"My foot is fine. I ran two miles this morning."

"What are you going to tell your audience about your miracle recovery? You going to tell 'em it was mint oil? Colloidal minerals?"

"I'm going to tell 'em nothing. The podcast is done. Speaking of miracles, Allie says you have a whole team of doctors now. Some of them are from Europe. They're saying you've done three months of healing in, what? Two weeks? She says when they walk by the door of your room, they look like little kids walking past a haunted house."

"I'm doing so well, I'm kinda getting the itch to jump out of bed, wander down to the geriatric ward, and smother a couple old ladies."

"Shut up," Donna said.

For a moment neither of them spoke.

"So Allie filled you in on my medical situation? You two are on speaking terms?"

"No. She was talking to Robin. I was just standing there. Allie has perfected the art of pretending she can't see me."

"Are those grackles?" Gwen asked, watching the birds hop on the other side of the glass.

"How the fuck would I know? Who cares?"

Gwen nodded at the chair next to the bed. "Sit down. I get tired easily. I want to say what I got to say and then you can go."

Donna looked pasty and tired herself. She looked, for the first time in her life, middle-aged. She settled into the black metal chair with her oversize purse in her lap.

"How are you doing about Colin?" Gwen asked.

Donna turned her head to regard the maybe-grackles out the window. "I liked the money. I liked the attention. He was so in control all the time, so calm. Van got killed and Colin was there. He had people to make sure I always had whatever I needed, whenever I needed it. Plane tickets. Quality coke. A PR team to book me on news shows. He took the weight of King Sorrow off my back so I could breathe. Colin could make it feel like the dragon didn't have anything to do with me. Bad people die every year, you know. Yeah, okay. We got together on the first day of every year and we went through the Enemies List. We'd say maybe this guy. This one self-appointed general in Southeast Asia stopped a bus full of Christian missionaries. His soldiers raped the teenage girls and a few of the boys, then his creeps shot them all and threw 'em in a shallow pit. A guy like that, you're only sorry he didn't die sooner. When you hear about him getting blown off the face of the earth on Easter morning, it's halfway around the world from you and he had it coming, and if he didn't get wiped out by King Sorrow, a counterrevolutionary would've got him, or a rival gang of thugs. Colin was like . . . like . . . noise-canceling headphones for all the terrible shit in my life." She sagged. "Only I guess some of the people we wiped out never killed anyone. Some of the people *I* wiped out. Like at Black Cricket. And some of the others weren't guilty of crimes against humanity, only crimes against Colin's interests."

"People like Arthur."

Donna lifted her gaze. Her eyes were watery and reddened. "Don't try to stick Arthur on me. I got enough to feel bad about. Arthur's on *you*. He loved you, and you kicked him to the curb."

Gwen said, "I didn't get you here so we can fight about who has the most to regret. That'd be a long conversation, and I only have the energy for a short one. So don't make me say this twice. Allie's right—there's a whole bunch of doctors in this building who can't figure out why my hip and my lung have healed so rapidly. The tracheostomy incision in my throat looks six months old, not three weeks. The Czech doctor said he's seen something like this only once before, ten years ago. A kid with bone cancer who washed himself in the waters at Lourdes and had a complete remission in four weeks."

"You said the hip and the lung are better. I thought you were hit three times."

"I was. I was shot through the abdomen and the bullet tore up some of my girl parts. There's an infection in a vestigial pouch next to the uterus. After you guys used the blood on me, that infection retreated, even seemed to go away. Now it's back. The bullet broke up inside of me, and there are pieces they couldn't find, still in there, still doing damage. They're draining the wound again right this instant." Gwen nodded to a length of tubing by the bed, filled with fluid the color of mashed eggplant. "And irrigating me with antibiotics. If they can get on top of it, they'll operate again, try and find the shards of bullet they missed. But it might take weeks to force the infection into retreat, and I don't have weeks."

Donna shook her head. "Robin dabbed all your wounds. You ought to be better. Goddamn it. Colin said it could fix anything."

"I'm sure Robin did a good job. I'm sure no one could've done better. I'm told the rectouterine pouch—sexy name, right?—has an elastic quality, and much like the placenta, medicines tend to bounce off it. St. Helen's Feelgood Juice did what it was supposed to on the *outer* wound. But the pouch probably shriveled up around the entry wound, sealing itself up . . . and sealing the infection in. The saint has been repelled by the female reproductive system."

"So what do we do? Are we all going to try and, I don't know, fight King Sorrow here? In the hospital?"

Upstairs, a baby made a mewling sound, and Donna's head snapped up to stare at the ceiling. When she looked back down, Gwen was smiling almost fondly.

"Newborn. Delivered last night. He's got a lusty pair of lungs, doesn't he? Kept me up past my bedtime. Kept me up thinking. No. We can't fight King Sorrow here in a hospital. Not unless we want a lot of babies and pregnant mamas and sick old men and tired overworked nurses to die. I won't allow that. We're still going to use my plan to try and cut down King Sorrow—I just don't think I'll be around to help. It'll have to be you, Donna."

"Fuck does that mean?"

"It's nine days until Easter Sunday. I'm going to check out of here the day before. They can't stop me. And I'll meet King Sorrow out behind The Briars . . . just like Colin planned. He can have me. Listen, though: He's at his weakest right *after* Easter. His weakest, his sleepiest, his smallest, and his most lethargic. You know the rest. Draw a loving spirit through in the form of a sword. Pull King Sorrow over from the Long Dark and strike off his head."

"Arthur won't come for me. Arthur didn't love *me*, Gwen."

"But Van did. And there was plenty of steel in him too, deep down. All the steel you need."

Donna opened her hands on her knees and spread her fingers and closed them into fists again.

"You fucking quitter," she hissed.

Gwen shut her eyes.

"I don't care if you quit on *me*. But you're going to quit on Allie? You're going to quit on Tana? Fuck you. Guess what? I won't do it. I brought you that bottle of holy bullshit so *you* could do it. You just want to die so you can be with Arthur again, and I think that's fucked. I could've saved Colin instead of you. *I could've picked Colin.*"

"Why didn't you?"

"*Because he didn't deserve it and you did,*" Donna said. "Because you rode around in that stupid ambulance for thirty years bringing dopers back to life, giving fat fucks mouth-to-mouth. Because I was going to let Colin wipe you out and then you jumped on top of me so I wouldn't get shot, which is the kind of cheap manipulative shit you're *always* doing. Because I thought *I'd* get to save *your* life for once. This is why I don't do good things! You give money to a hobo and he buys drugs with it! You make Thanksgiving dinner for your family and everyone fights. You douse the only really good person you've ever known in holy superblood and they say thanks but no thanks, I'd rather just die anyway, and by the way, here's an impossible job for you to do after I'm gone. Let me tell you something, Gwen. If you choose to die instead of fight? Then when next Easter comes around, I'm going to ask King Sorrow to eat someone *really nice*. Like Tom Hanks. Or Dolly Parton."

"Donna," Gwen said, and touched her hand, and Donna stood up so quickly her chair fell over with a crash.

"Don't touch me. You want to be dead? Don't wait for Easter. You're strong enough to get up, and the window is right there. It worked for Van."

Donna tried to slam the door, but it was on a pneumatic hinge and only sighed shut. Robin peeked cautiously in, and Gwen smiled weakly and turned away.

29.

Come Good Friday, she couldn't sleep. She finally dozed for a few hours on Saturday morning, between midnight and three. After that she was wide awake, staring at the drop ceiling. Her insides were sore. They were always sore these days.

She spoke to Arthur, sometimes, as had always been her habit.

Gwen said, "What else am I supposed to do? I couldn't beat him now even if I wasn't all rotten inside, Arthur. He's at full strength and he's ready for us."

He didn't reply because he wasn't there, not even the imaginary version she carried around inside her. She couldn't picture him, couldn't hear his voice.

She said, "I've done enough. I gave the others a way to beat him. They'll be all right. I'm tired and I'm sick and I don't want to do this anymore. I don't want to do any of it without you anymore. No one has the right to ask me to do more than I've already done."

This was met by a judgmental silence.

"I've been lonely ever since you left," she said. "It's not fair to me—that I had to do it all alone. My whole life. We were supposed to get forty years together. We could've had kids. We would've done the crossword together every morning. We should've had more time."

The quiet remained unimpressed with her.

"Anyway, I have it coming," Gwen said. "King Sorrow has killed hundreds in my name. And I let it happen. If I was really as good as everyone thinks, I would've asked King Sorrow to take me years ago. To take me instead of someone else. The only reason King Sorrow keeps killing is because we keep living, and how selfish is that?"

Someone—a nurse, maybe—laughed as she walked by in the hall.

She gave up trying to fall asleep again and sat up. It took ten minutes to pull all the tubes out of her back, all the needles out of her arm. By the time Gwen was free, her back was bleeding. She couldn't see where, but she could feel it, a sticky, lukewarm dribbling. She had, in the last few days, been making her way to the bathroom, hobbling along on a stainless-steel frame of the sort favored by arthritic old women. There was a crutch as well, with a foam pad for the armpit. She had, under the supervision of a physical therapist, made her way around the foot of the bed with the help of that crutch, and felt like she was being poked in the hip by a hot iron. She reached for it now, got it under the arm, and picked herself up.

A sweat sprang out on her face. She hopped three steps to a cupboard. She found pads of gauze and tape and a teensy pair of scissors. She cut herself a gauze pad and was just taping it over the leaking wound in her back when the door opened.

"What are you doing?" said the nurse, an older woman named Rachel, round faced and solid. She had been with the hospital maybe six years, had three years in the ER. Gwen knew all the nurses.

"Checking out," Gwen said. She was wearing a Patriots tee and gray sweats Allie had collected days ago, so Gwen would have some of her own things to wear. She didn't have shoes, but the hospital socks would do until her Uber got her home.

"You can't do that," Rachel said.

"Sure I can. Just watch."

She turned and began to crutch her way to the door. She could set her right foot down but didn't dare put any weight on it. The shattered bones in her hip had fused themselves back together—a medical impossibility, an Austrian doctor had told her—but it still sent an agonizing *twang* through her whole right side to bear down on it. That hip was mostly healed, but the nerve endings didn't seem to know it.

Rachel chased her down the hall. She was joined by another nurse, a distraught older woman named Inez, who was twisting her hands together.

"You have to sign here and here," Rachel said, waving a clipboard.

Gwen hit the button for the elevator. "Sure. Hold that still for me?"

Inez said, "You could be dead in a week, Ms. Underfoot. You have a serious infection and you're bleeding through your shirt."

"Not anymore. I threw some gauze on it."

"We could get a court order to compel you to stay."

"So get one," Gwen said. "Let me know when you hear from the judge." She signed her name on a release.

Rachel said, "This is suicidal. You belong in bed. *Healing*. For Christ's sake, Gwen. How many times have you taken an ambulance ride to someone's house and found them dead when you got there? Did you ever get used to it? Do you want to do that to someone else? Because whoever comes to pick up your corpse in a week, or three days, or tomorrow—they'll be a colleague. A friend. You want to do that to a friend? I never thought of Gwen Underfoot as a selfish person."

"I'd say I'm going through a midlife crisis," Gwen said, "but the way things are shaping up, it looks like the middle of my life was about twenty-two years ago. This isn't on you, Rachel. You did your best to keep me here. Now go and look after a patient who wants your help." The elevator doors opened. Gwen stepped in alone.

30.

Even here, even now, Gwen was an inveterate rule follower. Arthur had accused her of being a good little hobbit—by which he meant domestic and tidy and homey and rule-following. And he was right. There were signs warning visitors to keep their cells off in the hospital, to avoid interfering with sensitive diagnostic equipment, so Gwen did not activate her iPhone until she was making her way across the lobby to the sliding doors. Her insides felt stretched out and throbbed with pain. She supposed women felt much the same way after they delivered. She was pregnant herself, with her own death. The embryo was a shard of bullet, but it was never going to have a chance to grow to its full potential, because her abortion was scheduled for Easter morning. She felt clammy with sweat, her shirt already stuck to her back. The sliding doors opened and she made her way out into an unexpectedly sweet coolness, smelling of dew-soaked lawns. Her hand was damp and weak and she fumbled the phone while she was trying to open Uber. It slid through her fingers and cracked against the concrete.

"Piss on it," Gwen said. She bent to pick it up and the crutch slipped from under her arm and she knew she was going to eat it, she was going to face-plant on the concrete.

Robin caught her by the shoulder and steadied her before she could fall. "I've got it, you dumb cow." She collected the phone and handed it back to her.

Gwen's pulse thumped in her neck. She looked into Robin's good, cheerful face, and then past her. Donna sat behind the wheel of Colin's cherry '49 Caddy. Allie leaned against the side of the car, hugging herself against the chill. Tana had one haunch up on the hood and was sipping a coffee from Dunkin'.

"What's this?" Gwen asked.

"What's it look like?" Tana said. "It's a fuckin' ambush."

"We figured we'd practice our sneak attack on you," Allie said, "before anyone tried it out on King Sorrow."

Gwen opened her mouth.

"You want to plan your next words carefully," Donna said. "You can sit up front next to me or you can ride in the trunk. Up to you."

It surprised Gwen to feel the smile spreading across her face, the good feeling opening inside her chest.

"Okay," she said. "I know when I'm beat."

ONCE SHE WAS IN THE CAR, Robin took her crutch away and laid it across the floor in the back seat. Tana slammed the door on her, as if Gwen might change her mind and try to leap out. It felt good to get off her feet. There was a hot twist of pain in the small of her back and she wondered if she was bleeding through the gauze already. She was shaky from exertion and thought, *No way, NO WAY I can fight him like this.*

"Do you have to do this in the Brooks Library?" Donna asked.

"I think so. It survived the big fire a century ago—it was the only place on campus that didn't burn. The walls are a foot of solid stone. Even at his full strength, King Sorrow would have some work to do, knocking that down. Also, it's spring break. No students around to get hurt. Most of the on-campus staff will be gone too. It's a ghost ship."

"Arthur loved it there," Allie said.

"It's where all this began," Gwen said. "It's fitting to try and end it there."

"Okay then," Allie said. "It's only open from nine to six today and I checked the rotation. One librarian on duty and one volunteer. I booked Conference Room A for late morning. You know where that is? East wing, first floor. There's a door in there into a utility room. Bigger than a closet, but not by much. It used to be a break room for the custodial staff. Now they've got the library servers in there. You guys hide in the server room and I'll leave just before closing. I'll come back a couple hours later. Someone can let me in through one of the windows in the basement. There are bathrooms down there and—"

"Hang on," Gwen said. "Why would *we* all hide anywhere? Why would you come back?"

The Caddy glided along the broad avenue in a deep, leather-padded hush.

Allie began, "Gwen—"

Robin cut her off. "You can't do this alone, darling. Never mind battling a dragon like ye bold knights of old. How are you going to pick up a sword? You can barely hold your iPhone. You need us. We can help with the séance, and when the dragon shows up, we can run interference."

"You can get killed is what you can do. I told you to stay out of it. You all get burned up with me, there won't be anyone left to fight King Sorrow after Easter."

"If we all get burned up," Allie said, "King Sorrow will be done anyway. He can't keep coming back to our world if we're all gone. We win if we win. But we also win if we lose."

Tana said, "To be fair, it's harder to celebrate your big victory when you've been reduced to a pile of fackin' charred sticks."

"I don't want you there," Gwen said.

"Tough shit," Donna said. "You need the mirror and the martyr's robe, and I've got both. Wanna wrestle me for them?"

"Goddamn it, Donna."

Gwen felt ill from the motion of the car, from the racing motion inside her. She kept her hands pressed to the dash as if bracing for a crash.

Tana said, "What about campus security?"

Robin said, "I've been to the library myself, to do a little recon. The Special Collection has windows that face the lobby, but there are shades. We can roll them down. I think turning on the lights is out of the question, but we've got an almost full moon tonight—"

"'Course it's a full moon," Tana said.

"—and as long as we keep our voices down, I think we'll be

fine. Campus security might take a pass through the lobby once or twice, but there's no permanent presence in the library. Not that I've seen, and I spent most of one night parked on the street, where I could watch the place through the school gates."

"Is everyone in this car out of their minds?" Gwen asked, her voice shaking with emotion. "Can't you understand, I don't want anyone else to die for me?"

"Oh, will you unknot your panties?" Donna said. "No one is going to die for you. If things get too hairy, I'll just give your head a sharp twist and kill you myself. King Sorrow's gotta go away as soon as you're dead, and then we can all try again at our leisure." She drove for a moment, then added, "I hope that sets your mind at ease."

The car glided along the almost empty streets in silence. Gwen lowered her hands back to her lap and exhaled very slowly.

"Yeah, Donna," she said. "It's a load off my mind."

"See, and I'm always hearing I'm not a people person," Donna said.

31.

They turned into the parking lot behind the Brooks Library, and Donna rolled into a slot in a far back corner, the Caddy turned to face Rackham's Wood. They were almost the only car there.

Allie went in first. She climbed out of the rear, then leaned back in and pecked Tana on the cheek. She hurried away as if someone had just told her that her house was on fire. Tana cupped one hand to the side of her face, where Allie's lips had touched her.

Donna's gaze moved to the rearview mirror and locked on Tana's eyes. "I got one thing to say."

"Can't wait," Tana said.

"You break her heart, I'll rope you to the bumper of this car and drag you through the streets."

Robin said, "That's . . . highly specific."

Tana said, "You sure you're not from Gogan, McBride?"

"The Florida panhandle. It's like Gogan, but with alligators."

Robin went in next, about half an hour later. Allie thought they would attract less notice entering one at a time. If they walked in as a group, people would expect them to leave in a group.

"So let's say, hypothetically, things get bad," Donna said.

"I hate to update you on current events," Tana said, "but they got bad a while ago."

"I mean up in the tower when the dragon comes. Let's say it becomes clear this isn't going to work. Do you want me to tell you before I do it, Gwen, so you can prepare yourself, or is it better not to know?"

"*I'd* like to know," Tana said. "Be sure to tell me. Because the moment you decide Gwen has to die, you're going out the window."

"You won't have to tell me," Gwen said. "We'll both just know."

"No one is killing no one," Tana said. "The both of you can shut up."

"I don't shut up, I grow up," Donna said. "And when I look at you, I throw up. And then your momma runs around the corner and—oh, wait, I just remembered, your momma isn't running anywhere. Because you beat her head in. But go on, you were just about to give me a lecture on the sanctity of life."

"Jesus," Tana said, and got out of the car, and wandered out of sight around the library.

"You don't have to go out of your way to be nasty," Gwen said.

Donna said, "My best friend in third grade, Cady Lewis? She was the most adorable thing. Sunny and wide eyed and amazed by everything: a bald eagle in a tree, the ice cream truck, a gold star on a math test. Then she died and I spent the next thirty years feeling terrible about it. But when I'm gone, it won't hurt anyone the way Cady hurt me. The way Van hurt me when *he* died. That's why the world needs motherfuckers, I think. Motherfuckers hold the line. And if they get wiped out in the process, it's no big loss to anyone. The world dusts its hands off and moves on."

"Donna—" Gwen said.

Donna said, "I think you can go in now."

Gwen stared at her for a moment, then opened the passenger-side door. Donna got out on the other side to help her with her crutch.

There had been fresh clothes for Gwen in the car: a pair of sneakers and the ratty yellow hoodie Arthur had loaned her the last time they went sledding, the one with the face of Steve Biko on the back. Tana could've picked any of half a dozen sweatshirts out of Gwen's closet, but she had selected that one, for who knew what reason, and it was exactly right.

Donna offered her the crutch. Gwen flipped her hood up and took it and nodded.

"See you in there," Donna said.

Gwen shifted along the wet and cratered parking lot, hopping along on the crutch. The school was as still as she had ever seen it. With the students on leave, it belonged to the birds now. Juncos, they were called. She had looked them up.

She let herself in. The door fell shut with an echoing bang behind her. There was a librarian on the far side of the empty lobby, behind the counter, scanning books into the system. She looked Gwen's way, then dropped her gaze back to the work in front of her.

Gwen scooted along on her crutch, turning right and ducking into the east wing, then turning again into a darkened corridor. She ground her teeth against a fresh twist of pain in her hip. Conference Room A appeared on her left and she let herself in. The others were there, sitting anxiously around a table. The back of the room was a full-wall art piece, a blown-up photograph printed on white ceramic, rendered at such a large scale, it was possible to see the individual dots making up the image: it was J.R.R. Tolkien, the old man smiling in profile around his pipe, his eyes amused beneath shaggy eyebrows. It did not surprise Gwen to see him there. The old dragon fighter would not have wanted to miss out on a night like tonight. At the sight of him, it struck Gwen that Arthur was already with them, had always somewhat resembled a young Steve Biko, but with Tolkien's dress sense.

Donna joined them five minutes later. The door to the server room was almost invisible, a part of the white wall, hidden in Tolkien's shoulder. Donna felt around in that massive Michael Kors bag she carried over one shoulder, found something to stick in the little lock, and forced it with a savage twist.

She turned a small brass knob and opened the door on a warm, narrow, dark room, lined with Dragonware-brand servers on steel shelves. A few hundred lights twinkled and flashed, an alien cosmos of constellations in emerald and gold: a dragon's hoard of gleaming gems. So Colin was with them too, in his way. Gwen shivered, conscious of a clammy sweat on her back and sides.

"I think I'm going to try and nap," she said, crutching to the door and peering inside. She craved the warmth and gentle hum of the machinery, that twenty-first-century cavern of riches.

"Shouldn't we try to bring Arthur through now?" Allie asked.

"I don't know how long we'll be able to keep him here," Gwen said. "Once we bring him through, we'll want to pull King Sorrow straight into our world after him. Best if we wait until we have the library to ourselves."

There was a leather recliner in there, jammed in one corner, a stack of yellowing *Library Journals* piled in the seat. Gwen used her crutch to push the magazines to the floor. Her back was to the others, so she didn't see Tana and Allie trade a startled look, didn't know there was a blood stain as large as a man's palm on the back of the hoodie. She yawned.

"I feel like I could sleep a hundred years," Gwen said. "Don't let me snooze through anything interesting."

"Like what?" Donna asked. "Like a dragon kicking the roof off the place?"

"Yeah," Gwen agreed. "Like that."

THEY ARRANGED THEMSELVES on the floor of the server room, at Gwen's feet, while Gwen slept. She had dozed off almost the moment she hit the chair.

Tana had brought premade subs from Market Basket, but no one was hungry. Allie couldn't imagine eating. Her stomach was doing nervous backflips. She was going to have to leave soon, abandon them there, and return later with everything they needed for the night.

Donna sat with her back to a wall. In a low voice she said, "Do you think we can summon Arthur without Gwen? Or Van? If it's just you and me, Allie, we might have better luck calling for Van."

"Why would we summon either of them without her?" Robin asked.

"We might have to if she slides into unconsciousness. I can smell that wound from here. She's got something bad inside her."

Allie said, "She's not dying."

Donna stared at her.

"She's *not*," Allie said, wanting to cry.

"Maybe it's a good thing," Donna said. "That she's slipping away."

Allie wanted to punch her right in her big stupid mouth. "You were certainly hoping she'd die a month ago. You sound like you can't wait to snap her neck tonight."

Donna didn't flinch. She said, "Colin told me it's easier to bring someone through from the Long Dark if you're already on the bridge between life and death. She's our best chance of pulling Arthur through, not just because they meant everything to each other, but because she can meet him halfway. She's just about dead herself." She clutched her purse close to her stomach. "It's true I was going to let her die a month ago. Colin lied to me and used me . . . but I made it easy for him to turn me against her. I was angry. She told me I was inhuman for setting King Sorrow loose on Black Cricket, that I was as bad as the worst people we killed, and she was right. I couldn't bear for another single human being to see how bad I was. One of us had to go." She reflected another moment, then said, "I can't fix what I've done. I can't undo any of it, and I don't expect to be forgiven."

"But here you are," Robin said.

"But here I am."

"Why?"

"Because . . . it's not about me. It's about Gwen. It's about Allie. It's about the people who will live if we cut King Sorrow down." Donna's gaze found Robin. Her green eyes were as dull and disinterested as Allie had ever seen them. "What about you, Fellows? I can't think of one single good reason for you to be here. You could walk away."

"I walked away from Arthur Oakes," Robin said. "Or, rather, I allowed him to walk away from me. I knew it was a mistake, even then. I won't leave another friend. And you're all friends."

"You think so?" Donna asked. "Even you and I?"

"I know you've convinced yourself you're unlovable, Donna McBride, but when I look in your face, I see what your brother saw. Fierceness. An overwhelming urge to protect the people you care about. A lack of interest in being loved by anyone else. The yin to Van's yang. Can't love one and not the other: the both of you together made a whole."

"What about you, Tana?" Allie asked. "You d-don't have to stay." It appalled her, to feel so emotional she couldn't talk without stammering.

Tana heard the hitch in her voice and smiled. Winked. Allie thought she'd die of embarrassment and love.

"This woman here stood up for me for twenty-plus years." Nodding to Gwen. "She changed my son's diapers and wiped away his tears when I was getting sober. She wiped away some of my tears too. All of you turned your lives upside down just to save mine. Well—all right. To save Arthur. But I was a beneficiary. I always figured the bill would come due someday. Time to pay the check. What about you? You know, when you walk out of this library in an hour . . . you don't have to come back."

"Yes, she does. She's holding the robe and the mirror," Donna said. "But . . . maybe she shouldn't stay. It's hard to see how five women are going to achieve what attack helicopters and F-16s couldn't. Allie, you could try again, yourself, in a month, when he's at his absolute weakest. Get him while he's as small as a kitten and just as helpless."

"He's never that small and never that helpless, and don't you dare lock me out," Allie said, her voice shaking. Donna and Tana glanced at one another. Allie knew what was on their minds and jumped to her feet, her hands balled into fists. "I mean it. I see every thought you're thinking. Unthink it."

"Why, though?" Robin asked. "They're right. You could bring us what we need, to do tonight's work, and then go. Be ready to fight again if we fail."

"What do they say in those AA meetings? We pray for the strength to do the next right thing?"

Tana nodded.

"*This* is the next right thing. I'm part of this. One hundred percent."

Donna said, "You may be *in* one hundred percent . . . but you are sixty percent foolishness, twenty-five percent a chirpy pain in the ass, ten percent bullshit statistics, and about five percent adorable. Sit your scrawny ass back down and stop hyperventilating before you fall over."

Allie sat. And when Donna took her hand, Allie let her.

ALLIE LEFT JUST BEFORE FOUR, closed the door behind her, and turned off the light in the conference room. The others sat together in the whirring dark. Gwen snored. Tana smelled blood. *Sick* blood, a whiff of something coppery and rancid. Around four thirty her son sent her a text.

Went by the house. Where you at woman? I brought fried chicken. I've got the overnight shift.

I got a couple fires of my own to put out tonight, she wrote back. Eat it yourself. Leave me a leg. You know I like a tasty bit of leg.

Ew, gross, how many times have I told you not to text me about your sex life, dammit. Followed by a laughing face emoji.

She thought for a long time how to reply. Finally, she answered with three hearts, because it seemed for some emotions, some deeply held feelings, no words would do.

A few minutes before 7:00 p.m., Tana realized Gwen was staring at her, her eyes the brightest thing in the gloom. It startled her. She didn't know how long Gwen had been watching.

"This was a mistake," Gwen whispered. "I shouldn't have let any of you talk me into this. I was too weak to fight you off. If I can't fight off four middle-aged women, hell if I know how I'll fight off a dragon."

"If it's a mistake, it's not *your* mistake. It's *ours*. Let *us* make it." Tana put her head back against the wall. "Trust me, I made my share of 'em." She felt an anxious clench of anticipation, realized what she was about to say, hesitated, hung up on her own nerves, then decided to hell with it, if it was a foolish thing to admit, she wouldn't have to regret it for long. "I made one with Arthur, you know. Long time before you got together. He probably told you."

Gwen considered her with calm, untroubled features and said nothing. Tana prickled with worry, wished already she could take it back, kept her fool trap shut.

"Yeah, well. Don't worry. He wasn't ever in love with me. I made sure there was no chance of that. I told him—*ah*." Tana put a hand over her face, alarmed by her own sudden rush of feeling, a surge of loss and humiliation.

"What did you tell him?"

"That it was all part of the deal with Jayne. Something we were throwing in extra for stealing those books. I couldn't say Jayne had nothing to do with it. I couldn't tell him it was something *I* did—something I wanted for me—because he was a nice guy and I was never with a nice guy. Then Jayne found out I had been with him. She overheard me talking to him on the phone or something. She even complimented me, said it was a good move, gave us another way to control him. Do please forgive me, Gwen. It wasn't the worst thing I ever did in those days, but it was the worst thing I ever did to him. And a course I never said nothing to you. I needed you even more'n I needed him. So anyway. That's the kind of person you saved, Gwen Underfoot. Jayne Nighswander wasn't the only user in my family."

Gwen lifted herself up on her crutch. She came across the room, slowly, methodically, until she was leaning right over Tana. Tana lowered her head, her cheeks hot, and waited for Gwen to strike her. Instead, Gwen bent and cupped the back of her head and kissed her above the left eyebrow.

"Never let the thought trouble you again," Gwen said.

She slid to the floor to sit next to Tana and took her hand. The two women who had loved Arthur best sat side by side, with the crutch across their thighs. After a while, Tana let her head rest on Gwen's shoulder and wondered again how she had come through her life to this point, in the company of people who, against all reason and sense, still cared for her. That was a thing as fantastic and improbable as any ghost, any dragon.

They sat together for most of an hour, and then Donna said, "It's time."

Tana and Robin helped Gwen back up and they left Conference Room A in single file. Their hushed voices rose to the vaulted ceilings and banged around up there, so it sounded as if ghosts were whispering about them from the shadows. Tana had never been in the Brooks Library until today and felt as if she had stepped out of the conference room and into Westminster Abbey or the Tower of London.

She wished she had read more books. It had never come easy to her, was a struggle to fight her way through a thicket of words and into the story. But then, that was like wishing she hadn't been born in Gogan, that Daphne Nighswander hadn't been her mother, that Jayne hadn't been her sister. Sometimes, at AA meetings, Allie would read from the Big Book, and Tana felt she was hearing the words for the first time, felt as if the whole book had opened to her, as accessible as watching a woman speak on TV. She wondered if Allie would read to her sometime, then remembered they would all be dead by morning.

They descended to the basement. The other women flocked into the toilets, desperate for a pee, while Tana made her way to the radiator against the far wall. There was a narrow window up there, set with panes of frosted glass and hidden behind hedges on the other side. It was the exact same window Colin Wren had come through twenty-six years before, with a can of spray paint and a plan to frame townies for Arthur's theft of a quarter million dollars in rare books. Tana climbed onto the ancient, cobwebbed radiator and fought with the latch, which was painted shut. It snapped open all of a sudden, glossy shards of paint splintering and falling away. No sooner had she swung the window open than Allie pushed Gwen's messenger bag through. Tana leapt down and Allie wiggled through on her stomach, legs flailing for purchase. Tana took her thighs and helped her place her feet on the radiator.

"If your head was any farther up her ass," Donna said, "you'd have to get a hotel room." She had emerged from her stall and regarded them with something close to total dismissal. She bent and peeked under Robin's stall. "Oh, hey. You piss sitting down! I was wondering."

Robin laughed softly. "Yes, darling. Do you?"

Gwen exited her own stall on her crutch, moving slowly, grimacing slightly. "Take it easy on her, Robin."

"Yeah, that's right," Tana said. "Don't be too hard on her. Even I can see McBride is useful to have around in a fight like this."

"Useful for what?" Robin asked.

"Human shield," Tana replied.

32.

They went up the winding staircase to the Special Collection—Arthur had sometimes called it the treasure room, a name that seemed more apt that evening—with Donna leading the way, the ring of keys in one hand. Gwen was behind her, with Tana close on her heels, helping her along. Gwen needed the assistance. By the time she was halfway up, her hoodie was soaked through the back with sweat and her legs were shaking. Every leap to the next step sent a sick, piercing jolt through her insides. Something was very wrong in there. Her face was hot and sometimes the world went a little dark on her, as if someone were fiddling with a dimmer switch.

And yet, for all that, she felt an easiness in her heart she could not have imagined possible in such a moment. It was like the feeling when the last bell rang on the final day of school, and all of summer stretched out before a person. She had not wanted to believe that Arthur, in the unhappiest days of his life, had misused Tana, who had been so often misused by others. Although, in truth, she had never been able to hate him for anything. Arthur was perfectly capable of hating himself enough for both of them. He had lashed himself, loathed himself, all his life, for an act of moral stupidity he had not in fact committed. She wished he knew the truth of it. Maybe she would have a chance to tell him tonight.

Donna had the door to the treasure room open and stepped aside to let Gwen past. It was a small sort of door, and Tana had to let go of her. As she went through, lost in her thoughts, Gwen's left foot caught on the stone jamb. The crutch slipped free, spun, and fell. The floor rushed up at her. She got her hands up to keep from smashing face-first, but her knees hit the marble with a crack. Her elbows folded and she felt something tear inside her—like someone pulling apart a wet, rotting sheet. She tried to cry out but couldn't get any air. Pain flared in the damaged lung, as if she had inhaled hot ash.

In an instant, the other women were around her. Allie was trying not to cry, which vaguely irritated Gwen. She was the one who was hurt, not Allie, why did Allie always have to be half in tears? She wanted to bark at her. Instead, she reached out and found Allie's hand and patted it. It seemed one could not break a lifetime of habit—a lifetime of reassuring the distraught—without the sort of premeditated effort that was currently beyond her.

"It's all right," she said, although it most certainly was *not* all right. She could feel blood leaking down her back, through the bandage, staining the band of her sweatpants.

"Oh, this is fucked," Tana said. "This is so fucked. What is she doing out of a hospital bed? I didn't sign up to watch a sick woman die in front of us."

"If she was in her hospital bed," Donna said, her tone impassive, "she'd die for sure. And a whole lot of others with her. It's Easter Sunday in four hours. This is what's happening."

Tana twisted her head around, looked as if she were going to flare up . . . then visibly bit back whatever she was going to say. Robin Fellows patiently moved along the line of windows, which overlooked the library floor below, pulling down the shades as she went, hiding the treasure room from the sight of anyone who might pass through the lobby. Donna eased the door shut and locked it behind them.

Allie and Tana each took an arm and helped Gwen to her knees. Tana lifted the back of her shirt to look at the wound.

"This is sopping."

"I've got a kerchief," Robin said, sinking to her knees beside them and digging in her clutch.

Tana peeled off the bloody gauze. The smell made Gwen feel like gagging: the nasty-sweet fragrance of spoilage, like a bowl of rotting fruit. Tana used the strips of tape from the old square of gauze to stick down the thick pad of Robin's kerchief. Sparks were still whirling and flashing in front of Gwen's eyes. Tana approached Donna, whispering at her in an angry hiss. Donna put a hand on her chest and pushed her back a few feet, didn't deign to reply.

Gwen looked around the room, which she had never once entered, not even during her three and a half years as a student. It was a long and peaceful space for contemplation, with a few scarred wooden tables and straight-backed chairs. Someone had left a folded newspaper on one of them; it fluttered gently in a breeze that came from who knew where. The bookshelves were covered in wire grating, the grating secured with padlocks, a safety feature added in the years after the robberies. With funding from Colin Wren himself, the school had erected a glass wall in the back third of the room, and the most valuable books were now on the other side. One needed the correct keypad code to enter. The space in there was climate controlled, and a camera had been mounted in one corner to keep the glass vault under observation. Fortunately, it was pointed away from the rest of the room, the lens aimed at that back wall of precious volumes. The embrasures were narrow slits in the stone wall. Those slits were a full foot deep, and Gwen thought again that the place almost seemed to have been built to keep out a dragon.

Donna sank to her knees beside Gwen. "Hon, if you've got it in you, I think we better try to bring Arthur across now."

"How do we do this?" Allie asked, her voice fretful and uncertain.

"The same way we brought King Sorrow through," Gwen said. "The same way Llewellyn Wren brought Elwood Hondo into our world. Through shared belief . . . and shared magic. Do you have my cell phone? And the projector?"

Allison threw back the flap of the messenger bag. She set the contents on the floor, lining everything up in a neat row: the cracked Russian mirror, Gwen's phone, and the Bluetooth projector shaped like a black Coke can. Lastly, she removed the cloak made of itchy-looking brown and gray hair.

"Ugh," Allie said. "I think thirty percent of this thing was woven out of pubic hair. What do we do with it?"

"Put it over her," Donna said, and nodded at Gwen.

"No," Gwen said. "It'll hide me from King Sorrow, and I don't want to hide from him. Not yet. I *want* him to know where I am. One of you wear it."

"Allie," Tana said.

"Yeah, make Allie wear the pube cloak," Donna said.

"That makes it unanimous then," Robin said.

"It's *not* unanimous," Allie said. "I'm not voting for myself."

"You're not voting at all," Donna said. "Because we decided it's you."

"No. No, I—"

"Enough," Gwen croaked. "We need to do this thing. Put it on, Allie. You're our backup plan if this doesn't work tonight. If the rest of us get wiped out, you can try again."

Donna and Tana half wrestled the robe onto Allie. It had a mossy rope that could be drawn to bunch the collar up around the throat and create a hood. Allie squirmed and flushed, but at least she didn't rip it off. And while they were forcing her into the martyr's robe, Robin turned the projector on and pointed it toward the greenish wall of glass in the back of the room. Gwen opened the video on her phone and hit play, set to repeat over and over, until the battery ran out.

And Arthur joined them, there in the library.

Gwen is on the ground, covered in an ankle-length cape, a silky blanket draped over the arch of her back. A thug with a bulging Boris Karloff forehead stares stupidly down at her: he has just knocked her off her roller skates and down to the blacktop. He has his lacrosse stick in his hands. Some of the other lacrosse kids mill about, a bunch of pimply teens looking offended and confused about what just went down.

Allie screams off camera.

"Gwen! You're going to die!" Allie screams. "You're going to die!"

Allie skates into the field of view, wearing the head of a unicorn and rubber horse hooves over her hands. She seems intent on barreling right into the biggest of the lacrosse dumbbells, but before she can get to him, Van is there, sailing lightly and gracefully in to grab her around the waist and lift her right off her feet. Her hooves paw the air.

The biggest lacrosse player—the one who struck Gwen down—is saying something, trying to explain himself in a mulish voice. He isn't looking when Arthur Oakes glides into the circle of boys, hunched low, moving with purpose. Arthur has to be doing nearly twenty miles an hour when he throws his shoulder into the stomach of the boy who knocked Gwen off her feet. The kid barks like a dog and doubles over. His hands go loose, and it is the easiest thing in the world for Arthur to snatch the lacrosse stick out of his hands.

Arthur was a ghost. They were all ghosts. Projected upon the glass wall, the figures in the film assumed a brilliant transparency, shimmered like soap bubbles. It felt good to see him again . . . Arthur and Van both. *Hail, hail,* Gwen thought, *the gang's all here.* Even Colin was with them now, of course. He was the one behind the camera.

Donna took Gwen's left hand. Allie, kneeling on the other side, took her right. Without any discussion at all, the women in the tower had arranged themselves in a line facing that thick wall of soda-bottle green.

"Come back to us, Arthur," Donna said.

"Yo, Art," Tana called, holding Allie's hand. "Where you at?"

"Robin," Allie said. "Look for him in the mirror. Keep your eyes peeled for anything that doesn't make sense. Give it a few moments and if nothing happens, pass it on."

Robin lifted the cracked mirror, and turned her face this way and that, as if inspecting her eyelashes. "Are you there, Arthur? We miss you."

"So much," Gwen whispered. "Come back, Arthur. Let's go sledding. Let's go for a ride into the Long Dark."

"Let's go!" Arthur

shouts, in a laughing voice, whirling round and around on his skates, slinging that lacrosse stick like a knight laying into a crowd of his foes. A lacrosse bonehead catches it in his knee, shrieks, and hops around on one foot, holding his leg. A second lacrosse bozo gets thumped in the breastbone and is propelled, stumbling backward. His heels strike up against Gwen, who is still on all fours, and the bozo falls over.

Van's face appears in camera, filling most of the shot, his face jubilant. He wears chain mail and has a buckler on one arm—they had all dressed as characters from Dungeons & Dragons *that night.* "Take a knee, motherfuckers! King Arthur is back in town, and is he pissed!"

Van whoops and pitches himself into the action, circling Gwen in rapid swoops, his shield held out to one side. A lacrosse thug takes a run at Arthur from the side and catches a face full of Van's shield instead, is thrown onto his back.

And Arthur spins and spins, whipping that stick around and around, and he looks into the lens of the camera and his lips move, he's saying something, it's impossible to tell what, and that is where the video catches and freezes for an instant, before leaping back to the beginning to start all over again.

Gwen is on the ground, covered in an ankle-length cape . . .

The mirror made its way down the line. When it got to Gwen, she set it on the floor in front of her knees, the reflective side up. She held the hands of the women on either side of her and leaned forward to stare into the glass. A dying woman stared back. Her hair was limp and frail and there were dark satchels under her eyes and her upper lip was damp with sweat.

"Arthur," she said. "I know you're tired. I'm tired too. Come back. What do you say, old buddy? Old chum? Old *puh—p—*"

Something snagged in her throat and she coughed and felt another tearing sensation inside. She slipped a hand out of Allie's to touch her lips. It came away red. A drop of blood plinked onto the glass. She tried to wipe it away and only got it into the crack, making a kind of crimson shatter-line down the center of the mirror's face.

"*Christ*," Tana said. "She needs a doctor."

"I'm all right. Just—warm," Gwen said.

It was true. The room had a curiously airless quality. She might've been wrapped in the martyr's robe instead of Allie, she was so overheated. Gwen closed her eyes for an instant to recover herself.

When the flushed, swimmy sensation had passed, she glanced up and said, "Can we crack a window? Sorry, I know we just started."

Donna and Robin traded a look and Gwen got the idea she had said something unsettling.

"Sure, love," Robin said, and stood. Donna let go and got up with her.

Someone had moved the mirror during the few moments she had her eyes closed. It was in front of Tana now.

"How long was she out, you think?" Gwen heard Robin say, from a long way off.

"Half hour?" Donna said.

"These don't open," Robin said, gesturing to the thin panes of glass in one of the embrasures.

Donna picked up the newspaper that was scattered on a nearby study table, placed it over the window, and punched. Glass tinkled. When she tossed the newspaper down there was a cool, tender breath of green-smelling air coming in.

"Sure they do," Donna said.

They knelt again. Allie touched a wet cloth to Gwen's forehead. It was not that the cloth was chilly so much as Gwen's face was, she realized now, hideously warm. Where had the cloth come from? How had it got damp? It came to Gwen that she had been chanting for Arthur in a kind of trance, that she had not been entirely—or at all—conscious.

The ghost of Arthur Oakes rolled into view and began to fight again.

"What time is it?" Allie asked.

Tana replied. "Couple minutes after ten." But that was impossible. They had come upstairs at *seven thirty*, Gwen had only watched this little two-minute video play through twice. A fresh sweat prickled her face and sides.

The mirror went around and came back to Gwen. This time Gwen let go of Allie's hand to pick the mirror up and look into it. She was worried if she put it on the floor in front of her and bent forward to see her reflection, she would overbalance and go face-first.

"You there, old chum? You there, old buddy?"

Her hand was slippery with sweat and she couldn't hold the mirror steady. It jiggled to show her the wooden table behind her and to her left. The Y-shaped crack down the front of the mirror split that table in two, with the newspaper visible on the left-hand side. As Gwen watched, the breeze caught one corner of the newspaper, lifted it, and flapped it across the table. Only when it crossed the crack in the glass it became a storm of velvety black butterflies, a whirling cloud of them that rose in a whispering rush into darkness. Or maybe there was a crack running across her consciousness as well as the mirror and for an instant she was dreaming while awake.

She set the mirror on the floor with a shaking hand and turned her head. No butterflies, of course, but the newspaper had slid itself off the table and across the floor, wound up only a few feet away. Gwen left the line of kneeling girls. Donna twisted her head to see what she was doing, and Gwen waved a limp-wristed hand at her.

"Keep going," Gwen said. "I just need to—"

She didn't finish the sentence, didn't know what she needed. The newspaper had fallen open to the crossword. Someone had already penned in a few answers. *Hurts sharply*. SMARTS. *Sex cells?* GAMETES. *Where J. Nighswander died*. CALI.

Gwen stared at the puzzle, looking from the filled-in answers to the clues and back. A drop of sweat fell from her forehead, plinked onto the page.

"Gwen? Are you all right?" Allie asked.

Gwen nodded. "Keep calling for Arthur. I have to finish the crossword."

Allie was staring at her. Donna reached across the gap for Allie's hand.

"You heard her," Donna said. "Keep going."

"Arthur," Robin said. "I shouldn't have let you go under the bridge without me. Please come back."

"Yo, Artie," Tana said. "We had us some okay times, didn't we? Once more, for old time's sake? What do you say? You never forget your first?"

"Van," Donna said.

"Van," Allie whispered with her. "What's cookin', good lookin'?"

"You stood up for me once, Van," Donna said. "No, more than once. A thousand times. Can you do it again? One last time? Help me, Van. Come back to me."

Gwen ignored them and stared at the crossword. She was going to need a pen, but for a moment she just looked at it. Six across: *Property and coffee*. She knew that one, of course ... had spent some of her life caring for the one and fueled by the other.

"Grounds," she whispered, tracing her finger across the puzzle. She shut her eyes against a wave of dizziness.

When she opened her eyes again it had been filled in, in her own handwriting. Another drop of sweat plinked onto the newspaper. She wiped her brow, shook her head. One of the crosses was filling itself in, a down, building off GROUNDS. The clue was: *Elwood Hondo*. The answer, in Arthur's calligraphic handwriting, read GHOST.

"King Arthur is back in town!" Van shouted from across the room, his memory calling out over a gulf of twenty years.

Gwen searched the clues. *Internet troublemaker*. TROLL. *Deal with a psychic*. ZENER. As she thought the answers, they filled themselves in ... and at the same time Arthur was writing in answers of his own, from somewhere far away, somewhere on the other side of her pain and exhaustion. *Phone for spirits*. CONCH. *Cutest member of Mystery Inc*. VELMA. The answers wrote themselves, her words and his, a cat's cradle of what he knew and what she knew, the half of her that fitted perfectly against half of him. Across the room, Donna smashed another window to let in more air.

"Stop breaking windows, Donna," Gwen muttered. "Someone will notice."

"I didn't break it," Donna said. "It's Easter morning, babe. It's Easter morning, and he's here."

33.

Robin flew to her feet, banged her hip against one of the tables, didn't seem to notice, and reached an embrasure. She put her hands on the stone sill and gaped out.

"Oh, my God," she said, in a small voice.

Donna was prepared to yell at Gwen if she tried to set aside her crossword. But Gwen had hardly looked up, and then only with muddy, feverish eyes. Her gaze swiftly turned back to the newspaper open before her. Donna had a momentary look at it, in time to see letters scrawling themselves on the page, rising out of nowhere, much in the way lemon juice would reveal invisible ink. TEARS was just coming into being.

"Tears," Gwen muttered, pronouncing it as if it were the verb that meant *to rip*. Only Donna knew it wasn't "tears," *to rip*, but "tears," *what is wept*. She thought there would be plenty of those before the night was done.

Donna pushed herself to her feet and stepped into the embrasure to Robin's left, the one that had blown in as King Sorrow swept past the tower. Donna stared into the star-strewn night. For a moment, the campus was as still and peaceful as buildings in an undisturbed snow globe. A raft of silver cloud idled in the north.

Then the dragon swept across the moon, wings spread, vast enough to blot it out for an instant. King Sorrow banked like a stealth bomber and fell toward the library, growing in size, instant by instant, and Donna thought this was what it must've been like to stand at the top of one of the World Trade Center towers just as the plane was about to strike.

"Get the fuck down," Donna cried, shoving herself away from

the open embrasure and throwing herself at Robin, who seemed stuck in place.

They crashed to the floor as flame gouted through the embrasures, great jets of it, billowing right above them. The whole row of narrow north-facing windows erupted in a spray of glass. Fire poured through. Donna felt the heat of it on her back, as if she were lying beneath a kiln. Tana grabbed Allie and squashed her to the floor. Both of them disappeared under the spreading pool of the martyr's robe.

Gwen remained on her knees, her forehead almost touching the floor, like a woman of Islam called to prayer. The crossword was under her nose. Her face was almost serene, and the last answers were filling themselves in, although her eyes were so unfocused, who knew if she could even see them. Flame licked past her, inches behind her head. She didn't seem to notice.

When Donna lifted her gaze, the first thing she saw was the video projected upon the glass wall. It was glitching, playing the same second and a half of film, over and over. Arthur spun toward camera with the lacrosse stick, then snapped back. And again. And again. He was a shimmer and blur more than a person now, a smudge of light.

The jets of flame stopped as if someone had thrown a switch. The books on the far side of the room were afire. Smoke boiled through the chain-link grating. Robin struggled to wriggle out from under Donna.

"Get offa me," she cried.

Donna rose to one knee. Robin launched herself up and toward the door, and Donna thought, *Running, the fucking bitch is running, that fucking coward.* But Robin stopped before she reached the door to pry a slim fire extinguisher off the wall. She yanked it loose and turned to face the burning wall of books and began to blast away, the extinguisher propelling a sticky white foam into the smoke. From beneath the folds of the robe, Donna heard Allie's voice rising in prayer—not to God, but to Arthur and Van.

"Please Arthur please Van please Arthur please Van," Allie chanted.

But there was no Arthur, there was no Van, no magic sword out of a comic book and no help from the dead. There was only them, and they needed more time.

Donna stumbled up. She grasped for her purse and reeled to the embrasure in time to see King Sorrow blast past, thirty feet from the tower, in a rippling mass of black armored scales. The wind buffeted her. She could smell the lizardy reek of him. The force of his passing set off car alarms in the parking lot behind the building. Donna pushed one hand into the purse for the cold steel cylinder that had been there for weeks.

"King Sorrow!" she screamed. "King fucking Sorrow! More like King Chickenshit! Do you hear me? Do you fucking hear me? Donna McBride has a riddle for you! Come on over! Don't make me shout! Let's riddle for our lives, what do you say, big man?"

The dragon circled the tower—then tilted in, toward the library, and struck.

GWEN FELT KING SORROW HIT THE TOWER, felt the stones lurch, the floor shudder beneath her. It seemed to be happening a long way off. There was a grinding of old rock. Books fell off shelves behind the chain-link grating. The room was hazy with smoke and drifting spatter from the fire extinguisher. Gwen looked up, saw Donna's hand rising out of her purse, wondered if the woman had brought a gun. *Never bring a gun to a dragon fight*, she thought, and almost laughed, and looked back to the crossword. It was filled in, except for one last word in one last corner. *Bait for a shark but also your Arthur.*

"Chum," she whispered, and whether it was a drop of sweat or a tear that hit the newspaper, she didn't know. "I love you, old chum. It doesn't matter if I say it now. I wanted to say it a thousand times but King Sorrow wouldn't let me. I had to say it to you in my heart, instead, where I said it every day. Every time I thought of you. Come back to me if you can—and if you can't, I guess I'll come to you, soon enough, and that'll be all right too."

Letters began to write themselves in the last boxes.

C
H
U

And Gwen began to smile.

TANA LIFTED ONE CORNER OF THE ROBE to see what was happening and found that the Russian mirror had spun across the floor and wound up next to her elbow. Her gaze fell to the reflective surface . . . and she saw Arthur's hand pressed against the inside of the glass, his palm almost pink. It was as if he was right there, on the other side of a window. Tana reached out with her own hand, hardly knew what she was doing, to put her palm against his. Their fingertips met, separated by a quarter inch of glass. Tana felt a stab of pain travel up her hand into her funny bone—it was much as if she had brushed an electric fence. A loud, glassy pop caught her attention, and when Tana snapped her head up, she saw that a Y-shaped crack had appeared in the glass wall, at the back of the treasure room, a crack that mapped perfectly to the crack in the mirror, although it was six feet high instead of six inches long.

She glanced once more, wildly, into the mirror. Arthur's hand was gone, and the glass had healed itself, not so much as a scratch in its surface.

"*Come on!*" Donna screamed out the window. "*Show me your face and I'll give you a riddle. I've got a real fucking good one for you! I've got a real fucking stumper!*"

"Donna?" Allie asked in a frightened whisper. She had stuck her head out from under the robe as well, was staring across the room at the woman who had ruled her imagination for more than two decades. "Donna. What are you doing?"

Donna didn't look back at her.

"Guys," Robin whispered.

She pointed through the smoke at the glass wall. She stared with the stunned, blank eyes of someone who has been struck a ringing blow. Tana looked again and saw that the video was flicking back and forth over the same half second now, as Arthur Oakes wheeled about in a blur, slinging that lacrosse stick. Arthur's right arm was extended toward that new Y-shaped fissure running through the wall. By some trick of optical refraction, the handle of the lacrosse stick seemed to be pressing right through the crack, at the very point where the Y split in three directions, at the very spot where two lines joined to become one.

Gwen put the crossword down, rose from her knees, and began to walk, like one in a trance, toward the wall of glass.

KING SORROW GRIPPED THE OUTSIDE OF THE TOWER, claws sunk into the stone, belly pressed against the rock, like a salamander clinging to a stucco wall. His tail lifted to curl around the lower part of the tower. As he raised his face to peer through the embrasure, Donna unscrewed the top of the battered thermos, tipped her head back, and drank. It was, she thought, like drinking the brine in which they packed olives, so salty her throat wanted to seize up. She forced down the first swallow of dragon tears, and then the second . . . and abruptly the strength trickled out of her left hand. Her fingers tingled and numbed. The thermos fell and struck the floor with a bang and her right hand clutched the edge of the windowsill, in case her legs suddenly gave way.

King Sorrow's dark crown—that web of membrane, with its sharp ridges of cartilage—opened around his vast and terrible face. He turned his head to peer in at Donna with one eye, then swiveled around to stare in with the other. Those eyes were as big as the lenses of a lighthouse's beacon. Donna was reminded of a cat peering through a hole in the wall at mice.

"Why would I riddle with you, Donna McBride?" King Sorrow asked. His voice was so deep and powerful, it caused the chain-link grating over the shelved books to tremble and resonate. "You have nothing to offer me."

She felt it then: the moment the edge of her soul ignited. It was a thrill, a kind of shock—pleasurable and painful at once—that raced from the top of her skull to her toes. It was like being dizzy-drunk and freshly laid at the same time . . . a sensation of delight so powerful it threatened to stop the heart.

The tears were going to stop her heart. She could feel each new thud in her chest—sore but lovely—and count the long seconds in between. She coughed without opening her mouth . . . and tasted smoke.

"Solve my riddle," she said. "And you can have my life. I'll give it freely."

The edges of her vision warped and bulged. She rocked on her heels.

"I have your life already," King Sorrow assured her. "I'll tear this wall apart and burn you and these other fools to cinders. The only riddle worth pondering is what you imagined you might do—all of you—to stop me from killing you where you stand."

"Feed me and I live," Donna muttered. "Give me a drink and I die. What am I?"

"*That's* your riddle?" he sneered. "Oh, Donna. That makes me sad. That one was old when Judas Iscariot counted his silver. Everyone knows the answer to that one."

"Yeah," she said. "Fire. Okay. You knew it. Here's your prize, you cocky bitch."

She sucked a deep breath, her chest filled with sweet flame, and she blew with all her might. Fire flashed from her mouth and into King Sorrow's staring eye. She saw it blacken before he could snap his head away and to the side; a nictating membrane flashed up to protect the eye itself, but by then she had scorched it to ruin. She laid the flame down the side of his face, to the corner of his mouth, and along his throat, blackening and melting his gleaming coat of shifting scales. He let go of the tower and flung himself away.

He shrieked. The scarred wooden tables in the tower jittered as if a train were passing just feet away. The glass wall in the back of the room shook in its frame.

King Sorrow swooped out and away in a tight circle that launched him straight back at the tower, and he smashed into it with all his force. The entire library seemed to *jump*. Donna was lifted off her feet, flew back and to her right, crashed down on one of the tables, bounced and spun off, landed on her stomach. King Sorrow screamed again, a sound like attack jets screaming off the runway. He propelled himself free of the tower to circle and strike again.

And then, an awful thing. Allie cast off her robe, flung it aside, and leapt to her feet. Tana rose as well, grabbed her hand, tried to pull her back. Allie slipped loose and went on. She was halfway to Donna when King Sorrow smashed into the tower yet again. The shockwave of the impact lifted Tana and Allie both right off their feet. Allie landed hard, a few feet away. Tana went down on her back, her skull ringing off the stones with a sharp crack.

Donna reached for Allie's hand. It seemed a long way away. The thrill—that nerve-ringing thrill that had gone through her when she first swallowed the tears—was fading. Each time her heart beat, it was like someone bringing a hammer down on her chest . . . but the hammer didn't fall often now, no more than once every ten seconds or so.

"Donna," Allie said. "Stay here, Donna. Stay."

The hammer fell again and this time the pain was very bad. Donna squeezed Allie's hand and Allie squeezed back. Blood roared in Donna's ears, a tidal crash. She shut her eyes. She didn't think she could take much more. She needed air. She had never needed air so badly. This was what drowning was like.

Then someone was pulling, pulling hard, pulling her to her feet, out of the roar and tumble of the surf, and Van said, *You're all right, you're all right now, I've got you*, and she opened her eyes and found herself wading in the ocean, the waves falling in a bright crash of foam around her thighs, and while she caught her breath, her brother draped a necklace of sand dollars around her throat.

IT DIDN'T HURT ANYMORE. Gwen felt like a ghost of herself as she walked toward the wall of glass where Arthur was frozen, staring back at her, holding out his lacrosse stick. From the edge of her vision, she saw Robin snatch the martyr's robe from the floor. She leapt to Gwen's side and flung it around both of them as the room filled with fire, flame pouring through the windows in great red streams. Flame engulfed them, but Gwen felt no heat at all beneath the robe. That yellow Biko hoodie was soaked with sweat and blood, but she did not feel the sharp, tearing pain in her abdomen now. She might've been gliding on roller skates.

Arthur's face loomed before her, close enough to kiss. His lips moved. A thousand times she had watched this video and she had not been able to tell what he was saying, but now it was perfectly clear, so clear, she didn't know why she had ever been confused. *Take it*, he said.

He held out the lacrosse stick, and this time she saw two inches of golden handle extending through the crack in the wall. She reached and gripped the hilt and drew Arthur and the stick right out of the glass wall. Only when she pulled it free, it wasn't either. It was a blade of light, half the length of her own body. She should've been too weak to hold it, that shining yard of mirrored steel, but it seemed to have no weight at all.

"I'LL TEAR YOU APART," screamed King Sorrow. "NASTY BITCHES! I'LL BURY YOU IN STONE!"

Allie rocked back and forth, clutching Donna in her arms. Tana pushed herself up off the floor and stumbled toward Allison, caught her from behind. To what purpose Gwen couldn't know. Only to hold her, perhaps. Donna's body was twisted at the waist, her eyes open, her face blank, already gone. Her hair was windblown, prettily tangled, as if she had spent the day at the beach.

King Sorrow threw himself at the side of the tower for a third time. The floor shuddered. He gripped the outside of the stone and two talons slid inside an embrasure and he *pulled*. Stones grated and three big blocks of granite squalled free, flew into the night. His open mouth appeared on the other side of the hole for an instant, a maw filled with great teeth. He roared, producing a foul, hot shockwave of pulverized air that flipped tables and flung them against the far wall.

"*Where are you, Gwen Underfoot?*" he roared. One side of his face was blackened, the eye sealed shut, but he turned his head the other way to peer into the opening. His eye shifted this way and that, searching for her. "I may not *see* you, but I *smell* you. Do you really imagine whatever puny little enchantment you have will keep you from my grasp?"

He shoved his claw through the now four-foot hole, grasping inside the tower.

Gwen brought the blade out from under the robe, lifted it over her head, and scythed it down in a bright arc. It felt less as if she were swinging three feet of steel, more like she was only holding on while the sword swung itself, and she thought, *Of course, because it's Arthur, because it's my hands and his blade, my eyes and his strength*. At first she thought she missed, because the edge of the sword rang hard against stone and threw sparks. Then she saw the severed dragon digit, nearly four inches of talon, fall to the floor in a gush of blood.

King Sorrow shrieked again—a mad shriek of pain. Gwen was deafened by the sound of it. It was like a cannon going off. She recoiled, almost fell, and Allie caught her, having risen to steady her. When she had her heels under her, Allie let go and nodded and reached past her, reached toward the wall of glass.

"GWWWWWWEENNNNNN!" King Sorrow screamed. "*I'LL BITE YOU IN TWO, YOU WICKED WHORE! I'LL BURN YOU TO ASH!*"

Flame poured in through the ruin of a wall, but this time Allie repelled it, saved them all. She reached into the wall of glass, into the past, to take the shield from Van's outstretched hand, a great sheet of hammered steel, stamped with the image of a sand dollar, and she turned and held it up just as the fire flooded in about them. The blaze struck that shield—a shield as bright as the sea flaring in the morning light—and was repelled, thrown straight up toward the ceiling, where it blackened the stone roof. And Gwen thought Allie had never been more beautiful, her feet spread, knees bent, braced against that whirling blast of fire. With her jaw set and her eyes shut, it seemed as if Allie could stand there, repelling King Sorrow's flame, for a thousand years.

Gwen wasn't looking when King Sorrow's tail pulled away a yard of stone wall on the other side of the room, directly behind her—smashed through one embrasure and *yanked*, prying blocks loose in a shattering tumble. The tail coiled back and snapped in at them, striking Gwen and Robin both. Gwen felt a bitter, almost blinding shock of pain, a final fatal tear somewhere deep in her abdomen. She was driven straight back and struck the wall of glass behind her. It exploded, fissuring into a thousand pieces of green rubble. Robin was spun, whirled aside as if she had been clipped by a passing bus, hit a wooden table, and went down.

Gwen struck the floor with a bloody cough and dropped the sword. The martyr's robe fell upon her and she sprawled beneath it, a field mouse that has squirmed in beneath the carpet.

"*You're there, YOU'RE THERE,*" King Sorrow exulted. "*I felt you go smash.*"

Allie was screaming Gwen's name, but her voice was a mile away, hardly audible through the ringing in Gwen's ears. The tail rose, flailed about, and slammed down on her. Ribs shattered. The withered, half-healed left lung popped. Gwen could feel it go. It was like a paper bag, filled with air, when some class clown clapped his hand down on it.

"*There you are, you scrabbling chancer,*" King Sorrow cried.

She was bleeding badly now. Blood spread beneath her, expanding in a red, shimmering pool across the stones. His tail wavered in the air nearby, then dropped to the floor and began to move toward her, slithering across the floor like an anaconda.

"Killed you, bitch," King Sorrow said. "Happy Easter."

He pushed the unburnt half of his face to the hole in the north wall. Gwen thought he had been hurt quite badly, that the other side of his face had been scoured down to the muscle by Donna's flame. Gwen had an idea it had been centuries since anyone had hurt the King so.

Allie placed herself right in front of him—in that moment, Allie was fearless—and King Sorrow pushed one claw through the hole and batted her aside, his claw ringing off the shield. Allie was thrown end over end, like a child doing a somersault. Robin picked herself up off the floor and screamed and grabbed the fire extinguisher and ran at King Sorrow and was just as lightly swatted down. King Sorrow's mouth gaped open and Tana threw a chair into it. He crushed it in his teeth and then his tail snapped across Tana's back, threw her into a stone wall. Blood spattered.

Gwen turned on her side and swept her arm back and forth. Her fingers batted at the blade of the sword, caused it to rotate in a slow ringing circle. She flailed again and caught the hilt.

"I can *heeeeeear* you," King Sorrow shouted happily, and thrust his tail in her direction. The great serpentine length of it slid beneath the robe, joining her under the tent of that dark cloak. It probed the air a few inches from her face.

Gwen lifted herself onto her knees. She turned the sword to point the tip at the floor, squeezed both hands around the grip, and fell. The blade sank through King Sorrow's tail without any sense of friction. The tip of the sword found the mortar between blocks of stone and drove itself into the floor with a ringing chime, as if a silver bell had been struck with a silver hammer.

King Sorrow screamed again and all the world shook. Hardcovers trembled and leapt off the shelves behind the chain-link grating. Chairs danced about. The dragon tried to jerk his tail free, but the sword held him stapled to the stones, a pin pushed through a butterfly. The tail dropped into the spreading pool of Gwen's own blood, lifted and dropped again, smacking wetly against blood-slicked granite.

"You nasty little girl! You've stuck a needle into me! A nasty little needle!"

Gwen found herself too weak to even lift herself onto her elbows. She sprawled, chin on the rock beneath her and the robe spread over her. It was a struggle to breathe, and the want of air made her lightheaded and curiously calm. She had done all she could. Whatever would happen would happen. There was no more to worry about.

King Sorrow thrust his head through the hole on the opposite side of the tower. His black, forked tongue flicked out, searching for her. The tip flittered across the floor . . . and tasted the edge of that quivering pool of Gwen's blood.

"*Oh,*" King Sorrow murmured. "Oh, that's *good*. All that grief. All that loss. That's good, Gwen!"

He lapped at her blood, his tongue moving closer to her face, sliding under the edge of the robe. It twitched and vibrated a few inches from her nose, then turned and licked at the blood spattered upon his own tail.

"That's so good!" he cried again. "More!"

First his tongue lapped at his tail, then it curled around and around it. He pulled. The sword held his tail to the flagstones. King Sorrow grunted and pulled again, harder, and this time he dragged his tail toward him, the sword splitting him in two as he yanked himself along.

"Help yourself," Gwen said. "Dig in."

She spoke so softly she could hardly make out her own voice. But King Sorrow heard her fine. He chuckled, warmly, amiably . . . and then inhaled the tip of his own tail, like a graceless diner sucking up a length of spaghetti. The sword carved through the steadily thickening trunk of his tail, until only the hilt was still visible, which was when it came loose from the floor, still run right through him.

"*Oh, Gwen,*" he muttered, his voice clotted and thick. "*I never tasted better.*"

King Sorrow inhaled another yard of his own tail. He made a harsh, effortful choking sound as the Arthur-sword went into his gullet . . . and sucked again, pulling in six feet this time.

As he devoured himself, a kind of rippling convulsion passed through his tail. It began to pull itself through the wall, hitting blocks and knocking them free to drop away into the night. King Sorrow struggled to get more and yet more of himself into his mouth. He shoved a claw through the opening in the north wall, pulling away stone, widening the space.

"*Goot!*" he choked. "*Goot!*"

"Oh, God," Tana said, pulling herself off the floor on her knees. She was the only one of them to see what was about to happen. She scrambled, found Allie, got her in her arms and pulled her against one wall . . . then grabbed one of the study tables and pulled it over them, to hide beneath it.

In the next instant the dragon yanked the whole armored hoop of his body to the west, pulling himself right through the wall. Huge blocks of stone fell. Beams splintered and dropped through the dust. Allie and Tana disappeared into the rockslide, the great collapsing pile of granite blocks. Half the ceiling flew away, tumbling from the tower, down onto the roof of the library below. The other half of the ceiling was supported by the east wall of the tower, and what was left of the north and south faces. Dust whirled, a gush of powdered rock and ash exploding into the night, following King Sorrow up into the sky.

Robin reeled to Gwen's side, dropped to one knee, placed a hand on her shoulder. Her face appeared directly over Gwen's for a moment. She pushed hair back from Gwen's face, offered her a reassuring smile.

"Hang in there, Gwen," Robin said. "I hear sirens. There'll be some gents along to look after you in a jiff. Don't you dare die on me, now, I've been through that with you once already."

Gwen could hear the sirens herself, very dimly, through the hum in her ears. Robin lifted her head and scanned the night, possibly looking for the strobes of the emergency vehicles, possibly looking out for a frenzied dragon. A breath of fresh air moved across Gwen's face. When Robin sat up, Gwen could see into the night. The dust was already clearing, the evening breeze shifting it away in shimmering pale curtains, and she could see King Sorrow high above. He was a great black hoop, jerking first this way, then that, twitching across that map of stars spread over them. He wrestled with himself, his wings thrashing furiously at the darkness, while he swallowed one mouthful of his tail and another. His jaw unhinged—Gwen had heard snakes could do that—to force down his own hind legs. He was making sounds, great barking noises, as he rose into the dark. At first she thought it was the sound of the dragon choking. Then she believed she was hearing the sound of his laughter as he rose, and struggled, and rose, until at last, with one heroic effort, he inhaled an enormous bite and there was a kind of popping in her ears, as at a sudden pressure change, and King Sorrow swallowed himself, and was gone. Gwen's insides were all busted up, splintered bone sticking through her chest, through her lungs, the vital tissues in her abdomen torn down the middle. It was a lot of pain.

All the same: she had to laugh.

34.

When she shut her eyes, her nostrils were filled with the campfire smell of charred books, mingling with the cooling breezes of an ocean less than half a mile away. When she opened them, Van and Donna and Colin were down on the beach, burning the Christmas tree.

She was on the embankment above them, beneath a white spruce, the seagrass blowing about her legs. The wind, cold and fresh, caught at her hair, at the brown robe wrapped around her for warmth. Donna and Colin were dancing together while Van played something on a ukulele. He only knew one chord, as far as Gwen could tell, but it sounded pretty good all the same. Donna tossed her hair, and by the firelight, Gwen saw a necklace of sand dollars about her neck. Whitecaps surfed in with a crash and a hush, luminescent in the moonlight.

She wondered where Arthur was, and while she was scanning the rocks along the water, hunting for him, he stepped out from beneath the tree behind her. She smiled to see him, and when he put his arm around her waist, she rested her head on his shoulder.

They stood on their dune while the grass whipped at their legs. They stood and held each other. It was the most natural thing in the world to kiss, once, and twice, and then he pressed his lips to her temple.

"Can you stay?" he asked.

She put her head on his shoulder once more and stood with him at the very edge of the firelight and listened to the sweet boom of the surf and her friends laughing on the beach below, and she thought it over.

Epilogue

GWEN, OUT FROM UNDER

2016–2022

1.

Gwen was awake when they buckled her into the Stokes basket to lower her from the ruin. An improbably good-looking fireman with the cleft chin and blue eyes of a comic book Superman was bent anxiously over her, doing up the straps.

"Hey there, Jett Nighswander," Gwen croaked, and Jett's gaze darted to her face. "You want to leave this to someone else and go dig your mama out."

"Oh, God," he said in a watery, unsteady voice.

"Don't you worry," Gwen said. "Your mom is the kinda person just won't stay buried. She got under a table. Think she's all right. Go see."

"I got this, Jett," said his partner, a freckly woman who smiled down at Gwen to show the gap between her teeth. "Lady, you got so much grit in your hair, you look like you just come from the beach."

"How'd you know?" Gwen asked.

2.

When Jett heard his mother under the rubble and was persuaded she was all right, he returned to help winch Gwen down to earth. By then she was fading again. She could hear the surf in her ears, could hear the waves pounding the beach. The others were so close. She wanted to get back to them, while they were still dancing.

3.

As the ambulance turned through the stone gate and left the campus, she drew a sudden rattling breath as a spear of pain drove through her midsection—it felt as if she had been run through with a broadsword—and that was it. That was where Gwen died: a mile from the Podomaquassy hospital, thirty minutes from Eastern Maine Medical in Portland.

4.

They were three minutes reviving her. Her heart stopped again in the emergency room. It took five minutes that time, but after that they had her on oxygen and plasma, and it was safe to pack her on the helicopter and fly her to Portland.

"Wow, are *you* fucked up," said the EMT who placed her gurney on the helicopter. They had worked side by side at the prison disaster, but in the moment she couldn't remember his name. "It's easier to count the bones you *didn't* break, Underfoot."

"'Tis but a scratch," Gwen said.

5.

She was touch and go for most of six weeks. No blood of the saints to quicken her recovery this time. She wasn't at Donna's funeral in April, but she was able to attend the remembrance in August, at the Rackham College chapel. The Reverend Erin Oakes delivered the eulogy. She was as slim and pretty as ever, although her close-cropped hair was as silver as whitecaps in moonlight.

The reverend said Donna McBride had been angered by suffering and outraged by cruelty . . . and her anger, in turn, made her suffer; her outrage made her cruel. Donna, she said, drank hate's poison and hoped it would sicken her enemies; Donna had committed a thousand crimes to atone for the one she hadn't stopped, couldn't stop, because she had been just a child. Maybe she had never stopped being that child, in some way. But she had loved her friends as intensely and completely as she hated the rest of the world, and that love counted for something. It had kept her from consuming herself . . . as the worst always do.

It wasn't a pleasant account of one woman's life. But there was truth in it, a recognition of all Donna's pain and resentments and mistakes, and Gwen preferred that to a lot of comforting blab about some version of Donna that had never existed. It did Donna no kindness to falsely remember her. Maybe there was even some mercy in it, that Erin Oakes could look upon Donna's life the way a mother might look upon a child's skinned knee. And in the end, Donna had stood with them. Gwen knew it, even if no one else did. At the end, Donna had thrown off her whole ugly life like a rotten coat, which was, in a way, a thing as astonishing as seeing a dragon swallow its own tail.

Tana and Allie sat in the front row, and when they walked out, they were holding hands. Allie had a limp—a block of stone had crushed her foot, and it had not recovered—but Tana helped her along, every step of the way, and now and then Allie placed her head on Tana's shoulder and laughed.

6.

In the summer of 2018, fire raced through the blond, sere grass in the pastureland north of Hopland in Mendocino County, California. Red pines caught and went up like torches. A hot and dry wind pushed the fire steadily south and west. The blaze leapt dirt roads, creeks, highways. A thunderhead of black smoke, miles wide, mounted in the skies, above the helicopters dumping foam and water on the flames. As the heat climbed, redwoods began to explode like sticks of dynamite, the sap in them boiling and causing the wood to rupture. That night, the sky was filled with a billion whirling sparks, an alien constellation playing out against a long, smoky darkness. The fire would burn all summer and into September, consuming over six hundred square miles of farm and forest, hill and dale, incinerating thousands of animals and any number of unlucky Californians who failed to evacuate quickly enough.

The cause of the fire was never determined.

7.

A much smaller conflagration occurred on the opposite coast in December 2018, and while not as newsworthy as the Mendocino Complex Fire, the fire that destroyed The Briars—home of the late tech billionaire Colin Wren—was covered by the *Boston Globe*, NECN, and the rest of the regional press. The blaze began in the basement, where old, frayed wiring ignited some unsafe insulation that had been packed into the walls in 1973. The fire department put trucks on the road, but it was snowing heavily, coming down in fast white flakes, and they were a while getting there. Then they couldn't get up the drive—an electrical short had killed the power to the gate. The fire crews needed nearly ten minutes, working with the Jaws of Life, before they had it open and could drive up to the fully engulfed manor.

When the fire trucks had disappeared up the driveway, the pickup parked in the trees across the road turned on its headlights, and Gwen drove home.

8.

She didn't think she could sleep, so she rode out to the sledding hill in Gogan. She just thought she'd sit there for a while, watching the flecks of snow whirl and spin past, while the adrenaline subsided.

But some kid had left an inner tube leaning against the brick wall of the disused mill building. She spotted it in the passenger-side mirror and watched snow collect in the lower curve. Finally, she got out.

The cold air stung her scarred lungs, was like a chest full of splinters. But it was a good hurt. Her life was full of good hurt now: sore back, stiff joints, a bum knee. When it was particularly bad, she used a cane, had been leaning on that cane when she walked Allie up the aisle to greet Tana, waiting with her son, under an arch of roses. Erin had married Allie the first time and she married her the second, her eyes gem-bright with amusement, her voice full of barely suppressed laughter. There had been a lot of laughter that night.

Gwen limped now to the inner tube, put her mittened hands on it. She looked up into the snow, flakes catching in her eyebrows, kissing her cheeks: snow like falling ash.

"You want to go for a ride, old chum?" she asked. "One more time?"

"I wasn't doing anything else tonight," he said, the version of Arthur who went everywhere with her.

She carried the tube to the edge of the hill and looked down it, into a long dark. It would kill her leg, trudging back up with it. She placed herself gently in the center of the tube and reached over the side and pushed.

The darkness rushed up at her. She shut her eyes and let Arthur hold her.

Sure, it would hurt walking back up out of the darkness. Her life was full of good hurt, these days.

9.

It was three hundred steps to the attic, most of them through a narrow stone chimney, into the yellow reek of the smoke. The firefighters worked from the final landing, blasting at the flames beneath the roof of Notre-Dame with low-pressure deluge guns. Leonard Debois thought it was like using one of his son's Super Soaker squirt guns on a bonfire, but no one knew what kind of damage a higher-pressure blast of water might do to ancient stone, stained glass, and thirteenth-century oak. Leonard Debois was near the top of the stairs, holding the serpentine length of the hose—as thick as a boa constrictor—when he heard a terrible, squalling roar, and Jean Laurent, on the step above him, began to scream *Revenir! Revenir!* Men struggled back down the stone steps while the sound rose and rose around them, until Debois could hear nothing else, until his teeth vibrated from it.

The spire of Notre-Dame tilted slowly, inexorably, down into billowing sheets of fire. The spire might've been made of wax, at the end, the way it seemed to bend and collapse, shedding lead sheathing, which would soon begin to boil and fill the sky with toxic smoke. Debois was running by then, they were all running, away from the heat, away from the thunderous crash behind them. When the spire finally collapsed into the rest of the building, the entire roof erupted in a blast of super-oxygenated flame. It looked for all the world as if the cathedral had been struck with artillery, struck by a falling bomb. Debois ran, yelling *Putain ça, putain ça,* the whole way, but the sound of the roof collapsing behind him was too loud for him to hear himself.

Later, when he spoke to others of the 2019 inferno that had consumed Notre-Dame, Debois told his friends the fire sounded almost triumphant at the end: like a dragon screaming.

10.

A Goodreads review of *Toolkit for the Well-Prepared Dragonslayer*, by Arthur Oakes, PhD, with Gwen Underfoot, posted on November 4, 2019:

> svangur_bro
> 1,219 reviews
> 356 followers
> no stars

i was up for a good book about finding magical sords and stabbing dragons and rescuing hot babes in chainmail panties but instead i got a lot of WOKE nonsense. a dragon is just a dragon is just a dragon is what I say. it doesnt have to be a dum metaphor for drone strikes or whatever. THERE IS SO MUCH LIBERAL GILT in this book its as bad as watching rachel muddow (who i hate even if she is obvsly super hot). and UGH it just goes on and on, couldve been hundreds of pages shorter, who has the time for this shit, i didn't, quit before i got halfway. the only good thig here is the author photo of the girl writer, mmm, yummy, like velma in scooby due. anyway if you like me enjoy girls in chainmail follow the link in my bio for some totally unrated nasty medieval sxxxxx hahaha i promise it will be way more fun then this garbige.

11.

Warehouse 12 was on fire for less than twenty minutes before the explosion. Later, some of the (very few) survivors who lived along the harbor in Beirut said it hadn't sounded like a fire at all, not at the end. A child, a girl of eight named Adeline Hamoud, who was picked out of the rubble of an apartment building half a mile away, said in the last seconds before the detonation, there was a kind of rattling hiss, like a cobra, but *so* much louder. She said it sounded like a cobra as big as a plane, hissing and preparing to strike. It was the last thing Adeline heard before the building collapsed on her.

When Warehouse 12 exploded, it went off with over a kiloton of force, flattening houses, melting twelve-story cranes like birthday candles, flinging waterside bulldozers as if they were made of paper. The explosion was so powerful, it shook windows in the Gaza Strip, two hundred miles away. In Cypress, a mere 150 miles away, people in the streets of Nicosia threw themselves to the ground, taking shelter from what they believed was a nearby explosion. Later, the power of the blast was estimated to be far in excess of the explosion that destroyed Hiroshima.

Doctors concluded Adeline Hamoud was suffering from PTSD when she spoke of hearing a giant snake that hissed and rattled in the moments before her life quite literally crashed down around her, crushing her parents and older sister. They assumed much the same about the other dozen or so who reported hearing the shriek and roar of some tremendous animal, laying waste to the harbor.

12.

Gwen went to London in the late winter of 2022 for Robin Fellows's retirement party. She would've been there even if Robin hadn't published Arthur's book . . . a book that bore Gwen's own name as a coauthor, at Robin's insistence. Gwen hardly felt she had done anything. She had merely filled in the blanks Arthur had left behind, as she had done for a thousand crosswords they had shared. The book had done well enough. Some people liked it, some didn't, there were a few good reviews and a few bad ones, and if sales continued like they were, it might even stay in print awhile.

They celebrated Robin's forty years in the business on the roof of the publishing house, with a view of the Thames. There was a pyramid of glasses with champagne spilling over them and there were waiters in white bow ties carrying trays loaded with little cakes. There were speeches from celebrity writers like David Mitchell and Donna Tartt and Francis Spufford. An actor who had starred in *Friends* was there; Robin was publishing his memoir, although she would be well into her retirement before it came out. Gwen stood on the roof and watched the sunset behind the London Eye, the sky smoky and pink, the breeze pushing her hair back from her face. She shut her eyes and listened to the lively hum of conversation behind her, punctuated by the occasional shout of Robin's laughter. She thought the night was just about perfect, and she was filled with a desire for London, a wish to stay here, not for a few weeks, but for a few years. Of course, wanting England was much the same as wanting Arthur, she supposed. She walked Robin home after eleven, Robin tipsy and singing, and while they were crossing Westminster Bridge in the damp, chilly night, Russia invaded Ukraine.

In the days after the party, Gwen and Robin sat on the couch in her flat, parked in front of the TV, watching a line of tanks move toward Kyiv, staring at video of buildings with holes punched through them by missiles. On the ninth of March, something hit a maternity ward in Mariupol: a shattering blast, a gush of fire. A pregnant woman was killed; her baby was stillborn. Video of the sky, the night of the bombing, showed flashes of bright flame against a backdrop of smoke. Something detonated in a flash, and in the sudden, evil flicker of light, Gwen thought she saw a reveling dragon, its black bat-like wings open, its jaws agape. She grabbed for Robin's hand. Their fingers wound together and her old friend squeezed back and Gwen knew she had seen it too.

"It's another," Gwen gasped. Her chest hurt, where the ribs had been broken years before. She had to fight to get the air her old, beat-up lungs needed. "Goddamn it. It's another one, Robin! I *knew* there were more. I started thinking it after those fires, those insane wildfires in California a few years ago. There was something off about that, how big they got and how quickly. And then Notre-Dame. And there was that massive detonation in Beirut, remember? They said ammonium nitrate. Ammonium nitrate, my ass. How many more of these things are there, and what are we supposed to do about it? Don't we have to try and stop it? Don't we have to do something, somehow? You and me?"

"We can't fight all the dragons ourselves, love," Robin told her. "Let someone else have a turn. There are plenty of dragons to go around."

—Joe Hill
Good Friday, 2022

ACKNOWLEDGMENTS

2022? Wait, what?

No, that's not a typo—the first draft of this book was completed more than three years ago. Then I set it aside for most of a year. I used to do that quite often with manuscripts and, when possible (it's often not possible), I recommend it. When one comes back to a story after a long time away, it's possible to see it with fresh eyes. And then I needed most of a year to revise it, and the wheels of publishing grind slow but fine, so here we are in 2025, almost but not quite ten years since my last novel, *The Fireman*. I'll try not to take so long between books next time.

Speaking of that next book, I hired a research assistant to help me out with it—Ooh! Exciting! It's like I'm a big grown-up writer now! Only, the guy I employed wound up, of course, doing some legwork on *King Sorrow* as well. My thanks to Chris Del Santos for looking into a few things for me; that said, any errors of history or fact are entirely on me. Indeed, I consciously played a little loose with some small details of recent history. When there was a choice between strict adherence to the facts or making this scaly son-of-a-bitch move, I always erred on the side of speed.

One of my first readers on *NOS4A2* and *The Fireman* was the brilliant Gillian Redfearn, my extraordinary UK editor. We had to professionally part ways in 2016, which was a shame, but the lovely Gillian King stepped into the gap and took not one but two early passes at this manuscript. I love you, my darling. Thank you for marrying me.

Other first readers included my old *Locke & Key* editor, Chris Ryall, and a small squad of literary polymaths: Nick Harkaway,

Francis Spufford, Robin Hobb, Michael Koryta, and Tananarive Due. Each of them did their best to keep me from going splat on my face; although if I've gone splat anyway, don't blame them. The horror writer Bracken MacLeod gave me the joke about Milwaukee's Best, so now you know who to hate on, Milwaukee. I'm an innocent here! I love Milwaukee beers! My brother, Owen, offered several useful, clear-eyed suggestions, including one that he prefaced by saying, "I have one small suggestion if you want it, but it would involve you writing perhaps two paragraphs, and I understand if you'd rather take a chainsaw to your left leg." I thought through my options and finally wrote the two additional paragraphs. My parents, Tabitha and Stephen King, came in to provide their usual edits and, yeah, okay, holy shit, it's pretty insane to think I have two such gifted writers tuning up my prose. My ma and da have made every one of my books better. There's a line in one of those *Rocky* movies where Apollo Creed says, "I've taught you everything you know, but that doesn't mean I taught you everything *I* know." I'm still learning from my parents. I'll never be done learning from them—from their stories, their observations, their daily acts of kindness.

If this book works at all, it works because Jen Brehl solved the puzzle of Book One—how to make it do everything it needed to do, while steadily building in velocity and suspense. If it doesn't work, don't blame her; I'm the one who thought it would be a good idea to write 275,000 words about a big snake who talks like Robert Shaw. Jen has been my editor on every novel since the first and has vastly improved each one. She's made 'em *roar*. If you write a book about a dragon and it doesn't roar a little, you're in trouble.

King Sorrow had many faithful servants at William Morrow, toiling to do his snakey bidding. They include Kaitlin Harri, Jennifer Hart, Toby Luongo, and Paul Moore in the office; Hope Ellis, Dale Rohrbaugh, and Jessica Rozler in production editorial; Andrew DiCecco and Marie Rossi in production; and Emily Bierman and Miranda Ruoff in content development. Eliza Rosenberry handled the publicity on this book—as she did on some others of mine—with her usual good sense and enthusiasm. Tavia Kowalchuk prac-

ACKNOWLEDGMENTS

ticed her usual art of marketing magic, to great effect. This book was lovingly designed by the best of the best, from Jeff Freiert's copy writing to Brian Moore's art direction and jacket design to Leah Carlson-Stanisic's lovely interior design. Marleen Reimer, working in subsidiary rights, helped to spread King Sorrow's empire worldwide. Our audiobook producer, Suzanne Mitchell, created a whole prestige TV show for your ears. My thanks to them all and to the entire William Morrow sales team, both in-house and remote.

Greg Villepique faced this great sprawling beast of a book without fear, armed only with his metaphorical copyediting pen. Our heart-stopping cover art was crafted courtesy of Alan Dingman. Mi hermano Gabriel Rodríguez penned a perfect little King Sorrow icon for use throughout the book. Thank you, guys.

I'm grateful to my UK editor, Toby Jones, for taking this book on, and managing director Mari Evans, who went all out to make a happy home for me at Headline. I'm thrilled to be on the team. Marcus Gipps at Gollancz saw an early draft of this book and offered a happy mix of encouragement and insight. Thank you, man.

Laurel Choate of the Choate Agency handled the business end so that I could handle the creative end; Sean Daily of Hotchkiss & Daily has run absolutely amok selling my stories to the movie and TV people and, boy, has it been fun to watch. I've been so lucky to have them on my team.

Love to my sister and brother and my unflappable, reliable Redfearns, my UK family. I have five brilliant, hilarious, creative sons. No one makes me laugh harder or worry more—worry and laughter, that's what you sign up for when you become a dad. I won't stop doing either till I'm dead, I guess. Thanks for being such good boys, you lot. When I see how much you care about stories, it reminds me that this work isn't so unimportant after all.

And thanks to you, dearest reader, for riding with me once again. The dragons haven't got us yet.

Joe Hill
Exeter, New Hampshire
December 2024

RAISING READERS
Books Build Bright Futures

Dear Reader,

We'd love your attention for one more page to tell you about the crisis in children's reading, and what we can all do.

Studies have shown that reading for fun is the **single biggest predictor of a child's future success** – more than family circumstance, parents' educational background or income. It improves academic results, mental health, wealth, communication skills and ambition.

The number of children reading for fun is in rapid decline. Young people have a lot of competition for their time, and a worryingly high number do not have a single book at home.

Our business works extensively with schools, libraries and literacy charities, but here are some ways we can all raise more readers:

- Reading to children for just 10 minutes a day makes a difference
- Don't give up if your children aren't regular readers – there will be books for them!
- Visit bookshops and libraries to get recommendations
- Encourage them to listen to audiobooks
- Support school libraries
- Give books as gifts

Thank you for reading.
www.JoinRaisingReaders.com